DRUMS OF DESTINY

PETER BOURNE

DRUMS OF DESTINY

G. P. Putnam's Sons
New York

This edition of DRUMS OF DESTINY is especially prepared
for book club distribution with the approval of the author.

MANUFACTURED IN THE UNITED STATES OF AMERICA
AMERICAN BOOK—STRATFORD PRESS, INC., NEW YORK

CHAPTER ONE

THE valley was called Deil's Glen by all who lived within fifty miles of it. That was because the devil had an earthly home there, in The Cave.

The Cave held the valley in thrall. Its dark, yawning entrance was an inhuman scar on the face of Cairn Shee, whose granite peak dominated the chain of encircling hills. Like an evil eye, The Cave glared balefully down into every nook and cranny of the valley.

Save for that black scar on the cliff's face, the valley was beautiful in its serenity. The low-lying fields provided rich pastureland in which the Angus Doddies munched all day long, stuffing their black, shining hides to the bursting point. Where the ground rose toward the surrounding foothills, the lush grass ceased, and a carpet of purple heather masked the uneven lower crags. There, in contrast to the leisurely cattle, horned sheep wandered restlessly in search of food, now leaping as nimbly as goats from rock to rock, now eagerly craning woolly necks to nibble and pull at a sweet tidbit.

Set in this valley was the house of Malcolm Stewart. It was built of gray stone, low but roomy, and it had the rare distinction of a slate roof —green and mossy in parts. From a distance the house resembled a squat toadstool. Near by was a fine stone-built barn; farther off, a well.

Inside the farmhouse, in the year 1768, a woman lay abed in one of its two bedrooms. She might have been young, but all youth had been driven from her face, which was haggard and aged with hardship and pain. Her dark hair was drawn tightly back from her forehead, her face was lined by the ravages of sun and wind. Beneath her eyes the skin was pouched and deeply shadowed. Her forehead was wet with tiny beads of perspiration. There was stark fear in her eyes. She tossed and turned. Low quivering moans of pain disturbed the silence of the small room.

She turned once more and faced the open window from which she could see The Cave, leering at her with its single basilisk's eye.

"Elspeth, Elspeth," she called out in a weak voice.

There was an answer from the adjoining room—a rattle of pots and pans, and: "Coming, lass, coming."

Elspeth Macdonald bustled in. She was dumpy and plain, but her eyes and voice were kindly. She plumped herself down on the wooden stool beside the bed and with a corner of her apron wiped Jessie Stewart's forehead.

"Puir lass! Puir lass!"

"I canna bear the pain, Elspeth. How lang will it be, Elspeth?"

"It shouldna be mony hours now, Jessie."

Elspeth's words comforted the younger woman. She turned her eyes

3

toward the raftered ceiling, and the stricken misery in them was softened by a smile. Her hand stroked the coverlet as though, in imagination, she was already fondling the smooth skin of the child that her tortured body was struggling to expel.

The outstretched hand, which had been resting weakly upon the bed, closed convulsively. Fresh beads of perspiration burst from the sweat glands of the forehead, the sides of the nose. Once more a groan was forced from parched lips.

When the spasm had subsided, she whispered, "Am I gaun to dee?"

Elspeth took the clenched hands in her own. "Go on wi' ye, lass, what nonsense is this? Bless me, lass, but in twa hours' time you will hae a sweet bairn at your breast, whin you'll nae remember there is sic a thing as pain."

Jessie turned her head, this time toward the window. Her weary eyes stared at The Cave. "Elspeth, I am afeered. Where is Malcolm?"

"Caring for the beasties."

"Why doesna he send for a physician?"

Elspeth ominously tightened her lips. "Nor God nor deil could mak' Malcolm Stewart send for a man, whilk would cost him siller. Him what hae brung sae mony cattle into the warld, says he, dinna need a doctor fer the birth o' a mere bairn."

"I dinna want Malcolm here, Elspeth. Do ye hear me? I dinna want Malcolm here."

"Dinna fash yesel', my sweet. Malcolm Stewart winna hurt ye while Elspeth is here to tak' care o' ye."

"Look at The Cave, Elspeth. It's staring at me, it is. I am afeered. I am afeered. I want a physician." Jessie's voice rose as a fresh labor pang gripped her body. "I ken I am gien to dee. Oh, Elspeth! Elspeth!"

"Weel, lassie?"

"If I dee, and my bairn lives, will ye tak' it awa' frae Deil's Glen?"

Elspeth Macdonald was uneasy, alarmed. Her God-fearing nature shrank from making a promise which she would, in all probability, have no chance of fulfilling. She realized that Jessie was working herself into a fever that could do harm both to herself and her child. If such a promise would soothe her it was senseless to withhold it. Besides, there was little reason to fear for Jessie's life. She was a healthy, strapping woman who should be able to give birth easily enough.

While Elspeth hesitated, Jessie was seized with another pain. Her body fell limply back upon the pillows, but her grip upon Elspeth's wrist tightened until Elspeth had to choke back a cry of distress.

"My time is coming," Jessie screamed in an agonized voice. "Promise," she commanded.

Elspeth nodded her head. "God help me—I promise, lass," she murmured.

The September sun sank below the pine forests that straddled the western hills. The trees were a black outline against the golden light, which slowly melted into a vivid, angry crimson. A small, ominously dark cloud sailed up against the wind, seeming to appear from the very heart of the fiery glow.

The slight easterly wind that had helped to temper the heat of the day now died away. The lowing cattle huddled together in uneasy groups. Their eyes watched the stocky figure of Malcolm Stewart as he made his way through the grass to the distant house.

Malcolm stood five feet seven in his shoes, but what he lacked in height was compensated by his girth. His chest was massive. His arms were muscled, thick. His short legs were hairy, slightly bowed, with knees like huge oak knots. Deep-set eyes were surmounted by beetling eyebrows. His beard was matted.

As he trudged toward his home, he glanced up at The Cave, laughed loudly.

"The deil tak' ye, but you're looking evil this night," he called out. "Forby, I shall find anither Stewart awaiting me at hame, and ye ken the fact weel already, I doot nae."

As he came within earshot of his house, Malcolm heard the low quivering moan of a woman in torment. His disagreeable mouth spat out an impatient ejaculation as he realized that Jessie had not reached her time —Elspeth would have little leisure to attend to his wants. The door was shut to, but not on the latch. He kicked it angrily; it flew open with a crash.

Elspeth hurried out from the bedroom.

"Malcolm Stewart, it is time ye were here."

"What wad I be doing at hame when there is work to be doone in the fields?" he asked sullenly. "How is Jessie?"

Elspeth told him. "The bairn's lang due. Ye maun ride for a doctor mon. The twa o' ye could be here within the hour."

"Whisht, woman, are ye mad? What does Jessie want of a doctor when I am here?"

"Nae, nae, Malcolm. It is a doctor she maun hae."

"A doctor for to bring a child into the warld!" Malcolm glared angrily at the woman. "Hae I nae brought a thousand beasties to life not to help Jessie the noo?" He made a step toward the bedroom.

As his wife turned her head Jessie saw her husband standing in the doorway, like a huge, bloated toad about to spring. She shrieked her horror. The noise echoed round the small room.

Not realizing the reason for her shriek, he ascribed it to a different cause.

"Your time's come, Jessie," he growled. "I maun gie a hand to help the brat." To the accompaniment of his wife's shrieks, heedless alike of Elspeth's remonstrances and tugs, he rolled up the sleeves of his coarse shirt and advanced toward the bed.

In such a manner was Duncan Stewart born on the evening of the tenth of September, 1768. A moment later, with a sobbing sigh, Jessie died, victim of Malcolm's senseless brutality.

CHAPTER TWO

WITH a curt word to Elspeth to clean up the mess and attend to the child, Malcolm Stewart stumped out of the bedroom into the adjoining kitchen. A quantity of barley-meal bannocks, a wooden platter, a knife, a jug of ale, and a tankard stood upon the table, set there by Elspeth several hours previously.

Malcolm snatched up a ladle, crossed over to the wide, open hearth, and sniffed greedily at the savory mess of meat and pot herbs which simmered in an iron caldron slung above a smoldering log fire. He took up a ladleful of the pottage, tasted it warily, gulped down the remainder with noisy satisfaction, and heaped on his platter as much as it would hold. Then he sat down on a stool and began to cram food into his cavernous mouth. The bannock and the pottage disappeared, but he remained unsatisfied. He filled the tankard with ale, emptied it in two drafts, refilled it, then heaped more food on his plate.

"Elspeth!" he shouted.

There was a movement from the bedroom. Elspeth emerged, wiping her hands on her apron.

"What is it, Malcolm Stewart?" she challenged. "Hae ye forgotten the dee'd woman in there?"

"I havena. It is because o' her I maun speak wi' ye."

"What do ye wish to say?"

"Jessie is dee'd—"

"Thanks to ye, Malcolm Stewart," Elspeth cried out. "As sure as I stand here, ye killit her wi' your rough hands and your niggardliness."

Stewart hammered the table with his clenched fist. "What is doone is doone. Wi' Jessie nae mair who will ta' care o' the chiel? Ye ken I canna."

"Ye maun find someone to look after the wee ane."

"I ken that weel aneugh. Aye, and the richt ane to ask."

"And who might that be?"

"Naebody but yersell, Elspeth."

To Elspeth, Stewart's reply was the voice of fate. From the moment of his telling her to lay out Jessie's body she had known that Stewart would ask her to be foster mother to the child, housekeeper to the father. In her fear of him she had deliberately refused to consider what her answer should be.

Faced with the necessity for an immediate decision, she grappled with the problem. Since Jessie no longer needed her, her inclination was to leave Deil's Glen as quickly as possible. For the past two days she had stayed beneath the Stewart roof; already she disliked the sullen, brutish farmer who had no interests apart from his livestock. As she stared at his blue-chinned face it was in her mind to shout, "No, no, no!" at him and to rush from the kitchen, to lock herself in the bedroom that she was using, and hide her head beneath the patchwork quilt until dawn should light the way back to the town. But beside Stewart's face she saw Jessie's—drawn and haggard.

She had given her promise to Jessie, whose body was not yet cold, the distressed woman reflected. How could she now desert the bairn? She had sworn to take the boy away. That she could not, dared not, do—yet awhile—but she could love him as if he were her own child. That she could do so very, very easily.

Elspeth's glance traveled round the kitchen. If it were not for Malcolm Stewart's unbalanced nature—with which she felt capable of coping—the Stewart farm would make a pleasant home. Her duties would not be light, but she did not mind hard work when there were such compensations as rainproof shelter, an ample supply of wholesome food, and a real bed to sleep in. Undoubtedly there were many worse ways of passing the next few years . . .

"What wage will ye pay, Malcolm Stewart?" she demanded.

So Elspeth Macdonald settled in at the Stewart farm and mothered Duncan Stewart. The memory of Jessie's last moments faded. Though she loved the babe, Elspeth forgot her promise to take him away from Deil's Glen. She stayed on, daily growing more content with her task of caring for father and son.

Malcolm Stewart she handled with consummate tact. At first she subdued his wild moods, his sudden outbursts of temper, by threatening to leave the child. Later, when she had proved herself as excellent and thrifty a housekeeper as she was a foster mother, this threat became doubly effective. Stewart was so anxious to keep Elspeth with him that he contrived to control himself as never before.

Duncan grew. His hair showed promise of the brilliant red tint that had long distinguished the Stewart men. He began to crawl. Soon he reached the next stage of human motion. He crept from table to chair, from chair to door, from door to bed, holding on tightly to anything small enough for his fingers to clutch. Later, he was able to do without help; on his own two legs he toddled unsteadily across uncharted ground. One day when Elspeth looked for him, he was nowhere to be seen. She went in search of him. She found him seated by the well, gazing with serious eyes at The Cave. When he saw Elspeth he made a queer cooing noise and tried to point at the distant black patch which so closely resembled an enormous eye. Elspeth hastily snatched up the child and rushed into the house.

In bed that night Elspeth could not sleep. For the first time in a year she recollected Jessie's dying plea not to permit another Stewart man to grow up a victim of the vicious influence of The Cave. Elspeth shuddered with misgiving, for she realized that she had no intention of fulfilling that promise.

As she lay awake and listened for Malcolm Stewart to make his way into the next bedroom, she realized—perhaps for the first time clearly—whither her course was taking her, and that she was helpless to turn back. She lay rigid with fright, listening for the dead silence to be broken, tortured by his delay.

For a week now Stewart had retired to bed nearly thirty minutes later than usual. In the past he had gone to his bedroom as soon as he had eaten, leaving her to wash up the dishes, tidy the kitchen, and prepare the following morning's meal. Lately he had fallen into the habit of sitting down in the oak armchair and waiting there until she had gone to bed. While she settled herself for sleep, he whittled wood in the pretense that he was fashioning a cow for his son.

Elspeth listened for the scraping of the chair on the dried mud floor. The noise was usually the prelude to his returning the wood to an old press, and to other clumsy movements as he moved about the kitchen.

There it was, that long, dismal scratching and bumping noise as Stewart pushed the chair back to its accustomed place near the fire—he almost upset her spinning wheel as he did so; another recent habit. She waited anxiously for the next sound—she felt that she could not sleep until she had heard the bed in the next room knock against the intervening wall as he flung his heavy body down upon it.

There was a rattle of fire irons. Elspeth knew that Stewart had picked up the long poker, was thrusting it into the fire. Next he would pick up a shovel—ah! he was doing so. A noise of shoveling followed as he damped down the fire. From the fireplace he walked to the rough-hewn, shallow sink and scooped up a ladleful of water, which he swallowed down. From the sink he returned to the fireplace. He noisily cleared his throat, spat in the fire, placed the bellows handy for the morning, blew out the cruzie. Then he made his clumsy way toward the bedroom.

Elspeth's breath fluttered. For a week the sound of those dragging footsteps had haunted her dreams. Every step was subtly different; each one was slower, more deliberate, as they approached her door. She knew each one from memory. So now she counted them. One—two—three—four. He was by the corner of the table. Five—slower—six—slower—seven—eight—slower—silence!

An uneasy, tense silence. Elspeth stared at the door. Underneath she could see a ribbon of light, the reflection of the candle that he carried. Her lips were dry. The chill shiver that touched her spine failed to cool the rest of her body. Every night for the past seven Stewart had halted thus. She knew that the night would come when those reluctant footsteps would not pass on.

Elspeth felt she could bear the suspense no longer. She experienced an impulse to shriek. Then she heard the familiar shuffling footsteps again. She sighed with relief as her taut nerves relaxed.

Then the latch rattled softly—the ribbon of light beneath her door broadened at one end; then joined at right angles with another perpendicular ribbon of light that slowly widened . . .

CHAPTER THREE

B Y THE time Duncan was five, Elspeth had long since despaired of
managing him. She did not understand, and therefore could not
cope with, his solemn moods. Even as a baby he had smiled less than
most healthy babes. As he grew older, he seemed to live more and more
in a world of his own, secure behind a barrier of reserve that Elspeth
was unable to penetrate.

Had Duncan been her own child Elspeth could not have loved him
more. For the first two years she had tended him with affectionate detachment, but when Malcolm Stewart, unleashing the evil passions he
had deceptively held in check, revealed himself as a brutal savage lower
than any one of the beasts that it was his life's work to tend, all Elspeth's
gentle kindliness was lavished on the boy she had helped to bring into
the world.

Duncan treated her with good-humored tolerance. When she rebuked
him, his expression seemed to say, "I must listen to you because you love
me." There were times when this gratuitous forbearance goaded Elspeth,
and then she would beat him soundly. Her hard hand never succeeded
in making him cry. Nor did it alter his expression, except on occasions
when it grew terribly reproachful; then she would clutch him closely to
her and sob her regret for having lost her temper with him.

If his reaction to Elspeth was tolerance, the same could not be said
of his attitude to his father. The boy loathed Malcolm Stewart and never
attempted to dissemble. He would sit upon his stool and stare, unblink-
ingly, at the man.

Malcolm was amused rather than angered by his son's obvious dislike.
He would tantalize Duncan merely to rouse the hatred that glinted in
the boy's eyes. Then he would roar his laughter at his son's impotence,
whereupon the fires of hatred in Duncan's eyes would burn more brightly
than ever.

As soon as he was capable of walking Duncan broke loose from Elspeth's restraining hand. It was useless for her to order him to remain
wherever she might choose to put him. The moment she turned her
back he ran from her, out of the farmhouse. At first she was able to
catch him up, make him return to the house and obey her orders. As
he grew stronger and his legs speedier, he was frequently able to outwit
her. When she was unable to find him, no shouted appeal or threat
would induce him to reveal himself. He would return to the house only
when his stomach clamored to be filled. Nor would he disclose his hiding
places, or promise not to repeat the offense.

He rarely opened his mouth to speak. When he did, it was to ask
questions that Elspeth could rarely attempt to answer correctly. She was
amazed at, and not a little apprehensive of, his precociousness.

One day Duncan said to Elspeth: "Ye are nae me mither, Elspeth."

Elspeth was startled. She stared with consternation at the child who sat on the kitchen table, dangling his feet and playing curiously with the lifeless body of a wild rabbit that he had snared earlier in the day.

"Wha tellit ye that, Duncan? Was it your faither?"

"No," Duncan spat out in scorn.

"Then wha did tellit ye, Duncan? Wha?"

"Naebody, Elspeth."

"Then what made ye ask me?"

"Because I heer auld Campbell call ye Mees Macdonald."

"Aye, Duncan, ye did."

"Weel, if ye were ma mither wouldna ye be Mrs. Stewart?"

Elspeth shivered. "Ye shouldna fash yesell wi' sich matters. Why are ye nae playing in the sunshine?"

"Because I want to talk wi' ye, Elspeth," he replied calmly.

"What aboot?" she asked in despair.

"Ma mither. Did ye ken her?"

"Aye, weel. It was a sad day when the gude Lord took her awa' frae ye."

"Frae me, Elspeth? Was I alive whin ma mither dee'd?"

"Aye, lad," Elspeth admitted awkwardly.

"Why did she dee?"

"Because the gude Lord took her for His ain."

"The Lord doesna do that wi'oot reason, does He?"

"Nae, Duncan, 'twas for her happiness, the sweet."

"But Mither must hae been ailing, else she would nae hae dee'd."

"Aye, she was ailing."

There was a pause, Elspeth bustled about with her cooking, hoping to distract the boy from asking further questions, but fearing the worst; he stared out of the window with an air of concentration that, she had come to know, indicated that his childish mind was deeply engaged in thought.

Presently he transferred his attention to the rabbit. His fingers explored the stiff corpse. Then he looked at Elspeth again, his forehead creased with frowning lines.

"Elspeth?"

"Aye, lad?"

"How are lads and lassies born?"

Elspeth threw up her hands in dismay. "The gude Lord save us, what will ye be asking next? Gang awa' wi' ye, and dinna fash your brains sae."

He did not attempt to move from the table.

"I want tae ken," he told her obstinately.

"More's the pity," Elspeth retorted. " 'Tis nae natural for a bairn to ask sich questions."

"Are babies born like lambs?"

Elspeth looked distressed. "Aye," she admitted at length. "Aye."

"Is that how I was born?"

Elspeth nodded her head.

"Did it hurt Mither tae born me?"

The woman was at a loss to know how to handle the situation.

"Weel, did it, Elspeth?"

"Aye, it did. Your mither dee'd because o' ye, Duncan, and ye should foraye revere her memory."

"Tell me aboot it."

Why not? thought Elspeth. It could do the boy no harm to be told. Perhaps such knowledge might help to counteract the bad influence exerted on the child by his father. Besides, it seemed that the mystery of life was not unknown to Duncan, who had gained his knowledge from watching, with those grave, observant eyes of his, the herds that roamed Deil's Glen.

So she told Duncan of his mother, of the manner in which she had met her death.

"I am gien to be a physician," the boy said, baring his teeth. "Am I gien tae be a physician, or am I nae?" He picked up a knife from beside her and balanced it in his hand.

"Aye," Elspeth agreed. "Aye."

Duncan's suddenly aroused interest in medicine and surgery proved no passing phase. From the day he had learned the circumstances of his mother's death, he became absorbed in the study of anatomy. He begged Elspeth to give him an old knife. When she refused to do so, he accepted her refusal with apparent equanimity, but—so she learned many weeks later—he stole an old blade, took it with him to one of his hiding places, and there sharpened the cutting edge to razor keenness.

That knife never left him thereafter. With it he began a series of secret experiments upon the bodies of wild animals that he snared. On wet days he would pester Elspeth to pass on to him her knowledge of medicines and simples. He took to wandering afield, and tramped miles through neighboring valleys and over hilltops in his search for the herbs which she described to him. These he took back with him to the farm so that Elspeth should identify them, show him how to dry and preserve them, and instruct him as to their purposes.

As soon as he had assembled a stock of these herbs, he decided to begin a new series of experiments. One day Elspeth missed a small iron pot. Mystified by its disappearance, she asked him whether he had taken it. Blandly he denied all knowledge of it.

Yet he had lied. The caldron had joined the herbs in a little wooden hut he had built for himself in a small heather-concealed cave that, several centuries previously, some old Stewart had hollowed out of the mountainside as a retreat from the periodic raids of warring clans.

After he stole the pot his next job was to collect a quantity of kindling wood—an easy matter. The following morning, when Elspeth was out of the kitchen, he took a lump of smoldering peat from the fire, ran with it to the cave, placed it beneath the kindling, and blew upon it until the wood burst into flame. As soon as the fire was burning well, he rigged up the iron pot so that flames should heat it. Then he began to make some of the herbal concoctions of which Elspeth had told him.

11

Some days later he arrived at the farm with his face a pasty, greenish hue. As Elspeth opened her mouth to exclaim, he leaned forward and was violently sick. She sent him straight to bed, dosed him with her own mixtures, and anticipated that he would be well again by the morning. He was not. For two days he was subjected to violent spasms of vomiting until he was weak and helpless, and quite convinced, in his childish mind, that he would die.

By the evening of the fourth day he had fully recovered. When she questioned him, he would offer her no satisfactory explanation. She was not unduly perturbed, for she had already concluded that he had swallowed some poisonous berries, and she was comfortably convinced that his bout of sickness would teach him to be more careful thereafter.

That assumption was fully warranted. He was more careful in future. Instead of swallowing his own concoctions he administered them to wild rabbits that he snared and imprisoned in hutches. He carefully noted what effect his mixtures had on the animals, and stored up the knowledge in his retentive memory. In course of time he murdered a number of the unfortunate rabbits, but on the other hand he succeeded in saving the lives of many that he had first poisoned.

He also diligently helped his father during the mating and calving seasons. Until he had learned all he could about both functions, he asked his father questions. As Malcolm Stewart had neither niceties nor reticence he used to chuckle and answer the questions in great detail. He was proud and elated when he realized that his son understood all he was told.

CHAPTER FOUR

MALCOLM said to Elspeth one night, after Duncan had been sent to bed: "Elspeth, I want ye to make a change in the hoose."

"A change?"

"Aye."

Elspeth looked up from her spinning wheel, surprised by Malcolm's unusually hesitant manner.

"Weel?" she prompted.

"I want ye to put up the truckle bed in your room."

"For why?"

"For Duncan."

"For Duncan!" Elspeth stared at Malcolm with astonishment.

"Malcolm, ye are nae gang tae marry again?" she asked.

"Aye, but I am, and why shouldna I?"

"But Malcolm, do I nae mak' ye a gudewife?"

He laughed brutally. "Ye may be gude, but ye are nae wife o' mine."

"I will marry ye, Malcolm, if so ye'll hae me."

"I dinna want ye as a gudewife, Elspeth. It's Annie MacWhirter I want, and it's her I hae asked."

"Annie MacWhirter! That fliskmahoy! She's nae but a wee bit gowk

12

who scarcely kens wha' it is tae be a woman. Wha' can she gie ye that I canna, Malcolm Stewart?"

His answer was brutal. "Some more children. The more ma herds increase, the more help I need. Twa or three sons will save me a deal o' siller in the years tae coom."

Duncan stood with his hands clasped behind his back and solemnly watched his father harness the mare between the shafts of the cart. The boy was surprised. Never before had he known Malcolm to leave the farm on a Saturday. For some time he kept silent, but at last his curiosity prompted him to speak.

"Whare are ye gien, Faither?"

Almost for the first time Malcolm replied to his son with some degree of affability.

"To Clackenmuir."

"But there is nae market today."

"I ken that, Duncan. 'Tis nae cattle that tak's me there today. Tonight ye will hae a new mither, lad. I am getting marrit today."

"Marrit!" Duncan stared uncomprehendingly at his father. Then suddenly the storm broke. "I winna hae anither mither. I dinna want anither woman for ma mither. I love Elspeth. Faither, ye mustna get marrit." He clutched hold of Malcolm's arm and held on with all his strength to prevent the farmer's climbing up onto the driving seat.

Malcolm laughed as he pushed the boy away. "Dinna fash yesell aboot matters which dinna concern ye, lad. It will do ye gude tae hae anither woman in the hoose to teach ye manners. Elspeth's tae soft wi' ye." He sprang up on the cart, and cracked his whip. The mare stepped out.

With moist eyes and dragging footsteps Duncan returned to the house. He was aware of calamity; disaster had overtaken the tiny world in which he lived.

He entered the kitchen. Elspeth was not there as was usual at that time of the morning. As he crossed to her bedroom to see if she were there, he heard the sound of smothered sobbing. With his heart beating wildly with the terror a child feels before adult tears, he hesitatingly opened the door. Elspeth sat on the edge of her bed with her head buried in her hands; she rocked to and fro in her misery.

The sight affected Duncan's habitual and unnatural self-control. He gulped as the tears spurted to his own eyes. Unsteadily he rushed to her side, threw his arms as far round her ample waist as they would reach, and buried his head in her lap.

Elspeth removed her hands from her face; with one of them she stroked his bowed head and spread the tears that rolled off her cheeks.

"Puir lad! Puir lad!" she whispered. " 'Tis a sad day for us baith. Puir, puir Duncan. Wha' would your mither say if she could see ye the noo? The gude Lord tak' care o' ye, lad, for 'tis nae muckle longer tha' I shall be able tae keep my een upon ye."

Elspeth was bitterly aware, at that moment, of how terribly she had betrayed her promise. A feeling of guilty remorse shook her. Her tears continued to fall upon the boy's bowed head.

The day passed slowly enough for Elspeth, although there was plenty to do, what with shifting Duncan's clothes into her room and preparing the other room for the bride. When that work was finished Elspeth started baking; for Malcolm had ordered a wedding cake, and Elspeth knew the penalty of failing to carry out instructions. For that same reason she made Duncan do his customary farm work, though her heart longed to have the boy by her side to ease her loneliness.

The weather all day had been comparatively fine, but as the light failed, a heavy mist began to rise. The temperature dropped several degrees. When Duncan came in for the last meal, his hands and face were blue; he said he felt chilled.

Elspeth gave him a generous serving of the soup that simmered over the fire. While he swallowed it, she restored his circulation by stripping the clothes from him and giving him a hard toweling. As soon after as he would go, she put him to bed, for she was desperately anxious that he should be asleep when the bridal couple returned.

As one hour passed, and then a second, she realized that she need have had no fear on that score. When a third hour had passed, she decided to follow Duncan's example, and prayed that Annie and Malcolm would remain away all night. She squeezed her way round the door of her bedroom, for most of what little space there had been to spare was taken up by the truckle bed in which Duncan slept.

As she undressed she watched the sleeping boy. She did not remember having seen him thus for many, many months—indeed, she had seen him asleep probably not more than half a dozen times since the day when, after becoming Malcolm's mistress, she had transferred him to Malcolm's room and bed, to make room for Malcolm to share hers. Now, once more, the lad slept in her room. Above the bedclothes, which were pulled up to his chin, his face was turned toward her. She was amazed at the difference in the expression between Duncan awake and Duncan asleep. When he slept, the red, healthy cheeks, and the untidy hair that curled over his forehead and covered his left eye, made him look so much younger than when he was awake. It was the eyes, she decided, that changed him, for the closed eyelids hid the brooding, enigmatic expression that created the impression of an understanding beyond his years.

A wistful smile parted her lips as she gazed upon him. The impulse to kiss him was so strong that she tiptoed to the side of the bed and softly brushed his forehead with her lips. As she straightened up she noticed that he was smiling. She wondered whether he was dreaming that his dead mother had leaned down from Heaven to kiss him.

Then she regretted her impulse. The thought of Jessie revived memories of her broken promise, which all that day had tortured her conscience. She climbed into bed, blew out the candle, and prayed to God to forgive her for her trespasses. Then she prayed that her sleep should not be haunted by Jessie's accusing ghost. No sooner had she settled herself for sleep than she heard voices. Malcolm and his bride were returning.

As the voices grew clearer, she realized that the couple were singing. She could not distinguish the words, but the tune she dimly recognized. She trembled painfully and regretted that she had not retired an hour earlier so that she might have been asleep when this moment came about.

Singing, shouting, and raucously laughing in turn, Malcolm and Annie arrived at the farm. Elspeth knew they were drunk. No doubt they had been drinking steadily, she thought; and she murmured another prayer —that they would not awaken Duncan with their noise.

Presently the bride and groom stumbled into the kitchen. Annie started to sing again, but Malcolm stopped her with an exaggerated whisper of caution. Elspeth heard the door open, heard them enter, heard the door close again with a bang. Duncan stirred. She clenched her hands and stared into the darkness. From the other room came the noise of shuffling feet.

Elspeth sat up in bed as she heard a voice whisperingly call her name, a voice that she knew was Duncan's, but which echoed in her ears like the voice of his mother. She knew that the time had arrived to fulfill her seven-year-old pledge to Jessie.

CHAPTER FIVE

SHE lighted the candle that stood in a candlestick beside the bed. Duncan sat up and looked at her with wondering eyes. She leaned across the bed so that she could whisper to him.

"Dinna speak above a whisper. I nae want your faither tae hear."

The boy nodded.

"Your Elspeth is gien awa' frae the farm."

"For aye?"

"Elspeth is never gien tae return. Will ye come wi' me, lad?"

An expression of fierce exultation leaped into his eyes. He threw the bedclothes off and stood up between the big and the small bed. Then he impulsively threw his arms about her and kissed her wet cheeks.

It was all the answer she needed, but in a loud tremulous voice he confirmed his decision.

"Please, please, please. An' may I be a physician, Elspeth, instead o' a farmer?"

"Aye," she promised recklessly. "But saftly, lad, saftly. Do ye ken weel wha' I am saying? When ance I hae left Deil's Glen I shall never, never return, come what may. Are ye ready to gang awa' for aye?"

"Aye."

"Ye will never see your faither agin, do ye ken that weel?"

"Well aneugh," he replied with passion. "I hate my faither."

His words horrified her. "Hush, lad, hush! Ye shouldna say sich things. 'Tis wicked o' ye tae speak sae."

" 'Tis wha' I feel."

She shook her head with despair, as she realized that she would never come to understand the boy. There was a terse, bitter note in his voice

15

that convinced her that he had expressed no passing emotion. But it was no time to lecture him, she told herself. For the last time she tested the strength of his rapid decision.

"Things will nae be easy for us till I get work. Unless I do tha' soon, we may hae nae place to lay our heads, nae food tae fill our bellies wi'. Life may gae verra hard wi' us, ye may coom to regret ha'ing left the farm and your faither. Think on it wi' care, lad, for there can be nae turnin' back for us once we hae left Deil's Glen."

Duncan laughed in answer to Elspeth's appeal. "I am nae afeered, Elspeth," he whispered with confidence.

"Then hurry, lad, hurry and dress yesell," Elspeth urged, in a feverish anxiety to be gone.

The two fugitives hurriedly dressed in their warmest clothing. As soon as Elspeth was ready, she spread one of the blankets from her bed and made a bundle of her personal belongings and some extra things that Duncan might need.

Just as she finished there was sudden quiet in the next room. This was the moment she had feared. She paused, wondering whether to wait a while before venturing out. Then she shook her head, as panic urged her not to wait a moment longer than was necessary. She signaled to Duncan to be careful and not to make the slightest sound. Then she picked up the candlestick in one hand, the bundle in the other, and cautiously tiptoed into the kitchen.

As Duncan opened the outer door the in-draft caused wispy spirals of mist to eddy into the kitchen. The candle flame flickered weirdly and seemed to dwindle.

Elspeth gazed with dismay at the black wreathing void that faced them from the other side of the doorway. Her resolution faltered as she realized that the mist had thickened. To venture blindly into unknown country in such a mist could be perilous. With no means of seeing the country ahead or around there were a dozen dangers into which they might unknowingly blunder—forests, tarns, swift-flowing torrents, morasses, precipices. Unable to see the stars, they could not judge the north from the south, the east from the west. Nor would it be safe to proceed a short distance in the hope that the mist would lift with the dawn of a new day. Such mists, she knew, sometimes lasted for days. It would be wiser to wait for a clear, starry night before beginning a flight from Deil's Glen. After all, why should a short delay make any difference to their resolve? The few days with Annie would probably only strengthen their determination to leave the Glen forever.

Thus Elspeth hesitated, even though Duncan caught hold of her hand and tugged at it in an effort to pull her toward the door. Then she heard Malcolm say slurringly, "Gie me anither kiss, lass." There was a high-pitched giggle from Annie—movements . . .

A sob welled up into Elspeth's throat. Her eyes smarted. She blew out the candle with a gasp, and holding her bundle before her so that she could push it through the doorway, she stumbled forward into the mist, her head bowed. Duncan closed the door behind her and caught hold of her free hand.

The mist closed round them as though it were some tangible substance. It seemed to cling to them, almost to impede their progress. Elspeth, at any rate, had a momentary, ghastly conviction that she was swimming, a sensation that was not diminished by the wetness of the mist.

The blackness of the night was terrifying. Elspeth could feel Duncan's small fingers interlocked in her own, but when she turned her head in his direction she could not see him. He was as invisible to her as though he were not there.

Once again her spirit quailed. She was not without courage, but her almost superstitious fear of the unknown, combined with the strangeness of being abroad after dark, daunted her usual unimaginative serenity. For the second time she considered the wisdom of postponing their flight for a more suitable night. She looked behind her, but the farmhouse had disappeared from sight. She felt the boy tugging at her hand.

"Wha' is the matter?" he asked. His voice sounded distorted, and a long way off.

"I am afeered by this mist. We shall get lost."

"It doesna matter if we are. When the mist lifts we shall be able to ask oor way."

Uneasily she allowed herself to be pulled forward.

"Can ye nae feel the cart tracks beneath our shoon?" he continued manfully. "As lang as we fallow them we shall gang awa' frae the valley."

"Aye," she agreed. "And then we can mak' our way southeast for Strathyre."

Side by side, hand in hand, they stumbled forward along the cart track that would lead them out of Deil's Glen. Despite the darkness it was not as difficult to keep to the track as Elspeth had imagined, for Duncan's small foot fitted into one of the ruts; with each alternate step forward he felt for it with his left foot.

Progress was slow, but patiently they proceeded on their way until they grew aware that the cart track was bearing to the left. This fact told them that they were leaving the valley by way of the gorge at the north end of the Glen. As soon as the track ceased to bend, then would be the time to leave it, to proceed to their right for a few miles, then to face the south by again turning sharply to their right. If they were able to judge distances correctly, this course would bring them to a valley parallel with Deil's Glen but separated by a range of forest-capped foothills.

At last the cart track straightened out.

They left the track with regret and went forward into the unknown. It seemed to Elspeth that the long lush grass, the heather, and the undergrowth reached, not up to their ankles or knees, but up to their waists. The bundle that she carried no longer contained clothes and personal necessities, but iron weights that pulled her arm down and down.

Conditions could hardly have been more dismal. Their lower limbs were soaked from the wet grass and the heather; her arms and shoulders were drenched by the mist, which penetrated her thick shawl and home-spun gown. In spite of their exertions both their feet and hands were chilled and numb.

They plodded on, silent and weary, but stopped occasionally for Els-

17

peth to transfer Duncan and the bundle respectively from one arm to the other. Later, they realized that the ground was sloping sharply upward, and that it was no longer soft and yielding beneath their feet. She knew that they must have begun to climb one of the mountain peaks. Panic-stricken, she turned sharply to the left and proceeded downhill until sodden grass indicated that they were on lower ground again.

Urged by a terrifying conviction that if they ever stopped moving they would never have strength to rise, Elspeth and Duncan plodded on for hour after hour. Their brains stopped registering emotion, and their movements became automatic. They tried to follow a straight course, but obstacle after obstacle forced them to return along their own tracks or to detour, now to the left, now to the right. She lost all sense of direction and ceased to worry which way they went as long as they continued on and on; anywhere away from Deil's Glen and the vengeance that her hysterical imagination began to fear from a mad Stewart robbed of his only son. They wandered blindly from glen to mountainside, from mountainside to glen. Once they found themselves unexpectedly wading knee-deep in water that smelled foul in their nostrils. Turning, they fled from the tarn, only to find themselves presently among trees that surrounded them. Branches tore at their clothes, whipped their faces and their hands. Again they retraced their steps, and after a seemingly interminable interval, escaped from a forest that might have entrapped them.

Then came the final disaster, just as the dawn of a new day was beginning to lighten the awful blackness of the night. Elspeth lost her balance, disappered into space. There was a series of agonizing thuds, followed by the scraping noise of loose rubble sliding down a steep slope.

Duncan shrieked her name, again, again, and again. There was no answering call. The dawn remained as silent as the night had been.

CHAPTER SIX

THOMAS ANDERSON was a physician. He had a fashionable house in Leicester Fields, London, and an ancient mansion in Killin, Scotland. He was born in the latter and had lived there for the first fifteen years of his life. Later, when he inherited it from his father, his very natural attachment for the place drew him there year after year, usually for all August and as many weeks in September as his large and fashionable clientele permitted.

One morning late in the September of 1775, Dr. Anderson's coach waited outside his Killin home. Armstrong, the coachman, proud as always of the equipage that he had driven for so many years, sat up in his seat, as erect as his voluminous greatcoat permitted. Aware of the doctor's invariable punctuality, he did not anticipate any delay in setting out on the long, uncomfortable journey to London. His judgment was justified. The coach had been standing outside the house only three minutes when the door opened, and a number of people emerged.

For some minutes good-bys were kissed, shouted, and waved, but as soon as he judged that nobody had been forgotten, Dr. Anderson told the youngest of his three daughters to enter the coach. Three-year-old Elizabeth did so, seating herself in the far corner seat with her back to the horses. Margaret, eighteen months older, followed Elizabeth's example and seated herself close to her sister, Jean, the eldest, six years and five months in age, stepped into the coach and primly fitted herself into the vacant space by the front right-hand window. Then Dr. Anderson offered his hand to his wife. With a final wave Alice Anderson carefully mounted the steps into the coach and sat herself down opposite Elizabeth. Lastly, Anderson himself joined his family and occupied the other half of the back seat opposite Jean. The door was closed; the steps were smartly removed by Perkins, the footman, and stored away in the rear boot. Then he climbed up to Armstrong's side, folded his arms across his chest. To the accompaniment of last shouted messages the coach moved off.

As soon as Killin was out of sight, Dr. Anderson relaxed his upright attitude. He leaned back against the padded upholstery; with twinkling, benevolent eyes he surveyed each of his children in turn.

"Well, my chickens, have you enjoyed your holiday this year?" he asked.

"Yes, Papa," the three girls chorused.

"Are you glad to be going home?"

There was a slight pause. "Yes, Papa," Jean replied, a note of insincerity in her voice.

Anderson laughed boisterously. "I am afraid that is not the truth, my child. None of us wishes to return to London. It is always hard to continue work or lessons after happy weeks of leisure. I hope you have all memorized the verses Miss Frilby set you before we left for Scotland?" Miss Frilby was the girls' governess.

"Yes, Papa," they confirmed.

"Excellent, excellent." The doctor fondly inspected his small family— Jean, tall for her age, with lustrous hair so black, so thick, and skin so smooth and olive, that strangers frequently asserted their private conviction that a strain of gypsy blood must run through her veins—an opinion which was grossly libelous to both Dr. and Mrs. Anderson, for he came of an old Scottish family who had owned land in the neighborhood of Killin for as long as records existed, while Alice, his wife, was a member of the Tuke family of West Sussex; and those who knew anything of West Sussex knew, also, the exclusiveness of the Tuke family, whose titular head was one of the premier English earls.

Besides her hair, Jean owned another characteristic which was not immediately apparent but which later impressed one to the exclusion of aught else. It would have been difficult even for an artist to have faithfully described the color of her eyes, for they never appeared to be the same shade for two consecutive minutes. Sometimes they were faintly blue. Five minutes later they were hazel. Yet perhaps the very next minute they were pure gray. Whatever their shade, one had only to gaze into their depths to feel somewhat shocked that so old a pair of eyes could belong to so young a person. They were so serious, so suggestive of mental poise, that one felt that Jean was a person who never allowed life to ruffle her.

Margaret was utterly dissimilar. Alhough her eyes changed like Jean's, they were much bluer and reflected no such unusual poise and reserve. Every small-girl mood and impulse brightened or clouded them on the instant. When Margaret sulked, her eyes sulked. When she was sad, her eyes filled with tears. When some stroke of devilment entered her mind, telltale imps of mischief flashed in her eyes, so that long before anything happened, everybody knew she was up to some prank. Margaret had her father's hair—rich, flaming auburn shot with red and gold. Its color was indicative of her temperament.

Elizabeth, though hardly more than a baby, already gave every indication of being neither entirely like Jean nor entirely like Margaret, while being sufficiently like them both to make it obvious that they were sisters to her, even if not—apparently—to each other. Elizabeth had red hair, though of a far darker shade than Margaret's; but of her quick moods, not a sign.

Her nature, it seemed, would be more constant; even placid, except where loyalty was involved. For Jean she had an unquestioning adoration, no whit lessened by the fact that Jean was not very tolerant of her younger sister; in fact, far preferred the company of Margaret, with whom she could talk and play with that seriousness of purpose that was her special trait. Margaret, on the other hand, preferred to play with Elizabeth, because laughter rose more easily to Elizabeth's lips, and Margaret loved to laugh and to hear laughter.

In his family, Dr. Anderson felt immeasurably fortunate, but for one lack. His wife's affectionate, sunny temperament, consistent, pliant, yet strong, was a perfect balance to his own more brilliant, more turbulent nature; theirs was not only a sympathetic but a genuinely loving union. And the children—he loved them all; but if only one of them had been a boy, how much fuller would his cup of happiness have been. From the first he had always wanted a boy; a son to follow in the father's footsteps, a son to continue a career of medicine when the father died.

As Alice had given birth to one daughter after another Anderson had not despaired. Eventually Alice would present him with a son and heir. He was quite convinced of that. He could not believe that God would deprive him of the one thing he wanted to complete his full life. When, seven months after the birth of Elizabeth, he had learned that Alice was again pregnant he had been overwhelmingly happy. Alice was with a male child. It was impossible to believe otherwise. After three daughters he was, at last, to have a son.

Alas! The child was never born.

He realized the sad truth, that he could not hope for another child.

Presently Anderson noticed that the mountains on each side of them were obscured by a thick, swirling mist. But said nothing to his family for he could see they were not likely to reach its fringes for another thirty minutes. Meanwhile the day was growing older. Perhaps the mist might dissolve before they reached it.

Twenty minutes passed, while the children talked happily of the friends they had made and of the things they had done at Killin. But suddenly Jean said, "Papa, the horses are slowing."

He nodded his head. "We are running into mist." He peered out and noticed that the mist was thicker than before.

When the mist showed no sign of lifting Anderson considered the advisability of turning back. He was on the point of summoning Armstrong to a discussion when there was a shout from the old coachman, the noise of clattering hoofs as the horses stamped in alarm, and the coach came to a swaying halt.

CHAPTER SEVEN

W HAT has happened?" Alice asked anxiously.

"I shall see." Her husband opened the door and leaped down onto the road. "What is wrong, Armstrong?"

"There's a female and boy by the side of the road, sir. Fair gave me a start, and the hosses, too. The boy waved his arm sudden."

"Where are they?"

Armstrong pointed. The doctor peered through the mist. The other side of the road was bordered by mountainside that rose steeply up out of sight. Lying in a grotesque attitude at the foot of this cliff face was the motionless body of a woman. Seated on the road, with her head in his lap, was a boy; his back was against the rock, his legs outstretched. His arm was across the woman's breast, in a protective attitude—an incongruous picture, for he was quite small: a boy of seven or eight, no more, Anderson thought. The child's face was white and drawn, the eyes which stared back at the doctor through the mist were filled with misery.

The doctor quickly advanced a few steps forward until he stood beside the woman.

"What is the matter, boy? Is your mother ill?" Anderson asked gently.

"She isnae ma mither, an' she is dee'd."

He fell upon one knee, slipped his hand into Elspeth's gown.

"She is dee'd, I tellit ye."

"How do you know?"

"Her heart isnae gien mair."

Anderson stared into the steady eyes of the boy. "How do you know?" he repeated.

"Because I felt it. I ken when a body is dee'd as well as ye."

"What happened?"

Duncan pointed up into the mist. "She stepped into air up there. By the time I haed climbed doun she was dee'd frae a braken heid."

"When was this?"

"Aboot sunrise."

"Have you been here since?"

"Aye."

21

"Where were you going?"

"Onywhere."

"Anywhere! What do you mean?"

"Elspeth and me were rinnin' awa' frae ma faither."

"Is this Elspeth?"

"Aye."

"Who was—what was she?"

"Faither's woman until he marrit again last nicht."

Anderson had little need to ask further questions. He frowned. Now that Elspeth was dead the boy would have to be returned to his father.

"Is your mother dead?"

"Aye. She dee'd whin I was born because ma faither wouldna gang tae the village for the physician."

"What is your name?"

"Duncan."

"Duncan who? What is your father's name, Duncan?"

Duncan was about to reply when he was disturbed by a deep suspicion. "What dae ye want tae ken that for?"

Anderson was a truthful man. "Because you must go back to your father, Duncan."

The boy's face set into hard lines. His eyes gleamed fiercely.

"Then I'll nae tellit ye ma name."

"But you must, my boy. Your father will be worried by your absence. He may be looking for you at this moment, wondering where you are, why you are not at home. You do not want your father to be worried, do you?"

"Aye, but it doesnae worry me. I hate him."

"Duncan, that is not the way to speak of your father." Anderson was shocked by the virulence in the boy's voice.

"I dinna care. I hate him," Duncan repeated, his voice turning sullen again. "I am never gien back to ma faither. I hate him. He killit ma mither wi' his big, clumsy hands."

"But you must tell me where you come from," Anderson continued gently. "If you do not tell me you will have to tell the Sheriff."

"I willnae tell naebody," the boy repeated obstinately.

"Then where were you going?"

"Onywhere awa' from him and the farm."

"Ah! So your father has a farm?"

"Aye."

"Are you a farmer too?"

"I am nae gien tae be a farmer. I want tae be a physician."

Again Anderson was startled. There was no doubting the earnestness of the boy's desire. There had been a finality in Duncan's voice that convinced the doctor that no passing whim had prompted Duncan's decision. Strange that the boy should have chosen medicine.

He studied Duncan's face and was impressed by the character written on it. He was vaguely reminded of Jean, for Duncan's eyes were older than his childish features, and there was unusual depth in them. Like Jean's, Duncan's eyes suggested introspection and self-reliance.

Anderson heard his wife call.

"Yes, my dear?"

"What has happened, Thomas? Why are you staying over there? Is there anything I can do?"

"Would you come over here, dear?"

"Yes, Thomas. Perkins, the steps."

Perkins hurried forward and placed the steps. Alice stepped down and joined her husband. As she caught sight of Elspeth's still body an exclamation of pity rose to her lips. She sank on her knees beside her husband, caught hold of Elspeth's hand.

"Is there anything we can do, Thomas?"

"It is too late, my dear."

"Oh! God rest her soul!" Mrs. Anderson reverently crossed Elspeth's arms across the stiffening body. "What is to be done? Can we take her back to her home?"

"I do not know where it is."

"The little boy will tell us, will you not, my dear?"

"He will not," Anderson informed her irritably. "They ran away from home last night. Domestic trouble it seems. Duncan refuses to tell us the name of his home or his father as he is afraid of being returned there."

"Then he is a naughty boy," Alice rebuked. "Your family will be most anxious, Duncan, when they find you gone."

"He has no family, my dear, except a father, who appears to have recently remarried."

"Then what is to be done?" she asked plaintively.

"Heaven knows!"

"We cannot leave them here like this."

"Of course not. The boy looks wet through to the skin. He will take an ague."

Mrs. Anderson's sympathies were instantly aroused. "The poor lad! I wonder how far they have come." To Duncan Alice said, "Did you leave home early this morning, Duncan?"

"Last nicht," was the sullen reply.

"Heaven! Surely you have not been walking all night?"

"Aye."

"Then they may have come from Heaven alone knows where!" Mrs. Anderson said to her husband.

Anderson nodded his head. "Precisely. We may take them in the wrong direction whichever way we go. The only course I can suggest is to take them both to the next town and hand them over to the care of the Sheriff. The woman can go up on the box. Will you take the boy inside while I call Perkins to give me a hand?"

Alice nodded and rose to her feet. She smiled at Duncan and held out her hand. At first he regarded her with suspicion. Then his resistance wavered. He gave a sob, clambered to his feet, rushed toward Mrs. Anderson, and buried his face in her cloak. She placed a comforting arm around his shoulders, and slowly led him to the coach.

The three girls, meanwhile, had been eagerly peering through the coach windows, though there was little to see from where they were. As their mother approached they dutifully reoccupied their respective seats, but their faces vividly expressed curiosity, which was not lessened when their mother entered the coach door accompanied by a strange boy, whom she placed in the middle of the seat, next to herself.

"Mama—who is *he?*" asked Margaret.

"Why is he coming in the coach?" asked Jean.

"Hush, children!" Mrs. Anderson reproved, as she rubbed her fingers through Duncan's tousled hair, and her eyes filled with tears at the thought of the boy's misery.

The children were too excited to be easily repressed.

"He is soaking wet," said Jean.

"Look, Mama, he is getting the seat wet," said Elizabeth. "Papa will be cross."

"I do not think he will, dearest."

"But why is he so wet?" Margaret demanded.

"He—he has been lost in the mist."

This chatter of voices seemed at last to penetrate Duncan's consciousness. He stirred, extricated his head from the folds of Mrs. Anderson's cloak, sat up, rubbed his eyes, and stared at the girls opposite.

"Were you going to London?" Margaret asked.

Fortunately, explanations were spared him. Anderson opened the door and entered the carriage. He and his wife exchanged glances. The doctor nodded slightly as he sat down next to Duncan. "At the next village," he said in a low voice.

Perkins took away the steps, walked ahead into the mist. Armstrong made throaty noises, the four horses stepped forward with short, unsteady steps. The coach swung to and fro as it started forward.

"Well, children, this is Duncan," Anderson told the girls.

"We know, Papa," Jean announced.

"He is a naughty boy and a dunce," added Margaret.

Anderson laughed. "So you are soon acquainted."

"He is very wet, Papa," continued Jean.

Anderson's face grew solemn again. "I know. I hope he does not take an ague."

"Och! I shallnae tak' an ague," Duncan boasted, looking at the girls. "It's mony a time I hae been wet afore noo. I'll ta' a dose or twa o' camomeel and gill, whilk will put me tae reets by the marn."

Mrs. Anderson raised her eyebrows and looked at her husband. "The boy knows how to doctor himself, Thomas."

"Yes."

Duncan looked up at her. "Aye. I am a doctor," he boasted.

Margaret laughed scornfully. "You are not a doctor. You are a stupid boy and a dunce. Papa is a *real* doctor."

There was a moment's silence, but as Duncan appreciated the significance of Margaret's words, he uttered a wild cry and swung round to face the doctor.

Duncan caught hold of the doctor's breeches with a strength that made the doctor wince. "Let me help ye, Mister Doctor, please, please let me help ye. Larn me a' ye ken aboot physic, larn me how tae saw bones, haw tae mak' bairns coom mair easy frae thir mithers' wombs. Mak' me your mon, let me rin errants for ye, let me clean oot your crocks, mak' up your physic. Please, please, Mister, mak' me a physician. I'll dae a' ye say. I swear by the gude Lord I will. Dinna send me back tae ma faither. Tak' me wi' ye. Tak' me wi' ye, please, please."

Anderson looked into Duncan's pleading eyes, and the reflection crossed his mind that never before had he known so young a person possess such inflexible determination to follow a specific vocation.

If only he had been presented with the son for whom he had always craved! What unspeakable joy would have been his, if that son had been so eager to pursue the career of medicine as was this strange lad who had so mysteriously appeared from out of the mountain mist and was at that moment spoiling a sound pair of breeches with dirty, clawing fingers. Hastily Anderson tried to concentrate on things that were, and not on things that might have been.

He played uneasily with his watch chain and listened to Duncan's impassioned plea, now resumed with even greater urgency, because no answer had been vouchsafed to his first outburst. It was an impossible request, reflected the doctor. One could not take the lad away from his father without as much as a by-your-leave. One could not casually employ in one's house an uncouth farmer's boy of whom one knew nothing whatever. The boy said he was running away from his father, but how was one to corroborate his story? He might be a petty thief, endeavoring to escape punishment.

No, no. It was absurd even to listen to such a plea, the doctor angrily told himself. He had enough servants in the house; old, respectable servants in whose charge it was safe to leave his three daughters. As for training the lad to be a physician—who was to be responsible for the necessary outlay? It was quite obvious that the poor boy did not realize that much money had to be spent before one could obtain a diploma from the College of Physicians and thus become thoroughly qualified to act as a physician.

Anderson looked into the boy's swimming eyes. Certainly they were intelligent eyes. They seemed, also, to be honest eyes. If only Duncan were his son—Anderson forced himself to look elsewhere, not trusting himself to resist any longer the beseeching expression, which moved him deeply. Elsewhere chanced to be his wife's eyes. Startled, he recognized in them an expression similar to the one in the boy's eyes. Dear God! Now she was beseeching him. Beseeching him to do what? He stared hard at her, questioningly. Her gaze dropped, rested on the tousled, untidy head between them, was raised again, to meet his. Slowly Alice nodded as her lips parted in a sweet smile. The doctor knew that she, too, was thinking of the son who would never be born to them.

The doctor glanced at his three daughters in turn.

"Children," he asked, "would you like Duncan to come and stay with us, so that he could study to be a physician?"

"Would he be like our brother?" asked Jean, who liked to know the meaning of things.

"He would have to wash his face and speak nicely," said Margaret.

"Now he can be the papa when we play mamas and papas," exclaimed Elizabeth joyously.

CHAPTER EIGHT

TWO O'CLOCK in the afternoon. The hour of siesta was over, but the fierce sun still beat down upon the island of Grenada, southernmost of the Windward group of Caribbee Islands. It seemed as if an invisible curtain of fire were suspended from the blazing orb that dominated the white, molten sky; a fire that dried up the pores of the skin, blinded the eyes, and made one's senses reel. Even the purple petals of the bougainvillea wilted beneath the pitiless rays, and the flamboyant trees were dulled and drooping.

Merely to exist in that inferno of paralyzing heat was a veritable miracle of endurance, but from coast to coast of that tiny island, twenty-one miles, twelve miles broad, people did more than exist. They worked—not fitfully or lackadaisically, but with an amazing energy that would have been incomprehensible to one whose ears were deaf to the threatening sound of the cracking of whips, to the sibilant whish of leather thongs whistling through the air, to the groans of men and women whose backs bore bloody streaks.

Early-sown fields of sugar cane were being harvested. As a line of half-naked Negro men and women, armed with machetes, slowly worked their way forward into the high-growing cane, their arms rose and fell with a rhythmic motion as they dexterously chopped the pithy stalks from the roots. Behind them another gang of slaves gathered the canes and piled them into the waiting oxcarts. As soon as one of the carts was fully loaded it was driven off to the boiling-house, where sugar was extracted.

Poporla worked in the boiling-house, which was even hotter than the blazing sunshine, for the sugar mill furnace and the fires under the taches were burning fiercely.

Despite the terrible heat the stillroom was a hive of activity. At the far end was the sugar mill, a cumbrous piece of machinery comprising three large metal cylinders, which revolved noisily to crush the sugar cane and discharge a continuous stream of yellow juice along an iron gutter into large, round crucibles. Heated by the fire that roared under each crucible, the fresh juice soon simmered, whereupon the liquid was transferred to the taches—a series of shallow caldrons heated by wood fires. Here in these taches the pungent liquid, already attaining viscosity, reached boiling point, and a series of bubbles was constantly forced to the surface, there to burst with such force that each bubble sprayed a fountain of yellow spume into the air. By each tache stood slaves, clad only in trousers, who, at the constant shouted commands of the Negro headman to "skim light—skim light," used long-handled ladles to skim the boiling substance from one tache to the next until it was purified and on the point of crystallizing.

Yesterday Poporla had been a ladler. Today his job was to feed the fires. His ebony skin glistened with sweat as he ran from the cords, stacked outside the door of the boiling-house, to the furnace; from the furnace to the taches; from the taches back to the wood, the while a chorus of voices yelled for more wood, more wood. To and fro, to and fro—now out into the scorching heat of the sun, now into the fierce heat of the boiling-house. To and fro, until his ears were deafened by the grinding of the rollers, the roaring of the mill furnace and the tache fires, the orders of the headman, the babble of voices; and his face and arms were scorched by the heat of fires and by the spray of bursting bubbles; until his muscles were weary and slack.

At rare intervals, when the attention of the headman was otherwise occupied, Poporla would snatch a moment's rest. Then he would take one of the sugar canes that were piled near the mill, ready to be fed to the grinding rollers, and leaning up against the wall, he would chew the sugar cane for its refreshing, sustaining juice and think of Marie, his wife, who was close to her time.

Marie, too, was a slave of M. Bellanger. Marie knew no other country but Grenada, for she was born in slavery and had remained a slave. M. Bellanger insisted that all his slaves should be baptized. So when Marie was born she had received a good Christian name and was taught the rudiments of Christianity by a priest who tried to drown his horror of heathen religions in liberal potions of rum.

When Marie reached a marriageable age she was fortunately too plain to attract M. Bellanger's notice. No objections, therefore, were raised to her marriage with Poporla. Indeed, M. Bellanger cheerfully gave his blessing to the marriage, since he trusted that it would be a fruitful one and thus increase his assets at no cost to himself.

Even though the first pangs of labor were already upon her, she still worked in the fields, for M. Bellanger was a good Christian and had promised to subscribe handsomely for a new church. The slaves' time, therefore, could not lightly be wasted.

The cutting of the cane continued merrily, for in spite of hardships the slaves sang as they worked, and often laughed with a dazzling flash of white teeth. The eyes of those who remembered Africa sometimes clouded over when they thought of their past freedom, but even their overburdened hearts were glad of the opportunity to forget the miseries of life in song and laughter.

The long line of machetes flashed in the sun, and the long line of slaves moved slowly forward. But Marie knew that she could no longer continue. She approached the overseer and asked permission to abandon work. The overseer glanced at her swollen body and her pain-stricken eyes, then nodded his head. It was a nuisance to lose Marie's strong arm and cheerful spirits, but then one wanted the child to be born alive and fit.

Marie stumbled across the cane fields in the direction of a saman tree. There, beneath the welcome shade of the outstretched branches, played a score of very young children, cared for by aged mammies, too old for physical labor. These were the children of slaves; gaily unconscious of their weary future, they romped away the carefree hours while their mothers toiled, pausing only for brief moments to suckle their infants in the shade of the saman tree.

As Marie approached the tree, the two old crones looked inquiringly at her.

"Is it time?" asked the older of the two, whose wrinkled skin resembled a cracked, dirty mask of grayish clay through which peered two tired, dull eyes and two shriveled, toothless gums.

"Yes, Mama Gi."

"Come then." Mama Gi rose laboriously to her feet and waddled toward a deep ditch that bordered the cart track. Marie followed, moaning softly. They clambered into the ditch; thereupon Mama Gi looked about her and selected a suitable spot. Marie went there and loosened the coarse shift that clung to her body. Her solitary garment fell to the ground, leaving her naked. She lay down in the dust, and bracing her feet firmly against the side of the ditch, raised her arms and caught hold of the roots of a *bayahonda* bush above her head.

"Pull, pull," the old woman admonished. "Pull hard, my cabbage. The harder you pull the sooner the little one will show itself."

Marie pulled with her arms and pushed with her feet, until her body was curved and rigid, and every nerve and muscle trembled and quivered with the convulsive spasms which shook her. Then, suddenly, her torture ended. As a tiny, black morsel of humanity made its appearance Marie gave one last happy gasp. Her body relaxed; she sank back into the thick dust and closed her eyes. Her breasts rose and fell with unnatural rapidity, but gradually their motion grew steadier, and her breathing easier. As a feeble wail told her that her child was alive, a tremulous happy smile parted her lips.

Mother Gi reached out her withered arms for two small, sharp-edged pieces of flinty rock. With these she severed the umbilical cord. She picked up the child, cleansed it after a fashion with leaves and a corner of its mother's robe, and fondled it.

"It is a boy," she informed Marie.

Marie smiled again and opened her eyes. "Poporla will be glad." She held out her arms for her baby and kissed the black, shiny face.

For some minutes they remained in the ditch; Marie, Mama Gi and the baby. Mama Gi sat down on her haunches and rocked to and fro, mumbling a prayer to African gods. A wagon, laden with canes, rumbled cumbrously past. The two men who walked beside it cracking their whips to urge the slow-moving oxen forward, saw Marie and the baby and chanted a spell to frighten off any evil spirits who might be in the neighborhood.

As soon as Mama Gi considered that Marie had rested long enough she motioned the younger woman to rise. They had been absent from the fields long enough, Mama Gi said. Marie rose unsteadily to her feet and donned her shift. With movements that became firmer with each step, she accompanied Mama Gi to the saman tree, laid her baby down upon a heap of trash, and then crossed the fields in the direction of the flashing machetes.

"What shall we call our son?" Marie asked Poporla that night.

"Henri, after our master," replied Poporla, who could only speak in bastard French, although the English had captured the island from the French five years previously.

The next five years were happy ones for Henri, as he played with other children beneath the shade of the saman tree. How could one be other than happy when one's whole life consisted of eating fruit when one was hungry, sucking sugar canes when one was thirsty, and drowsing in the hot sun when one was tired of playing?

Henri's first awareness of slavery came when he was nearly five, for he was claimed by the pickaninnies' gang. Henceforth, instead of playing he had to work with other children of his own age. Under the supervision of an elderly slave woman armed with a vicious-looking switch, the pickaninnies picked up trash and wood for the boiling-house furnaces, collected cane leaves and other edible substances for the cattle, and performed many other light and useful services. But although the children were no longer free to play, the work was not arduous; and the days continued to ring with their shrill laughter as they raced one another to see who could collect the most wood, or teased the slave woman in charge to find out who was the most dexterous in avoiding her stinging switch.

Henri grew up a sturdy youngster, his tall, well-knit frame already showing promise of extraordinary strength. He was not long a member of the pickaninny gang before he became their accepted leader, even though several boys were older than he. Henri proved that he could carry more in one load than any of the gang, could run farther and leap farther than the rest and showed an intelligence far keener than the average slave's. He evolved a game from work. Whenever the boys of the gang gathered wood they secretly split into two forces, one under the leadership of Henri, the other under the leadership of Henri's rival, a slow-witted mulish boy named George. Unknown to the slave woman who had charge of them—and whose switch frequently raised a red weal across their black buttocks—the two forces engaged in a series of mimic warfares: so long as the woman was directly watching one group of boys, its members busily occupied themselves in gathering the wood, and thereby lulled her vigilance. But the moment the woman looked toward the other group, members of the first team would seize a piece of wood, and using it as a spear, would hurl it at a member of the opposing force. Any boy touched by one of these wooden spears was thereafter considered dead and was forbidden, under pain of punishment, to take part in the battle—which raged until every member of one force was "dead."

The side commanded by Henri was invariably victorious. George and his followers never understood the reason, though it was simple. In the first place, Henri maneuvered his troops into a partly protected position, while ensuring that the enemy were left exposed. Secondly, Henri himself was equal to at least half a dozen extra warriors.

His brain was unusually receptive. There was no schooling for slaves; their place in life was to spend their waking hours working for the benefit of the planter who lived in the big white house on top of the hill. But Henri learned many things besides native lore and the ways of the jungle. Without consciously realizing the fact he analyzed and memorized everything that met his inquisitive glance.

For two years Henri remained in the pickaninny gang. Then he was taken away from the pickaninnies and sold to a Negro mason.

All joy left Henri's life when that happened. The mason, who called himself Rougnon, had spent the first forty years of his life as a slave to M. Bellanger's father. As a slave he had been surly and rebellious. Floggings and starvation alike had failed to make him tractable. Had he not shown himself to be an excellent mason, the elder Bellanger would have ordered his death. Instead of having the man executed Bellanger gave Rougnon his freedom and employed him on the estate.

Neither Bellanger père nor his son had had cause to regret having freed Rougnon. As though to prove that he possessed one spark of humanity in his twisted body, Rougnon tried to express his gratitude for his freedom by well and faithfully carrying out all work entrusted to him. But only toward the Bellangers did Rougnon reveal any sign that his heart was softer than the blocks of granite which his fingers cleverly carved into ornamental shapes. He treated his workmen with unparalleled harshness.

For no apparent reason Rougnon felt that he had an antagonist in Henri. Perhaps it was because the boy looked more intelligent than most slaves. From the day Henri was apprenticed to him the mason wasted no opportunity of inflicting some of the horrors that had embittered his life. Each morning Henri was allotted more work before dusk than a grown man could have accomplished. Each evening the boy suffered punishment for his laziness—sometimes he was flogged; sometimes he was hung in ropes from the roof so that he could not lie down all night; sometimes he was merely deprived of food and drink. The very uncertainty as to his inevitable punishment was additional torture.

But there could be no redress for the unfortunate boy. He was a slave, to be treated as his master willed.

CHAPTER NINE

IN Brienne, France, in the year 1779 young Buonaparte was entering the Brienne military academy. A career was opening in accordance with Nabulione's own unswerving intent.

In Paris, recently, an old man, Jean Jacques Rousseau, not wholly sane, struggling to complete his *Confessions*, had died. A life was finished; but the voice echoed on. And in many a country and far island of the world, unaccustomed, unsettling words were in the air: tyranny, equality, liberty, justice.

Henri knew nothing of the war that was shaking Great Britain and her overseas possessions, of which the 133 square miles of Grenada was a small part, until one morning in July of 1779. M. Bellanger's plantation was high up Richmond Hill. From it one could see below the landlocked harbor of St. George, with its line of careened vessels awaiting refitting or repair, the roofs of the harbor town, the squat, gray fort at the end of the promontory that formed the eastern arm of the harbor, and the red roofs of the other part of the town that nestled beneath the promontory on the seaward side. Beyond the gray of the fort, the green vegetation of the promontory, and the red roofs of the town, one could see the blue Caribbean Sea.

Soon after dawn on this fourth of July, 1779, Henri trudged off to M. Bellanger's house, where Rougnon was rebuilding a wing that had been razed by fire the previous April. As he looked out to sea he saw an unusual sight. A mile or two out, making for the island were twenty-four sail that, even to Henri's inexperienced eye, appeared larger and strangely different from the merchantmen that usually visited the island.

It was the French West Indies fleet commanded by Comte d'Estaing. Later that day Henri watched a strong force of French soldiers land to attack the small British garrison.

As soon as the French landed Henri fled from the Bellanger plantation and hid himself among the wild vegetation. There were ships in the harbor, ships that could carry him away from Rougnon, M. Bellanger, Grenada, to some country across the blue Caribbean Sea.

Day was dawning when Henri made his way to the harbor. In the gray light of the thick mist, which was rapidly being dispersed by the cobalt and purple beams of the rising sun, he saw a number of craft idly straining against their hawsers and bumping gently against the quayside. One ship attracted his attention because the deck seemed deserted.

With a quick, shuffling gait he ran across the gangplank and stepped down onto the deck. For a moment he stood irresolute and fearful, for he heard a warning noise from the forecastle. He made for some bales that were waiting to go ashore, but he was too late. Captain Moreau stepped out from the poop door behind him.

"Mother of God! What are you doing here?" Captain Moreau lazily lifted his foot and pushed Henri in the back. The boy reeled across the deck and crashed against the bulwarks. His feet tripped over a bollard, and he fell into the scuppers with a force that brought a chuckle of amusement to the captain's thin lips.

Henri turned to face Moreau.

"Excuse, monsieur," he pleaded. "I want to speak to the captain."

"You are speaking to him, you black-skinned son of Satan. What do you want? If I find out that you came aboard to see what those sooty fingers of yours could pick up, I'll have you tied up to the mizzen there, then I'll flay your filthy back till the skin hangs in ribbons."

"I swear I have taken nothing, Monsieur le Capitaine. May God wither my bowels if I do not speak the truth, monsieur."

Moreau laughed. "A fine heathen you are to swear by God."

"I am good Christian, Monsieur le Capitaine."

"May my own bowels wither if a black-souled son of a heathen like you could be a Christian even if your skin were as fair as the white of your coward's eyes. What do you want?" Moreau repeated irritably.

"I want to leave Grenada, Monsieur le Capitaine."

"By heaven! If you are a God-damned English pig then I am going to pitch your rascally carcass to the sharks." The captain took a threatening step forward.

"No, Monsieur le Capitaine," Henri called out in terror. "Not English. I am a good Frenchman."

"Then why do you want to leave the island, now that our brave sailors have filled the bellies of those cursed English with good French lead, you black-tongued liar?"

"I want to see the world."

"Do you think you can pull the wool over my eyes, you limb of Satan? You are a runaway slave who thought to take advantage of a skirmish to slip his bonds, eh? Back you are going to your lawful master before the sun sets again, and if I do not see as juicy a flogging as ever a man could desire, then I know nothing of West Indian planters."

Moreau laughed hoarsely, stepped across the deck, and caught hold of Henri's arm. With a cruel jerk he swung the boy to his feet.

"What is your name?"

"Henri."

"Which plantation do you belong to?"

"Monsieur Bellanger's."

"Bellanger, eh!" Moreau let go and stepped back a pace. "That is a different story. Bellanger and I are no cronies. He did me a bad turn once, and I should not say nay to repaying that debt with interest. So you are one of Bellanger's slaves, are you?" Moreau's ice-blue eyes inspected the Negro lad and noted with admiration Henri's tall, straight body, his sturdy limbs, his swelling muscles. "You are as fine a specimen of a slave as I have seen for some years. How old are you?"

"Close upon twelve, monsieur."

"Twelve, eh! And you are one of Bellanger's slaves—" A gleam of suspicion revealed itself in Moreau's pale eyes. He grasped the boy's shoulders in his stubby fingers and pressed with such force that the sharp edges of his broken fingernails pierced the black flesh. As tiny drops of blood rolled down Henri's heaving chest and fell on the deck the Negro cried out in pain.

"How do I know you are telling the truth?" Moreau snarled. "How do I know that you haven't heard that Bellanger and I aren't friends and are telling lies so that I shouldn't send you back to your master?"

Henri fell upon his knees. "I swear I tell the truth. I am a Christian, Monsieur le Capitaine. God knows I tell the truth. I was sold to Monsieur Bellanger's mason."

"Rougnon, eh? I know the swine. Why have you run away from him?"

"He beat me and starved me, monsieur. See my back, monsieur."

Henri turned so that his festering, deeply scarred back was visible to the Frenchman.

Moreau examined the countless weals and stripes that puckered the flesh of Henri's back, from the top of the neck to below the buttocks, then shrugged his shoulders.

"That is what comes of freeing slaves," he said contemptuously. There was no sympathy in his voice; only anger that Negroes should be freed and allowed to vent their spleen upon other slaves. Moreau's world was one in which white men were supreme; they alone were fit to possess power of authority. "By God! When I see your back I can well believe that you were Rougnon's apprentice. But no matter whether or no you spoke the truth. I have just thought what to do with you."

"You will not take me back to Monsieur Bellanger?" Henri asked, scarcely able to comprehend his good fortune.

"No, nor to anyone else in Grenada."

"You will take me away, right away?"

"Yes, you lump of ebony! To Saint-Domingue. I'll get good money for you there. We sail at dawn tomorrow so stow your black carcass down in the aft hold."

Henri needed no second bidding. Before the sound of Moreau's last words had died away, the boy was scuttling for the aft hold. Fearless of consequences he leaped down into the black, noisome hold that yawned beneath the hatch.

Henri lay on a bed of tattered sailcloth and listened to the commotion overhead; the noise reverberated through the half-empty hold like the beating of a huge tom-tom.

The atmosphere in the hold was unbearable; only one hatch cover had been lifted, and the stale air hung heavily with little chance of escape. When the sun rose, its fierce rays seemed to penetrate even through the thick timbers of the sunward side of the vessel, and through the calked deck planks. His body broke into a sweat that made his cotton pantaloons cling damply to his body. His stomach rumbled with emptiness. But Rougnon had long since inured him to periods of starvation. Though his throat was dry, his tongue swollen, and his stomach sick, he endured the hardships cheerfully; was he not soon to leave his hated work, and the even more hated mason, forever?

That his future could be other than one of slavery did not occur to him. White men were masters, Negroes were slaves. That fact was an ordinance, it seemed, of Christian God and African gods alike. He had been told stories of another land far, far away where black men were not slaves; but was never able to believe such stories. Black men could never hope to be as white men. A black man could hope for no more than to save enough to buy his freedom, or so to earn the gratitude of a master that freedom was voluntarily conferred.

All that Henri prayed for was that, when he arrived in the new country, he would be lucky enough to find a master who would beat and torture him less than Rougnon had done.

Presently the hatches of the aft hold were removed. Two of the crew

33

climbed down into the hold, for some cargo had come aboard, and they had been sent down to stow it—Moreau had warned them of the boy's presence.

"Hullo, *petit*," greeted François, who lacked one eye, two fingers, and half an ear. "Are you hungry?" He tossed a loaf of bread to the boy and slammed down a pitcher of water which the captain had ordered him to bring down. He saw Henri seize the loaf and bite into it ravenously, so François considered he had been sufficiently answered. He laughed humorously, for this was his first trip to the new world. Indeed, it was his first trip as a sailor. He had been a soldier, until there had been trouble about his stabbing a comrade during a drunken fracas. He had fought in so many battles that parts of him were scattered over half the world—the eye he lost fighting against Clive in India; the two fingers were buried in Ireland, where they had been trampled underfoot while François throttled the man whose saber had severed them. To his dismay, he had been unable to locate the other half of his ear; it had been carried off at Rossbach on the tip of a Prussian's sword; François had failed to catch up with his adversary, although he had run hard, in the hope of recovering and pickling the half of his ear. Because François—until this voyage—had always been a soldier and knew little of life. He had not realized that all white men were masters, all black men slaves. His simple mind believed that all men, whatever their color, were born free.

"So you are going to Saint-Domingue, the captain says," François continued, as he pushed some rubbish out of the way and cleverly squashed a rat to pulp with a hearty kick.

"Yes, monsieur," Henri mumbled, his mouth full.

François gave the other sailor a heavy clap on the back. "Do you hear that, Pedro? He called me monsieur." François laughed loudly. "He is a *petit* after my own heart. He knows quality when he sees it."

Pedro was a Spaniard and had often visited the West Indies. "I would have kicked the hide off him if he had spoken otherwise," he said sourly, speaking in atrocious French. "The boy is a Negro."

"So I see, I am not blind," grunted François as he labored with a heavy sack of cacao that had come from St. Lucia. "What difference does that make?"

"*Madre de Dios!*" Pedro exclaimed in a startled voice. "He is a slave who has run away from his master. If Moreau had any sense he would have returned the boy. He couldn't escape punishment if he were discovered helping a slave to escape."

"A slave!" François repeated and rubbed his blue chin with the three fingers of his left hand. "Why mustn't he go to another country if he wants to?"

"You make me sick with your dullness," spat out Pedro. "Help me with this sack. It weighs like lead."

"I am a simple man. I do not know what a slave is."

"He! He! He!" Pedro roared in a high-pitched laughter. "Haven't I told you that you are a dullard?"

"You will tell me once too often," François threatened, "but I still have five fingers on my right hand capable of squeezing the breath out of

34

your windpipe. One day I'll tell you what happened to the man whose saber cut off these fingers." He held up his left hand.

"You have told me a dozen times already since this voyage began," Pedro pointed out in a conciliatory manner, for he was shorter than François by half a head and weighed many pounds less—and for a man with a simple mind, François was known to possess a murderous nature when his temper was roused. "Do you want to hear what slaves are?"

"Yes, by thunder."

But Pedro did not get an opportunity to supply an explanation. There was an angry roar from the deck above, and the sailors saw Moreau's sharp-featured face framed in the hatchway.

"Below there, you swabs. Get a move on with that cargo. The nigger boy can give you a hand. Get up, you black bastard of Beelzebub, and help if you want more bread."

Henri rose obediently to his feet and assisted François and Pedro to shift some sacks, which smelled sweetly with the aromatic perfume of spices.

CHAPTER TEN

ALL day Henri toiled with François and Pedro—and even the sour-hearted Spaniard recognized the strength and willingness of the young Negro. François, who was extremely garrulous for such a simple-minded man, made the boy blissfully happy by talking to him as man to man. There was no end to the strange stories François would relate to a willing listener; he spoke of a score of things; of life in cultured France; of the strange habits of the shopkeeping English; of the barbaric customs of the savage Irish; of the fabulous fortunes of Indian princes—into Henri's ears he poured a wealth of garbled fact and fancy which made the boy's brain reel. Yet much of what François told Henri that day was stored away in a young brain that never forgot details.

When the hatches were replaced over the hold, Henri made a nest for himself among the sacks of sugar and was asleep before the last stevedore had left the ship.

As a new day dawned a medley of unaccustomed noises awakened Henri from his deep sleep. High above all other sounds he heard Moreau's voice barking a series of orders, but he also distinguished the voices of the sailors—who lustily bawled chanties as they turned the capstan, or sang heaving choruses while they hoisted the topsails and the jib; the high squealing of the blocks; the screeching of the capstan; the explosive flapping of the sail not yet in the teeth of the wind; the stamping of feet upon the deck; the lapping of water against the ship's side. Presently the vessel heeled slightly, as the sails bellied out in the wind, and the lapping became more pronounced; he realized that the voyage to Saint-Domingue had begun.

The passage out of the land-locked harbor was a tricky one, but of the series of tacks that carried the ship to the open sea he saw nothing. For long after the quayside had been left behind he was left in the black hold. But at last a streak of light penetrated the hold, and François's friendly voice bellowed down: "The island's well astern now, *mon petit*, and the captain says you may come up on deck."

Henri stepped out on deck. Above his head full sail was billowing out to a fine, steady breeze. Before him some of the crew were coiling halyards and shrouds or swabbing the deck. One man was at a tub, busily scrubbing clothes; another was hanging out clean clothes on a rope strung from the port to the starboard shrouds. Outside the galley a white boy of his own age was preparing sweet potatoes.

Behind, he saw the outstretched, mountainous island of Grenada. In the foreground, on the poop, the helmsman stood stolidly by the steering wheel, now gazing at the misty horizon ahead, now looking up at the sails, ready to take advantage of any shift of wind by altering course. By him stood Moreau, fierce-eyed and unshaven.

"Get forrard there, and set that black bastard to work, you, François," the captain roared. "And if he slackens off give him a lash on that back of his to remind him he's not yet in his heathen heaven."

"Aye, aye, captain. Come along, *mon petit*, there are ropes to splice." As they hastened along the deck François added in a lower voice: "After a few bottles of rum the captain is none too gentle."

The warning did not alarm Henri. He knew no man could equal the cruelty of Rougnon. Besides, his skin was black. All black men were slaves; to work or be whipped, at the whim of their white masters.

Le Roi de France, skimming across the placid Caribbean Sea, made good time. About noon on the fifteenth day after leaving Grenada—and after having called first at St. Christopher—the vessel rounded Fort Picelot and sailed into a wide bay. Standing on the starboard cathead, Henri had his first glimpse of a town that was one day to be named after him, and of a country that was to ring with the echo of his deeds through-out the centuries.

Stretching out from the cape on their port bow, which the ship had just rounded, the bay swept in a deep curve of palm-fringed coral beach. Its gleaming, dazzling whiteness was emphasized by the peacock blue of the sea, which gently lapped its edge, and by the variegated green of the jungle beyond. Over all towered an ominous, dark mountain mass; it stretched into the dim distance, in ever bleaker, ever mightier ranges, which hid their massive heights in perpetual cloud.

The bay was crowded with merchantment, cutters, caravels, coracles, French men-of-war. Merchantment and innumerable smaller boats, some being rowed, some being sailed, some carrying passengers, some goods. In all directions the bay was in a bustle of activity.

The town beyond sprawled along the seashore, at the foot of the mountains. On the outskirts to the right of the town Henri distinguished the caserne of the French troops. On the peak of a high hill behind these barracks, he saw a square building that—as he afterward learned—was the powder magazine for the batteries that occupied a slight promontory to the left of the caserne, in front of the town. Still farther to the left he saw, high above the roofs of the surrounding buildings, the single spire of the church and a long building with a wing at either end that was the Jesuits' college. Behind, and on the extreme left of the town, he saw a large, artificially protected mound, the Fossette of the Compagnie des Indes.

As *Le Roi de France* approached nearer to land Captain Moreau, dressed more smartly than Henri had yet seen him, began to rasp out orders. The sails were furled. When the bows of the bark no longer moved, the anchor was let go.

Captain Moreau bellowed for the cutter to be lowered. When it was riding the water he signaled to four of the crew—François being one of the four—to take the oars. Then he motioned to Henri.

"Get in there, you black son of Satan. We'll see whether we can find you a new, kindhearted master. And remember one thing—" Moreau glared fiercely, and stabbed a threatening forefinger into the boy's stomach. "If you tell anyone I helped you to escape from Grenada I'll carve that black heart out of your body as sure as I'm captain of this ship. Do you understand?"

"Yes, monsieur."

"You've not come from Grenada but from Saint Christopher. Is that clear? I bought you in Saint Christopher."

"Perfectly, monsieur."

Henri climbed down and took his place in the boat. Moreau—carrying a flat, black leather case crammed with papers—followed him down. One of the oarsmen pushed off, and the four seamen pulled for the shore.

They landed at a jetty at the south end of the town. As Moreau stepped ashore he tossed the leather case to François.

"Carry that, and accompany us to the agents."

"Aye, aye," François growled, pleased at the opportunity of stretching his legs.

"You, too," Moreau barked at Henri.

Henri joined François. Side by side, with Moreau in front, they walked toward the center of the town.

They soon found themselves in the midst of an indescribable medley of noise and color, turmoil and commotion, that astonished Henri and François alike. The streets were crowded with people. There were French soldiers from the casernes, in cocked hats, long buttoned tunics, breeches, and gaiters; sailors from the men-of-war in cocked hats, pea jackets, petticoat trousers, and buckled shoes, and their officers in blue coats with white facings and gold buttons, over long white waistcoats, white knee breeches, white stockings, buckle shoes, and gold-braided, three-cornered cocked hats. There were planters—European and Creole—dressed in the latest Paris mode. There were the planters' womenfolk in fine muslin dresses with long, pointed waists, laced bodices, elbow-length sleeves frilled with lace.

These, for the most part, comprised the white people, but they represented by far the smallest proportion of the occupants of the streets of Cap François, for the planters numbered but 15 per cent of the popula-

37

tion, though they owned 90 per cent of the land. There were the people of color, of every shade ranging from the rich chocolate brown of the sacatra to a sickly white of the *sangmêlé*, dressed in clothes which varied from the silks, the satins, the muslins, the lace, and the embroideries—in gaudier, brighter shades—of the planters, to the cotton, the broad-cloth, and the trash of the slaves.

Lastly, there were the Negroes. Many of the men wore only a pair of tattered trousers; women, dressed in coarse Osnaburg chemises, their heads bound with gaudy blue and white scarves; and children, naked as the day they were born. These were the slaves of the white population, come to Cap François to haggle in the markets, to buy or sell, to convey messages, to carry goods, to transport produce to the warehouses, to return to the plantations with goods imported from Paris, to do one or more of a thousand tasks.

Though confused enough by the medley of sensations, Henri had further cause for wonder in the size and the length of the streets, the stateliness of the buildings. As they proceeded along paved streets through the town, they passed beautiful churches; gardens laid out with brilliant, tropical plants; private houses, stone built, of considerable size and magnificence, with cupolas and balconies; squares decorated with statues and cooled by fountains; shops displaying incredibly luxurious merchandise; cafés filled with noble clients. For such was the town of Cap François in the year 1779—the Paris of the West Indies—a town of luxury and refinement, of unprecedented trade and commerce—the rich center of the richest country in the rich new world.

Captain Moreau's business with the shipping agents took him only thirty minutes. Meanwhile, François and Henri stood in the street, awaiting him. Both, in their own way, were still amazed, though to François the refinement of Cap François was the refinement of a Europe to which he was no stranger, even if he could marvel at the luxuriance and the coloring of the vegetation. But Henri had only seen the town of St. George from a distance, and St. George was far smaller, less blatant than Cap François. He had not realized there could be so many buildings, so many white masters, so many slaves in the whole world. The bustling turmoil of his surroundings stirred him. He offered up a childish paean of thanks to God for having allowed a poor slave boy to escape from Grenada and come to Saint-Domingue. Surely Saint-Domingue must be the most marvelous place in the world. He would be happy, being a slave in Saint-Domingue.

When Captain Moreau left the agents he made for a building at the northwest end of the town. Accompanied by the same two companions, he led the way across rue Espagnole and continued as far as the rue Sainte Avoile, whence they could see the Fossette. Afterward he returned through the town in an easterly direction, past the Jesuit college and grounds and then down the rue Marie into the Place d'Armes.

There an amazing scene presented itself. The square was dotted with awnings under which tables had been placed. At each table sat French naval officers in bright blue and gold uniforms, busily engaged in filling up papers that were spread over each table. Surrounding the tables were clustered men of all colors—white men, black men, mulattoes.

"Mother of God!" Moreau exclaimed. "What is happening?"

"Monsieur le Comte d'Estaing has arrived with the French fleet, monsieur."

"I know that," Moreau said irritably. "I saw his ships in the bay. What are his officers doing at those tables?"

"The French Government is sending an army to America to help the colonists defeat the cursed British. Saint-Domingue has been ordered to supply a quota of fifteen hundred men. The officers are taking down the names of men willing to go and help the American colonists fight for liberty and independence." There was a faint sneer in the voice of the mulatto with whom he spoke.

Moreau's thin lips parted in a grim smile. "Are you volunteering?"

"Not I, monsieur. I have a small plantation, a wife, and two children. I am content, and I have my freedom. Why should I risk my life fighting for the American colonists?"

"The world could afford to lose a few of you and your kind," Moreau barked. He walked on and pushed his way through a crowd of shuffling Negroes toward one of the tables. Upon arriving close to the table he halted and chuckled at the sight of the young officer who scratched away with a pen that spattered the ink in all directions. He heard Moreau laugh, and looked up.

"Well, have you come to volunteer for the American war? We want fifteen hundred men. There is still time for you to enlist."

"Not I," Moreau said. "I am no friend of the American colonists. They can sizzle in hell, for all I care whether they stick the cursed English in their bellies, or whether the English carve the scalps off their heads. Let them murder one another to extinction, say I, and leave us in peace."

"If the colonists win the war it will mean the downfall of England," the officer declared.

"So much the better."

"Then why not help a good cause?"

"Me and my barque are my good cause. Why not send the mulattoes and the Negroes to fight with the colonists?"

"We are doing so." The officer looked critically at Henri. "What about the boy? He looks as if he should shape up to be a good fighter."

"Maybe, but you cannot enlist him."

"Why not?"

"He is a slave."

"We are enlisting slaves."

"Not this one. I paid good money for him in Saint Christopher a few days ago. I want to sell him."

"Well, the navy is not buying slaves," said the officer curtly. With a mocking laugh Moreau turned away.

"One moment, monsieur," the naval man called out.

"Yes, monsieur?"

"Do you say the boy is for sale?"

"At a good price."

"Is he strong and healthy?"

"Look at him, monsieur. He is already a well-built boy. He will be a strapping man in two or three years' time."

"I could do with a servant. What is his name?"

"Henri," replied Moreau. Then he added: "Henri Christophe, after Saint Christopher, where I bought him."

"I will buy him, if we can agree on a price."

"What is the market price for slaves?"

The naval man shook his head. "I do not know."

Moreau smiled crookedly. "Then I will take four thousand livres for him," he said, naming double the market rate ruling at that time.

And so Henri Christophe changed hands and became the property of Cornet Jourdain of the French frigate, the Ville de Paris.

CHAPTER ELEVEN

JOURDAIN took Henri with him when he sailed with D'Estaing's fleet on France's abortive expedition against British-held Savannah in the American colonies.

Within two months, D'Estaing had returned with his fleet to Cap François. There after a time he received orders to return to France. Jourdain sold Henri to M. Coidovid, the free Negro who owned the hotel in which Jourdain had stayed. Thus Henri Christophe became stableboy at the Hôtel de la Couronne.

Henri's life, though monotonous in daily tasks, was now filled with interest by the goings and comings at the hotel. One day, soon after the French fleet had sailed away from Saint-Domingue, he cleared out the hotel stables. A dark shadow crossed the patch of sunshine just inside the door where he was scraping the baked earth free of some freshly dropped dung. He looked up.

"Good morning, Monsieur Toussaint," he murmured as he recognized the face of the Comte de Bréda's coachman.

Toussaint was some thirty-six years of age, of moderate stature, his shoulders broad, his limbs straight and firm-fleshed, and by his upright carriage one gained the impression that his body was supple and healthy. His face was particularly striking. Its firm contour, the keen expression in the dark, intelligent eyes, and the high forehead above suggested unusual character. Here was no ordinary slave fit only for the most elementary tasks of menial labor. His alert expression suggested intellectual powers of a high degree.

"Good morning, Henri," Toussaint greeted him in his gentle voice. "Monsieur Coidovid informs me that you are now his slave."

"Yes. When Monsieur Jourdain returned to France he sold me to Monsieur Coidovid."

"I am glad that you are working here. I think you will be happy. Is that his young daughter he is playing with at this moment?"

"Yes. Monsieur Coidovid plays often with Mademoiselle Marie Louise."

Toussaint nodded. "I often pass by here, Henri, so I'll hope to see and talk to you frequently."

Henri was surprised and flattered. "Thank you, monsieur," he acknowledged, and wondered why his older man should wish to waste his time talking to one so much younger than himself.

Toussaint smiled as he realized the trend of the boy's thoughts. Upending a wooden bucket he sat down.

"Do you wonder why I am interested in you? I'll tell you. I was born on one of the Comte de Bréda's plantations and was baptized in the Holy Catholic Church; a Negro, Pierre-Baptiste, was my godfather. He was a man of piety and intellect. He had been educated by a missionary who taught him to read and write French, Latin, and some geometry. Though I am healthy enough now, as a child I was nicknamed Fatras-Bâton, because I was so weak. Fortunately I had an indulgent master who took as much care of his slaves as he did of his other property. I was not made to work very hard, so Pierre-Baptiste saw that I spent some time in study. The knowledge that Pierre-Baptiste had learned from the missionary he passed on to me, Henri. Now I, in my turn, will pass it on to you."

Henri grimaced. His plans did not include having his brain stuffed with Latin, geometry, reading, and writing.

His expression revealed his thoughts only too clearly. The coachman leaned forward and held the boy's arm.

"Listen, boy," he began earnestly. "The world is changing. A new spirit of tolerance is spreading. Other people are beginning to share the views of Abbé Raynal."

"What does Monsieur l'Abbé say?"

"He says that liberty is everyone's property; that there are three kinds of liberty—a natural liberty, civil liberty, political liberty."

"What does he mean?"

"Natural liberty is the liberty of the man; civil liberty is the liberty of the citizen; political liberty is the liberty of the community. Natural liberty, he says, is the right that nature has given to everyone to dispose of himself according to his own will. Without liberty, or the possession of one's own body and the enjoyment of one's own mind, one has neither wife, father, relation, nor friend. Without liberty one can have neither country, friend, nor God. The slave, an instrument in the hands of wickedness, is less than the dog that the Spaniards let loose against runaway slaves."

Henri repeated one phrase, which burned itself indelibly on his young memory. Natural liberty is the right that nature has given to everyone to dispose of himself according to his own will! "But we cannot dispose of ourselves according to our own wills, Monsieur Toussaint."

"Only because white men have robbed us of our natural rights."

"Why doesn't God punish the white men for defying Him?"

41

"The Bible says: 'Have confidence in the Lord with all thy heart, and lean not upon thy own prudence.' It is not for mankind to ask God for an explanation of His mysteries."

"But Monsieur Toussaint: If one white man says that we should not be slaves, why do other white men keep us in slavery?"

"Because, boy, the Abbé Raynal is a God-fearing Christian, which not all other white men are."

He felt Henri tremble with excitement. "Don't mistake me," he warned the boy. "The time is not ripe. As yet, for every one who would free the black man from his bonds, there are ten financially interested in keeping us slaves, but one day the half a million slaves of Saint-Domingue will be freed. But the black people of this country must have leaders to guide them in the ways of wisdom and direct their footsteps along the paths of self-control to prosperity, else their freedom will prove as empty an advantage as Esau's mess of pottage.

"Who among us is worthy of such a responsibility? Alas! I know of none. Nevertheless, we should try to prepare our people for that day of emancipation by instructing our leaders now, that they may be able to use that liberty when it comes."

Toussaint held the boy's gaze with his own steady eyes. "I believe that you, Henri Christophe, should prepare yourself for that leadership. You are young, and have more intelligence than most of our people who have been degraded by slavery. If you are willing I will teach you, but what about you? Are you ready to sacrifice your leisure and to study hard?"

Henri nodded.

Thereafter Toussaint Bréda and Henri Christophe met frequently. Toussaint had a receptive student. Yet, strange to say, he never succeeded in teaching the boy to read or write. Perhaps Henri was too impatient, too old in experience to learn to walk before he ran. Nevertheless Toussaint was not dissatisfied. With great care he nurtured the bud that was already straining to burst into bloom.

Another incident occurred soon after the French fleet had sailed for Europe.

A white man who for some hours had been drinking steadily at the hotel bar reeled into the courtyard to relieve himself. As he unsteadily crossed to a far corner he whooped with joy.

"By thunder! If it is not my little blackbird I see before me then the rum that black rogue has been selling is fouler than it tastes." His hearty slap made Henri reel.

"Good evening, Monsieur François," he spluttered.

"What are you doing here? I thought you had gone to France with that whippersnapper officer of yours."

"Monsieur Jourdain sold me to Monsieur Coidovid, who is the inn-keeper here."

"Then you are a lucky devil, my boy, for who wants to go to France when they can stop in this paradise of wine and women?" François hic-cuped loudly. "My lad, I never knew there were such women in the wide world. Their breasts are like the mountains of Saint-Domingue, hard and large, with peaks to make a man long to scale them. And what is more, *mon petit*, the girls don't say no to a man who likes mountain climbing." François roared with laughter. "As for the rum, I can get drunk here for less than half what it costs in France. This to France"—he belched so explosively that the boy chuckled.

Presently he reeled back to the bar, and Henri did not see him again that night. But the next morning, François, none the worse for his carouse, strode round to the hotel stables.

"Ah, my young blackhearted son of a heathen, I'm glad to see you working hard. Hard work never hurt man nor beast." He chuckled loudly. "And François is no man. He is an old soldier—and what old soldiers do is for nobody to ask questions about."

"Monsieur François, would you tell me about France?"

"What do you want to know about France, you little bastard?"

"What is the King like, and all the people who rule the country?"

"King Louis! You have asked the right man to tell you about him. Haven't I fought for him and his father since I was your age? Many a time I've seen him in his palaces at Fontainebleau and Versailles."

"Then tell me of him, please, Monsieur François," Henri pleaded.

"God's thunder! What is the world coming to? A nigger boy with a thirst for knowledge?" François roared with good-natured laughter, but presently he began to speak of King Louis XV and his mistresses, of King Louis XVI, his queen Marie Antoinette, of Fontainebleau, of Versailles, of the Prussian Frederick's palace of Sans-Souci, and other palaces in different parts of the world; for François, being a simple-minded man and having no prejudices about slaves and the color of a man's skin—and having no children of his own, at least none that he knew of—was fond of the young slave.

So François often spent an hour or two describing a world where only white men lived, and where there were kings and queens, and dukes and counts, and palaces and fortresses.

And Coidovid, who grew genuinely to like the boy, permitted him to talk to François and Toussaint; and, later, removed him from the stables, gave him a suit of good clothes, and promoted him to the billiard room, where he served drinks to the white planters and marked up their scores as they played.

CHAPTER TWELVE

THE events of Duncan Stewart's first week in London passed as in a dream, in which hard work played no small part, for Dr. Anderson, most indulgent of men while on holiday, was a martinet thereafter. He spared nobody, least of all himself. At first, the boy was affected by this rigorous application to work in which every member of the household conspired. Confused by the noise from cobbled streets that everlastingly echoed with the clatter of traffic, bewildered by the constant meeting with strange manners, strange habits, strange people, strange talk; fatigued by the softer air, dismayed by the lack of boundless scenery to gaze at, Duncan thought that life consisted of little but work. From the moment he placed his head on the pillow in his attic room at night, he slept soundly until old Blodgett awakened him early the following morning.

On the morning of the eighth day, Duncan awakened of his own accord. The day had only just dawned, and Blodgett was not likely to appear for at least another half hour.. Happy in this knowledge, for the bed was comfortable and warm, which the room was not, the boy stared through the small, sloping skylight at the gray, cloudy sky, which reminded him of Scotland. He thought of the home that he had deserted, of his father whom he hated. Nothing could change that hate, which had become part of him. He thought of Elspeth less as someone whom he had loved than as someone who had served his purpose and was now dead.

With somber eyes he inspected the bare attic; its one redeeming point was its cleanliness. The contrast between the cheerlessness of the attic and the splendor of the rooms below was so startling that it set his probing, eager mind to wondering whether there could be other people as rich as Dr. Anderson. He thought of the many pairs of fine boots that the servants had daily to clean, of the silver salvers, tea sets, vases, tantalus, all of which had to be kept in a state of dazzling spotlessness. He thought of the fragile porcelain ornaments that filled two whatnots in the withdrawing room and overflowed onto the mantel and the top of the harpsichord.

Then there were the pictures—dark, stately portraits of bewigged men with staring eyes, and big-bosomed women clothed in classical draperies. There were the heavy velvet and brocade curtains, the heavy brass fenders, the chandeliers at night twinkled not with the one homemade tallow "dip" he had always known, but with six, nine, even twelve wax candles.

Above all, there was the surgery. Its cleanliness and tidiness had become Duncan's special responsibility. It was this room that claimed his attenion almost to the exclusion of all else. It was large, and lighted during daylight hours by two high, narrow windows, out of which Duncan could see nothing but the sky, for the sill was well above the level of his eyes. At night, two chandeliers, each holding six candles, were available, but they were rarely used, for Dr. Anderson seldom remained in the surgery after dark. Three of the walls were almost entirely covered with shelves. In one part of the room, the shelves were devoted solely to books, where Hippocrates rubbed covers with Caelius Aurelianus and Galen, and countless other works. The remainder of the shelves contained supplies for compounding the remedies that a physician commonly found himself in the necessity of prescribing, and also the requisite ingredients for preparing the famous gout alleviator, and the particular syrups and unguents, of which Anderson alone knew the secret formulas and from which he derived considerable profit and neatly arranged were a small regiment of scalpels, probes, forceps, and graded pestles and mortars.

44

Against the general impression of stern physic and stale blood there was a reminder of sweeter things in the faint tantalizing aroma of the gentler herbs and spices.

Stretched along the entire length of the wall beneath the two windows was a plain wooden bench, which Anderson used for dissecting purposes. He was a great admirer of William and John Hunter. Some years previously he had visited John Hunter's famous menagerie and museum at Earl's Court. Thereafter, Anderson had devoted most of his spare time to studying surgical pathology and comparative anatomy, in the more modern principles and practices of which he found it difficult to believe with wholehearted enthusiasm, but which, notwithstanding, he sought to confirm or contradict from his own research and experience. On this bench the doctor was in the habit of disjointing the carcasses of rabbits, cats, dogs, monkeys, lambs and even parts of horses which had died in the near-by stables. In the course of years the bench had become blackened from the stains of blood, excrement, urine, bile, and the like.

These dissections Anderson usually caried out on the best lighted part of the bench, which was the middle. At one end was a wooden box in which he placed his surgical instruments after use. At the other was an ewer of water, a basin, a cake of soap, and a towel.

A massive wooden chair stood in the middle of the floor, directly facing one of the two windows. This was the chair where patients sat for examination. Those who wanted teeth extracted also sat in this chair and had their arms securely bound to the arms, to prevent interrupting the doctor at the crisis of the operation.

Duncan's thoughts were interrupted by the opening of his bedroom door. Boldgett entered and stumped across the floor to the bedside with rheumatic limbs. He was old and no longer fit for physical work, but he had not lost the knack of directing the toil of others, and his eyes were almost as sharp as Mrs. Jones's, the housekeeper.

As soon as Blodgett reached the bedside he stretched out a shaky arm toward Duncan's shoulder; but it did not reach its destination, for the old man saw that the boy's eyes were open and staring gravely at him.

"So you are already awake, Master Duncan, are you?"

"Aye," Duncan answered shortly.

"Not aye," Blodgett reproved. "You must say yes. You do not hear the Master saying aye, do you, Master Duncan? And he is a Scotsman, the same as yourself."

"Nae, I havenae heard the doctor saying aye."

Blodgett shook his head. "Master Duncan! Master Duncan! Not 'havenae.' 'Have not! Have not!' Bless my soul, no wonder you try Miss Frilby's patience, and she so good as to try and teach you handwriting and reading and sums, like the young mistresses learn."

"I dinna want tae learn handwriting and sums. I want to be a physician. And surgeon," he added, as an afterthought in the light of recently acquired knowledge.

"And who has ever heard of a physician that could not write and do sums? You will never be a physician if you do not pay attention to what

45

Miss Frilby tells you. But 'tis time you were up and doing, my boy. Rouse yourself." Blodgett caught hold of the bedclothes, and pulled them back to expose Duncan's curled-up body.

The boy rose from the bed and padded across the floor to the wash-stand. Taking care to keep his back toward Blodgett he bent over the tin basin and made a pretense of energetically lathering his face with the bar of crude soap. At the same time he noisily splashed the water with his finger tips.

Blodgett was not deceived. He chuckled mirthlessly and stumped nearer to the door, from which position he could plainly see the boy. "Dip your face into the water, Master Duncan. Right in, now, or you will find me doing it for you. Now use the soap. Plenty of it. Plenty of it. What will Miss Frilby say to me if she sees you with that streak of dirt round your ears? And the Master, too. He can't bear the sight of dirty young varmints."

With a sigh Duncan resigned himself to the ice-cold water and washed his face and hands clean. When he was dry he attired himself in the serge suit, the open-necked shirt, the white worsted stockings, and the shoes, all of which the doctor had bought for him in Stirling. As soon as he had finished dressing, and Blodgett was satisfied with the boy's appearance, they left the bedroom and proceeded downstairs to the breakfast room. Breakfast was laid, but the room was empty. With a warning to Duncan not to touch any food until Miss Frilby's arrival, a warning that Duncan's behavior on the first few days made necessary, the old servant went out.

Five minutes later Miss Frilby, accompanied by Anderson's three daughters, entered the breakfast room.

"Good morning, Duncan," she greeted primly, with a quick, critical inspection of the boy's face, hands, and clothes.

"Gude marning, Miss Frilby," he replied sullenly. He did not like Miss Frilby.

"Now, Duncan, how many more times must I tell you to say good morning, and not 'gude marning'? You are no longer in your own bar-barous country. You are in London and must try to behave more like a little English gentleman and less like an uncouth peasant. Say, good morning."

"Good morning," he repeated.

"That is better. Now, girls, say good morning to Duncan."

"Good morning, Duncan," Jean and Margaret said together. Elizabeth dreamily added her echo.

"Good morning," Duncan replied.

Miss Frilby marched to the head of the small table. The four children meekly followed. When each was standing in his place, Miss Frilby bowed her head, closed her eyes.

"For what we are about to receive may the Lord make us truly thank-ful. Amen. Be seated, children." Miss Frilby rang the tiny hand bell that stood on the table. Blodgett and Jackson entered, the latter carrying a bowl of steaming oatmeal porridge. Under Miss Frilby's watchful eyes the meal proceeded quietly, decorously. None of the children spoke, unless previously spoken to by the governess or to ask for something to be passed.

At last the meal was over. Miss Frilby gazed at the four eager faces in turn. "You may now talk, children," she said graciously. "But remember what I have told you, Duncan, about speaking and behaving like a little English gentleman."

Miss Frilby's words were a prelude for an outburst of conversation, but high above Jean's quiet questions and Elizabeth's plea to Miss Frilby for "a stowy" rose Margaret's chanting voice. "Duncan cannot spell dog, Duncan cannot spell dog. D-O-G, dog. D-O-G, dog."

"Hush! Stop, Margaret, this very moment," Miss Frilby reproved. "You are a very rude girl."

"And a cruel girl," Jean added.

"I am not cruel, Jean."

"You are."

"I am not. Duncan cannot spell dog."

Miss Frilby stamped her foot. "Be quiet, Jean. Be quiet, Margaret. You, Jean, must not interrupt me when I am speaking to Margaret."

"But she is a cruel girl for saying Duncan cannot spell dog."

"That is for me to point out. As for you, Margaret, I am ashamed of you. It is no disgrace for Duncan not to know how to spell dog. He has not had the advantages which you have had. Duncan is only beginning his education. You have been learning how to spell for a long time."

"I ken many things she doesnae ken," Duncan boasted.

"Know, Duncan, know. Not 'ken.'"

"What sort of things do you know, Duncan?" Jean asked.

"I know why you cannae—cannot milk a coo—cow until she's had a calf," Duncan boasted. "And how to tell when she's ready to calve—"

Miss Frilby's cheeks flamed. She interrupted with a sharp, "Duncan Stewart!"

Duncan shuffled his feet, stared sullenly down at his plate. "Weel!"

"It is monstrous that a boy of your age should possess such knowledge, but that, I suppose, is what comes of a child having an upbringing such as yours. But listen to me, Duncan Stewart. Such subjects are not for the ears of young ladies. You are never, never to mention these and kindred matters to anyone. To anyone, do you understand! Unless you give me your promise to be careful in future I shall recommend to Dr. Anderson that you leave the house."

The threat made Jean unhappy.

"Miss Frilby! Please, please do not say anything to Papa," she pleaded.

"Hold your tongue, Jean. This is my business." Miss Frilby stared sternly at Jean through her spectacles. Jean's lips trembled, and her eyes began to fill with tears. Then Miss Frilby turned toward Duncan again. "Give me your promise never to speak of such things."

"What things?"

"Of—of—farm animals and—and their habits," she stammered.

Duncan hesitated before replying, because he could not properly understand the demand. Jean stretched out her foot and lightly kicked his leg. When he glanced up Jean nodded her head affirmatively.

47

"Aye," Duncan agreed shortly. Then he corrected himself. "Yes."

Miss Frilby's severity relaxed. "That is a good boy, Duncan," she said.

Elizabeth tugged at the governess's sleeve. "What is a—a calf, Miss Fwilby?" she asked.

After breakfast came, for Duncan, the happiest period of the day. While the three sisters went with Miss Frilby to the schoolroom for their morning lessons, Duncan proceeded to the surgery. It was empty, for Dr. Anderson was not due there for at least another hour, but there was plenty of work awaiting Duncan.

He swept the surgery floor, cleaned the instruments and then started dusting the books.

Until he had come to London Duncan had known nothing of books, but he had quickly learned to love them; especially those in the surgery. Merely to touch the tomes gave him exquisite pleasure, an inexpressible thrill that surprised Anderson every time he was made aware of the fact by the eagerness in Duncan's voice when he asked a question about the books, by the light in his eyes whenever he gazed at the shelves, by the gentleness with which he handled the volumes.

Duncan was still dusting the books when Anderson entered the surgery.

"Good morning, Duncan."

"Good morning, sir."

"I see you are dusting the books again. You must be careful not to rub away the covers, my boy. Do you wish you could read them?"

"Yes, sir."

"The more attention you pay to the lessons Miss Frilby gives you, the sooner you will be able to read and digest the contents of those books." His manner became brisker. "Now to work. We have a busy morning before us. There is a plaister to be made up for Robert Day, a troche for Lord March, and we must not forget Mrs. Charles Montagu's medicine, Duncan. She is sending a footman for it at eleven of the clock precisely."

After dinner came the most detested period of the day, when Duncan had to accompany the girls to the schoolroom, there to share in their lessons, but he rebelled secretly, for he knew that open defiance would result in his conduct being reported to the doctor. Only from spelling did he derive any pleasure, for he recognized that the quicker he could spell, the sooner he would be able to master the secrets of medicine locked up in the doctor's library. In his spelling Duncan made a quick and steady progress that gratified the conscientious Miss Frilby.

Dr. Anderson's three daughters enjoyed the company of their adopted brother—as they chose to regard the newcomer, though his exact status in the household was still somewhat obscure to everyone concerned, including Anderson himself. Each regarded him in a different light—Jean, as a companion with whom she could exchange confidences and secrets, and a playmate with whom to play mother and father, and tag, and hopscotch, and seesaw. Margaret was just as eager to play with Duncan, but she used him as a convenient butt for all her varying moods. She derived immense satisfaction from teasing him; from seeing his cheeks redden and his lips tremble with anger as he glowered at her. More especially did she derive a malicious satisfaction from her mischievous pranks when she discovered that, never mind how many devils she succeeded in luring into his eyes, never mind how incoherent he became with savage fury, he never (by deed, at any rate) attempted to retaliate. In Jean, some sense of this restraint of Duncan's may have been the reason for her often defending him. To Margaret it was a chance to make him dance to her tune.

Elizabeth accepted Duncan's presence with an equanimity that was natural to her. When he played with her, she was delighted. When he was not able to do so, she did not repine. She played with her dolls instead.

CHAPTER THIRTEEN

WITH the passing years, Duncan came to be accepted as one of the family. He worked hard in the schoolroom and quickly mastered all the knowledge that Miss Frilby had to impart. He became a scholar at Westminster School and spoke with an accent that was no more pronounced than Anderson's. He worked equally hard in the surgery, and Anderson derived the pleasure he had anticipated from teaching the boy the rudiments of medicine and the science of surgery.

Duncan frequently accompanied Anderson on professional visits. Anderson was inviarably dressed in the full wig and the black velvet coat of his profession, and he carried with him the professional gold-headed cane containing preventives against infection in the cupped handle. Together they went to the Hall of the Masters, Governors, and Commonalty of the Art and Science of Surgery, which was situated in Old Bailey; there, they frequently watched the dissection of bodies of executed criminals. They often visited the hospitals—Guy's Hospital, the Westminster Dispensary, the City of London Lying-in Hospital, the Lock Hospital, the Smallpox Hospital.

Thus Duncan added to his store of knowledge and enthusiastically prepared himself against the great day when he would apply to the Court of Examiners sitting in Surgeons' Hall for their diploma.

CHAPTER FOURTEEN

ARMAND DE GALINIERE, a dilettante spendthrift of the court of Louis XVI, awoke one morning in 1788 to the uncomfortable knowledge that he must precipitately flee his debtors or languish forever forgotten in the Bastille. Bemoaning his harsh fate, he arrived in London. From the moment the Dover-bound packet boat had lifted its bows to the mountains of creaming water that hurled themselves landward from a Channel violently agitated by a freshening southwesterly storm he was sick. As the clouds rotated in dizzy circles, and his stomach sank to depths far below the heaving surface of the water, he lost all interest in his past. Only the dismal present remained to him—a dreadful, nauseating present. With each swift lurch into the trough of the waves, Armand died anew—and vomited afresh. All that he had eaten that day, and the day before, he gave back to the ungrateful world.

The arrival of the packet in Dover harbor was insufficient to reassure Armand that he was still in the land of the living. Two burly seamen carried first his luggage, and then Armand himself, to shore, where they put him into the coach for London.

The journey to London served finally to convince Armand that he was a doomed man. When the coach drew up at the Golden Cross Inn, Charing Cross, the Frenchman remained seated long after the other travelers had left the coachyard. Presently the head drawer espied and shook Armand's knee. Armand groaned loudly but did not open his eyes.

"This is the Golden Cross, sir. The coach goes no farther."

"I cannot move. I am dying."

The drawer was startled. "Bless my soul!" He scarcely knew what to do with dying men. He stood still and stared at the handsome face, which looked very white in the dark, grimy interior of the coach. "Bless my soul! You mustn't die in the coach, sir. 'Tain't seemly, to my way of thinking, a-dying in a coach. You would be more comfortable in a bed." The drawer saw the coachman come out of the inn and wipe his mouth with the sleeve of his greatcoat. "Hey! Come here, Bill."

Bill lumbered across the cobbled square. "Yus, Joe," he wheezed, tainting the air about him with the smell of onions, beer, and horseflesh.

Joe pointed to the traveler inside the coach. "That there gent says he's a-dying. A coach ain't no place to die in, is what I says. Help me to carry him inside and put him to bed."

The coachman struggled with his greatcoat and presently succeeded in pulling a huge red handkerchief from the pocket of his breeches. "If he be a-dying, why not let him die in the coachyard instead of a-mucking up a clean pair of sheets?" He loudly blew his nose.

Joe shook his head. "That's what comes of having no imagination, Bill. He brought luggage with him, didn't he?"

"Yus."

"Then, if a man dies and owes a reckoning for board and lodging, ain't it fit and proper to collect just dues by helping ourselves to a bit of luggage?"

Bill pulled off his triangular hat and scratched his greasy head. "Some people knows how to many money, some people does."

"And there are some as doesn't," Joe explained. "That's why they stays coachmen."

Together the two men assisted Armand to a bedroom and laid him on the bed.

"He do seem bad. Worse'n he was at Dover," Bill said.

"Un médecin, vite! Dieu! Je meurs! Un médecin—"

"What's he saying?" Bill asked, with relief.

"Sounds like he's asking for some medicine." Joe slapped his knee. "I'll get him a physician. There's that young gentleman in the taproom—" Leaving Bill to watch the traveler, Joe hurried from the bedroom and stumped downstairs to the taproom.

There he peered through the blue haze, and tried to distinguish among the numerous occupants the face of the man he thought was a physician. The low-ceilinged room was crowded.

Presently Joe espied the party for whom he was looking. Four young bloods, who had arrived too late to secure a private room, were seated at a table near the door that opened onto the coachyard. They were all of an age, dressed in the extravagant clothes of the London rakes, of luxurious cloth lined with contrasting satin, edged with sable and ermine, and befrogged with braid; with waistcoat and tight breeches of the same satin as the coat lining, and as lavishly ornamented. On the table around which the four men sat were several bottles; neatly arranged before each man was a line of small and large tankards. The large tankards were filled with the highly intoxicating Yorkshire brewed and matured beer and each of the smaller vessels contained a different liquor: brandy, port wine, rum, the increasingly popular champagne, and the newly fashionable sherry. Some of the contents of each glass had already disappeared; already the four men were hilarious as they beat time on the tabletop and chanted scandalous lampoons that were the rage of London taverns and coffeehouses.

The head drawer elbowed his way toward that table. "Excuse me, gentlemen—"

Ignoring Joe's presence, one of the young men jumped to his feet and began to sing.

"Gentlemen, *please*."

The singing tailed off. The four men looked at Joe.

"It's our friend, Joe," the rhymer called out gaily. "Joe, my man, have you heard the latest Peter Pindar?"

"Mr. Fletcher, please—"

Joe was not allowed to finish the sentence.

"More Peter Pindar! More Peter Pindar!" shouted Edward Dayes.

"Gentlemen, please listen to me," the drawer entreated.

Fletcher shook his head at Dayes. "Edward, I am ashamed of you. Tonight we are gathered together to celebrate the acceptance of your picture for public exhibition at the Royal Academy, and all you can think of is ribaldry and Peter Pindar."

"More Peter Pindar! More Peter Pindar!" Dayes demanded.

The cadet shrugged his shoulders with a resigned air. "You see, Joe, my public demands it of me." Swaying unsteadily he leaned nearer to the drawer. "My good man, have you heard about the death of Lady Mount-Edgcumbe's favorite pig?"

"No, sir, but I want to ask a question—"

" 'But me no buts,' my man, but listen—:

> "O dry that tear, so round and big;
>   Nor waste in sighs your precious wind!
> Death only takes a single Pig—
>   Your Lord and Son are still behind."

51

Once more Pindar's scandalous verse received acclaim. Fletcher tried to bow, but sat down heavily. "A toast!" he called out. "A toast to our most notorious satirist."

"To Peter Pindar!" his companions toasted.

Each man in the party drank deeply, then replaced the tankard on the table. For a moment there was a brief lull in their hilarity, of which Joe took quick advantage.

"Isn't one of you gentlemen a physician?"

Callcott laughed hoarsely. "In my youth I studied the noble profession of medicine. But the sight and smell of blood sickened me, my man. I am no doctor. I am a musician, having the degree of Musical Bachelor—"

"And composer," Fletcher added thickly.

"And composer," Callcott agreed. "Winner of many Catch Club prizes—but I am no physician. Nor, mark you, my man, is my dear friend Edward Dayes, who pretends to be an artist so that he may have the excuse of disrobing succulent females and seeing them as Nature has molded them. As for Dick Fletcher, shortly to be gazetted to the Royal Artillery, we pray, he is a Woolwich cadet because he has no brains to be anything else."

"Gentlemen—"

Callcott dug his forefinger into Joe's ample stomach. "Lastly, my man, we have our friend—" As Callcott turned to the man on his left, his lower jaw dropped. "Zounds!" he gasped. "But we have, after all, a physician in our midst, none other than our bosom friend, Duncan Stewart." Callcott solemnly rose to his feet and bowed.

Duncan laughed gaily. "Not yet, John, but next year when I come of age—"

"A toast to Duncan," Fletcher called out.

"To Duncan Stewart, M.B. to be," Duncan's companions toasted.

Joe desperately pushed his way past Callcott's chair to Duncan's side. "If you are a physician, sir," the drawer said hoarsely, "there is a man upstairs like to die, and needs attention."

"A man dying!" the laughter vanished from Duncan's eyes. "I cannot let a man die if I can be of assistance to him." He rose to his feet, steadied himself. "Gentlemen, my services are required. I present my apologies, especially to you, Ted, and beg to be excused."

"We shall not excuse you," Callcott roared. "Your glasses are still but half emptied."

"Nay," shouted the irrepressible Fletcher. "We shall not excuse you, but we shall accompany you. Shall we not, gentlemen?" he appealed.

Dayes attempted to rise to his feet. After an effort he succeeded, but only by leaning heavily upon the table. "Yes, Duncan, let us all attend this dying man. I warrant I have not forgotten to bleed a patient, even if I cannot bear the sight and smell of blood."

"No, gentlemen." Duncan shook his head decisively. "A physician has a sacred duty to his patients. I shall go alone and see if there is anything I can do for the poor fellow upstairs. I shall join you later."

"When you have killed him?" Fletcher asked.

Duncan did not heed the quip. He turned to the drawer. "Lead the way, Joe."

With an utter lack of courtesy to those whom he pushed aside with his powerful arm, Joe forced a passage for Duncan. Together the two men proceeded upstairs to Armand de Galinière.

On his way Duncan conscientiously sobered himself by plunging his head into cold water. The Frenchman had already recovered sufficiently to engage in conversation with the scurfy-headed coachman. Upon seeing Duncan and Joe enter, Bill sidled toward the door.

" 'Tain't nothing much wrong with him," the coachman said hoarsely. "Not even them Frenchies die that easily." With this enigmatic remark he disappeared.

Duncan nodded to De Galinière and took hold of his wrist.

"Are you a physician, monsieur?"

"I practice medicine."

"The coachman tells me that I have sent for you unnecessarily," Armand said in a weak, halting voice. "I thought I was dying, but he said I was suffering only from the sickness of the sea, and then of the diligence. Dieu! That diligence, it was terrible, monsieur. It swayed this way, that way, this way, that way." With a groan of anguish he waved his free hand about. "My—my—what you call it, my estomac, he is gone from me. I have him no more."

Duncan smiled as he released the Frenchman's wrist. "Assuredly you are not dying, sir. A bleeding and a decoction of mint to appease the ill humors of your stomach will quickly set you to rights."

De Galinière sighed his relief.

"I am vastly relieved. I have no wish to die." With an effort he sat up. "Permit me to introduce myself, monsieur. I am Armand, fifteenth Sieur de Galinière, in the province of Provence, Knight of the Blue Ribbon and Hereditary Keeper of Her Majesty's Stables at the Court of Versailles. At your service, monsieur." Armand bowed ceremoniously.

"And I, sir, am Duncan Stewart, adopted son of Dr. Anderson of Leicester Fields." Duncan bowed. "Are you staying long in this country?"

"Alas! For many years, I fear. I have had the misfortune to offend a more influential man at court than I. Monsieur, you see before you a ruined man. I, Armand de Galinière, Keeper of the Queen's Stables, must seek employment in a foreign land."

"Employment, sir! Of what nature?"

Armand shrugged his shoulders. "By birth and education I am a nobleman, entitled to mix only with noblemen, but I have thought that I should teach the cultured tongue of France."

Duncan chuckled at the pompous demeanor of the young idler who was so devastatingly handsome. Nevertheless, his humor was good-natured. De Galinière, Duncan thought, appeared, with due allowance for his foreign affectations, to have a likable character, which should go far in assisting him to obtain a clientele.

"I think it worth considering, sir."

"Do you think I shall find people of good breeding anxious to remunerate me for my time in teaching them my beautiful language?"

"I do. Moreover, sir," Duncan added, acting upon impulse, "I should feel honored if you would consent to accept me as your first pupil. I know but a few words learned from my governess. It would give me very great pleasure to speak French fluently."

"But your kindness is overwhelming, monsieur," murmured De Galinière, gratified to have so quickly formed a connection.

"I believe, sir, that I could promise you other pupils."

Armand's white teeth revealed themselves in a flashing smile; his black, expressive eyes joined in. "It must have been le bon Dieu's goodness that sent you to this bedroom, monsieur."

"But they would not be men, sir."

"Not men!" The Frenchman, not understanding, raised his eyebrows.

"No, sir. Would you consider instructing three young ladies—the Misses Anderson, my adopted sisters?"

"After your kindness, monsieur, how could I refuse?"

"Is that settled, sir?" Duncan asked eagerly.

De Galinière nodded.

CHAPTER FIFTEEN

"GOOD morning, Duncan," Anderson greeted, after he had been dutifully kissed by the three daughters. "You must have returned late last night. I did not hear you come in." Anderson had altered little in the passing years, save to develop a prosperous-looking paunch and an irritable temper that everyone was careful not to arouse.

"No, sir. Last night was a special occasion."

"Indeed, what was that?" Anderson asked, as he made his way toward the head of the breakfast table.

"Edward Dayes has had another landscape accepted for the Royal Academy."

"That is welcome news. Perhaps his continuing success will banish the melancholy expression from his eyes. I confess, Duncan, that there are times when I fear he is not destined to have a long life."

"Poor Mr. Dayes!" Elizabeth said sympathetically. "Papa, may we go to the Academy to see his pictures?"

"We usually do go to the Academy, Elizabeth. I can see no reason for not doing so this year." Anderson raised his hand for grace. "For what we are about to receive, may the Lord make us truly thankful." He sat down, the family did the same.

Duncan laughed. "Edward was not melancholy last night."

"Who else was with you?" Jean asked.

"Dick Fletcher and John Callcott."

"How strange!" Margaret murmured.

"What is strange, my dear?" her mother asked.

"I was playing some of Mr. Callcott's music last night."

"Stranger things than that happened last night," Duncan said gaily. Everyone was immediately attentive. "What happened?" Elizabeth asked.

"We were at the Golden Cross, celebrating Edward's success, when Joe, the head drawer, came to the table and asked if one of us was a physician."

"A physician! And you offered your services, I suppose?"

"Yes, sir. According to Joe a man was dying in the hotel, so I agreed to visit him, with the intention of seeing what I could do until he was sent to the hospital."

Anderson's professional instincts were immediately aroused. "What was the matter with him, Duncan?"

"Nothing, sir. He was merely suffering from a severe attack of sea and travel sickness."

"Seasickness, eh? Was he a foreigner?"

"Yes, sir. From the Court of Versailles. He was a Frenchman, by the name of Armand de Galinière, who has fled his country to escape the vengeance of a powerful nobleman who covets Monsieur de Galinière's post, the Keepership of the Queen's Stables."

"Does he contemplate living in London?"

"For a time, until it is safe for him to return. Unfortunately, owing to the conspiracy against him organized by the other noblemen, the poor fellow is almost penniless. He will have to earn a livelihood."

"For the first time in his life, no doubt," commented Anderson, whose British insularity caused him to detest all foreigners. "What does this French gentleman propose to do?"

"Teach the French language. I have offered myself as his first pupil."

"Humph!" Anderson nodded his head several times. "A commendable plan, Duncan. I approve it highly. A physician should be erudite. A thorough knowledge of the French tongue should help you considerably to improve your knowledge."

"Thank you, sir. But, of course—" Duncan hesitated, then hastily continued, "Monsieur de Galinière must have other pupils."

"Of course," Anderson agreed dryly.

"It has occurred to me, sir—"

"Well?"

"That—that Monsieur de Galinière might also teach Jean, Margaret, and Elizabeth the French tongue."

"Bless my soul!" Anderson stared at Duncan. "What gave you that suggestion? The girls learned all the French they need to learn at Miss Howland's Academy."

"Oh! Papa, please do as Duncan suggests," Jean appealed wistfully. "I would love to know French well enough to read Molière and Rousseau."

Margaret clapped her hands. "Please, please, Papa, let us learn French. Jean is right. We ought to be more fluent with that cultured tongue."

"Anne Seymour can speak the language like a Frenchwoman," Elizabeth added. "She has been taught by a Frenchman."

The doctor frowned. "I do not approve of the idea."

"Why not, Papa dear? Anne Seymour is not the only girl who speaks French very well. Elizabeth North, and Mary Ryan, and Mary Philpotts, and Angela—"

Anderson stilled Jean with a wave of his hand. "I am not interested in your friends, Jean."

"The girls are learning music from a music master, sir, and dancing and deportment from a dancing master. Why should they not learn French from a French master?"

"Because he is a Frenchman," Anderson snapped. "I am sure you are well aware that I do not approve of my daughters coming into contact with foreigners."

"He is a reputable French nobleman, sir, and a thoroughly amiable person to boot."

"You would not want your daughters to be considered ignorant, would you, Papa?" Margaret daringly asked.

The doctor's expression grew indecisive. He turned toward his wife. "What is your opinion, my dear?"

"I think, Mr. Anderson, that it would be a kindness to the girls, and to the unfortunate Monsieur de Galinière," she answered placidly.

Anderson was still not happy. "I shall interview the foreign gentleman and give you my decision later." He raised a warning finger. "But mind, I make no rash promises. Duncan, will you arrange to have Monsieur Whatever-his-name-is to call upon me one evening?"

"Certainly, sir." With twinkling eyes Duncan surveyed each sister in turn.

Jean, at nineteen tall and slim, with her dark gypsy coloring, and at rare moments a brilliance flaring in her eyes to betray the high-strung spirit under the reserve that was so mysteriously attractive—and so disconcerting; . . . Margaret, changed from a young mischief to a young beauty, her rippling burnished-copper curls seeming to imprison and reflect every stray gleam of light, and her astonishing self-possession, too, taking fire now and then in shows of temper that had lost all the petulance and kept all the liveliness; . . . Elizabeth, still girlishly plump, so likable for her easygoing gaiety, for her quaint and comforting habit of instantly realizing the humorous aspect of any dramatic situation, and above all for the sympathy that could shine out so sweetly from the depths of those very blue eyes—Duncan enjoyed thinking how the sisters would be interested, or challenged, or awed, or amused, by such a person as Armand de Galinière.

As events shaped, Dr. Anderson was not at liberty to interview Armand de Galinière until nearly two weeks later.

In the meantime Armand and Duncan met frequently, for Duncan found himself inexplicably drawn toward the other man. What formed the basis of this attachment was a mystery to all who were aware of it, for the two men were quite dissimilar. True, they were sufficiently of an age to be companionable; Armand was twenty-one, just a year older than Duncan. True, they were both dandies in matters of dress; both were young bloods and fond of the type of roisterous nocturnal adventure that was fashionable among the younger members of London society. But there the resemblance between them ended. Armand's temperament was Latin, Duncan's Scots. Armand was an idle, dissolute waster. Duncan, for all his sowing of wild oats, was passionately determined to allow nothing to obstruct his career.

The two men became firm friends. Every hour that Duncan could snatch from his work he spent with Armand, who, flattered by his easy conquest, was not blind to the possible advantages of the friendship. He gave Duncan many hours of recreation by relating the past and current gossip of the French court and depicting the mode of life there.

For his part, Duncan introduced the Frenchman to London, London society, and London ways. He took Armand to Boodles, where the Frenchman was, only with difficulty, prevented from risking his meager capital on the turn of a card; to the Cheshire Cheese, in Fleet Street, where they were fortunate enough to hear Boswell recount an unpublished adventure of his tour to the Hebrides; to the Theatre Royal in Drury Lane, to hear Mrs. Siddons in her new part as Queen Katharine; to Ranelagh Gardens; to the Oxford Street galleries for pistol-shooting practice—to most of the haunts frequented by the macaronis, the rakes, and the bucks.

At last Dr. Anderson arranged an evening for Monsieur de Galinière to call. The appointment was fixed for a late hour, after the three sisters had retired to bed, for Anderson was determined that there should be no likelihood of their meeting the Frenchman until he had had an opportunity of approving the prospective French master. Duncan grew ever more nervous of the result, for Anderson's prejudices were not lightly overcome.

His fears were unnecessary. Incredibly discerning as a result of a life spent in social diplomacy, Armand de Galinière set himself to impress the doctor. The Frenchman succeeded. Before he returned to the rooms that he had rented in Maiden Lane, he had received Anderson's grudging consent to instruct his three daughters in the French language on two afternoons each week.

On the following Tuesday De Galinière arrived punctually to give the first lesson. Duncan was busy in the surgery and was unable to greet Armand upon his arrival, but he joined the party later, as Armand was bidding au revoir to Mrs. Anderson and the three girls.

"How did the lesson proceed?" he asked gaily.

Margaret answered for Armand. "Until today I did not know French was such a beautiful language. Monsieur de Galinière has been reciting Racine to us."

"I am afraid monsieur found us very stupid," observed Jean.

Armand bowed. "Mesdemoiselles, if all my pupils were so understanding and perceptive, my poor efforts to teach my tongue to others would become a recreation rather than a laborious undertaking."

Mrs. Anderson smiled. "I am afraid you flatter my daughters, monsieur." Then she added sadly, "I wish I could have learned my French lessons from so excellent a teacher. Do you think you will succeed in teaching my daughters to speak fluently?"

"If it is your wish that they should do so, madame, how could I fail?"

After the exchange of further compliments Duncan escorted the visitor to the street. There Armand caught hold of his arm. "Why did you not tell me? How did you keep the secret for so long?"

"Tell you what? Keep what secret?"

"They are *ravissantes*." Armand paused. His expression grew puzzled as he looked at Duncan. "Do you not think they are beautiful?"

Duncan laughed. "Certainly. But this ecstasy of yours surprises me."

De Galinière threw up his hands in despair. "You English! Are you blind, or is your heart made of stone? Are you a man or just a marble statue?"

Duncan grew irritable. "I am neither blind, nor made of stone. Why should you think so?"

"Because, my friend, if you were not blind, or if you had blood in your veins, by now you would have made your choice."

"My choice of what?"

"Your future wife!" Armand laughed scornfully. "From three such beautiful mesdemoiselles a man would have chosen one for his wife. But you—" He shook his head. "You choose medicine. *Mordieu!*"

Duncan turned and stared at the house from which they had just emerged. "A wife!" he murmured. "I have never thought of marriage in connection with my adopted sisters."

CHAPTER SIXTEEN

DUNCAN was the only person under the doctor's roof who had not thought of his marriage to one of the sisters. The discussion as to which sister he would ultimately marry was a perennial one in the Anderson household; it had begun as soon as it became evident that Duncan was to remain.

Margaret was Dr. Anderson's choice for Duncan. Of the three girls Margaret was the fondest of Duncan, who, for his part, preferred Margaret to either Jean or Elizabeth. He refused to admit that this conviction was founded upon his own feelings toward his daughter, for he had a preference for Margaret with her glorious hair, her assurance, and her quick temper. Margaret, he felt, would make a better wife for Duncan than either of her sisters. She could manage him better, see that he was not led astray by his rakish companions.

Mrs. Anderson did not agree with his choice. Margaret and Duncan were good friends now, but should they ever marry, they would inevitably quarrel. Duncan, she maintained, would treat his wife more as a chattel than as a human being; although it was customary for most men to treat a wife in that spirit. Margaret was likely to rebel. Both children were strongwilled; a good enough reason in itself for thinking they should not marry. Now Elizabeth was different. She possessed a character that would agree admirably with Duncan's. It was to be hoped that Duncan would have sufficient sense to realize that fact. So argued Mrs. Anderson, who had a special tenderness for her youngest child.

Mrs. Jones was another who believed that Margaret would be Duncan's choice. Perkins—who had stepped into Blodgett's shoes—disagreed. Elizabeth would be Duncan's bride, he maintained. Trust a good-looking gentleman to pick the youngest girl in the family! A man liked a wife to be younger than himself, and he would bet a month's salary on Elizabeth. Of the other servants, four were convinced Duncan would choose Margaret (one of them accepted Perkins' bet), and two voted for Elizabeth. Only one small voice was raised on Jean's behalf. That was Annie's, the tweeny's, and nobody paid any attention to her. What did she know about the family? she was asked scornfully. And Annie, who had joined the staff soon after Duncan's sixteenth birthday, meekly agreed that she could not possibly know as much about such matters as the other servants.

The seed which Armand de Galinière sowed in Duncan's mind took root. From that moment the camaraderie that had previously existed between him and the girls was destroyed. He grew ill at ease, not only with Jean but with Margaret and Elizabeth as well. And soon, from asking himself: Should I marry one of them? he began to wonder: Which? Jean, Margaret, or Elizabeth? Mysterious Jean, capable Margaret, or merry Elizabeth?

Duncan's changed demeanor did not pass unnoticed by the three girls. Their attitude grew even more constrained than his own. They were not flattered by the instinctive knowledge that they were being weighed in the balance. They fell into the habit of veiling their eyes whenever they were aware that he was watching them. Their conversation grew stilted and unnatural, which made Duncan wonder unhappily what had so altered his foster sisters—and just at a time when he was trying to discover which one of them he loved the most!

That all three girls were beautiful, each in her own special fashion— Jean, for her haunting sense of mystery; Margaret, for the glamour of her richly auburn hair and incomparable complexion; Elizabeth, for her smiling eyes and lips—only made the choice more elusive. Which was the most beautiful? Which did he care for most? And, more cautiously, which would make the best wife? Which?

The French lessons proceeded apace. By the end of the sixth month Duncan and Jean could speak fluently. Margaret was not so fluent, but her accent was better. Poor Elizabeth, however, lagged behind. Although she found it easy to translate French into English, she found it difficult to translate English into French, and harder still to carry on a long conversation that did not consist of the few sentences which she had, parrotwise, learned by heart.

One day De Galinière suggested the performance of a play. "One of Racine's plays," he continued with enthusiasm. "You could all play a part, mesdemoiselles. And Duncan. I, too, could play a part, and also madame, your mother—"

"Oh, no, monsieur," Mrs. Anderson interrupted, flushed with joy. "My French is not good enough."

"But I assure you, madame, that you would have no cause to fear playing a part. A little extra coaching, madame, and I swear that the audience will take you for a Frenchwoman co-opted especially for the play."

"Then a small part, monsieur, a part of not too many lines—"

"It shall be as you say, madame."

As Armand turned, Margaret said breathlessly: "You spoke just now of an audience—"

"But yes, mademoiselle. A play needs an audience. I shall try to persuade monsieur, your father, to permit us to give our performance at his next reception. I feel sure—"

A babel of chatter drowned his words. Agog with excitement at the idea of performing a French play before an audience of their friends, the girls clamored for further information: When should they give the performance? In which room could it best be held? What play did monsieur suggest? Who was to play the biggest part? Jean? Margaret? Would they have to make special costumes? What—why—which—when—

So, after considerable diplomacy had been exercised in persuading Dr. Anderson to give his consent to the scheme (he, secretly, being highly delighted at the thought of displaying his daughters' talent to his friends), all arrangements were completed. De Galinière chose as the play to be performed Racine's tragedy *Bajazet;* the part of Bajazet was allocated to Duncan, that of Atalide to Margaret, with Jean as Roxane, Elizabeth as Zatime, Mrs. Anderson as Zaire, and himself as Acomat. Edward Dayes was co-opted to play the part of Osmin.

A blissful period followed. Even the servants felt proud to know that the young mistresses were to perform a play, "and in French, too," so that all the extra work entailed was accepted with ungrudging enthusiasm. The large drawing room on the ground floor was prepared for the occasion. A raised platform was built, curtains erected, candle footlights fixed, and a number of chairs arranged for the audience.

At last the day of reception arrived. So tense with excitement were Jean and Margaret that after breakfast Anderson felt constrained to bleed them both, and ordered them to keep *sal volatile* handy to prevent the possibility of a disconcerting fainting spell. Fortunately, the day passed without incident. Toward five o'clock the guests began to arrive. Anderson received them in the smaller reception room across the passage from the drawing room. Footmen handed round cups of coffee or chocolate to the ladies, but for the gentlemen there were glasses of mum, port wine, sherry, or brandy. Also trays of pastries of marinated lamb seasoned with eschalots, anchovies, and nutmeg; Shrewsbury cake; jumbles; Yorkshire parkin, cheesecakes, and ices.

When the last of the guests had arrived Dr. Anderson gave the signal for everyone to proceed into the other room. He, with Mrs. Seymour on his arm, led the way. The moment was one of the proudest in his life, but not even to himself would he admit the fact. Behind him followed half a dozen Tukes; one Anderson; Sir Joshua Reynolds, who lived at number 47 Leicester Fields; John Hunter, from number 28, whence he had lately moved his museum from Earl's Court; Mrs. Hogarth, widow of the engraver; and a number of Anderson's social friends and influential patients.

As soon as everyone was comfortably seated, Perkins, with his long-handled snuffer, extinguished the candles. When the room was dim John Callcott played, on one of Mr. Broadwood's grand piano-fortes, a composition of his own, *Dance of the Sultan's Slaves* (especially written for the occasion and dedicated to Elizabeth Anderson).

The piece was generously applauded. Then Anderson called out, "Hush!" The drawing room grew quietly expectant.

The curtains were drawn back—Armand de Galinière, dressed to represent Acomat, the Grand Vizier, stepped forward and addressed the very unhappy and obviously nervous Osmin.

The play (abridged by Armand) proved him to be not only a good French teacher but an efficient stage producer. The scenes followed one another smoothly, and the prompter was rarely heard. Duncan, as much to his own surprise as to that of everyone who knew him, played his part of Bajazet with great success. He entered into the spirit of the play. He forgot that he was Duncan Stewart and became the Sultan's brother, the long-imprisoned victim of his brother's spite.

Bajazet, loving Atalide, is loved by Roxane, the Sultan's favorite, who offers Bajazet freedom and power if he will marry her.

Bajazet refuses, but Atalide, so that his freedom shall be attained, persuades Bajazet to pretend love for Roxane. Bajazet agrees. He makes love too convincingly. Atalide becomes jealous, and taxes him with having fallen a victim to Roxane's charms. Bajazet reaffirms his love for Atalide.

> "N'exigez rien de plus. Ni la mort, ni vous-même
> Ne me ferez jamais prononcer que je l'aime,
> Puisque jamais je n'aimerai que vous."

Duncan faltered. As though another—the prompter perhaps—were translating the lines he had just declaimed, he seemed to hear a whispering echo saying:

> Ask no more than this. Neither death nor even you
> Shall ever make me say that I love her
> Since I shall never love anyone save you.

Past and future merged into a present that bore no relation to the Byzantium of Racine's play. Atalide vanished. Bajazet vanished. Unsteadily, Duncan saw, not Atalide's, but Margaret's face before him, wistfully appealing. Unaware of his own actions he stepped closer to her, took her hand in his own. Then, to the prompter's consternation, Duncan repeated the three lines. And in speaking, he found the answer.

It was Margaret he loved; Margaret he would marry.

61

The voice of Bajazet grew warmer, more sincere, as the play continued. At the end, out of compliment to their host, the audience clapped Jean and Margaret the most. But, secretly, the ladies considered Duncan the best player of all. He had made love so convincingly.

A long evening followed the finale of the play. To Duncan the subsequent events became a dream in which only two characters possessed reality—himself and Margaret. The guests were shadowy, unsubstantial beings who spoke meaningless words to him and appeared to expect a reply. What gibberish he spoke, what he did, what he ate, what he drank —none of these things could he subsequently remember. To him the passing hours were a hiatus that lasted from the moment of his declaration of love for Margaret until he found himself in bed, lying flat upon his back, staring at the flickering candle.

So it was Margaret he loved! As he softly spoke her name aloud, he realized that from boyhood he had always loved Margaret the most. Margaret! He repeated the name caressingly. Margaret! How lovely she was; how enchanting she had looked on the stage, dressed in the diaphanous draperies of an Ottoman woman. He had seen by the expression that had flashed into her eyes when he repeated Bajazet's declaration of love for Atalide, that she had recognized that he spoke, not to Atalide, but to her. Her eyes had responded to his; as he hurried on, joy had filled his heart as he had understood, by their shy gladness, that she welcomed the inference underlying his passionate words. That joy had not been dispelled with the passing hours. A dozen times he had managed to look into her eyes, and what he had seen in them had made him feel stifled with happiness.

He wondered how he could have been unaware of his love for so long. With amazed delight he saw coming into his picture of the future—till now holding nothing but work and the triumphs of a difficult skill—this new tenderness and joy. Even the prospect of confronting Dr. Anderson with an unlooked-for and probably unwelcome proposal—after all, why should Anderson, wellborn, rich, successful, accept the penniless son of a farmer for son-in-law when he could pick almost whomever he pleased?— this chilling thought only sharpened Duncan's determination to pose the question at once.

To his amazement Anderson made no demur about the marriage.

"If Margaret wishes to marry you, Duncan, I shall have no objection. My only comment will be, 'God bless you both.' "

"Then I have your permission to speak to Margaret, sir?"

Anderson raised a warning finger. "I must make certain conditions."

"What are they, sir?"

"That if Margaret says yes, your engagement shall not be officially announced until you obtain your diploma from Surgeons' Hall."

"I shall do that within the next six months."

Anderson sighed. "The confidence of youth! But I have faith in you, Duncan. I am convinced that you were born to be a man of medicine. I can still see your face, my boy, as it was then. White and blue with cold, with the moisture of the mist dripping from your tousled hair, and your eyelids heavy with the tears you had shed for that poor woman's death—what was her name?"

"Elspeth."

"Yes, Elspeth. And later, when you were in the carriage you pleaded with me to take you to London. You had no other thought than that, Duncan. You wanted to be a doctor. And soon you will be." Anderson sighed once again. "I am a good physician, as physicians go, my boy, but you already know more of medicine than I do, for all my thirty years of practice." He saw that Duncan was about to protest. "Do not contradict me. I am not blind to the truth, Duncan. Medicine is beginning a new era. Unheard-of theories are being propounded and substantiated. In the next century medicine will make a great advancement, and much of it will be due to the courage and intelligence of youth. You have in you to be one of the pioneers in a new age of medicine—perhaps not in five years, or in ten years, but sometime. Inevitably sometime."

Anderson smiled happily. "I am glad to know you want to marry one of my daughters. It will make me proud that Margaret will share in the fame and success that I am convinced you will attain. And if I live to see you successful I shall feel even greater pride in the knowledge that I had a share in helping you along the road to that success." Anderson turned away and noisily blew his nose. "And now," he continued, "run along and ask the girl. And do not come back until she has said yes. I think she will," he added to himself as the door closed behind Duncan.

He was right.

CHAPTER SEVENTEEN

ALTHOUGH no announcement was made of the engagement, every member of the household was aware that Duncan had at last made his choice and everybody was pleased.

Armand, in company with others who visited the Anderson home, knew nothing of the understanding. Having a pair of eyes and an instinct for sensing romance, he would quickly have become aware of the state of affairs but for the fact that he rarely saw Margaret and Duncan together. When Armand called upon the Andersons, Duncan was usually in the surgery or out with Anderson. For this reason, when he began surreptitiously to court Margaret, he did not realize the extent of his treachery to his friend, but all the same, he set about his task in the methodical, subtle manner that long practice at the Court of France had made perfect. A few whispered words of flattery, when the inflection of his voice inferred more than his words; a swift touch of the hand; a posy of flowers sent clandestinely; a passionate French verse sent anonymously—Margaret permitted these attentions, for she was a woman and reveled in the homage of so attractive a cavalier. Besides, she was grateful to Armand, for was it not he who had suggested the French play that had opened

Duncan's eyes? She was fascinated by the secrecy necessitated by Mrs. Anderson's vigilant chaperonage; enthralled by his ingenuity in overcoming this obstacle.

It was Elizabeth who first drew Duncan's attention to Armand's intrigue. She and Jean were alone with Duncan, for Margaret had retired to bed with a migraine, and Mr. and Mrs. Anderson were at an entertainment that was being held at the Pantheon.

"Have you told Monsieur de Galinière of your coming engagement to Margaret?"

"Naturally not."

"Because of Papa's stipulation?"

"Yes."

"I think it would be wise to make an exception and inform Monsieur de Galinière of your understanding."

"What are you saying, Elizabeth?" Jean protested.

"You know what is happening, Jean, as well as I."

"What is happening?" Duncan asked, amused.

"Monsieur de Galinière is making advances to Margaret."

"What!"

"It is true, Duncan."

Duncan frowned at Elizabeth. "Those are the meanest words I have ever heard from you, Elizabeth. How could you say that about your own sister? Besides, your parents would be ashamed of you if they were to know that your mind was engaged with thoughts of that nature. You are too young to know of such matters."

Elizabeth's eyes misted with tears. "If you do not believe me, ask Jean."

"Duncan is quite right. You should be ashamed of yourself," Jean protested loyally.

"Well, I am not, so there! I have seen the flowers Monsieur de Galinière sends Margaret through that nasty Wilkins. I have seen him touch her hand when he thought nobody was watching. The other day he kissed her hand, when Mama's back was turned. They are always whispering together. You know they are, Jean."

Duncan turned toward Jean. His face was white. "Is it true, Jean?"

Jean loyally tried to protect Margaret. "Elizabeth has too vivid an imagination for a child of her age."

"I asked, is it true, Jean?"

Even loyalty was not stronger than truth. Jean glanced down at the carpet. "Yes," she admitted unhappily. "But please, Duncan, do not treat so trivial a matter too seriously," she pleaded. "Monsieur de Galinière does not realize his perfidy. As for Margaret, she is a stupid girl who is merely pandering to her vanity. I am sure that, if you speak to Monsieur de Galinière, he will cease his attentions."

Duncan spoke to Armand that next night. In a brusque manner he informed the Frenchman of his unofficial engagement. Armand's congratulations were so generous and sincere that Duncan decided that Elizabeth and Jean had been exaggerating.

During the next few days Duncan tried to forget Elizabeth's insinuations, but suspicion, once aroused in a dour, forthright mind, is not easily dislodged. He found himself watching Margaret covertly, he neglected his work in the surgery to be present at the Friday French lesson, and found difficulty in sleeping because his brain was occupied with jealous visions of Armand whispering secrets into Margaret's ear

In his calmer moments Duncan admitted that Margaret's conduct gave him no cause for anxiety. She greeted Armand no more warmly than she customarily did old Franklin, her dancing master, or Signor Guiseppi, her music master. She did not allow Armand to approach her closely enough to touch her hand. The only whispering she did was into Jean's ear. Nor had Margaret's attitude toward himself changed. The light in her eyes was no less tender, her dazzling smile no less warm than hitherto. To reassure himself Duncan repeated: "She loves me. She does not love Armand. She does not love Armand." His faith was not without effect. His mood grew more tranquil when he succeeded in convincing himself that Elizabeth and Jean, influenced by the measure of their loyalty to Margaret and himself, had drawn baseless inferences from commonplace happenings.

A week later at five o'clock Duncan was due to go with Anderson to number 40, Berkeley Square, where Mr. Horace Walpole was giving a reception, but with darkness he had a return of his anxiety as torturing as before. He tried to excuse himself, but Anderson brusquely overrode all objections and told Duncan to prepare himself.

Duncan drank deeply of the port and sherry that were offered at the reception, and the alcohol induced an artificial courage and joviality. He was sorry when two hours later Anderson announced that he was anxious to leave, since he and Mrs. Anderson were to visit Mrs. Montagu at her new home, Portman House. Duncan returned home by himself. He went direct to one of the upstairs sitting rooms, which the girls were in the habit of occupying. He found Elizabeth alone.

"Where is Margaret?"

"Jean is out with Aunt Mary Tuke."

"I asked where Margaret is, not Jean."

"Margaret is out, too."

"With Aunt Mary Tuke and Jean?"

"No."

"Then where has she gone?" he asked in a loud voice; the effects of the port wine made him feel truculent.

She glanced at him with uneasy eyes, then bent her head over her needlework. He crossed to her chair and placed his hand on her shoulder. "What is wrong with you, Elizabeth? Are you feeling ill?"

"Nothing is wrong with me, Duncan," she stammered. "It's Margaret."

His grip on her shoulder tightened. "Is Margaret ill? Why wasn't her father told? I must fetch the doctor back without delay. Why did Mrs. Anderson—"

"Margaret is not ill," she interrupted, checking his flow of words. "She has gone out."

He gave an angry laugh. "Why should that upset you?"

"Duncan, I am afraid to tell you."

"To tell me what?" He raised his voice. "For goodness' sake, Elizabeth, don't sit like a stuffed doll and stare at me."

"Have you been drinking?"

"What has that to do with Margaret."

"Because you must keep calm."

"The devil! Where is Margaret, I say?"

"I do not know."

He laughed unsteadily. "I must be drunk, otherwise I should understand what you are trying to tell me. Once and for all, Elizabeth, where is Margaret?"

She caught hold of his arm. "I do not know where she is, Duncan dear. Late this afternoon she received a note. After Mama and Papa had gone Margaret slipped away, without saying where she was going."

"But the note, Elizabeth! Do you know where it came from?" he appealed.

She bowed her head. "From Monsieur de Galinière," she told him.

CHAPTER EIGHTEEN

MARGARET threw away the note," Elizabeth explained presently. "I found it, Duncan, and read it."

"Where is it?" he demanded.

"Do not ask to see it. Please, please take no notice of it."

"You must be mad, Elizabeth. How could I take no notice of a man who is trying to steal Margaret from me?"

"Because Margaret is not worth your love," Elizabeth answered quickly. "Margaret is my sister; I love her. But you are my adopted brother, and I am very fond of you. I do not want to see you hurt by Margaret's waywardness and coquetry. You are blind to her faults, because you are a man and think you are in love with her. No woman, not even a younger sister, is ever blind to another woman's fault. Give Margaret up; try to forget your love for her; think of her only as your adopted sister. Margaret is not in love with you. She only pretends to be, because your attentions satisfy her vanity."

"You are a liar, Elizabeth, Margaret is in love with me."

"If she were she would not have allowed Monsieur de Galinière to have penned a note to her, couched in such terms."

"Show me the note."

"Please do not ask me to do that."

"Show me the note," he shouted.

Elizabeth turned away as she lifted her skirt to search her petticoat pocket. When he saw a crumpled square of paper in her hand, he snatched it from her and unfolded it. Through a blurred haze he saw De Galinière's angular writing.

Ma chérie,

I have learned that tonight Monsieur and Madame Anderson are to dine at Mrs. Montagu's. Could you not slip away from your home and meet me at the place of assignation that I suggested to you a week past? Be there by nine of the clock, and I shall quickly join you thereafter. Until that hour I shall lull suspicion by being seen in my usual haunts. My sweet! My sweet! The hours will pass all too slowly until that blessed moment when I shall be able to gaze into your eyes without fear of interruption. Let none know of these plans, and above all be discreet. Neither your sisters, nor your parents, nor Duncan must hear of our meeting. Neither must the servants know of your leaving the house, for fear of their disclosing the fact to your parents. Pretend to go to bed with a migraine, as upon other occasions. Au revoir. I am all impatient for our meeting. A.

Some ten minutes later Duncan was on his way to De Galinière's lodgings in Maiden Lane. He was wrapped in a full, thick overcoat that was buttoned up to his chin above and cut away to behind his knees below; his hands were covered with heavy gauntlets. His head was protected by an ample triangular hat; his silken hose, by knee-high boots. Despite this amount of clothing he would have felt the sudden, bitter cold had he not been fired by his resentment against the Frenchman. De Galinière and Margaret! The names echoed in his head like the uneven, slow, ticktocking of a clock with a badly hung pendulum. De Galinière and Margaret! Damn them both, he thought. Damn the Frenchman for a philandering scoundrel. Damn him! Damn him!

De Galinière was not in his rooms. Duncan began to search the taverns, going first to the Ship. From the Ship he went to the Crown and Anchor, thence to Palsgrave's Head. At each tavern he ordered a drink, for his thirst raged. Armand was at none of the taverns, so Duncan proceeded eastward to Fleet Street. He must find De Galinière. He must prevent the assignation with Margaret before it was too late. As he proceeded from one tavern to the next his walk became ever more unsteady. Once he tripped over an uneven cobble and nearly fell. Another time he did fall, but by good fortune dived into a bank of snow. He struggled to his feet with the help of a passer-by, who attempted to pick his pocket without success. He staggered on; Armand de Galinière must be found. Nothing else in all the world mattered.

The Devil, the Globe, the Mitre. Another brandy. Another brandy. Another brandy. On to the Queen's Arms in St. Paul's Churchyard. Another brandy. Dolly's, in Paternoster Row. Another brandy. The Salutation and Cat in Newgate Street. Mulled ale there, for a change, to slake the thirst that was still raging. On to Cornhill and the Pope's Head. Yes, mulled ale. Mulled ale was good to cool the head while warming the blood. One must keep a cool head when chasing a phantom Frenchman. Elizabeth had said, "Keep cool." He must do what Elizabeth said. She was a sweet child. But for her he would never have known how treacherous a foreign nobleman could be. To the devil with noblemen. To the devil with Frenchmen. To the devil with all foreigners. Anderson was right to detest foreigners. To the devil with everybody. Armand de Galinière must be found.

So to Bishopsgate-Street-Within and the Green Dragon. And there Duncan did indeed find Armand de Galinière.

The Frenchman had also been drinking. "*Nom d'un nom!* But is it you, *mon ami?*" He turned to a man who sat beside him. "May the Blessed Virgin send me straight to purgatory if my friend Duncan Stewart does not stand before me."

The stranger who sat beside De Galinière burst into loud laughter. He was dressed in a coarse but substantial serge suit with a rough jersey of homespun to complete his practical attire. His own black hair fell untidily around his head. Small gold rings were set in his ears. His complexion was ruddied from a lifetime's exposure to the elements. His teeth were chipped and brown with tobacco juice. His hands were large and callused. One of them, the left, was tattooed on the back with an elaborate monogram intertwined in a heart. His nails had been so pared away that it was difficult to distinguish whether or no he possessed any.

"Zounds! But you'll go there, my cock sparrow, without you offering up any prayers," he roared. "If Beelzebub hasn't already marked you for a special pit in hell, may me name never be Tom Beard, Captain of the *Pride of Bristol.*"

Armand bowed drunkenly. "Your humble servant, Captain Beard. Meet my best friend, Mr. Duncan Stewart."

Beard thrust out one of his horny hands. "Glad to meet you, Mr. Stewart."

Duncan ignored him. "I must find Armand de Galinière," he mumbled.

The Frenchman giggled. "Here I am, Duncan. Can you not see me?"

Duncan rubbed his eyes, trying to focus them. The image grew clearer. He rested his hands upon the table and leaned unsteadily forward.

"Where is Margaret?" he mouthed.

De Galinière wagged his head. "How should I know, Duncan? I have not seen her."

"You lie, De Galinière. You have an assignation with her tonight."

"Ho! Ho!" Captain Beard's broad chest heaved; he bellowed with laughter and dug his forefinger into Armand's side. "So your stories about wenches were as true as they were amusing, monsoor. Oddsfish! Your best friend! Where is Margaret? Ho! Ho! You sly rascal. What have you been doing with Margaret?"

The Frenchman disregarded the captain's remarks. He rose to his feet and tried to stand upright. The effort was not very successful. "Monsieur, I cannot think that I have heard you aright."

"Where is Margaret?"

"I repeat that I have no knowledge of the whereabouts of Mademoiselle Margaret. Why should I possess such—such—" He hiccuped. "Such knowledge?"

"And I repeat that you lie," Duncan shouted. "I have seen the note you addressed to her."

A leering expression revealed itself on Armand's flushed face. He giggled. "Ah! My note to Mademoiselle Margaret. That is different. That is—" The Frenchman checked himself as he realized what he was saying. "I do not know what you mean, Duncan. I have sent no note to your sweetheart."

Captain Beard's robust laughter bellowed out once more; its blast seemed to thunder against the disputants, imprisoning them in a small world of noise, deafening them to other sounds that might have penetrated their fuddled minds for their own good.

"What of that wench in Versailles?" the captain choked. "Ho! Ho! You didn't send her no notes, neither, monsoor, to bring her hotfoot to your house in haste for your warm kisses to set her heart pounding, your warm hands to stroke her sleek black hair. What of those other wives in Versailles and in Paris you've been telling me about these past two hours? And you didn't send no notes to Margaret!" He leaned back in his chair and gasped for breath.

The sound dinned in Duncan's ears. Armand's face jumped out of focus again. It grew hazy, then hazier, but larger. Armand's mouth drooled open, but Duncan saw only a jeering, salacious smile of triumph.

He swayed backward and felt something against his back. Something he could use as a weapon. He gripped the chair with his hands, raised it above his head. The face of Armand de Galinière taunted him—mocked him— There were two faces. One face. It was revolving in dizzy circles.

Duncan lurched forward. The heavy chair smashed down upon Armand's head. The Frenchman collapsed onto the table and scattered pewter tankards in every direction.

A sequence of events followed that for Duncan remained forever a hazy nightmare—a nightmare of the sudden silence that followed Armand's collapse upon the table; the subsequent commotion of shouting voices, a solemn "He is dead"; a second silence; a voice that called upon someone to fetch the peace officers; a shout of "Here comes the watch"; a sudden darkness; more commotion; the pain of a huge hand that clutched at his arm and pulled him along with it; a mass of people; the night air; shouts; a chase through the streets of London.

When Duncan recovered his senses he found himself in a room no larger than a wooden box with bunks on each side, a folding table in the center; a box that was blue with tobacco smoke. Duncan watched a lamp that was suspended from the low roof. It swung to and fro, slowly and rhythmically. He could not think why it should swing so. He had never seen a lamp that swung from side to side.

Then the room filled with the noise of herculean laughter. He looked in the direction of the terrifying noise. A man stood by the table, stooping to avoid the roof. His face was vaguely familiar.

"So you are awake at last, my hearty. And about time, too. How are you feeling?"

"Where am I?"

"Aboard the finest, trimmest craft that sails the seven seas, the *Pride of Bristol* by name—outward bound for America, first stop, the Caribee Isles."

"What am I doing here?"

"Ho! Ho! That's a fine question to ask, shipmate. You are saving your neck being stretched by the gibbet at Tyburn or Tower Hill."

"I do not understand."

"You killed a man last night. If it hadn't been for me, and the fact that I likes the look of your face better nor the one that belonged to that French froggie, what I have no time for, you would be in jail now, my cockalorum, instead of lying pretty in that there bunk."

Duncan struggled to a sitting position. "Is the ship moving?"

"She is. At a fair eight knots, too."

"You must land me, Captain," Duncan demanded. "Is it morning yet?"

Captain Beard grunted his amusement and expertly spat a quid of tobacco juice into a cuspidor on the floor. "Nay, boy. It's more than morning. It's nearly evening, and as for being landed, you'll have to wait a few weeks, when we are due to arrive in Saint-Domingue. I'll put you ashore there, and if you've good sense, there you'll stay. The Bow Street runners don't follow a man to Saint-Domingue. It's French, and the King's Writ don't run there. It's the best place for you, lad. Aye, and there's rum and fine women in Saint-Domingue."

"But I don't want to go to Saint-Domingue."

"I fear you must, lad," Beard pointed out dryly. "I'm not going to lose precious hours putting back to land you in England so that you may be strung up to a gibbet as a murderer."

Duncan tried to understand the situation, but the effort was not successful. "Whom am I supposed to have killed?" he asked.

Captain Beard told him. With horror in his eyes Duncan stared at the other man.

"Oh, God!"

"Cheer up, lad," Beard said, with irritation. "You should be glad you are a free man aboard this ship instead of being a prisoner in jail. If you're breaking your heart about leaving Margaret behind—don't. There are as good Margarets in Saint-Domingue as any in London."

"I am not thinking of her."

"Then what are you thinking of? Do you lack courage to start life anew? Zounds! You are still a youth. You've all your life ahead of you."

"But, Captain Beard, I must land." Duncan's voice grew hoarse with anxiety. "I am to be a physician. I am soon to apply for my diploma. I must be there. I will be a physician. I must land, I tell you."

"Understand this once and for all, lad," Beard growled. "Firstly, I'll be damned if I'm going to upset my passage to land you; and secondly, that if I was to land you, the hangman would string you up quicker nor you could say Jack Robinson. You have killed a fellow being. The punishment is death. You'll not see England again for many years—not if you want to live—and that's final."

Duncan stared at the swaying lamp, as he slowly grasped the purport of what Beard had just said. Never to practice medicine! Never to practice medicine! The phrase repeated itself in his mind as tonelessly and monotonously as the swinging of the lamp. Never to practice medicine! After thirteen years of apprenticeship, study, practice; after thirteen years of plans, of promise, of hope— Never to practice medicine.

"Captain Beard."

"Yes, lad?"

"Have you any liquor on board?"

"Aye. Barrels of it—mostly rum. Trust Captain Beard. He don't never travel without his tot of rum. Why?"

"Give me some," Duncan demanded.

CHAPTER NINETEEN

ABOUT eleven one January morning of the year 1789 the *Pride of Bristol* dropped anchor off Cap François. Duncan climbed down the swaying rope ladder into the bow of the boat that rode almost motionless upon the dazzling blue surface of the sea.

During the past weeks he had seen his fill of sailors, of Captain Beard's face, of the *Pride of Bristol*; he welcomed this moment of leaving the ship. Already in his mind he had left a life behind—all that he had, all that he hoped: now let the severance be complete. Slowly through days and nights of stupefying anguish he had grasped the finality of his situation. Toward the Andersons, for all of whom, save one, he felt a devotion only heightened by his remorse and his terrible need, he could make no gesture. To them and to his friends he was dead, and that part must become dead within himself—the memories be fought down until he would not remember. It was well he had come so far, to another world.

He shifted so as to face in the direction of the town of Cap François. The town was merely a blurred mass of white against a background of green and black. Then, as his vision gradually adjusted itself to the shimmering, distorted heat, he was able to distinguish certain landmarks— those same landmarks that Henri Christophe had first seen from the deck of the *Roi de France*, and more; for in the intervening ten years the town of Cap François had grown; much of the money paid out by the French war chest had flowed into Saint-Domingue coffers, for the island had been used as a vast supply depot for French and American soldiers fighting in the American states.

Now that he was beginning to recover slightly from the carousals of the previous night, he recalled some facts about the West Indies. But, although he recollected an account of the prosperity of the islands, he had scarcely anticipated quite so magnificent a town, even though Beard had told him that the inhabitants of Cap François delighted in calling their town the Paris of the West Indies. From what one could see of it, their claim was not unjustified. Even at a distance the fine architecture, statues, fountains, busy warehouses, cultivated gardens, and other amenities of a wealthy town were plainly visible.

71

"Welcome back to Cap François," Captain Beard's shipping agent, one Garreau, greeted Captain Beard, speaking English with an atrocious accent. "Time passes quickly in these days. It seems but a few weeks since you were last here."

The captain guffawed. "I haven't forgotten that night, m'soo. Have you seen that girl again? What was her name?"

"Clémentine? But no! A few nights after you and I had the pleasure of entertaining Clémentine, Monsieur de St. Just saw her. Monsieur de St. Just is a wealthy and a selfish man. He installed her as his mistress. I have not seen her since."

"Damn his hide!" Captain Beard growled. "But now, M'soo Garreau, allow me to present my friend, Mr. Stewart. He is a passenger aboard my ship."

"I am enchanted to meet you, Monsieur Stewart. Welcome to Cap François. But I did not know you carried passengers on your ship, Captain Beard."

"I don't, but Mr. Stewart now—" the captain winked broadly. "Well, he was in a hurry to go abroad, if you know what I mean, m'soo. He appealed to my sense of justice. And me, not being the sort of man what could see another man trying to fight half a dozen scurvy Bow Street runners, I said to Mr. Stewart: The *Pride of Bristol's* as good a ship as the next to take a trip in, so get ye below, and I'll tell those sons of bitches a tale what will make their heads split. And here he is, m'soo, safe in Saint-Domingue."

"Do you propose to settle down in Saint-Domingue, monsieur?" Garreau asked Stewart.

"If I can find work."

"Ah! That should present no difficulties. Saint-Domingue is a prosperous country. There is wealth and riches for all who care to work. What work have you had experience of, monsieur?"

Duncan frowned. "None I can take advantage of."

Garreau remarked the expression of anguish that his question evoked. "I shall be happy to do anything in my power to assist you, monsieur," he said courteously. "Do you speak French?"

Duncan answered the other man in his own tongue. "Sufficiently, I believe, monsieur, to have no difficulty in making myself understood." There was a bitter taste to the language he had learned from De Galinière—but he must forget that here.

"Excellent, excellent," Garreau cried out with delight. "It is so rare to find an Englishman speaking a foreign tongue. Has monsieur brought his luggage on shore?"

"I have nothing but the clothes I stand up in," Duncan told him sourly. "As Captain Beard has explained, I left England in—in a hurry."

"Of no importance," Garreau quickly assured Duncan. Then he continued, more hesitantly: "And if you will forgive a personal, and impertinent question—you have money, monsieur?"

"Enough to last me for a week or two."

"I am glad. At the end of that time if you would permit of my being temporarily your banker—"

At this point, Beard, becoming impatient of conversation that he could not understand, interrupted.

"I hope you are not engaged for tonight, m'soo."

Garreau smiled. "When the *Pride of Bristol* was sighted I sent word to my wife not to expect me home at the usual hour."

Beard chuckled loudly, and smote the Frenchman heartily on the back. "A man after my own heart, m'soo. Tonight we will show Mr. Stewart what happens in Cap François when the sun goes down, eh?"

"It will give me great pleasure, Captain."

The captain craned his head forward and sideways, reminding Duncan of an inquisitive parrot.

"Are there any new haunts of vice to visit, m'soo?"

"Ah, Captain, since your last visit to this city I have learned of the Casino François."

"Is it hot stuff?" Beard asked coarsely.

"It is a little more than it should be," Garreau admitted. "But it is—" He blew a kiss into the air. "It is owned by an old French campaigner who lost half an ear, an eye, and two fingers of his left hand, while fighting for France in different parts of the world. Then he fought in the American War of Independence at Savannah. When the volunteers returned, François—as everyone calls him, for nobody knows his other name—settled in Cap François. He obtained a position as a commission-aire at one of the hotels here. A year ago he opened the Casino François —one does not ask from where he obtained the financial backing, but one suspects a certain fair charmer of color, who now has to buy where once she sold. The casino is a great success, for François has an eye for beauti-ful women, Negresses and mulattoes alike. But it is of no use arriving there before midnight."

"That's the place for us all tonight, eh, Mr. Stewart?" Captain Beard asked boisterously.

Duncan's nod was disinterested. What matter where they went so long as the drink was strong enough to make one forget the past?

CHAPTER TWENTY

THE *Terre d'Or* from France dropped anchor, and a number of people landed at Cap François. The hotels, the cafés, and the restaurants were busier than ever that night, as they always were when a vessel ar-rived direct from France; there was always the chance that a traveler from Paris might enter one's favorite bar, and then one might hear the latest news and gossip to augment the meager and often distorted information contained in the newspapers.

The Hôtel de la Couronne was full. Perspiring waiters ran as quickly as they could from one client to another. There were continual shouts for Henri or for Marie—for Marie Louise Coidovid helped her father when he was busy. Though she was barely eleven years old she was exceptionally quick and intelligent; and her lithe body, with tropical precocity, already betrayed her budding womanhood. She was a favorite among the whites who frequented the Hôtel, and more than one of them had already envisaged the day when she would be old enough to seduce, and had privately computed the sum he would bid for the right to proclaim her as his mistress.

"Ah, there you are, Psaume!" said Cazeaux with satisfaction as, having made his way through the crowded bar, he reached a small group of men already seated. Cazeaux owned one of the large plantations situated in the immense and incredibly fertile Plaine-du-Nord, some miles to the southeast of Cap François. Turpin, the planter whose table he was joining, bellowed:

"Henri!"

Henri Christophe hurried to his side.

"Monsieur?"

"Four of the usual."

"At once, monsieur."

Henri hurried to get the rum punches. Turpin turned to Psaume, who had just returned from Paris on the *Terre d'Or*.

"We are impatient for the news, Psaume. What are the latest developments in Paris? Matters are not too satisfactory in France, are they?"

"Name of God! They are not. France is no longer the country it used to be. It was a sad day when the government decided to help those damned American colonists to fight the British."

"Why?"

"Why?" Psaume surveyed the circle of interested faces. "Even before America began that cursed War of Independence the French treasury was in a bad way, what with the extravagance of Louis XIV, and the cost of the mistresses of Louis XV. But now the national debt amounts to nearly four billion livres."

There were gasps from several of the men standing around. "It is not possible," one of them murmured.

"Is it not?" continued Psaume. "Even in 1781, Necker warned the government that the country was drifting into bankruptcy. You know the reward he received for his pains."

"Necker has been recalled."

"Yes, but the damage has been done. There is unrest in the country from Normandy to Anguedoc. Our soldiers helped the Americans set up their cursed republic; ever since their return to France, our peasants have been grumbling at the expense of keeping a king and court, and discussing the advantages of a republic."

"That is treason!" Sarrus said wildly. Sarrus was an effeminate young dandy who had arrived in Saint-Domingue as secretary of Duchilleau, governor of the French portion of the island. "It is treasonable even to repeat such rebellious sentiments."

"Maybe it is." The interruption made Psaume look sour. "But they are not my thoughts. I would not hurt a hair of the King's head, God bless him! But there is trouble in store for France, I tell you. Trouble."

"You are not suggesting revolution?"

"No, no," Psaume denied with an emphatic headshake. "Matters are not as bad as that. But there will be trouble of a sort. The peasants are openly demanding an amelioration of their living conditions."

"It's to be hoped that the government will ignore their demands," Turpin growled. "If I had my way I would flog peasants as I flog my damned niggers. A good flogging is the most salutary lesson I know for restless canaille—peasants and niggers alike."

"Unfortunately, notice is being taken of the people," Psaume stated somberly. "Before I left France I heard that the States-General had been summoned for next May."

There was grim silence, broken, a moment later, by excited conversation. Here was news indeed.

Psaume held up his hand. "I've far worse than that to tell you."

The hubbub died away.

"Too many of us have sent our bastard sons to be educated in Paris," Psaume continued—with commendable tact, for he had no bastard sons by black women. His three mistresses were in France, and his five bastards were all white. "The affranchis are worming their way into official favor. A number of interfering, mischievous, cant-ridden fanatics have formed themselves into a society called 'Les Amis des Noirs,' and they are—"

Psaume's last words were lost in a shout of rage that rose from the assembled company. Les Amis des Noirs! The Friends of the Blacks! It was incredible. White people befriending Negroes to the detriment of the white planters of the West Indies!

Oaths were shouted, fists brandished in the air. A surging wave of anger against the motherland roused the planters to frenzy.

"The Governor must be informed instantly," Turpin yelled. "Monsieur Duchilleau should be warned of what is happening. You, Sarrus, go to the Governor and tell him about those rats, Les Amis des Noirs. Name of God! I wish all 'friends of the niggers' were here now. They should share a flogging with their precious protégés."

"But Turpin—" Sarrus expostulated.

"Go. There is no time to waste."

Turpin's contorted face frightened the foppish secretary. With nervous reluctance he picked his way through the excited throng of white men.

When the clamor subsided Psaume answered further questions.

"What do these friends of the blacks hope to gain for the Negroes?"

"Emancipation," he replied. "They want the affranchis to have equal rights with us; that there should be no distinction in society; that no man shall have a right to possess or acquire anything to the exclusion of others—therefore the mulattoes should not be compelled to serve three years in the constabulary—or in the corvées; that they should be paid for serving in the militia; that they should not have to provide their arms, ammunition, and accouterments at their own expense; that in future they should be allowed to hold public office, and if they wish, become priests, lawyers, physicians, surgeons, apothecaries, or schoolmasters. All these things, which we say the mulattoes shall not do, those cursed Friends of

75

the Blacks would have them do. Lastly, the Friends demand the abolition of Negro slavery."

Once more his words were greeted by clamor. The furious shouting was renewed. Men milled around, careless of their behavior. A table crashed on the floor, and the clatter of broken glass added to the uproar. Coidovid and Henri tried to force their way to the debris, but they were roughly pushed aside; the bits of broken glass were ground into powder by restless feet.

"We must protect our rights," Turpin bellowed. "The King must be made to realize that the white colonists have rights and the black filth none. The affranchis must be warned to keep their place."

"Turpin is right," Cazeaux agreed. "Duchilleau must be made to understand our feelings."

"Let us hold meetings of protest."

"Yes, yes," chorused several of the planters.

"Let us declare the right of the colonists to send deputies to the States-General," called out Turpin.

"A toast to that idea," someone shouted.

There were calls for glasses to be recharged and Psaume jumped up on a chair.

"To the right of white colonists to send deputies to the States-General," he toasted.

The great shout which greeted the toast was heard in all the surrounding streets.

Captain Beard hiccuped. "Where's that confounded row coming from?" he demanded in a loud voice, as he walked unsteadily along the street, arm in arm with Duncan on one side and Garreau on the other.

"From the Hôtel de la Couronne, my friend," Garreau replied.

"Have we had a drink there yet?"

"Let me think, Captain. Have we yet had a drink at the Hôtel de la Couronne?"

"I want a drink," Beard shouted.

"But certainly, monsieur. We all want a drink. Let us enter the Hôtel de la Couronne."

Staggering unsteadily, first in one direction, then in another, the three men pushed their way into the barroom of the hotel. Few saw them enter, for most of the white people crowded about Psaume, who was now declaiming angrily against the French government.

Captain Beard led the way to a vacant table; the three men sat down.

"Service," Garreau shouted, as he hammered on the table with his closed fist. "Service, you pestiferous nigger," he repeated—for the time being he had lost the veneer of gentlemanly deportment that years of studied application normally enabled him to simulate.

Henri Christophe heard the summons. He hurried to answer it.

"Messieurs!"

"Three rums and lime juice," Garreau ordered.

"At once, messieurs." He hastened away to execute the order.

Captain Beard saw Marie Louise and lost interest in his companions.

76

Garreau giggled and leaned forward. "I am sure you are the son of a nobleman," he said to Duncan, in a confidential voice.

"I am the son of a physician."

"A physician!" The shipping agent gravely considered this information, then nodded his head in patronizing manner. A physician was of consequence among people of quality.

Garreau waved to Henri Christophe to put the drinks on the table.

"And are you, also, a physician?"

Duncan stared with drunken solemnity at his questioner. "Yes," he muttered craftily. "Yes. Physician and surgeon." He fingered his glass of rum with a caressing air. If the man opposite should ask any more questions he would throw the contents of the glass into Garreau's face.

But Garreau was silent—he was not quite sure what he and the stranger from England had been talking about. It would soon be time to leave for the Casino François, he decided. It would be far more interesting to watch beautiful women than to listen to men who shouted and argued about such unimportant subjects as Colonial Assemblies and National Assemblies.

"Ogé has sent a message from Paris by the *Terre d'Or*," Chavannes, a mulatto leader, told his followers. "A new society has been formed in France known as 'Les Amis des Noirs'—"

"Damn!" exclaimed Pétion. "Why should the French people befriend the cursed niggers?"

Chavannes held up a restraining hand. "One moment, my friends, Les Amis des Noirs wish to befriend the mulattoes—"

There was a howl of rage from his friends. "How dare they class us with the Negroes?"

"Because the white swine know no better," Chavannes pointed out. "But listen to what Ogé has to say. These Friends of the Blacks are sympathetic to the cause of the mulattoes. They want us to have our rights—equality with the whites."

"Real equality?" asked Rigaud.

"Absolute equality," confirmed Chavannes. "These people are agitating for our right to become priests, surgeons, lawyers, schoolmasters. No more serving in the constabulary, to spend our time hunting for runaway slaves. No more demeaning ourselves by compulsory roadwork in the *corvées*."

"Are Les Amis des Noirs trying to bring about all those reforms?" Riguad persisted.

"All. Ogé and our other friends in Paris are doing good work. Our time may come sooner than we believe."

"But I still do not like being classed with Negroes," Pétion muttered.

Chavannes revealed his teeth in a wolfish grin. "I agree, Pétion, but that is no reason why we should spite ourselves. Let us use this organization in France to serve our own ends, then when we have all we want—" He revealed his white teeth in a flashing smile.

"We can take care to see that the dirty niggers are kept in their proper places," Rigaud finished.

77

"Precisely, my friends, precisely," Chavannes assented.

For hours Toussaint impatiently listened to the sound of the wild shouting in the Hôtel de la Couronne. He was rarely impatient, for a life of slavery had taught him to be patient. But for once he was unsettled. For the past few hours wild rumors had circulated among the Negroes in the French portion of Saint-Domingue. He listened to the drums, whose throbbing disturbed the stillness of the night—tom-ti-ti-tom; tom-ti-ti-tom; tom-titi-titi-tom-tom; tom-titi-titi-tom-tom. The rumors he had already heard were being passed on from town to town, from plantation to plantation, from settlement to settlement, across the plains, over the mountaintops, through the depths of the jungle. Tom-ti-ti-tom; tom-ti-ti-tom.

Toussaint was happy to know that the Negroes were awakening to a sense of their own future, but he paid no serious heed to the message of the drums; he preferred to wait and hear the truth from the lips of Henri Christophe, who had the opportunity of learning the real facts from the white men who gathered in the Hôtel de la Couronne—he knew that he could rely upon Henri to repeat what he overheard without embellishment.

"Henri, my son, you are later than usual!" he warmly greeted the younger man. "What is the news from Paris?"

"Wonderful news, Toussaint."

"Tell me."

"A society of white people has been formed in Paris to obtain emancipation for the Negroes."

Toussaint's lips moved as he closed his eyes.

"I thank You, O Lord, for this, Thy handiwork. Thou has listened often, O Lord, to my prayers for the freedom of Your beloved people who are born in unnatural slavery. Listen, I pray, O Lord, to my further prayer: that the merciful white men whom in Thy graciousness Thou hast seen fit to make heed the pleas of the Negro may influence their fellow men. Grant, O Lord, that the spirit of goodness may soften the hearts of all white men as Thy gentle wind softens the heat of the noonday sun. Grant Thou this, O Lord, in Thy infinite grace and mercy. Amen."

Deeply moved, Toussaint embraced Henri.

"The years pass slowly, Henri, but the time will come when we Negroes will be free."

Henri scarcely had patience to listen. "I have other news, Toussaint."

"Well?"

"I have just collected the last livre that will enable me to purchase my freedom."

In the bright light of the moon Toussaint's gentle face evinced his satisfaction.

"I am glad, Henri. You have earned the right to be free, for you have worked conscientiously and industriously. One day you will make a worthy leader. And now—" He took hold of the young Negro's shoulders in his strong grasp.

"Yes, Toussaint?"

"When that day arrives, remember all that I have tried to teach you. Always thank God for His everlasting mercy. Work always for the good of your fellow Negroes. Remain friends with the white men, for they are not all bad. Be gentle with those who are less worthy than yourself. Be humble. Use your leadership wisely. Do those things well, and you will be revered among the black races of the world. Will you promise me that if ever you have the opportunity to do these things that you will do them?"

Henri thought: I wish all my dreams were as pleasant as Toussaint's. But aloud he said, in all sincerity: "I promise, Papa Toussaint."

CHAPTER TWENTY-ONE

WHILE Henri gave Toussaint the latest tidings from Paris, Duncan, Garreau, and Captain Beard arrived at the Casino François. It was a large, square, stone-built house of some thirty to forty rooms, which had once been the home of a wealthy planter. Its architecture was ornate; every simplicity had been rigorously eschewed. A loggia over which were carved mahogany architraves supported by slender columns of grained marble, stretched from the front entrance to each end of the façade. This entrance, like the columns of the loggia, was built wholly of marble and consisted of a semicircular stairway, six fluted columns, and a cupola above. The doors at the rear of this entrance were of carved wood and studded brass.

Formal gardens surrounded the building. These were planted with exotic plants, cacti shrubs, and colorful trees indigenous to the island, and with an immense variety of less spectacular flowers that had been imported from the Old World. These gardens were enclosed by railings of wrought iron, which permitted entry only by way of the twin wrought-iron gates that were directly opposite the main entrance into the house. Halfway between them and the entrance was a large, circular fountain, fed from the mouths of four sculptured dolphins.

Duncan had seen few houses in London that could compare with the Casino. He marveled silently at the immense sums of money that must have been expended. Captain Beard marveled too, but not silently.

"This is not a casino, this is a palace, fit for the King of France himself," he commented in his usual blunt manner.

Garreau laughed his pleasure. "There are many houses finer than this in Cap François, Captain. To say nothing of the remainder of Saint-Domingue. Did I not tell you that Saint-Domingue is the richest country in the New World?"

Garreau pushed open one of the iron gates and motioned his two friends to precede him. Together they proceeded along the paved path that led to the house. As they passed the fountain, Duncan listened to the splashing of the four jets of water. The sound was soothing but was almost drowned by other noises from the house—voices raised in loud conversation, song, and laughter.

Both the loggia and the entrance were lighted by lanterns of colored glass. As the three men stepped up toward the doors, Duncan saw that the architraves were smothered with masses of frangipani, poinsettia, and bougainvillea, which filled the surrounding air with a cloying scent. He saw, too, discreetly hidden among the low-hanging, intertwined branches, high-backed semicircular seats of stone, just wide enough to accommodate two people. Some of these seats were occupied by couples whose shadowy forms merged almost into one. . . .

Garreau pulled a bell rope. Almost at once the doors were opened. In the blaze of light Duncan saw a huge Negro, in a flunky's uniform of bright blue and scarlet, bowing low.

"Welcome, messieurs, to the Casino François."

They moved forward past the twin doors, which the flunky closed behind them. There they found themselves in a short, wide corridor, brilliantly lit by a chandelier burning forty wax candles. At the far end of the corridor were double doors, painted white and gilt, guarded by another brilliantly uniformed Negro. As the visitors approached, the second Negro bowed too. Then he threw wide the doors, and an extraordinary scene greeted the three men as they stood on the threshold of a huge ballroom.

This room, which occupied at least half the total length of the building and more than half the width, was lavishly decorated. Three chandeliers, each burning fifty-two candles, illuminated the room. The ceiling from which they were suspended was painted to represent Biton and Cleobis dragging the chariot of Cydippe to the temple of Hera, and other scenes from classical history. The walls were hung with mauve brocade and decorated with portraits of Louis XVI, Marie Antoinette, Louis XV, and Madame du Barry, interspersed with richly gilded mirrors. One half of the floor was occupied by tables. In a far corner five Negro musicians played throbbing, barbaric music.

While the visitors stood still, waiting to be directed to a vacant table, a man approached from across the ballroom. He was dressed modishly in clothes that looked incongruous on his thick-set, stocky body; for though the colors and the cut conformed to the latest whims of Paris tailors, the rough, horny hands below the lace ruffles—two fingers of the left hand were missing—the bristly, iron-gray hair, the lined, grizzled face with but one eye and half an ear, the stamping, unwieldy gait, were ill-suited to such fine raiment.

"Welcome, Monsieur Garreau. You see, I haven't forgotten your name," François greeted in his gruff, good-natured manner, but shouting so that he could be heard above the music. "So you could not keep away from my Casino for long, eh, monsieur? Old François knows his business. By thunder! Who would dare to say otherwise?" Ungracefully he swept his arm round in a circle, to indicate the crowded room.

"Not I," Garreau hastily assured him. "I hope you have a spare table, François, for I have brought two Englishmen with me tonight, as you see."

"Englishmen!" François laughed his pleasure. "I've spent all my life fighting against you, messieurs from England, but now you've come to buy a drink from me, and perhaps the kisses of one of my women, eh, messieurs?" The old soldier winked broadly. "Name of God! One never knows what is going to happen next. Now if one of you had come here to return to me the half of my ear, which an Englishman shot away from me when I was fighting in Spain—"

"What about a table, François?"

"Ah, yes, messieurs, of course, you wish a table. Follow me." As François threaded his way through the tables, he carelessly brushed aside anyone, guest or waiter, who got in his way, shouted loud greetings, exchanged coarse jokes. Presently he spied a vacant table, led them to it.

"What better table could you wish for than this one?" he lied unblushingly. "From here, messieurs, you will be able to see everything that happens—everything that happens in *this* room, I mean." He leaned forward in a confidential manner. "The games are proceeding in the usual rooms—"

"I doubt whether we shall want to play," Garreau told him.

François beamed. "You are like me, messieurs. By thunder! say I, who would play cards while there are the other rooms to use, the pick of all the girls in Saint-Domingue to choose from? Why, messieurs—"

"They will soon be seeing for themselves, François," the shipping agent pointed out with impatience.

The understanding François nodded his head. "Another time, messieurs, another time I must tell you of how I lost my fingers in Russia—"

"It was Italy last week, François."

"It was Russia," François contradicted firmly.

"And next week it will be Prussia," Garreau jeered.

François remained unperturbed. "We must meet again, monsieur," he said to Duncan. "It will be a novel experience for François to be friendly with an Englishman. But someone else has arrived. I must hurry off." With a friendly chuckle François stamped away, colliding with a Negro waiter as he did so.

"What has that carved-up piece of mincemeat been saying?" Beard growled in English.

CHAPTER TWENTY-TWO

DUNCAN looked round the ballroom at the fantastic ensemble of which he had become a part. With two exceptions every table was fully occupied by a mixed company of men and women, but the men were white, the women mulattoes. Many of the men were richly dressed in high boots, short trousers, tail coat adorned with large metal buttons, cut-away waistcoat with pendant jeweled watch chains, and a peruke with tail tightly rolled and fastened with a bow of black silk. Some of them, though obviously of white birth, had darker complexions than the mulatto women who accompanied them. These were the planters who paid scrupulous attention to their colonial interests, or who lived permanently on the island from which they drew their immense wealth; others were creoles, white descendants of earlier white settlers. Some men, noticeably attired in the utmost extravagance of fashion, still had the ruddy complexion of the sun-burned European. These were the planters—and they were a numerous company—who chose to spend most of their time in Paris and their money in idleness and riotous living.

The gowns of the women showed greater variety; though some were dressed as fashionably as their partners, the majority showed a superb dis-regard for stultifying modes and emphasized their slender lines and superb carriage with diaphanous draperies. All possessed seductive beauty and perfect bodies; they smiled or laughed incessantly, with a flashing of white teeth, alike to confidences whispered in their ears as to remarks shouted from other tables.

Presently Beard rose from the table and left the ballroom. Garreau watched him go.

"The capital wealth represented in this ballroom would pay off a con-siderable share of the French national debt," he observed moodily. "There is Monsieur Turpin over there by the window—he must have come here from the Hôtel de la Couronne, for he was there when we first entered. Sitting next to him is Monsieur Marilys. Marilys has more money than sense. Two years ago he wished to punish some of his slaves, so he invited his friends to a game of bowls. When the friends arrived they found a number of slaves buried up to their necks in the ground. Marilys then pro-duced a number of cannon balls, and invited the visitors to bowl them at the heads of the Negroes. It took more than an hour to kill them all."

"To kill them!" Duncan stared incredulously at Garreau.

"Yes."

"God!" Duncan felt sick. "The fiend."

"The fool, you mean, monsieur! He could have sold the slaves instead of killing them. Strong, healthy slaves are selling for the equivalent of sixty pounds in your English money. That game of bowls cost him more than five hundred pounds. My God! Had he given the slaves to me I should have known what to do with the money."

The music blared loudly. A clown appeared and began to sing, but the din drowned his words, and his poor pantomime passed almost unnoticed.

"The woman with Marilys is his mistress. Of course, as you see, no white woman comes to the Casino François. Every woman here is the mistress of her cavalier—or even of them all. You see that ravishing beauty at the table next to Turpin's. She is Louise Nanette, the most successful strum-pet in town. She will not reserve herself to any one man. She has had many offers, but she declares for variety and makes more money by re-maining free. It would be cheaper for you to buy a dozen slaves, monsieur, than to spend a night in her bed. The man with her is the Comte de Sara-mon. He came out to Saint-Domingue for his amusement. Now he swears he will not leave the island unless Louise Nanette accompanies him. It is said that he has already paid her one hundred thousand Saint-Domingue livres for her kisses."

The music blared loudly. The men shouted uproariously. The mulatto women laughed.

"Guilbaud is another rich planter," Garreau continued. "He owns more

82

slaves than the year has days. The man in uniform at his table is Colonel Mauduit, who commands one of the French regiments stationed on the island. With them is Thionnet. Thionnet spends most of his money buying female slaves. He has thirteen bastards, each by a different woman. They are all in Paris, being educated. Sometimes Thionnet holds a ball at his château, which is halfway up the mountains behind Cap François. His guests are men only. Before they dance Thionnet calls in his slaves. At a signal the girls throw off their clothing. The men then choose their dancing partners."

Duncan's soul revolted at the things Garreau was telling him. He told himself that the shipping agent was lying; that the tales he was telling of Saint-Domingue were products of a vivid, diseased imagination; that Garreau had a vicious mind, which attributed to others practices which he himself secretly craved. The more Duncan tried to persuade himself that petty-minded lies had been poured into his ears, the more his dour common sense assured him of the contrary. During the past few hours he had had an opportunity of appraising the character of Garreau, and he knew Garreau for a kindly soul whose narrow mind was uninterested in anything that did not immediately concern him. Garreau merely made the best and the most of what life offered.

The shipping agent was too interested in describing the people at the Casino to notice Duncan's expression of repugnance. "Over there are some of the other men who were at the Hôtel de la Couronne," he continued. "Do you see the one with a birthmark on his left cheek? That is Cazeaux. He produces indigo. The man with him is Psaume, who has just arrived from France. The woman with him is Madeleine. Rumor says that while Psaume has been in Paris, she has had an affair with Lambion, who runs a banking business in Cap François. If Psaume hears of it he will kill Madeleine. But Lambion will be safe, because most of Psaume's money is handled by Lambion et Compagnie."

The countrymen of Armand de Galinière! thought Duncan, with disgust. And still Garreau chattered on.

"At the next table, sitting with his back to Psaume, is the Baron de Vincent. The Baron has the ear of the King, so it is said. The man with him is Binoche. Binoche's favorite method of disposing of slaves is by flogging them to death. He lost a very dear friend, killed by Negroes in Africa. From that moment Binoche has never ceased to revenge that death. He has a greater percentage of maroons—runaway slaves—to his credit than anyone else on the island. He has four bloodhounds. Every time a slave flees from his plantation Binoche invites his friends to a hunt. They hunt the slave, and those in at the kill receive a gift. I was at the kill once. Binoche sent me a case of champagne."

"Do you mean—the—the hunters killed the poor devil for running away?"

"Hush, monsieur!" the nervous Garreau cautioned. "You mustn't call slaves poor devils. No, the huntsmen do not kill the maroons. The dogs do that."

"The dogs?"

"Yes. They are starved and ill-treated by their Negro keepers into a state of savagery. Those dogs have only to see a Negro to tear him to bits and eat him."

"Great God! And did you enjoy 'the kill,' Monsieur Garreau?" Duncan asked with scorn.

Garreau moistened his lips with the tip of his tongue. He looked about him; then, observing that nobody appeared to be paying particular attention to their table, he leaned forward. "Between ourselves, monsieur," he admitted fearfully, "I did not. To watch a man torn to pieces is not my idea of amusement. I never could stand the smell of raw meat. But in the name of God, monsieur, never tell anyone what I have said. If it were thought that I was weak enough to sympathize with slaves I should be ostracized, and ruined."

"I'm not likely to, but are all the runaway slaves from the plantation of Binoche hunted in the same fashion?"

"Most of them."

"Then why do they run away?"

"They prefer the risk of being torn to pieces by the jaws of savage dogs to the misery of remaining with Binoche."

"The man must be a bloodthirsty fiend."

"I do not like him," Garreau confirmed, with an uneasy glance about him. "But for God's sake, let us not talk of Monsieur Binoche any more. Let me tell you of some of the other men here."

"You have told me enough."

The shipping agent shook his head. "I don't want to give you a wrong impression of Saint-Domingue, monsieur. I do not approve of torturing slaves, but beyond that, well, after all, slaves are just—slaves."

Duncan frowned. "They are men and women. And I, who am a physician and have studied human anatomy, say that men and women, whatever their color, are the greatest of all God's miracles. He did not make men and women to be used as ninepins, to be flogged to death for amusement, or to be torn to pieces by maddened dogs for the recreation of white men and women."

"What do you want?" Garreau asked abruptly in a loud voice.

Duncan turned and saw that a waiter stood behind him.

"Your orders, messieurs."

It seemed to the Scot that the voice was familiar. He looked up at the waiter's face and recognized the man who had served them at the Hôtel de la Couronne.

"Have you been listening to our conversation?" Garreau demanded in a hectoring manner, behind which Duncan distinguished a note of fear.

"No, monsieur," Henri Christophe replied with servile haste. "How could one overhear anything in this noise, monsieur?"

In spite of Henri's denial Duncan believed that the Negro lied. He first scrutinized and then admired, as a medical man, Henri's fine, powerful body, his firm Negroid face, his unusually intelligent eyes. The man must have terrific physique and stamina.

"Did you serve us at the Hôtel de la Couronne?" he asked.

Henri nodded. "Yes, monsieur."

"Are you also a waiter here?"

"I am, monsieur."

Garreau clutched at Duncan's arm. "Don't talk to the man. He will become impertinent," he entreated.

"Surely I am doing no harm in asking him a few questions?"

"You are new to this island. You should allow me to prompt you as to what a white man should or should not do."

Duncan recognized the truth of this observation and appreciated the agent's feeling of anxiety, but the fumes of the alcohol which he had been steadily drinking all the evening had not entirely dispersed. He felt reckless, defiant.

"I insist upon satisfying my curiosity. I am a doctor. I am interested in knowing how a man can work so many hours without tiring."

"Slaves are not permitted to feel tired," Garreau pointed out naïvely.

Duncan disregarded the Frenchman. "Doesn't the work tire you?" he asked Henri.

The Negro prevaricated. "I am the slave of Monsieur Coidovid, of the Hôtel de la Couronne. The work there I am compelled to do. This work, with the permission of Monsieur Coidovid, I do voluntarily."

"Voluntarily?"

"The tips I earn here, monsieur, help to buy my freedom. Besides, I am anxious to help Monsieur François. He has been kind to me since I was twelve years of age."

Garreau could restrain his patience no longer. "Bring three rum and limes," he shouted.

"Three, monsieur?"

"Yes, fool. Our friend has only left us for a moment."

"Certainly." Henri departed.

"Insolent rascal," Garreau muttered angrily. "So François has been kind to him, has he?"

Duncan feared that Garreau might make trouble for François and Henri. "You'll not pass on the information?"

Garreau shrugged his shoulders. Then a swift smile chased away his annoyance. "But no, why should I try to do harm? Besides, I do not want the Casino to suffer. I enjoy coming here occasionally. François is making a remarkable success. You must understand that this is not the only room. There are many other, smaller rooms. In some of them one gambles. In others—" The agent smiled slyly. "One makes up one's own parties. Many things happen in the private rooms that one would not like one's wife to hear about.

"I was born in Marseille," he continued. "Marseille is a gay city. So is Paris, I am told, monsieur. But Cap François offers everything to a man that gaiety and love can offer, and of the many places of entertainment the Casino François is the most interesting. In the private rooms here, monsieur, one does not embrace one woman, but many. One can hold bacchanalian feasts such as the Romans never dreamed of, my friend. Life in Saint-Domingue can be very pleasant."

The music blared. The men shouted uproariously. The mulatto women smiled. The clown waved his hand and departed through a concealed door behind the musicians' stand. The people laughed and cheered his departure, though none had heard his song.

François appeared from the concealed door, and as he stamped forward into the center of the cleared space, there was a whispering sigh that traveled like a wave, from table to table, until it was drowned by huzzas of welcome.

"That is what everyone has been waiting for," Garreau explained.

François raised his arms. The shouting died away.

"Good evening, messieurs," François announced with gruff good humor. "I am delighted to see so many familiar faces at my tables, and to know that the slight entertainment with which I try to amuse my audience—"

"Is being appreciated," several voices chanted.

"Quite right, messieurs. But now—"

"I have a surprise for you," the revelers shouted in unison.

François beamed. "Yes, messieurs, as a special surprise I am going—"

"To present an entirely new and unique entertainment," his cheerful hecklers called out.

"We know the speech by heart, François," Thionnet shouted thickly. "Start the music."

"Yes, yes, waste no time, François," several other visitors echoed.

"So now, messieurs," he continued, smiling broadly, "the Casino François has the pleasure of presenting to its honored guests the *Danse Françoise*, followed by the *Danse Saint-Domingue*." As he shouted the last word he raised his hand, and the band broke into violent discord. The old trooper stumped away, and from what apparently was the artists' door, twelve dancers ran out into the ballroom.

Their appearance was a signal for a terrific shout of laughter, in which Duncan joined as loudly as any in the ballroom. All twelve dancers were full-blooded Negresses. Their hair was frizzed like a black halo, reminding Duncan of the golliwogg toy he had seen Elizabeth playing with in the past; the whites of their eyes were brought into high relief as they rolled them about with abandon; their white teeth flashed as they parted their full lips in sly laughter. To the Negro eye they were probably beautiful; judged even by the standards of white men they were not distasteful, for the perfect bodies, laughing lips, and white teeth were seductive, the expression in their roving eyes frankly inviting. But their attraction was discounted by their costume. They wore full ballet dress—white satin shoes, white silk tights, tight bodices that concealed their busts, frail shoulder straps, and voluminous knee-length skirts with numerous petticoats beneath.

The burlesque was cruel, for the vivid white of the dresses served to accentuate the coal black of the Negresses' flesh, while their bearing accentuated the incongruity of their costume. Wave after wave of hysterical laughter shook the audience. The extraordinary antics and the infectious laughter of the dancers completed the burlesque. As the band distorted the music of Vestris' ballet *Hero and Leander*, the dancers flung themselves into the air with floundering movements; they collided, they tripped, their every movement was a deliberate travesty of grace. The audience held their aching sides.

The music ceased. With the last note each dancer held her pose. There was a bewildering silence, followed by gasps as the audience gazed at the unmoving picture, which now resembled a waxworks tableau. The seconds passed by. Still no man in the orchestra, no dancer on the floor moved. Excitement rose higher as the audience wondered how much longer the tableau could last.

Then the music blared out afresh, but no longer discordantly. The Negresses began to dance again, but gracefully. For a few minutes they danced a stately minuet, until the ballroom was hushed with appreciation of the exquisite artistry. Presently, almost more quickly than the eye could follow, the dancers executed two strange movements, but it was not until they pirouetted, and a shower of ballet shoes fell against the wall behind, that many of the onlookers realized that the Negresses had removed their shoes. A slight ripple of laughter traveled through the room, but it was short, uncertain; no one knew whether the movement was to be accepted seriously or as a renewal of the burlesque. The dancers continued to dance correctly. Once more only the music and the sound of the girls' feet were to be heard.

Again there were two strange movements, this time slower, as the dancers stripped the tights first from their right, then their left legs. The ballet continued with a mounting of excitement as some of the audience anticipated the next move. A pirouette, a dexterous twist of the arms, and tight bodices, freed from twisting bodies, were flung against the wall. When the dancers turned again they were nude to the waist.

The sigh became louder, for each young, taut breast stood proudly erect from its smooth body. But still the massed white petticoats billowed from their waists. Somebody called out drunkenly: "Strip off the skirts, too," but even as the words echoed through the ballroom, the skirts, too, were flung away. The Negresses posed, proudly naked; every coal-black figure was physically perfect.

The black bodies began to sway with sinuous, stamping grace. The movements grew quicker. Men leaped to their feet and pounded upon the tables. The women with them clapped; their rolling eyes seemed to grow larger and to glisten whitely with desire. Their bodies swayed with the music.

Then again a sudden, abrupt, alarming silence. For ten seconds the dancers remained motionless. A chair clattered to the ground as a man stumbled toward the center of the floor. Before he had gone far his friends seized hold of him and forced him back.

The music began again. Duncan believed that he was hearing discords again, but then realized that this was not so. The tune was barbaric but rhythmic and reminded him of the throbbing notes of drums amplified by the addition of cymbals, horns, and conch shells. The dancers retired to the wall and stood there in repose. The artists' door opened, and a dancer appeared, clad in a loose hooded robe that concealed all save her eyes. To the clash of cymbals, the shriek of conches, she ran to the center of the floor and stood poised, waiting for her cue. The cymbals and conches faded away. The throbbing of the drums grew louder. The crescendo ended in a terrific boom. With a vivid gesture the dancer threw away her cloak, to stand revealed as a mulatto woman, naked from head to feet.

She was greeted by a loud shout that died away as she began to dance. The movements were not those of the graceful ballet of European derivation, but a dance of primitive Africa—savage, violent, lustful. Her sinuous body weaved and twisted in undulating movements that traveled from her toes to her head, until every muscle rippled.

Excitement mounted. The mulatto mistresses surrendered their bodies to the rhythm; their hips and breasts undulated with increasing abandon. Breath escaped from their lips with a hissing sound; they clapped their hands to the beat of the drums. The white men joined in; the noise became louder, faster, louder, faster. The dancing Negresses joined in; their bodies swayed sinuously.

Duncan gazed with burning eyes at the solo dancer. Together with the others he clapped his hands in rhythm and pounded the floor with one foot. He was not aware of doing so. He was aware of nothing save that he had never seen a more beautiful body than the mulatto's. "It is perfect," he whispered aloud, again and again. He had seen many bodies, but none such as hers. He gazed entranced at her provocative eyes, at her crimson, sensuous lips, at the pointed tip of her tongue, at the sheen of her honey-colored flesh, at her round, molded breasts with crimsoned nipples, at her swaying hips, at her slim buttocks and thighs. He felt desire sweep through his body, overpowering every other thought or urge.

Faster, faster, faster. She could not dance much longer, she could not, she could not. But still she twisted, laughed, turned, swayed, to the shrieks of the conches, the thunderous accompaniment of her audience. Presently she danced forward toward the tables, threaded her way among them, still twisting, laughing, turning, swaying. The tips of her fingers lightly caressed the chins of the men who stood up; the crimson nipples of her breasts kissed the cheeks, the eyes, the lips of the men who still sat down, the laughing, inviting, tormenting devil in her eyes challenged the staring eyes of those farther off.

The Negresses followed her. In every direction were taut, black breasts, slim buttocks, crimson lips, taunting eyes. Laughing, twisting, turning, swaying. Louder, faster, louder, faster—

The music stopped. Duncan gasped as he closed his weary eyes. Presently, when he felt sanity return, he opened them again. The mulatto with the crimsoned breasts was gone; the Negresses were gone. So were Captain Beard and Garreau!

CHAPTER TWENTY-THREE

DUNCAN struggled into complete wakefulness. He opened leaden-weighted eyelids and stared up at a white plaster ceiling. He shifted his head slightly and saw a pleasant woman of middle age. Her eyes were dark brown, kindly. Her skin was as brown as a berry. Her figure was pleasantly plump, and she wore a white muslin dress. So much he observed, but the effort of keeping his eyes open was painful. A spasm of vertigo attacked him. His head became a reverberating battleground of drums. His throat was afire and parched.

He spoke in French and finished with a forlorn moan of misery. "Who are you? I do not remember your being on the ship. Where have you been hiding all this time?"

"Ship, monsieur? Ah!" The speaker laughed softly as she realized the trend of his thoughts. "You are no longer on board the *Pride of Bristol*."

"Not on board——" Regardless of the pain he opened his eyes and gazed at the woman who stroked his forehead. "Where am I?"

"In a house in Cap François. My husband Simon brought you here some hours ago."

"I know no Simon. Simon who?"

"Simon Garreau, the shipping agent."

The name set the machinery of memory into motion. He knew he had lately heard the name. Garreau—shipping agent—a short, dark man with salacious eyes, nervous fingers—

"Now I remember," he announced. "Captain Beard introduced me to him last night. We went out together, the three of us."

"A roistering time you must all have had," Mme Garreau commented without resentment. "It is always so when Captain Beard comes to Cap François. On such nights I do not see my husband until the following morning. And when I do—*la! la!*—what a state he is in. But I rejoice that he does not see yellow dogs. Captain Beard broke my beautiful vase while trying to kick a yellow dog out of the way."

"Where is Captain Beard now?"

"On his way to America. He helped Simon to carry you into the house and into this bedroom. He told Simon that you intended to stay in Saint-Domingue."

Affected by the misery which she glimpsed in his eyes, she sat down on the bed and clasped him to her.

"The poor one!" she murmured in a caressing whisper. "The poor Monsieur Stewart! Life has been unkind to him. He has killed a man and has had to leave his own country. But one does not need to tell Annette Garreau that the man he killed deserved to die. Doubtless he was a villain?"

There was a note of interrogation in her voice.

"He was a thief," he replied with a viciousness that was the more intense for his having been deprived of any sympathy for so many weeks. "He was a foul ingrate who repaid my kindnesses to him by seducing my beloved. I killed him for what he did to Margaret and me. I killed him, do you hear? I struck him on his head. I made his stinking blood stain the sawdust red, and I'm glad. He robbed me of all I wanted from life. Now he can burn in hell for all eternity."

"Hush, oh, monsieur, hush!" Mme Garreau glanced about her with frightened eyes. "You must not call thus upon the powers of evil, lest they claim you, too, as their victim."

His laughter was bitter. "Hell hasn't any terror for me, madame. What more could I suffer than to be robbed of my ambition? Within a few months I was to be a physician. All my life I have worked and studied to be a physician. Now I've been robbed of that joy by that cursed thief of a Fren—of a foreigner."

She wept in sympathy. "The poor one! The poor one! How well I can appreciate your sorrow, monsieur. Many years ago I, too, left my native country. When I saw France vanishing in the distance I thought my heart would break. Behind me were all my friends, and my relations. Before me was an unknown country where I should know none save an uncle whom I had never seen. When I landed in Saint-Domingue I cried all night because of what I had left in France. But my sadness quickly passed. Now, monsieur, there isn't a happier woman in all Saint-Domingue. Not one."

Garreau returned home at noon. Save for a slight listlessness there was little evidence to be seen of his previous night's carouse. Duncan, on the other hand, although considerably recovered since his awakening, was in a sorry condition. Although reddened by the wind and sun during his passage through the Caribbean Sea, he was pale, listless and dispirited.

Garreau greeted his guest with outstretched hand. "So you are up, Monsieur Stewart. How are you feeling? Not very cheerful?"

"What reason should Monsieur Stewart have for feeling cheerful?" Mme Gareau asked with asperity. "You should be ashamed of yourself, you worthless man, making monsieur the worse for liquor on the first night of his first visit to Cap François. You should have realized that monsieur is not as seasoned a rum drinker as yourself."

"Is he not?" The shipping agent chuckled. "Captain Beard gave me an excellent report on his capacity for rum."

"That Captain Beard! He is no fit person to associate with. I thank the good God that he does not call here more often. Moreover, Simon, life has been unkind to Monsieur Stewart. It is little wonder that he drinks too much rum. Had I been a man when I left France I should have found forgetfulness in rum."

"Yes, my pet," Garreau agreed easily, having heard many times of his wife's distress at leaving France. "Are you ready for food, monsieur? If not, you will be when you see and smell the meal which is nearly ready. For all her faults Annette is a marvelous cook."

"I am quite hungry," Duncan lied gallantly.

The Frenchman chuckled, as though well aware of his guests's insincerity. "Are you feeling the heat?"

"I'm sweating like a pig. Is it always as hot on the island?"

"As hot! My friend, this is the cool season of the year. During August the days are half as hot again. And we, in Cap François, consider ourselves fortunate that we do not live in Port-au-Prince. Here, at least, we are cooled by a north wind each evening, but Port-au-Prince faces west and is deprived of that slight advantage by chains of mountains."

Duncan dried his forehead. Not ten minutes previously he had bathed his face with chilled water, but beads of perspiration were again oozing from the pores of his skin and trickling into his eyes and down his cheeks.

"If it is like this in the cool season how do you live through the heat of August?"

"One becomes accustomed to it," Garreau replied carelessly. "During the first few months of his stay here the newcomer sweats every drop of moisture from his body. After that his skin is like leather and all but immune from perspiration. By this time next year you will be grumbling at the cold."

"Saint-Domingue is a difficult place," said Duncan.

"But money can be made in Saint-Domingue," said Garreau. "A man can grow prosperous."

"You are not one to talk so blithely of being prosperous," Mme Garreau interrupted.

"I have hopes, my pet. I do not intend always to remain a shipping agent."

"Ever since our marriage I have heard the same story. Hopes, hopes, hopes! Do you know that Madame Gauchez has twice as many house slaves as I? Even Madame Emery has two more slaves than I, she whose husband has not lived five years on the island."

"Monsieur Emery was fortunate in buying a cotton plantation from a shiftless bankrupt."

"Are there not other worthless people willing to sell their plantations?" Mme Garreau demanded. "Monsieur Pegois has not long to live, and that colored bastard of his has but one thought—to go to France to arouse the sympathies of decent white people for the mulattoes. If I had my way all mulattoes would be slaves like the Negroes."

"Aren't some of the Negroes free?" Duncan asked.

"Yes, many of them, more's the pity," Mme Garreau snapped.

Her husband shifted restlessly in his chair. He did not like the manner in which Annette had spoken of the mulattoes. It made him wonder whether she suspected that he was the father of a mulatto girl-child by a handsome black wench, daughter of one of the slaves who worked on the company's wharf.

"Some of the Negroes are not bad creatures," he murmured.

Duncan tried to distract the attention of his host and hostess from their conjugal argument. "How many white people are there in Saint-Domingue?"

Garreau welcomed the excuse to change the conversation. "About thirty thousand."

"And nearly as many mulattoes," Mme Garreau added. "The mulattoes now number more than twenty-four thousand. Such figures speak more adequately than I can of the white man's proclivities!"

"Are there as many Negroes?"

"Nearly half a million," Garreau replied. "And that number is being swelled yearly, by birth and importation. The year before last slave vessels brought thirty-one thousand Negroes into the French colony. Of those, Cap François received approximately six thousand men, more than two thousand women, one thousand five hundred boys, and nearly one thousand girls."

"Half a million Negroes to thirty thousand whites!" Duncan glanced at the shipping agent. "Then the Negroes outnumber the whites by nearly seventeen to one?"

"Yes."

"Isn't there danger of the black man rising against his white master?"

"Danger!" Garreau laughed scornfully. "If you were a farmer would you fear danger from a herd of sheep? Negroes are born to be slaves." He broke off and glanced at Duncan. "It is time we spoke of you instead of ourselves. First of all, we must help you to find a nice hotel where you can stay."

"Indeed, no," Mme Garreau interrupted. "How dare you suggest we should be guilty of such inhospitality? Why should Monsieur Stewart have to occupy a room in a hotel when there is a vacant bedroom in this house?"

"But Madame Garreau—" Duncan protested.

"An excellent idea, monsieur," Garreau supported warmly. "It would give us the greatest pleasure to have you as our guest until you desire to make your own establishment."

Duncan glanced at his hostess. She nodded her head.

"Please stay with us, monsieur. You can more than repay us by telling us of England. We have heard so much of your country."

Still Duncan hesitated. A few hours previously he had been anathematizing all Frenchmen. How could he now accept hospitality from a French family, even though he liked Mme Garreau and was almost ready to tolerate her husband?

Mme Garreau sensed his indecision and decided to press home the advantage that she felt was already hers.

"We have so few visitors, monsieur," she added in an embarrassed whisper. "We are not rich enough for the planters to be friendly with us, while, on the other hand, we are quite certainly not trade."

"Most certainly we are not," Garreau echoed. He wanted to forget that he had been born the son of a Marseilles butcher and not the son of one of the original settlers.

Duncan told the Garreaus that he would be delighted to stay with them.

CHAPTER TWENTY-FOUR

AS Garreau prepared to return to the office he said to Duncan: "Why not come with me for the afternoon, monsieur? I can give you an insight into the commerce of Saint-Domingue. A large proportion of its exports pass through the hands of Dumestre et Fils. I could tell you more in one hour of the cause of this island's prosperity than many a planter could if he talked to you for a week."

"Yes, go with Simon," Mme Garreau urged. "You will realize what a fool of a husband it is my misfortune to possess. He knows how easily money is to be made in Saint-Domingue, yet he has not the ability to make some for himself."

"Peace, Annette, for the love of God! For ten of our twelve years of married life you have nagged me to gamble my future by purchasing a plantation. Do I not occupy an important position with Dumestre et Fils?

Shipping is safe. Why should I throw away such good employment? My father was a butcher."

"As long as the world lasts, men must eat. Butchering is a safe business. If safety is your only thought in life, why did you forsake your father's business? Isn't the ownership of a plantation as safe as shipping or butchering?"

"No," he denied sulkily. "But there is no further time to waste. Do you care to come with me this afternoon, Monsier Stewart?"

"If I may."

The two men stepped into a fiacre after Garreau had ordered the Negro driver to drive them to the corner of the quay overlooking the Place de Brasseur.

"The portion of this island owned by France is divided into three departments," Garreau explained, as he leaned back against the carriage seat and lazily fanned himself. "They are known as the North, the West, and the South. Cap François is the capital of the northern province and the seat of the French government in time of war. At all other times Port-au-Prince is the metropolis of the colony, though heaven alone knows why, for it is but two thirds the size of Cap François and certainly less attractive."

"Is Port-au-Prince also in the northern province?"

"No, my friend. Port-au-Prince is in the western province. The southern province is the least important and has only two towns of note, Aux Cayes and Jacmel." He waved his free hand at the magnificent mansion that they were passing at that moment. "The home of De Saint Just, of whom I spoke to Captain Beard. Until you have met him, you will not have seen the greatest elegance of our island, monsieur. The small building to the right is his also. He bought it some months back, for his mistress, Clémentine.

"There, opposite the beautiful Clémentine's villa," Garreau continued, "is Monsieur Psaume's establishment, rarely inhabited by him, for he spends most of his time in Paris. Farther along this road is the Cap François villa of Monsieur Turpin, who is one of the six richest men on the island. Now glance at the building to your left, monsieur. You might well imagine it to be the palace of His Excellency the Governor, Monsieur Duchilleau. But you would be wrong. The Comte de Saramon lives there. His ancestor was one of the buccaneers who seized this part of the island from the Spaniards."

As they arrived at crossroads, Duncan glanced along the intersecting avenues. Many fine buildings of varied architecture and design were to be seen, most of them quite as magnificent as Psaume's or De Saint Just's.

"Are there many roads as prosperous as the one we are in?"

"Many. Besides shops, offices, and warehouses, there are nearly one thousand homes in Cap François, of which a high proportion belong to men of wealth." The agent paused. "How many domestic slaves would you imagine there are in Cap François?"

"Three to four thousand," Duncan ventured.

Garreau laughed. "My friend, there are twelve thousand domestic slaves in this town, and eight thousand free inhabitants of all colors. Those figures do not include the French troops, the seafaring people, and the actors who perform at the playhouse."

Presently they came within sight of the sea. Upon reaching the water front the carriage turned to the left, to stop outside one of the largest buildings Duncan had yet seen in Cap François. It was a plain, brick building, square, two stories high, with three large entrances.

"The warehouse of Dumestre et Fils. Is it not a building of which the New World has reason to be proud? Can your London boast many greater buildings?"

"Please don't remind me of London."

Garreau was instantly contrite. "Forgive me, monsieur. For a moment I had forgotten your circumstances." He indicated a slave who had hurried forward to assist the men to alight. "Will you descend?"

Duncan did so, followed by his host. Together the two men entered the warehouse, where they were greeted upon all sides by flashing teeth and rolling eyes.

Fascinated, Duncan gazed about him. From floor to ceiling every available inch of room had been put to the fullest possible use. Goods were stacked in long, straight avenues, in square bales, long, narrow bundles, rough wooden cases, or casks, according to the commodity, and the strong, mixed odor of perfume, spices, tobacco, and cacao permeated the building in such profusion that he could distinguish no specific smell. The cloying fragrance was wafted about his nostrils until his head threatened to swim.

The noise was deafening. In every avenue slaves were at work. One group wheeled away bales of goods to be loaded in the holds of one of the ships that lay out in the wide bay, another group filled up the vacant space with a fresh consignment of produce newly arrived from one of the plantations. Other slaves stitched canvas for the bales, sawed wood for the cases, or hammered nails home. All these separate noises, loud and incessant, were accompanied by a pandemonium of shrill chatter from the slaves and shouted orders from the overseers.

"Sugar," Garreau shouted in Duncan's ear as he pointed to the bales that lined both sides of an avenue down which they strolled. "Muscovado is unrefined sugar, monsieur, and in quantity is Saint-Domingue's largest product. We produce and export annually eighty-six million pounds of muscovado, valued at thirty-five million Saint-Domingue livres. But muscovado is not our most valuable commodity."

The agent pointed to an avenue of bulky sacks. "Coffee exports total seventy-one million Saint-Domingue livres, for that same number of pounds. A valuable business, is it not, Monsieur Stewart? Since the cost of feeding the slaves is practically the only charge against that sum, it is not surprising that this colony is one of the richest in the world."

The two men moved on. "Purified sugar," Garreau next pointed out. "Or, as we call it, clayed sugar, because it is purified by water percolating through a layer of clay spread over the surface of the sugar. The water carries away with it the residuary viscid syrup, and by a slow process the sugar is thus whitened. Nearly sixty million pounds of clayed sugar are produced annually, realizing more than forty-one million livres."

"Is the Colony given up exclusively to sugar and coffee?" he asked presently.

Garreau laughed. "By no means. There are eight hundred plantations producing sugar and more than three thousand producing coffee, but sugar and coffee plantations combined make up less than half the total of plantations contained in the French part of Santo Domingo. Come with me, monsieur."

Duncan followed Garreau past a number of avenues. At the far end of the warehouse Garreau pointed to stocks of larger size bales.

"Cotton," he announced. "The Colony produces annually seven million pounds of cotton, valued at more than twelve million livres, from nearly eight hundred plantations. Those hogsheads that you see beyond contain molasses, a by-product of the sugar cane. Annual production of molasses approximates twenty-three thousand hogsheads, worth about three million Saint-Domingue livres."

"If only twenty-three thousand hogsheads of molasses are produced annually, then you must have a year's supply in stock."

The agent chuckled. "You make a joke, eh, my friend? There seem to be thousands of hogsheads, no? True, there are many in this warehouse, but not as many as twenty-three thousand. Besides, they do not all contain molasses. Follow me, and I will show you."

Once again the two men proceeded for what seemed to Duncan a considerable distance.

"Look!" Garreau presently ordered. "These hogsheads contain tafia, an inferior quality of rum. Do you notice several mulattoes loitering near by? Their only duty is to guard the tafia against theft. Tafia is the black man's drink. The slaves who work here would quickly rob us of tafia worth many thousands of livres if we did not take stringent precautions to guard the liquid. What is more, despite all those precautions, a large quantity still disappears."

"How?"

Garreau raised his arms in gesticulation. "The good Lord knows! They have more tricks of stealing tafia than a cat for stealing fish. Sometimes we catch the guilty. They are flogged to the point of death, but their sufferings do not act as a deterrent.

"Perhaps some of the mulatto guards act as accomplices."

"No. Mulattoes loathe their black brethren. I don't know why. It is only a question of a degree of color."

"Do you acknowledge the lighter-skinned mulatoes as almost the equal of the white man?" Duncan asked maliciously.

The mere suggestion made Garreau indignant. "No. Even a sang-mêlé, who is a child of a white man by a quarteron, who has only one-quarter black blood in her veins—even a sang-mêlé is a man of color."

"And therefore beyond the pale?"

"Of course," the agent snapped. Then his momentary spasm of temper vanished. He linked his arm with Duncan's. "When you have been longer in Saint-Domingue, my friend, you will realize the existence of a barrier between the white man and the colored man that may never be surmounted or passed."

95

"Not even by humanity?"

"Are you a cynic?"

"I am—or hoped to be—a physician. A physician should be color-blind in the cause of humanity."

"Not a physician in Saint-Domingue. Not a physician who hopes to maintain a practice among the white people."

"Does a white physician never treat a Negro?"

"The Negroes have their own physicians, monsieur. I have heard of one—his name is Toussaint—who is reputed to have performed a number of cures. The Negro is like an animal. When he is ill he applies to Nature for a remedy. These Negro physicians have only to boil up a handful of herbs gathered from the interior to cure a Negro of any sickness."

"That is what our physicians in Europe believed until the beginning of this century, but now we—they—are beginning to turn more and more toward surgery. The progress of anatomy and physiology has made many advanced thinkers prefer to cure an increasing number of ills by opening up the body and treating the complaint from the inside, instead of relying too much upon dosing the patient with herbal concoctions. Have the Negroes surgeons to care for their bodies?"

"No! Their flesh is probably too tough to cut. For myself, I could never be a surgeon. I hate equally the sight and the smell of blood. It is distasteful to me even to look at those rawhides over there." Garreau urged Duncan toward the masses of stacked hides. "We import rawhides to the value of fifty-two thousand livres, and tanned hides amounting to more than one hundred thousand livres."

They walked past the hides, to see more hogsheads beyond.

"More rum?" Duncan questioned.

"No. Indigo. Indigo is fifth on our list of exported commodities. Last year, my friend, we exported more than eight million livres' worth of indigo, somewhat to Lambion's benefit, for his plantations produce nothing else but indigo. Cazeaux is another big producer of indigo. Turpin prefers sugar and cotton. Monsieur Bayou de Liberas of the Bréda plantation— Toussaint, whom I mentioned to you just now, was his coachman—is another big sugar-producer. Monsieur le Comte de Saramon, on the other hand, relies upon cacao for his riches."

"So cacao grows in Saint-Domingue?"

"Anything grows in Saint-Domingue. Its soil is the most fertile in the world."

"But surely Jamaica—"

"We export more than Jamaica," Garreau interrupted. "Chiefly because the French planters have a better system of irrigation. But speaking of cacao, or cocoa, as you English say, we can boast of fifty-four cacao plantations. De Saint Just grows cacao. So does Marilys."

"What does the Pegois plantation raise?" Duncan slyly questioned.

"Muscovado. Shall we go up to my office?"

Duncan nodded and accompanied Garreau up a narrow flight of stone steps to the floor above. As they reached the landing a slave messenger jumped up from the stool on which he had been sitting and touched his forehead; his huge mouth gaped open in a smile that stretched from ear to ear. Garreau paid no attention to the man, but Duncan could not resist the Negro's cheerful friendliness, so he nodded back. Then he gazed at the office, which consisted of a large open space filled with high wooden desks and a large ornamental table on a raised platform at the far end. Fifteen to twenty mulattoes worked at the desks; some stood, some were crouched up on high wooden stools. All of them, bending over papers or immense ledgers, gave the impression of intense industry. The majority, Duncan noticed, were engaged in writing of some sort or another, and the large quill pens they used combined to create a loud scratching sound that could be heard whenever there was an occasional lull in the noise from below.

When they reached the far end of the office Garreau drew Duncan toward a window and with a sweep of his arm indicated the vast bay of Can François, which the office overlooked.

"Count the ships that lie in this harbor, my friend, if you wish to gain an even better insight into the trade of Saint-Domingue. On the right *Saint Pierre et Saint Paul*, sailing for Marseille with a full cargo of sugar, coffee, and tanned hides. Next to her, *Santa Maria* from Africa, with three hundred slaves aboard. To her right is *Louis Quinze*, from Bordeaux, with wine and preserved fruit. Next to her *Terre d'Or* from Nantes, with a cargo of salt beef, butter, and hams. Farther on, *Nancy Perkins* from Boston, with codfish and timber.

Garreau waved his arms in his enthusiam. "Twenty years I have worked in this office. Every day during that time I have gazed out from these windows at the harbor below. I have seen ships arrive and depart again for every port in France, and for Spanish, English, and American ports. Some of the ships I have come to recognize by their silhouettes. Some of their captains are my friends, like Captain Beard.

"Not a day goes by, monsieur, that I do not stand at this window and gaze out at the shipping," he repeated. "For me, the fascination of commerce never fades. When the books of Dumestre et Fils inform me that profits have increased I am glad, though I earn no more because of it. When I see Cap François growing ever more prosperous I rejoice, though no share of that prosperity comes my way. But I still cherish the sight of the trade ships as they lie in the harbor. You see, I love my business, and I like Cap François. With such sentiments as these, would I be happier for owning a sugar plantation twenty miles distant from the sea, thirty miles distant from Cap François?"

Though he stared defiantly into Duncan's face, there was a note of entreaty in Garreau's voice that warned Duncan what his answer should be.

"I doubt it," he replied awkwardly. "Wealth is not the alpha and omega of life." A bitter note tinged his voice as he continued: "I would not trade the richest plantation on the island for the right to manipulate a scalpel."

"You are right," Garreau affirmed as he thrust out his weak lower lip. "Why should we men renounce our happiness for the sake of a woman's whim? And what creates that whim? Snobbery, monsieur. The desire to have more slaves than Madame Gauchez or Madame Emery. Just snobbery!"

97

Duncan smiled, remembering some lines that a fellow countryman of his by the name of Robert Burns had recently published:

> Oh wad some power the giftie gie us
> To see oursels as others see us!
> It wad frae monie a blunder free us,
>   An' foolish notion.

CHAPTER TWENTY-FIVE

THAT evening at a meeting of prominent planters, over which Turpin presided, with many loud words the planters resolved to send a deputation to the States-General in France, demanding colonial representation, although Sarrus, the Governor's effeminate secretary, warned that M. Duchilleau would oppose such action.

Duncan only half listened to a succession of fervid speeches insisting upon the planters' rights, punctuated now and then by quieter, more cautious arguments. It was during one of the latter that a glance at the tensely listening Negro waiter, Henri Christophe, suddenly brought him to full attention. The Comte de Saramon was imploring his fellow planters to delay, for the state of opinion in France, he said, was more unfriendly to the planters' cause than many realized. Antislavery sentiments overseas had reached such proportions that they must seriously be reckoned with.

Duncan was startled by the blazing hope that flared into Henri's eyes at those words. Long after the meeting the powerful impression the waiter made would recur to him. The man had the body of a bull—but the face of an idealist: a combination that in some circumstances, Duncan told himself, could be dangerous.

The warning of Sarrus, that the Governor would oppose the sending of colonial deputies to the States-General, was quickly justified. Although M. Duchilleau was reputed secretly to favor popular pretensions, he issued proclamations forbidding all parochial and provincial assemblies. Despite opposition from the Governor General, from all French officials, and from the group of colonials who supported the Comte de Saramon; despite, too, M. Duchilleau's official ban, assemblies were held throughout the Colony, at which a series of resolutions were passed declaring the right of the colonists to send representatives to the States-General. Thirty-seven representative deputies were elected, and a full statement of grievances was drawn up, together with a specific demand for certain reforms in colonial administration.

Duncan remained the guest of M. and Mme Garreau, neither of whom would hear from him any suggestion of impatience to settle his future. "Show yourself at ease. Make acquaintance. By and by opportunities will fall to you," said the shipping agent. Mme Garreau mothered him with so obvious a pleasure that Duncan had not the heart to repulse her. "You are still a boy. It is now that you most need the consolation of a mother. This the good God has denied you, just as He has denied me children. Be my son, Duncan," she pleaded. "Let me take the place of that poor soul whom you do not remember."

Like a hen clucking over a single chick, she fell into the habit of following him about the villa to see that everything he needed was to hand. She bullied her two slaves unmercifully to insure that everything possible was done for his comfort. She wheedled from him a list of his favorite dishes; thereafter, none other was served at table. She took him visiting, especially to friends who possessed daughters of marriageable age. She even took the risk of being snubbed by some of the wealthier inhabitants by introducing Duncan to them so that he might widen his circle of acquaintances. Strangely enough, these tactics were successful. As a gentleman from England, a country that the French detested but respected, Duncan possessed a key that opened doors closed to his hostess. Poor Mme Garreau had the mortification of seeing her guest receive the invitations that, during ten years, she had craved, but she did not begrudge Duncan his social victory, because she had come genuinely to love him. He, for his part, was not blind to the inference lying behind those invitations that ignored his kindhearted hostess. Every day increased his secret contempt for the social tenets of Saint-Domingue.

Garreau proved, on the whole, an agreeable host. Duncan found nothing heroic in the shipping agent. His outlook on life was narrow and unimaginative, but he was pleasant and certainly inoffensive. Besides, he had one redeeming feature that it was impossible to overlook—a passion that he shared equally between his work and the Colony. He loved both, and anything that lay beyond the confines of either held no interest for him. There was little about the Colony with which he was not familiar —its history, geography, commerce, personalities. Given the opportunity, he would talk for hours about Saint-Domingue.

Garreau took Duncan riding or driving. They visited every street and avenue in Cap François. They went to the theater, where they saw a performance of Voltaire's Mérope. They visited the Jesuits' college, the barracks, the royal arsenal, and the two hospitals.

They traveled far along surfaced roads to the great Plaine-du-Nord, where most of the wealthier planters had their plantations. Here Duncan received his first impression of the incredible fertility of the Colony, and also added confirmation of its prosperity; amid scenes of magnificent beauty were set the country houses at which the planters spent so little of their time—large, rambling houses of pink and white plaster, containing scores of rooms, lighted by immense windows, surrounded by enormous verandas, and set in gardens of unsurpassed loveliness.

CHAPTER TWENTY-SIX

LATE one night Garreau knocked on Duncan's door. Duncan was almost asleep. "What do you want?" he mumbled.

Garreau entered. "Duncan," he began, scarcely able to conceal his curiosity, "there is a Negro outside asking for you."

"A Negro! For me!" Bemused by his nightcap of rum and the first flush of sleep, Duncan stared stupidly at his host.

"Léon ordered the man away, but he refused to go. He calls himself Pierre Dominique Toussaint Bréda, freed slave of Monsieur de Libertas, and asked to see you at once. A matter of life or death."

"Toussaint! Do I know the man, Simon?"

"Why should you know him? If I had known that you were asleep I should not have disturbed you; but I did not think you could have fallen asleep so quickly."

Duncan's eyes closed. "Tell him to come back tomorrow."

"If you wish, but I wondered—" Garreau paused.

"What?" Duncan mumbled.

"Perhaps Monsieur de Libertas desires your presence."

"Why?"

"I cannot imagine why. But if I were you I should go. Monsieur de Libertas, who supervises the great plantation of the Comte de Noé de Bréda, is a very influential colonial."

"What difference does that make?"

"If you were to oblige Monsieur de Libertas—"

Duncan interrupted with a laugh. "My dear Simon, at heart you are just as much a social climber as Madame Garreau. Perhaps, after all, you will buy the Pegois plantation."

"God forbid!"

"Why? It is not far from Turpin's property."

"Please be serious. If Monsieur de Libertas really wants you to visit him, why not go?"

"At this time of night?"

"It is not late."

"Would it give you pleasure, Simon, to have De Libertas under an obligation to me?"

Garreau did not reply, but Duncan knew that were the shipping clerk to speak the truth, the answer would be yes.

Duncan sat up. "For your sake, Simon, I'll speak to this Negro."

He clambered out of bed and accompanied Garreau to the back door of the house. There, in the uncertain light of a flickering candle, he saw a Negro of medium stature, whose wrinkled face and gray hair revealed advancing years.

"Monsieur Stewart?"

"Yes."

"My name is Pierre Dominique Tou—"

Duncan interrupted with a curt: "I have been told your name. You come from Monsieur de Libertas?"

"I work for Monsieur de Libertas. I do not come from him."

"Then why are you here?"

Toussaint delayed his reply while white man and black looked deep into the eyes of the other. For the second time within a few days Duncan was resentfully aware of a Negro's appraising glance. At the same time he was strangely stirred by the black man's dignity and serene expression.

Presently Toussaint spoke. "To appeal to your charity, monsieur."

Duncan laughed. "Then your appeal fails. But for Monsieur Garreau I should myself be in difficulties. I am poor, not rich. Though why I should be explaining this to you—"

"I do not ask for money."

"Then what do you ask for? What else have I to give?"

Toussaint ignored the question. "Henri Christophe has told me that you are different from other whites. You do not despise us."

"No." Duncan's manner turned brusque. "You mentioned the words life or death to Monsieur Garreau."

"With good reason. My friend, a young man of your own age, lies, I fear, close to death. I have come to you for help."

"To me! Why to me?"

"Because you are a physician, monsieur."

"Who said so?" Duncan demanded sharply.

"Henri Christophe."

"I do not know this Henri Christophe."

"Henri Christophe is a waiter at the Hôtel de la Couronne, monsieur. He has often served you."

"Ah! That Henri! But, Toussaint. I am not a physician."

The bitterness in Duncan's voice made Toussaint glance strangely at the white man. "Henri Christophe is not a liar," he stated.

"Do you insinuate that I am? By God, this is intolerable!"

"Forgive me, monsieur," Toussaint hastily interrupted. "That was not my meaning." His shoulders seemed to droop with disappointment. "Christophe must have been mistaken. I beg you to overlook my presumption in coming here tonight. Only desperation gave me the courage."

The Negro turned to leave. Acting upon impulse, Duncan restrained him.

"I cannot call myself a physician, Toussaint, because, in my country, it is necessary to pass certain examinations before one is entitled to be called a physician. But I have studied medicine for many years."

An expression of joy spread from Toussaint's eyes to his lips. "Then come with me to the bedside of Henri Christophe, monsieur, for he needs your advice."

"Impossible!"

"But Monsieur—"

"I say it is not possible to do as you suggest," Duncan interrupted unhappily. "I have no right to assume the duties of a physician. Besides, why do you not call upon the Negro physicians to attend your friend Christophe?"

"I am a physician," Toussaint retorted gravely. "God be praised, I have successfully treated hundreds of my fellow Negroes. That is why Christophe sent for me when he became ill. But, monsieur, I am afraid. I have treated Christophe with herbal poultices, but he grows not better but worse. He can no longer walk."

"Then apply to a white physician."

Toussaint sadly shook his head. "It would do little good, monsieur.

There are so many Negroes in Saint-Domingue. The death of one means little to our masters."

"Do you mean that no white doctor will attend a Negro?"

"It would be untrue to say that, Monsieur, but there are several receptions tonight. Many of the physicians are there. If I were to go to them now they would say: 'Tomorrow is soon enough. I will attend the man tomorrow.'"

"Is tomorrow not soon enough?"

"I have seen men die suddenly when such swellings have burst."

"A swelling!" Duncan's attention was held. "Where?"

"In the hollow behind the knee."

"How big is the swelling?"

Toussaint clenched his fist and held it close to the candle. "Bigger than that."

Duncan's lips tightened. "If the aneurism is as large as you describe, an immediate operation must be performed. You must find a surgeon, and force him to listen to your description of Christophe's illness. He will recognize the danger of death if an operation is not performed immediately. If he has a spark of humanity in his heart he will go with you to Christophe's bedside."

"Will an operation cure Henri Christophe?"

Duncan turned away from Toussaint's anxious eyes and gazed into the darkness beyond. Far away, high up in the mountains, flickering lights betrayed the existence of large fires. The air reverberated with the muffled beating of drums.

"If knowledge of John Hunter's operation for popliteal aneurism has traveled to Saint-Domingue, there is a chance of Christophe's life being saved," Duncan muttered. "But it was only three years ago that he discovered the possibility of that operation."

"I know nothing of surgery. I cannot tell you whether the surgeons here know anything of the operation you mention, but I can tell you that many men—white men and Negroes—have died of swellings behind their knees."

"Lately?"

"Two months ago a friend of my master died from that cause. But he was an elderly man, monsieur."

"Yes, of course," Duncan muttered. "Mostly it is elderly people who suffer from aneurisms. It is unusual for a young man to be so afflicted."

"But many young Negroes have that kind of swelling."

Duncan recollected something which John Hunter had said during a lecture. "You are right. Younger men suffering from a certain disease are susceptible to aneurisms," Duncan explained. "But time is being wasted, Toussaint. The sooner Christophe is operated upon, the more chance there is of saving both his life and his leg."

Toussaint's voice trembled. "May Christophe lose his leg?"

"Unless the surgeons here practice Hunter's operation, Christophe may lose either his leg or his life."

"Poor Henri Christophe! He was becoming a fine man." The Negro paused, only to continue with added vehemence: "God forgive me, monsieur, but I cannot return to Christophe without making one more appeal. Monsieur Stewart, won't you perform this new operation upon my poor young friend? Neither Christophe nor I could reward you, but God would do so." Regardless, for the first time in his life, of a Negro's enforced respect for the person of a white man, Toussaint placed his shaking hands on Duncan's arm as though to pull him forcefully to the Hôtel de Couronne.

Duncan shook off the frantic, clutching hands. "Impossible. Even if I were a qualified surgeon I could not perform such an operation. I have neither sufficient knowledge nor sufficient skill."

Tears sprang into the Negro's eyes. "You spoke of the operation as if it were known to you."

"So it is," Duncan explained impatiently. "I was in Saint George's Hospital in London when John Hunter performed his first popliteal aneurism. But I am not sufficiently experienced to perform on Christophe. If he should die his death would lie heavily upon my conscience."

"The twelve apostles were not qualified physicians or surgeons, monsieur, but Jesus Christ gave them power to 'heal sickness, and cast out devils.' Won't you heal the sick? Christophe will probably die unless he is quickly tended. Where would be the sin if he should die while you were trying to save his life?"

Duncan stared at the distant fires. What had he to lose from an attempt to cure the aneurism? If Christophe died, who would pay heed to the tragedy, with the possible exception of the innkeeper, Coidovid? Slaves were always dying. What mattered the death of one more Negro? Nearly half a million Negroes cooped up in a colony smaller than Ireland and there were still millions left in the jungles of Africa. If, as was possible, Christophe was condemned by neglect to die of his aneurism, would it not be an act of humanity to use every possible means of curing him, even if such an attempt meant hazarding his life? A score of arguments in favor of operating began to formulate themselves, but Duncan tried to dismiss them; he was sufficiently honest to admit that he was being swayed by one factor only—the opportunity of experimenting with a difficult operation without the risk of any blame attaching to himself in the event of failure.

Ignoring Toussaint and the waiting Garreau Duncan began to pace up and down the veranda as he wrestled with the problem. His blood warmed to the prospect of experiencing the thrill of handling surgical instruments again; he imagined Christophe's naked body lying on a make-shift operating table, the ugly tumor distorting the handsome line of his leg. Joy! It would be more than joy to become once more, if only for a brief hour, a practicing surgeon. The mere thought made his heart beat faster. Would it be so wrong to wield the scalpel, to experiment, to enjoy so short a period of bliss in so many weeks of desolation?

Presently his exultation was chilled by the warnings of common sense. What would happen when the physicians and surgeons of Saint-Domingue came to hear of his unauthorized and unorthodox experiment? At the very least he would be liable to immediate deportation. Well, he could go on to America, as Captain Beard had sometimes urged. A more important obstacle was his lack of the necessary surgical instruments.

"I have no instruments," he began.

"But I have," Toussaint told him. "My master purchased them for me from a surgeon's widow."

"Can you use them?"

"For little operations, yes, monsieur."

"If I perform this operation I might be punished, since I am not a qualified surgeon."

"I am not punished for treating slaves. But, monsieur, if you wish, none shall hear of your attempt. That I swear," Toussaint promised with simple dignity.

It seemed to Duncan that the night drums beat louder. Their throbbing rhythm echoed in his ears, bemused his thoughts, and weakened his power of resistance.

"You will come to the Hôtel de la Couronne?" Toussaint urged.

"I will come," Duncan agreed.

Duncan briefly explained the situation to Garreau who begged him not to meddle, but Duncan, having reached his decision, was intolerant of advice. He told Garreau curtly that a life saved was of more importance than any possible consequence to himself. When he was dressed he rejoined Toussaint. Together they proceeded to the Hôtel de la Couronne.

Toussaint led him to a small straw-thatched, wattle and mud hut overlooking the stableyard of the hotel building. "Christophe is in here," he explained as he opened the door.

There was a murmur of voices from within, which stopped abruptly as Duncan stepped inside, followed by Toussaint. The only light was that shed by a single guttering candle. Three people were bending over the mat on which Christophe was outstretched. One of the three, a white man, was holding the Negro's wrist, and he realized that his visit had been forestalled.

The white physician was a stranger to Duncan. The other two people he recognized. One was Coidovid. The other, a soft-eyed demure Negress of eleven years of age, was the hotelkeeper's daughter, Marie Louise.

Coidovid glanced at Toussaint with apology. "Monsieur le docteur asked me why Henri was not serving. I explained that he was ill, so Monsieur Deschenel kindly offered to see him."

Deschenel turned. He glanced inquiringly at Duncan.

"Good evening, monsieur," he greeted, in a voice that conveyed his unspoken surprise.

Duncan inspected Deschenel, who was a thickset individual with slightly bulging eyes, a large nose, and an obstinate mouth.

"Good evening. I heard from Toussaint that Christophe was ill with a popliteal aneurism—"

The Frenchman interrupted with an exclamation of amazement. "Is an aneurism an anévrisme?"

"I did not know the French word, but if an anévrisme is a swelling of an artery, then that is the word."

"How did you know that Christophe was suffering from an *anévrisme?*"

"Toussaint explained the symptoms."

"Are you a physician, monsieur?" Deschenel demanded in a sharp voice.

"I—" Duncan's lips tightened. "I am a medical student."

"Ah!" The Frenchman exclaimed scornfully. "Perhaps you have come here to examine a particularly ripe specimen." He bent over the mat, pulled the coverlet from off the patient, and pointed to the hideous protuberance behind Christophe's left knee. "Have you seen a bigger tumor than that?"

"No," Duncan gravely admitted. "How will you treat it, monsieur?"

"Amputate the limb, naturally."

There was a cry of horror from Marie Louise, a moan of despair from Christophe.

"He would not be the only Negro in the Colony without a leg. If there were less disease there would be more legs."

"Save his leg, monsieur le docteur, I beg you," implored Marie Louise.

Deschenel shrugged his shoulders. "If he keeps his leg he will lose his life. The tumor will burst. Then—pouf! He can take his choice."

"Can you not operate, monsieur?" Duncan inquired.

"I have operated on some *anévrismes*," the physician said carelessly. "The result is usually fatal, even when they are only half as bad as this one."

"Which operation do you perform?"

"There is only one," Deschenel asserted. "That of tying the artery above and below the tumor, and cutting down upon it to evacuate its contents."

"John Hunter established a safer method, monsieur."

"Well?" the physician sneered.

Duncan flushed with anger at the supercilious note in the other man's voice, but he forced himself to continue. He dropped to one knee beside the Negro.

"I saw Hunter ligature the femoral artery here, in the lower part of the thigh, where the artery was still sound. As a consequence the pure blood stream continued circulating through collateral vessels, while its absorbents gradually destroyed the poisons of the tumor. In six weeks the limb had recovered sufficiently for the patient to leave the hospital."

Deschenel laughed scornfully. "I have seen too many men die of *anévrismes* to believe they can be so simply cured."

"The operation was sufficiently successful to excite the attention of all the surgeons in Europe. Ligature Christophe's femoral artery where I suggest, and he has a chance of becoming a sound man again."

The suggestion excited Marie Louise. With shining eyes she faced Deschenel. "Will you not do as Monsieur Stewart suggests, monsieur le docteur? Please, oh, please save Henri's leg!"

Deschenel angrily thrust the girl to one side. "A fairy story. Men's lives are not so easily saved. I shall amputate the limb tomorrow."

Moaning with pain, Christophe shifted his position. "Save my leg, Monsieur Stewart," he gasped. "You save my leg."

The furious Frenchman faced Duncan. "How dare you come here, monsieur, and flout your ignorance before one who practiced medicine before you were born? I demand that you leave here immediately."

"Please, monsieur le docteur. I want him to save my leg. I want my leg, I need it." Christophe's voice rose. The perspiration on his face gathered into rivulets that trickled down his face.

"I warn you not to interfere in this affair," the physician declared pompously. "If you touch this Negro I shall make myself responsible for seeing that you suffer the consequences. You are a foreigner, a mere youth who has not even taken his degree. You would not be lightly treated if you were to usurp the prerogative of a qualified medical man. Do I make myself clear?"

Duncan glanced from Deschenel's choleric face to Marie Louise. The girl stared at him with so tense a pleading that he had to look elsewhere, at Coidovid. When he did so the innkeeper looked down at the floor and uneasily shuffled his feet. Duncan glanced at Toussaint. In Toussaint's eyes was the sadness of understanding.

Lastly, Duncan looked at Henri Christophe. The Negro's body was naked. Duncan was more than ever impressed by the Negro's magnificent physique, the broad chest, the firm, healthy flesh, the bulging rippling muscles. Everything about the Negro proclaimed his physical perfection. It was marred only by the loathsome tumor.

To think of the fine body's being mutilated, to foresee its degenerating for want of proper exercise, saddened the Scot. If only Christophe were in England, or John Hunter were in Saint-Domingue. If only he, Duncan, were qualified. If only he had the courage to risk the Negro's life. If only Coidovid had not brought the bullying, obstinate Deschenel to Christophe's hut.

If—if—if— But for the ifs the Negro might be permitted to live, to keep his magnificent body intact.

Duncan faced the physician.

"I'll operate," he announced.

CHAPTER TWENTY-SEVEN

SILENCE followed Duncan's words. He removed his coat and handed it to a radiant Marie Louise. Then he rolled up the sleeves of his cambric shirt and turned to Toussaint.

"Can you apply a tourniquet?"

Toussaint shook his head. "You mustn't perform the operation, monsieur."

"But it was you who begged me to."

"Circumstances have changed," the Negro protested, with resigned despair.

"Because of Monsieur Deschenel?"

"There is no reason for you, a white man, to suffer on account of a Negro, monsieur."

"That is my affair."

Duncan faced his patient. His throat was dry; his heart beat uneasily. The hand that would have to perform the operation shook slightly. His unaccustomed sense of panic was not lessened when Deschenel laughed. Could he remember every detail of the operation? the laughter inferred. Would he be able to control his hands? What if he were unable to locate the femoral artery? What if he failed to perform a successful ligature?

In a husky voice he said to the patient: "Henri Christophe, you heard me tell monsieur le docteur that I am or was a medical student. I have never been more than that. I am neither a qualified physician nor a qualified surgeon. I have never previously performed an operation for an anévrisme. I have only watched another man at work." He held out his hand. "Look at my hand trembling. That is because I am uncertain of myself. I have no right to operate upon you without your realizing the consequences. I may—I may kill you."

Christophe's tormented eyes started up at Duncan. "I would rather die than lose a leg, monsieur."

Duncan moistened his lips with a tongue that was almost as dry. "Fetch me some rum," he ordered in a croaking voice. "The strongest you have. Plenty of it."

"Yes, monsieur," Marie Louise said eagerly and hurried from the hut.

Duncan tried to ask Toussaint for the surgical instruments, but the only sounds he made were unintelligible. But Toussaint understood. He proceeded to a corner of the hut and picked up a small wooden box, which he opened and handed to Duncan.

With anxious eyes he inspected the instruments. They were woefully antiquated, and badly scarred as though from having suffered damage at some time or other. Fortunately, they still looked more or less serviceable, so he took those he needed out of their case and handled them to accustom himself to their feel, weight, and balance.

Marie Louise returned with a large glass of rum. He took it from her and passed it on to Christophe. "Drink this," he ordered. "Every drop of it."

The Negro struggled painfully to a sitting position and swallowed the contents of the glass. Then with a moan he sank back again. Duncan signaled to Toussaint. The two men knelt down beside Christophe, gently eased him onto his back, and deftly pinioned his arms. Duncan then attached thongs to Christophe's ankles to prevent his kicking. Then they turned him over.

"Are you ready, Christophe?"

The Negro's body was damp with perspiration; his eyes were filled with fear. But he nodded his head and muttered in a thick voice, "Yes, monsieur." So Duncan opened the man's mouth and thrust a thick pad of cloth into it.

All was now ready for the application of the tourniquet. Duncan placed his hand on Christophe's thigh. Then impulse caused him to turn and glance at Deschenel. The physician had moved nearer to the door, the better to see the performance of the operation. His lips smiled contempt. His eyes burned with fury.

Duncan realized that he had made an implacable enemy. The knowledge strengthened his resolution. When he turned back to Christophe, both mind and body were steady.

The operation was successfully performed. Afterward, when Duncan stood up, his legs felt unsteady, so he leaned against a wall.

Deschenel prepared to leave. "In two or three days' time, my young friend, if your ridiculous operation has not killed the man, it will necessitate the amputation of the limb. But you will not perform the next operation." With this last warning the physician departed.

"Christophe must not move, whatever happens," Duncan warned Coidovid. "Absolute rest is essential for at least six weeks."

"I'll nurse him myself, monsieur," Marie Louise interrupted.

"You can be sure that she will carry out her promise," Coidovid confirmed. "If Christophe recovers he is to marry her."

"Then you will give him every chance to recover?"

"Yes, monsieur. For the sake of Marie Louise. Besides, I like the lad. He is hard-working and intelligent. He will make her a good husband."

So it was arranged. Shaken by his ordeal, tired and dispirited by the reaction, Duncan bade Toussaint and Christophe good night, though the sick man was too far sunk in a drunken stupor to know what was happening.

Duncan found Garreau waiting up for him.

"What happened?" the shipping agent inquired eagerly.

"I operated."

"Successfully?"

"Yes."

"I am glad," Garreau acknowledged with sincerity. Then he added: "What a pity it was only a Negro whose life you saved."

Deschenel carried out his threat. At the first opportunity he reported the matter of Duncan's operation to the Governor General. But Deschenel had overlooked one important fact. As an ardent supporter of Turpin and the Colonial party, Deschenel was no longer in the Governor's favor. Having listened with polite boredom to the physician's complaint, M. Duchilleau observed dryly: "I thing the matter is of too great importance to warrant action on my part, Monsieur Deschenel. I suggest that you request your friends the deputies to draw the attention of the States-General to the backwardness of the New World in matters of scientific knowledge. It is intolerable to think of a European's performing an operation unknown to Saint-Domingue's leading man of medicine."

Scarcely able to control his indignation, the physician retired from the Governor's presence and repaired to the Hôtel du Cap for liquid solace. There, meeting friends, he related how Duncan had insulted another white man in the presence of Negro witnesses. As time passed Deschenel added highly colored interpretations of the Governor's attitude, and the consequent slight to the Colonial party. The physician's wrath communicated itself to his friends. The story, further distorted, spread rapidly from mouth to mouth; whipped up by the wind of prejudice, the tiny ripple that had disturbed the center of the lake dashed itself in a violent storm against the rockstrewn boundaries.

Nor were the Colonials the sole retailers of the news. The slaves of the Bréda plantation whispered the story that Toussaint had told them of the strange white man who, for no reward, had defied his fellow white man, and was trying to save a Negro's life and limb. News indeed for those slaves who did not work on the humane plantations of the Comte de Noé, and who had never encountered a white man's humanity. Told in the beat of rhythmic drums, the story throbbed its course along fertile plains, through savage jungles, across impenetrable valleys, and over impassable mountain peaks. The slaves heard, whispered, and wondered—would Henri Christophe live? Never before had they heard his name. But they wanted him to live. He must live—to prove to the white physician that a Negro's life could be worth the saving. Offer prayer to Jesus Christ, to Maîtresse Erzulie, to the Virgin Mary, to Damballa Ouedo, the serpent god, to Papa Legba, the god of generation and fecundity, to Agoué, the sea god, to Piè Jupitè-Tonnè, the thunder god, to Ogoun Badagris, the warrior—to gods of the tribes of Dahomey, Arada, Congo, Nago—Henri Christophe must live! Henri Christophe must be healed!

And Henri Christophe lived. His limb would heal. When Duncan next visited the Negro twelve hours later, Christophe's leg was warmer than normal. The blood was freely circulating.

That same night Garreau's slaves were summoned to the kitchen door by a single knock. Upon opening it they found only a plucked fowl, plump and expertly trussed. Of the one who had left it on the veranda there was no sound, but from the darkness of the night there was a muffled: "Pour papaloi blanc." So the slave gave it into Duncan's keeping, while an uneasy Garreau explained that some unknown Negro must have intended the fowl to be accepted as a present for saving Christophe's life.

Some hours later, when the slaves awoke to the dawning of a new day, there were many articles laid out upon the bare boards—three more chickens, potatoes, a small box of corn, a heap of fruit—and a torn piece of paper on which was written in crude, uncertain lettering: "Pour le papaloi blanc Dcan."

"What does papaloi mean, Simon?" Duncan asked.

Garreau loosened his collar. "A papaloi is a Negro medicine man or voodoo priest," he answered in a scared voice. "It means that the Negroes now regard you as a kind of witch doctor. I do not like the idea, Duncan. I do not like it at all."

"Why not?" Mme Garreau demanded. Like a mother hen ruffling her feathers in aggressive defense of her chicks she stared angrily at her husband. "Is there anything disgraceful in the Negroes' being grateful to Duncan? I am not surprised they look upon him as a white witch doctor. He is. Hasn't he performed an operation that was not even known to our surgeons?"

"Maybe!" Garreau agreed grudgingly. "But what are you going to do with that food, Duncan?"

"What else should I wish to do with it but present it with all my gratitude to one who has looked after me with such loving care these last few weeks." Duncan raised Mme Garreau's hand to his lips and kissed it.

Her plump cheeks dimpled. "Thank you, Duncan."

"No," Garreau called out. "You cannot accept, Annette."

"Why not?"

"You, a white woman, cannot be beholden to Negro slaves for the food we eat."

Mme Garreau bit her lips. She half turned to Duncan. He read in her eyes agreement with her husband's remark, but her affection and pride in Duncan proved to be stronger than her own pride.

"Don't be ridiculous, Simon," she snapped. "As far as I am concerned, Duncan has offered me the food. Where he got it from is his own affair."

"It makes no difference," her husband persisted, displaying unusual obstinacy. "You know how the slaves talk among themselves. If you accept the presents Léon will tell Placide. Placide will tell Jules. Before noon the story will be known from one end of the Cap to the other. What will your friends think? What will my business clients say?"

Mme Garreau's lips quivered. "I am afraid Simon is right. I do not mind what my friends think, but—but Simon dare not prejudice the business." Unable to face Duncan's reproach, she gazed down at the tips of the shoes.

"Isn't a surgeon entitled to his fees?" Duncan demanded. "What does Deschenel live on, if not the fees of his unfortunate patients?"

"That is different," Garreau mumbled. "A white man can accept money or presents from another white man."

"The Negroes who left those chickens and those potatoes probably have no money. Instead of money they have given me food and fruit to express their gratitude. I am not ashamed to accept their offerings," Duncan asserted with canny Scots dignity.

"You are not a colonial," the other man pointed out sulkily. "In Saint-Domingue slaves are classified as animals. Cattle may only graze in their own fields."

"By God! Where is your Christian sense of humanity?" Duncan stormed. "Isn't a Negro a human being like any other man? What does the color of his body matter if the man is sick? A physician who loves his work doesn't care a damn about the color of his patient's skin. He knows that blood is always red. Don't some of the larger plantations maintain their own white physicians to care for the slaves? Why, even Deschenel was ready to operate upon Christophe."

"But the white master, not the slaves, maintains the physician. As for Deschenel, I don't doubt but that he would have sent in the bill for the operation to Coidovid, who is a free man."

"Coidovid is a Negro. Besides, Christophe is soon to be free."

"The chickens and the other goods came not from Coidovid, nor from Christophe, for that matter, but from slaves. Once show kindness to a slave, or accept a gift from him, and he begins to look upon himself as your equal. When that happens it sometimes takes the lash to make him work again. But come, Duncan, my dear chap, don't let us quarrel. You are a rebel. But you cannot alter existing conditions. Nobody could —even if there were a good reason for altering them."

Thus the incident was passed over as far as the Garreaus were concerned, but within the hour Duncan was to find the shipping agent's uneasiness had not been unwarranted. On his way to the Hôtel de la Couronne Duncan came face to face with De Saint Just, that most polished, most brilliant of island aristocrats, whom he had met not four nights previously in Psaume's home.

"Good morning, Monsieur de Saint Just."

De Saint Just's face became a mask. He continued his swaggering walk and passed Duncan by with neither word nor gesture.

No more invitations addressed to M. Duncan Stewart arrived at the Garreau household. No white man spoke to him as he walked or drove through the streets of Cap François. No lace handkerchief fluttered a greeting to him from passing carriages. Even the *petits blancs*—the obsequious tradesmen, the commercial employees, the lesser ranks of government servants—anxious to follow the lead of their social superiors, ignored Duncan; or, if forced by circumstances to speak to him, interjected a note of supercilious scorn into their voices.

Since Duncan had enough money to last him, with care, a few weeks more, he expressed his desire to leave the Garreaus, and stay at one of the cheaper hotels in the town. This move Mme Garreau strenuously refused to countenance, maintaining stoutly that Duncan's presence was causing her no trouble whatever, that she was happier for his company, and that, never mind what anyone else said or thought about him, she was his dear friend.

Dear, kindhearted, loyal Annette! Two nights later, returning home at a late hour, he found the house in darkness. He entered as quietly as possible and crept toward his bedroom. As he passed by the Garreaus' bedroom he heard a murmuring of voices and overheard his own name mentioned. Acting upon impulse, he stood still and listened.

"I know you are fond of Duncan, my pet. I know he has taken the place of the son the good God has denied us. I, too, like him."

"Then why should he not continue to live with us?"

"Unless he goes, several of the planters will refuse to deal with Dumestre et Fils. They say that his behavior is beginning to unsettle the slaves."

"You know that is a lie," Mme Garreau interrupted. "It is the news from France that disturbs us all, whites as well as blacks."

"Maybe you are right, my pet, but the planters are using Duncan as an excuse to give their business to Plissons, who are undercutting our freight rates. Besides, it is not fair to you that he should remain here. Why were we not asked to Madame Delaire's reception last week?"

"There is no reason why we should always be asked to her receptions."

"Never since her marriage has she omitted to invite us. It is because you persist in upholding Duncan that we were not invited."

"It is because you are not a planter, Simon."

"Do not deceive yourself. The Negroes are acting scandalously. They are making a god of Duncan because of the way he treats them. Soon they will be wondering why they are not being treated the same way by other white men. They——"

Duncan continued along the passage to his room. For the next two hours he busied himself in writing a letter to the Garreaus, tidying up the room, and making a parcel of his pitifully few belongings. When he had finished he picked up his parcel, left the bedroom, and tiptoed his way to the back veranda. Once outside the Garreaus' house he made his way to the Hôtel de la Couronne.

CHAPTER TWENTY-EIGHT

TOUSSAINT visited Duncan at the Couronne. Toussaint's attitude toward Duncan had changed in one respect only: the suggestion of timid uncertainty so common to all Negroes and slaves when addressing an unknown white man had gone.

"Monsieur, is it true that you have left Monsieur Garreau, and come to live at the Hôtel de la Couronne?"

"It is."

"But it is monsieur's ambition to be a surgeon?"

"Yes."

"Then practice surgery here, in Saint-Domingue, monsieur." Toussaint's eager voice failed him as he observed Duncan's startled eyes. "I am sorry, monsieur. Please forgive my impertinence."

"You are foolish, not impertinent. There are many reasons why I may not practice medicine in Saint-Domingue, not least of which is the fact that I should starve if I had to rely upon what fees I should obtain from white men who won't even acknowledge my existence."

Toussaint hesitated. "I was not thinking of white patients, monsieur."

Duncan stared at the Negro.

"The Negroes," Toussaint continued. "We could not pay you much, but——"

"Impossible!" Duncan snapped.

"Are you quite sure? I beg of you, monsieur, to think! Would it not make you happy to have an immediate opportunity to practice medicine and surgery, and to save the lives of Negroes? Would not our love and gratitude compensate for what we could not give in money?"

"Why do you infer that Negroes die for want of a physician to attend them? The larger plantations retain their own physicians for that purpose."

"I know, monsieur. But they care for slaves as they would for any property of value. They have little sympathy, and less knowledge. They save fewer lives than I, who know only the cures of nature that my ancestors have used for generations. There is a slave on the Turpin plantation who is suffering from the same illness as Christophe's. He knows that we shall soon be holding a *manger des morts*—a death feast to comfort a dead man on his way to the next world."

"But, surely, if slaves are valuable—" Duncan gazed at the Negro with puzzled eyes. "I do not understand the ways of the people who live on this island."

"Turpin's slave is no longer valuable. He is getting old, no longer capable of heavy labor. But he has a wife and daughter who love him. They do not want him to die. You could save him as you are saving Christophe."

"What you suggest is impossible."

The Negro hurriedly continued: "Monsieur, within a week your scalpel might save a dozen Negro lives. Dronné is in terrible agony because he is unable to pass his urine. Monsieur Joubert, his master, is too poor to pay a surgeon's fees, so he sent Dronné to me, but I cannot cure him, monsieur. Magaud, who is Monsieur Clément's slave, has a poisoned foot that must be quickly amputated if he is not to die. But Monsieur Clément has gone to Port-au-Prince, so yesterday his superintendent flogged Magaud for malingering. Finet's wife will die tonight if a scalpel is not used to help the birth of her baby. The woman is far away at a small settlement high up on Le Haut du Cap, and no white surgeon will travel that distance to save a slave woman's life. But I think you would, monsieur. I think that you would willingly travel to that woman's bedside if it were to save her life, and perhaps also the life of her baby."

Duncan felt that he was fighting a losing battle. "Aren't there any Negro midwives capable of helping a child into the world?"

"There are *mamalois* up in the mountains who brew herbal concoctions, monsieur. Sometimes they save lives, but often Negro men and women die because the *mamalois* have no knowledge of surgery such as you possess, monsieur."

"Don't you believe in *mamalois*, Toussaint? You are a Negro. Are your beliefs different from theirs?"

"I am a Christian, monsieur."

"Aren't other Negroes Christians?"

"Many are Christians only by the will of their Christian masters. They are but half Christians, for they believe also in Damballa, the serpent god of their ancestors."

"And you, Toussaint, do you believe in Damballa?"

"I am a good Christian. Pierre-Baptiste, who instructed me in Christian principles, taught me to despise heathen deities. Monsieur, for the sake of Jesus Christ, who suffered in death that mankind might be cleansed of their sins, won't you work to save our bodies as the good Jesuit fathers work to save our souls?"

Duncan rose from his seat and approached the window, which overlooked the cheerful, busy street below. "You do not realize what a sacrifice you are asking me to make, Toussaint." His voice became anguished as he saw Cazeaux and his two daughters pass by in their carriage. "I am neither a hero nor a Jesuit father. I am a young man, not a hermit to shut myself away forever from the company of my fellow white men."

"I hoped—for the sake of practicing medicine and surgery—" Toussaint began diffidently, but observing Duncan's grim profile the Negro stopped short and bowed his head. "By tomorrow Finet will be a widower."

As Duncan stared down at the street below Psaume passed by in a carriage. It seemed to the watcher that he could see a mocking, taunting expression on his face. Scarcely had he disappeared than Gallifet walked past. Gallifet's eyes were mocking—or so Duncan was convinced.

Gallifet was followed by a Jesuit father, whose rough brown habit was in sharp contrast to the gay colors of the white men and women who bowed respectfully as they passed him. The priest's deportment was upright and dignified, his expression serene; it reminded Duncan of Toussaint's. But as the priest arrived opposite the hotel window the harassed man within was convinced that the priest's face grew no less mocking than Psaume's had been.

Then came an old slave, bowed and white-haired with age. He wore rags. His feet were bare. He leaned heavily on a thick, gnarled stick. His pace was slow, for one foot was twisted and crippled, as a result, perhaps, of some injury that medical treatment might have ameliorated or cured. But the eyes of the slave were not mocking or taunting or scornful. They were weary with the sadness of one for whom life held no peace or happiness—the sadness of resignation.

The world passed by in ceaseless cavalcade. Planters and priests, soldiers and slaves, mulattoes and merchants. Enjoying the last hour of sunshine, they came into the orbit of Duncan's vision and passed out of it again, some in carriages, some on horseback, some afoot. A cavalcade of contrast: of joy and sadness; of the cheerful clop-clop of horses' hoofs and the soft padding of naked black feet; of the arrogance of armed might and the serenity of Christian peace; of flamboyant silks and faded cottons; of hard, intellectual white faces, of docile, childish black faces, of sullen, disdainful brown faces.

This was the world Duncan was being asked to abandon for the sake of Negro slaves whose lives and health many white masters were too dissipated or too heedless to safeguard. There could be no question of half measures. There could be no running with the hare and hunting with the hounds. The gulf between white man and black could not be spanned save by way of the bridge of profane love, trodden solely by black mistresses and their white lovers.

He was shaken by a growing realization that he must quickly choose between the alternatives that faced him. The first meant living his future life among Negro slaves for whom he felt no other emotion than compassion; they could offer him no companionship, and would be unable to reward his sacrifice with any more substantial fee than their gratitude. But there would be offered to him the opportunity of fulfilling his ambition. He would be able to practice medicine and surgery to his heart's content. He might even be able to experiment, to take chances with the hardy slaves that he would not have dared to take in London hospitals or private homes.

What was the alternative? He might go to America. An unknown country, but one where he would meet his own kind and speak his own language. A country where he would be able to follow a career of some kind. Perhaps even a medical career. But he mentally underlined a word. Perhaps! For America, following the example of the European countries, had established a medical college at Philadelphia. If he went to America, would he, an unqualified physician, be permitted to practice even on the outskirts of the civilized parts of the continent?

A black world or a white? A life of medicine in Saint-Domingue, or some other, problematical career in America? He rubbed his fingers against his moist palms, as though stroking a scalpel. Then, as he gazed at the Negro faces, some void of expression, some sad, some bleak, some childish, he felt distaste. They were entitled to humane treatment, reasonable care, and personal liberty. But they were black. He was white. He had not the courage to leave his own world and become an inhabitant of theirs.

Outside, the leaves of the poinsettias and the bougainvillea rustled with the first stirrings of the evening breeze. The soughing of the wind was like the whispering of a warm, comforting, cheerful voice—Elspeth's.

"Ye mither wou'd hae lived if Malcolm Stewart had gien for a physician—ye mither wou'd hae lived—ye mither wou'd hae lived—ye mither wou'd hae lived—she might live, monsieur, if a physician went to her—"

Duncan wiped away the perspiration that misted his eyes. "Monsieur! Monsieur!" It was not a voice from the past whispering "Monsieur" in his ear, but Toussaint—a strangely different Toussaint with compelling eyes and coercive voice which pleaded for his fellow Negroes with unsuspected audacity and assurance, a Toussaint who seemed suddenly and mysteriously to be the equal of a white man.

"You still ask me to abandon my own world?" Duncan asked in a toneless voice.

"Only for a short time. It will not be for always. Later, when the white men have had time to appreciate your skill and kindness to us Negroes, I am sure they will become your friends again."

"Have you so much faith in the white man, Toussaint?"

"I have." The decision in the voice convinced Duncan of Toussaint's sincerity.

"Then you have more faith than I have."

"I respect and admire the white man, monsieur. Some may be bad, but more are good. The white men are far kinder than the mulattoes to their slaves." Toussaint glanced anxiously at the window. The western horizon was tinged with the burnished golden rays of the setting sun. "Labor may begin soon. If Finet's wife is to live you must operate before dawn tomorrow. Will you save her life, monsieur?"

Black world or white? Duncan chose.

CHAPTER TWENTY-NINE

DUNCAN was now living alone in a small house at the end of the rue du Pet au Diable, on the outskirts of the town, within a stone's throw of the civil prison. One day he received a visitor, a white man whose face was vaguely familiar.

"Monsieur Stewart?"

"Yes," Duncan admitted curtly, for white men usually spoke to him only to make insulting remarks.

The visitor fidgeted uneasily with his cane. "Would you forgive me, monsieur, but is it true that you are a physician and surgeon?"

"It is not true."

"But I have been told—" With an expression of distress the visitor glanced at the mountain immediately behind him, and then at his two sweating horses. "I have come all the way from Petit Goave because I was told that you had performed some marvelous operations and effected some extraordinary cures."

"I have been fortunate in saving the lives of several Negroes."

Hope shone again in the other man's eyes. "Then you are a man of medicine?"

"I am not qualified, and I treat only Negroes and mulattoes."

"Ah, monsieur!" Prompted by relief, the visitor seized Duncan's hand and shook it up and down as he would a pump handle. "Then I pray you to come with me to Limonade, and see somebody who is very dear to me. My name is Ferrand de Beaudierre—"

"Ah!"

De Beaudierre dropped Duncan's hand. "What is it, monsieur?"

"I have seen you before, at the Hôtel de la Couronne, one night when Turpin was inviting the Colonials to send a delegation to the States-General."

"It is true. I happened to be there because I was visiting the Cap. Now I remember you. You were sitting at the next table. Monsieur, are you aware of the prejudices against me in this colony on account of my marriage?"

"I have heard the question of your marriage referred to. We are fellow victims of that prejudice, because I, too, am blind to the color of a man's flesh."

"Thank God for that, monsieur. It is my wife who is ill. I cannot persuade any physician to see her, because I chose to offer her marriage instead of maintaining her as my mistress. I have traveled from the far side of the colony to beg of you, to see her. She could travel no farther, so I left her at Limonade. I am not a poor man. I will willingly pay you any fee you ask. For pity's sake, come with me, Monsieur Stewart. See, I have even brought a spare horse in the hope—"

De Beaudierre's distress was painful. Only pausing to recall the list of his patients, so as to be sure that there was none whom it might be dangerous to leave, Duncan agreed to accompany De Beaudierre. Within thirty minutes he was packed and ready for the journey. With a lighter heart than he had possessed for many a week he swung himself onto the saddle.

"At your service, Monsieur de Beaudierre," he announced with a note of gaiety.

The two men turned their animals southward, toward the Chemin de la Vigie, the road to Port-au-Prince. For a short distance they skirted the town by keeping on the inside of the entrenchments, but presently they turned to their left and passed beyond the boundary, onto the Chemin de la Vigie. Almost at once they began climbing.

"How far is it to Limonade?" Duncan presently asked.

"About twenty-five leagues, monsieur. We shall not reach there before tomorrow night. Pray God madame will be no worse by then." As though in a deliberate effort not to allow his thoughts to dwell too long on that subject he went on: "It was kind of you, monsieur, to consent to undertake such an arduous journey for a complete stranger."

"Nonsense. Besides, I have reason to feel grateful to you."

"To me?"

"It is only upon rare occasions that I have the opportunity of talking to a white man. In all Saint-Domingue there are only two white men who condescend to speak to me. The first is a shipping agent who was once a butcher's son, but secretly yearns to be a social lion."

"And the other?"

Duncan smiled at the obvious curiosity in his companion's voice. "An old reprobate of a French soldier who has lost an eye, two fingers, and half an ear somewhere in Europe, and what was left of his morals in Saint-Domingue. He has a brusque manner but a heart of gold. He fears neither man nor devil, and talks to white man, mulatto, and Negro alike. Strangely enough, he is respected and liked by all."

"You speak of François?"

"Yes. You know him?"

"I have heard of him. His fame—or ill fame, if you please—and that of his casino, has traveled even as far as Petit Goave. So you see François sometimes?"

"I do, thank God!"

Beaudierre glanced at Duncan. "Do you not speak to the Negroes?"

"Do not mistake me. I am friendly with the black men. I do not ignore them, as the other whites do, nor do I despise them, as the mulattoes do. Psychologically, I find them a fascinating study. I have noticed, for instance, that contact with white civilization sharpens their intellects. The Negroes newly imported from Africa have the intelligence of sheep, but their sons—and more markedly their grandsons—are decidedly more intelligent. The average Negro whom I have been meeting for the past few months is slow-thinking. His interests are confined to working, eating, dancing, and sleeping. He has neither thought for yesterday nor tomorrow. He would like to be as free as the white man, but he is not resentful of his servitude. He accepts his lot with a philosophical resignation that it is not easy for the white man to comprehend. He is not aware of his own power—"

"Power!"

"Certainly. His power to fight for that freedom of which he does nothing else but dream. There are sixteen Negroes to every white man in the Colony, monsieur! If the Negroes were more intelligent, and chose to rise against their white masters, do you not think such odds would be terrifying?"

"For a time—but France would soon send troops—"

"You and I know that such a rising would probably be soon crushed, but the Negroes have not sufficient imagination even to conceive the possibilities of an insurrection in the first place. But I was speaking of exceptions. I know two Negroes, monsieur, who possess unusual intelligence. Their names are Toussaint and Christophe. It is a pleasure to converse with them."

"Do these two men, Toussaint and Christophe, comprehend the possibility of an insurrection?"

"No," Duncan answered. "They dream of the day when their fellow Negroes shall become free, but all their hopes and plans are peaceable. They are not blood-minded. On the contrary, Toussaint is one of the gentlest men of any color I have yet met. He is loyal alike to his black brethren and to his white master. He is generous, kind, a truer Christian than I."

"And Christophe?"

"Christophe has a different character," Duncan replied. "Christophe has an extraordinarily facile brain for matters of commerce. He knows how to make money, and, having made it, how to continue using it to the best possible advantage. His is an analytical brain. Toussaint would not encourage an insurrection, because he would not like to see blood needlessly shed. Christophe would likewise discourage the use of force, because he appreciates the consequences of an uprising. He has seen war —in Grenada and in America. He knows the power of the white man, and for that reason would be afraid to risk challenging his power. Yet he is one of the most courageous men I know. He is sensible enough to keep his reckless courage under control, because he realizes the uselessness of pitting black brute courage against white force and cunning."

"You speak as though you possessed a liking for the two men, monsieur."

"A liking!" Duncan shook his head doubtfully. "Admiration, respect, and sympathy for their ideals—but a liking—I cannot answer that question, Monsieur de Beaudierre. Perhaps because I cannot, or prefer not to, analyze my own feelings."

"You say you have sympathy for their ideals—"

Duncan laughed. "Because I have always been a rebel."

"But you do not put that sympathy into practice?"

"No," Duncan spoke with decision. "I am a physician, not a politician. I am neither a Frenchman nor a creole. I am a Scot. I should consider any intervention on my part in colonial politics both reprehensible and unjustifiable."

De Beaudierre, interested, persisted in his questions. "But suppose, monsieur, that the Negroes were to rise against the white man. On which side yould you fight? Would you take sides against men of your own color?"

Duncan frowned suddenly. "You will forgive me if I say that I owe nothing to the white people of this colony, monsieur. Nothing! They have slighted and insulted me because I treated a Negro humanely. Moreover, a Frenchman robbed me of the woman I loved, and of my career. I have no cause to love your countrymen—but I should not fight against them."

"Then you would fight against the Negroes?"

"No," Duncan denied. "I should remain neutral. As a physician I should treat white man and black. Why do you ask, monsieur?"

"Because I should like to take your hand." Ferrand de Beaudierre leaned near to Duncan, and held out his own.

Duncan said, "Slavery will not be abolished in our time."

"But the French government may officially abolish slavery."

"Surely the planters have too much influence at the French court. Their delegates to the National Assembly will fight for their rights."

De Beaudierre glanced at his companion. "Have you not heard the latest news from France?"

"Only that which is printed in the Cap François newspapers. Remember, monsieur, I meet no white men to acquaint me with current events."

"Ah! Then you have not heard that the people of Paris have revolted, and stormed the Bastille?"

The news startled Duncan. "Indeed, I have not. When did you hear this news?"

"Yesterday, when I reached Limonade."

"That must have been the message sent by the drums last night. They were busier than for many weeks past. Why did the King not call in the Army to quell the revolt?"

"I am told that the Army is no longer to be relied upon. If the soldiers join the populace—" He finished the sentence with a shrug of his shoulders that spoke his thoughts more eloquently than words.

"Revolution?"

"Who knows, Monsieur Stewart? Meanwhile, the news is causing the white people of Saint-Domingue acute anxiety. Nobody can forecast what may happen next. Monsieur Cazeaux, of whom you must have heard, has received a letter warning him that Les Amis des Noirs are to press the National Assembly to abolish slavery, and to grant mulattoes equal rights with the white race. He and Turpin are for forming a second delegation to join the first in Paris, but the planters of the other two provinces oppose them. Perhaps you have heard of the jealousy that exists between the northern and the western provinces. Each desires to be predominant in matters of counsel and trade. Generally speaking, however, the Colonials hope to take advantage of French unrest to secure more ind¬pend- ence for the Colony. The *petits blancs*, on the other hand, may be encouraged by the example of the Paris mob to pursue a somewhat similar course here, in Saint-Domingue."

"How does the government party regard the information from France?"

"They are perplexed, and uncertain in what light to consider the rising supremacy of the National Assembly. While they rejoice at the rebuff that the National Assembly delivered to the Colonials by admitting only six of the thirty-seven delegates, they are naturally aghast at the means employed by the people of Paris to flout established law and order. They look upon the creation of the National Assembly and the storming of the Bastille as dangerous precedents.

"You must realize from what I have been telling you, monsieur, that the white people of Saint-Domingue are divided in sympathies. The rich Colonials wish to secure independence for the Colony, the *petits blancs* want independence and pickings for themselves, the government party works to keep the *status quo*. The North is jealous of the West and the South. The mulattoes are not all fools. Their leaders are quite aware that the various white interests are squabbling with one another. They further realize that a house divided against itself cannot stand. Sooner or later they will seize the opportunity to press their own claims—and I shall sympathize with them."

De Beaudierre paused, but as if apprehensive of interruption, he continued in an uncertain voice:

"I do not know why I speak to you of such matters, monsieur. Perhaps because you, too, feel compassion for people of color. I say, you *too*, which is strange, for until now I have hesitated to admit such a sympathy even to myself. I have been loyal to my race at the expense of my conscience, even though I am married to a mulatto woman." His voice grew firmer. "Monsieur Stewart, if you save the life of my wife, as I pray you will, for I love her dearly, I swear that I shall assist the mulattoes in securing equality, and the Negroes in achieving freedom. So help me God!" The magistrate turned away from Duncan to conceal his emotion.

CHAPTER THIRTY

THE operation on Mme. de Beaudierre was a simple one. After the seventh day of his stay Duncan was able to leave Limonade with the knowledge that his patient would soon be well enough to return with her husband to Petit Goave. He was glad to find his affairs in Cap François much as he had left them. All his patients were proceeding satisfactorily, and of the new patients who had visited his house during his absence, apparently none of them had a complaint that suffered overmuch by the delay.

One week later Suzanne entered Duncan's life. He noticed her as he strolled through the slave market. A sale was in progress, and bidding had been brisk up to the moment when Suzanne mounted the platform. Her appearance was greeted with laughter, for she was enormously fat, enormously ugly, and obviously enormously useless for any save the lightest manual labor.

Suzanne was a treasure, the auctioneer announced heartily (a costly one to keep, shouted a wit). As a cook no one on the island was her equal (but any three others were, suggested the same wit). She was a widow, having been married once (four times, called out a fresh voice), had given birth to two children (or twelve? chorused several onlookers together); she was willing (to sleep? and what else? asked yet another heckler, amid uproarious laughter).

So the ritual of proclaiming her virtues, and the interruptions, had continued until the people were almost hysterical with amusement. At last the auctioneer lost his temper. With a shrug of his shoulders he angrily demanded offers for Suzanne. An offer of one French livre caused renewed laughter. So did the man who asked what Suzanne's present owner offered to be relieved of such an appetite. The auctioneer pleaded for a sensible offer, but none was forthcoming, for everybody realized that such an enormous body would eat more than it could earn—and the earning capacity of slaves was all that mattered. As the auctioneer was roughly ordering Suzanne to stand down, Duncan bought her. He was attracted by her enormous smile and the kindly, gentle expression in her eyes.

He never regretted his impulse, although she cost him one quarter of his available capital. She cooked, cared, mended, and mothered him until he had come to thank God for her. She even put him to bed and nursed him upon those occasions when he drank himself into a stupor. Such bouts became rarer as the weeks passed, for he immersed himself in his work and was happier. But occasionally some incident would evoke a poignant recollection of the past, and whenever he could endure his memories no longer he sought forgetfulness in tafia.

One afternoon he walked down the rue Saint Pierre to the Cours le Brasseur. The Cours was situated between the rue Neuve and the Quay Saint Louis, and from its tree-shaded gardens one could enjoy a pleasant view of the bay. As usual, the Cours was crowded with people enjoying a brief interval between the rains. As usual, De Saint Just was the conspicuous ornament of promenading society. He was startlingly dressed, as befitted the acknowledged leader of Saint-Domingue fashion, in a jacket of vivid plum velvet with cuffs of gold lace and buttons of large cabochon emeralds, and waistcoat embroidered in gold. A matching tassel of plum-colored silk and gold thread was suspended from his sword hilt. He sauntered along with an air—superbly affected—of total unconcern for the attention he attracted; he paused often, turning now toward some friend who passed, now toward his companion, achieving a variety of graceful poses.

With him was a woman whose face was unknown to all De Saint Just's friends, and though it was no novelty to see him with a new woman, this time the men of his acquaintance made little attempt to conceal their resentful envy. For she was startlingly, vividly beautiful, even on an island that could boast of many beautiful women.

A slight crinkle in her raven-black hair betrayed her mulatto blood. But for that telltale clue nobody would have suspected her of being other than a white woman—though perhaps the fire in her eyes and a lithe, panther-like movement in her walk were warning enough to men who knew, from experience, the subtle difference between a white woman and a woman in whose veins flowed some heritage of fierce, hot African blood. Her complexion was faintly olive, her large, brilliant eyes were richly brown, her lips were warm, perfectly shaped, her teeth exquisitely white and even.

"God! When did you last see a woman like that?" Joubert asked his companion, Gallifet. "Why should De Saint Just have all the good luck?"

"Because he has all the wealth. What a fascinating face!"

"What a shapely ankle!"

"What an exquisite body! What perfect breasts!"

"But who is she?"

Still rhapsodizing about the charms of De Saint Just's companion, Joubert and Gallifet passed beyond Duncan's hearing; and to the scornful look he gave to the backs of those arrogant idlers he added a quick shrug of annoyance with himself. He, too, had caught his breath; had almost whispered—"Who is she?"

Others whom he recognized were Louise Nanette, Marilys's mistress; Turpin, looking resentful, with Sarrus, the dandy, hovering close behind; Dubois (walking alone, and greeted only by the *petits blancs*); Deschenel; Turpin's neighbor, Clément, who accompanied the Comte de Saramon; and Mme. Cazeaux and Mme. Psaume walking together.

None of these acknowledged him, though all had met him at one time or another. All save Deschenel passed by him as though he were a stranger. Deschenel greeted him with a low, mocking bow, and called out in a loud voice so that many could hear, "Good afternoon, Monsieur l'Ami des Noirs."

Duncan had become impervious to slight and insult alike. With contempt he compared Deschenel with Toussaint, Turpin with Christophe, Mme. Cazeaux with Suzanne. Could one believe in all honesty that the hectoring, callous Deschenel was a better man than Toussaint, who was serene, intensely responsive to the sufferings of his race, and above all, used his penetrating wisdom to improve their conditions? Or that Turpin, physically as magnificent as Christophe, was superior in intellect? True, Turpin was educated, cultured. He was a natural leader of men, but he was the descendant of a long line of educated men, and learning, no doubt, had come easily to him. Christophe could neither write nor read. His brain was quick, accurate in its reasoning and retentive. So he learned quickly—and many of the lessons he learned from the whites were taught unwittingly. Christophe was cultured, not comparably with Turpin, but in view of his youth and the yoke of slavery that had oppressed him, his achievement was all the more credit to his ability. Christophe was a better man than Turpin, Duncan decided, because the Negro was using his intellect to construct where Turpin was endeavoring to destroy. Christophe was raising himself, where Turpin, because of his unreasoning attitude to slavery, was descending in the scale of humanity.

Presently Duncan left the Cours le Brasseur and emerged on the Quay Saint Louis. He continued his stroll along the quay, passing Dumestre's warehouse. He glanced up at the windows, wondering whether Garreau were to be seen watching the ships in the bay. Garreau was not visible, so he continued on and passed Delaire's warehouse. When he was nearly at the far end of the town, within sight of the slave market, he saw Garreau and François gazing with rapt eyes at the line of shipping stretched across the bay.

CHAPTER THIRTY-ONE

G OOD afternoon, Simon. I did not expect to see you here."
François laughed gruffly. "The very words, monsieur, I said to him fifteen minutes ago, when I came to see how the unloading of the *Louis Quinze* is proceeding. There are several hogsheads of wine aboard her consigned to me, and badly needed they are."

"How is the Casino, François? Is it making your fortune?"

The old soldier spat dexterously into the sea. "There is a certain madame who worries, but not me. There is a nest egg hidden, where nobody but me is going to find it, that will last me for the rest of my days if the worst comes along."

"What worst, François?"

"One never knows. Although a Swiss bastard sliced off half my ear, the other half is still capable of hearing a few things that are not intended for my ears. Funny things are happening in Saint-Domingue. My girls complain because they have only to satisfy one lover every night instead of several. When men forget what women are made for, I tell myself that their minds are busy with other matters."

"With politics?"

"Yes, monsieur. There is soon going to be an explosion in Saint-Domingue, the same as there was in Paris, or I still have the eye I lost in Portugal. Trust an old soldier like me to scent trouble when it's about."

Duncan laughed. "Be careful to keep out of it or you may lose that other eye of yours."

"There are other parts of me I would sooner keep. But you take Monsieur Garreau, here. He is not downhearted. And why should he be, I ask? Why? Because, like old François, he is making his way in the world."

Garreau's doleful expression belied François's words. Anticipating that Garreau would answer quip for quip, Duncan remained silent. So did the shipping agent. Apparently unconscious of being the subject of conversation, he continued to stare at the ships as though he were bidding them a farewell.

"He has been like this ever since I joined him," François grunted presently.

"What is the matter, Simon?"

"Old man Pegois died suddenly a month ago," Garreau answered with a dismal sigh.

"Well?"

"Before Pegois was cold in his grave his bastard sold the plantation so that he might journey to Paris, where he has wanted to go these several years."

Duncan was mystified. "I know Madame Garreau urged you to purchase the property, but you did not want to. Why should you worry now that it is sold?"

"Because I am the man who bought it."

Remembering Garreau's determination never to buy the plantation, Duncan could not resist a chuckle. So, after all, Mme. Garreau had achieved her ambition! At what cost to her husband's happiness? Garreau's miserable expression as he stared across the bay was sufficient reply. Duncan checked his laughter.

"Cheer up, Simon. I am sure matters cannot be as bad as your looks portend. You will not be so far away from the sea that you will be unable to take a look at the shipping now and again. Why, once you have the plantation properly organized you may be able to spend as much time in Cap François as most of the other planters. If you prefer to be here, on the quay, instead of at the Hôtel de la Couronne, that will be your affair."

"What do I care about watching ships if I no longer have a personal interest in them? Besides, I cannot bear to think of that Pilon sitting in my seat, at my desk, doing my work. He is a fool!" Garreau shouted. "He will ruin the business."

"That is no longer any worry of yours, Simon." Duncan placed his hand on Garreau's shoulder. "You will soon find consolation in your new plantation. Is it a prosperous one?"

"No."

"Then you will be able to occupy yourself in making a success of another person's failure. Besides, now that you are a planter you may find yourself too busy attending or giving receptions and musicales to think of the ships in the harbor."

Garreau grew more cheerful. "Do you think that Lambion and Cazeaux and Joubert and Psaume will ask Madame Garreau and myself to their soirées?"

"I am sure they will," Duncan replied.

Rumor succeeded rumor. The King had been assassinated! Paris had become a battleground! The King had ordered his foreign troops to fire on the National Assembly! Civil war was raging! Whence these rumors originated nobody knew, but a ship had only to be seen tacking round the cape for a new story, supposedly emanating from that particular vessel, to go the rounds of every salon.

Each rumor was denied, or corrected, but no sooner was it killed than a new version would breathe fresh life into the rotting carcass. All realized the incalculable harm wrought by these inventions, yet none seriously attempted to put an end to them. A spirit of restlessness came into being, and it grew more intense with each passing day.

The mulattoes and the *petits blancs* were the worst offenders. Convinced that only a matter of weeks separated them from equality with the white men, the mulattoes began to anticipate the proclamation by provocative acts that aroused the tempers of white man and mulatto alike.

Until this time they had been allowed to use only seats in church that were especially allocated to them. Now they began daringly to seat themselves in the pews reserved for the whites. Many scuffles occurred, which served to fan the fires of hatred.

Insolence became the keynote of the *petit blancs*. Where they had once greeted the wealthy colonials with subservience, and had displayed their goods with the pride and enthusiasm of men anxious to trade and prosper, now they raised their prices and made sneering reference to the nobles in France who had been thrust back into their rightful place by the National Assembly. One Barbedette, who for years past had derived handsome profits from his sale of jewelry to Clémentine, De Saint Just's mistress, actually turned his back upon her and contemptuously announced that he was no longer obliged to have dealings with colored people. Enraged by this insult, which he recognized as being directed as much at himself as at Clémentine, De Saint Just stormed into Barbedette's shop and thrashed the jeweler until the whip broke in halves. Barbedette dared to bring an action in the courts for this assault, and was awarded minimum damages. The murmurings of his fellow traders grew louder.

Only the Negroes remained undisturbed by the increasing unrest.

"Why, the good Lord bless my soul, Ti Rouge," Suzanne said to Duncan one day, addressing him by the familiar corruption of Petit Rouge, by which, on account of his hair, he was affectionately known to the Negroes. "What does it matter to us Negroes what happens in France? Some of us have been slaves so long now we do not want to be set free."

"Would you not be happier if you were free?"

Suzanne laughed so heartily that her enormous body quivered like a monstrous black jelly.

"Happier!" she gasped as tears streamed from her eyes. "Could anyone be happier than us slaves, Ti Rouge? Do you ever see us miserable as long as the sun shines?"

What Suzanne said was true. There were but few moments during the day when Duncan's small house was not cheery with her rich laughter, or with the sound of her deep voice singing the songs that had accompanied her mother from the African jungle. Nothing ever worried or disturbed her, and what work she was able to do she did willingly and heartily.

She was no exception. The majority of the Negroes, he had observed, worked with the same carefree irresponsibility. So long as their labors were not too arduous, so long as their bellies were satisfied, so long as the sun shone, then the majority of the Negroes lived their lives with joyful, childish abandon. Only when their masters were exceptionally cruel were they genuinely discontented with their fate.

Nobody in Saint-Domingue gave thought to the Negroes. The Colonials worked for independence. The *petits blancs* dreamed of another fourteenth of July. The mulattoes plotted for equality with the whites. Only Toussaint and Christophe, and perhaps a dozen other Negroes— Dessalines, Bouckman, Biassou, Jeannot, Jean-François—and, in distant France, Les Amis des Noirs, had dreams that included the Negroes. And the main preoccupation of Les Amis des Noirs was political—the sub-version of the French government!

The people of France were in a mood to reprimand the Colonials. Any system that had the appearance of despotism must be destroyed. On the tenth of August, 1789, the National Assembly abolished all agrarian abuses and feudal privileges. Ten days later the Assembly promulgated the "Rights of Man," wherein it was declared that "all men are born and continue free and equal as to their rights."

Equality for all men! At first the white people of Saint-Domingue could not believe the news. It was just one more of the hundreds of such rumors that had preceded it. Equality for the mulattoes! No! It could not be true. The National Assembly could not have intended *that* interpretation. Even though most of the members knew nothing of the conditions of the colonies, they could not have intended mulattoes to claim equal rights with whites.

Immediately upon hearing the sensational news, Turpin hurried to M. Duchilleau, the governor general, from whom he demanded an official denial. This His Excellency could not give.

"On the contrary, my dear Turpin, I must confirm the veracity of the story. I am today in receipt of a letter from the Minister of Marine giving me the gist of the principal clauses of the declaration."

"Is it true that all men are to be free and equal as to their rights?"

"Undoubtedly."

"Then the cursed mulattoes are now our equals, Duchilleau. The equal of you and me."

The Governor winced. "The declaration does not say so specifically."

"But the inference is there?"

"I am afraid so."

CHAPTER THIRTY-TWO

LIKE the first note of a tocsin, news of a proposed provincial assembly of the Colonials traveled the length and breadth of the Colony. It was accorded a mixed reception. The Governor General condemned the plan in outspoken language and described it as unconstitutional and revolutionary in character. He was automatically supported by those of his fellow citizens who held office. In consequence, the estrangement between M. Duchilleau and the Colonial party grew more acute than ever.

The news of their exclusion from the proposed assembly caused the mulattoes intense dismay. However unjust their treatment under the French, they knew that once the Governor's restraining authority was overthrown, the status of the colored people would become infinitely worse than it was already.

News regarding ferment among the mulattoes was given to Duncan by Toussaint and Christophe; they were frequent visitors in these days of political unrest.

"Since the departure of Pétion and Riguad to France to plead for the cause of the mulattoes the hotheads are gaining ground," a grave Toussaint told Duncan. "Both Ogé and Chavannes are firebrands. Lacombe is more cautious in advocating armed insurrection, but he is reckless and may influence others."

Duncan shook his head. "If enough steam escapes from the boiling pot there is no fear of its blowing up."

"Many, many years ago, Ti Rouge, when I was a boy, Pierre-Baptiste used to read stories to me from Montaigne. There was one about a worm that turned—"

"I know it, Toussaint."

"The worms are turning. I know, because the slaves have told me so when they have come to me for advice."

"How do the Negroes know of the mulattoes' plans?"

"Because the mulatto's contempt for the black man is not so strong as his hatred of the white. In every parish in the Colony, Ti Rouge, mulattoes are spreading sedition among the slaves and trying to obtain their support in an uprising against their white masters."

"My God! Toussaint, that's damnably serious," Duncan exclaimed.

"It might be, if the Negroes had not asked me for my advice."

"What did you tell them?"

"Listen to the drums. They are passing on a message that Toussaint Bréda sends to his fellow Negroes—'Do not listen to the smooth-tongued mulattoes who seek to shed your blood for their own selfish purposes.'"

"Will the black people listen to your advice, Toussaint?"

"I don't know. When the slaves want to be healed they come to Papa Toussaint. They like and respect Papa Toussaint—but there are other Negroes. I am afraid of Bouckman's influence. He is one of Monsieur Turpin's slaves. We Negroes have no reason to feel kindly toward Monsieur Turpin. He scorns us and hates the mulattoes. If it were not for Monsieur Turpin and his like, we Negroes might hope to obtain our freedom by peaceful means.

"Bouckman is an impatient man. He is huge and strong—a man bull. He practices voodoo worship and is a man of violent impulses. I have told you, Ti Rouge, of the voodoo dances, which I abhor because I am a good Christian, and because their effect on my people is evil. These dances deliverately rouse passions to fever heat. Usually the dancers slake their passion with sexual orgies, but the more intelligent Negroes might divert that passion from sex to war.

"Bouckman is not the only Negro whose influence among the slaves is dangerous. A maroon, Jean-François, who fled into the mountains from Monsieur Papillon's plantation. One of Monsieur Bullet's slaves, by the name of Jeannot, has an implacable hatred for the whites. Biassou, who belongs to the Fathers of Charity, is another who is ready to free himself from the yoke of slavery by violent means."

"Are these the men whom the mulattoes hope to make their allies?"

"No, for the men I have mentioned distrust the mulattoes, Ti Rouge. No, the mulattoes are confining their attention to the less important slaves."

"With what success?"

"None. We Negroes do not want strife or trouble. We do not hate the white man. All we ask for is our liberty."

"Not all ask for that," Christophe muttered contemptuously, speaking for the first time.

"Do not scorn others slower-witted than yourself, Henri," Toussaint chided.

"Surely any man should be able to comprehend the difference between freedom and slavery." Christophe turned toward Duncan. "Most slaves are too lazy to think for themselves. I worked hard to buy my freedom. When I became a free man I worked still harder. I have prospered. But when I tell others that they should try to do the same they stare at me as if they did not understand me."

"Nor do they. But they realize that you and I are striving to better their lives and are content to follow where we lead."

"Or Biassou, or Jean-François, or Bouckman, or Dessalines," Christophe pointed out morosely.

Duncan had heard Toussaint and Christophe argue about Negro mentality and had never failed to derive interest from the sharp contrast in character between the two men who, while both striving to obtain freedom for their fellow Negroes, were so strangely different. Toussaint possessed many of those traits that one associated with the Old World: serenity, dignity, a traditional sense of justice, and patient determination —characteristics that he must have assimilated through the Comte de Noé, and his overseer Bayou de Libertas, two men who were held in universal respect. Christophe, on the contrary, seemed essentially a product of the strange New World. He had an acute perception in all matters pertaining to commerce. He was virile, intolerant of sloth and mental indolence, blunt, and courageously headstrong. Duncan often wondered to what extent these tendencies had been developed by Christophe's sojourn in America at the time of the War of Independence.

Today Duncan had no desire to hear a repetition of old arguments. He was worried by Toussaint's news.

"Will the mulattoes act, even if they are unaided by the slaves?"

"I fear so," Toussaint stated.

"Then the authorities must be warned, Toussaint, so that the conspiracy can be checked before it spreads."

"That is why I have told you of it, Ti Rouge."

"Told me?"

"Nobody would listen to me, or to Christophe. They would to you."

"Why do you think anyone would listen to me—the pariah, the Friend of the Blacks, the *blanc papaloi?*" Duncan said bitterly.

"You must make them," Toussaint urged. "I swear to you, Ti Rouge, that unless proper precautions are taken, the mulattoes will rise. There will be revolution, civil war. Hundreds of lives may be lost. For the sake of those lives you must make the whites realize how dangerous the mulatto question is becoming."

Toussaint gazed at Duncan's face, anxious to read there the first expression of agreement. Christophe looked up at the white plaster ceiling, out of sympathy with Toussaint's plea, for Christophe would gladly have seen a few unwanted mulattoes dispatched to their doom. Duncan himself gazed through the open door at a white building standing on the summit of the nearest mountain—the Hospital for Free Colored People. It was a building at which he frequently gazed with wistful eyes and an intense desire to be allowed the use of their surgical equipment so that he might continue the series of experiments he had started two years previously. He was so keen to save lives that many a time he had daydreamed of being asked to go to the hospital in the mountains to save mulatto lives. Toussaint offered him that opportunity—and perhaps the possibility of saving the lives of white people as well—but not as a physician. No, only as a friend of the blacks, a man regarded as a pariah by those he sought to warn. At what cost to his pride and esteem would such an errand be? Probably he would be insulted, even compelled to suffer the humiliation of being treated as a renegade.

His memory bridged the gap of time and took him back to Anderson's surgery. "Remember, Duncan, my boy, it is the physician's sacred duty to try to save life. Once a man becomes a physician he no longer belongs to himself; nor even to his wife and his family. He becomes a public man at the beck and call of his patients, or of anyone in need of his services. Regardless of what dangers he may have to face, no matter what the consequences to himself, he must try to save a life whenever God honors him by granting him that opportunity."

Save life! Again and again Dr. Anderson had drilled that sense of sacred duty into the attentive ears of the red-headed lad he had adopted. So, in different circumstances, had Hunter. So had Hernon, the apothecary, and Henry Cline, the surgeon. Save life! It was the creed of medical men, to be followed blindly, selflessly, inexorably.

Toussaint could not interpret Duncan's expression and was anxious.

"You have been kind to us Negroes, Ti Rouge. You have saved black lives. Will you not save mulatto lives?" he urged.

Christophe gave a scornful exclamation, but Duncan ignored it.

"I shall do my best," he promised. Then he added: "Though I doubt whether any effort of mine will succeed."

He soon discovered how well justified had been his misgivings. Turpin, whom he visited first, condescended to see him.

"What do you want with me, Monsieur l'Ami des Noirs?" the Frenchman taunted. "I regret to say that none of my slaves requires your services." He laughed disagreeably when he saw the anger flare in Duncan's eyes. "I am told that you have a larger practice than any other physician in the Colony. What a pity that it should be such a poorly paid one! But you never want for bananas, eggs, and chickens, I am told?"

"I have not come here to discuss medicine, Monsieur Turpin," Duncan began in an unsteady voice. "I have come here to warn you—"

"To warn me! Alas! I am beginning to tremble for my life," Turpin mocked. "Surely it is a new departure for a physician to threaten life instead of saving it."

"Damn you, Turpin! Why not listen to what I have to say?"

"My dear fellow, I am listening. With all ears, I am most apprehensive and alarmed. I have always understood that redheaded men were to be feared on account of their violence. I find it quite a new experience to be afraid of a man."

Duncan was unable entirely to control his resentment. "I wish to God only you and I were involved in the business that has brought me here, Turpin. I would give you damned good cause to have every reason for fearing a redheaded man—"

"Would you prefer swords or pistols, I wonder? No, of course not. You Britons are famous for your vulgar bouts of fisticuffs. Let me see. I am a good half a head taller than you, much heavier, and have a longer reach. But then, I am not used to brawling. I am satisfied to use a sword —or a horsewhip," he finished viciously.

"Perhaps I am a vulgar Briton, compared with a courteous Frenchman," Duncan remarked. "But even savages, I have learned, respect their guests."

The mockery quickly left Turpin's expression. He was courageous enough to admit his own faults.

"I apologize, monsieur, for overlooking the fact that you are a guest in my house," he said curtly. "You have warned me. What else have you to say?"

"I did not come here to warn you personally, but the white people of this colony."

"Of what, may I ask?"

"Of the mulattoes."

"The mulattoes!" Turpin was obviously surprised by Duncan's reply. His voice sharpened with temporary interest. "I do not understand."

"I have reason to know, Turpin, that some of the mulattoes are contemplating an armed coup to enforce what they believe to be their right of equality."

"How do you know this?"

"From the Negroes whom the mulattoes have been trying to seduce into rebellion against their masters."

"Why are you telling me this?"

"So that you many warn the military authorities to take necessary precautions against such an uprising."

"I appreciate the spirit that brought you here, monsieur, but—" Turpin shrugged his shoulders. His mocking smile adequately expressed his opinion of the warning.

"But what?"

"I am afraid your black friends have taken advantage of your credulity to recount an improbable story."

"Do you not believe what I tell you?"

"Frankly, no. The mulattoes would not dare to rise against the white population of this colony. Still less the slaves."

Conceiving it to be useless to prolong the conversation, Duncan rose to his feet. Then his dour, dogged nature asserted itself. He sat down again.

"Monsieur Turpin, the white people of Saint-Domingue have little interest in me. Believe me, I have less in them. It would cause me no grief if every one of you were to die tonight. But I happen to be a physician—"

"An unqualified student, I believe," Turpin murmured.

"An unqualified physician, if you prefer. But I have a conscience. I should not care to have a death on my conscience that any warning of mine might help to prevent."

"Very considerate of you, monsieur."

Duncan glared at his tormentor. "I came here to warn you, Turpin, and, by God, warn you I will. Unless you prevent them, the mulattoes will rise."

A sardonic smile parted Turpin's lips. "They will go to their graves if they do," he murmured, his eyes sparkling wickedly.

"If the Negroes were not so easygoing and stupid they would join the uprising. They may yet do so," Duncan continued doggedly. "One of your own slaves, Bouckman, is inciting the Negroes to violence—"

"Bouckman!" Turpin lingered over the name. "My overseer, Sickard, shall deal with him."

Duncan laughed. "So you do place some credence in my warning?"

"No, monsieur, I do not." Turpin stood up. "Nor, I imagine, will any other white man in the Colony. Bouckman has always been an unsatisfactory slave. I can believe that he might try to make trouble, but not the others. That the mulattoes want equality we know. But that they would fight for that equality—the mere suggestion is too ridiculous to be heeded."

"Is there nothing I can do to convince you?"

"No, monsieur. We who have lived our lives in this colony know what we have to fear—and what we do not have to fear," he concluded, unable to resist one final sneer.

In Paris the mulattoes were not slow to take advantage of the Rights of Man. A petition was presented to the National Assembly requesting an assurance that their recent declaration envisaged the rights of *all* men to full and equal citizenship. In answer to this petition the president of the Assembly declared: "Not a single part of the nation shall ask in vain for its rights from the assembly of the representatives of the French people."

As soon as the news of this pronouncement reached Saint-Domingue, the jubilant Lacombe presented a petition to the Northern Provincial Assembly demanding its recognition of the rights of the mulattoes to equality. The fury of the Colonials surpassed any previous mood. Lacombe was seized, his petition was declared to be incendiary and traitorous, and without formality of trial the unfortunate man was summarily hanged.

The sparks of the insurrection blazed into flame. Disgusted by the arbitrary treatment of Lacombe, several Colonials, and many of the French led by Dubois, openly proclaimed their sympathy with the mulattoes, and demanded equality for free men of color and the abolition of slavery. In the South, Ferrand de Beaudierre, true to his vow, drew up a memorial to the parochial committee of Petit Goave that claimed for the mulattoes the full benefit of the rights granted to them by the French National Assembly. At Jacmel, on the Caribbean coast, and in the Artibonite valley, on the border of the northern and western provinces, the mulattoes acted as Toussaint had prophesied, and revolted. Courageous in their reckless disregard of weakness in numbers and arms, they established bases and confidently waited for the rest of the colored people to follow their example.

But the influence of Pétion and Riguad was strong. Some of the mulattoes were wise, some were cautious, some were cowardly. The call to arms trumpeted by the mulattoes of Jacmel and Artibonite was not answered. The revolutionaries were isolated. After a short engagement the two pitifully small forces were defeated, and the combatants taken prisoners.

The sparks of insurrection having been stamped out, the year 1789 passed slowly to a peaceful end—but only the very optimistic, or the very foolish, failed to realize that the merest breath of wind would fan the kindling flame into a conflagration that might destroy the Colony ere it was quelled.

CHAPTER THIRTY-THREE

ONE late afternoon in September Suzanne disturbed Duncan's siesta. "Wake up, monsieur," she rumbled in a loud voice as she shook his shoulder. "There is a man here to see you."

He yawned and shielded his eyes from the white glare of sunshine that streamed into the bedroom through the door, which fat Suzanne had neglected to close.

"You have left the door open, Suzanne," he mildly reproved her.

"Because you must not drop off to sleep again, master. The man says the matter is urgent. He comes from Monsieur François."

"François! Is he ill?"

"He is a stupid fellow, this Negro, master," Suzanne replied scornfully. "I can get him to answer nothing else but that Monsieur François wants Ti Rouge to visit him as soon as possible. He is a ninny."

"I shall see him in two minutes, Suzanne."

Suzanne eyed her master doubtfully. "If I leave you, you will fall asleep again."

"If you were to stay, my gazelle, you would see a sight that would bring a pink blush to your coal-black maidenly cheeks."

An immense blood-red, ivory-white gash divided Suzanne's face as a thunderous rumble of laughter welled up from her huge belly. Her eyes disappeared behind rolls of flesh; her bosom heaved like two empty barrels floating in a rough sea. She placed her hands on her swelling hips and rocked to and fro.

"Bless my soul, master!" she wheezed presently. "Fancy Suzanne's cheeks blushing pink, like those of a white! Oh, master, that I, who have undressed you a score of times to put you to bed, should blush like a white—" Unable to finish the sentence for laughter, she waddled from the room, heavily, like a young elephant. She did not close the door behind her, but having taken three or four steps into the next room she turned round and caught a glimpse of his white body as he rose from the bed, whereupon she rumbled afresh until she was breathless. Presently, when she had recovered her meager store of breath, she retailed the story of her pink cheeks to the waiting Negro.

In daylight the Casino was sordid and depressing, like a glimpse of a prostitute after one's appetite has been sated.

The only human was an old white-haired Negro, dressed in a tattered shirt and disreputable trousers, who sat in a gilt chair. His head lolled upon his shoulder. A gentle, contented smile on his lips convinced Duncan that the old man's dreams were peaceful and happy. Perhaps he was dreaming of the mysterious future where there would be no slaves, where every soul would be its own master, whatever the color of its skin.

Duncan gently shook the old man. The Negro jumped to his feet and stared at the visitor with eyes still bleary with sleep.

"What do you want, monsieur?" he quavered. "The Casino is not yet open."

"I want Monsieur François, Augustin. Where is he? In bed?"

Augustin peered more closely at Duncan. "Ah! Monsieur le docteur. Monsieur François waits for you. He sent me here to accompany you to the bedroom."

"To his bedroom?"

"But certainly not. Monsieur François is well. Monsieur François is always well." Mumbling to himself, the old man stumped along the dim corridor toward the ornately gilded double doors that a few hours later would be thrown open to visitors by gorgeously uniformed Negro flunkies, but that now remained grimly closed as though in a sullen mood at being surprised en déshabille. One of these doors Augustin forced open with difficulty, for it was of indigenous mahogany and heavy for an old man to push.

"Pass through, if you please," he wheezed.

Duncan passed into another corridor and continued to walk toward another pair of doors at the far end, which opened into the ballroom. He had only moved a few steps when he heard Augustin behind him.

"Not that way, monsieur."

He turned and saw the slave holding open a small door that was normally inconspicuous to passers-by because of the gilt scrollwork that edged it. On the other side was a narrow staircase in a small hall hung with portraits. He let Augustin take the lead, and the Negro climbed the flight, groaning at each separate stair as if the effort of lifting one foot higher than the other were a painful one.

When he reached the floor above, Augustin turned to his right and knocked softly at the door that faced the stairs. After a pause it was opened by François, who, seeing Duncan, stepped out into the passage and closed the door behind him.

"Ah! There you are, my boy. Thank you for coming so quickly. I have a patient for you."

"I feared it was you, François."

"Me!" François laughed huskily. "Who ever heard of an old soldier having megrims?" He glanced at the door behind them, leaned near to Duncan's ear, and whispered, "It's the old woman. She's sick."

"Madame Vroux?"

"Yes."

"What is the matter with her?"

"Nothing that a little blood letting will not banish. She has been worrying herself sick because the Casino has had a smaller turnover than usual for the past three months—the old usurer."

Examination assured Duncan that François had more or less faithfully described Mme. Vroux's symptoms. Duncan cupped the patient, and left with a promise to send her a cooling medicine later on. Downstairs he found François awaiting him.

"Duncan, lad, it is weeks since we have seen much of each other. To-night you must dine with me here at the Casino. We can eat before the place becomes too crowded, though God knows the ballroom is no longer as crowded as when you first came to the island. Will you stay?"

Duncan nodded. "I shall be glad to, François."

The two men strolled toward a smaller passage that led to the gardens surrounding the Casino.

"Let's sit in the pagoda where it is cheerful, my boy. Augustin will bring us drinks there."

Soon they were seated in a comfortable summerhouse that was shaded from the hot glare of the sun by imported vines. On the table by their elbows stood cooled drinks. The air was fragrant with the sickly sweet perfume of frangipani and fragrant tobacco.

"Why is business decreasing, François? Has the pendulum of fashion already started the contrary swing, or are your girls losing their allure?"

François swore a lewd oath that brought a twinkle to Duncan's eyes. "If you were less content to lead a hermit's life in that house of yours, you would know that the Casino François remains as fashionable as always," he boasted. "As for the girls, they are more succulent than ever, my lad. And so they will remain as long as François keeps his remaining eye. I haven't lived my life without recognizing a tasty morsel when I see one. What's more, I don't have to search for them; they come to me, and beg on their knees for an opportunity to work at the Casino."

"It's not my fault that less money is being spent here, though that old bitch who lies abed with her megrim would have you believe that the blame is mine. I tell you, lad, that business is bad because the people here have lost confidence in the immediate future. Thy are afraid their moneybags are threatened, so instead of doing what old François would do, and spending while the money is still theirs to spend, they are burying their treasures and telling the Casino to go hang itself with a rope of debts.

"Now, just what do we have, to regulate our affairs? Well, we have a governor who is at odds with the provinces and does not know from day to day where he stands with France. We have a new Colonial Assembly— by agreement of three provincial assemblies that agree in nothing else.

"When the members of the Colonial Assembly sailed aboard the *Léopard* for France, everyone who wished well of the Assembly rubbed hands for joy and said: 'You will see, the situation will improve. The Colonial Assembly will soon make the National Assembly see reason. Nothing but good can come of the journey to France.' But they took good care to sew up their pockets and their purses in case they should be proved false prophets. And they who derided the Colonial Assembly rubbed their hands and said: 'Now those upstart legislators will be put in their proper places. Wait until they appear before the National Assembly. They will wet their pantaloons in terror.' But they, too, aren't convinced by their own arguments."

"Do you think the Colony is at peace, my boy?" he asked.

"It seems so to me."

"That is because you are living solitary. What about the Negroes? Are they quiet and contented?"

"The Negro has a happy nature, François. He doesn't ask much more of life than to eat, drink, sleep, love, and dance."

"He wants freedom too, doesn't he?"

"Yes, but he will not struggle for it. He lets others do that."

"Your friends Toussaint and Christophe, for instance?"

"Yes, and others too, unfortunately. Hotheads, voodoo worshipers, fugitives like Bouckman, Jean-François, Biassou. But I don't think they are making much progress as yet."

"It is a pity one can't say the same of the mulattoes. Jacques Ogé has left France, Duncan."

"For Saint-Domingue?"

François revealed his brown teeth in a jeering grin. "For America, so he makes out. But he's going there to buy arms. Afterward he means to come on here, in the belief that the mulattoes only await his leadership to rise against the whites."

Duncan was startled. "All this is news to me, François."

"It is supposed to be a secret."

"Then how did you come to hear of it?"

The old soldier chuckled. "Haven't I told you before, my lad, that the Prussian who cut off my ear at the battle of Wilhelmstadt did only half a job? This one ear of mine is all the sharper for being on its own. I have heard things—" He winked his eye.

"It was Les Amis des Noirs who persuaded Ogé into sailing. They flattered him by procuring him a lieutenant colonelcy in the army of a German princeling"—François spat his contempt—"and sent him packing for the New World, with the blessing of God and the French people. Pah!" he ejaculated violently.

"Do the authorities here know of Ogé's intentions?"

"Of course they do, lad. How else should I know? The planters have their spies in Paris. The Governor has received warning of the conspiracy, and a likeness of the man. The moment he attempts to land in Saint-Domingue he will be arrested and tried for treason."

"Poor devil!"

"Troublemakers ask to be exterminated," he grunted.

CHAPTER THIRTY-FOUR

NO propaganda could have better suited the purposes of Les Amis des Noirs than the story of Ogé's death. Jacques Ogé, a mulatto, returned from France, had landed despite the watch set against him on Saint-Domingue and had led an abortive revolt of mulattoes against the dominant planters. Defeated and captured, executed by breaking on the wheel, he became in France a symbol of martyrdom, of the Rights of Man. Paris was shocked. Paris was made acutely conscious that the members of the ruling class of Saint-Domingue were detestable monsters, vicious libertines, tyrannical brutes, medieval torturers. On the fifteenth of May, 1791, a decree was passed enacting that all people of color in French colonies, born of free parents, were entitled, as of right, to all the privileges of French citizens, including that of being eligible to seats in both the parochial and colonial assemblies.

The effect of this decree, news of which reached Cap François on the thirtieth of June, was catastrophic. Seething with discontent, all classes of white people united to resist its enforcement. The cry spread—seize French ships, confiscate French property, prohibit the entry of further French goods. The national cockade was spat upon.

With the mercury rising to its mid-August maximum, the temper of the white inhabitants sharpened to unreasoning frenzy. Reports circulated of some mulattoes being threatened, of some being fired upon, and of the death by lynching of others. The colored people, alarmed by fears of a pogrom, fled from the town and the villages and once again assembled in armed bands.

Uneasiness lay like a pall over the Colony on the twenty-third of August. Duncan was about to retire for the night when Christophe arrived. His expression was strange.

"What is it, Henri? Is somebody ill?"

"No, Ti Rouge. Nobody is ill, but I have come to ask you to make a journey."

"Where to?"

"A voodoo dance at Monsieur Turpin's plantation."

Duncan was astonished. "I have been to several voodoo dances, Henri. Besides, I have no particular wish to get drunk tonight."

"Toussaint is coming."

"Toussaint! I thought he abominated voodoo ceremonies."

"He does, Ti Rouge, but he is afraid of tonight's. So am I."

"Afraid of what?"

"I don't know, but neither Toussaint nor I have been told of the dance tonight . . . perhaps it is because you are my friend."

"I! What connection is there between me and a voodoo dance?"

"You are a white man."

"What of it? Many white men, including myself, have witnessed voodoo ceremonies."

"Do not ask me questions but come, Ti Rouge," Christophe urged.

Becoming fearful of what the night would disclose, Duncan agreed to accompany Christophe.

Five months previously Duncan had purchased Jenny. Jenny was a blood mare, bought by Duncan for a mere song from a mulatto coffee planter who had overworked and ill-treated the poor beast to the point of death. The mare had repaid the cost of generous feeding and kindly attention; now the Colony knew few more capable animals.

Duncan saddled Jenny and told Christophe he was ready, adding, "Which way are we going, Henri?"

"To the Plain—but where, I do not know. The drums must lead us." Christophe swung onto his own horse. "Come, Ti Rouge."

The crescent moon was high in the heavens, luminous, shimmering, fairly-like; and every star sparkled with a sharp brilliance. The two men had no difficulty in seeing the road ahead of them; at a steady pace they made their way toward the track that branched away from the town on the far side of the retrenchments, and wound its way through the encircling mountains toward the great plain.

From every direction the drums throbbed unceasingly. From nearer valleys, from distant mountaintops, tom-tom-tomitty-tomitty-tom-tom; tom-tom-tomitty-tomitty-tom-tom. Now the loud bellow of the monster of drums, which, hollowed from a tree trunk and covered with a head of bull's hide, stood higher than the tallest man, and was beaten by men standing on a raised platform. Now the deep reverberating zoom of the maman drums, three feet high, beaten by a man using a stick and the base of his palm. Now the high-pitched, impinging note of the boula, a "baby" drum, manipulated by flat palm, finger tips, clenched knuckles, and a rosin-coated thumb.

Tom-tom-tomitty-tomitty-tom-tom; tom-tom-tomitty-tomitty-tom-tom. The noise traveled through the air in waves of sound. At one moment it seemed to come from a point no more than a stone's throw from them; the next, from a distant eyrie. Drums to the east, to the south, to the west of them; drums from every direction save that of the town they were leaving behind them; drums from the plantations, drums from the forests; drums from the mountains, drums from the valleys. Unceasing, barbaric, mysterious.

Even to Duncan's untutored ears the rhythm of the drums was unusually frenzied. The sensuous night air was throbbingly alive; the ground beneath their horses' hoofs vibrated with the thunder of rhythmic sound. The horses seemed nervous and uneasy.

"What is happening tonight, Henri?" Duncan asked sharply. "The Colony seems awake from end to end."

"I cannot tell you more than I have already done."

"But you can read the message of the drums."

"The only message that the drums are sending out tonight, Ti Rouge, is one calling the slaves to a Petro sacrifice."

"A Petro sacrifice?" Duncan was startled. "Why does Toussaint propose to visit a ceremony that he professes to abhor?"

"Because neither of us has been told anything about tonight's sacrifice. Two weeks ago a Petro sacrifice was held on the Noé plantation. Toussaint did not go, but since then the Negroes have avoided Toussaint and me, because it is known that you are my friend, the friend of Toussaint. . . ."

"And the friend of many other Negroes," Duncan interrupted.

"That is true, but none has better reason to be grateful to you than I, and I have never failed to tell the Negroes of my feelings for you."

"Thank you. But why should the Negroes have avoided you?"

"So that neither Toussaint nor I should hear of the sacrifice until too late—and through one of us, you, Ti Rouge. You are a white, and the Negroes cannot forget that, though you have befriended them and saved their lives."

"But am I not a white to you, Henri?"

"I have no hatred of the whites." There was a contemptuous tone in Christophe's voice. "I am intelligent enough to realize that the white man and the Negro can live side by side to the benefit of both. Each needs the other. I have seen more than most Negroes of white men, Ti Rouge. I admire them. They have faults, but they know how to organize industry and how to promote trade. Without the white man to oversee him, the Negro would sleep his life away. He is no more than a happy, contented child. No, I ask only one thing of the whites—the freedom of the Negroes from slavery."

"But this ceremony tonight—"

"There are others, Ti Rouge, who are as anxious for freedom as Toussaint or myself."

"Bouckman, for instance?"

"Yes. I warned you of his activities, but no stop was put to them."

"I passed your warning on to Monsieur Turpin, but it was not believed."

"Many white men are blinded by their overweening conceit," Christophe commented. "Monsieur Turpin had Bouckman flogged, but took no other steps to prevent the man from spreading sedition. The flogging merely served to aggravate his bitterness."

"Is the dance tonight a cloak to hide conspiracy?"

"I know nothing. I have only my suspicions. That is why Toussaint and I propose to be at the ceremony—as unseen witnesses."

"And what part am I to play, Henri?"

"Who knows? Perhaps that of a savior."

"Are you joking, Henri?"

"Am I in the habit of joking?"

"You have a sense of humor—but that is beside the point. Who am I to save, Henri?"

"Perhaps your fellow white men."

"Good God!" Duncan leaned in the direction of Christophe, stretched out, caught hold of his bridle, and brought both horses to a standstill.

"Henri, you must be more frank with me. What is it that you fear?" Duncan demanded.

"I know nothing definite. But as I listen to the drums I fear what may happen tonight. We Negroes are a patient race. But our blood is African. If ever it should become really inflamed we might become like the mad bulls the Spaniards make sport of across the border. We might try to follow the example of the mulattoes, and seek to secure our freedom by force of arms."

"The mulattoes have failed to overcome the white men, not once but several times."

"The mulattoes!" Christophe's voice filled with scorn. "They are neither fish, flesh, nor fowl. They are cravens; cowardly bastards who shelter behind the soldiers of their white betters. The Negroes might succeed where the mulattoes have failed."

"How?"

"There are sixteen Negroes to every white man. If every slave were to rise, how could the white men hope to defend themselves?"

"In France there are many millions to avenge every death of a white man in Saint-Domingue," Duncan warned him.

Christopher chuckled. "From the news one receives from France, Ti Rouge, Frenchmen have too many troubles of their own to pay much heed to what happens in Saint-Domingue. Besides, Les Amis des Noirs are favorably disposed toward the slaves."

"They would not tolerate the death of white men at the hands of slaves. They would send another army to maintain peace."

"Do you think that the slaves are blind to what is happening in this colony? They know that the white men are so divided among themselves that they foolishly ignore all danger. They have seen the mulattoes rise in insurrection, and have not failed to notice that all but a few of the mulattoes have remained unpunished. But enough, Ti Rouge. The arguments are not mine, but those of Bouckman and Jean-François. Toussaint has converted me from belligerent ways."

"As much as the fact that you now own the Hôtel de la Couronne?"

"Perhaps," Christophe admitted. "But what do my reasons matter? I believe that the hour of emancipation is drawing near, the hour that I have dreamed of all my life, prayed for since I fought in America, and worked for since I obtained my own freedom. But I believe that the hour must be peaceful, not bloody."

"You speak as though the slaves are restive."

"Of course they are restive, Ti Rouge. How could they be otherwise, considering the events of the past year? In the towns they are quiet, but away on the plantations, where they have had less opportunity of appreciating the power and might of the white man, they are becoming dangerously unsettled. But we are wasting time. Toussaint expects us."

Duncan nodded agreement. The travelers spurred their animals forward. As they advanced deeper into the countryside the booming of the drums grew louder and more frenzied. Christophe urged speed. The forest through which they passed rustled with restless life and sparkled with a million fireflies.

They reached the highest point of the track. Below them the great plain stretched for miles, bathed in a silvery radiance and streaked with ribbons of steel where the rivers and irrigating water channels reflected the bright moonlight. In the distance, on the mountains bordering the far side of the plain, twinkling lights, glowing redly, revealed brush-wood fires.

As the track descended their speed increased. They dashed forward through the bright night toward the Bréda plantation, which they reached while the moon was still below its zenith. As they neared the long palm-fringed drive, which stretched from the road to the home of the Comte de Noé, a shadowy figure on horseback emerged from the shadows of a bayahonda bush. It was Toussaint.

"There is menace in the drums," he said. "We must hurry if we are not to be too late."

"Have you heard more news, Toussaint?"

"Only that a black pig is to be sacrificed on the Choiseul le Marquis plantation tonight."

"Then come." Christophe spurred forward again, followed by Duncan and Toussaint.

They lost count of time and distance. On, on, on, to the accompaniment of the zooming drums. On past estate after estate, now coffee, now cotton, now indigo, all looking orderly, well cared for, in the cold light of the moon. On past prosperous, handsome homes and slave compounds. On, on, on to the Choiseul le Marquis estate, along a road constructed and excellently maintained by French engineers. On, with the horses beginning to falter in their long stride.

Presently Toussaint, whose fresher animal had taken him to the fore, raised his arm. The two men behind reined in.

"We are reaching the outskirts of the Turpin plantation," Toussaint told Duncan. "We must tether our horses and proceed on foot."

The men dismounted. Toussaint led the way into a grove of banana trees, where they secured their animals. To Duncan Toussaint continued: "The sacrifice will be held as far from the road and the household as possible. Beyond the far corner of the plantation is an uncultivated valley that is part of the Choiseul le Marquis estate. It is there I shall expect to find the heathens. Will you be able to find your way back to your animal in case of necessity?"

"Yes," Duncan replied shortly.

They proceeded along the banana grove until they reached the vast fields of coffee. As they progressed the booming of the drums decreased in sound . . . a secret in acoustics known only to the Negroes . . . but Duncan thought he heard the chanting of voices.

They reached the edge of the plantation. In front of them they saw the black shapes of gnarled trees etched sharply against the silver-blue-black of the sky—the fringe of unclaimed jungle. Toussaint took Duncan's hand and led the way into the mass of trees and undergrowth that turned the silver night into dense blackness. Christophe followed in the rear.

Duncan was thankful for the hand that guided him through the jungle, for he could see nothing. Alone he would have forced a way through the tangled growth, probably at the cost of tearing his clothes and lacerating his flesh. But Toussaint, as if by instinct, led the way along a narrow path that was little better than a tunnel. All round them they heard the scuttling of animals, the hiss of disturbed snakes. Glowworms and fireflies flashed before their eyes.

Soon the chanting of many voices grew clearer. Some distance ahead they saw the red glow of a vast fire. They advanced another five hundred yards. As the undergrowth thinned out there was exposed before them a picture of primeval savagery.

The scene, set in a clearing that formed a natural arena, was redly lighted by leaping flames from a high cone of burning brushwood, which scorched the surrounding air with its fierce heat and scented the neighborhood with the smoke of aromatic woods. High on the edge of the arena, to the left of the watchers, were the drums; these were beaten by half-naked, frenzied men whose fine bodies glistened with sweat. Around the fire were three or four hundred Negroes and Negresses, who squatted on their haunches, swayed in unison to the rhythm of the drums, and wailed a melodious chant. To the right of the bowl a magnificent black boar pawed the ground and squealed with fear as it tugged, bent-headed, at its halter; its eyes were red-rimmed with its instinctive fear of imminent doom. Beside the boar were two goats, which bleated shrilly and reared up in the air in an effort to break loose. Beyond was a wooden case in which squawked half a dozen pure white cockerels, also destined for sacrifice.

The rhythm of the drums accelerated as the drummers pounded their instruments with movements quicker than the eye could follow. The swaying movement of the squatting Negroes kept time to the increasing beat; their voices rose raucously as frenzy rendered hoarse their wailing chant.

Duncan gripped the branches of the trees in front of him. His ears throbbed with the sound of the barbaric music; he was conscious of elemental impulses, of orgiastic desires, of a compelling urge to join in the rites of sacrifice to Damballa Ouedo, the serpent god. To what lengths these influences would have carried him was, ever after, a matter of conjecture, for the spell was broken when a red-robed woman sprang up from among the foremost ranks of the Negroes. The drums stopped; the drummers reeled from their instruments and collapsed to the ground in a state of exhaustion. A sigh like the whisper of wind traveled round the arena; rigid bodies relaxed; for some moments the uncanny quietness was disturbed only by the loud crackling of burning wood and the echo of distant drums.

The silence did not last long. Fresh drummers leaped to take the place of their tired comrades. The drums crashed out in a new rhythm. From out of the jungle appeared a retinue of weirdly garbed celebrants; men and women—dressed in fantastic scarlet and white robes, feathered headdresses, serpentine symbols, and cabalistic emblems—pranced in animalistic postures and chanted a dirge to Ogoun Badagris.

The chant finished; the celebrants took their place among the worshipers. A white-haired, serpent-crowned Negro stood up, stretched his arms upward, and mouthed an incantation in an African dialect that Duncan did not recognize. As the echo of his last word died away the worshipers shouted a response. The old man sank to his haunches; a young Negro leaped to his feet and seized a large bundle of firewood, which he hurled into the heart of the fire. A thick cloud of blazing sparks rose into the air, and was blown by the wind among the worshipers. A smell of scorched flesh and burned hair filled the arena, but not a man or woman moved. The flames leaped higher. The young Negro began to dance; sometimes he disappeared from sight among the flames, which seemed to lick his body; finally he stood firmly upon the soles of his feet and vibrated every limb and muscle in his body in a quivering, sensuous mimicry of the procreative act.

The drums ceased. Once more the serpent-crowned priest rose to his feet, chanting. A number of women joined the circle of worshipers, bearing bowls of food and large gourds of tafia, which they laid down close to the fire. The drums paused, the priest shouted a single word, then they began again in a maddening staccato rhythm that grew faster and faster. Into the circle of worshipers leaped a naked, sinuous woman, who held her arms above her head to make her pointed breasts stand out rigidly from her bosom like black marble. In her hands she held a black squawking cockerel. She leaped and postured as she passed through the ranks of the worshipers, and lustfully pressed her quivering body against men and women alike, arousing them to delirious passion. With glazed eyes they stared at the dancer's mad contortions, and at the feathers that showered down upon her from the wings of the flapping cockerel.

With an obscene gesture she stopped dancing. The drums boomed louder. The muscles of the woman's arms tautened as she slowly exerted a sideways pressure, and tore the neck of the cockerel from its body. The blood flowed down upon her upturned face and breasts. Then she pushed the bleeding neck of the cockerel into her open mouth, and drank the fresh warm blood in deep gulps.

The worshipers leaped to their feet and surged forward toward the food and drink that awaited them. The dancer spattered the nearer ones with the blood that overflowed from her mouth. A dancing, twirling papaloi waved a loud rattle to clear a pathway; papalois and mamalois carried the white cockerels and led the hornless goats and the struggling pig to the place of sacrifice. With swift blows of his machete the white-haired papaloi severed the heads of the cockerels and allowed the blood to gush into a wooden trough. When the birds were blooded, the goats, and afterward the pig, were pushed to the trough so that the papaloi could slit their throats. When the trough was full of blood the white-haired papaloi blessed it, and the celebrants danced among the worshipers, spattering them with blood. Small gourds were dipped into the trough, filled, and passed on after each in turn had drunk deeply of the blood that their gods had blessed. Purified, ecstatically maddened, god-possessed, the worshipers began to dance to the quickening beat of the drums. Duncan, who had witnessed Petro sacrifices, knew that the climax was approaching. Soon the dance would become a Corybantic saturnalia of sex-drugged religious fanatics, who would leap and twirl and scream in erotic posturing until the surging tide of passion sought its natural relief.

That moment would arrive soon now, he thought. It must arrive soon. Passions were already at straining point. At any moment the weakest-willed man among the milling crowd of gasping, exhausted dancers might seize the nearest woman and fall with her, wrestling, to the ground. . . .

The drums ceased, the dancers shuffled to astounded immobility. A huge black figure elbowed his way nearer to the fringe of the crackling fire, leaped upon a fallen tree trunk, and spread his arms in an appeal for attention. As the flickering light of the leaping flames illuminated the face Duncan recognized Bouckman.

CHAPTER THIRTY-FIVE

THE slave shouted a dozen sentences in the dialect that the white-haired *papaloi* had used earlier. Men and women who had been struggling together, limbs interlocked, disentangled themselves, stared at the man on the tree trunk. The arena grew quiet.

As soon as he had captured the attention of the worshipers, Bouckman continued. The sound of his harsh voice traveled through the still night air, accompanied by the explosive crackling of the burning brushwood. With voice, grimace, and gesticulation the man harangued his audience; his thick, dark lips mouthed the words.

He used no trick to hold his audience. It was evident that what he lacked in subtlety was compensated by his forthright vigor, which forced his meaning into slow-thinking, heated brains. Shouts, acclamations, gesticulations began to punctuate his speech as the inflamed passions of the slaves were diverted into channels whose ominous implications Duncan could only surmise.

Alarmed by his fears, Duncan turned toward Christophe, who stood on his left.

"What is he saying, Henri?"

Christophe did not reply. His face was illuminated by the leaping flames, and Duncan was shocked by the transformation in Henri's expression. The man's mouth was open in a mirthless, canine grin. His eyes stared at the distant Bouckman with no less eagerness than that expressed by the slaves in the arena. He was no longer the intellectual thinker of Duncan's acquaintance, but a stranger; a passionate Negro expressing all the elemental emotions of his savage ancestors.

Fearful of the change that was taking place in Christophe, Duncan turned sharply to his right with the thought: Surely Toussaint was not similarly affected—the erudite, anti-voodooist Toussaint? But Toussaint was. His eyes were fanatical, bright and red in the reflected light, as he held his head sideways at an angle, as if not to miss one word.

The white man asked himself anxiously: What was Bouckman saying to affect two such rational beings as Christophe and Toussaint? What could the stabbing, hammering words be that so easily destroyed learning and intelligence and stripped off the veneer of civilization? However momentarily, these two men had assumed kinship with the exulting mob in the arena, who were under the influence of erotic excitation, warm blood, and raw alcohol. If that were the effect of Bouckman's bellowing delivery on Christophe and Toussaint, what must those same words be doing to the frenzied slaves?

The slaves themselves answered Duncan's unspoken question. Again they stamped on the ground and yelled, but it was patent to Duncan that the motive force was no longer sexual. The womenfolk were ignored. So were the *papalois*, the *mamalois*, and the celebrants. Bouckman held the stage. Bouckman, and the ubiquitous gourds of tafia.

The tumult grew fiercer. Bouckman's voice boomed louder with triumph. His sentences grew staccato, compelling, as he questioned the slaves, who continually shouted back a single word that signified their agreement.

Duncan turned to Toussaint. "What is Bouckman saying?"

Toussaint answered tonelessly: "Bouckman demands the abolition of slavery. He is telling the people that now is the time for them to press for their demands. He is asking them whether they wish to be free; if so, he will lead them to freedom. He is a clever man, Bouckman. He has aroused the passions of the slaves, and is goading them on before they have the chance of slaking their desires."

Duncan shook his arm, for Toussaint was like a man in a coma. "What more is he saying? Tell me, man, is he inciting them to action?"

"He is, and why not?" Toussaint asked. "Why shouldn't we seek liberty? Why should a few thousand men possess half a million slaves? The mulattoes have struck a blow for equality. Now is the time for us to do the same. Aren't the people of France themselves preaching liberty and equality?" Toussaint laughed with excitement. "Listen to what Bouckman says now: 'Rise, slaves, rise against the tyranny of the whites. We are sixteen men to their one. In Guinea we have been mighty fighters, we Negroes. In Saint-Domingue we can be as mighty. Descendants of the fighting tribes of Guinea, rise against the whites. Fight for freedom. Fight for liberty. Fight, kill, burn, ravage'—"

Both Toussaint's shrill interpretation and Bouckman's bellow were drowned by the deafening thunder of drums, stamping feet, and the shrieking of frenzied voices. As one man the slaves in the arena formed into a series of concentric rings round the blazing fire. Instinct warned Duncan what had happened. The contagion of revolt had supplanted the sex lust in the inflamed brains of the slaves. The milling, screaming dance no longer heralded an orgiastic explosion of sexual passions, but a lust for blood. The slaves were dancing the war dances of their native Africa. Before long they would probably lose what little self-control remained to them, and erupt from the arena. When that happened they would spread across the great plain, perhaps to leave death and destruction in their wake.

Duncan knew at last why he had been brought to witness the scene of sacrifice. Toussaint and Christophe had suspected what might happen, and had hoped, through his eyes and testimony, to convince the white rulers that they must guard against the black tide that threatened to rise. What his two companions had not anticipated, he felt sure, was that they too would become victims of the contagion.

Convinced that he must escape without delay, he clutched at Toussaint's arm. "Take me back to the horses, Toussaint," he shouted. The man did not hear a word, for the drums made an inferno of the night, but he guessed what was demanded of him; sanity returned to his eyes, and with sanity, alarm. He nodded his head and caught hold of Duncan's hand with the intention of returning to the horses.

Before they could move Bouckman's volcano erupted its human lava. The slaves surged out of the bowl-like arena. The three witnesses of the voodoo rites were engulfed in a mass of struggling, screaming men and women. In the flickering light of torches white teeth gleamed in thick-lipped wolfish grins; red-tinged eyeballs rolled in the mad lust for destruction.

None paid attention to the white man, for the slaves were incapable of coherency. Besides, Toussaint and Christophe shielded him as best they could. The maddened slaves caught up with the three men and passed quickly by them like a swarm of locusts. "To Monsieur Turpin! To Monsieur Turpin!" was their parrot-like shout, and what lay between them and their quarry was of no consequence. They crashed through the jungle, insensible of the thorns that punctured and tore their black skins. To the Turpin home was their only thought—before word of their coming could reach that hated master.

Duncan followed in the wake of the slaves in the hope that some miracle might delay them long enough for him to warn the white people of the danger that menaced them. Guided by Toussaint, he floundered through the jungle and emerged at a spot where the fringe of the jungle fought to reinvest and destroy the cultivated fields of cotton. Some distance ahead the slaves continued their wanton progress; they trampled down the growing plants and dropped the ends of burning torches upon the inflammable vegetation. Already in a dozen different places the cotton was afire, and the flames, fanned by the cool night breeze from the mountains, spread rapidly.

"Which way is Turpin's house? Is there a shorter route?" Duncan appealed.

"No, Ti Rouge. The slaves are taking the shortest route to the plantation house," Toussaint replied. "There is no way of reaching Monsieur Turpin before they do."

"Then we must follow behind to try to rescue the white people there."

"That would be too dangerous, Ti Rouge," Toussaint pointed out sharply. "They are crazed with blood lust. They won't listen to commands or discipline. They are still under the influence of the drums. They believe that the gods have possessed them, that they are invincible and immune from harm. Until the effects of the sacrifice have abated it will be unsafe for a white man to approach them."

"But we cannot stand by and witness murder. Can't you do anything to help, Toussaint? You don't **want white** people to be massacred, **do** you?"

"The good God knows how I abhor bloodshed."

"Then speak to them as Bouckman did," Duncan urged. "You are known to them. You have influence with your people, Toussaint. Use it to save the people in the Turpin household."

"I don't think they will listen to me, Ti Rouge, but I will try."

Christophe interrupted. "If we do not move quickly there will be a wall of flame between us and the house," he pointed out. "The fools! They are destroying thousands of livres' worth of good cotton. Destroying property will do them no good and will harm our cause."

His two companions could see for themselves that Christophe was not exaggerating. Fire was meeting fire and creating a blazing, crackling inferno that was already turning the silver-black sky a dull red.

The three men ran toward the nearest opening in the flames, already so narrow that the three of them could not pass through abreast. Toussaint went first, but as Duncan followed through the draft caused by the passage of his body attracted the flames. Long, curling streaks of stinging heat burned his face and hands and singed his red, unruly hair. Acrid smoke blinded his eyes, and, filling his nostrils, made him choke and splutter. The noise deafened him, and he did not hear Toussaint's shout. He was blundering straight toward the heart of a new outbreak when Toussaint caught hold of his arm and pulled him away from danger.

Roaring flames turned night into red day. Ahead of them new fires sprang up in a dozen different places. Their leaping flames were reflected upon the shiny black bodies of the slaves, who had begun to destroy everything that stood in their way—imported plows, native carts, their own compounds, stables, storehouses. In screaming, shouting ranks they advanced upon Turpin's magnificent house. Willfully they trampled down all the fine plants and bushes he had imported from France, hacked with their machetes at the ornamental trees, which had also come from Europe, fired a gazebo. In a few minutes the work of decades was ruined.

Armed with machetes, thick branches, anything, in fact, upon which they could lay their hands, the howling mob surrounded the house and slowly advanced upon it. The nearer slaves were within twenty yards of it when the door opened and Turpin stepped out, dressed in loose shirt, breeches, and slippers. His hair was tousled, his eyes heavy with sleep, but in spite of his appearance his attitude was threatening. He held his broad shoulders squarely, carried a vicious-looking slave whip in his hand, and faced the slaves with an abandoned recklessness that made his huge sturdy figure starkly impressive.

"Back, you dogs! Get back to your quarters, you black-skinned swine, back before I flog the skin off every one of you!"

His bellowing voice overshouted the yelling of the advancing slaves, and the crack of his whip echoed sharply. The habits and fears of years were not easily cast off. Shouting died away as the slaves shuffled to a halt. In a timid semicircle about him they faced the man who possessed power of life and death over them.

146

Turpin stared contemptuously at the ring of black faces around him.

"You filthy swine!" he shouted. "Field slaves! Get back to where you belong before I set my house slaves and dogs upon you. Get back, and put out those fires. Do you hear me? Get back, or by the Lord God above, I swear I'll break every one of you on the wheel."

He cracked his whip again and stepped forward a pace. The cowed Negroes shuffled uneasily. Turpin laughed, and with a flick of his wrist curled the lash round the legs of a woman within reach of his whip. The woman shrieked, and the foremost slaves scrambled away to a safer distance. Turpin advanced a pace. The line of Negroes wavered, and Duncan, watching from a distance, believed that the revolt was over before it had begun.

Turpin's indomitable courage might have had effect but for one person, Bouckman. Bouckman, whom Turpin had flogged for insubordination and for inciting unrest. Bouckman leaped forward. The Frenchman raised his arm, but the slave darted beneath the curling lash and with his machete struck swiftly upward at the hand that held the whip. Hand and whip fell upon the ground. Turpin, with his arm still upraised, stared down stupidly at his own hand.

There was a scream of triumph from the slaves. The whip, the symbol of the white man's power and authority over them, had fallen to the ground. An omen from the gods. An omen of victory. In a body they rushed upon the defenseless Turpin, machetes flashing in the red reflection cast by the flaming gazebo. Turpin staggered, recovered himself, then fell for the last time. There was a shriek of horror from the house. A slim figure, clad only in a shirt, rushed from the house and clawed his way through the crowd toward Turpin's body. The slaves let him by. Sarrus fell, weeping, upon the mutilated body, and passionately kissed the bloody lips of the man he loved. Bouckman laughed hoarsely. A dozen machetes, dripping redly, flashed downward. Then followed a concerted rush upon the house, where there were other white victims.

Horror succeeded horror with such startling rapidity that Duncan's sanity trembled. Nor were his companions unaffected, though Christophe to a lesser degree than Toussaint. The three men saw Turpin's house burst into flames from a dozen places, then heard the slaves shout: "Gallifet next." Gallifet's plantation was on the road to Cap François. So were Joubert's, Pascal's, Clément's, Flaville's, and a host of others, to say nothing of poor Garreau's ill-fated property. All these people might be warned by three men on horseback; Duncan turned to Toussaint and Christophe, and begged them to help him warn the planters.

"If we can reach Joubert, Pascal, and Clément, they can warn their neighbors in turn," he urged. "When we have done that we can ride on to the Cap and advise the Governor."

"Will Monsieur Blanchelande send troops to attack the slaves?"

"Of course."

"Then Christophe and I cannot go with you."

"But Toussaint—"

"Do not reproach us, Ti Rouge. We are Negroes. You must not ask us to betray men of our own color. If Monsieur Blanchelande sends the militia to re-establish order there will be fighting. Lives will be lost. Negro lives. Negro lives are as precious to us as the lives of white men are to you."

"But whenever the news of this revolt reaches the Governor he can do nothing else but send soldiers to protect the white population."

"True, but you, not Henri or I, must warn him. You are a white man. Already, perhaps, we have betrayed our people by bringing you here to-night. Go, Ti Rouge, while you may."

"What about you, Toussaint, and you, Christophe?"

"There is work for me to do," Toussaint replied. "I must protect Monsieur de Libertas and his family from harm, and use what influence I may have to restrain my people from committing more terrible deeds."

"I'll not stay, Toussaint," Christophe anounced suddenly. "It will not be safe for Ti Rouge to travel alone tonight."

"But on horseback——"

Christophe waved his hand. "None of us will see his horse again."

Toussaint turned hastily. The banana grove where the horses had been tethered was on fire.

"Then go now, Ti Rouge," Toussaint urged in an anxious voice. "Go while you may, and you, too, Henri. God be with you both."

Keeping clear of small bands of Negroes, who were scattering in all directions, Duncan and Christophe set off at a run for Joubert's plantation. Joubert had horses. If they could reach his stables before the slaves, there might still be an opportunity of warning the neighboring planters of the terror that was on its way. Those hopes proved abortive. Long before they reached Joubert's plantation they saw that it was already a mass of flames, buildings and fields alike. Presently Duncan stumbled over Joubert's body, mutilated and burned black by the flames that had passed over it. In the distance the slaves, their numbers increased by the addition of Joubert's slaves, were moving in the direction of Pascal's plantation.

With a feeling of horror Duncan realized that Pascal, too, was doomed. The slaves were too near his home for warning to reach him in time. But away to their right, where Flaville's plantation lay, the sky was still silver-black.

"The slaves haven't reached the Flaville plantation, Henri. We might reach him in time. But we must find horses. Unless the militia arrive soon, the great plain is doomed. The slaves must be halted and brought to their senses."

Christophe did not reply, but at a steady loping gait set off for the Flaville plantation, one of the richest in that part of the plain. Duncan followed him, his chest heaving. They pounded forward, keeping to the bridle paths and cart tracks that intersected the plantation. Soon they saw the house in the distance, for it was set on an eminence higher than the countryside immediately surounding it. Then, from their right, they heard the shouts of a band of slaves who were advancing upon the house from a different direction. Christophe increased his pace. Duncan could not keep up with him. He dropped back.

"Hurry, Ti Rouge. The stables are this side of the house. If we can reach them before the slaves we shall be able to take horses and get back to Cap François before we are cut off."

"We must warn Monsieur Flaville first," Duncan gasped.

"No. If we do we shall never reach Cap François. Hurry, hurry."

Duncan tried to increase his speed, but the combined effects of the emotional stress of the night's events, the excessive perspiration that soaked his heavy clothing, and his general condition were not conducive to sustained physical effort. His pace grew slower and slower; before the two men could reach the stable doors they were obliged to witness the crowning horror of seeing the wife and three daughters of the *procureur* of the estate on their bended knees before their own slaves imploring mercy for the *procureur* and the other four male occupants of the house. The plea was of no avail; all five men and the women were butchered.

Duncan fled from the scene as fast as he could run.

CHAPTER THIRTY-SIX

WITHOUT Christophe's help Duncan could not have lived through the night, for his anxiety to reach the town made him blind to danger, deaf to warnings, and reckless of his actions. Again and again he would have found himself face to face with a roving band of blood-crazed Negroes. Again and again, had he been alone, he would have sacrificed his mission to help a fellow white man or woman. Even if a kindly fate had guided him safely past such dangers, he would still have fallen by the wayside, utterly exhausted. But Christophe was mindful of his debt of gratitude. Whenever his acute ears heard the approach of a band of slaves, he forced Duncan to hide until the Negroes had passed by; it was his hand that persistently restrained Duncan from going to the aid of doomed men and women; it was his strength that supported Duncan as the two men struggled to reach the town fourteen miles away, a distance almost doubled by their enforcedly circuitous route.

Everywhere about them the drums continued to make the night hideous. There was no longer any rhythm in their pounding throb; the symphony they played that night was a call to bloody massacre, a primeval spur to savage desperation. Everywhere about them the slaves screamed aloud their drunken triumph as the red glow in the sky spread and smothered the moon in spiraling smoke. Everywhere about them were enacted scenes of unprecedented horror.

As soon as they dared they paused to look behind them. The crescent moon was about to disappear, but where the sky should have darkened it glowed redly with the reflection of the flames below. Vast, sweeping fires burned in a dozen directions, as they consumed carreau upon carreau of valuable produce. Farther off, in the more distant plantations and upon the mountainsides beyond, twinkled many more, smaller fires—the normal fires of the slave compounds that should have died away hours since, and the fires of mulatto encampments. The black and colored population of the northern province was awake from end to end, as the people listened to the message of the drums and debated their decision—peace or war!

Toward the hour of dawn the first refugees began to straggle into the town of Cap François. Occupants, these, of the nearer plantations, who had fled before the terror had reached their homes. They knew little of what had actually occurred, but fear fired their imaginations. Rumors spread toward the heart of the town and at last reached the ears of M. Blanchelande, the governor, who was awakened by an officer of militia and told that field slaves in the Plaine-du-Nord had revolted and were massacring their masters.

"A nonsensical story!" M. Blanchelande shouted in anger, for no man is at his best when awakened unduly early. Nevertheless, he dressed and dispatched orders to his military officers commanding them to assemble immediately at Government House. Other messengers were sent to bring in persons who had newly arrived in the city, but their stories were uniformly vague. The witnesses had heard the drums beating more wildly than usual ("But the drums are never silent in Saint-Domingue," testily interrupted the Governor, who loathed the sound of their throbbing); they had seen flames in the distance ("A plantation on fire is not necessarily a plantation in revolt," M. Blanchelande pointed out caustically); they had heard alarming noises, seen white men galloping past with terrified faces— There was hearsay evidence in abundance, and a score of theories as to what was happening, ranging from M. Gallien's, who was convinced that the wrath of God was ravaging the Colony with fire as a divine punishment for the iniquities of its society, to M. Pajot's, who asserted that an army of one hundred thousand Negroes, officered by mulattoes, was marching upon Cap François. But there was not a single eyewitness of the events of that night; the bewildered Governor was at his wits' end.

About this time Duncan and Christophe came in sight of the soldiers who manned the entrenchments, for the sun was just below the horizon and warm, crimson-shot daylight was turning the night gray.

"Here are two more coming, Captain," observed a cornet to Captain Maryse.

Maryse regarded the two men staggering toward him. "They are Negroes," he said, but added presently: "No, one of them is not dark enough for a Negro. He must be an *affranchi*."

"Do you know any *affranchis* with red hair, Captain?"

"Red hair! But you are right, Boubon. The smaller man has red hair. The only man with red hair that I know is that dirty Englishman, the man who physics the Negroes."

"Is that Christophe with him, of the Hôtel de la Couronne?"

"Yes," Maryse agreed presently. "You have sharper eyes than I, Boubon. Then the red-haired man must be the Englishman, for he and Christophe are often together, I'm told."

"Only an Englishman would be friends with a Negro," Boubon muttered.

Upon the arrival of Duncan and Christophe, Maryse stepped forward. "Monsieur?"

Duncan looked at the French officers with weary eyes. "Yes, Captain."

"Do you know what has happened on the plain tonight?"

"Revolt, massacre, rapine, monsieur. We've come to warn the Governor to send troops. We should have arrived sooner, but our horses were burned, and we could not obtain others."

"We have heard many rumors, but nobody knows for certain—"

"I do," Duncan interrupted. "God knows I wish I didn't!"

"Monsieur Blanchelande is anxious for definite news. Will you accompany me to Government House?"

"I am at your service, Captain."

"Then I shall return to the hotel, Ti Rouge," Christophe interrupted.

Duncan nodded wearily; his head seemed too heavy a burden for his body to carry. "I shall come to see you soon, Henri, to thank you for saving my life tonight. But for you I shouldn't have reached Cap François."

"Please, monsieur," Maryse urged impatiently. "If matters are as bad as you say, there is no time to waste. I have a carriage here that can take us immediately to His Excellency."

As the blue-shaded night turned to a rich golden hue, Duncan drove with Captain Maryse to the seat of government, where they found Blanchelande in the audience chamber; he bit his nails and paced up and down a lane of military officers and important townspeople who conversed among themselves in low voices.

"Well, Captain, what is it?" the Governor demanded irritably when Maryse and Duncan were brought before him.

"Another witness, Your Excellency."

"We have heard many witnesses. They all know nothing, except what is in their cursed imaginations. I want only the truth of what is happening, Captain, not more theories about God's sending a visitation to punish the Colony for its sinfulness."

"I think you will find monsieur's report a full one, Your Excellency."

M. Blanchelande turned to Duncan. "Who are you? Where do you come from?"

"I live in Cap François. My name is Duncan Stewart."

"Are you an Englishman, monsieur?"

"A Scotsman," Duncan corrected dryly.

A fleeting smile revealed itself on the Governor's face. "As an ancient ally, that nationality rings more pleasantly in a Frenchman's ears." His face assumed a more severe expression. "Stewart! Stewart! The name is familiar."

"Perhaps you have heard Dr. Deschenel speak of him as L'Ami des Noirs, Your Excellency," somebody murmured in the Governor's ear.

"That I have. So you are the man who coddles the Negroes?" Blanchelande queried in a cold voice, as he stared with hard eyes at Duncan. "Is it true that you have news for me?"

"Yes. The slaves on the plain have revolted and are spreading death and destruction. If you wish to prevent the revolt from growing worse, Your Excellency, you will dispatch a military force to the Turpin plantation without delay."

"The Turpin plantation! Monsieur Turpin's slaves wouldn't have dared to revolt against him," De Saint Just interrupted scornfully.

"Unhappily they have dared, so Monsieur Turpin lies dead at his ruined plantation."

"Dead!" The word echoed round a room that grew tensely silent. "Who killed him?" Blanchelande demanded. "The man shall be broken on the wheel."

"Monsieur Turpin died from a score of wounds. And Sarrus, too," Duncan said wearily.

"His death is no loss to the community," Psaume muttered with contempt.

"But Sarrus was a white man, monsieur," Blanchelande said quickly. Then, to Duncan again: "How can you vouch for the truth of your statement?"

"I witnessed his death with my own eyes."

"And did nothing to aid him, monsieur?"

Duncan's wan cheeks flushed. "What could one man do against three hundred, Your Excellency? Besides, I was chiefly occupied in trying to reach this city in time to warn you to send the militia."

"About what time did Monsieur Turpin die?"

"Soon after midnight."

"It is now after dawn. You have taken your time about returning with the warning," Blanchelande accused.

"Our horses perished in the conflagration."

"Why did you not apply to Joubert, Turpin's neighbor, for the loan of a horse?"

"I had hoped to, but I was too late. Joubert was killed before I reached his home."

"Joubert too! My God! Monsieur, tell us the worst—"

Before the Governor could continue a man stepped forward from behind the Governor and seized Duncan's arm in a fierce grip.

"My plantation is near Turpin's. Is it safe? For God's sake, tell me that my slaves have remained loyal to me. There are women there—my cousin and her three daughters—"

Duncan recognized Flaville. Instinctively he placed his hand on the Frenchman's shoulders. "Prepare yourself for bad news, monsieur," he replied huskily. "From Joubert's I went to your plantation, hoping to warn your procureur and find horses there. Again I was too late. Your slaves had also risen. The five white men at your home were butchered before my eyes."

Flaville's expression was terrible. "But the women, monsieur, the women?" he pleaded in an anguished voice. "Are they safe?"

Duncan could not face the tormented eyes. He bent his head. "They were killed."

Flaville listened, like a man bereft of his reason. Then he turned, and without a word to anyone shambled from the audience chamber. As the door closed behind him the men present indicated their sympathy, each in his own particular fashion. Some openly expressed their horror, others relieved their feelings by indulging in fluent blasphemy. All grew thin-lipped, vengeful-eyed.

With the passing of the hours the full story of the insurrection became known. Men and women who had escaped from different plantations began to stream into Cap François, where they related stories of incredible horrors. Name upon name was added to the list of those plantations that were known to have been destroyed: Gallifet's, Clément's, Pascal's, Psaume's, Legrand's. Gallifet's was the largest plantation in the plain, and had been so noted for its kindly treatment of the slaves that *petits blancs* had come to speak of a person being *heureux comme un Nègre de Gallifet*. Clément, another who had always shown consideration for his slaves, was among those massacred.

As the toll of death and destruction mounted, less was heard of those who asserted that the insurrection was a purely local affair. When news of revolt arrived from every quarter of the plain the fact became recognized, with increasing consternation, that the Negroes had risen in force, and that military operations must be organized on a large scale to stamp out the insurrection. Volunteers were called for and armed. Women and children were sent aboard ships in the harbor; so were hundreds of house slaves, where they were closely guarded lest they should rise in sympathy with the field slaves.

Morning dragged on into afternoon. Fresh refugees arrived, to report that the outrages had not stopped with the rising of the sun, but were continuing. The estimated number of revolted slaves increased every hour, and with it the temper of the townspeople. A white butcher in the rue de la Boucherie shot and killed a mulatto who entered his shop to buy a joint of pork. In the rue Penthievre another mulatto was stoned to death by a party of young men who were on their way to volunteer for service. In the rue des Vierges, not a stone's throw from the Barracks, a third mulatto was chased by a small crowd, and owed his life to the fact that he ran into a troop of soldiers who were exercising.

The *petits blancs* remembered the earlier insurrections of the mulattoes and began to murmur against the colored people, saying that the *affranchis*, having failed to organize themselves, had encouraged the Negroes to revolt. When reports reached the Governor that a massacre of the mulattoes was being planned he hurriedly issued a proclamation giving them protection.

Watchers stationed at Le Haut du Cap reported that fresh fires were breaking out in all directions. A fresh stream of refugees reported increased violence instead of the hoped-for diminution. In the morning seamen from the ships were landed to strengthen the city's fighting strength, and a demand was made that a large force of soldiers should be dispatched to attack the Negroes.

A force was assembled, under the leadership of De Touzard, and marched to the plantation of Latour, where the slaves were encamped, four thousand strong. De Touzard was not insensible to the advantage of position. He selected his own field of battle, then gave the order to fire. A score of Negroes fell with the first fusillade. But there were a dozen slaves to take the place of every one who died. Weight of numbers carried their yelling, screaming ranks constantly nearer to De Touzard's line. The alarmed commander realized that, if he remained in his present position, it would be only a matter of time before his thin white line was swamped by successive black waves. He ordered the retreat to be sounded.

The white forces retired in good order, and reached Cap François without further loss. But none realized better than De Touzard himself that if the slaves had been properly led they could have followed up their victory by overtaking and sweeping through the ranks of the white soldiers, whereupon the defenseless town would have been open to their ravaging.

Cap François was saved because the man who would become the most brilliant Negro general in history had not yet joined the insurrection; Toussaint was intent upon saving the life of his master's superintendent, Bayou de Libertas.

CHAPTER THIRTY-SEVEN

THE circumstances of De Touzard's return to Cap François warned the townspeople that the revolt of the slaves was developing into civil war, and made them tardily aware that their beautiful town was wide open to invasion from the land; all existing fortifications faced the sea. In an effort to correct his weakness immediate measures were taken to fortify every avenue of approach. Troops and artillery were stationed on the heights of Le Haut du Cap, which commanded the approach from the south. A battery of cannon was mounted on pontoons and floated on the river, which formed the eastern boundary. An embargo was laid on all outward bound shipping in order that sailors might be impressed for the defense of the town, and their vessels used as a possible means of retreat. A letter was sent to implore the aid of Jamaica's governor, Lord Effingham. Messengers were dispatched to all parishes to advise them to take precautions against surprise attacks.

In face of the common danger all the contentious factions of Cap François abandoned their political enmity and united to erect the palisades. There was one man who did not work at the palisades—Duncan. The news spread that he had been the first to convey the news of the uprising to the Governor; that he had been an eyewitness to the Negro atrocities. Because he was a foreigner, because he lived a solitary life and received and visited only two or three white men, because the volatile French folk and creoles failed to comprehend how a man could be happy in deliberately shunning the society of women, he had long been viewed by his neighbors with some dislike and considerable suspicion. In consequence, his name was readily associated with the revolt. It was rumored that he had first encouraged the Negroes to rise, and afterward had reported the news of the rising to the Governor not as a friendly warning but as a red herring across the trail of his own guilt. The *petits blancs* scowled as they passed him. Young children grimaced, or, at a safe distance, shouted insulting abuse.

At first Duncan was not disturbed. He had always been aware of his unpopularity and had not been troubled by it, because he never felt lonely or in a mood for company; that much at least he owed to his Stewart ancestors, who had lived solitary lives for generations. But when he joined a company of men who were erecting a section of the palisades near his home, he learned that unpopularity had become something more.

"We have plenty of slaves working for us," the overseer sneered. "We can do without the help of a white Negro."

"L'Ami des Noirs!" one of the workers jeered—it was Barbedette, whom De Saint Just had thrashed. "Have you come here to see whether your Negro friends on the plain will be able to smash their way through the palisade?"

"Dirty foreigner," shouted out the man next to Barbedette. "We don't want your kind working with us."

"Spy!" shouted another. "English spy!"

"Who encouraged the Negroes to revolt? Who watched them kill Monsieur Turpin? Who did nothing to save them?"

Fury swept along the line of workers. Many of them dropped their implements and picked up dirt, stones, pieces of wood, anything within reach. A volley of missiles bombarded Duncan. A stone knocked off his hat, another bruised his chest, a length of timber rapped his right ankle.

"Get away, you, before you cause a riot," the overseer rasped. "Can't you see what we think of you and your kind?"

Duncan paid no heed to the man. He did not hear the vicious words. He stared at the line of jeering, angry men, and was unable to believe that they could mean what had been said. True, he was a Scot, they were French or creole. But Scot, Frenchman, or creole, they were brother white men. Surely they could not be thinking that, because he was keeping to the spirit of the Hippocratic oath, he was a traitor to his birthright.

Misery changed to anger; the quick temper that so often goes with flaming red hair was not lacking in him.

"Liars!" he shouted back at the men. "Not one of you could have done more than I did. I was one among hundreds. If I had gone to Turpin's assistance I should have been massacred. My only thought was to warn the Governor—"

The rest of his words were drowned by a chorus of catcalls, whistles, and angry, scoffing shouts. A fresh volley of missiles was flung at him. A sharp flint cut the flesh above his temple. A third volley followed the second. He staggered.

"Get away from here while you can," the overseer shouted. "Clear out, you dirty white Negro." He gave Duncan a violent push. Duncan stumbled back behind a near-by house, where he was hidden from the angry men.

He returned home, holding a handkerchief to his bleeding forehead. When Suzanne saw him she waddled to his side, her huge belly and breasts wobbling violently beneath her coarse cotton shift.

"Lord have mercy upon us!" she wailed. "You are hurt, master. What has happened? Sit down, my lamb. Suzanne will take care of you. She knows what to do. Sit quietly, my pet, while Suzanne fetches water." Tears dripped onto his face as she leaned over him and smoothed his hair away from the wound.

He leaned back against the chair and closed his eyes while Suzanne stamped out to fill a ewer from the nearest fountain. His physical hurt was little; the wound, he knew, was no more than a slight abrasion. The mental hurt was more acute. White men had rejected his help. With sticks and stones and coarse abuse they had driven him from among them as though he were no better than a mad dog. They had jeered at him, called him a white Negro, accused him of cowardice, of treachery, and of other things too vile to remember.

The contrast between his treatment by the Negroes and that accorded him by the whites was emphasized and contorted beyond reasonable perspective. He thought of Henri Christophe. Christophe had taken him to the Turpin plantation that he might warn the white population of the seriousness of the projected revolt. On the return journey Christophe, at the risk of his own life, had protected and supported him for mile upon mile. These things Christophe had done though they were inimical to the Negro cause.

Compare this act of gratitude, Duncan thought bitterly, with the reception accorded to him by the Governor and his officers. Insults, scorn, contempt were his only thanks, because he had chosen to dedicate his knowledge of medicine and surgery to Negroes.

Fate was conspiring to show him how wide was the rift between the white man and the black.

That night Christophe visited Duncan.

"I have heard what happened to you at the palisades, Ti Rouge. Why did they pelt you with stones and rubbish? You are not a cursed mulatto, like the others they have stoned. You are a white man like themselves. Do they hate you because you come from Great Britain? Do all other peoples hate your people? The Americans do. The French do. But why? We Negroes like you. In Jamaica you treat your slaves more kindly than the French do in Saint-Domingue."

"The French people do not hate me because I am British, Henri, but because I am different. They do not think it natural for a man to prefer his own company to theirs, and they cannot understand why I do not care for women. They resent my treating Negroes and saving the lives of slaves."

"But why? The life of a strong slave is valuable. In saving the lives of slaves you have saved many a white master the cost of a new slave. They should be grateful to you."

"Some of the planters are too rich to possess a commercial instinct such as yours, Henri. They would rather lose a slave than be under an obligation to me."

"I do not understand the whites, although I try hard."

"Why do you wish to understand them?"

"Because they know how to make money, Ti Rouge. I want to make money, not just to be rich but to prove myself the equal of the white man." He glanced defiantly at Duncan. "Don't forget that centuries ago your country was as primtive as Guinea, and that the white men who lived there were no better than the people of Guinea. It is true that the white savage bettered himself; that, as the centuries passed, he built towns and cities, manufactured clothes, and built large ships—while the Negro remained ignorant and uncultured. Now, because the Negroes are the slaves of white men, the whites despise the black men as savages, and believe them to be incapable of following the example of the white men."

"Well?"

"I think the whites are wrong," Christophe continued vehemently. "What is the difference between the white man and the black other than the color of their skin? Beneath his skin the Negro has a finer body than the white, he has a strong heart, and he has a brain. Hell! Isn't the brain of Toussaint superior to that of the jeweler, Barbedette? Barbedette has never read Epictetus, or Guischard's *Military Memoirs of the Greeks and Romans*, or Marshal Saxe's *Military Reveries*, or D'Orléan's *History of Revolutions in England and Spain*, because he hasn't the brain to read such books. But Toussaint reads and understands them, and many others besides. And have I not a brain, too, Ti Rouge? Am I not making a better success of my hotel than Monsieur Duplan, whose Hotel Paris was seized by the bailiffs last week?"

"You are a good businessman," Duncan acknowledged.

"I know. I am a better businessman than many of the whites. And Toussaint is more learned than many white men. If I am a good businessman, why shouldn't many other Negroes be equally good, Ti Rouge? One might find other Toussaints among us if all Negroes were taught as Toussaint and I were taught."

Christophe's eyes burned. "I can speak to you as I would not dare to speak to any other white man. I tell you that if the Negro is ever allowed an opportunity he will prove to the world that he can fight as well as the white man, trade as well, learn as well, build as well."

"What does this lead to, Henri? Are you proposing to leave Cap François and join the insurgents? Your experience as a gunner with the Colonial Artillery should be useful to them."

Christophe's fire and enthusiasm died. He shook his head sullenly, as though he believed that Duncan were laughing at him. "No," he grunted. "I shall not fight with the insurgents. Nor shall I volunteer to fight against them, as some of the other free Negroes are doing."

"But Toussaint—" Duncan began.

"I love Toussaint," Christophe interrupted sharply. "But Toussaint is an idealist. I am a practical man. Toussaint can be of great service to the insurgents as a physician, and as a man of brains, to give their leaders good counsel. For myself, I can do better for my people by carrying on my work in Cap François as a hotelkeeper. I shall continue to make money." His voice grew excited. "I believe that money means power. With power I could do more for the Negroes than by loading cannon— which they do not possess."

Before Duncan could reply Toussaint arrived.

"Toussaint!" Christophe stared at the coachman. "What are you doing here? I thought you were with the insurgents."

Toussaint sat down. "I had work to do, Henri. My mistress was at the plantation. As long as her life was in danger my place was by her side, to protect her."

"What of his own slaves?" Duncan asked.

"Praise the Lord! I was able to persuade them to remain faithful to her long enough for me to make arrangements for her escape. Monsieur and Madame Bayou de Libertas have always been kind to us slaves, and we have not forgotten."

"Is Madame in Cap François?"

"Yes, Ti Rouge. My brother Paul and I brought her here in her carriage. Madame is now with her husband." He smiled. "It was good to see his happiness when he saw his wife alive."

"Will you stay in Cap François, now that you are here?" Christophe asked.

"No, Henri. My place is with my fellow men. Out on the plain hundreds of Negroes are dying for want of a doctor's care. One or two white physicians are doing what they can—" He stopped short, seeing the surprise on Duncan's face. "Yes, Ti Rouge, white physicians. They are prisoners; their lives were spared so that they can look after the wounded. But more physicians are needed, for there are many casualties, and there will be many more."

"You think the insurrection will last, Toussaint?"

Toussaint nodded gravely. "Yes, Ti Rouge. It is war between the white and the Negro. Thousands of slaves are joining the army that Jean-François is forming. There will be no peace in Saint-Domingue until slavery is abolished."

The Negro's eyes shone, not with the excitement that Duncan had earlier glimpsed in Christophe's eyes, but with a quiet exultation that reminded the white man of the eyes of a Virgin with Child he had seen on the walls of Garreau's house.

"As a Christian I deplore bloodshed. I should not have lifted a hand to bring about this civil war. But now that war has broken out, Ti Rouge, I am glad, because I believe that it will lead to the emancipation of the slaves. We shall fight, we must fight until that day when the Negro can lift up his head and say to himself: 'I am as free as the dog that scratches the fleas from his hide, as free as the mulatto, as free as the white man.' Think of what the Negroes are fighting for, and ask yourself whether we shall capitulate without attaining it."

There was a magnetic quality in Toussaint's voice that astounded Duncan, for he had never heard it before. Toussaint's demeanor had invariably been that of a well-trained, deferential servant. Now he was no longer a slave, but a free man who still possessed the vigor of youth in his bearing and the wisdom of age in his thoughtful eyes. He was a dreamer awakened, an inspired leader.

He continued: "I have done my duty to my master. I can do no more, for the war will be sure to sweep over his plantation as it will over every other plantation in Saint-Domingue. I leave my master's affairs to devote myself to the Negro cause. War is being fought between the white men and the black, Ti Rouge, but if I can use my influence with Jean-François and Biassou it shall be a Christian war, and not a savage massacre of unarmed and innocent people." He raised his arms; his voice rang out sonorously. "We are without weapons, without officers. We are untrained, ignorant of warfare. But we'll win our fight for liberty because we are many, because our cause is God's cause. We can't lose. Victory will be ours, Ti Rouge, and then—" his voice rang with confidence. "The Negroes will be free men!"

Before his hearers could recover from the spell of his oratory, Toussaint spoke again.

"Do you accompany me, Henri? Are you with us?"

"I am staying here."

"Henri—"

A significant smile slowly parted Christophe's thick lips. "Are there cannon on the plain?"

"No."

"There are cannon and ammunition in Cap François, Toussaint." Dark-brown eyes stared into dark-brown eyes.

"I think I understand, Henri. You are offering us neutrality and secret help. Your hotel is important in your life. But one day you will join the Negroes. Sooner or later your heart will overcome your head. And you, Ti Rouge? Will you accompany me?"

"Where?"

"To the plain."

Duncan stared at the Negro unwilling to believe that Toussaint could be speaking seriously. But Toussaint's eyes were solemn.

"Are you mad, Toussaint? Are you suggesting that I should fight for the slaves against the whites?"

"Not fight, Ti Rouge. You are a physician. There are hundreds of lives to be saved. Perhaps thousands. Here in Cap François men of your own color drove you from them with stones."

"So you know that already?"

"The Negroes love you, Ti Rouge. There were some who saw what happened and passed the news on to me while I was still two hours' journey from the city. You have cast your lot with us Negroes once already. Do so again. Your influence and your presence would help to check the brutality of the more lawless leaders—you see, I do not seek to deny its existence—"

"God knows you couldn't! I saw horrors of which I thought no man, white or black, was capable."

"Are the atrocities that we committed in the heat of passion worse than those that the whites perpetrated in sport? We have not forgotten the slaves of Monsieur Marilys, who were buried up to their shoulders so that white men could roll cannon balls at their heads. Slaves have been whipped to death, broken on the wheel for insignificant offenses, hunted down and killed by wild, starved bloodhounds. We have learned many evil lessons in white schools, Ti Rouge." He raised his hand, seeing Duncan about to interrupt. "But I do not seek to excuse them. My prayer is that I may prevent further brutalities. We can do that, you and I. Come with us, and you will save not only the lives of wounded Negroes but the lives of white prisoners."

Duncan shook his head in confusion. "You have an uncanny gift, Toussaint. You almost make the incredible sound convincing."

"Then you will come?" Toussaint urged.

Duncan thought of the Governor's contemptuous attitude, of De Saint Just's sneers, of Barbedette's vulgar abuse, of the volley of stones that had greeted his offer of assistance. He glanced round the bare rooms of his hired house. It was not a home. It never could be a home. It was no more than a roof and a shelter, a place where he could eat and sleep. What had he to lose from leaving Cap François? Not a home. Not friends, for he had none among the white people save old François. Not a happy existence. Not truly a practice, for his Negro patients were poor and what they paid him, either in money or kind, did no more than pay his rent and feed Suzanne and him.

What was the reverse side of the picture? He had little, but Toussaint offered him less. A bed beneath the sky, a home in the jungle, hardships, the daily risk of an inglorious death if the white men should take him prisoner, or death from disease or snake poison—Toussaint offered him nothing but the solace of fulfilling the Hippocratic oath, with no promise of reward or even glory. None but a fool would consent to exchange little for less. None, that is to say, but a mad Stewart, or a flaming-haired rebel whose hatred for all Frenchmen had been fiercely revived by the studied insolence of M. Blanchelande and his friends, and the acts of the jeweler Barbedette and his cronies.

Duncan glanced at the bottle that stood on the floor beside his chair; a third of its contents remained—enough for a toast. He emptied the remainder of the rum into three glasses.

"Here's to Dr. Stewart," he laughed unsteadily. "Physician Extraordinary to the Negro Army of Saint-Domingue." He drank deeply, then added: "And damnation to the French."

CHAPTER THIRTY-EIGHT

THE Negro army increased rapidly as the slaves of the more distant plantations revolted and flocked to the encampments that had been set up on the Plaine-du-Nord. One of the largest of these was established at Gallifet's plantation, and thither proceeded the two physicians, white and black. Duncan was appalled. Hundreds of men needed attention, most of whom suffered from wounds received when De Touzard had attacked Latour's plantation. Duncan and Toussaint worked tirelessly to save lives, but many died before they could be treated. Each day Duncan rose at dawn and retired only when darkness intervened to prevent further work.

Meanwhile, the scattered bands that at first could only be entitled an army because of their numerical strength were slowly molded into a militarized body. Jean-François was elected its commander and at once proclaimed himself Grand Admiral of France. Generalissimo Biassou was appointed *Maréchal de Camp*; Bouckman and Jeannot were created brigadiers. Cannon mysteriously apeared and were mounted on the walls of the Gallifet buildings where they were controlled by a white prisoner—a gunner from the frigate *La Prudente*, who had been taken prisoner and his life spared because he was an officer of the King. Crude military tactics of a guerrilla nature were devised and practiced. Skirmishes with the white troops were frequent; the Negro loss of life was heavy (Bouckman was among the earliest victims), but there were always more slaves to take the places of casualties. The white losses were proportionately as great.

In the weeks that followed, Duncan saw the man Toussaint gradually emerge from the slave chrysalis. In a compelling, resonant voice he encouraged the black men to continue the fight for freedom. They were not fighting entirely for themselves, he told them. They were fighting also for the King of France who wanted all his subjects to be equal, to live at peace with one another; white, colored, and black. The King was anxious for the emancipation of the Negroes. These wishes had been defied by the planters of Saint-Domingue. The interests of the planters conflicted with the interests of the King and the French people. Therefore, in fighting the planters, the Negroes were fighting for their white King.

These arguments astonished Duncan, but he quickly appreciated that Toussaint used them in all sincerity. The Negroes believed wholeheartedly that Louis XVI was their benevolent patron. The reflection was a comforting one, for was not the King a god? And if the gods were pleased with their fight for freedom, they could not lose. *Vive sa Majesté! Vive Les Amis des Noirs! Vive l'Amiral Jean-François! Vive Toussaint!*

Toussaint enthralled his audience. "Have courage, my children. You are fighting a noble cause, for liberty and equality. You are not fighting all whites. Many whites are good men. Monsieur de Beaudierre was a good man. Many planters were good men. Monsieur Clément was a good man. Shame upon you for killing him! Many of the French were good men, as good as Monsieur Dubois, who was sent back to France because he wanted to help the slaves. Your enemies are the bad planters who want to retain slavery. When we have defeated the bad men the good men will make peace with us. We shall be freed, and live happily. So fight the bad men with a good will, but do not kill your prisoners, protect them so that they may understand that we Negroes respect them and wish to be friends with them. Besides, we can exchange white prisoners for black. So heed what I say. Fight strongly, protect prisoners, and God will bless our cause."

Jean-François and Biassou encouraged him to talk to the Negroes because he was instilling courage in the hearts of the black men. His advice was worth asking and following. He seemed to have so much knowledge in that head of his. Knowledge of how battles should be fought, knowledge of the art of leading men, knowledge of horses and horsemanship, knowledge of medicine.

Ammunition and artillery continued to arrive on the plain. White prisoners were mystified by the Negroes' possession of such arms, having believed the black men to be armed only with machetes, scythes, and other plantation implements. Duncan had his suspicions, which one day Toussaint proved well founded.

"Some of it comes from Cap François, Ti Rouge. From Henri Christophe. That is one of his reasons for remaining there instead of fighting with us."

"How does Henri get it?"

"Negroes in Cap François steal it from the Arsenal, and Henri arranges its secret dispatch to us."

"Surely not all of it comes from the Arsenal?" Duncan protested. "The ordnance would miss such a huge quantity."

"Not all of it comes from the Arsenal, or from other towns. We exchange stocks of rum and sugar from the plantation warehouses for supplies of powder and ball."

"With whom?"

"Merchants in North America. They send the ammunition to us in small vessels, and accept rum and sugar in return. Henri Christophe arranges such matters—he has a head for trade."

With the help of this supply of arms and ammuntion the Negroes succeeded in confining the white forces within the district immediately surrounding Cap François. Meanwhile, in the hope of localizing the revolt, the remaining whites of the island assembled in two camps, one at Grande Rivière, the other at Dondon. Perhaps they had forgotten that both places had been the scenes of mulatto defeats. The mulattoes had not forgotten. Those who had been forced to flee from the towns and cities of Saint-Domingue and had established their own camps now, for the first time, joined forces with the Negroes in the hope of avenging past defeats. A mixed force of Negroes and mulattoes attacked the two white encampments. Bloody carnage followed. The whites suffered a heavy loss and were decisively defeated.

The first weeks of September saw the welter of bloodshed, carnage, and destruction persist with uncompromising severity as whites and blacks continued to vie with one another in committing unspeakable cruelties. The Negro army grew daily more fantastic. While the rank and file were practically naked and had to fight with what they could procure—broken swords, machetes, rusted muskets, dueling pistols, and other odd weapons collected from the field of battle—their leaders did not scruple to wear plundered uniforms. Marshals, colonels, commanders, and lieutenants strutted in ill-fitting but brilliant jackets, cocked hats, white pantaloons, and spurred jack boots. The highest orders glittered upon their breasts; jeweled sabers hung from their waists.

Even Toussaint was unable to resist that attraction. He appeared before

Duncan one night dressed in the uniform of a colonel of the Normandy Regiment.

"Congratulate me, Ti Rouge. I have been appointed a brigadier under Biassou."

Duncan gazed with weary eyes at the bright blue jacket with flaring lapels of white silk, decorated with gold braid and buttons, gold epaulets, and gold chevrons on the sleeves.

"A brigadier!" he repeated shortly, feeling that Toussaint's acceptance constituted an act of disloyalty to himself. He had been persuaded to leave Cap François so that he and the Negro might work together saving life. But now, it seemed, instead of devoting himself to saving life, Toussaint proposed to mete out death.

Toussaint was quick to sense Duncan's disapproval. "Are you disappointed?"

"The wounded need you."

"That is the truth, but not the whole truth, Ti Rouge. If I desert the wounded I do so because I am needed for a greater cause—the cause for which we fight. The wounded number thousands, but all of us number hundreds of thousands. Is not the whole greater than the part? I must try to make you understand. You know what the Negro cause means to me, Ti Rouge; you, more than any other man. All my life I have had one ideal —Negro emancipation. For that cause there is nothing I would not do.

"The cause that I would cheerfully die for is in danger. We have an army of nearly one hundred thousand men, we have some artillery and some ammunition. What we don't possess enough of is food. On the first night of the uprising Henri Christophe realized what would happen. He told us that the Negroes were harming themselves more than the whites. Henri was right. The fire that was started that night swept across the plain from one end to the other. Crops of cotton, coffee, sugar, and— more important to us—fruit and vegetables were destroyed. Now, because the men are starving, they are becoming turbulent and mutinous. Only severe discipline will prevent large-scale desertions, which might bring about the collapse of our army."

"I thought Jean-François was keeping his men under strict watch. Wasn't a man hanged yesterday for stealing cattle?"

"Yes. Jean-François is a good leader. So is Biassou. But they are already in disagreement. How can discipline be maintained if our leaders quarrel?"

"Whom does Jeannot support? Jean-François or Biassou?"

"Neither. I abominate that man, Ti Rouge. He is a bloodthirsty tyrant who uses the past as an excuse for torturing and massacring his prisoners. Now that I am a brigadier I shall try to influence Jean-François to put a stop to Jeannot's barbarity."

"Jeannot is one of your best leaders," Duncan pointed out dryly. "From what I hear there isn't another man in the Negro army with more daring and courage. If it's true that he has turned several impending defeats into victories, wouldn't your cause suffer if his leadership were lost?"

"True," Toussaint admitted. "It would. But our cause would be lost even though won if, when we have achieved victory, the whites should hate the Negro instead of respecting him. We want emancipation, God knows, but not at such a price, Ti Rouge. The emancipation of which I dream is only a beginning, not the end. My dream is of a new Saint-Domingue shared equally by white and black, in which slavery would be merely a memory of an unhappy past, where the Negroes would work, not for the benefit of a few, but for the community as a whole. I dream of a new colony arising from the ashes of the old, with Negroes sharing not only the work and the rewards, but also the government. For this dream, Ti Rouge, there is no sacrifice I would not make. Do you understand now why I am ceasing my work as a physician in order to be a leader?"

Duncan nodded as he wondered how he could have known Toussaint for more than two years without having become aware of the spell that the ex-coachman seemed able to exercise upon even the most sober-minded.

Toussaint quickly fulfilled his promise to curb Jeannot's savagery, and Duncan himself was the indirect cause. The following night, as he sat alone in front of the fire, his head nodded with weariness. There had been another sharp skirmish that day between the whites and the blacks, as a result of which more than fifty Negroes had been killed and one hundred wounded. Most of the wounded men had somehow managed to drag themselves to the tent in which Duncan had established his crude surgery —reports of his skill as a surgeon had spread among the scattered bodies of Negro fighters, so the wounded were anxious for him to operate upon them; the succession of cases, following one after the other, unceasingly, day after day, was responsible for his attaining an unusual proficiency. Moreover, necessity, added to the knowledge that many of his patients were destined to die whatever happened, had encouraged him to experiment; to perform hitherto unthought-of operations. Some of these were unsuccessful. But in several instances the results were amazing, and by dint of experiment with scalpel, herbs, and raw spirit he evolved new methods of combating gangrene and extracting awkwardly placed pistol balls.

While he reflected that he might as well sleep lying on a bed of leaves as sitting up before the fire, he became aware of a commotion in the vicinity of another fire, some hundred yards distant. Commotions of this sort were not unusual, for the Negroes quarreled among themselves, or played strange games that were often noisier and more alarming. Duncan shrugged his shoulders and rose to his feet, but as he moved toward his tent he heard a cry of terror, followed by high-pitched laughter. He turned. The cry was repeated; he realized that a white person was somewhere hidden among the group of black bodies shuffling round another, larger fire.

Anger hastened his movements. White prisoners had been executed and even tortured, but he had been unable to check the evil because he had never been near enough to the scene of execution. Mostly, indeed, he had known nothing of such matters until many hours afterward. Now that the opportunity of saving at least one victim was his, he intended to take advantage of it.

He reached the larger fire and pushed his way through the crowd. As he reached the circle of men nearest to the fire he saw the man whose cry he had heard. Body and clothes were brown with filth and grime, hair unkempt, chin covered with bristles of many weeks' growth, cheeks were blood-stained and sunken, reddened eyes were glazed with fear. He was on his knees before a slight, slim Negro with a repulsive face, who held a burning brand before his nose and laughed with savage glee whenever his prisoner flinched from the flaming wood.

Duncan rounded the fire and knocked the brand from the man's hand. "Stop torturing this man, Jeannot!"

Jeannot said sullenly: "He is my prisoner. I am going to kill him."

"Who took him prisoner?"

"I helped to, Ti Rouge," one of the men behind Jeannot said. "We found him hiding in the jungle."

"There is no reason to kill him, Jeannot. He is a prisoner of war."

"I take no white prisoners of war," Jeannot sneered. "I am going to kill him as I have killed every white man brought before me." He spat into the face of the kneeling man. "Canaille!" he shrieked. "Pig! We will tie you on a spit before the fire and roast you alive. Then we will drink your blood and eat your heart and liver, and the gods will make us safe from white musket balls and white sabers."

The men behind Jeannot chorused excitedly. Duncan noticed that many faces possessed the features of the Mina and other Dahomey tribes of Africa. They chattered excitedly in a foreign dialect, instead of the bastard French commonly in use. These men, with the Ashanti tribes, were the backbone of the army, for they were generally of fine physique and capable of sustained physical labor, their intelligence was above the normal, they were fierce in attack, steady in retreat. Warriors all, untamed by servitude, they automatically gathered round the leader who possessed similar characteristics—Jeannot.

Duncan stood his ground. "Jean-François has commanded that white prisoners shall remain alive and unhurt. I order you to leave the white alone and turn him over to your generalissimo."

Jeannot laughed scornfully. The crowd echoed his laughter, though they did not properly understand the white man's words. "Jean-François! Is Jean-François a god?"

"He is your leader."

"Today he is a leader, but yesterday he was a maroon. Today I am a brigadier, but tomorrow I may be the leader of the army. The men will follow me because they know that I am a better fighter than Jean-François. I am not afraid of Jean-François, nor of you. I say that this prisoner shall die the death we have planned for him. What do you say?" He appealed to the Dahomeys behind him, and the men shouted fiercely, "Yes, yes." The men on the other side of the fire, behind Duncan, remained silent, their indecision mirroring their confusion as to the issues involved.

Before Duncan could reply to Jeannot's challenge Jean-François himself did so. He thrust his way through the Dahomeys, followed by Toussaint and his personal bodyguard.

"So you are a better fighter than I am, are you, Jeannot? Tomorrow you may be the leader of the army!" He turned to Duncan. "What has been happening? What is that white man doing here? Why is he on the ground?"

"He was captured in the jungle, Jeannot was proposing to roast him and eat his heart and liver."

Jean-François's face was contorted with passion as he faced Jeannot. "You know my commands about white prisoners."

"They were Toussaint's orders, not yours," Jeannot replied sullenly. "Toussaint is a psalm-singing renegade who saves the lives of whites for the sake of what he can get from them. I hate the whites, Jean-François. If I had my way not one should live, not even the red-haired one who stands by your side."

"Silence, dog," Jean-François shouted. He signaled to his bodyguard. "Take and hang him from the nearest tree. As long as I am in command there shall be no mutiny in the army. Hang him now, and give his uniform to Dessalines, who can have his rank."

Jeannot was seized and hustled away. The Dahomeys made no attempt to prevent the bodyguard from carrying out Jean-François's orders. If Jean-François were a more powerful chief than Jeannot, then they would follow Jean-François. With emotionless faces they watched Jeannot's body dangle from a tree.

"See that the man remains unharmed," Jean-François ordered as he slouched away; with difficulty he prevented his plumed hat, which was many sizes too big for his head, from falling over both eyes. There were smaller hats for the choosing, but none quite so magnificent.

Toussaint and Duncan turned toward the prisoner, who was seated wearily on the ground. For the first time Duncan recognized the face. It belonged to Garreau.

CHAPTER THIRTY-NINE

DUNCAN took Garreau to his tent and offered the exhausted man his only chair—an ornate piece of furniture of delicate carving, brocade, and gilt. A few weeks previously it had stood in one of De Saint Just's salons, but it had been looted before the flames had done more than scorch one of its carved rosewood legs. Biassou had wanted the chair for his own tent. So had Jeannot. At the height of their quarrel Jean-François had intervened with a judgment worthy of Solomon: the chair should go to the white *papaloi* as a sign to the Negro patients that Duncan enjoyed the patronage of the Grand Admiral of France and Commander of the Negro Army. Whenever he thought of De Saint Just Duncan enjoyed sitting in that chair.

He handed Garreau a cup of coffee, a small piece of manioc cake, and a portion of breadfruit, the remains of the day's rations. Garreau's sunken, black-rimmed eyes stared up at his rescuer, but he made no move to take the proffered food.

"Here is food, Simon, and a cup of coffee to warm you." Duncan spoke gently, for the expression in Garreau's eyes made him fear for the other man's sanity. Garreau was still sane, he believed, but any kind of shock—even that of being treated kindly, if such treatment were too precipitate—might cause the ex-shipping agent to lose his mental balance. "Take the bread, but do not eat it too quickly."

Still Garreau made no move, but continued to stare at Duncan.

"Come, eat, Simon. The food will do you good."

"No," Garreau muttered, in a voice barely recognizable.

"You must be hungry—"

"I am starving," Garreau interrupted. "I have not eaten for three days."

"Then here is food, my dear fellow. The coffee is not good, but it is hot, and will revive you. The manioc is two days stale, and tastes more like ship's biscuits, but it is food and will help to sustain you."

"I do not want it."

Duncan fidgeted beneath Garreau's crazed, unfaltering stare. "But you must eat something, Simon. Come, as a physician I order you to try to eat the food. Dip the bread in the coffee. It will help to make it more palatable."

"I do not want it," Garreau burst out. "Take it away. It is yours. I want nothing of yours. I would rather die."

"Simon, you are ill—"

"Ill!" There was a note of hysteria in Garreau's laugh. "Perhaps I am, but not ill enough to accept the charity of a white renegade." He attempted to rise, but was not strong enough to keep his balance. With a moan of despair he collapsed. "I am too weak to leave this tent, but if I were stronger I would get out of it rather than stay here."

"But we are friends."

Duncan had chosen his words unfortunately. "You are no friend of mine, damn you!" Garreau shouted in his weak, cracked voice. "No white man who helps an army of black swine could be a friend of mine. They killed Annette before my eyes—my own few slaves. One night they armed themselves with machetes, forced their way into our bedroom where we were sleeping, and then— Oh, God! Annette was a lovely woman. I loved her. I swear that I loved her from the day we first met. But those black fiends—" A choking fit stopped his words, and Duncan saw that he was coughing blood.

"Afterward they tried to kill me. I wanted to die, but something stronger than myself made me fight for life. I caught hold of a brass candlestick and hit the slave who was holding me. He staggered away. I hit another slave, then another. I reached the window and jumped out. I ran and ran—anywhere to escape. I reached the jungle. I was there until last night. Then the devils dragged me league after league, stabbing me with their machetes to make me walk—" With a last effort he tried to spit upon Duncan, but failed because his lips were cracked and his mouth dry. "Get away from me. Poor Annette loved you as she would a son. So did I. Now I hate the sight of you—you are helping the black devils who —who—killed—Annette—"

His head sank forward upon his chest. Duncan waited, hoping to see tears flow—which would have meant a welcome relief. But there were no tears left in Garreau.

"You are unfair to me, Simon," Duncan began bitterly. "I am a physician. I do not help the Negroes to fight against the whites. My assistance to the black men is restricted to healing their wounds."

"Don't white men suffer wounds that need healing? Isn't their suffering of more importance to you than a few Negro lives?"

"But I treat the whites too, Simon. Any wounded white man taken prisoner is brought to this tent for treatment. [When the poor devils are not murdered on sight, he reflected miserably.] I save white men first, Negroes afterward. The Negroes know this but don't begrudge the white lives I save, partly because I have saved so many Negroes."

"If you had remained at Cap François you could have saved the lives of Negro prisoners," Garreau sneered.

Anger reddened Duncan's cheeks. "You forget, Simon, that the white inhabitants of Cap François aren't as tolerant as the Negroes. The planters taunted me; the *petits blancs* jeered and threw stones at me when I offered my assistance."

"They would have forgotten their anger when they realized the sincerity of your offer."

Duncan laughed scornfully. "Nonsense! Besides, you know as well as anyone that I had no cause to love the people of Cap François, damn their petty little minds."

Duncan replied, his voice commanding understanding. "When I first came to Saint-Domingue I looked upon a Negro as just a slave, a black man. I thought of them all as alike, as two peas in a pod. Too many white men think like that, Simon. Do you, as a Frenchman, consider your characteristics those of the Prussian? Do you see any similarity between me and a Greek? Do you think you could mistake a Russian peasant for a Portuguese merchant? Yet the half million Negroes in Saint-Domingue are as dissimilar, mentally and physically, as Europeans. They speak different tongues, worship different gods, have different characteristics. Around us at this moment are Negro Dahomeys and Ashantis, Bantu Nkomis and Mobalis, men from Ama-Zulu tribes and from the Hottentot territory. Is the tall strong Zulu Matabele a brother of the smaller Bantu Nkomi? Is there any relation between the Negro Dahomey warrior and the Hottentot bushman?"

Duncan stared at the fire and continued: "I think that slavery should be abolished, that all men should be free. Whether, in consequence, the free Negro would make an honest, hard-working citizen of the Colony is a matter of speculation. But he should be freed. Freedom is the birthright of every man. It is similarly the right of every sick man to demand the help of a physician." Duncan moved close to Garreau and placed a hand on his shoulder. "I am not a renegade," he continued in a strained voice. "I want you to believe that, Simon. You and François are my only white friends—" Embarrassed by his own display of emotion he turned away and strode to the flap of the tent.

Presently he heard a welcome sound as Garreau's unnatural restraint at last gave way.

"I have always hated the sight of blood," the Frenchman sobbed. "I hated it enough to leave France. And now I have seen rivers of blood. Lakes of blood. As long as I live I shall never forget these last weeks. They'll haunt my dreams, Duncan. I'll see blood—blood—all the time—Oh, God! I wish I were dead."

Garreau buried his face in his hands as the tears began to flow again. His shoulder shook with deep, gasping sobs. Duncan was glad to hear them for he believed Garreau's sanity was saved. He turned away to re-warm the coffee.

The insurrection that had crossed the border into the western province reached the outskirts of Port-au-Prince. The defenseless town awaited its doom. But the mulatto leaders, having failed to win the general support of the Negro slaves, withdrew from the town with the announcement that they had no wish to war against the Colony, but only to enforce the decree of the fifteenth of May. Thus a truce between affranchis and the whites of the western province was signed, and was quickly followed by a proclamation of the general assembly, which declared an end of their opposition to the same decree. This was dated the twentieth of September, 1791. A general truce was arranged which gave both sides an opportunity to count their losses. They were heart-rending. In two months more than two thousand white people had been massacred; one thousand plantations had been destroyed. On the Negro side, ten thousand had died from wounds or starvation, and some hundreds on the wheel.

It was a heavy price to have paid for victory, but the Negroes were satisfied. The decree of the fifteenth of May, although it benefited mostly the hated mulattoes, was nevertheless a step toward Negro emancipation. The twentieth of September was a day of rejoicing.

CHAPTER FORTY

IN October Duncan returned to Cap François with Garreau, having obtained his release from Jean-François. Indeed, the Commander was more willing to release Garreau than Duncan, for, though fighting had ceased, the Negroes were still dying in great numbers from pestilence and famine. But Duncan had adhered to his demand, despite the danger of returning to a town where he might be subjected to the insults, and even the vengeance, of white people who would look upon him as a renegade and traitor to his color. The fact that he lived in a poorer quarter of the town, inhabited almost entirely by Negroes, would lessen the risk. Moreover, he was dangerously exhausted.

All the white people who had managed to escape from the Plaine-du-Nord had flocked to Cap François. Many had been completely ruined and were subsisting as best they could, while the more fortunate, whose entire capital had not been invested in their plantations, shipped with their families and remaining possessions to one of the American colonies, or, preferably, to Louisiana, which had remained essentially French in spite of its having been ceded to Spain. In consequence of this upheaval trade was slack, and though Garreau spent day after day trying to find employment, his efforts met with no success. During this time he stayed with Duncan, to whom the city Negroes quickly came for medical attention as soon as they heard of his return. To them, as to the revolted slaves, Ti Rouge had become almost a god. To him they made offerings of food and money as they did to the Christian God—and the heathen gods, too, which many of them worshiped whenever they could be sure that the good Jesuit fathers were not about.

One night Garreau protested against receiving such long hospitality, but Duncan refused to listen.

"Nonsense, Simon," he said dryly. "I am merely returning the hospitality that you extended to me when I arrived here. I was practically penniless then, but you sheltered, fed, and even clothed me. I should be an ungrateful devil if I were unwilling to do the same for you now that you are in need of help."

"But it may be weeks, even months, before I find work."

"I disagree. Trade may be bad at the moment, but nearly everybody is convinced that it will improve when the commissioners arrive. Not everyone is as pessimistic as the traders you have been talking to. I have heard from Toussaint. He writes that most of the Negro leaders are alarmed by the news that more French soldiers are on their way here. He thinks that Jean-François will offer terms of submission to the commissioners as soon as they arrive."

Within three days of Duncan's note of optimism *La Reine de la Mer* arrived from France, bringing calamitous news. The National Assembly, having received alarming reports from Saint-Domingue of the disorders that had followed the decree of the fifteenth of May, and being unaware of the subsequent Negro insurrection, had annulled all decrees affecting the rights of the planters, including particularly that of the fifteenth of May granting equal status to people of color.

The situation deteriorated rapidly. The mulattoes, unable or unwilling to believe that the Colonials had had no part in these annulments, were driven to take a final, irrevocable, and desperate step. With a declaration that either they or the whites must be exterminated, they rose in force against the whites, and the long threatened civil war was at last an accomplished fact. In the southern province Port St. Louis fell quickly into their possession, but at Port-au-Prince, thanks to the reinforcement of troops recently arrived from Europe, they were driven from the neighborhood with great loss of life, but not before they had started a conflagration that eventually destroyed a third of the city.

War raged furiously throughout the entire colony. All the atrocities that had characterized the revolt of the northern slaves now became a feature of the hostilities. Barbaric cruelties were inflicted upon their prisoners by the contestants on both sides.

Such was the internal state of the Colony just before Christmastide of the year 1791, when the three civil commissioners Mirbeck, St. Leger, and Roume, newly appointed by the National Assembly of France, arrived at Cap François.

As the ship approached the quay the inhabitants of Cap François raised a cheer for the commissioners. There was good will in their voices, for had not these three men come to their colony to settle all differences between the whites, the affranchis, and the Negroes? They were bound to succeed, for they stood for the government of France. The motherland.

The same night Duncan and Garreau visited the Casino. Some tables were occupied, but many remained empty. Few familiar faces were to be seen. Of the old patrons Lambion alone appeared, and though he was half-drunk, and laughed and shouted more loudly than anyone as he hired half a dozen mulatto girls to sit at his table, there was a note of artificiality in his jubilation. His laughter reminded one unpleasantly of ghosts.

"How can he afford to be here?" Garreau asked François.

"He was fortunate enough to have a plantation in the southern province that remained unaffected until the last rising."

"But now?"

"A week ago he received news that it had been destroyed."

"And yet he still has money?"

"Enough, he says, to last him two more weeks. After that—" François shrugged his shoulders.

"If I were he I should husband my resources."

"For my sake I am glad he does not," François observed bluntly. "But I do not blame him, Garreau. He has always spent money freely. He cannot face the future as a poor man, so he is going down with his flag flying."

"I think he is a fool!" Garreau insisted scornfully.

"In his own way he is a brave man," François contradicted. "The circumstances of the Comte de Saramon are much the same, but Monsieur le Comte has become niggardly, and lives miserably."

"There is misery in Lambion's laughter."

"It is not for himself, but because his friends are not here to share his last two weeks. He tried to bring them, but they were too proud."

"De Saint Just—?" Duncan asked.

"Has not been here for many weeks," François replied moodily, thinking of how much De Saint Just had spent in the old days.

Duncan was vaguely disappointed. If De Saint Just had come, Phebe might have accompanied him—and Duncan would have liked the opportunity of seeing Phebe again. With its burning eyes, high prominent cheekbones, and full lips, hers was an extraordinarily attractive face.

François rose to greet a party of six men who had just entered. Duncan glanced indifferently in their direction, then stiffened. Among them was Mirbeck.

"Your commissioners have begun work," Duncan caustically told Garreau. "One of them has just entered. Does he consider it his duty to study life in Domingue from every angle?"

Rumors began to circulate; Mirbeck was more interested in debauchery than in promoting peace; St. Leger was exacting heavy bribes from the mulattoes on the pretext that he was their friend; Roume was inefficient and incapable. But the white population masked their increasing contempt for the commissioners—peace and prosperity were of greater importance than private morals.

In January the commissioners issued their second proclamation—a general amnesty for all rebels, irrespective of color, who, within a prescribed time, laid down their arms and took the oath required by the new constitution.

This act first bewildered and then angered the white population, who considered the proposal intolerable. They recalled the white planters who had been massacred, tortured, or ruined. They asserted that clemency would be construed as weakness and create a dangerous precedent that would influence those Negroes who had hitherto remained faithful to the white race.

The mulattoes were infuriated. For them the amnesty was futile, since it was coupled with the order that all men of color were instantly to disarm, which rendered void all their striving for equality. As a bloody gesture of their contempt for the commissioners the mulattoes at Petit Goave executed thirty-four white prisoners by breaking them on the wheel. Mulattoes who had remained loyal to the whites overlooked their hatred of the black man and flocked to the Negro camps.

The Negroes alone welcomed the proposed amnesty. In a letter dictated by the Abbé de la Haye, curé of Dondon, and signed by "Jean-François, général; Biassou, maréchal de camp; Desprez, Manzeau, Toussaint, et Aubert, commissaries ad hoc," the Negroes reiterated their desire for a peace conditional on the amelioration of their treatment. The letter was conveyed to the Colonial Assembly by two representatives who traveled with letters of safe conduct granted by the three commissioners. When Jean-François's letter was read, the Colonial Assembly arrogantly refused to treat with the Negroes except on terms of unconditional surrender. When news of this reply reached Jean-François's camp, the Negroes were so enraged that only Toussaint's unremitting efforts succeeded in preventing a wholesale massacre of white prisoners. Thanks again to Toussaint, these prisoners were subsequently released in exchange for free pardons for four hundred of the Negro leaders.

One night Toussaint and Christophe called on Duncan. While he greeted Toussaint and made him welcome, Duncan was astonished by the change that had taken place in the short interval since their last meeting. Toussaint's attitude was that of a powerful and confident man. There was determination in his intelligent eyes; authority in his voice.

"I am glad to find you safe and well, Ti Rouge. When you returned to Cap François after the truce I was nervous for you."

Duncan shrugged. "I am hated more than ever, which disturbs me less than ever. Garreau and François remain my friends. Suzanne cares for me. My patients show their gratitude. I am content."

If there was a gruffness in Duncan's voice and an expression in his eyes that belied his words, Toussaint chose not to notice. "I am glad," he said simply.

"So you have come to Cap François to arrange terms of peace?"

"That was the purpose of my visit, but it has failed."

"Surely not without hope—"

"How could it be otherwise?" Toussaint demanded passionately. "I came to treat with the three commissioners, but they have no power to promote peace. Or if they have that power, the members of the Colonial Assembly decline to acknowledge it. They arrogantly reject our overtures because they are relying upon reinforcements from France, and, if necessary, English help from Jamaica."

"And if they do not rely in vain?"

"We are not afraid, Ti Rouge. We are preparing for a long war. Food is being grown for our troops on distant mountains beyond easy reach of the white men. Our men are being drilled, and are daily better armed. It would take a very large army to defeat us now, for even if their artillery and their cavalry should drive us from the plains, we can retire among the mountains where they would be unable to follow us."

Duncan glanced keenly at the Negro. "But you still want peace, Toussaint?"

"I do. I desire peace with all my heart, but it must be an acceptable peace, which will entitle us, in future, to be treated as men and women, not as cattle." Toussaint shook his head sadly. "War may be necessary sometimes, but it is none the less detestable. Biassou, now, would rather fight than have peace, for he is enraged by the insolence of the Colonial Assembly, but I have attained influence, and my advice is often sought and taken."

"And you, Christophe, do you agree with Toussaint?"

"Certainly I want peace," Christophe answered morosely. "A year ago my hotel was always full. Now it is half empty."

"Suppose that you cannot have peace on your terms?"

Christophe's eyes glowered. "Then I, too, will fight."

"You will be fighting, Henri, before the war ends," Toussaint told him.

Before three months had expired the commissioners realized that to prolong their stay in Saint-Domingue would be useless. They returned to France, where the extremists, headed by Robespierre and Marat, were gaining the ascendancy in the National Assembly. Again and again the affairs of the West Indian colonies came up for discussion. On the fourth of April 1792 a new decree was passed that provided that all people of color and free Negroes should enjoy political equality with the whites, have the right to vote in all primary and electoral assemblies, and be eligible for the legislature and other positions of trust, further, that the authors of the disturbances be sent to France for trial. It was then ordered that a sufficient force, composed chiefly of national guards, should be dispatched to the Colony.

Robespierre and Marat who had forced this decree through the National Assembly appointed as commissioners two of their most notorious party men, Santhonax and Polverel. Ailhaud, a moderate, was the third member of the commission. Together with six thousand troops, the three men sailed for Saint-Domingue. Santhonax and Polverel, insanely revolutionary, viciously hostile to anyone or anything connected with ci-devant aristos, rapaciously ambitious, discussed ways and means of humbling the haughty planters.

On their arrival the new commissioners dissolved the Colonial Assembly and arrested M. Blanchelande; he was relieved of his post as governor and sent home for trial. After months of confusion, the National Assembly sent a former planter, Galbaud, to Saint-Domingue as governor. Santhonax and Polverel promptly rejected his authority.

CHAPTER FORTY-ONE

DUNCAN was awakened from a doze by Garreau's energetic shaking. "Fighting has broken out in Cap François," he gasped.

Duncan sat up abruptly. "The Negroes—"

"No. Galbaud has landed with more than a thousand seamen. He is being joined by hundreds of townspeople. They are marching upon Government House—" Garreau paused, breathless.

"What about the garrison at the Arsenal?"

"They have joined forces with Galbaud."

Duncan laughed shortly. "I'm not surprised in view of the number of their officers the commissioners have deported. I suppose Saint-Domingue can now say good-by to Messieurs Santhonax et Compagnie."

"If only that were true!" An expression of dismay contorted Garreau's face. "The commissioners have a force of mulattoes on guard at Government House, and one piece of cannon. But there is worse news than that, Duncan. The National Guard is joining the commissioners."

"Good God! By the time the two forces have finished fighting one another this city will be a shambles. Heaven help the women!" He raised his voice. "Suzanne."

Suzanne wobbled in, looking scared. "Master, I can hear the sound of guns."

"Fighting has broken out," Duncan told her crisply. "It is not safe for women to remain in the city. Pack your things and get as far away as you can. Go to the convent and ask the good mothers for shelter, and take as many other women as possible with you."

"But master, I am only a fat Negro woman. Nobody would want to harm me."

"No woman is safe when men smell blood and get the lust for killing."

"Will you come too, master?"

"No, Suzanne. There will be work for me to do here."

"Perhaps the fighting will finish soon."

"If it does you may come back again. If not, I will come to the convent to find you."

"Who will care for you, master?" the Negress continued to argue. "Suzanne must stay to look after you."

"Go," he ordered impatiently. "As quickly as you can. And do not forget to take other women with you."

Suzanne turned away with reluctance. Through the open door Duncan saw her run to the next house and hammer on the door with her huge, fat hand. A slave came out, white-eyed and trembling. Suzanne spoke to him. He disappeared. Presently two mulatto women came out, each carrying a huge bundle of goods. With hurrying steps they made their way toward the ford north of Government House. They were soon followed by other women. Before long the road was choked with a crowd of refugees, women, children, and old men of all shades of color from pure white to the darkest black, most of them staggering along with as many personal belongings as they could carry, some wailing and sobbing their fear and misery.

The noise from the center of the town became increasingly tumultuous. Musket shots, shouts, the clash of steel, the pounding hoofs of frightened horses, the roll of drums, bugle calls, and the boom of cannon intermingled indescribably. Duncan and Garreau sprinted down the rue de Michel, but their progress was slow, for they had continually to dodge charging fiacres, recklessly driven by terrified slaves, whose only thought was to escape from the scene of conflict. The bouncing, swaying carriages were steered on the shortest course, regardless of obstructions. Human beings were crushed and mangled beneath iron-shod roofs and ironbound wheels. Fiacres interlocked, to be overturned or smashed to pieces against the buildings. The streets echoed with shrieks of pain and terror and the neighing of horses.

Men of all colors milled hither and thither, the unarmed seeking arms, the armed seeking enemies, the terrified seeking safety.

Duncan and Garreau spent the night in the small villa that De Saint Just had built for Clémentine. Under Duncan's direction the door had been forced and the wounded of both parties carried into the building and laid upon the floor to await attention. With Garreau and three slightly wounded soldiers to help, Duncan painstakingly progressed along the lines of wounded men, doing the best he could with plain water, the instruments he had had in his pocket, and rough bandages that his helpers made by ripping up all the loose material in the villa upon which they could lay their hands. Many of the patients died from lack of medicine or from the excessive heat, but Duncan stubbornly persevered, although he had only two candles at a time to light the rooms for him.

Thither came De Saint Just, with Phebe. De Saint Just's face was drawn and pale, but his eyes sparkled maliciously as he apprehended what Duncan had done. Phebe was dressed in clothes as exotic as those she had worn on the day Duncan had first seen her, but her crimsoned, seductive lips bore a sulky expression that was new to him.

"What are you and these men doing in this villa?" De Saint Just asked.

Duncan was kneeling on the floor, probing for a musket ball that had become lodged in the right arm of one of the seamen from La Normande. He stared back at De Saint Just.

"It is obvious, is it not, monsieur? These men were wounded during

175

the fighting today. I am trying to treat their wounds before gangrene sets in."

"But these are white men. I understood that you only treated Negroes, Monsieur l'Ami des Noirs?" De Saint Just taunted.

Duncan flushed, but he controlled his temper, and disregarded his audience as he bent over the groaning seaman and continued his search for the musket ball.

"It is strange to see you back among white people," his tormentor continued. "I had expected that by this time the slaves would have crowned you their white emperor. Or at least have made you Physician Extraordinary to the Negro Army of Insurrection. After all, your bosom comrade Toussaint has done so well for himself that he now bears the surname 'L'Ouverture.'" De Saint Just laughed his contempt. "'He who makes openings.' Nom de Dieu!"

Duncan remained silent.

"Some weeks ago I heard that you were making use of some furniture that your black companions plundered from my plantation. You should have informed me that you coveted my goods; I should gladly have made you a gift of all you wanted. Perhaps then it would not have been necessary to burn down my house."

"Your sarcasm is wasted upon me, monsieur," Duncan growled, provoked against his better judgment into answering back.

"Sarcasm! My dear Monsieur Stewart, please do not take my words in that spirit. After all, why should I begrudge a few pieces of furniture if they could have prevented my ruin? But there! I do not harbor malice. A year ago I was one of the richest men in Saint-Domingue. Today I am penniless, owning nothing save two villas that I cannot afford to maintain, and a mistress whom I cannot afford to lose." He slipped his arm round Phebe's slender waist. "But is that any reason for harboring bitterness? Of course not," he continued mockingly. "These are days of liberty, equality, and fraternity. And I, Armand de Saint Just, am now the equal of the meanest slave."

"Kill the aristocrats!" the sailor muttered hoarsely.

"Quite, my friend, quite," De Saint Just agreed lightly. "Now that I own nothing, I too can add my voice to the common cry. But if those are your sentiments, my dear fellow, you should be fighting for the revolutionary commissioners, not against them. But perhaps you are. Nobody knows who is fighting whom. I give you a toast, my poor wounded fighting friend: Vive la Révolution! Vive les Nègres! Vive les Amis des Noirs!"

"Is this the incredible Monsieur l'Anglais who physics the slaves?" Phebe asked, speaking for the first time.

Duncan looked up sharply into Phebe's burning eyes, but before he could speak De Saint Just answered her.

"It is, my brown cabbage. This is the Briton who anticipated France's declaration of war upon England by himself declaring insurrection against a French colony."

"You lie, monsieur," Duncan snapped violently.

De Saint Just's eyes sparkled angrily, and the arm that embraced Phebe tightened, causing her to gasp for breath. But he continued, derisively:

"No doubt, Monsieur Stewart, you have returned to Cap François to curry favor with Messieurs les Commissionaires. With the revolutionary canaille on their side, and the black men on yours, all Saint-Domingue might become yours. Who knows! You, and those swine from Paris, would command unlimited power. You could commandeer for your personal use anything that escapes destruction. It might not amount to much, but no matter! You could have me deported, or better still, have me broken on the wheel. Would such a sight bring pleasure to those blazing eyes of yours, Monsieur Stewart? You might even command the kisses of my little rabbit here. With a careless gesture De Saint Just ruffled Phebe's hair.

"I should kill myself first," she hissed, revealing her white teeth and tossing her head so that her long earrings jangled.

"Not if monsieur were rich enough. You are too fond of luxury to kill yourself, my pet."

"I hate him," Phebe said in a piercing voice. "I hate him for what he did to you, Armand, and more so for what he has done to me."

"To you?" De Saint Just asked, with uplifted eyebrows.

"This was my villa," she replied shrilly. "You gave it to me, Armand. The bed was mine, the furniture mine, the carpets mine. Now everything has been ruined by these dirty rats. Look how everything has been torn to shreds and the floors stained with blood. This was my villa, Englishman. That's why I hate you." She leaned across the wounded seaman and spat at Duncan. Her spittle splashed his face, rolled down his cheek, and fell upon the bared chest below.

The seaman growled admiringly: "The bitch! What couldn't I do to her if I wasn't wounded!"

For two days the battle raged between the white inhabitants entrenched in their houses and the prowling bands of Negroes and mulattoes; a battle watched from afar by the horrified eyes of those who had escaped to the mountains, or had fortunately reached the fleet of ships in the harbor, among whom were the commissioners themselves, strongly protected by a large bodyguard of troops from the mother country, for Santhonax and Polverel had as much reason to fear the vengeance of the white townspeople as they had to distrust the good faith of their Negro allies.

Among the buildings to hold out was the villa that De Saint Just had built for one mulatto mistress and redecorated for another. The wounded men who occupied it fought off attack after attack. The pile of black corpses that surrounded it mounted hourly, until at last Macaya's Negroes lost heart and decided to concentrate on the less defensible houses. These capitulated one after the other, their remaining occupants were butchered, their contents looted, and the buildings fired. Day was turned into night by the pall of black smoke that hung over the city, but when the real night came the streets were bright with flames.

Odd scraps of news reached the men beleaguered in Phebe's villa, brought to them by refugees from other buildings. One of these, a man who had been sabered several times and yet still lived, told Duncan and Garreau of the fate of Dumestre's warehouse.

"It was blazing from end to end when I last saw it," he gasped. "Nothing could have saved it. By now it's probably gutted."

Garreau turned slowly and stared, dry-eyed, in the direction of the quays. His body seemed to wilt, as though his last tie with life was severed. "I loved my work," he murmured tonelessly. "I loved the sight of ships riding in the bay. And now—" His lips moved spasmodically. With dragging feet he shuffled into another room.

Then came more news: Delaire's warehouse was in flames—the Hôtel Paris—the Hôtel du Nouveau Monde—Cazeaux's villa in the rue Vaudreuil—Lambion's home in the rue Daujon—the coffeeshop in the Place d'Armes. News, also, of people: Delaire and his family were safe on board one of the ships in the harbor—Lambion was dead—De Saint Just and Phebe were in Psaume's villa, which was still holding out.

Next came Henri Christophe, haggard and bloody. He was nearly shot by one of the seamen who saw him running toward the window, but fortunately the seaman's aim was bad, and the musket ball missed Christopher and hit one of the Negroes attacking Turpin's house opposite, held by a platoon of the Cap Regiment.

"Christophe! What are you doing here, man? If you leave your hotel—"

"The hotel is gutted," Christophe interrupted bitterly. "The devils set fire to it."

"But Henri, it was your hotel. Surely your being—being—" Duncan faltered.

"A Negro!" Christophe finished grimly. "Yes, I am a Negro, but no friend of Macaya's swine, Ti Rouge. I tried to calm them, but they jeered at me, the canailles." The veins in his forehead throbbed. "Because I am a Negro they left my hotel alone until they discovered that there was a white man sheltering inside. Then they attacked, set fire to it, and killed him."

"Who was he?"

"Deschenel."

"Not the physician?"

"Yes. Deschenel, of all people. He has always had a deep grudge against both of us since you saved my life, yet it was in the Hôtel de la Couronne that he sought safety. In my hotel! Curse his black soul, he has carried out his threat of ruining us both, Ti Rouge."

"How did you know I was here?" Duncan asked abruptly.

"Garreau told me."

"Garreau! That is impossible. Garreau is here, in this villa."

Christophe's harsh voice softened. "Monsieur Garreau is dead, Ti Rouge. I found him by my side just as the Hôtel de la Couronne collapsed. He asked me to try to rescue you, and then—"

"And then?"

"He wrenched a saber from the hands of a dead soldier and attacked a party of six slaves. He killed three of them before he died. Poor Monsieur Garreau. He loved ships."

CHAPTER FORTY-TWO

AMONG the buildings in Cap François that had escaped damage during the three days' battle was Duncan's small home; as it was empty, both of occupants and plunder, the pillaging Negroes had contemptuously ignored it, as they had all the neighboring houses. The Casino François, too, although damaged, was still intact, as Duncan discovered when he went along to see how François had fared. As for François himself, the old soldier had a bloody gash up his left cheek that stretched from his chin to his blind eye, but otherwise he was unharmed and as blustery as ever.

After the two men had appraised each other rejoicingly, Duncan said: "So you are still alive, François, thank God!"

"But yes, my boy, of course I'm alive. Do you think an old warrior like me would let a bunch of black bastards pop him off so easily? But I feel happier now that I have had a sight of you, lad. I was planning upon visiting you tomorrow. Have you heard what's doing?"

"Only rumors. There's one being passed on that hundreds of slaves who swore allegiance to obtain their freedom have deserted, established themselves in the mountains, and are now making raids on all the outlying plantations."

"I've heard that something is happening on the Spanish border."

"Spanish troops are pushing across. Did you know, by the way, that Jean-François, Biassou, and Toussaint have joined the Spanish army? Jean-François has been made a general, Biassou a field marshal, and Toussaint a colonel. They are fighting for Spain against France."

"The damned renegades!"

Duncan shook his head. "Don't judge too harshly, François. All their lives they have been taught to look upon their king as a god. Almost as soon as reliable news reached them that Louis was dead they deserted to Spain, so that they could still serve under a king. Many white Frenchmen, monarchists at heart, have changed their nationality."

It was shortly after this conversation with François that Christophe appeared at Duncan's house, his black face beaming.

"I am going to be married next week," he announced joyfully.

"To Marie Louise?"

"Of course. Who else should I wish to marry?"

Duncan congratulated the Negro, adding: "What has decided you so suddenly, Henri, now that you no longer have a hotel? Are you going to join Toussaint?"

The smile left Christophe's thick lips. "No, Ti Rouge," he replied gravely. "Toussaint and I both hope and plan for the freedom of Negroes from slavery, but we work in different ways. Toussaint hopes to conquer the white man and force Negro emancipation as a condition of peace. I have less faith in the whites, and, as you know, more fear of them."

"Why?"

"As a white man, Ti Rouge, will you answer this question: If we Negroes were to drive you out of the Colony, what would you do? Would you swallow your pride and do nothing? Or would you be ashamed of being conquered by a black race, and raise an army to avenge your defeat? Don't be afraid to answer frankly."

"I am a Scotsman, not a Frenchman," Duncan equivocated.

"If you were a Frenchman you would try to regain control of the Colony, wouldn't you, Ti Rouge?" Christophe insisted.

"Yes, but France is too unsettled. She is in the throes of an internal reign of terror. She is at war with three great countries. I doubt whether she could spare the men for such an expedition."

"The reign of terror will come to an end. So will the wars. One day, when France has recovered, her leaders would think: It is time to regain our lost colony. They would dispatch a great army. Perhaps they might conquer the Negroes. Then they would make the Negroes slaves again."

"I don't think the French would do that now. There are too many Frenchmen friendly to the Negro cause."

"If we were to drive the French out of Saint-Domingue that cause would soon be forgotten," Christophe commented shrewdly. "No, Ti Rouge. I want the white man to emancipate the Negro willingly, for I am convinced that only a peaceful emancipation can remain permanent. I want the gratitude of France, not her enmity. François has told me too much about warfare. That is why I respect the power of France, and mean to continue to work peacefully for emancipation."

"Perhaps Toussaint does, too, Henri. Perhaps that is his reason for joining the Spanish flag."

"Maybe," Christophe agreed. "But Spain still recognizes slavery." He scowled angrily. "I can tell you this, Ti Rouge: Jean-François, Biassou, and Dessalines are selling their black prisoners to the Spanish as slaves."

"Toussaint, also?"

"No. I'll admit that Papa Toussaint is still faithful to his ideals. He has no hand in enslaving his fellow Negroes. But I have not told you the rest of my news, Ti Rouge. I am starting business again."

"What do you propose to do?"

"Open a butcher's shop," Christophe answered surprisingly.

Santhonax, on the twenty-ninth of August, proclaimed the absolute abolition of every kind of slavery for the Negroes of the northern province; all Negroes, henceforward, to consider themselves, and to be considered, as free citizens.

At the time of this proclamation, his fellow commissioner Polverel was at Port-au-Prince. He was aghast at this unauthorized and dangerous expedient, but he had no option but to issue a similar proclamation, granting equal freedom to the slaves of the two remaining provinces.

That same night Christophe called upon Duncan. The Negro was scarcely able to control his jubilation. His eyes and teeth flashed whitely; he spoke in a high-pitched voice.

"Did I not say that my method was the better one?" he shouted excitedly, without prefacing his remark with the formal greeting. "We are free, Ti Rouge. No longer are we Negroes to be treated as human cattle. Now we are the equals of the scurvy mulattoes. We are free, and more than free. We are citizens. This is a day in Negro history to be celebrated in future years."

"Why did Santhonax make such an unexpected decree?"

"Why shouldn't he have done so?" Christophe demanded angrily. "Do you begrudge us Negroes our freedom?"

"You know that I do not," Duncan pointed out.

The Negro was immediately contrite. "Forgive me, Ti Rouge. I do not mean what I said. I am so pleased I scarcely know what I'm doing. Why has Santhonax proclaimed our freedom? Because he needs our help. He must have many more men to—" Christophe paused, then continued slowly: "Have you not heard the news?"

"What news?"

"Of your countrymen?"

"What do you mean, my countrymen?" Duncan asked with asperity.

"I may have to fight against them. Monsieur Santhonax has heard that the British are preparing to send an army to annex Saint-Domingue."

"So Saint-Domingue may become a British colony!" Duncan laughed dryly. "The possibility appeals to my sense of humor. If the British were to conquer Cap François, then De Saint Just and Marilys and Psaume would have to mend their manners toward me, Henri, and be pleasant to me for the first time, because of my nationality." Presently his expression of amusement faded. "If the British came to Cap François I should have to leave, Henri, in case I should be recognized. In British justice a murderer always remains a murderer," he explained bitterly. With an effort he directed his thoughts into a different channel. "So Santhonax released the slaves that they might fight the British." He glanced up suddenly as he recollected Christophe's previous words. "Are you going to fight, Henri?"

"I served as a soldier before you arrived on the island," Christophe explained. "I was first gunner in a regiment of colonial artillery. Now I have been offered a captaincy in the infantry if I will volunteer for service."

"Which you propose doing?"

"It is better than butchering." Christophe pulled a paper from his pocket, which he unfolded and showed Duncan. "Look."

Duncan read the crudely printed pamphlet:

In Camp Trivel, August 29, 1793

Brothers and Friends:

I am Toussaint l'Ouverture; my name is perhaps known to you. I have undertaken to avenge your wrongs. It is my desire that liberty and equality shall reign in Saint-Domingue. I am striving to this end. Come and unite with us, brothers, and combat with us for the same cause.

Your very humble and obedient servant,

Toussaint l'Ouverture,

General for the Public Welfare

"Perhaps Santhonax's proclamation is in answer to that rather than a measure of defense against the British," Duncan pointed out.

A frown momentarily revealed itself on Christophe's forehead, but it quickly vanished. "I still believe it is better to be manumitted freely than to achieve freedom by conquest," he maintained.

On the ninth of September the first British expeditionary force left Port Royal, Jamaica, for the island of Santo Domingo. It consisted of 677 rank and file under the command of Lieutenant Colonel Whitelocke, and was escorted by the *Europa* and four other frigates. Ten days later they landed in Jérémie, in the southern province, which was surrendered to them without a shot having been fired. From the southern province a party of English mariners sailed to the Mole of Cap St. Nicholas, northern province, where the garrison, consisting of some Irish battalions and national guards, had offered allegiance to the English flag. The town of St. Nicholas was less amenable. From having been monarchist in sympathy, at the threat of foreign interference the local inhabitants at once joined the republican forces, and for two months held up any further advance by the British in that neighborhood. Nevertheless, the loss of the Mole was a severe one to the commissioners, for it was the strongest military port on the island, and contained a large supply of necessary stores. Even more harmful were the moral effects of the British landing. By their rash emancipation of all slaves the commissioners had already incensed their mulatto supporters. Rendered nervous by the British successes, they now deserted the commissioners, and under the leadership of Rigaud and Pétion they made war against the commissioners on their own account.

It was little wonder that General Laveaux wrote despairingly to the mother country:

We are in a country where, by the course of events, the white man is detested. The guilty have fled, it is true; but the hatred toward the whites, borne by the Africans, is not in the least assuaged thereby, and who can force these new citizens to do their duty, once they have abjured it? Will they respect the handful of white troops that yet remains?

Laveaux was soon to have further proof of Negro power. Spanish and Negro troops, the latter still under the command of Jean-François, Biassou, and Toussaint, pressed steadily forward into French territory. It was not long before the people of Cap François realized that the French colony of Saint-Domingue was doomed. Unless a miracle intervened, England and Spain intended to chase the French from the island and divide the spoils.

CHAPTER FORTY-THREE

OPPRESSED by the prospect of revisiting the Casino, empty and cheerless, a mockery of its past glories, Duncan nevertheless decided to go for the sake of a chat with François. Since the death of Garreau and the departure of Christophe with his Negro infantry, François was the only man with whom Duncan could enjoy an interesting conversation.

He dressed himself in clothes he had recently acquired cheaply, from a white widow who, to raise passage money, had sold all the possessions salvaged from her home. The suit was highly fashionable, for the jacket was double-breasted and the tail was replaced by a short, square back. The lapels were still exaggerated, but the sleeves were longer. More revolutionary still were the pantaloons, which were appearing for the first time in generations, and were tightly fitting round the calf. As he strolled along the rue Espagnole, Duncan unwittingly attracted the attention of many startled people to whom pantaloons were still a novelty after the breeches of the past century.

If his dress surprised many whom he passed by, he was no less startled by what he saw about him. He began to realize more fully the effects of Negro emancipation. Where the streets of Cap François had once been filled with white inhabitants, barely noticeable slaves, and a sprinkling of mulattoes, now the whites and the mulattoes were in the minority. The thousands of Negroes who had been inconspicuous as slaves were now, as freemen, fantastically outstanding. They strutted boldly where once they had slip-slopped apologetically. They congregated in groups, and forced white people to step round them. They talked in loud, blustering voices. They wore uniforms, brightly colored clothes, or uniforms of scarlet, black, gold, and blue; cocked hats, plumed hats, feathered beavers. Every other Negro was a soldier; every other soldier was a captain, or a brigadier, or a colonel.

It was plain that the demeanor of the Negroes angered their late masters. The Negroes were not insolent. Nor were they rude, nor in any way offensive. Yet their atttiude radiated an unspoken, and possibly unconscious, sense of triumph, a vague suggestion of familiarity, a definite assumption of equality and fraternity.

It was a strange freak of fate that Duncan, who was better dressed than at any time since his arrival in the Colony, should come face to face with De Saint Just, who was shabbier than he had ever been. As De Saint Just recognized Duncan he halted and touched his companion on the arm.

"The devil burn me if I do not recognize our Englishman, Psaume, my dear fellow," De Saint Just drawled as his glance traveled the length of Duncan's body. "And dressed in the very latest mode from Paris. Apparently there is more money to be made from purging Negroes than we suspected. Behold, our ugly duckling has blossomed into a swan. My dear Stewart, you must certainly allow me to congratulate you upon your tailor. If I did not dislike you so heartily I should have no hesitation in asking you for his name."

Duncan stared angrily at De Saint Just, and wondered why it was that the Frenchman always succeeded in placing him at a disadvantage, like a truant scholar face to face with his master.

"I purchased it secondhand," he retorted dourly. "It probably cost less than one of your cravats."

"You forget that I am now penniless." Once again De Saint Just inspected the suit. "Dear me! Since you mention the fact, the suit has a familiar appearance. There was only one other person in Cap François as modish as I in the matter of clothes. Chobert! Am I right? Did poor Chobert once wear that suit?"

"Madame Chobert certainly sold it to me."

"So! So!" De Saint Just nodded his head. "How symbolic! Do you agree, Psaume?"

"How is it symbolic?"

De Saint Just smiled mockingly. "The passing of the old order, the coming of the new. A few days ago I saw a Negro wearing Chobert's uniform. The slaves of yesterday are the masters of today. Damme if the events in Europe are not paralleled in Saint-Domingue! There, the white canailles chop off the heads of the nobles; here, the black swine torture us to death. I cannot decide whether or no we should be grateful for the Negroes' dislike of the guillotine. It is a quick death, and so very aristocratic."

"It is a wonder Monsieur Stewart is not wearing a military uniform," Psaume interrupted.

"But of course not," De Saint Just reproved smoothly. "Surely you would not expect an Englishman to fight against his fellow countrymen at the Mole, or his Negro friends at Limonade?"

"No," Duncan slipped in quickly before Psaume could speak again. "But I should expect a Frenchman to fight against his foes, English or Spanish."

De Saint Just's drawn face reddened. "Fight for Santhonax! If I did not abominate you so heartily, my friend, I should feel more tempted to fight for the English than against them. At least some Englishmen are gentlemen. But I find it hard to decide whom I abominate the most—the English, the Spaniards, the Negroes, or the republicans."

"There is not a tittle to choose between them," Psaume murmured carelessly as he attempted to draw De Saint Just forward.

"One moment, my dear Psaume, if you please. I have one more matter to mention to Monsieur Stewart."

"Well?" Duncan queried shortly.

"Do not forget to make use of my villas whenever you feel inclined." De Saint Just laughed, and strolled on with an assured poise that was in no whit altered from the days when he was in the habit of accompanying his latest mistress along the Cours le Brasseur. By merely watching his walk a stranger would have found it hard to believe that he was not still one of the richest men on the island, and the acknowledged leader of men's fashions. Thinking of him in that light Duncan lost some of his resentment, and experienced instead a feeling of admiration for the Frenchman. Whatever else he might be, at least De Saint Just was a man, and faced his misfortune with courage. A man to be likened to the nobles of France who went to the guillotine with a smile on their lips and a sneer in their eyes for the canaille who had ordered their execution.

Within the hour Duncan was to meet with another example of this defiance of fate's buffets. Upon arrival at the Casino he found François a very joyful person.

"Ah, lad! It is about time you showed up again. You are going to enjoy yourself tonight."

"Why?"

"Because the Casino will be full again. Every night for the past week the ballroom and the gaming rooms have been crowded."

Duncan was astonished. "Where are the people getting the money from?"

"From the same bank as mine—the stocking."

"But why should they rob their stockings? One would think that the Colony was at peace instead of being engaged in a disastrous war."

"It is the war that is making them spend their money."

"But why?"

"Why? Because the people mean to have their last fling. Don't you know that the Negroes are marching on Cap François? I am an old soldier, lad, and can see that it will not be long now before the Negroes will have surrounded this city. The people are not all fools. Some of them can see as well as I that the Negroes will march into Cap François a second time. What is the use of having money in the stocking if your house is burning, and your dead body is in the heart of the flames? One can't take money to heaven."

"Toussaint wouldn't permit this city to be sacked again."

"Toussaint isn't the general."

"He has his own army now, François."

"Maybe he has, but I still say he isn't the generalissimo of the Negro forces."

"Agreed. Jean-François still commands the Negroes, but Toussaint's influences increases every day."

"Aye, he has made progress. But I've heard that Jean-François is becoming jealous of Toussaint's successes. I should not be surprised to hear there's been a mighty quarrel between the black leaders. If Jean-François crushes Toussaint, the Cap will fall to the Negroes."

"You really fear that?"

"I do," François admitted gravely. Then he showed his black teeth in a crooked grin. "If you want to leave the Cap you had better do so while there is still time. You could seek refuge with your fellow countrymen."

"What about you? Are you proposing to leave?"

"While I am still making money?"

Duncan chuckled. "What is the use of having money in the stocking if your house is burning, and your dead body is in the heart of the flames?" he quoted.

"I have had my day, and a good long day it has been, too," François growled. "I am getting too old to look for new pastures. If the Negroes come, well, I am ready to die as long as I can take a few of those sons of Beelzebub with me to Valhalla. But let's be cheerful while we can, for I can promise you a surprise tonight. A new solo dancer," he explained with a lewd chuckle. "She costs more than I dare tell old Vroux, but she is worth every livre, and more. My clients are mad about her."

"Who is she, François?"

"That is a secret that has filled the ballroom every night this week."

Later on, as the ballroom began to fill up, Duncan realized that François had not exaggerated in saying that the Casino was its old self again. Loud voices, boisterous laughter, the shuffling feet of Negro waiters, and the noisy band combined to create a cheerful clamor in which normal conversation was impossible. Food, drink, color, laughter, gaiety—all these things reminded Duncan of the Casino as it had been in prerevolution days; with this exception: though the atmosphere was enough to intoxicate one, yet to the acute ear there was about it an undertone of strain, of hopeless resignation. The people of Cap François were celebrating their own wake.

In spite of the sad undercurrent it was difficult not to be affected by the noise, the music, and the laughter. The combination reminded him of the first night he had spent there, when he had been accompanied by poor Garreau and Captain Beard. (What had happened to Beard? He had not visited the Cap since.) He smiled as he remembered his emotions of that night. He had been drunk, of course, with rum and misery, and so had only a very hazy memory of naked dancing girls, painted breasts, sinuous buttocks, fevered shouts, frenzied excesses. The events leading up to the disappearance of both Beard and Garreau were just as uncertain. Sometimes he could dimly remember some mulattoes (or were they Negresses?) coming to the table, one, two, three of them, and the repellent scarlet lips that sought to capture and imprison his own. But the rest was nebulous. Two memories alone remained clearly etched in his mind: the first, that of the emotion that prompted him to struggle against the mulatto girl's enticement; the second, the extraordinary sensation that he had experienced upon witnessing the expression on the faces of Garreau and Beard when they rejoined him in the ballroom.

Duncan stared at the bubbles that rose in the champagne before him. Partly, it had been the memory, not solely of Margaret, but of Jean, and Dr. Anderson also (perhaps Mrs. Anderson and Elizabeth, too), that, drunk though he had been, had prompted him to resist the temptation to seek forgetfulness in the arms of the mulatto girl. But chiefly an impulse stronger than his own inclinations had urged him not to break one link that bound him to the past. A strange link, and one that often made him jeer, but there it was, puissant and undeniable. Celibacy was that link. A twisted reasoning, based on the theory of the male's superiority over the female. He would remain faithful to Margaret, because she had been faithless to him. Virginal, he had loved her; virginal, he would hate her for her betrayal of his love. He would avenge her weakness by proving his strength.

Presently he looked up from the champagne and gazed round the ballroom. To his surprise he saw that, while he had been dreaming of the past, the room had completely filled, as François had forecast. Every chair at every table was occupied, and newcomers, who were still arriving, had to stand aganist the mirrors or take themselves off to the gaming rooms. Among those present were some who had often frequented the Casino in the past—Marilys, Thionnet, Gallifet, Cazeaux, the Comte de Saramon, and others.

François moved among the tables and exchanged words with his guests. His face was wreathed in smiles—and why not when one considered how much money the Casino was taking?—but none who did not know him could have realized that fact, for since the saber cut had sliced open his left cheek his lined, weather-beaten old face, which never had been angelic, now looked positively ferocious, an impression that his rasping voice and blistering language did not help to mitigate. But the old rascal was too well known and affectionately liked for anyone to heed his bark. There were shouts of: "Hurry up with the performance, old soldier. We haven't come here to see your face."

"I know what you have come to see, and it isn't anyone's *face*," François bellowed back, amid roars of laughter.

"Then get on with the show."

"Patience, messieurs. All in good time. All in good time. The longer you have to wait, the more you will appreciate what I am offering you tonight."

"Who is the dancer, François? Tell us her name."

"If I told you her name she would no longer be a mystery."

"She would still be as beautiful."

"But not so provoking."

As the hour wore on the excitement mounted. The hubbub became terrific as the men shouted for the new dancer, though they well knew that François's plans were not to be hurried on by a single minute. But finally François gave a signal. There was a cheer from everyone who knew what it portended. The band struck a barbaric chord, and the performance began.

Duncan was presently amused by noticing an essential difference between the new ballet and the dozens that had preceded it over a period of years. Hitherto the chief attraction of the dances had rested in the nudity of the dancers, but tonight the ballet master (whom everyone suspected was François himself) had conceived an entirely new techique for provoking excitement. Instead of appearing as a fully dressed ballet, as in the past, tonight the dancers appeared clad in diaphanous draperies that titillated the senses by concealing much and suggesting more. Those who had not recently visited the Casino anticipated the speedy discard of these draperies. Instead, during the progress of the dance the mulattoes reversed the usual procedure, and to the accompaniment of groans of disappointment gradually attired themselves in garments that successively covered more and more of their lovely bodies.

With a crashing discord the dance finished; the girls disappeared. From different parts of the ballroom there were loud shouts of disapproval and calls for François. François appeared, his face alight with malicious amusement. With a wave of his hand he commanded silence.

"Messieurs, I am delighted to see some familiar faces in the ballroom tonight, and to know that the slight entertainment with which I try to amuse my audience—"

"Is being appreciated," chanted several voices.

But others called out: "Is *not* being appreciated."

"Quite right, messieurs. But now—"

"I have a surprise for you," the old habitués shouted.

"But yes, messieurs, as a special surprise I am going—"

"To present an entirely new and unique entertainment," his guests finished for him.

"The last dance was unique enough," loudly growled Legrand, who had not visited the Casino for months.

His remark was greeted by loud laughter.

"Get on with the dance, old man," Cezeaux shouted.

"I will, messieurs. Messieurs, the *Danse Extase.*"

At François's signal many candles in the body of the room were snuffed out. The band struck up; the ballet entered, carrying candles shielded by silks of different colors. These they placed upon the floor and retired. There was a moment's silence. As the band blared out again a solo dancer entered, swathed in gossamer veils, colored to represent a brightly plumaged hummingbird. With rapid, graceful movements imitative of the bird, she darted from candle to candle, dipping, weaving, and swirling. Now, as she danced about a red-shielded candle, she was a red flame; now a blue mist rising from the ground; now a splash of golden sunlight; now a green pool. With exquisite personality she held her audience entranced, though it was not the dance of perfection they had come to see, but something quite different. She held them until the novelty wore off, and they became restive. Then, with a cunning sense of timing, she began a new movement. As she passed by a red-shaded candle she tossed one of her veils into the air. It writhed this way and that, like a tongue of living flame, until it fell, extinguished, on the floor.

One by one the veils floated in the air, then disappeared. Soon it became possible to glimpse the woman beneath the hummingbird. The music quickened, and with it her movements. Another veil. Another. And another. The lines of her body became clearer. So, too, the color of her flesh. It was almost white. Exciting.

Duncan leaned across the table as he stared at the twisting, turning dancer. Veils still shrouded her head and concealed her face, though her body was now plainly visible beneath the draperies. One more veil fluttered into the air. He wet his dry lips with his tongue. He had only to stretch out an arm to touch one of the tantalizing breasts that now stood out firmly from her body.

Then more veils until her head alone was covered. Every line of her perfect, exquisite body was revealed to his staring eyes, but through a mist that he could not brush away with his hand. He had seen many naked women—white, mulatto, black—in Guy's Hospital, in Edward Dayes' studio, in the Casino François, at voodoo ceremonies. But never one to equal the dancer's, for this woman was a goddess among women; the perfection of exotic desire. Her face! What was it like? Was it as beautiful as her lovely body? It must be. So consummate a body could not have a face that was not faultless. He had to fight against an impulse to snatch at the one remaining veil.

He was unaware that many men present were affected with the same tantalizing curiosity. But one of the drunken men at the next table lost control. He rose unsteadily to his feet, and by extraordinary chance succeeded in catching hold of the veil. The force of his pull spun the dancer around. As she fell against Duncan's table the veil split open. He found himself staring into eyes that were filled with alarm. As soon as she had recovered her balance she covered her face with her hands and disappeared, after knocking over a candle in her hurried flight. The candle set light to its silken shade, and the flames had to be stamped out by a Negro waiter who shuffled onto the dance floor to do so, and jostled the ballet, who had come out for the finale of *Danse Extase*. Most of the diners laughed.

But Duncan stared at the door through which the dancer had disappeared, for he had recognized her as De Saint Just's mistress, Phebe.

CHAPTER FORTY-FOUR

DUNCAN slept well enough that night, but when he awoke the following morning he felt that overnight he had passed another milestone along the road of manhood. Life was strangely different, but he was unable to account for this disturbing sensation, for he could recollect nothing that had taken place between his leaving the small house and his return to make him feel as though he had walked from one world into another. The spring of life within him was bubbling to the surface, seeking an outlet, and Phebe was the divining rod that had penetrated the hard crust of bitter isolation; she was succeeding where the tropics had failed.

Thereafter his thoughts dwelled constantly upon her. Quite clearly he visualized her as he had seen her upon three separate occasions. The first, the second day after his return from Limonade, where he had treated M. de Beaudierre's wife. He saw her walking alongside the foppish De Saint Just, her large, brilliant eyes excited by the knowledge that she was causing a stir among Saint-Domingue society. He saw again her scarlet lips, her white teeth, the cluster of jewels in her corsage, the panther-like walk. Even in a town of beautiful women she had been outstandingly beautiful.

Then the second occasion, when her eyes had become tigerish, and her bold lips had spat at him because he had dared to turn her deserted villa into a temporary dressing station.

Lastly, he saw her again as he had seen her the previous night, with every beautiful line of her body sharply etched against a background of blue-gray smoke and color-shaded candles. Although this particular image was the most vivid, it did not cancel the others. What he really saw was a composite picture, tormentingly real.

During the next few days this vision of Phebe continued to haunt him. When he examined the bodies of his Negro patients he did not see the hairy, black torso of a Dahomey, or the swollen stomach of a pregnant woman, or the diseased back of a youth. He saw the breasts of Phebe, the thighs of Phebe, the gently swelling buttocks of Phebe. He no longer troubled to deny to himself that he desired her more than he had ever desired anything in his life, but he did try to subjugate what was becoming an obsession because he felt degraded that he could feel so intensely for a mulatto, a woman who was the mistress of at least one man, a woman who nightly exposed her naked body to the lusting eyes of white men and black.

On the evening of the third day after his visit to the Casino, Duncan capitulated to his desires. As soon as it was time for the Casino to open he hurried there and looked for François. He noticed at once that François's expression was less jubilant, but before he could comment upon the fact François said:

"What is the matter, lad?"

Duncan started. "What do you mean, François?"

"You look as if you hadn't slept well for several nights. You haven't had another touch of fever?"

"No."

"Then—" François paused. "You've had bad news—from England?"

"How could I?" Duncan demanded bitterly. "Nobody in England knows where I am."

François's face brightened. "Then it must be rum. That doesn't matter much."

Duncan glanced away uneasily. "I haven't touched rum for days."

"Name of God! Then what has come over you? I haven't seen you looking like this since the time you landed at the Cap."

"It is—I want Phebe."

"Phebe!" François stared at his friend, but the hoarse laugh from which Duncan had winced in anticipation was not forthcoming. "Do you mean you want her as your woman?"

"Yes."

"Hell! It is my fault. I promised you a surprise. I put you in the best place for seeing the dancers—though I was offered an extra hundred livres for that table—because I thought you might become interested in that baggage."

"Well, I did, François, so I've come here tonight to see her again. I can't get her out of my thoughts. I want to meet her—"

"I should have known better," François growled. "The fever is always worse when it attacks those who have never had it before. I was a fool, a blundering idiot."

"I tell you I am not suffering from a fever," Duncan protested.

"There are many kinds of fever," François continued uneasily. "What you are suffering from now is woman fever."

"Well?" Duncan challenged. "Haven't you urged me a score of times to find a mistress?"

"Yes, I have, because a man needs a woman to keep him human. But why did you have to choose Phebe?"

"Why not? Isn't she one of the loveliest women you have ever seen?"

"The loveliest," François interrupted.

"And if she is one of your dancers, doesn't that mean that she is agreeable to selling herself?" Duncan demanded impatiently.

The old soldier groaned dismally. "I warned you, Duncan, not to defy nature. Men aren't made for continence, especially in the tropics, which are dangerous to all white men, particularly to the overweak ones, who kill themselves quickly, and the overstrong ones, who resist for so long that eventually they all but explode in consequence."

Duncan glared angrily at the old soldier. "It isn't too late for me to fall in line with other white men, is it?" he rasped.

"Of course it is not," François agreed eagerly. "Haven't I always told you that you could have any girl in this establishment? Tonight you shall have your pick before the other clients—"

"I have made my choice. Phebe."

François shrugged his shoulders despairingly. "She's no longer here, Duncan. You remember that cursed fool tearing the veil from her face—"

"That is how I recognized her. If she isn't here, where is she?"

"You were not the only man who recognized her. The next morning someone told Monsieur de Saint Just that his mistress was dancing at the Casino François. He came here and threatened to kill me if I ever allowed her to enter the place again. I have not seen her since."

"Why did she come here?"

"For the money I paid her, Duncan. Phebe's beauty is eclipsed only by her greed. Since the revolution Monsieur de Saint Just has not been able to give her the same luxuries as in the past."

"Then I'll find her, and buy her love. I'll make my Negro patients pay me more money. I'm going to have her, and to hell with De Saint Just."

François placed his mutilated hand on Duncan's shoulder. "Steady, lad. You must keep calm. Monsieur de Saint Just has left the Cap and taken Phebe with him."

"Where have they gone?"

"Nobody knows."

Duncan stared at the waiters who were giving the ballroom the finishing touches before the arrival of the first guests. François is lying to me, he thought. Fate couldn't be so mean as to rob me for the second time of the woman I want. It wouldn't be fair. If Phebe is no longer to be found, it is because François wants her for himself and is hiding her. The old reprobate. Damn him!

"Where is she, François? Where are you hiding her?"

"I don't know where she is."

191

"You must know. You are hiding her for yourself. Tell me where she is."

"Want her for myself! I shouldn't say no to her—but not at your expense. Have you ever known me to lie to you, lad?"

Duncan did not reply.

"Have you?" François urged. "Do you think I should deceive a man I care for more than any other in the world?"

"No," Duncan admitted bitterly. "Damn De Saint Just! He has always hated me. Why should it have been he who had to rob me?"

"I do not think it was a question of *his* robbing you," François pointed out dryly.

"What does it matter what the cause? I want that woman, François. I must have her."

The old soldier gazed compassionately at Duncan's strained expression. "You have the fever too badly for your own good," he muttered uneasily. "You put me in mind of young Berneron. He was an idealist when he came out to the Colony from France about ten years ago or more. He wasn't going to his marriage bed with sullied lips, he said, not meaning his lips. His friends all laughed at him, but they did not succeed in making him alter his mind. For three years he lived an exemplary life, which is a long time for a man to remain celibate in this country. At last he became affianced to Cazeaux's daughter—a mariage of convenience. A week later he fell in love, and the silly young fool had to choose for his beloved a married woman. He caught the fever so badly that it didn't worry him that she did not care a tittle for him. He lost his head, and pestered the woman so much that his conduct became a scandal. Eventually the husband came to hear what was happening. He threatened to give young Berneron a horsewhipping if he ever spoke to the woman again. That night Berneron forced his way into the house of his beloved, killed her, and then committed suicide over her dead body. That was the end of a nice young man."

"How does his story concern me?" Duncan demanded irritably.

"Because you will lose your senses too, if you are not careful." François shook his grizzled old head. "I tell you, lad, the air of Saint-Domingue is poison to white men. The heat of the sun, the sea air, the moonlight nights, the sound of the drums—they are all bad for a white, especially one from the colder countries. I'll tell you the name of the poison—woman fever. If the fever isn't cured in time something goes wrong with the brain."

"I shall follow her."

"You will not do that yet a while, lad. Not now. Not with the Negroes closing in on the city. I doubt whether you could get past their lines in time."

"They would not touch me if I told them my name. There isn't a Negro who would dare to kill Ti Rouge."

François grunted. "Maybe not, but sometimes the Negroes have a way of killing a white man without finding out who he is. You are not going out on any wild-goose chase if I can prevent it."

"You can't prevent it," Duncan pointed out.

"Yes, I can," François contradicted. "Tonight I am the physician, and you are my patient. You are going to stay here and pick out your own medicine—Cléopâtre or Eléonore or Valentine. Any of those three baggages is capable of curing your fever."

Duncan stayed at the Casino, and for his special benefit François slightly rearranged the dances so that each of the three girls could reveal the full measure of her charms. The old soldier further arranged to sit at Duncan's table and extol upon the particular qualities of each girl. Eléonore was the first of the three to make an appearance.

"Now, lad, keep your eye on that beauty. If you can find a more graceful dancer in all Saint-Domingue, then bring her to me, for I would make her my star girl within the week. She is a haughty-looking wench, that Eléonore, and well she might be, too. Her father was a Spanish grandee, my boy, whose ancestors had been established in Castile for generations. She is fiery, that girl."

Duncan gazed through the haze at the dancing mulatto girl. François was right. The dancer was graceful; her profile bore unmistakable proof of classical Spanish blood. But she was not Phebe.

"She is not Phebe," he protested.

The old soldier shrugged his shoulders. "Then wait for Valentine. She should please you."

Presently Valentine came upon the floor. Although she had not the grace of Eléonore, she had the prettier body; for there was a freshness about her that made her comparable to a frolicsome gazelle.

François's eyes glistened as he eulogized the dancer. "If you want young virginal curves, Duncan, then pick Valentine. She is still shy and simple."

The sight of the slim, chocolate body was a torment to Duncan, but when his gaze reached her face he was repelled by the thick lips, the flat nose, and the crinkly hair, all of which, though light in shade, were of the pure Negroid type.

"Look at her face!" Duncan pointed out resentfully. "Is that a beautiful face?"

"My God!" François stared at his companion. "Is it a face you want, or a body?"

"I want Phebe."

The old soldier vigorously scratched his head. "You want Arcadia," he grumbled.

CHAPTER FORTY-FIVE

IN JUNE 1794 the French commissioners, sure that Saint-Domingue would soon be lost to the Spaniards and English, sailed for France. They left General Laveaux in command. When he learned that rivalry between Jean-François and Toussaint had broken out in open fighting, he sent for Henri Christophe.

"Christophe, you have proved yourself a faithful friend of the Republic."

"I thank you, General.

"Tell me, is it true that Toussaint, who now entitles himself l'Ouverture, was your friend?"

"Is my friend," Christophe corrected.

"Then how come you to be fighting on different sides?"

"Because, General, although we both seek one end, we do so by different paths."

"What is that end?"

"The emancipation of the Negro."

"And the different paths?"

"His was the way of war, mine of peace."

"But the objective has been attained. The National Convention has approved the abolition of all slavery, and the equal citizenship of all men, irrespective of color."

"I know, General. That decree decided me to volunteer for service with the French Republic, because I do not wish to see Saint-Domingue in the hands of England or Spain, for both of them still recognize slavery."

Laveaux had grown old in the service of France. His was a character that subjugates self to duty. As a soldier of France he interpreted that duty as allegiance to the men who ruled France. If he held private opinions unflattering to his republican masters, he carefully stifled them. He studied the strong face of the Negro before him, and was satisfied that he could trust Christophe to execute a secret mission.

"Do you think that Toussaint would have deserted to the Spanish if the decree abolishing slavery had been promulgated earlier?"

"I know he would not."

"In spite of his love for monarchy?" Laveaux asked dryly.

"We Negroes respect our chiefs, and all kings," Christophe replied with dignity. "But to Toussaint one cause was important, as it is to me. The freedom of all black men."

"I see!" Laveaux nodded. "Have you heard of Jean-François's plot to kill Toussaint l'Ouverture?" he asked suddenly.

Christophe scowled. "I have, General. I wish I had been near enough to Toussaint to go to his rescue and punish Jean-François for his treachery. The quarrel was inevitable. Toussaint is a wise and clever man. It is he, and not Jean-François, who should be leading the Negro army. Though, for the sake of France, I am glad he is not."

"I agree," Laveaux said, smiling wryly at the double-edged statement. "But now that France has abolished slavery, why does Toussaint continue to fight against her on behalf of a country that still recognizes slavery? Especially when he has reason to fear a stab in the back from his own allies!"

"I cannot say, General."

"Toussaint l'Ouverture is now fighting against his cause instead of for it. If Spain drives us French from this part of the island the whole of Santo-Domingue will be Spanish, and slavery will flourish again."

"It seems thus to me," Christophe agreed.

Laveaux leaned forward. "Listen carefully to me, Christophe. I do not have to hide from you that Saint-Domingue is desperately hard-pressed. She is attacked on the east by Spain, in the west by England. Internally she is riven by a mulatto army and guerrilla bands of Negro ex-slaves. Even the white inhabitants of the Colony are subdivided into monarchist and republican parties, French and creole parties. Unless I receive reinforcements from France, the Colony of Saint-Domingue will fall into the hands of the English and the Spanish."

"Yes?" Christophe queried noncommittally.

"Such reinforcements are unlikely to be forthcoming. While Frenchmen are busily killing one another, Austria, Prussia, Spain, and England knock at the gates of France. Robespierre has little time to waste upon this small part of the French Empire. I have writen in vain for aid and succor. Saint-Domingue, I repeat, is doomed, unless—"

"Unless?"

"Toussaint l'Ouverture returns to his old allegiance."

Christophe shuffled his feet as he glanced at the floor. "I do not think Toussaint would do that, sir, unless he could be sure that the decree abolishing slavery would not be annulled."

"Why should it be annulled?"

"Other decrees have been annulled."

Laveaux pursed his lips. "Suppose that one could guard against that possibility?"

"How, General?"

"By giving him high rank in the French army—shall we say, a general of brigade? Then, do you think, Christophe, that Toussaint l'Ouverture might consider fighting for the French flag, instead of against it?"

Christophe's eyes shone. "I think he might."

Laveaux toyed with his pen. "Will you undertake such a mission for me, Christophe? If it is successful—" He paused, smiling significantly. "You will not find France ungrateful, Christophe."

In May Toussaint proclaimed his allegiance to France by pulling down the Spanish monarchist flag and hoisting the republican tricolor of France. Within a few weeks of his allying himself to Laveaux, Toussaint had relieved the French general and recovered for France a large part of the northern province that had fallen to the Spaniards. Wherever he appeared the Negroes hailed him as hero and conqueror. Those who had previously served under Jean-François and Biassou hastened to serve under Toussaint l'Ouverture, the man who had sworn to drive the British from the French island of Saint-Domingue.

The rise of Toussaint l'Ouverture inspired the Negroes with passionate jubilation. It did not displease General Laveaux, who was fanatically loyal to France, and therefore ready to use any stratagem likely to drive the hated British troops out of the Colony. But there was one section who regarded with increasing alarm the achievements of the Negro and his alliance with the French general—the mulattoes, who despised the blacks even more than they hated the whites, and who abominated the prospect of having to acknowledge and accept the leadership of a Negro.

Cunning lips spread dissatisfaction among the people of Cap François, where Laveaux had his headquarters. Chocolate-colored faces secretively leaned near the white faces of the *petits blancs*. "Are you going to submit to the orders of a black man, an ex-slave coachman? What do you think of a white general who favors a Negro by making him a brigadier general? If this sort of thing continues, the Negroes will oust the white men from the Colony."

"What can we do about it?" the *petits blancs* asked nervously.

"Do what the slaves did. Revolt. Rise up against this Laveaux. Make him understand that he is in the Colony to fight the English, not to promote ex-slaves into brigadier generals."

"How can we revolt? Laveaux has soldiers to protect him."

"White soldiers," the mulattoes pointed out. "Do you think the white soldiers are anxious to salute black officers? Win them over and they will quickly make General Laveaux understand that he has gone too far. There need be no bloodshed. Talk to the soldiers, and see if they are not of the same opinion."

The white soldiers were of the same opinion. Wasn't Laveaux supposed to be a monarchist at heart? Why should he have promoted Toussaint—another self-proclaimed monarchist—to be general? Was General Laveaux planing a royalist coup, such as the seizing of the island in the name of the cursed brat Louis Capet?

The words loyalty and duty having lost all significance for the sons of revolution, the campaign gained many adherents. In the following March a group of officers was ordered by the mulatto general Villatte to arrest General Laveaux and his intendant, Perroud. That night the drums throbbed loudly. When news of the arrest reached Toussaint l'Ouverture, he called a meeting of his officers.

"The inhabitants of Cap François have revolted," he announced grimly. "General Laveaux and Monsieur Perroud have been arrested."

There was an angry growl from the other men. "General Laveaux is our friend," Christophe said bluntly. "Who has taken his place?"

"Villatte."

Dessalines thumped the table with his clenched fist. His ugly, bestial face glared malignantly. "The cursed mulattoes! They have done this to the General because he made you a brigadier general, Toussaint. They want to keep all the power in their own hands."

"Of course, Dessalines. The mulattoes have always hated us Negroes."

"Not more than I loathe the colored swine," Dessalines shouted.

"Do you propose to do something about it?" Maurepas questioned.

"Undoubtedly," Toussaint agreed decisively. "General Laveaux must be released."

"Damn!" Dessalines exploded. "It is more necessary to punish the mulattoes for their interference than to have Laveaux released. He is of no more use to us. We can do without him."

"There you are mistaken," Toussaint pointed out quietly. "We Negroes are now a powerful party, I agree, but we still need the cooperation of France."

"Why?" Dessalines interrupted contemptuously. "Of what further use to us are the French people?"

"For trade, if for nothing else. You must remember that this is a French colony. If General Laveaux should die, then France would send out another general to take his place. His successor might not be so friendly. We might have to renew our fight for freedom from France, instead of fighting for France against the English."

"You are too softhearted," Dessalines stormed. "Why not let us keep Saint-Domingue for the Negroes? Let us kick out all the whites, French and English alike, and the mulattoes as well. Give me a few thousand men, Toussaint, and I will clear the island of everyone who hasn't a black skin."

"You are a foolish boaster," Christophe interrupted. "You should know that the whites are not so easily defeated."

"Nonsense!" Dessalines sneered. "Because you and Toussaint like that white doctor Ti Rouge, is that any reason why we should believe all white men to be angels and call them brothers?"

"To a point, yes. For the sake of future trade," Christophe replied calmly.

"Trade! Trade! Trade! That is all some of you think of."

"There has been enough argument," Toussaint stated with authority. "I called you together to consult you about the arrest of General Laveaux."

"What do you suggest?" Clervaux asked.

"I'll undertake to release him, but I'll butcher a few mulattoes before I do," Dessalines growled.

"That is why I shall not send you. We may be able to avoid bloodshed."

"How?" asked Maurepas.

"By using threats, Maurepas. If one of us marches with an army to the Cap, Villatte may be willing to listen to reason."

"Am I to go, Toussaint?"

"No, Clervaux. Christophe is the best man to go, because I can trust him to keep his head. Besides, he knows the Cap better than most of us. Will you go, Henri?"

Christophe's eyes shone. "As soon as you say."

"And if you should see Ti Rouge, tell him that I hope he keeps well."

"That man is an Englishman, and one of our enemies," Dessalines growled.

"He may be an Englishman, but he is not an enemy," Toussaint pointed out sternly. "The Negroes could not wish for a truer friend than Ti Rouge."

"Any man who is an enemy of Ti Rouge is an enemy of mine," Christophe added belligerently. "He saved my life."

"So we have often heard," Dessalines muttered as he strode out of the tent.

CHAPTER FORTY-SIX

CHRISTOPHE marched upon Cap François at the head of a formidable force. They were an incongruous body of men, for scarcely two had a like uniform; their arms were as ill assorted. Some carried French muskets, some English, some American, some Spanish. There was even a sprinkling of German-made muskets to be seen. The men marched in ragged formation, and the noise they made was terrific. Still, they were quite unlike the recklessly terrified slaves who had originally revolted against their white masters. They conducted themslves with some discipline and considerable confidence.

General Villatte heard of Christophe's coming, and also the reason for the strength of the army. He assembled his officers and members of the municipality in the audience chamber of the battered Government House, and there confidently awaited the impertinent Negro chief who was proposing to dictate to the Cap authorities what they should or should not do.

Accompanied by his own officers, Christophe marched to Government House. There he was ushered into the audience chamber, an impressive figure in resplendent uniform. He stared insolently at the assembled dignitaries, then saluted perfunctorily.

"Messieurs," he began loudly in a sonorous voice. "I have the honor to bear a letter from Brigadier General Toussaint l'Ouverture with reference to the arrest and imprisonment of General Laveaux, General in Chief of the armies of Saint-Domingue. On behalf of Brigadier General Toussaint l'Ouverture and the officers of the Negro army of Saint-Domingue, this letter demands the instant release and restoration to their posts of General Laveaux and Monsieur Perroud."

"You may leave the letter, Brigadier Christophe, and its contents shall be noted," Villatte sneered. "You will convey to the Brigadier General Toussaint l'Ouverture the direction of the Municipal Assembly that he should concentrate his undoubted abilities upon the military services for which he is responsible, and leave the handling of civil affairs to those who are competent to conduct them in a proper manner."

There were murmurs of approbation from the men assembled about Villatte, but these died away as they glanced at Christophe's angry face. To the accompaniment of his jangling scabbard and spurs he strode toward the men facing him. His huge, stalwart figure was menacing as he towered over them, and his blazing eyes sought to capture and to hold their wavering glances.

"I am not here to bandy words," he declared harshly. "I came here to demand the liberty of our general, not to plead for it."

"By what right?" Villatte asked.

"By right of arms," Christophe retorted. "Outside the walls of this city are several thousand trained soldiers, hardened by years of fighting and loyal to their commander in chief. At a word from me they will attack this city, force the defenses, and march through the streets to the prison where General Laveaux is confined."

"Threats will not turn us from our duty," the mulatto asserted. "Besides, Jean-François could not penetrate the defenses of this city, though he besieged it for months. Why should we fear your succeeding where he failed?"

Christophe laughed grimly. "Because then I was helping to defend the city. And because Jean-François's men were rabble."

"While your men are fighters, as you have already told us," the mulatto gibed.

"Have you forgotten what happened to this city nearly two years ago? Its streets ran with the blood of thousands of its inhabitants. What happened then will happen again if the men who are outside the city come into it. Unless General Laveaux is released it may be you—or you—or you—" with each spat-out word Christophe stabbed a rigid forefinger toward one or another of the men in front of him—"who will die this time."

"The fortifications—" Villatte began uneasily.

"My men would smash down your trumpery fortifications like sugar cane," Christophe sneered. "Take your choice. Restore General Laveaux and Monsieur Perroud, or my men will do so over your bloody carcasses." With every word he spoke his words became more impassioned, his eyes more ferocious. The primeval was uppermost in him, and the men who witnessed the phenomenon of this change realized that the cloak of French veneer had dropped from the shoulders of Christophe, to reveal the naked African.

"We must have time to consider your proposition," mumbled one of the municipal councilors. He had a wife and a fourteen-year-old daughter at home, and a mental picture flashed before him of what might happen to them.

"I make no propositions," Christophe retorted. "I make demands. For time you shall have no more than that necessary to sign the prison releases." He caught hold of the slighter Villatte by his tunic, lifted the man effortlessly, and shook him as he might a dog. "Your choice?"

There were indignant murmurs from the councilors, who regarded Christophe's conduct as an outrage, but not one lifted a hand to assist the mulatto general. They were cowed by the Negro's awe-inspiring presence. They remembered his threats, and the army of men who only awaited a signal to massacre and spoil. Several mulatto officers stepped forward protestingly, but the Negroes behind Christophe smiled grimly and touched their swords. The sullen mulattoes stepped back again.

Christophe released Villatte. "Well?"

"I vote for releasing General Laveaux and Monsieur Perroud," called out the man with wife and daughter.

"And I," seconded another man, who had daughters at home.

"And I," echoed a third, who valued his own skin.

With considerable reluctance the councilors and the rebel officers agreed. Before another hour had passed, Laveaux and Perroud had been released and several minor instigators of the coup imprisoned.

Later Christophe visited Duncan.

"I have just come from Marie Louise," he announced joyfully, after Duncan had made him welcome.

"Then you found your son and heir well."

Christophe laughed happily. "Never have I seen a finer baby than my little François-Ferdinand. He is strong and strapping, like me. He recognized me, Ti Rouge. He caught hold of my finger and smiled. He is the image of me," Christophe went on proudly. "When he grows up he will be as big and strong as me. Then I shall tell him of the white man who brought him into the world, and François-Ferdinand will grow to love Ti Rouge as I do."

"Nonsense!" Duncan muttered.

"It is not nonsense. I do love you, Ti Rouge. So does Marie Louise and so shall François-Ferdinand, or I'll not call him my son." Presently Christophe said: "So you have been having further trouble in the Cap?"

Duncan shrugged his shoulders. "The inhabitants of Saint-Domingue are like the Irish—unhappy unless they are fighting. There's been little peace in the Colony for years now."

"Nor will there be peace again until the English are driven from the island, mulattoes subjugated, and a strong man at the head of the executive. I am sorry, Ti Rouge. When I spoke of the English—"

"There is no need to apologize," Duncan interrupted tonelessly. "I am a man without nationality."

"Don't say that," Christophe urged.

"Why not?"

"I like the British. I am glad you are British."

"But they are your enemies!"

"Yes, and that is why I hope they are driven from the island. I fear the British. But I also respect them. They are good fighters and good tradesmen, and I didn't think that possible. If I obtain any say in the government of this colony, I shall vote for opening up trade with England and America. They make things we need, and could use our products."

"France needs your products too."

"I believe England and America would give us higher prices for cotton, sugar, and coffee."

"Possibly. So you are still a trader at heart, Christophe, even though you are now—what are you? A colonel?"

"A brigadier," Christophe said proudly.

"A brigadier! You have advanced quickly, and your uniform is magnificent," Duncan said, unsmiling, for he knew it would please Christophe to have his rank and uniform praised. "I am glad to know that both my Negro friends are prospering. I hear that Toussaint is the hero of your people."

A reverent expression revealed itself in Christophe's eyes. "Toussaint is a wonderful man, Ti Rouge. Do you know that he is more than fifty years of age, and can still ride faster and farther than any man serving under him? Whenever his men are threatened with danger he goes to

them and fights by their side. That's one reason why he has achieved one victory after another.

"But he is more than just a fighter. When he is not riding from post to post to cheer his men, or drill them, he dictates letters, organizes the cultivation of land, and maintains discipline. He is severe toward idlers and traitors, but is kind and considerate to his enemies. He has saved many white prisoners from death. Even the whites admire and respect him and know that his word is to be trusted."

"I wonder if the Spaniards would agree with you," Duncan murmured.

"Do you reproach him, Ti Rouge?" he questioned, in a voice more hurt than angry. "He had the greater cause to consider—the future of his fellow Negroes. He put us before the Spaniards. I should have done the same," he concluded challengingly.

"So Toussaint is as much a hero to you, Henri, as to any of his men?"

"Yes," the Negro agreed defiantly. "He is to anyone of his own blood."

"I have been told he is a fine orator."

Christophe laughed. "Once he swayed you into saving my life, Ti Rouge, so you should appreciate the power of his voice."

Duncan nodded. "Perhaps I do," he admitted slowly. "I often remember that night and think how strange it is that the slave who pleaded with me to try to save your life is now the acknowledged leader of hundreds of thousands of Negroes—while the *blanc papaloi* with whom he pleaded is one of the dregs of the white people."

The Negro frowned. "You must not speak so of yourself, Ti Rouge. To many Negroes you are a hero only less than Toussaint himself. Why is your voice so bitter tonight? What has happened to you?"

"The trouble is that nothing has happened. I am in one of life's dead ends. Nothing lies ahead of me but a blank wall. I am a piece of human flotsam that has been flung high and dry upon an island that charms a man's senses while robbing him of his soul."

Christophe shook his head in a puzzled mood. "I don't know what you mean. But if there is anything I can do for you—"

Duncan began to shake his head but stopped as he changed his mind. "Perhaps there is something you can do for me, Henri," he admitted. "François tells me I am suffering from fever—"

"You are a physician, Ti Rouge. Can't you cure your fever?"

"I cannot, but there is someone who can. Do you remember De Saint Just?"

"Very well."

"And Phebe—his latest mistress?"

"Yes."

"De Saint Just and Phebe disappeared from Cap François many months ago. I can find nobody who knows where they have gone. If you should have news of them, Henri, would you let me know?"

"Gladly." The Negro looked more puzzled than ever. "But how can De Saint Just cure your fever?"

"De Saint Just cannot—but Phebe can."

Christophe's large white teeth flashed. "Now I begin to understand," he announced with a throaty chuckle.

General Laveaux was grateful to Toussaint for having sent Christophe to the rescue. This gratitude later took a concrete form, for shortly after his liberation Laveaux received news from France of his appointment as Governor General of the Colony. Laveaux's first official act was to appoint Toussaint l'Ouverture his chief aide with the official title of Lieutenant Governor.

Whites and mulattoes alike received this news with stunned amazement. It could not be true that they had to acknowledge as Lieutenant Governor a Negro. Laveaux could not be intending to subject them to the culminating indignity of having to bow low before a black man, of having to present their wives and daughters to a black woman! When it was realized that Toussaint was indeed Lieutenant Governor of the Colony, Cazeaux committed suicide in despair and shame.

Toussaint used his new power to pursue a triple policy—of benefiting the conditions of Negro labor, of recultivating the Colony and restoring it to its past prosperity, and of ending the British invasion.

Shortly afterward an election was held at Cap François to elect deputies to fill the two seats in the Council of Five Hundred that had been allotted to the Colony of Saint-Domingue. Toussaint circulated his wishes: that one of those seats should be occupied by General Laveaux as a signal mark of the Colony's gratitude to the General for his outstanding achievement in saving the Colony from foreign invasion. At the same time he let it be known that if his good friend Laveaux were not elevated to that post of honor he would have much pleasure in burning what remained of the city of Cap François. Of course Laveaux was elected by a large majority and sailed for France. Not until he had left the island did the majority of the Colonials realize that, by his departure, Toussaint l'Ouverture had become commander in chief of the French forces in Saint-Domingue.

However, Santhonax was still left. White and mulatto alike disliked and mistrusted the treacherous commissioner, but at least he was a white man, and, as a commissioner of the motherland, was still vested with some authority. The whites and mulattoes looked to Santhonax to keep Toussaint under control. Such were Santhonax's intentions, for everything had worked out precisely as planned. Under cover of Toussaint's military authority he would govern (and plunder) the Colony as never before.

Alas for Santhonax's hopes! In his machinations he had overlooked one very important point—that two seats in the Council had been allotted to Saint-Domingue. Despite a desperate resistance on his part, Santhonax awoke one morning to find himself elected to the Council by the use of exactly the same ruse that had caused Laveaux's departure for France. So Santhonax sailed back to France, victim of his own craftiness, and Toussaint l'Ouverture came into virtual control of what, eight years previously, had been the richest colony in the new world. Toussaint l'Ouverture, Negro and ex-slave. The First of the Blacks! By uncanny foresight and a deft use of circumstance, those wild, seemingly impossible dreams (and they had been no more) had come true. Why, therefore, should he not dream again? A dream of an island that was no longer a French colony, but a free, independent Negro country.

CHAPTER FORTY-SEVEN

LATE in the day, when the heat was tempered by the cooling wind from the mountains, Captain Beard, master of the *May Queen of London* and Nathaniel Martin, an American, manager of Saint-Domingue's branch of the firm of Roncin & Co., drove from the warehouse to the rue St. Louis, where Stewart had his house. Beard had not touched at the island since '89—since that morning twelve years ago when he had brought the *Pride of Bristol*, and a wretched young fugitive from London, into harbor. With astonishment and indignation he observed, along the once familiar streets, the scars left from the sack of the town by the black troops. Many of the beautiful houses that he remembered from past visits were no longer inhabited. Some were just a mass of blackened rubble, concealed by greedy tropical vegetation. Others still stood, open to all winds. Others, again, had been demolished to provide large sites for the erection of temporary houses for the use of the American and other foreign merchants who had landed in the city soon after Toussaint had decreed a measure of free trade. Smaller sites had been used for the erection of ugly little shops owned and frequented by Negroes.

In striking contrast were those houses that the conflagration had spared. These houses still stood as mute reminders of a glorious past, their paintwork fresh, their windows curtained, and their canopied balconies occupied. But no longer by white people. Fat, gaudily dressed Negro women sat on gilt chairs and stared languidly down, waving handkerchiefs at their neighbors or at any friends who passed along the street below.

Toward the center of the town as on the quays, the preponderance of black faces over colored and white was marked. Uniforms flashed in every direction, while many civilians were dressed in clothes that were obviously luxurious and modish, though, to Beard's way of thinking, utterly incongruous. Yet there were a number of white people who, because of their fair skins, blue eyes, and blond hair, were obviously neither French nor creoles. One or two, indeed, waved to Martin and called out a greeting to him in English.

"Are there many Americans at Cap François?" Beard asked at last.

"Quite a number, Captain. Several of the younger men who arrived here as bachelors have subsequently married mulatto women." Observing Beard's expression, Martin continued: "I suppose mulattoes were beyond the pale when you were last here?"

"Yes," Beard replied bluntly.

"All that nonsense has been dropped. In Saint-Domingue white, colored, and black now mix in absolute equality—except that the Negroes hold nearly all the important offices," Martin continued with a chuckle. "I don't say that I personally would care to marry a Negress, or even a mulatto, but I believe in minding my own business—and business is my business, if you follow me, Captain—and what other people do is their affair, not mine. If one of my friends marries a mulatto, well, I remain as friendly with the wife as if she had been a white woman. Same with the Negroes now. I dine with Negroes, do business with them, even play games with them. I sometimes play billiards with Governor General Toussaint or General Christophe."

"Last time I was here they was slaves," Beard muttered in a bewildered voice. "How is it that an American is ready to mix with slaves? I thought you was against the abolition of slavery."

"In the north we Yankees are for the abolition of slavery. It is the southerners who regard slavery as an American institution."

The Captain pulled at his lower lip. "I have no opinion about the rights and wrongs of slavery, but I don't like the idea of a white man having to pull his forelock to a bloody black."

Martin chuckled. "Then you are fortunate in not having to live in Saint-Domingue. Otherwise, one of the Negro generals would soon find an excuse for having you executed. But here we are."

Beard did not move. He stared at the four-story building opposite which they had stopped. In the past he had seen other, finer buildings, but not many. Every upper window opened its brightly colored shutters onto a stone balcony; the twin doors that comprised the main entrance were of carved mahogany decorated with iron scrollwork; masses of potted blooms filled the shallow entrance porch; the curtains that draped the lower windows were sumptuous. The house obviously belonged to a man of wealth.

"What's this place, mister?"

"Stewart's house."

"Duncan Stewart's house!" Beard laughed hoarsely. "All right, mister. It's a good joke, and I ain't a man not to like a bit of fun now and then. And the more I think about it the funnier it is. Duncan Stewart's house! Ho! Ho! Ho!" Beard's stentorian laughter echoed along the street. Many of the Negroes near by started to laugh too, for laughter is infectious among the black people.

"But I assure you, Captain, that I am not joking."

Beard's laughter slowly died away. "But Stewart was penniless when he landed here."

"No doubt, but he befriended the Negroes before they revolted. Gratitude is a characteristic of the Negro. When the men whose lives he had saved in the past came into power, they did not forget the white physician who had been insulted by men of his own color. They heaped rewards upon him, including this house. Once it belonged to a wealthy planter by the name of Cazeaux, who committed suicide some years ago, so Toussaint forced the city councilors to buy the place from the heirs and present it to Stewart. Now he is physician to the Governor General, General Christophe, General Clervaux, General Dessalines, and nearly all the important Negroes in the northern province."

Like a man lost in dreams Beard stepped out of the fiacre and walked slowly toward the entrance, muttering something to himself.

In answer to Martin's knock the doors were opened by an immense Negress whose fat face beamed a welcome when she recognized Martin.

"Good afternoon, sir," she said in slurring English.

"Good afternoon, Suzanne. Is Mr. Stewart in?"

"No, sir, Mist' Duncan is done gone to the Hôtel de la République. He ain't reckoned for you to come so soon."

"Probably not. We got through our business sooner than we expected. Suzanne, your English improves every time I come here. I suspect you have been seeing too much of that good-for-nothing Jonas. Before you know where you are he will be wheedling you into coming to take care of me instead of Mr. Duncan, and then what would Mr. Duncan say?"

Suzanne laughed self-consciously. "Lord, sir, you do say sich things! I wouldn't leave Mist' Duncan not for all de niggers in town."

"Good for you, Suzanne. Mr. Duncan needs somebody to look after him. Now we'll follow right after him to the hotel."

The two men turned. Martin hailed another fiacre. As soon as they were on their way Martin told Beard something of Suzanne's history and continued: "When I came here from America I brought Jonas with me. He was a runaway slave from South Carolina who, as he was passing by, saved one of my father's stallions from being burned to death. Father was so grateful that he purchased Jonas's freedom and made him my servant. He has been with me ever since. He is too lazy to learn the bastard French that the Negroes here talk, so he has taught Suzanne to speak English instead, in order to enjoy her company."

Presently they reached the Hôtel de la République. At one of the long tables sat five full-blooded Negroes, three of them in military uniform. Next to them sat three white men talking in English, two of whom Beard judged, by their accent, to be American, and the third an Irishman. Beyond the American sat some creoles, beyond the creoles several Englishmen and a few light-colored mulattoes. Other tables were equally mixed, so that one heard simultaneously pure French, the thick-lipped sibilant patois of the Negro, the American drawl, and the broad vowels and clipped consonants of the British.

Across the far side of the room were open doors through which one could see a billiard table and two men, one black and the other white. As the white man bent over the table to make a stroke Beard recognized Duncan, not by the profile, for the face was mature and burned a deep brown, but by the red hair, which was still the brilliant, untidy mop the captain remembered on board the *Pride of Bristol*.

"Come along, Captain. Duncan is playing billiards with His Excellency the Governor." Martin led the way through the crowded tables to the adjoining room, which they entered quietly. As they did so Toussaint applauded Duncan.

"Bravo, Ti Rouge! Another break of nine cannons, which makes game. I cannot keep pace with your skill. I shall soon be demanding that you set me forward twenty-five." Looking round, the Negro recognized Martin. "Ah! Your friend Monsieur Martin has arrived."

Duncan turned quickly and saw Beard. He tossed his cue to the Negro marker and hurried across to the Captain, both hands outstretched.

"Welcome back to Saint-Domingue, Captain!" he greeted, his face reddening with pleasure, and then with embarrassment as a tumult of memories quickened his breathing. "It's been— I looked to see you again long before this."

"Spent most of the time on a Pacific island," he reported dryly. "The old *Pride of Bristol* what brought you here was wrecked, and I was there for nigh on eight years before I was rescued by His Majesty's sloop *Favourite*. When I got back to England I was given the *May Queen* with a cargo for Saint Domingyew, and here I am."

"And welcome, too." Duncan turned to face Toussaint. "Your Excellency, may I have the honor of presenting my friend Captain Tom Beard, who has landed here today with a cargo for Roncin's."

"Any friend of yours, Ti Rouge, is a welcome visitor," Toussaint said cordially, in halting English, as he held out his hand.

Beard found himself facing a man of medium stature who, because of his upright bearing and his recently acquired habit of standing with his shoulders squared, looked both taller and broader than, in actual fact, he was. His face was very black, but smaller than many Negro faces. His nose, though pronouncedly broad, was finer than most Negro noses. So were his lips. His black curly hair was streaked with gray. The general expression of the face was, at that moment, kindly, but, taking everything into consideration, the Captain thought, rather unfathomable. Meanwhile, was he supposed to shake the Negro's hand? He had never shaken hands with a nigger, and he didn't feel disposed to start doing so at his time of life—one can't teach an old dog new tricks—but if he didn't it might prove awkward for Duncan Stewart, who apparently didn't object to calling the Negro "Your Excellency," and awkward for the American, Nathaniel Martin—rather a nice fellow for an American—and after all, business was business. There would be a fine to-do in London if it reached the ears of the owners that Captain Beard of the *May Queen* had insulted the Governor General of Saint-Domingue. Beard reluctantly pulled off his blue cap and shook the proffered hand.

"Thank you, mister," he growled.

"Trade is deeferent now, *mon commandant*," Toussaint continued easily. "Once upon a time very few sheeps other than French, or sheeps from Santo Domingo, were allowed to land cargoes here, but since the revolution, and particularly since your clever, daring seamen have captured so many French vessels, and even prevented neutrals from coming calling, *alors!* we are glad even to have Engleesh cargoes. Tell me, *mon commandant*, what is the latest news from Europe? Is Napoleon still busy with his European wars?"

Beard rubbed his chin. "I don't know much about what is happening in Europe, but the people of Kent seem fair upset that old Bony intends to try and land there one day."

"Surely your new hero, Admiral Nelson, will nevair allow that to happen? Is it not *vrai* that Nelson has recently won a big naval victory over *les Danois*—" Toussaint glanced at Duncan.

"The Danes," Duncan interpreted.

"Aye! He showed them furriners they'd best leave England in peace.

But for all that, the Kentish people are building stone forts along the coast, and a canal behind to hold old Bony up if he tries any of his frog-eating tricks on us English."

"So the British fear the power of Bonaparte?" the Negro commented.

"The British don't fear no plaguy furriners," Beard retorted wrathfully.

Toussaint's eyes twinkled. "That I can well believe, *mon commandant*. I have fought against them so I can appreciate their fighting qualities. But Napoleon has other enemies besides the British: *les Russes*—ah, yes, the Rooshians, the—the Germans, the *Italiens*, and *les Autrichiens*—Surely so many enemies keep the armies of the First Consul busy?"

"I suppose so," Beard admitted, but in so dubious a voice that Toussaint realized that the seaman was almost entirely ignorant of what was really happening in Europe. He sighed, and turning to Duncan, said in French: "Perhaps the wish is father to the thought, Ti Rouge. It would be pleasant to hear that the First Consul was too occupied with European affairs to concern himself with what is happening in the West Indies. Within the next few days, my friend, I shall be publishing an important document—"

"The constitution?"

"Yes. That constitution, besides creating me Governor General for life, will mean the virtual independence of Saint-Domingue." He was quick to observe the fleeting expression on Duncan's face. "You share Christophe's doubts as to the wisdom of that move?" he accused.

"How can I do otherwise, Excellency? France has a powerful army and a strong leader. If the First Consul felt provoked by such a declaration of independence, he might send an army to reconquer the island."

"Against my Negro warriors?"

"Yes, Excellency."

"You English sent an army to conquer us, and we repelled it."

"The English force was little more than an expedition, a halfhearted attempt—too little, too late. France would strike with determination. Where the English sent hundreds of soldiers, France would send thousands."

"There are thousands of Negroes in my army. But there, Ti Rouge," Toussaint continued, appreciating Duncan's embarrassment. "I have listened to all your arguments from Christophe's mouth. He is no coward, as we both know, yet he has a persistent respect for French might that I do not share. Not because I underrate the French, Ti Rouge, but because I respect the English more."

"The English?"

"Yes. England and France are at war. As long as an English navy sails the Atlantic Ocean France cannot send an army to recover Saint-Domingue. And now that I am encouraging trade with England, she will be very pleased to see that France does not have an opportunity of regaining her lost possession, for France's gain would be Britain's loss."

"True. But England and France will not fight forever."

"By that time the independence of Saint-Domingue will be an accomplished fact," Toussaint said.

"From what one hears of Napoleon Bonaparte, he is not a man to relinquish French possessions so easily."

"Even if England and France should sign a treaty of peace, even if the First Consul could spare an army from Europe, I should still have faith in my Negroes, Ti Rouge. But come, we are being rude to your guests, and I have an appointment with my generals. Good-by, Ti Rouge. We must play another game of billiards very soon; I shall not rest content until I have defeated you again."

Toussaint turned to Beard. "I bid you good day, Capitaine Beard," he greeted in English. "And wish you many more treeps to Saint-Domingue."

"I won't say no to coming again."

"And you, too, Monsieur Martin, I shall hope to see again soon." With a courteous half salute of his hand, which embraced all three men, Toussaint left the billard room. As soon as he had gone Martin said: "I'll leave you two Britishers alone. Beasley is outside. I want to speak to him about the review next week. See you later, Duncan."

Duncan turned to Beard. "The usual, Captain?"

"Aye, mister. I've traveled the world over, but I've yet to find a better drink than rum."

Duncan gave an order to the Negro waiter, then led the way to a sofa at the far end of the room where the clamor from the salon was less noticeable. The two men sat down. "Tell me about England."

Beard gazed into eyes that stared at him with passionate intensity from a lean, brown face.

"Homesick, lad?"

Duncan laughed mirthlessly. "The sound of the old cockney lingo does something to one." His voice became urgent. "Have you seen her, Captain?"

"Aye, I've seen her, but not until a few months ago."

"Where? At home? In Leicester Fields? Did you speak to her? Did you tell her about me? Did she ask after me? Did she just say one word to prove she wasn't entirely heartless? Did she—"

"Steady, my boy. I've said that I only saw her a few months ago. Twelve years is a long time for a woman—half her love life. You couldn't expect a woman to spend her years mourning a ghost, could you?"

"Good God! I'm no ghost," Duncan exclaimed sharply.

"How was she to know that?"

"Of course not. I scarcely know what I am saying. Why should I expect her to remain single on my account? Why should I?" he repeated, as if to reassure himself. "Besides, if she had really loved me she would not have intrigued with that cursed Frenchman. But did she say anything about me? Did she ask any questions? Is she still beautiful? Is her laughter as musical as ever? Is she still a spitfire?"

"I did not speak to her."

"But you saw her?"

"Aye, I saw her, my boy, but from a distance. I was in the pit. And she was on the stage."

"The stage! In God's name, what are you trying to tell me?"

"That your Margaret Anderson is now the famous Eulalia," Beard replied gruffly. "The harum-scarum witch of Drury Lane. She's your Margaret, and though it ain't none of my business, it's my opinion that there French lover of hers did you a good turn instead of a bad one." The Captain spat his disgust, expertly, into the nearest spittoon.

CHAPTER FORTY-EIGHT

THE fame of Eulalia had reached even Cap François. Since Toussaint had opened up trade with Britain, several Englishmen had taken to living in Saint-Domingue. These English residents frequently received parcels of magazines and news sheets from London which they gladly passed on to Duncan after reading.

Eulalia—Margaret! Margaret—Eulalia! Margaret, daughter of Dr. Anderson, the conventional father whose persistent refusal to allow his young daughters to visit a playhouse was as characteristic as his own partiality for the drama. Eulalia, the notorious actress whose association with the rakes of London society was the butt of the pamphleteers, the caricaturists, and the gossip mongers of the scandalous daily sheets!

"Are you still in love with her, lad?"

Duncan took time to answer, uneasily: "I don't know, Captain. There are times when I cannot forget her. I remember how she used to torment and tease me, quarrel with me, and—and kiss me." He turned an uncertain face toward his companion. "At other times she means nothing to me. Then I think of her only as a stepsister—one of three stepsisters—and she means no more to me than the other two. Especially Jean. Although I loved Margaret, I always liked Jean. She was so quiet and reserved. She never quarreled with me or said cruel things. Nor did Elizabeth, but then Elizabeth was such a child—" He stopped, to add in embarrassed surprise: "Why am I telling you all these things?"

"Because I have reminded you of home. You're homesick, just as you were on the old *Pride of Bristol*."

"I am not homesick," Duncan contradicted, a little too much decision in his voice. "I wouldn't return to England even if I could. This island is my home now."

Beard laughed his unbelief. "You can believe that if you like. I don't. You would return home tomorrow if you thought Miss Margaret wanted you back."

"No." Then again, in a louder voice, as if to make certain that he would not be misunderstood: "No."

The captain stared keenly at the face of the younger man. "There's something else worrying you."

Duncan swallowed down his rum. "Very well, there is, and it's a woman! Another woman! A woman ten times more beautiful than Margaret Anderson," Duncan continued, defiant, challenging. "A woman with eyes to drive a man to hell, with the face of Helen of Troy and the body of Cleopatra."

"Gawd!" Beard muttered, enviously, as he appreciated Duncan's meaning without comprehending his metaphors. "Who is she? She sounds like one of the Casino women."

"She's a mulatto."

"Then, swelp me! She'll be a hot-blooded baggage." A salacious grin. "She's your woman—"

"I don't know where she is, Captain. She has disappeared, with her lover, De Saint Just."

"Him that owned a coffee plantation? One of the richest men on the island?" Beard interrupted.

"Yes. He took her away some years ago. Nobody has seen or heard anything of either of them since. Toussaint promised to return the plantation to him providing he returned to Cap François to claim it, but he never came, and Toussaint granted the land to Christophe. Ever since I last saw her I have wanted her. Perhaps that's why I can sometimes forget Margaret. Phebe has taken her place."

"If I was you I should find another woman," Beard advised bluntly.

"That is what François suggests, but I don't want any other woman."

"You seem to be badly struck, lad, and the best thing you can do is to take yourself off to a cooler climate."

"You have been talking to François," Duncan accused.

"If you mean that old soldier what keeps the Casino, I haven't seen him since I was last here, though Mr. Martin said something about going there tonight."

"Yes, I want you both to be my guests." Duncan passed a weary hand over his eyes. "I have no right to bore you with my troubles, Captain."

"My shoulders are broad enough to carry the worries of half a dozen people," Beard joked. Then, "All the same, Mr. Stewart, you have been here twelve years now, and that's too long for any man to live in a festering heathen land. Why not sail with me when I go?"

Duncan shook his head, although he felt immensely grateful to Beard for his offer. "No, Captain, I meant what I said just now about being unwilling to leave Saint-Domingue. I belong here now, and despite what I have been telling you about Margaret and Phebe, I am not unhappy. After all, I have been fortunate. I arrived here a penniless student of medicine. Now I own a fine house—"

"A fine house, d'you call it? It's well-nigh a blasted palace."

"Scarcely that, but it is quite a sumptuous home. I am moderately wealthy, and becoming wealthier every day, and I am a physician and surgeon of note, not only here in Saint-Domingue but in America as well. One American physician who came to this island a few months ago has written a short book about my surgery. All the leading Negroes are patients of mine, and all the richest mulattoes. Even some of the white residents, who used to look upon me as something less than dirt, call me in if they're really ill. That's a record to be proud of, isn't it, Captain?"

"Yes."

"Not that success is all that keeps me here. Even if I were still living in the little house near the river I should choose to stay in Saint-Domingue. Captain, a revolutionary chapter in the history of the world is being written in this island. Toussaint is trying to fuse a score of races into one, the Saint-Dominguan Negro; a score of religions into one: Roman Catholicism. But the Negro has two religions, the Catholicism of the white man and the pagan beliefs of Africa. Today he genuflects to Jesus Christ. Tomorrow he sacrifices a white goat to Damballa, the serpent. Today the Catholic religion is supreme, for Toussaint is a devoted and sincere Christian and not solely because he fears the influence of voodoo. But tomorrow—what? In the answer to that question lies the future of Saint-Domingue," Duncan stated didactically. "What do you think, Captain?"

"That it's time for more rum," Beard replied, rather bemused by Duncan's unusual eloquence.

CHAPTER FORTY-NINE

THAT night at the Casino, Beard swore loudly with astonishment. By the Beard of the Prophet! Mr. Stewart was right. The place had changed.

He stared round. When he had last visited the Casino the only black people in the ballroom were the waiters and the dancers. But now many of the tables were occupied by Negroes in resplendent military uniforms. They sat there as the whites had sat in the old days, drinking, smoking, singing, shouting, caressing mulatto women, hammering on the tables for waiters, staring with lustful eyes at the sinuous torsos of the naked dancers. Mulattoes, too, sat at some of the tables, dressed in the latest fashion, talking and laughing loudly, ogling the women at other tables. Lastly, Beard noted, there were also white men present. Fewer in number than the Negroes, but more than the mulattoes. Of them more than half were foreigners; Americans, Germans, some British. The remainder were French—one-time *petits blancs* who, in the chaos of civil war, had snatched positions for themselves, and now, in their turn, stared contemptuously at the new *petits blancs*, who were few in number, for most minor jobs were now held by Negroes or mulattoes.

Duncan looked around for François, but the old soldier was nowhere to be seen. A waiter hurried forward.

"Your usual table is free, monsieur." As Duncan and his two guests crossed the floor, Duncan was welcomed upon all sides. White, mulatto, Negro, all greeted Duncan. Some as friends, some as patients. Some (the white) with camaraderie. Others (the Negroes) with respect. Captain Beard marveled, and realized that Duncan was probably wise to stay in Saint-Domingue. Any man would be a fool willingly to leave a place where he was so obviously a respected and notable citizen.

"Where is François?" Duncan asked the waiter as they reached the reserved table.

"He left a message for you, monsieur, that he would not be long."

Duncan ordered rum to be served, then turned to Beard. "You were saying earlier, Captain, that on your last visit to the Casino all Cap François society was present. Well, all Cap François society is here tonight, too, but as you can see for yourself, it is a mixed society. Do you see the table beneath that picture of Greek heroes? Look at the man on the right, facing us. The uglier one."

"Devil take them! They are both ugly," Beard growled. "But perhaps you are right," he conceded presently, as he studied the characteristics of the face on the other side of the room—thick blubbery lips, broad nose, flashing teeth, and large, dark, white-rimmed eyes. "He's a real buck nigger. I can knock out most men with my fist, but if he came at me aboard the *May Queen* I wouldn't stand on me reputation; I'd clout him with a belaying pin, and ask questions afterward. What is he? A king of somewhere or other?"

"He's General Dessalines. 'Butcher' Dessalines. Except for Toussaint, he has more influence than any other man on the island."

Beard picked his nose. "Toussaint ain't such a bad-looking cuss now, but that other devil—I like the looks of the woman with him, even if she ain't no chicken."

"She isn't. She was probably here the last time you came. Her name is Louise Nanette. At that time she was a free-lance, sought after by every wealthy white man. As times grew bad, and she grew older, she sank lower and lower. Then Dessalines saw her and took her away from the *petit blancs*. He won't keep her long. Then she will have to start her downward course again."

"Serves the trollop right!" Beard exclaimed righteously, who despised all such ladies although he gladly slept the night with them. "What's the man at the next table? Another general?"

"General Christophe."

Beard studied Christophe with added interest. Although the Negro was not so immense as Dessalines, he was still an imposing man. His shoulders and chest were broad, and his massive arms looked capable of great strength. His face, though possessing the usual Negroid characteristics, was finer than Dessalines's. His chin was decisive, his eyes steady, intelligent.

"I remember that name, Mr. Stewart. And the face."

Duncan laughed dryly. "Then you must have been less drunk than Garreau and I thought you were, Captain. Do you recollect the man who served us with drinks at the Hôtel de la Couronne?"

"We had drinks at a number of hotels. Aye, that I do now, for it comes back to me. Didn't he also attend us here at the Casino?"

"He did. Now he is a general, and commandant of this town and the surrounding district. He has done well for himself."

"I think he deserves his success," Martin interpolated.

"Undoubtedly, Nat," Duncan agreed. "In my opinion Henri Christophe has the shrewdest brain in the island."

"Better than Toussaint's?"

"I think so. Toussaint allows his idealism to sway his judgment. Christophe has as many ideals, but has also the more practical approach to them." Duncan turned back to Beard. "You see the mulatto at the same table?"

The seaman glanced at Christophe's companion, who was fair-skinned, slight in build, and dapper in appearance.

"A bit of a spark, isn't he?"

"Yes. His name is Pompée Valentin Vastey."

Beard chuckled loudly. "No wonder he's a dandy with a name like that."

"Vastey is one of Christophe's secretaries, and another astute individual. The two mulattoes sitting at the third table on Christophe's right are two old enemies of Toussaint's, Rigaud and Pétion. If their wishes could kill, Dessalines would be a dead man by now. And there sits Paul l'Ouverture, brother of Toussaint." Duncan nodded to another part of the ballroom. "Here comes François."

Beard glanced across the room. He had a good memory for faces, and recollected the old soldier who had welcomed him to the Casino François twelve years previously. He thought that François's grizzled head was grayer, his face more lined, his shoulders a little bowed.

François greeted the party boisterously. Duncan looked at him. There was an air of mystery about the old soldier that aroused the Scot's suspicions. "What mischief are you hatching?"

"No mischief, Duncan. I want your advice about a new dancer. It will all depend upon your opinion of her as to whether I hire her or not."

This answer did not satisfy Duncan. "That is the first time I have known you to seek someone else's opinion where a woman is concerned. Are you still trying to find a remedy for tropical fever?"

François looked embarrassed. "It isn't natural for a man to have lived to your age without having had pleasure from a woman," he grumbled. "But you'll come upstairs?" he urged.

"What do you say, Nat?"

"Count me in. I should hate to miss something good."

Duncan then explained to the captain the gist of the conversation with François. When he heard of the reason Beard immediately announced his willingness to follow wherever Duncan led.

"I'll come back for you later," François told Duncan. "About the middle of the entertainment."

During the next hour the three men thoroughly enjoyed themselves. François, for a man who had spent the best part of his life soldiering, possessed a positive genius for inventing provocative ballets—probably based upon shows he had seen during his campaigns, argued his critics. Whenever taxed about the justification for this accusation, he merely laughed and said nothing.

Tonight his girls performed a ballet that he announced as "Evolution, or Completing the Circle." The first scene was one representing the Garden of Eden. A log of wood was the Tree, a girl, with rouged breasts and a skirt of green leaves, was the apple. Both Eve and Adam were naked. Six other girls, dressed in colored silks, danced about in Indian file, as the serpent. The ballet closely followed the story of the temptation of Adam.

The next scene represented mankind in the stone age, in which the ladies of the ballet wore animal skins round their waists. In the third scene waist and breasts were clothed, and the audience realized that they were witnessing a caricatured history of mankind told in ballet. Duncan's eyes twinkled as he began to appreciate François cynical humor. No doubt the girls would continue to wear more and more clothes until the present was arrived at, the circle completed, and the dancers were once more naked. Duncan judged the circle to be almost complete when François returned to their table.

"Are you ready, lad?"

The three men rose and followed François out of the ballroom, up the ornate staircase that led to the floors above, and into a dimly lit, over-decorated bedroom. The bed had been pushed to one side, and three chairs occupied its place. A table, with a bottle of rum and tankards on it, was there, too. From below they heard, quite loudly, the clamor from the ballroom and the noise of the band tuning their instruments.

François's hoarse voice gave an explanation for the chairs.

"You will see the finish of the ballet up here. It will be danced exactly as before, but by different dancers."

"Why?" the American asked.

"You will see," François replied as the music struck up below.

From a door communicating with the next bedroom three dancers glided out, swathed in veils. They danced, with sinuous movements, in time with the music below. Presently they each unwound a veil, which was tossed into the air. Then a second veil, and the third.

Duncan was disappointed with François's lack of originality. The dance of the veils had been performed many times at the Casino. The only reason he could think of for François's mysterious manner was the discovery of another girl who, introduced to him in the dance Phebe had once made famous, might affect him in the same way. Duncan chuckled dryly; François was an intriguing old reprobate, but his scheme was doomed to failure. There was not another Phebe in the world.

The veils disappeared one by one until the girls' breasts were bared. Beard chuckled lewdly. Martin shrugged his shoulders, but Duncan leaned forward and gripped the arms of his chair. In spite of his conviction he felt obliged to admit to himself that the body of the swathed dancer before him did, to some extent, remind him of the one that had haunted his dreams for years. Its curves were more pronounced, fuller, perhaps, than Phebe's, but they were almost as voluptuous, almost as enticing. His excitement mounted as more veils were discarded, until just as Phebe had been, all three dancers were naked save for their heads, which remained entirely concealed.

Duncan barely glanced at the dancers in front of Beard and Martin. All three girls were mulattoes, all three had fine, attractive figures, but he had eyes only for the one girl who reminded him of Phebe. He watched her dance closer to him, her veiled head thrust forward to within inches of his. He half rose, but she pushed him back into the chair, and he heard the sound of her low laughter. She thrust one end of a veil into his hands, and when he grasped it she pirouetted away from him, unwinding it. With increasing clearness he saw crimsoned lips and large eyes, which more and more resembled Phebe's. Yet it could not be she. . . . A barbaric clash of music, a final pirouette, and the last fold of the veil dropped away from the dancer's face. She was Phebe. A rounder, fuller Phebe, but a Phebe more beautiful, more desirable than ever.

"Phebe!"

At the sound of his voice her crimson lips parted; her eyes flashed him a welcome. She ran forward, knelt on the floor, leaned against his knees in a half-twisted position, and by winding a willowy arm round his neck, forced his head down so that she could imprison his lips with hers.

"Do you love Phebe, Ti Rouge?" she whispered presently.

"Yes—no—the devil! I don't know what I'm saying," he exclaimed, distraught. "You are beautiful, Phebe. More beautiful than ever." He encircled her supple, yielding waist with his arms. "Of course I love you, Phebe. I have loved you for years, ever since I saw you dance."

"François has promised to let me dance at the Casino."

"But De Saint Just—"

Her face darkened with fury. "He is a beast. I have left him. I never want to see him again."

"Where is he?"

"What does that matter? I don't care for him any more. He is penniless. He has no money to buy food, let alone the beautiful things I must have."

"Is that why you have left him—because he is penniless?"

"Of course."

When she felt him stiffen, she laughed mockingly and pressed her body against his.

"Aren't my kisses worth anything? Does the innkeeper give away his finest vintage wines? Why should I give my love for nothing? When Phebe loves, she loves as no other woman, Ti Rouge."

His impulse was to thrust her away, but resolution was weak.

"Why have you come back to Cap François? Why didn't you go to Santo Domingo, or Port-au-Prince, or Jérémie?"

"Because I knew François would give me much money to dance for him." She rightly interpreted his expression of angry jealousy, and laughed in triumph. "But I'll not dance for François if someone nice will keep me. You love me, Ti Rouge. Why don't you keep me?"

"Do you remember spitting at me?" he asked dryly. "Now you are willing to sell your love to me."

"Because you are rich and famous," she replied with utter candor. "If I become your mistress I shall be the envy of other women again. They will say: 'There goes the beautiful Phebe. What lovely jewels she wears! What lovely clothes!' Say that you want Phebe, my Ti Rouge. Tell me that I'm to be your woman."

He looked into her tempting unscrupulous eyes, and, for answer, pressed his lips against her sensuous mouth.

CHAPTER FIFTY

L'ANGE DE L'AFRIQUE arrived at Cap François on the 15th of December, 1801. One of the first men to land was a young Negro about twenty years of age. To one of the Negro officers who was standing about on the quay he asked, "Where shall I find the General Toussaint?"

"Look for him first at the Hôtel de la République."

With a curt word of thanks he called a fiacre and instructed the driver to proceed to the Hôtel de la République.

"Is the Governor General here?" he questioned one of the servants.

"In the billiard room." The man lazily indicated the direction.

The visitor entered the billiard room. Besides the marker there were three men in the room: Toussaint, Christophe, and Dessalines. Christophe and Dessalines were playing, Toussaint watching.

"Monsieur le Gouverneur Général?" the visitor asked, looking at all three in turn.

Toussaint nodded his head. "I am General Toussaint."

"My name is Pierre Thionnet, General. I have just arrived from France on board *l'Ange de l'Afrique*. I bring you a message from your sons—"

Toussaint interrupted, his face transfigured with joy. "You know my sons, Thionnet? Are you their friend? Then I am happy to welcome you here with news of them. Ah! I am as impatient for their message as their mother will be."

"General. They are well and studying admirably to prove themselves worthy of their illustrious father. But the message they have asked me to convey to you concerns the future of Saint-Domingue."

"I do not understand, monsieur," Toussaint said slowly. "What do my young sons know of such matters?"

Thionnet hesitated before replying and diercted suspicious glances at the other men present. "It is an affair of state, General."

With a gesture Toussaint told the marker to leave. "Close the door behind you, and see that nobody interrupts." Then, to Thionnet: "You may speak frankly, my young friend. I have no secrets from anyone present."

Thionnet continued to look doubtful, but having been commanded to speak he did so. "I was born a slave on Monsieur Thionnet's plantation, General, but one day, when Monsieur Thionnet was passing by the slave compound, he saw me, and by God's grace was moved to manumit me. He settled a sum of money on me so that I could be educated in Paris. I took his name for my own. Last year, while I was in Paris, I met your two sons. We became firm friends, so when the completion of my law studies made it necessary for me to return to Saint-Domingue, your sons entrusted me with many messages for you and their mother. Two days before I left Paris for Bordeaux I saw them. They said: 'Tell our father that the First Consul has learned of the Declaration of Independence, that France and Great Britain have agreed to an armistice, and that Napoleon Bonaparte intends to subjugate Saint-Domingue.' "

Before Toussaint could speak Dessalines interrupted with a loud oath and a crash of his clenched fist upon the billiard table. "By the great serpent, those cursed planters have reached his ear, Toussaint. If we had exterminated them they could not have gone to France to stir up trouble. I always said you were too softhearted."

"Peace, Dessalines. Why must you always try to build a house with a handful of bricks? Thionnet has spoken of Bonaparte's intentions, but intentions are not always actions. It was only to be expected that France would resent our declaration of independence, but that is not to say that she will take any steps to recover her lost colony."

"England sent an army to America when the American colonies declared their independence," Christophe pointed out.

Toussaint laughed easily. "With what result? England was defeated. Perhaps Bonaparte will profit by England's misfortune."

"General," Thionnet interrupted hastily, "you have not yet heard the full message. Napoleon Bonaparte believes he is destined to be master of the world. He is not a man to put up with defiance."

Toussaint frowned. "I have heard others speak like that of Bonaparte."

"With reason," Thionnet urged. "You are a thousand leagues from the scene of his military successes. In Europe, where he has defeated enemy after enemy, he is feared."

"But he is, as you say, a thousand leagues distant," Toussaint remarked dryly. "I still do not believe that he will send an army to reconquer Saint-Domingue."

"But, General, when I left France that army was already being assembled at Brest, Lorient, and Rochefort, under the command of Bonaparte's brother-in-law, General Leclerc. It may sail at any moment."

The Negroes were shocked into silence. Anxiously they scanned Thionnet's face, as if they hoped that his expression might belie his words. When they were satisfied that they had heard aright, Christophe and Dessalines turned to Toussaint with a question in their eyes that he did not attempt to answer.

Presently Christophe spoke. "I warned you, Toussaint, not to promulgate that constitution," he said bitterly.

"Are you afraid of Bonaparte?"

"I don't forget the months I spent in the camps of the whites, fighting with and against them. I am nervous of the power of the white man. Have I ever pretended otherwise?"

"No, Henri."

Once again Thionnet broke into the conversation. "General, your sons urge you to take every possible precaution to prepare Saint-Domingue for hostilities."

Consciously or otherwise Thionnet stressed the words "your sons." Toussaint glanced at his visitor with curiosity. "Are there others who do not share my sons' views?"

"Bonaparte has attempted to make sure that you should not share them," the younger man answered meaningly. "On the morning I left

Paris your sons were placed under arrest by Bonaparte's orders, to serve as hostages for your capitulation to General Leclerc."

Toussaint's expresion of quiet confidence vanished. In that moment he aged visibly.

The other men gazed with compassion at the Governor General. Christophe placed his hand on Toussaint's shoulder.

"We cannot fight the French now, Toussaint."

The Governor General raised his head. "Why not?"

"If you resist General Leclerc he may execute your two sons."

"If he does we Negroes will not fight with less courage but with more, and they will not die in vain."

"But Toussaint—"

"Enough, Henri! Can I, who have encouraged our people to risk their lives and the lives of their families for the sake of liberty, now desert them because of a personal threat? Have I not sworn that nothing shall prevent my fighting for Negro independence? I shall pray to God to direct Bonaparte's ambitions away from this pitifully small part of France, but if in His infinite wisdom my prayers remain unheard, and this French upstart sends an army to Saint-Domingue, then we must resist him, fight to the last man."

Dessalines laughed loudly. "That is the way to talk. It sounds sweeter to me than Christophe's bleatings."

Christophe scowled. "I am not afraid to fight if need be."

"We know that. You would be as good a warrior as I if you were not so fond of the whites."

"Because the whites are good to trade with. If you had your way I believe you would massacre every white and colored man on the island."

Dessalines scowled. "And why not? If this is to be a Negro country, why not keep it for black men?"

"If Saint-Domingue is to be a Negro country it must first be defended against Bonaparte's army," Toussaint interposed. The distress had vanished from his face; once more he was the man of decision who had led the Negro armies to victory. "We will show this Bonaparte how we Negroes can fight." He continued crisply: "General Christophe!"

"Excellency."

"You will make yourself responsible for putting the northern province in a state of defense. See that all forts are properly manned. Give your troops constant exercises, and prepare routes of retreat to the interior. Even if we should fail to hold the French at the coast, we shall be able to halt them inland. General Dessalines!"

"Sir?"

"You will hold the southern province, General Maurepas the western. You have heard my instructions to General Christophe. They apply equally to you."

"Trust me to make it warm for the French if they land," Dessalines growled. "What about the whites who are already here?"

"They are to remain unmolested and unharmed."

"But they are already discontented," Dessalines protested vigorously.

"Even Christophe must admit that. They'll welcome any opportunity of harming you, Toussaint. Let me deal with them first."

"No."

"Many Negroes are equally discontented," Christophe pointed out.

Toussaint sighed. "I know that the laborers do not realize that many of our apparently harsh laws were passed for their own good, but surely, Henri, they would not fight for the French against us?"

"I wish I could share your good opinion of them. You can leave it to me to handle those in the northern province, and I don't doubt that Dessalines can keep the malcontents of the south under control."

Dessalines eyes shone evilly. "They had better not play any tricks. I will show them who their master is."

"You must control your impetuosity," Toussaint reproved. "Soldiers who love you will fight better than those who fear or hate you."

"The soldiers love me well enough," Dessalines asserted boastfully. "I have disciplined them."

"With cocomacacque."

Dessalines laughed slyly. "You have forbidden the use of the whip on Negroes, Toussaint, so one must find other means of tickling their hides."

Toussaint felt suddenly weary. Were these changes to be the only sweets of the Negroes' fight for independence—the forced cultivation of land instead of slavery; the cocomacacque instead of the lash?

On the fourteenth of December, 1801, fifty-six sail and twenty-five thousand men sailed for Saint-Domingue. With them left General Leclerc, his wife, Pauline, his brother-in-law Jerome Bonaparte, General Rochambeau (an erstwhile proprietor in Saint-Domingue and a notorious supporter of slavery), and Admiral Villaret, in command of the fleet.

On the twenty-eight of January the fleet reassembled in the bay of Samana, off the eastern coast of the island. Here Leclerc divided his forces, dispatching General Kerverseau with one division to capture the city of Santo Domingo, the capital town of what had once been the Spanish portion of the island, and General Boudet, with a second division, to Port-au-Prince; Rochambeau, with a third division, was ordered to effect a landing at Manzanillo Bay, while the commander in chief himself, with the remainder of his troops, sailed for Cap François.

This news reached Christophe in Cap François. He sent for Duncan, for he had come to rely upon the physician's advice.

"The French have arrived," Christophe announced grimly. "Thirty-five men-of-war, twenty-one frigates, and twenty-five thousand fully equipped soldiers. More than a quarter of that number are on the way to Cap François. The city has never been besieged by so large a force. I cannot hope to hold out against that number."

"Why not, Henri? As long as Fort Picolet commands the bay, the French will find it difficult to land sufficient men to obtain a footing in the city. If they land in successive small parties you should be able to defeat each party in turn."

"If you wished to capture Cap François, Ti Rouge, how would you plan to do so?"

"I am not a military man."

"But how would you?" Christophe persisted. "If you knew that the bay was commanded by a fort with cannon, and that there were sufficient defenders—though no more—to fight off small landing parties, what would seem to you to be the best method of attacking the city?"

Duncan pondered upon the problem. "Attack by land."

"That is what I am afraid of. Bonaparte is clever enough to have sent men who know the island—white men and mulattoes who hate the Negroes. Among them are sure to be some who know Cap François and can appreciate that it is weakest from the land side."

"Then strengthen the mountain forts."

"If I do that we shall be too weak to repel landing parties. Besides, there are several thousand whites in the city who might rise against us if they knew that the French were near."

"What do you propose to do?"

"Retreat to the mountains and the jungles," Christophe replied. "There we shall be on equal terms with the French. But before I retreat I shall make the cursed invaders regret the day they sailed for Saint-Domingue. They won't land to find a city of houses, theaters, hospitals, and barracks all ready for them to walk into."

"What do you intend to do?" Duncan asked, startled.

"Destroy the city by fire," Christophe rasped. "If we cannot have the benefit of Cap François, neither shall the French." There was a deeper hatred in his thick voice than Duncan had ever known him to express. "Why must Bonaparte invade us, Ti Rouge? If Bonaparte had treated with Toussaint and promised us good will and trade, then Bonaparte might have regained the island without war."

"He can think only in terms of war, or the threat of war."

"Then he shall have war," Christophe raved. "War as he has never known it. We will burn the cities and towns, lure him into the jungle, kill off his men one by one, poison the rivers—"

A fierce light that was part fear, part insane fury, flamed in Christophe's eyes. Duncan realized that Bonaparte's aggressive militarism had converted at least one friendly ally of the French into an implacable foe.

That night Duncan idly watched Phebe. She was dressed in a long, white silk robe, cut away at the throat to reveal the perfect sheen of her smooth olive skin beneath a jeweled pendant whose crimson brilliance matched her high-waisted sash.

Her face was in repose; a rare occurrence, for usually her vivid expressions revealed every passing emotion; her face was, indeed, an ever changing screen that rarely failed to enchant him, for, whatever her expression, she remained beautiful, even when her crimson lips were drawn back in temper. So beautiful was she that sometimes he felt humbly grateful to fate for having granted him months of happiness with her.

Happiness! Was his choice of word the right one? That Phebe had given him physical satisfaction was undeniable. She had taught him ecstasies of love previously beyond his imagining. She had brought extraordinary contentment into his life. But did physical satisfaction allied to contentment spell unadulterated happiness? Not for him. One thing at least marred his complete happiness. Conscience! He was tormented by the knowledge that he had allowed inherent scruples to be swept aside by a profane passion and had come to regard his liaison as something indecent because at heart he sternly believed that their association was immoral. Whenever he did so he remembered Margaret and Jean and Elizabeth and Dr. and Mrs. Anderson. This was one memory that hurt, for he knew that the austere outlook of that comfortable household would prefer him dead rather than know that he was living in sin.

There were occasions when he hated his mistress. Once or twice he had tried to summon up enough courage to send her away, only to discover that he had not the moral strength to deny himself. He had also tried appealing to his self-respect, arguing that, by taking a mistress, he had become an object of derision among the inhabitants of the town, but this attempt at self-deception was equally unsuccessful; he was well aware that the unexpected appearance of Phebe in his fine home occasioned no comment save that of envy. Such liaisons had been too commonplace in the history of the Cap for anyone to pronounce judgment, and the change of government from white to black had not brought about a new morality. Toussaint, it was true, led an exemplary life, but the other Negro leaders were less praiseworthy. Dessalines had two known mistresses. Even Christophe, though he was devoted to Marie Louise and his family, sometimes distributed his favors. Among the lesser Negroes concubinage was a recognized status.

"Are you happy, my sweet?" Duncan asked abruptly.

She was invariably and immediately responsive to any mark of attention. The repose disappeared; her eyes filled with a light that he could have sworn was loving adoration had he not known that it was the one emotion she was incapable of feeling. She hurried across the room, curled herself on his knees, and snuggled up against him.

"I am happier than I have ever been, Ti Rouge," she cooed.

He felt unreasonably jealous. "Happier than when you were with De Saint Just?"

She laughed. "De Saint Just is a beast. I hate him."

"You did not always hate him."

"Not when he used to buy me nice clothes and lovely jewels. Not when he said yes to everything I asked him for. He was more generous than you are, Ti Rouge," she added petulantly. As though to take the sting out of her words she rubbed her fingers through his hair. "But sometimes Ti Rouge is a nice, nice man, and then Phebe loves him, oh, so much! So very, very much."

"If you lived with De Saint Just only for what he would give you, why did you remain with him when he had to give up his villa?"

"I was afraid he would kill me."

"Aren't you still afraid he may kill you?"

"He does not know where I am."

"What if he finds out?"

He saw by the shadow that crossed her face that she had not exag-. gerated her fear of the Frenchman. She clutched him closely and replied in a low voice: "I shall go to a *papaloi* for an *ouanga* against him."

Duncan knew of these *ouangas*, charms manufactured of dried blood, hair, herbs, roots, ashes, semen, liver, entrails, and what not, according to requirements, for there was a different *ouanga* for each of a hundred uses or demands: one to ward off the evil eye, another to win a virgin's love, another to cure fevers, another to produce them, another to bring harm, and so on. At first he was astounded to think of Phebe's having faith in *ouangas*; she seemed otherwise so vital and self-reliant. Some other time, he decided, he would question her about her superstitions, but for the moment he had another purpose in mind.

"Are you quite sure that you only lived with De Saint Just because he was rich?" Duncan persisted.

"Why do you keep asking me the same question?"

"Because I know that you are a mercenary little devil, but I am anxious to find out just how mercenary."

"Why?"

"Suppose I were to tell you that I was not going to live in this house any more, would you leave me?"

A startled expression appeared in her eyes, but she pulled his head close to hers and kissed him on the tip of his nose, on each cheek, on his chin, and finally upon his lips—a lingering, exciting kiss.

"You are teasing Phebe," she accused lightly. "Why should you wish to leave this lovely house?"

"I do not want to leave it—willingly." He stressed the last word.

"Then why should you leave? You are rich enough to maintain it. Aren't you, Ti Rouge?" she asked, her voice sharp with anxiety.

"Yes, but—" Now that he had reached the point where he must divulge the bad news he hesitated.

He felt her body stiffen. "But what?"

"It is just possible, Phebe," he explained slowly, "that the government might order us to leave this house. A few hours ago I was talking to General Christophe. He told me that a French squadron has arrived."

"The French!" she whispered.

"Yes. If it becomes evident to Christophe that the Cap may fall into French hands, he is going to set the city on fire."

"Oh!" She sprang from his lap shaking with agitation. "No, no. You are not telling me the truth, Ti Rouge."

"I wish I were."

She realized from his set face that he was in earnest. Her voice rose to a high pitch. "No, no. Christophe cannot give such an order. He must not. It would be wicked to burn this lovely house. What about my beautiful furniture, and all my clothes, my jewels? What would happen to them? You are Christophe's friend, Ti Rouge. You must forbid him to commit such a crime."

"Do you think I shall not mind this house being razed?" he asked gloomily. "Do you think Christophe is anxious to see his house going up in flames? War is likely to break out again. Haven't you seen enough of war to know that the wishes of the individual cease to be considered when the existence of the state is at stake?"

"War, war, war! It is all you men think about. What is to happen to the women and children if the town is burned down?"

"They will have to follow the men into the interior."

"Are you going into the interior?" she demanded swiftly.

"Years ago I threw in my lot with the Negroes. I am not going to desert them now and join the French."

"Do you expect me to accompany you?"

"I was hoping you would, Phebe. The war may not last long. Times will improve as they have in the past. When they do I shall be able to buy you another house, more clothes, more luxuries."

"Fool!" she shrieked. "I am sick to death of living on mountain-tops or in jungles, wearing filthy rags, sleeping in hovels, and feeding on wild vegetables. You know I adore nice things. If you really loved me you would not ask me to leave Cap François. You would try to persuade Christophe to change his mind."

"You know that I love you, Phebe," Duncan explained patiently, trying to catch hold of her so that he could make her sit on his lap again. She angrily stepped beyond his reach. "As for my trying to dissuade Christophe from his course, you are being very childish, my sweet. I have explained to you that Christophe will not give orders for the town to be burned until it is evident that it will fall into French hands. I should not expect the French to show much mercy to Monsieur l'Amis des Noirs, as they called me once, including your precious lover, De Saint Just."

"I will not go into the jungle," she raged tearfully, stamping her tiny feet. "I will not. I will not. I hate you, Ti Rouge, I hope you take fever and die. I hope the French hang you."

"Little spitfire!" he muttered. Surely you must hate her, he thought. How can you do anything but hate her? Think of the things she has been saying to you. She doesn't care a fig for you, only for your money. Send her packing now. After all, the French might not land, and that would serve her right, the mercenary little devil. Go on, you coward. Tell her to clear out and go to the devil.

"Of course, the French may not come after all," he said dryly. "Then this house would not be burned down. But, naturally, you are welcome to anticipate events by leaving me at once."

With a grim smile he watched her changing emotions. Fury was succeeded by doubt, doubt by slyness, slyness by mischievousness. She danced to his side, covered his face with kisses. "Don't be cross with your little Phebe," she whispered. "She doesn't mean what she has been saying. She loves you too much to leave you."

You brazen little liar! he thought as he buried his face in her shoulder and bruised her flesh with his lips.

CHAPTER FIFTY-ONE

EARLY on the morning of the first of February the inhabitants of Cap François were startled by the reverberating boom of cannon from the direction of Fort Picolet. Work ceased in an instant, and all that neighborhood erupted a surging mass of Negroes and white men who ran to the waterside to see what was happening. Those nearer the center of the town rushed to upper windows, or any spot that afforded a view of the bay. There was a second boom from the fort, then a third. Two clouds of black smoke spiraled into the air and slowly dissolved. Anxious eyes stared seaward, but the only vessels to be seen were merchantmen at anchor and the small Negro man-of-war that Christophe had once commanded. Two more cannon fired. Still there was nothing to be seen, so many concluded that General Christophe had ordered the garrison to practice firing. Only a few of the wiser shook their heads and pointed out that the cannon must be firing at a target beyond the headland because there were no telltale splashes to show where the cannon balls had struck the water.

Sure enough, some minutes later the sharp prow of a frigate nosed its way into sight and gracefully heeled over to the breeze that blew from the ocean. The cannon boomed again. The water fountained into the air some distance short of the vessel. There was a second cascade, even farther from the moving target. The crowd laughed derisively. Nathaniel Martin, who was watching the scene from one of the upper windows of Roncin's office, said to his companion: "If that is their best shooting, God help Cap François."

Webster, his chief clerk, pointed out: "It's only for effect. That ship is 'way out of range."

The frigate was followed by a second vessel, another frigate, then a third, this time a cutter. The guns of Fort Picolet boomed at quick intervals, fountains of water cascaded in all directions, except near the ships, which sailed serenely on. Upon course being altered to take them into the bay, the foremost ship came within striking distance of the fort guns, for a cannon ball passed over its bows and struck the water beyond. A stream of flags fluttered up to the masthead as the frigate tacked away from that dangerous spot. All three vessels luffed and took a tack to carry them out of the bay. As soon as they were out of range they turned and tacked their way back toward the headland from which they had recently appeared. When they were lost to sight the cannon stopped booming, and the crowd of curious onlookers slowly dispersed.

"Here endeth the first lesson," Martin chuckled. The fort wasted a lot of good ammunition on a mere reconnoitering party."

Webster shook his head. "It has warned the French that anyone who tries to land here will get a warm reception."

"It can't be too warm, as far as I am concerned," said Martin viciously.

"Why couldn't that upstart Corsican keep his wars in Europe? Whether he wins or loses, our trade will be spoiled."

"It will be more than spoiled if he wins. It will be ruined," Webster commented sourly. He was in no hurry to return to the United States. There was a girl in the rue Taranne whom he was hoping to marry; as she was a mulatto he doubted the wisdom of taking her back to America.

That morning there was little work done in Cap François. Since a brief appearance of the French men-of-war many rumors had started to circulate. Some of these were passed on only to Frenchmen, creoles, or trusted mulattoes. Strike a blow now for Bonaparte, for France, and for ourselves, said the whispers. When General Leclerc attacks, make General Christophe divide his forces by causing a diversion in the town. M. César Télémaque, the mayor, is at one with us.

Another rumor emanated officially from Government House: If there is any danger of the French landing a force, the city will be fired and its white inhabitants massacred. There were many still living in the Cap who remembered that black June when Macaya's hordes had deluged the city in blood. Their reaction to the threat of invasion was undecided. Toussaint's mild and wise government was surely better than fire, rapine, plunder, and massacre. Their fear became contagious and spread.

Once more the Fort Picolet cannon gave warning that the enemy was in sight. The French fleet swept majestically round the headland; frigates, cutters, corvettes in grim procession, their cannon projecting ominously through the gun ports. Soon they were assembled in formidable array where the roadstead entered the bay. Across the still water the silent citizens heard the clanging of anchor chains.

Christophe watched, from the ramparts of Fort Picolet, the fleet maneuver into the anchorage. From the high poop of the flagship General Leclerc examined the town he intended to capture. Each used a telescope. Presently Leclerc saw a boat put off from the slipway nearest to the fort and skim toward him across the gently heaving, sun-speckled waters of the bay.

Leclerc turned to the company assembled about him and waved his hand in the direction of the boat. "The black pigs are offering their capitulation," he drawled. "My dear, does the prospect of queening it over so enchanting a city fill you with ecstasy?" This to Pauline, who stood near him, surrounded by several admiring naval officers.

"I have been told that the Negroes are cannibals," she said with a shiver of disgust.

"Of course. All Negroes are cannibals," Leclerc agreed casually. "The fact need not worry you, my precious. I have no doubt but that they will cringe to the crack of our whips, and that before long we shall have reduced them to their proper station in life."

The boat danced alongside the flagship. A rope ladder was dropped. A few moments later a Negro in bright uniform clambered over the bulwarks.

"Port Captain Sangos, with a message from General Christophe to General Leclerc," he announced.

Leclerc, who had stepped forward, accompanied by his aides-de-camp and his second in command, indicated that the messenger should be brought before him.

"You have a message for me?"

Sangos saluted. "Henri Christophe, General of Brigade, Commandant of the Arrondissement of the Cap, to the General in Chief, Leclerc, his compliments. General Christophe begs to acquaint General in Chief Leclerc that Governor General Toussaint l'Ouverture is absent from Cap François, being on a mission to Dondon. In these circumstances General Christophe would advise General in Chief Leclerc that it is necessary to await the return of a courier dispatched to His Excellency the Governor General before any steps are taken to disembark a military force. On a refusal to await the permission of His Excellency for such a landing General Christophe will consider the white inhabitants of his district as hostages for the conduct of the French force, and that an attack upon any town or village under the command of General Christophe will be the signal for its immediate conflagration."

Surrounded by his officers Christophe received an emissary from Leclerc. After an exchange of compliments Christophe accepted the letter from the emissary, dated February 3, 1801, which he passed on to a mulatto who stood by his side.

"Read it to me, Vastey."

The mulatto opened the letter and read out the contents slowly.

"The General in Chief of the Army of Saint-Domingue, Captain General of the Colony, to the General of Brigade, Christophe, Commandant at the Cap.

"I learn with indignation, Citizen General, that you refuse to receive the squadron of the French Army that I command, under the pretext that you have no order from the Governor General.

"France has arranged peace with England, and its government now sends to Saint-Domingue forces capable of subduing rebels if there should be any in Saint-Domingue.

"As to you, Citizen General, I should be loath to account you among the rebels. I warn you that if, today, you have not handed over Forts Picolet and Bel-Air, and all coastal batteries, tomorrow at dawn I shall land fifteen thousand men. Four thousand are at present landing at Fort Liberté, eight thousand at Port-au-Prince. Enclosed you will find my proclamation, which embodies the intentions of the French government.

"But remember that, no matter how your conduct in the Colony may have impressed me personally, I must hold you responsible for all consequences."

Christophe's face became grim as the message progressed and when Vastey read out: "Signed, the Captain General, Leclerc," Christophe thundered: "Toussaint l'Ouverture is my chief, not this Leclerc, this French general whom I have never met, who pretends to esteem me. Write this Leclerc that we Negroes are no longer slaves," he bellowed, striding heavily up and down the room, his scabbard clattering. "Tell him that we have trained fighters who can give a good account of themselves against his fifteen thousand troops. Tell him that hostile intentions will make us fight even more fiercely against France. Tell him that we shall never submit. Do you hear, Vastey?"

"If it is true that four thousand men were landed at Fort Liberté, you will not be able to hold the city against the French General," Vastey pointed out quietly.

"Then we shall fire it. Impress upon the Frenchman that none of his troops shall enter the Cap until it is reduced to ashes."

"It is a lovely city, General, to be consumed by flames."

"I'm not blind to its charms," Christophe asserted angrily. "Do you think I'm Nero to enjoy burning a town? I love Cap François because it's my home, and the home of my wife and my children, and because it was here that the emancipation of slavery in this island was first declared. But a long time ago that old soldier, François, told me that the best way of defeating an enemy is to scorch the earth before him, so as to destroy anything he can make use of. Toussaint's told me that, too. He's read about it in books."

"Who would rebuild the Cap?"

"If the French hold it, let them rebuild it. If we drive the French from the island again, we'll build a bigger city than ever." Christophe's eyes blazed. "We'll build a town of palaces, Vastey, lovelier than the world has ever known. We'll take the best from Paris, London, Rome, Cologne. We'll employ all the best architects, stonemasons, sculptors. Rome rose from the flames; why not Cap François?"

"And where will the money come from to pay for the new town?"

Christophe grunted. "We are discussing the answer to Leclerc. Say this to the general—"

Boom! Boom! Boom! The dread sound of the cannon from Fort Picolet and Fort Bel-Air was the first warning received by the terrified inhabitants of Cap François that the French were attacking. Soldiers hurried to their posts. Civilians ran to places of vantage from which events in the bay might be viewed. The more nervous left the town and proceeded to the village of Haut-du-Cap, in the mountains high above the city.

The ships in the bay deployed so as to bring their guns to bear upon the forts. The sea was churned up by the several cannon balls that fell short of their mark, but three balls fell on land. The first fell in the quadrangle of Fort Picolet but did no harm. The second knocked the head from the shoulders of a Negro soldier. The third fell in the town and wrecked a baker's shop. But the fleet also suffered casualties. A mast crashed down on the deck of a frigate, killing two seamen and knocking two others overboard. A cutter shuddered with the impact of a projectile that smashed through its timbers just above the water line. Another frigate lost an entire gun crew.

Presently the people on land saw a fleet of small boats putting off from the men-of-war. Each was crammed with soldiers and equipment. The cannon boomed out. Fountains of water cascaded all round the oncoming boats. One was hit and sank almost immediately as its occupants were flung into the water. Several men sank with the weight of their equipment. Others reached and clung to the nearest boats. The early afternoon was noisy with the reverberating echo of spasmodic explosions, and the bluish smoke gathered into a low-lying cloud that drifted slowly above the surface of the water. A second boat was hit. Again some soldiers were drowned, and some rescued. A third boat was just missed, but the force of the water that was flung up knocked three men overboard, and all three were drowned.

Despite casualties, the boats steadily and inexorably approached the land until they came within musket range. The men died by the score, but others took their places. The first boat reached a slipway; the soldiers disembarked and rushed up the slope at the black defenders, who fired at point-blank range. There was a hand-to-hand melee in which most of the Frenchmen were killed or mortally wounded, but meanwhile a second boat had landed its complement of men. The Negro defenders died in their turn, so the French pushed forward to Fort Picolet, which General Humbert, commanding the landing force, hoped to reduce before the arrival of General Leclerc, who would attack by way of Limbé.

Presently Christophe learned that the French, firmly established, were strongly attacking the fort. The news did not dismay him. Reserves were in readiness to cut the French line, not only to relieve the offensive on Fort Picolet, but also to entrap the enemy between two forces. He stood waiting to give the signal for this move.

A gasping messenger hurried to his side. A strong force of French had landed at Acul Bay and was making a forced march upon the Cap from the west.

CHAPTER FIFTY-TWO

A DOZEN Negroes were posted in different parts of the city, waiting to carry out Christophe's threat to start a general conflagration. Christophe had only to command the cannon of Fort Picolet to fire the prearranged signal and the city was doomed. Yet Christophe hesitated to give the word to the waiting messenger. Scarred though it was from the previous conflagration, Cap François was still beautiful and prosperous, still the finest town in the West Indies.

Here he had purchased his freedom from slavery—the most precious moment in his life. Here he had worked hard, prospered, even gained the respect of the whites. Here he had met Marie Louise, his wife. Here three children had been born, François-Ferdinand, then François-Améthyste, four years later, and the year before last, Anne-Athénaïs. Here slavery had finally been abolished, and here, until now, he had governed as commandant of the arrondissement. It was no ordinary city. It was almost his. He could no more order its doom than he could execute one of his own children.

He gazed about him with somber eyes at the breathless messenger who had brought him the news of the landing at Acul Bay, at other runners who stood by to transmit his orders. Then he stared at the buildings, scarcely less magnificent than they had been in the heyday of Saint-Domingue prosperity, for the new ruling order, the Negroes, readily adopting the standard of prerevolt days, had furnished their homes with sumptuous elegance. His glance dwelled longest upon his own home, which occupied a southwest corner of the rues Dauphine and du Hazard. There was not a more magnificent home in Cap François, for he had furnished it with choice paintings and fine furniture purchased for a mere song from bankrupt heirs of murdered planters. Nor could any other establishment boast of a more adequate domestic service, for he ran the house with that smooth efficiency which had ensured his success as an innkeeper. Strangers to the island, invited to Christophe's home for the first time, usually found it one that many European nobles might have envied. Such was the house that his signal would destroy. It had taken him many months to furnish, and more money than he cared to reckon.

Christophe scowled, thinking of French officers sleeping in his bed— that handsome bed from De Saint Just's villa. And French officers dining at the delicate table from Cazeaux's home. And French officers drinking the champagne, the Burgundy, and the rum that the Comte de Saramon had sold from his cellars. In a paroxysm of rage Christophe shook his clenched fists in the direction of the quays from which came loud echoes of musket shots, bugles, drums, and the despairing shouts of the wounded. Never should the cursed French lord it in the home that he had assembled with such care and love. Better to see it in ashes than to be tortured by the thought of Frenchmen's reaping what he had sown. Besides, with the resources of the Cap at their disposal, the enemy would be in a better position to wage war. If the Cap were destroyed the French soldiers would be deprived of their plunder—they might become dissatisfied, even mutinous.

"Give the signal for retreat," he commanded.

Christophe's officers, who knew what his words portended, stared, sullen-eyed, at their leader. They too had homes in Cap François, so they failed to appreciate the wisdom of setting fire to one of their own towns —for they no longer considered that the island was French. It now belonged to the Negroes, gained at the cost of their blood. But Christophe was their leader, and the Negroes had long since discovered that, without a strong supporting clique, defiance of their leaders was the signal for their own execution. So, when Christophe left, they proceeded to their allotted duties.

Insensible to his officers' disapproval, Christophe hastened in the direction of his home. He found the great door wide open. Scared faces peered at him from shaded corners. With his own face set and grim, Christophe passed through into the kitchen, where a fire was burning. From a pile of cordwood he picked up two long stakes, one in each hand, and plunged their ends into the flames. They were soon blazing furiously, so he withdrew them from the fire, and holding them before him he entered the dining room, after thrusting the door open with a kick that splintered the gilded rosewood panel. He looked about him for the most inflammable material.

The acrid smoke from the flaming brands filled the room and made Christophe's gloomy eyes smart. He flung one of the brands on the carpet, pulled down the curtains with a ferocious tug, and threw them across the brand. The flames flickered uneasily as if they had no wish to start a conflagration. Christophe believed the brand was being stifled. If so— by Damballa, if so, it was an omen that his home was not to be burned, the city not to be destroyed. With fascinated eyes he watched the smoldering brand. If the Cap were to be saved he would have to work quickly. The officer in charge of the fort cannon would have to be warned—

The smoke became thicker; the sun-baked material flared up. The flames reached almost to the ceiling. Simultaneously cannon in Fort Picolet gave the signal. The city burst into flames at a dozen different places. Then at a dozen more as the Negroes rushed from house to house.

CHAPTER FIFTY-THREE

CHRISTOPHE'S black army retreated in good order. With them went Duncan, Phebe, and two thousand white people as hostages, Martin and Webster among them. "What is your friend Christophe going to do with us whites?" Martin asked Duncan at the first opportunity. "Does he really mean to have his revenge on us for what the French are doing? It was bad enough to have him destroy my business, but I'm damned if I want to lose my life as well. And I am sure Webster doesn't." He glanced at the clerk who trudged the rough mountain road alongside him. "Though to look at his face you wouldn't expect that any such fate overhung us. He looks as pleased as a cat with a bowl of cream. As far as you are concerned, I suppose anything is better than working at Roncin's?"

"It isn't that. It's the—the girl."

"What girl?"

"The girl I was telling you about—the one I'm thinking of marrying."

"A fine time to talk of marying anyone. What about her?"

"She's with us, just ahead."

"As a hostage or as a refugee?"

"I don't know. Shall I try to find out?"

Martin laughed shortly. "I should, if I were you, while there is still the chance. But don't hurry too much or the Negroes might think that you were trying to escape, and take a pot shot at you."

As soon as Webster had set off to make his way up the straggling column Duncan answered Martin's question. "No white need worry about his life on account of Christophe's threats. He was trying to outbluff the French."

"Setting fire to Cap François wasn't a bluff," the American pointed out dryly.

"Perhaps not, but Christophe has always respected the whites—especially those who are not French. He is particularly fond of Americans and English."

"Thanks to your influence."

"Not entirely. Christophe was born with a shrewd brain for trade."

"Then why in the name of glory did he burn down the chief trading center of Saint-Domingue? That was the craziest notion a man ever got into his head."

"That is what I told him right away. I did my best to turn him from his purpose because I was selfish enough to regret the loss of my own home. Do you know, Nat, as soon as it was necessary to leave the place I realized I was more attached to it than I had suspected."

"Human nature," Martin grunted laconically.

"But Christophe had considerably more to lose than I," Duncan continued. "You know that lovely home of his. But what he did was consistent with the rules of defensive warfare, and the French army, four thousand miles from its base, will soon have reason to curse Christophe's courage in destroying the town. Even if Christophe had not burned your goods the French would have seized them."

"Father should have known better than to start trading with this crazy country. Where is Christophe making for?"

"To meet Toussaint at Bréda. When we arrive there, Christophe will probably release his hostages."

Duncan's words proved prophetic. Christophe and Toussaint met to discuss the campaign against the French. The Governor General ordered Christophe to proceed to the mountainous district of Marmelade to organize defense, and announced his intention of continuing to Héricourt, thence to Bréda. Before the two generals parted, the white hostages were released. As soon as Martin heard this he spoke of returning to the Cap in the hope of catching the next vessel outward bound for the United States.

"Why not come with me, Duncan?" he urged. "I should welcome the chance of introducing you to Salem society, and with Father's influence, and your own surgical skill, you would soon establish yourself—especially when it became known that you have had a book written about you."

"A thin book, Nat."

"Maybe, but a book for all that. We may be citizens of a republic but we are still snobbish about some things—and the next best thing to being a famous author is to be the character written about by a famous author. Why, I'll wager that you would make your fortune in no time."

Duncan shook his head.

Martin grimaced. "I thought so."

"Why?"

"There is something devilishly fascinating about this country. Like Circe. She lures you by her charms, and then degrades you. Rots your soul, or give you yellow fever, or sends you mad with sunstroke. Does everything but treat you as a white man should be treated."

"The creoles are healthy enough."

"Yes, the strong survive and become inured—but only the strong. I shall be sorry to leave the Cap—to say nothing of François, the old reprobate, and his Casino."

231

"If the bug has bitten you, Nat, you will come back to Saint-Domingue before I reach America."

"If there is a chance of trading I shall return." He laughed shortly. "Three of us came out together. I shall be the only one returning."

Duncan stared at the American. "What do you mean?"

"Cupid has been playing tricks, Duncan. Webster, if you please, is going to marry his mulatto girl or die fighting the French."

"Well, I'll be damned!"

"And Jonas—" Martin shrugged his shoulders.

"Suzanne?"

"Yes. The rascal came to me last night and said: 'Ah is gwine ter ask you a fevver, Mist' Nat. Ah wants ter stay hyah in Saint-Domingue. Huccome it hap'n Ah ain't aiming ter know, but dis hyah black hairt of mine is sho' set on that Suzanne, an' she won' leave dis country, not fer anythin' long as Mist' Duncan stays.' When I reproached him for thinking of deserting me the tears sprang to his eyes, because he thought I was going to insist upon his returning with me. He tried to explain that not for any other person in the whole wide world would he have left me, and indeed, I believe that only a woman could have tempted him from my service."

Duncan ruefully ruffled his hair. "You and I seem to be experiencing a similar fate, Nat. You have lost a warehouse and are about to lose a man-servant; I have lost a home and am about to lose a woman servant. I shall miss Suzanne. She has been almost a—a nurse to me."

"You're not losing a servant, Duncan. On the contrary, you stand to gain one. Suzanne has refused to leave your service, so if Jonas wants to marry her he will have to join your staff if you are agreeable."

"Agreeable? Need you ask? From what I have seen of Jonas he is an excellent servant."

"Thanks—but shall I be able to pay his wages?"

Martin chuckled. "You have nothing to fear on that score. If you find yourself unable to support Jonas you will very soon find him supporting you. He can be a cunning rascal if needs be, capable of stealing an egg from under a hen without the bird's knowing."

Thus the matter was arranged. Martin returned to the Cap, leaving Jonas with Duncan. That night Jonas took Suzanne to wife without the benefit of clergy—a not uncommon occurrence in a country where a man might possess as many concubines as he was capable of supporting. The following day the newly enlarged household—Duncan, Jonas, Suzanne, and Phebe, who was by turns sullen, petulant, and pathetic in her protest at the rough conditions of this life—accompanied Christophe's soldiers to a mountain some fifteen miles southwest of Cap François.

Leclerc had underrated his opponent when he had hoped to secure co-operation first by blandishments and then by using Toussaint's sons as hostages. The Governor General resolutely resisted all attempts to seduce him from the cause of Negro freedom, and prepared energetically to resist the French invaders who fanned out from the Cap in three divisions, advancing triumphantly across the plain. But the farther the French advanced the wilder the country became; they had to contend with densely wooded valleys, precipitous mountainsides and fever-impregnated jungles, through which the defending Negroes moved easily, exploiting the swift thrust and parry of the guerrilla tactics that Toussaint had perfected. Every inaccessible height was used as a base for operations and fortified. Between heights every stretch of uneven ground unsuited to French cavalry was made untenable for infantry by a series of ambuscades, formed by lines of Negro soldiers who had become expert in concealing themselves in the luxuriant undergrowth. Every forest became a death trap for the unhappy invaders. Moreover, the Negroes rarely allowed themselves to be forced into a pitched combat, but relied upon fierce skirmishes and lightning raids to harry the French troops into a state of fatigue and dangerous exasperation. The French were further confused by the difficulty of establishing whether a troop of blacks were allies or enemies, a perplexity of which the defenders took ruthless advantage; and scorching sun and miasmic night air played havoc with the Europeans.

Leclerc's position became less tenable each day; so he resigned himself to the more negative satisfaction of attaining his object by means of chicanery.

He issued a new proclamation addressed to the people of Saint-Domingue.

CHAPTER FIFTY-FOUR

IN THE name of liberty, equality, and the French government the islanders were informed that a provisional organization be set up, of which the basis was to be liberty and equality to all inhabitants, without regard to color. The organization was to debate the administration of justice, defense, the imposition of duties, regulation of agriculture and commerce, and the administration of natural domains; to comprise seven citizens, proprietors and merchants (without regard to color), from the South and seven from the West, to be chosen by the generals of those divisions, and eight from the North, the choice being reserved to Leclerc himself.

This document of specious promises and scarcely veiled threats received considerable attention. For all their natural shrewdness the Negroes overlooked the cunning provision for retraction contained in the words: "the provisional organization . . . shall not be definite until approved by the French Government," and weighed the promises against the threats. They are threatened with "measures disastrous to the Colony." Should they gamble on the good faith of the French general in chief and agree to live in peace under the French flag? Or should they fight for black independence at the risk of possible disaster?

The Negro decision was influenced by two circumstances: the arrival, during April, of French reinforcements, in the shape of two squadrons from Le Havre and Flushing; and the constant defections of the cultivators, who were willing to fight neither for Toussaint nor for the French but only to secure their own liberty, which they believed was menaced by the warfare between Toussaint and Leclerc. Such men listened readily to the blandishments of the French propaganda agents and willingly pledged their loyalty to the French government.

One day in mid-April Christophe said to Duncan: "I have received a letter from Vilton, commandant of Petite-Anse. Read it, Ti Rouge."

My dear colleague,
I heard with deep regret of your persistent refusal to submit to the good offices of the French general whom the First Consul has sent to Saint-Domingue to effect the maintenance and consolidation of that order which you have established so well in the town of Cap François, the dependency of the North, where you have gained the respect of all the colonists. You have often told me that you looked forward to the arrival of the French, so that you might place in their hands the authority with which you were invested; by what fatality have you so suddenly changed your good intentions? You have renounced your happiness, your fortune, and the magnificent destiny that was in store for your delightful family.

A strong hint followed that having adopted this course, Henri would best serve his own interests by leaving Saint-Domingue and settling in any country he chose, where he would be assured of a comfortable fortune and the protection of France.

Duncan returned the letter to the Negro. "Well?" he observed, non-committally.

Christophe's face became expressive with exultation. "They fear me, Ti Rouge. The French fear me so much they want me to leave the island. We have shown the French, Toussaint, Dessalines, and I, that we are better soldiers than they are, man for man. They know now that they can't defeat us in battle so they want to buy our friendship. I don't want French friendship. I don't want to be called by a French Christian name any more. Henri is a French name, isn't it?"

"Yes."

The Negro scowled. "I want an English name. Is there an English name like Henri?"

"There is an English equivalent of Henri, which is Henry."

Christophe was delighted. "Say it again, Ti Rouge."

"Henry."

With his face beaming Christophe tried to pronounce the name, but he had difficulty with the aspirate. "En-ry. En-ry."

"Hen-ry," Duncan corrected.

"Hen-ry. Henry. Henry. Is that right, Ti Rouge?"

"Yes," Duncan agreed, generously.

"Then I'm always going to be En—Hen-ry. You will call me Henry, won't you, Ti Rouge?"

"If you wish."

"I do wish. Everyone must call me Henry in future. People shall know what I think of the French."

"Then you are going to defy General Leclerc?"

The unexpected question dissipated the Negro's childlike pleasure. During a long silence his expression turned sullen.

"Why do you ask that?" he demanded.

"If you loathe the French to the extent of changing your name, isn't it natural to assume that you intend to continue fighting them?"

"No," Christophe snapped. "I don't think it is wise for us Negroes to continue resisting."

Duncan was astonished. "Just now you were boasting that, man for man, the Negro was as good a fighter as the Frenchman."

"So he is, but how much longer will it be man to man? My troops are beginning to desert in large numbers. Do you know how the French are treating all Negroes who have not agreed to co-operate with the Republic? They are made to dig their own graves, then they are buried alive. Others are shot down without a chance of fighting. The blacks are becoming terrified, especially the cultivators."

The French have thousands upon thousands of white soldiers already here," he shouted wildly. "More arrived a few weeks ago, and for all we know still more are on their way. Now that cursed Leclerc is bribing our own people to fight against us. How much longer can we hope to carry on fighting if we continue to lose men while our enemy is reinforced, not only with soldiers, but with new artillery, ammunition, and equipment?"

"If your enemies were as pessimistic as you are I doubt whether they would have taken the trouble to try and bribe you. They probably realize that their best chance of obtaining mastery is by dividing Toussaint's forces."

Christophe was perfectly aware of Duncan's reproach. His voice and face became still more sullen.

"You are not trying to see things from the Negro point of view," the black man accused unjustly. "Toussaint and I have always shared the same dream, Negro emancipation. General Leclerc's proclamation confirms emancipation and promises equality as well."

"You had both those things under Toussaint's governorship."

"Of course we had," Christophe agreed impatiently. "But if we continue fighting most of us may be killed. Of what use is liberty and equality to us if we are dead?"

"If you are so sure the French will win, why did you oppose them in the first place?"

"I didn't think our leaders would desert," Christophe replied bitterly. "Laplume, Maurepas, Clervaux—all have gone over to the French. Only Toussaint, Dessalines, and I remain."

"Do you trust Leclerc's promises?"

Christophe hesitated a short time before replying. "I am not sure."

"If you capitulate to Leclerc, then Toussaint and Dessalines will be left on their own, in a worse position than ever to defy the French."

"I should never desert Toussaint. If I agree not to fight any more it will be on condition that similar terms of peace are offered to Toussaint and Dessalines."

Duncan realized that he had misjudged Christophe in fearing that his nerve was failing, and that he was prepared to ensure his personal safety at the cost of deserting Toussaint l'Ouverture. Christophe believed sincerely that despite recent successes the Negro cause was doomed. He had concluded, with good reason, that the Negroes could not hope to match the resources of a powerful white nation.

Duncan understood now that Christophe's shrewd brain had carefully weighed the prospects offered by the choice of alternatives and had decided that capitulation, while he was still in a position to dictate terms, was the wiser course. As long as the Negro leaders lived, and retained their rank and authority, Negro influence would still remain a power with which the French must reckon, but if Toussaint, Dessalines, and Christophe were to die or become outlaws, bereft of power, it was certain that the French would take advantage of their superior strength to impose on the blacks conditions little better than slavery.

"Shall I be right, Ti Rouge, to open negotiations with Vilton?"

"Yes," Duncan presently agreed.

Shrewdly, Christophe did not immediately accede to Vilton's request for peace negotiations. He wrote a letter vilifying the French general for suggesting that Christophe should desert Toussaint l'Ouverture, who was his leader and friend. This produced a brief note from Leclerc that Toussaint would be treated equally generously if the Governor General so desired. After further correspondence had passed between Christophe and Vilton a meeting between Leclerc and the Negro was ultimately arranged, at which Christophe formally agreed to lay down arms on condition that a general amnesty should be extended to all Negro troops, that he should retain his rank and property, and that the same terms should be offered to Toussaint and Dessalines. These conditions being agreed, Christophe proceeded to Marmelade, where he informed Toussaint of his capitulation and passed on a letter from Leclerc.

During the first week of May, Toussaint expressed his willingness to make peace. However, he did not stipulate that he should keep his rank or position. The truth was that Toussaint was tired of war. He wanted peace and the opportunity of retiring to his estate at Ennery, there to enjoy the serenity of family life. To this modest request Leclerc was only too pleased to agree. Toussaint thereupon laid down his arms and advised Dessalines to follow his example. His last official act was to hold a review of his troops. Amid the acclamations of the people Toussaint made his last speech to the black army and embraced his officers one by one, after praising them for their heroic courage. His departure for Ennery was greeted by a salvo of artillery.

Peace at last. And the price? Saint-Domingue had made submission to the sovereignty of France. Napoleon Bonaparte, archdreamer and imperialist, had quickly put an end to Toussaint's dream of a Negro country. Christophe—and Duncan with him—retired to Bonnet-à-l'Evêque; Dessalines to St. Marc. Leclerc, the victorious, in the belief that he could safely leave his generals in charge, retired to La Tortue, an island off the north coast of Saint-Domingue, to recuperate after his strenuous campaign and, more particularly, to place himself as far as possible from his fever-ridden troops.

Peace?

"I am uneasy, Ti Rouge," Christophe told Duncan one evening.

"About what?" Duncan asked.

"Do you hear the drums?"

Duncan listened. The drums were throbbing and booming from the mountaintops and distant valleys.

"The drums are uneasy," Christophe explained. "The witch doctors say that the gods are angry. When the gods are angry with us Negroes they punish us."

"Be damned for a tale! Surely you do not believe in all that nonsense, Henry? You, who call yourself a Christian?"

"Of course I am a Christian, Ti Rouge, but—" He paused.

"But you do not altogether disbelieve in the gods of Guinea?"

"How can we be sure that the Christian God is not God only of the white man? He was white, wasn't He?"

"Yes, but He preached universal brotherhood, and when He did that He was speaking of men of all color."

"He was a good god, your Jesus Christ, but for every good god there must be a bad one. Nothing is ever singular. All nature is plural. Living things are male and female. There is sun and moon, light and darkness, day and night, mountain and valley. Perhaps the black gods are the bad ones. If we blacks do not sometimes make sacrifice to our gods, troubles overtake us, and then we know that we are being punished. If you had seen some of the miracles performed by the witch doctors, you would believe as I do. They could not perform such miracles if the black gods did not give them the power."

Duncan wondered despairingly if he would ever really understand the Negro character. Christophe's brain was so clear and concise, it was difficult to think of it as being cluttered up with dark, unreasoning taboos. Yet apparently it was so.

Duncan recollected the mysterious manner in which news traveled from one end of the island to the other, even when the drums were not throbbing. The gift of black gods! "What do the witch doctors say?"

"That General Leclerc is making plans."

Duncan started. "Leclerc is still in La Tortue. How could anyone in Saint-Domingue know what he is doing?"

Christophe laughed slyly. "You must ask your white God to explain." His face sobered. "The *papalois* do not know what he is planning, but it is something treacherous to do with us Negroes."

"Why should he commit treachery?" Duncan expostulated. "He has attained the object of his expedition. Unless—" He glanced keenly at Christophe. "Are the Negroes conspiring against Leclerc?"

"No," Christophe indignantly maintained.

"Then your witch doctors must be mistaken. Leclerc probably welcomes peace as much as you do, Henry."

"The witch doctors are never wrong," Christophe asserted obstinately. "Mark my words, Ti Rouge, something will soon happen that will cause trouble. I'm not taking risks. I'm going to protect myself by keeping a company of soldiers with me."

"Will Toussaint and Dessalines do the same?"

Christophe smiled grimly. "Dessalines will take care of himself. I am not so sure of Toussaint. He still has faith in Leclerc's promises."

"Haven't you?"

"Not since the drums have spoken," Christophe replied viciously.

One May night, after the moon had waned, two vessels set a stealthy course for the Bay of Gonaïves. The two vessels were the frigate *Créole* and the *Héros*, a ship of seventy-four guns. As the two ships neared the shore, orders were given and passed on in hoarse whispers.

Boats were filled, their crews pulled for the shore. Their muffled oars made a minimum of noise; no man spoke under penalty of disciplinary punishment. With the leading boat went Brigadier Brunet; in another, Ferrari, aide-de-camp to Leclerc.

The boats nosed gently onto the shelving shore. The troops disembarked at speed, with primed muskets and swords loosened in their scabbards. But no attack followed; Leclerc's perfidy had been well and cunningly organized. The distant drums throbbed with suspicion, but they gave no warning of the danger threatening Toussaint l'Ouverture and his family, who slept peacefully in their home a short distance away. In fact, Brunet encountered no difficulties; he marched his silent men to Toussaint's house at Ennery, surrounded it, and then, accompanied by Ferrari and a company of grenadiers, forced his way in.

Leclerc's treachery, in alliance with Toussaint's confidence in the Frenchman's good faith, succeeded only too admirably. In the face of odds that threatened the lives of his elderly wife and his youngest children the Negro was forced to surrender his sword, whereupon he was curtly informed that he was under arrest for conspiracy and that he and his family must prepare instantly for an enforced journey to France. To his protestations that the arrest was dishonorable; his denial that he had been engaged in any conspiracy against the French commander in chief; his plea that he alone should suffer Brunet remained unresponsive save only to order the Negro family to gather together a few belongings; for the impatient brigadier was anxious to return to the safety of the warships before an alarm could be given.

As soon as Toussaint and his family were ready, they were hustled out into the night and hurriedly marched toward the shore. But the raiding party was not to escape entirely unmolested. As soon as the last Frenchman had left the house, servants spread the alarm. Local chiefs hurried after the French in the hope of being able to rescue their beloved leader. They were too few. They died manfully but uselessly. Before other Negroes could reach the district, Toussaint had been embarked on one vessel, his family on the other.

The hated French had achieved the last laugh.

CHAPTER FIFTY-FIVE

CHRISTOPHE brought Duncan news of Toussaint's arrest in the middle of the night. The candle beside his bed had been lighted; its flickering light enabled him to recognize that the Negro's white-rimmed eyes were filled with alarm.

"What do you want, Henry? François-Ferdinand is not worse?"—for Christophe's eldest child had been sickly for the past few days.

"The boy is better. I have more impotrant news. The French have arrested Toussaint."

Duncan raised himself on one elbow. "Impossible!"

"It is true, Ti Rouge. A few hours ago the *Héros* and the *Créole* landed troops off Gonaïves. The men marched on Ennery, surrounded Toussaint's house, forced their way in and arrested him."

"On what charge?"

"Of conspiring against General Leclerc."

"Is the charge justified?"

"I swear it is not. If it had been Dessalines or me—everybody knows what we think of the French. But Toussaint— The cursed French hate Tousaint because he defied them successfully; now they are afraid to leave him peacefully at home. They want him in France so that they can avenge themselves upon him for their defeat at his hands."

"There must be some other explanation—" Duncan began.

"There is not," the Negro interrupted. "Listen to the drums."

"They have often repeated unfounded rumors—"

"Not this time," Christophe shouted impatiently. "If I had not been sure of the facts should I have awakened you at this time of the night?"

"Why didn't you wait for the morning?"

"I am not staying here to meet the same fate as Toussaint. I am off to join Dessalines while there is still an opportunity of doing so."

"You have sufficient troops here to resist a small force."

A cunning expression flashed into Christophe's eyes. "What makes you think that the French would send a small force to arrest me, Ti Rouge? They know that I am not so trusting as Toussaint."

"A larger force would take longer to reach you. You would have warning of its approach and ample time to escape in daylight."

"I am taking no chances. I would rather spend the rest of my life in the mountains of Saint-Domingue than rot away in some filthy French dungeon. Will you come with me?"

"You do not need me, Henry."

"But I do," Christophe asserted fervently. "I should be afraid to take Marie Louise, poor François-Ferdinand, and the other children with me unless I knew that you were near to care for them. Besides, you are my mascot, and I love you, Ti Rouge."

Suspecting blandishment Duncan glanced swiftly at the black figure by his bedside. Christophe was in a full-dress uniform that added inches to his height and his already broad chest. But Duncan had seen the uniform on many occasions; it was the face that held his attention. There was sincerity, not guile, in Christophe's warm eyes. Sincerity and an unembarrassed devotion. And presently, as though he sensed Duncan's indecision, a pleading.

"Please come with me, Ti Rouge," he urged. "I know how much I am asking of you, because you've had enough of wandering among the mountains of Saint-Domingue. But we have been through too much together to part company now. Toussaint told me that your life was bound up with mine, and he was right, even though you are a white, and I am a Negro. The gods want us to be together, Ti Rouge, and they will be angry if we defy them."

Duncan, thinking over the strange, staunch friendship that seemed to have grown up almost without the seeking of either man, was touched. In the thirteen years since he had operated on Christophe—and although the debt had long since been balanced, in that frightful night of the first slave insurrection—Henry had never asked another favor. Until now.

Christophe's purpose in visiting Dessalines was obvious. With armed resistance as the two Negroes' only protection against possible arrest, war was liable to break out afresh in Saint-Domingue. By accompanying Christophe, Duncan would again be involved. The prospect was not enchanting, but could he refuse since Christophe asked?

"I will come," Duncan agreed.

Anxiety left Christophe's eyes; his white teeth were revealed in a dazzling smile.

"Thank you, Ti Rouge. If I return at dawn can you be ready?"

"We'll be ready."

The Negro nodded his thanks, turned, and left swiftly. Duncan eyed a connecting door. He smiled grimly, not relishing the task before him. In the next room slept Phebe—his beautiful shrew. What would she say when she heard of his decision to accompany Christophe? Indolent, luxury-loving Phebe.

He softly crossed the room, opened the door and looked in. She lay on the bed, naked. Phebe was happiest when she was naked.

This night he compared her with a sleek, contented cat. She was stretched out neither on one side, nor on her back, but in a graceful posture that combined something of both positions. Her right eye and cheek were buried in the down pillow, so was one smooth shoulder. One arm was upflung on the pillow, the other hung loosely over the side of the bed, with her long fingers just reaching the floor. One leg was stretched out at full length, hiding all but the knee of the other, which was curled underneath. Her firm rounded breasts stood out from her body prominently, arrogantly.

His woman, Duncan thought contentedly, proudly. His woman! A creature of moods, and passion. A gorgeous creature with the temper of a vixen, the grace of a panther, and the sharp claws of a cat. A beautiful, happy, hot-blooded, selfish, vain creature who had brought to him contentment alternating with exasperation and had filled his home with laughter, barbaric song, and animation.

He crossed to the bed and sat down between her curved leg and trailing arm. He stroked her shoulder caressingly, thinking for the thousandth time, how velvety-smooth was her skin, and how seductive.

She moved and lazily turned her head so that she could look up at him. Her eyes began to flame as she caught hold of the hand stroking her and slipped it under her yielding waist; the other arm she raised to his neck, to pull his lips down to hers.

He resisted her pull and shook his head.

"You must get up, Phebe. We must leave by dawn."

"Leave here! For Cap François?" she asked joyfully.

"No, for St. Marc."

Her eyes became sharp with suspicion.

"For Dessalines's house! Why?"

"Toussaint has been abducted by the French and taken aboard a man-of-war. Christophe fears that the French may try to treat him in the same manner, so he is going to Dessalines to discuss the situation."

"I'd like to see every Negro in Saint-Domingue taken aboard a French man-of-war. Just because Christophe wants to join Dessalines, is that a reason for you to go along as well? You know that Dessalines hates you as much as any other white man."

"François-Ferdinand is in poor health. Christophe is afraid that the journey might make the boy worse and wants me to be on hand to physic him," Duncan explained, talking to her as he would to a child.

"There are plenty of black physicians to dose the brat. Are you content to be the servant of a nigger slave?" Her anger waxed rapidly, as it usually did when her wants and desires were thwarted. "Why should you be always at Christophe's beck and call?" she demanded shrilly. "No white man has ever taken orders from a black pig before—why should you be the first to do so? Who does he think he is to travel with a suite? A king or an emperor?"

"Christophe looks upon me as a servant no more than I regard him as a master. He believes me to be his friend, and I am his friend. You have lived with me long enough for it to be unnecessary for me to point that out to you."

"If he is your friend why does he want to drag us away from here?" she demanded swiftly. "It is not so pleasant as our house at Cap François—" She paused, as tears dimmed her eyes at the memory of the luxurious home they had left, but she continued: "But it is better than a tent. I hate tents," she shrieked. "I hate tents and slave hovels and the jungle and the mountains. Why can't we stay here, Ti Rouge? We've been happy here, haven't we?"

"I am no more anxious than you to leave here—" he began.

She swiftly interrupted. "Then we are going to stay?"

"No," he contradicted sharply. "If Christophe's suspicions that the French are on their way here are true I should be no safer than he. The French have no liking for me."

"They would not dare to arrest you."

"Would they not? Probably I should disappear, and nobody would ever find out what had happened to me unless my corpse should drift inshore with the tide."

Fear gleamed from her expressive eyes. She caught hold of his right hand and pressed it against her cheek. "I should die if anything happened to you, Ti Rouge."

He smiled unbelievingly. "Only in imagination, my sweet. Within an hour of my death you would be flaunting your beautiful body before the richest French officer you could find. Probably General Leclerc himself."

She pouted. "I do not like married men; their wives watch them too carefully."

"If you played your cards wisely you would not have to worry about Leclerc's wife; if rumor does not lie, Pauline has no difficulty in finding consolation for her husband's long absences."

"Is General Leclerc very rich?" she asked, with an eagerness in her voice that her assumed indifference failed to conceal.

Usually he was able to overlook Phebe's mercenary nature and forget that she had deserted Armand de Saint Just as soon as he was penniless, to become the mistress of a man he—and she—had previously scorned. This was not so difficult since Phebe was generous with the commodity she sold at so high a price. She did not stimulate passion; she had no need to; she was passionate to the last drop of her hot African blood. Without a mate she would have been a lifeless being; with one she was a pulsating, stimulating hetaera. Her insatiable demand for ever increasing physical proof of his desire for her was matched by her equally insatiable demand for ever increasing financial proof.

Duncan rose abruptly to his feet. He recognized that the original fault was his, for having been foolish enough to open the subject. Even while she kissed his hand with her soft, full lips, he knew that her mind was occupied with the problem of whom to select as his successor, and the knowledge made him hot with jealousy. He stared down at the smooth sleek lines of her body and imagined other hands caressing her lovely breasts, other lips pressing against her vivid, seductive mouth, other arms clasping her yielding body. He was insanely resentful of the past, of Armand de Saint Just. How much more reason had he to be jealous of the future? In a surge of possessive emotion he bent over her, lifted her from the bed, crushed her roughly to him, and pressed his lips behind her ear.

"If ever you leave me for another man I'll kill you," he threatened.

She laughed tauntingly. "That is what Armand said to me, but I am still alive."

"You'll come with me to Dessalines whether you wish to or not. And your damned luxuries shall accompany us. I'll buy wagons, and oxen to pull them. You shall have a curricule to ride in when you tire of horseback, and servants to wait upon you. You shall travel like a queen, my sweet. You shall be a queen. My queen."

She lifted her head, drew the lobe of his ear between her sharp, white teeth, and bit hard.

CHAPTER FIFTY-SIX

WITHIN two hours of dawn a long procession left Christophe's plantation and set off for St. Marc, whither Dessalines had retired after signing the peace treaty with the French. It was not only a long procession, but also a bulky one, for Christophe took with him his family, his domestic servants, his considerable bodyguard of Dahomeys, and everything of value that could be transported.

The long line was headed by a small advance guard of warriors whose duty it was to discover a possible ambush. Christophe and Duncan headed the main party, accompanied by another small body of warriors. Next came Christophe's wife and family, followed by Christophe's chattels. Then Phebe, accompanied by Suzanne and Jonas, Duncan's loaded wagon, the main force of Dahomeys, and lastly a rear guard consisting of picked guardsmen— obsessed by the conviction that the French intended to try to abduct him also, Christophe was careful to take every precaution to avoid sharing Toussaint's fate.

Further news concerning Toussaint's arrest soon circulated.

"I was right to leave my home, Ti Rouge," Christophe told Duncan. "The French have arrested nearly all Toussaint's friends. Two of his captains have been shot for trying to rescue their chief. If they can, the French will not allow one of Toussaint's friends to escape. They would not even listen to Toussaint's pleas that his wife and family should be left in peace."

Duncan felt shocked. "The French haven't arrested them?"

"They have," Christophe shouted, so loudly that his animal pranced and was not easily quieted. "Napoleon has no mercy on those who oppose him, still less on those who defeat him. One might have excused him for the arrest of Toussaint's children, for they would have been anxious to avenge this last act of treachery. But why should Napoleon want an old woman like Madame l'Ouverture? Does he fear that she might raise the banner of revolt?"

"It was a contemptible act, to arrest Toussaint."

"Contemptible! It was madness!" Christophe corrected. "Do you realize what effect Toussaint's arrest will have on the Negroes? Like myself, they will lose both faith and trust in the word of the French."

Christophe reined in his horse; at the same moment he raised his free arm in the air as a signal for those behind to halt. He nodded to his left. Duncan saw two men some fifty yards from the road. They stared curiously at the passing cavalcade and had evidently been engaged on digging the weed-encumbered land, for they leaned lazily forward, resting their weight on spades in front of them.

"Hey, you men, come here," Christophe shouted.

The cultivators stared at the mounted Negro but made no move.

"Come here," Christophe repeated. "I want to speak to you."

This time the men seemed to understand the meaning of Christophe's hail. They dropped their spades and shuffled forward to the road and stared up, with bovine eyes, at the mounted man.

"Do you know who I am?" Christophe asked them.

"No," answered one of the men. "No," echoed the other.

"I am General Christophe. Have you heard of me?"

"Yes," answered the first man, somewhat dubiously. "Yes," confirmed his companion.

"Have you heard of Toussaint l'Ouverture?"

As though a spring of intelligence had been suddenly tapped, expression flooded their eyes. "Yes," the younger man asserted. "Once my brother and I were slaves. Now we are free men. We love Toussaint."

"That is so," confirmed his brother.

"There were others you owe your freedom to," Christophe pointed out jealously. "Do you know what has happened to General Toussaint? The French have arrested him and are taking him to France."

"Without Toussaint to protect us the French will make us slaves again," the older brother wailed. "They will take our land from us, beat us, place chains upon us and steal our women."

"Have you fought against the French?"

"Yes, General. My brother and I both fought against them. My brother was wounded in the leg. Show the general your wound."

"Never mind about your wounds. Are you willing to fight them again?"

"But if they have captured Toussaint l'Ouverture, who is to lead us?"

"I will lead you. I have often defeated the French," Christophe boasted. "It is better to die in battle than to become slaves of the cursed French. Do you want to join my army? I will feed you well, and pay you well when we are victorious."

The brothers gazed at each other in dismay. "We have had our land less than a year. We do not want to leave it again. All the work we have done will be wasted."

Christophe stared at the overgrown land. "You do not seem to have done much to it in twelve months."

"Clearing land is hard work," mumbled the elder man.

"But we do it because Toussaint gave us the land and told us that we must raise coffee," added his brother. "Do you think the French will take it away because Toussaint gave it to us?"

"They will unless you fight and send their soldiers back to their own cursed land beyond the sea."

"Then we might as well fight."

"Say good-by to your family and join the men in the rear."

At a signal from Christophe the procession moved on, but during the succeeding hours that interview, with innumerable variations, was continually repeated. Upon learning from Christophe that their hero had been arrested many of the Negroes volunteered to join Christophe's army. Some did so because they believed that with Toussaint no longer able to lead them, the French would once more swarm over the Colony and enslave the black men as in the past. Others were moved by a genuine spirit of vengeance, for they had come to look upon Toussaint as a lesser god.

As the ever increasing army progressed further south news of Toussaint's arrest, and of Christophe's approach, traveled ahead of the army. From every district within easy walking or riding distance the Negroes flocked to the road as soon as the leading warriors approached the cavalcade grew steadily longer. Each face wore an expression of grim determination. Their beloved Toussaint had been arrested and was already on his way to France. For that heedless crime they would take vengeance on the treacherous French and at the same time protect the freedom they had won at so bloody a cost.

By the time Christophe's small army had reached the Dondon valley it was already half as large again. There Duncan found Christophe astride his horse staring at the mountain ranges of the Masif du Nord and the Montagnes Noir with rapt intensity.

"What are you staring at?"

Christophe waved his hand at the mountains, which danced and shimmered in the heat.

"Do you see that highest peak of all?"

"Bonnet-à-l'Evêque?"

"No, Ti Rouge. Bonnet-à-l'Evêque is not the highest peak. La Ferrière is."

"Well?"

"Do you notice how it overlooks the surrounding countryside? If a man built a fortress there do you think it would ever be taken?"

"Not by surprise."

"Or even by attack?" Christophe persisted.

"Not even then," Duncan agreed. "For the simple reason, Henry, that I doubt whether an army could reach there in sufficient strength to organize an attack. But I cannot imagine a fortress there."

"Why not?"

"Because of the impossibility of building it in such an inaccessible spot."

"Nothing is impossible. The rock to build a fortress could be quarried from the very mountain on which it was built."

"It would take thousands of men to quarry the rock."

"There are thousands of Negro laborers in Saint-Domingue."

"It would take years to build."

"What are a few years in a lifetime?"

"Of what use would a fortress be without food, water, armaments, ammunition?"

"Food, guns, and ammunition could be stored there," declared Christophe testily. Criticism was making him sullen, as it so often did.

"If guns had wings they could fly there, but otherwise—" Duncan stared at the precipitous incline that sloped up to the mountain summit. "From here it looks as if even a mountain goat would have difficulty in reaching the top."

"Toussaint would not be a prisoner of the French had he built a fortress there." Christophe's voice warmed with enthusiasm. "Why, a handful of my Dahomeys could defend such a place against Napoleon's whole army."

"Certainly," Duncan agreed. "If it were possible to build a fortress there."

The morning brought many more recruits to Christophe's growing army. Drawn together by the drums, they had assembled in small companies and set off for Marmelade. Christophe gazed with exultant eyes at the mounting total of his following.

"Look, Ti Rouge, Toussaint's faith in the black man is justified. The Negro still fears enslavement, but he's no longer afraid to meet the French in battle. He is ready to defend his freedom. There will be no more peace treaties. The French will have to accept our terms, for we shall fight on until they are conquered."

"If there is any fear of that happening, Henry, Napoleon will send a second army to support the first, and, if necessary, a third to support the second."

A shadow passed over Christophe's eyes. "What if he does? We must fight and conquer his armies as quickly as he sends them. Now that we Negroes realize that the French are treacherous dogs whose word cannot be relied upon, we'll fight on until every French soldier is driven into the sea, or every Negro a corpse. The next war with the French will be à outrance, Ti Rouge. The future of the black man is at stake."

"What if Dessalines has different views?"

Christophe laughed his scorn. "Then I will fight the French on my own. But you know Dessalines. Do you think he would be content to stand aside from any war in which the French were engaged? He might still be fighting the French but for me. It was I who persuaded Dessalines to agree to the peace terms. I haven't doubts about Dessalines even if I have about Clervaux, and some of the other generals." He raised his voice to call to a group of passing officers.

"Poux! Bigaye! Magny!"

The officers approached. "Yes, General?" asked one of them.

"Tell me, Colonel Poux, will General Dessalines join us in fighting the French?"

"Of course General Dessalines will fight the French, General. General Dessalines hates the French as much as we do, and besides, isn't he the most feared of all the enemies of the French?"

The answer was scarcely diplomatic; the frown grew more pronounced.

"What have you to say, Captain Bigaye?" Christophe snapped.

"I agree with Colonel Poux in believing that there can be no doubt about General Dessalines's fighting the French, General, but as long as General Christophe is fighting, the French can never hope to enslave the inhabitants of Saint-Domingue."

The frown disappeared as if by magic; Christophe's cold, ferocious glare gave way to an expression of childish pleasure. "Thank you, Captain Bigaye." He glanced at the third man. "Do you agree, Colonel Magny?"

"Emphatically, sir," Magny answered promptly. "There are not many Negroes who fail to realize their debt to General Christophe."

The officers saluted and departed, wondering why General Christophe was so anxious about Dessalines. With scowling eyes Christophe watched them depart.

"I shall keep my eyes on that Poux," he muttered.

CHAPTER FIFTY-SEVEN

CHRISTOPHE and his followers arrived at Dessalines's plantation an hour before dusk. They found a large part of it already occupied by many local chiefs who had heard the news of Toussaint's arrest and had hastened to seek Dessalines's advice.

Having commanded Poux to settle the men in for the night, Christophe asked Duncan to accompany him to the house. Duncan refused, pointing out that his presence would be resented and that he had no interest in the deliberations. Christophe overruled all objections, so Duncan agreed, with the secret determination to do his best to divert the Negroes from a course that might lead to a worse disaster than any the black men had hitherto suffered.

As the two men approached the large house that Dessalines had seized for himself, they heard the loud buzz of conversation. The house was packed with brilliantly uniformed officers of the regular army, less resplendent officers of the irregulars, and local chiefs, attired in civilian clothes. They stood about in groups wherever they could find room, argued noisily, and exchanged the latest rumors. The task of forcing a way through the gathering appeared a formidable feat, but Christophe was equal to it. He advanced arrogantly into the house and summarily thrust aside all who stood in the way.

Dessalines saw Christophe approach.

"Welcome, Henry," he greeted in his harsh, guttural voice. "I heard that you were on your way at the head of many men. You were wise not to remain—" He came to an abrupt stop as he caught sight of Duncan's flaming hair. "Who's that behind you?"

The question traveled round the room; the loud chatter abated as the surrounding men stared in the direction of the two newcomers.

"Ti Rouge," Christophe replied impatiently. "You have seen him often enough, Jean-Jacques, to recognize him."

"I do, but he is a white. There is no place here for a white."

There was a confused murmur from the far corner of the salon, but the majority were silent, content to watch events with interested eyes.

Christophe scowled. "Who are our enemies, the whites or the French?"

"The whites, if I had my way, for they include the French."

"Then it is fortunate for us that there are others with more sense, Jean-Jacques. Neither the English nor the Americans are our enemies. Didn't the English help us to fight the French?"

"Only because England and France were at war."

"Perhaps, but who were the first to raise their voices against slavery? The English!"

Dessalines laughed sourly. "The English have not abolished slavery in Jamaica."

"They will soon do so. Mr. Wilberforce is seeing to that."

"There are still slaves in the American states."

"That is the Americans' business, not ours here in Saint-Domingue," argued Christophe, who felt that he was being driven into a corner. "We need the friendship of the Americans and the English in order to trade with them."

"Trade! That is all you think of. We Negroes worked enough when we were slaves; what is the sense of working as hard now we have our freedom?"

This remark was greeted with loud approbation.

"Only fools encourage laziness. If Saint-Domingue is to be prosperous again we shall have to work as hard as we did when we were slaves. But what purpose does this argument serve, Jean-Jacques? I have come here to discuss what is to be done about the capture of Toussaint."

"General Christophe is right," called out one man.

Dessalines faced him. "I agree, but are we to discuss our business in front of the white man?"

Silence followed this question; some of the men shuffled uneasily.

"If Christophe says he is to be trusted let him stay," the man answered at last.

"Ti Rouge is a good man; we all know him," shouted a man by the door.

"He saved my life when I was wounded," called out another.

"He saved my brother's life," continued a fourth.

Three others added their approval of Duncan. Dessalines gazed about him with disagreeable eyes.

"I suppose you may stay, Ti Rouge," he answered presently. "I have nothing against you except that you are white." He looked at Christophe. "Which do you vote for, Henry? For war against the rotten French, or peace—and trade?" he added with a sneer.

"Why do you think I brought an army with me?" Christophe replied.

The majority were for war. The arrest of Toussaint horrified them, though not on account of the treacherous nature of the arrest. Treachery was recognized as a handy method of augmenting one's income or bettering one's position. Few among the chiefs in Dessaline's house that night had not, at some time or other, betrayed their immediate chief by selling out to the enemy.

The cause of horror was the knowledge that the gods had betrayed Toussaint. So often had Toussaint escaped death, by battle, ambuscade, treachery, and the like, that his followers had come to regard him as almost superhuman; a man whom the gods had taken under their protection. That the gods had failed to protect him as soon as he had relaxed his usual precautions was, to these superstitious people, a presage of doom to their cause that could only be warded off by fighting, and conquering, the obvious instrument of that doom—the French.

There was also another cause for alarm. The list of Toussaint's friends arrested by the French was growing hourly, and none knew where they were being taken, or what was happening to them. They were being dragged away to France, declared several, but none could name the ship being used for that purpose. Others had a more tragic story to tell. The prisoners were taken out to sea at night, and there flung overboard to drown. This rumor was more readily credited than the first, for, they argued logically, of what use could Negro prisoners be to the French?

Feeling ran high, but there were some present who advocated caution. Wait, Dupuy advised, for General Leclerc to reveal his plans, before rashly renewing the war.

"By Damballa!" Dessalines mouthed angrily. "Time is the ally of the French, not of us Negroes. Unless we strike quickly, we shall disappear one at a time until none of us is left to fight the French."

Many shouted their approval, but Christophe was not among them; he was more interested in studying Dupuy, who was on the far side of the room. Dupuy was young, and his skin was of a lighter shade than most of his friends; but what particularly attracted Christophe's attention was the keen, intelligent expression of Dupuy's eyes.

"One moment, Dupuy," Christophe called out. "Have you a reason for counseling against war?"

"Several," Dupuy answered promptly. "As many as the fingers on one hand." He held up his hand in illustration.

"What are they?"

"Here is the first." Dupuy placed the forefinger of his right hand on the little finger of his left. "French soldiers are not easily defeated. They are well armed, well drilled, there are many already here, and more are on their way."

"We've defeated French soldiers before," Dessalines boasted.

"If our soldiers were capable of defeating the French why did we have defeat after defeat? Why did you and Christophe and Toussaint sign a treaty of peace instead of driving them back into the sea?"

"If my leaders had not deserted me the story would have been a different one," Christophe called out angrily.

"I am not criticizing you, General. But did we, or did we not, capitulate to the French?"

A shuffling silence answered Dupuy's question, so he continued: "What we could not do a few months ago, we cannot expect to do now with less than a quarter of the warriors we had then."

"Thousands are volunteering," Dessalines objected.

"And many thousands more will yet do so, no doubt, but until they do we are not strong enough to attack."

"Dupuy is right," Christophe agreed loudly.

Dessalines glared, first at Christophe, then at Dupuy. "The other reasons?" he demanded.

Dupuy transferred his forefinger to the third finger. "The longer we wait before fighting the French the better opportunity we shall have, not only of enlisting a larger number of men but of arming and training them."

This argument appealed to many present and was greeted with approval.

"Thirdly," continued Dupuy, "it has yet to be proved that the French intend to harm us."

Dessalines scowled ferociously. "Do we need more proof of French intentions?" he raved. "Haven't Toussaint, and a score of Toussaint's friends, disappeared?"

"Yes," Dupuy answered calmly. "I dislike the news of the arrests as much as any man here. But we should be stupid to overlook the nature of the white man. The idea that a Negro and a one-time slave could successfully defy him for many years was an intolerable blow to his pride, which he could not forgive. Toussaint's arrest is a sop which will satisfy his egotism, placate his pride, and make him more amenable to our demand for liberty, equality, and fraternity. Ask Ti Rouge if I am not right."

A score of dark faces turned in Duncan's direction.

Duncan thought of the aristocrats who had ridden in the tumbrils to the Place de la Concorde, a sacrificial symbol of victory, vengeance, and power. Many heads had fallen beneath the keen blade of Madame Guillotine, but the lust for blood had been quickly sated—if one compared the Reign of Terror with the centuries of oppression which had preceded it—and the hated aristocrats no longer went in fear of summary execution. Dupuy's analysis of the Frenchman's nature was shrewd; he must win, and his enemy's defeat must remain manifest. It was conceivable that with Toussaint no longer a constant reminder of past defeats, the French might be more sympathetic toward the rights of the Negroes.

"There is some truth in what you say," he admitted.

"Would you care to risk your life on it?" Christophe asked shrewdly.

"No, but it is a sound argument for not acting hastily."

"Thank you, Ti Rouge," Dupuy said in a loud voice as he placed forefinger upon forefinger. "Now for my fourth reason. Yellow fever is already ravaging the French troops," he proclaimed. "And the greatest heat is yet to come. Disease will kill them off quicker than a dozen battles, and at no cost to us. If we wait until the end of the year our task of annihilating the French will be halved."

A storm of excited discussion followed. The majority opinion had changed, and was now for the postponement of hostilities. Dessalines alone remained unaffected by Dupuy's argument. From a superior height his eyes scornfully surveyed the packed throng.

"Continue, Dupuy," he shouted.

"Continue what, General?"

"Your reasons for being against war."

"I have given them to you."

"You said you had as many as the fingers on one hand. You have given us only four."

"I did not mention thumbs, my general."

The listeners welcomed this sally with a burst of laughter, but Dessalines was in deadly earnest. He scowled.

"I am against waiting," he bellowed. "A small army is already assembled on this plantation. Within a few days we could double it, treble it. We could seize Port-au-Prince; one victory would secure us the support of every Negro in Saint-Domingue. And this time there would be no defections."

"Could you guarantee that, Jean-Jacques?"

"I could." The Negroes have learned their lesson. They will never again trust the word of a French pig. Let us fight now, I say, for when the sun is at its hottest, the white man isn't so good at fighting. Besides, Bonaparte may send reinforcements before the autumn."

Once more the council wavered. There were convincing reasons for an immediate attack upon the French. There were as many good reasons for waiting. Which course was the best?

The crowded rooms grew noisy with discussion.

Despite the support for Dessalines, Dupuy's arguments won the day.

Duncan threaded his way between sleeping forms and past the glowing ashes of fires lighted several hours past. When he reached the tent which Jonas and Suzanne had erected he entered quietly, believing that he would find Phebe asleep. To his surprise she stirred.

"Ti Rouge," she whispered. "I am glad you have come. You have been away so long."

"Why aren't you asleep?"

"I cannot sleep. I am frightened."

"Frightened! What has happened?" he demanded sharply.

"I will tell you when you are undressed."

"What happened?" he repeated angrily.

"Please wait, Ti Rouge," she pleaded. "I do not want to tell you until I can feel your arms around me. I shall feel safer then."

Duncan was exasperated, but he recognized that she was in one of her obstinate moods from which she could be diverted only at the cost of an embarrassing scene. Besides, her fears were probably groundless; her emotions, he had discovered, were not to be trusted, for her childlike imagination invariably magnified them beyond all reason.

He undressed and lay down upon the grass-filled paillasse. She clutched him with frenzied arms and pulled him close to her. He felt her body quiver.

"Hold me, Ti Rouge." He did so. "Tighter, tighter," she ordered.

He began to suspect an ulterior motive. "What did you want to tell me?" he asked patiently, for he was tired, and anxious for sleep.

"Armand de Saint Just is living on a plantation less than a league away," she whispered.

"De Saint Just!" He stiffened. "I thought De Saint Just was dead," he muttered.

She shivered. "I wish he were. I am frightened, Ti Rouge. If he hears that I am here he will come to kill me."

"Ridiculous—"

"He will," she contradicted hysterically. "I know he will. He always swore he would kill me if I left him."

"You did leave him, and he did not kill you."

"He didn't know I was leaving him. He had gone on a two days' visit to Jérémie. By the time he had returned I was on my way to Cap François. Please take me away before he hears we are here."

There might be no immediate reason for apprehension, but there was no doubting the intensity of Phebe's fears. Her body trembled from head to toe, her voice was shrill with terror.

"You have no need to worry," he assured her. "I have already made plans to leave here tomorrow morning."

She gasped her relief. "Early?"

"Soon after dawn."

The trembling ceased abruptly, her breathing grew steadier. Presently she asked, in a voice from which every suggestion of fear had been banished: "Where are we going, Ti Rouge?"

"We are going to Cap François," he told her.

"Cap François!" The joy in her voice was emphatic. She kissed him fervently until he gasped for breath and was compelled to push her away. "That news makes me happy."

"So it seems. Now perhaps we can go to sleep." He climbed onto the second paillasse, and stretched his limbs in voluptuous relaxation.

For sime time there was silence. Then came the question which he had been expecting, for he was convinced that her insatiable curiosity would allow neither of them to sleep until it had been satisfied.

"Why are we returning to the Cap, Ti Rouge?"

"Because Christophe is going there."

"To attack the town?" she asked in a sharper voice.

"No, to pay his respects to General Leclerc."

"But I thought the Negroes were going to fight the French."

"The generals have decided not to do so." He did not add the words: "For the time being." That was news which, for the sake of the Negroes, he dared not entrust to her, for gossip was the breath of life to her.

"In which hotel shall we stay?"

"In none of them. I propose asking François whether we can stay at the Casino until we find a place of our own. Does that please you?"

"Yes," she replied joyfully.

There was a long pause. Duncan was almost asleep when she asked, softly: "Does General Leclerc visit François's Casino, Ti Rouge?"

CHAPTER FIFTY-EIGHT

ON Duncan's return to Cap François, he made a new discovery about himself, one that startled him no less than the knowledge of how happy he had been among the Negroes. He had been homesick for Cap François.

François's delight upon seeing Duncan was affecting. He embraced the younger man with fervor and winked delightedly at Phebe from behind Duncan's back.

"It does this old eye of mine good to see you again, my boy. I have often wondered what happened to you after the fire. I heard that your place had gone up in flames, like many others, but when I tried to find out whether you were dead or alive, and where you were, why, bless my soul! I could not meet a body who knew anything about you. You have not changed much, Duncan."

"Did you expect me to change so much in three months?"

"Three months! Was the fire only three months ago? It seems longer to me, but there, when one gets older time plays strange tricks. Three months! Well, a lot has happened in that time." A crafty expression lighted up his solitary eye. "It is an ill wind that blows nobody any good, and it's not for me to grumble at the coming of the French army. The Casino is its old self once more. Every night sees it packed to suffocation with white men again, and a sprinkling of the mulatto generals. What are you doing back at the Cap?"

"The Cap is my home, François."

François looked astonished. "Then your house was not burned—"

"Its walls had fallen in before I left," Duncan interrupted. "I have come back to try and start another home."

"That will not be easy, my boy. There are not many buildings intact, and the French officers are occupying most of them."

"I can have one rebuilt. Meanwhile, have you a spare room?"

François smote Duncan a hearty blow on his shoulder. "As long as there is a room under François's roof it is yours." His eyes gleamed as he appreciated the slim, graceful lines of Phebe's body.

"But a word of warning to you, Duncan," François continued. "If you are coming to stay with me at the Casino, see to it that your woman remains unseen."

Phebe's laughter turned to anger. "Why should I remain unseen, old man? I want to see life as much as Ti Rouge."

François ignored her. "She is too pretty a piece of goods to be seen by some of the young fire-eaters who visit the Casino every night. They would outbid you."

"I should kill her first."

"That's the spirit. But you haven't told me what happened to you after the fire. Did you accompany Christophe?"

"Yes. Afterwards, when Christophe made peace with the French, he offered me the use of a house on his plantation, where we have remained until now."

François glanced uneasily about him as if he feared eavesdroppers. "I suppose you have heard the news?"

"About Toussaint?"

"Yes. I am still a Frenchman, even if I have lived in this hellhole for the past twenty-three years," he began, "and if I had thought there was any chance of the General's troops being beaten by a pack of dirty niggers I should have polished up my old saber and have sent my share of black bastards to hell. I know how you feel toward the blacks, Duncan, but when an old soldier has lost half an ear in Italy, an eye in Austria, and a couple of fingers in Switzerland, while fighting for his country, he can't stand by and watch French soldiers being killed."

"I understand, François."

"It isn't for me to question the General, but it doesn't seem right to sign peace with a man, and then arrest him as soon as he's off his guard. Especially General Toussaint, who was not bad for a Negro, though he didn't spend any money at this Casino. If I had been General Leclerc I should have said to myself: 'The Negroes look upon Toussaint l'Ouverture as a hero. If I ship him off to France, one of two things will happen. Either the Negroes will be cowed by the loss of their leader, or else they will rebel again so as to avenge him.'" His single eye stared keenly at Duncan. "Wouldn't I have done right in asking that question if I had been General Leclerc?"

"Yes," Duncan admitted guardedly.

François seemed disappointed. "And if I had been General Leclerc how should I have answered that question, Duncan?" he persisted.

Duncan remembered François's words of a moment ago: "An old soldier . . . could not stand by and watch French soldiers being killed." Why was François so anxious to learn the Negroes' reaction to the arrest of their hero? As an old soldier was he anxious to warn the expeditionary force of the Negroes' intentions?

Duncan felt stifled. "It is hot in here, François," he temporized, loosening his cravat.

"Hot! No more than usual at this time of the day, lad. But there, I'll let some air in if there's any to let in."

The Frenchman stumped across the ballroom floor toward the long, narrow windows that lined one side of the room. Duncan watched, and wrestled with his conscience. The French might anticipate that the blacks would rise up against them, but he, Duncan Stewart, was probably the only white man in Saint-Domingue who knew the Negroes' plans. There was a vast difference between guesswork and knowledge, a difference of life and death. One word from him would put the French on their guard. But could he give that word, even in the form of a hint to the probing François, without betraying men who trusted, respected, and honored him, and tried to repay the debt they owed him? Could he be their Judas Iscariot?

François flung open three of the windows. Hot air, sickly with the cloying perfume of exotic plants, flowed into the gilt and plush ballroom. Through the interlaced branches of the vine which shaded the windows Duncan gazed at the dazzling, molten-white sky. How hot he felt. Hotter, indeed, than he remembered having been since his first summer in Saint-Domingue. He thought of the dispirited French troops who were to be seen in every street in the Cap. If he felt the heat, inured though he was to tropical summers, how much worse must those other poor devils, straight from a temperate clime, feel.

He saw that François's keen eye was watching him with curiosity.

"Anything wrong, lad?"

"The heat seems worse than usual."

"That's because you've been living on the plain for the past few months. My eye is still as keen as ever," he grunted. Then he went on: "Those fellows from France are feeling the heat badly. They are dying off in their scores. Think of them, and be glad you are dressed for the tropics, which is more than they are, in their military uniforms."

Duncan was thinking of the French soldiers. Once more, it seemed, Fate was forcing him to decide between the white world and the black: a white world composed of Frenchmen whom he hated, and a black composed of simple-minded men who trusted him.

He realized that François was speaking.

"Where is that rascal Christophe?" François asked with forced humor, trying—not too successfully—to dissimulate.

"On his way to the Cap."

Though his disinterest had been feigned, François astonishment was genuine enough.

"On his way here!" he repeated. "Then he doesn't intend to rise against the French?"

"No."

"You surprise me, lad. He always pretended to admire and respect Toussaint l'Ouverture, so I thought— But there, he has his head screwed on the right way, has Christophe. But Dessalines now—I shouldn't care to rely upon his keeping the peace—" He gazed questioningly at Duncan.

Duncan temporized. "I have not heard that Dessalines plans to make any immediate warlike move," he said, consoling himself with the reflection that, if necessary, he could disclose more at a later date. Tomorrow, maybe—

CHAPTER FIFTY-NINE

TOMORROW!

On the morrow the May Queen dropped anchor in the roadstead beyond Cap François. Captain Tom Beard found Duncan at the Casino.

"I have news for ye, Duncan," he announced.

"Of—of the Andersons?"

"Aye, of one of them. Eulalia is on her way to the West Indies."

The captain's announcement was a shock that bridged the years as though they were days. With disconcerting vividness Duncan saw a vision of the Margaret he had known so intimately: red hair tousled, blue eyes sparkling with mischief, cheeks flushed with health, lips pouting for his. That was how he had seen her on the morning of the fatal night when he had forced Elizabeth to show him De Galinière's note. He had been proceeding along the hall from the surgery; she had just returned home from a visit to Mrs. Hogarth. In her impatience (assumed, as he now knew it to have been) she had snatched off hat and overcoat, dropped them carelessly on the hall chair, and had rushed helter-skelter along the polished floor to meet him. She had hugged him tightly and raised her face for him to kiss.

So real was his memory of those minutes that he still seemed to feel the coldness of her cheeks, which had been whipped by the keen, snow-laden wind; and the twin blocks of ice at the back of his neck—her hands. Above all, he could feel her body nestling within his arms, and her warm lips resting softly against his in a kiss that was sweet ecstasy.

Margaret was coming to the West Indies! No more need he think of her only as a memory; if he took pains to see her she could become for him once more the living personality to whom he had given his first love.

"How do you know?" he asked Beard.

The captain frowned. Drat the woman! he thought. There was no mistaking Mr. Stewart's agitation, nor the reason for it.

"I read a paragraph in the *Courier*," he replied.

"Yes, yes, but what did the paragraph say?"

"You'll understand that I disremember the exact words, Mr. Stewart, 'cause I haven't a head for keeping all the tiddily-bits I read in the journals, but it said something about a celebrated actress paying a visit to the New World, where it was not to be doubted that she would add a considerable number of admirers to an already overlong list—"

Duncan wanted to shake the seaman by his short, stocky shoulders. "Go on, man," he urged impatiently.

"Then it went on to say that they referred to the fascinating toast of the town, the beautiful Eulalia. Eulalia had been invited to play in some of Sheridan's plays at Charleston, Philadelphia, and New York, but that on the way to Charleston she proposed to give several performances at Kingston, Jamaica."

Duncan caught hold of the captain's arm in a fierce grip.

"When was she due at Kingston?"

"I don't rightly know, Mr. Stewart. All the paper said wus that she would be leaving England in about three weeks' time."

"Three weeks! Then that allows me time, Captain."

"For what, if I might be so bold as to ask, Mr. Stewart?"

"To arrive in Jamaica before she does."

Beard rubbed his chin. "You are the hurryingest man I've met in a few years, but I kinda thought you might want to be visiting Kingston, sudden-like—" He paused. "If you can wait a day or two while I unload, I wus thinking that you might like to come aboard the old *May Queen*. I have some salted beef fer Kingston, and that short distance won't take us so much longer—"

"I'll come. Gladly," Duncan interrupted impulsively.

"And right welcome you'll be, too, as far as I'm concerned, Mr. Stewart. But there is one thing—"

In spite of his agitation Duncan was astonished to note that the captain showed signs of being unusually embarrassed.

"But what, Captain?"

Beard rubbed his blue chin reflectively. "But this is what I'm trying to say, Mr. Stewart. We are as we wus made. You're one that feels things worse. You've burned yourself once and taken until now fer to get well agin. Don't go and burn yourself again at the same fire. You are happy in Saint-Domingue. You've told me so yourself. Don't go to Kingston. Stay here. That's my advice, and I hopes you don't take it amiss."

"I am going to Jamaica," Duncan asserted with a finality that warned Beard that his efforts had been wasted.

Duncan realized in his joy at the news of Margaret's imminent arrival in the West Indies, there was something—someone—he had entirely overlooked. Phebe!

Phebe! *She* could not go with him to Jamaica. The mere idea of taking his mistress—especially a colored woman—on a journey, which he joyfully hoped would result in his meeting Margaret again, was so positively indecorous that he laughed cynically. Duncan realized that the task of telling Phebe that he was going away was not likely to be pleasant.

Duncan moved slowly to his bedroom. He opened the door quietly, but Phebe was already awake and out of bed. She stood naked in the path of sunshine streaming in through the open window and bathed in its golden radiance while she combed her black, lustrous hair.

She smiled happily. "Why are you up so early, my Ti Rouge?"

"Captain Beard has arrived at the Cap."

"Captain Beard?"

"The man who brought me here from England. He brings goods here. You have seen him before. He was with me here at the Casino on the night you came to me."

She smiled lazily. "Was he that short man with large shoulders, red face, and rough hands?"

"Yes."

"I remember him, Ti Rouge. He speaks no French and shouts at everyone who cannot understand what he says." She shrugged her beautiful shoulders. "But I am not interested in ugly men, especially when they are seamen. Seamen have no money to spend," she added with scornful finality. "Why did he want you?"

Without answering he crossed the room toward the wardrobe, which was beyond the window. As he passed she caught hold of his arm, pulled him toward her, and wrapped her own arms about him.

"Kiss me," she commanded.

Kiss me! Kiss me! Kiss me! Her appetite for kisses was as avid as her curiosity. It was never sated.

Hitherto she had not found him unresponsive. If her appetite was naturally insatiable, his was developed by long repression. There had been no damming its turbulent rush—until now! Now, as he saw her deep smoldering eyes, her open, moist lips, and compared her exotic beauty with the fresh innocence of Margaret, he experienced a revulsion of feeling. The one was like the flamboyant orchid, bred and living in the poisonous atmosphere of a miasmic swamp; the other was as sweet as the simple woodland violet.

He disentangled himself from her arms. "I am going to Jamaica."

"To Jamaica! Why are we going to Jamaica, Ti Rouge?"

"We are not going. You are remaining behind.

She did not understand. "What do you mean, Ti Rouge?"

"What I said: you are not coming to Jamaica with me."

He almost regretted his words, for her hurt expression reminded him of the reproach in the eyes of animals when they are unjustly punished.

"I am sorry, Phebe, I cannot take you with me."

"But you must, Ti Rouge. You cannot leave me behind."

"It is a question of business."

"Business! Why should business prevent your taking me?"

"I cannot go into that, Phebe. The point is that in two or three days' time I am going to Jamaica."

"What about Suzanne and Jonas—"

"They are going with me."

His words shocked her. She shook as though he had dealt her a physical blow and stared at him with eyes that could not understand.

"Why are you taking Suzanne and Jonas, and not me—" she began pitifully, like a frightened child. "You are planning to go to another woman," she accused.

"I am not," he denied harshly.

Her voice rose shrilly. "You are, but you shall not go. You are my man. No other woman shall have you, Ti Rouge. You shall not go. I will not let you."

He interrupted her tirade. "I am going."

She recognized the finality in his voice; her temper changed from frenzied incoherence to ice-cold hate.

"You are going to another woman," she accused for the third time.

He made no further attempt to deceive her. "Yes, I am. Captain Beard has brought me news that my sister is on her way to Jamaica."

"Your sister!" she repeated with a sneer.

He was angered by her scorn. "It is true," he shouted. "If you do not believe me, ask Captain Beard. He is still downstairs."

"You have no sister. You have told me again and again that you were an only child."

"Foster sister, if you must be precise. I have always looked upon her as a sister."

"Ah!" The flames in her eyes intensified as she realized the significance of the relationship, but she did not upbraid him. "How long are you going for?"

"I cannot say. Perhaps for a week or two. Perhaps—longer."

"What is to happen to me while you are away?"

What was to happen to her during his absence? In his excitement to make preparations for sailing to Jamaica, he had not paused to consider her side of the parting. What was to happen to her? If she were to sell the jewels she had exacted, first from Saint Just and then from himself, she would no doubt be able to maintain herself in moderate style for a number of years. But Phebe would starve before parting with the jewels to which she was so passionately attached. Besides, it was difficult to envisage her living save in luxury. She was essentially a tropical flower. Once exposed to a cool wind of adversity she would wilt. Her beauty would fade. She would become a lifeless husk of something that had once been extravagantly alluring.

Duncan realized what would happen to her. She would take to herself a fresh lover to keep her in pampered indolence. Straight from his bed she would step into some other man's bed, just as she had stepped from De Saint Just's into his. The possibility—no, the probability—made him resentful. He was unaware of the etiquette of the occasion, but he decided to try to buy her chastity so that he would not have to suffer the knowledge that his late mistress was in the arms of some other man.

"I will make you an allowance through François. He will pay you a fixed sum each week. Suzanne will find a woman to take care of you."

"How much?" she asked eagerly.

"Five English livres."

Her forehead wrinkled as she tried to calculate the purchasing power of five livres. Values were meaningless to her. Five did not sound many; she only had that number of fingers on one hand, so she suspected that the same number of livres could not mean luxury.

"I want more."

"I will make it six."

"I want much, much more," she demanded rapaciously.

He converted the offer into the equivalent local currency—35 livres to the pound.

"Two hundred Hispaniola livres and no more," he offered, disgusted at having to bargain and haggle over the price of her faithfulness. Besides, he could not afford more. Even the payment of that sum each week might prove a drain of his resources if circumstances developed as he hoped they would.

A strange expression flashed into her eyes as she nodded her head in agreement.

CHAPTER SIXTY

THAT night the *May Queen* left for Jamaica. She reached Kingston the following day, about seven A.M.

"Will you come ashore with me now?" asked Captain Beard. "It won't take me long to finish my business with them blasted authorities, and then we can have a look at the town and book a room fer you at one of the inns."

Duncan found it strange to hear his own tongue spoken so freely. For so many years he had heard nothing but French spoken generally that he felt as if he had stepped from one world into another. A Scots accent acutely reminded Duncan of the physician. Nostalgic memories beseiged him. At that moment he would cheerfully have sacrificed half his remaining wealth in exchange for the presence of that lovable martinet, whose kindness and patience could not have been surpassed. Dear Dr. Anderson! Dear Mrs. Anderson! Dear Jean! Dear Elizabeth! If only a miracle could transport him back into their midst, even without Margaret. Better still, if that miracle could not only restore him to the Anderson family, but re-establish life as it had been before the cursed Armand de Galinière had come upon the scene. Aye, even before the betrothal. He had been very happy living with the Anderson family, when he had looked upon Jean and Margaret and Elizabeth just as joyous, quarrelsome foster sisters and no more.

As Duncan gazed about him he was vividly reminded of the Cap François that had vanished. There were the same docile Negroes going about their work with easygoing unconcern and curiously contented faces; the same aggressive foremen, barking a lot but biting little; the same prosperous-looking masters.

If one closed one's eyes to the numberless black faces and the dazzling whitewash of the square, squat buildings, one could almost imagine oneself back in a district of London. The white women looked homely. Their complexions were browner than in England and they held sunshades over their heads, but otherwise they were the same busybodies he remembered so well. How many times had he seen them so in that past that was infinitely less distant than it had been several days ago? Some of them carried shopping baskets as in London. Some of them gazed at the shopping stalls with calculating eyes; it was not hard to guess that there were limited purses in Kingston as well as in London.

Eventually the two men drove to the Royal George Inn, which the captain recommended as a quiet, respectable place to which Duncan would not be ashamed to ask any woman. "A bit different from the Casino Frongswa, but you will eat well there, have a clean, comfortable bed, and won't be overcharged."

From the exterior the Royal George Inn looked a friendly place. It was wooden built and stood in its own grounds, which were surrounded by a tall iron railing. Trees and bushes shaded the building from the direct glare of the sun. On the left was a pleasant, flower-bordered lawn that reminded Duncan of Leicester Fields.

Beard kicked open the ornamental gate and pushed Duncan before him with a friendly slap upon the shoulder. "You and Mr. Williams will hit it off," he stated with certainty. "Mr. Williams is a man of learning."

Williams was a tall thin man with an almost academic bearing.

"Good morning, Captain Beard," he greeted in a cultured voice. "Welcome back to Kingston. Are you here for long?"

"No longer than usual, but this time I've brung a friend with me who would like to stay with you fer a few days. Mr. Duncan Stewart his name is, and he comes from Cap Frongswa, Saint-Domingue."

"That unhappy city!" He extended his hand to Duncan. "I shall be very happy to accommodate you, Mr. Stewart. Any friend of Captain Beard's is always welcome at my humble inn. Would you care for a cooling drink, gentlemen, or is it too early in the morning?"

"It is never too early for a drink," Beard said heartily.

Williams began to ask questions about Saint-Domingue, which Duncan answered with impatience. When Williams paused to ring for more drinks, Duncan introduced mention of Eulalia into the conversation. The seed fell upon fertile ground. Williams knew all there was to be known about Eulalia. Did not the monthly mail packet bring him out issues of the London *Morning Post?*

Was it true that Eulalia proposed to visit Kingston in the near future? Of course it was true. Was not every inhabitant of Jamaica anxiously awaiting the arrival of the notorious Eulalia? Why, her visit was likely to prove the event of the year 1802. Everybody knew that she was still unmarried, and though she was no longer as young as she used to be, well, she was still beautiful. Or so said the *Morning Post.*

Duncan gathered the impression that the smooth-tongued Williams did not propose to confine his interest in Eulalia to touting for her patronage. In a sharp voice, which made the innkeeper glance at him in surprise, Duncan asked when Eulalia was due to arrive at Kingston.

Williams' enthusiasm waned. Her visit to the New World had been postponed, he explained, for another two or three months. . . .

CHAPTER SIXTY-ONE

DURING the first few days of his stay at Kingston Duncan spent a considerable portion of his time with Williams. Not on account of any liking for the other man. He felt that Williams was not entirely to be trusted. Yet he enjoyed the hours they spent together, because the innkeeper had a profound knowledge of many subjects, which made him a thoroughly diverting conversationalist.

When it was too late Duncan learned that Williams was also an inveterate gossip. As soon as he had discovered that his guest had been an eyewitness of the original revolt of the slaves, and of the many subsequent dramatic episodes in the unhappy history of the French colony, he gratified his taste for drama by spreading the news, and at the same time basked in Duncan's reflected glory. For the visitor the consequences were of a not unhappy nature; he began to receive invitations to numerous soirees, not only to houses in Kingston but to some of the outlying properties. There were many people, he found, who were anxious to hear the truth of what had happened to that other island, rather less than two hundred miles to the east.

The days passed quickly, for which he was thankful, for he was impatient for Margaret's coming. This impatience increased daily. Now that he found himself among English people once more, that part of him that belonged to England revived. He found himself not only speaking in English, but thinking English again. And in thinking English, he remembered England and the Anderson family.

He seldom thought of Phebe. When he did, it was with a sense of unease. In Saint-Domingue he had lived with a mulatto woman without shame; in Jamaica the thought of his liaison was distasteful.

News from Saint-Domingue trickled into Kingston, sometimes weeks late. Christophe had returned to the Cap and had expressed his allegiance and Dessalines's to the French. Leclerc had assumed Toussaint's title of General in Chief. Acting upon instructions from Leclerc, both Christophe and Dessalines were moving against the insurgents. In seeking an explanation to account for these puzzling moves Duncan decided that Christophe, Dessalines, and the more important Negro leaders must have altered their plans in favor of collaboration with the French, and that some of the lesser chiefs, in defiance of this agreement, were organizing petty revolts. Duncan's acquaintance with the French forces in Saint-Domingue assured him that they had nothing to fear from such haphazard warfare.

On the afternoon of the eighteenth of August, following the arrival of the mail packet from England, Williams visited Duncan's room.

"By now she is on her way to Kingston—"

"Eulalia?"

"Yes, Mr. Stewart, Eulalia. The master of the packet has claimed his hundred guineas for a fast run. The latest issue of the *Morning Post* is dated the twenty-fourth of July and states that Eulalia will definitely leave for the West Indies before the end of the month."

Williams babbled on excitedly, but Duncan did not listen. If it were true that Margaret had left England before the end of July, then she was already nearing the island.

Time no longer passed as speedily as it had before Williams had received the latest news of Eulalia from London. Duncan was unable to check his impatience. He called again and again at the office of the shipping agent although he knew already what the clerks confirmed each time, that their ships could not be bespoken because they were faster than any other vessels bound for Jamaica. He spent hour after hour gazing out to sea in the hope of being the first to sight the packet boat.

He sighted the approach of several beating a course for Kingston, but none of them was English. Two were American, two Spanish, three French, and two came from the Low Countries.

Time passed still more slowly. He stopped accepting afternoon invitations lest he should miss Margaret's arrival. He tormented himself. He aggravated Williams. He made Jonas so miserable that the Negro began to mutter under his breath at receiving orders that were not to his liking. Suzanne—monstrous, happy Suzanne—alone among the people who surrounded him remained unaffected by his black moods. That was because nothing ever affected Suzanne. She was as unchangeable as Morne du Cap itself. Besides, she had known Duncan in the days when he had drunk himself to sleep to blot out the past, and had loved him then. It was not likely that an occasional unpleasant mood would affect her now.

One day, from his usual lookout spot at the end of the quays, he saw a ship tacking across the bay. She was a rakish, speedy-looking craft and news of the ship's arrival spread with rapidity. Within a few minutes of Duncan's first sighting the bows of the vessel townspeople began to converge upon the quays from all directions. Tiny cockleshells skimmed across the turquoise-blue surface toward and around the approaching packet, and avoided the creaming wash of the bows with miraculous skill. Other boats, each containing two or three Negro lads dressed in a loincloth, awaited the arrival of the packet at the quays.

The shouts of the master echoed through the still air; the remaining sails flapped, as the vessel luffed, and were hastily clawed up by the men in the yardarms. The bow wash slowly vanished as the ship's speed slackened and the vessel crept closer to the quay. As the faces of the passengers became discernible to those on shore, handkerchiefs fluttered gaily. Shouted greetings were exchanged. The Negro boys in the boats clamored for money to be thrown into the water.

Duncan recognized Margaret as the ship's side thudded lightly against the quay.

CHAPTER SIXTY-TWO

HER hair flamed in the brilliant sunshine like burnished gold. No one else could have possessed that precise shade. It was personal to her. He could have picked it out from among a score of redheads.

The face was Margaret's. Every sweet line was Margaret's. So was the little, pointed chin, which could be thrust out defiantly whenever the occasion demanded; the shapely lips, which embraced rather than yielded; the dimple just beside, on the left; the smooth translucent cheeks, glowing pinkly with the health of a northerly clime; the nose, which possessed no classical beauty but in its perky, indefinite shape imparted to her expression a hint of mischievousness.

His glance traveled downward, avoiding her eyes—for he was, just then, very much like the child who leaves the best tidbit on its plate for the last mouthful. At once he was conscious of a change in her physical appearance. The Margaret he remembered had just budded into womanhood, but the Margaret before him had matured. Her breasts were full, her hips pronounced; there was a suspicion of plumpness about her body that was attractive.

The moment had arrived for the ultimate delight. Slowly, almost shyly, his glance traveled upward toward the eyes that had once gazed so trustingly into his. That was, before the cursed De Galinière—

To hell with Galinière! he thought angrily. Why should he allow the memory of the damned Frenchman to spoil this moment for him? De Galinière belonged to an era that was past and forgotten.

He hesitated for one last moment while he thought of her eyes as he had always known them; their blueness, which was deeper than that of the ocean or the sky, and their ever changing expression; how by looking into them one had always known what mood she was in, and what she would do next—whether she would scold, or laugh, or cry.

At last he questioned them, now.

Disillusion followed. The hair was Margaret's. The chin was Margaret's. The dimple was Margaret's. The nose was Margaret's. But the eyes were not hers. The eyes belonged to a stranger to him.

Margaret had had faults enough for two; she had had a spitfire temper, a spiteful mischievousness, a long memory for real and fancied wrongs— With all these faults she had possessed a soul. A turbulent, vital, woman's soul. She had laughed when her heart was gay, cried when it was despondent, raged when it was angry. But the eyes of the woman aboard the packet boat were the emotionless, calculating eyes of a hoyden who had no heart, a creature who molded her world and everyone within it to suit her own selfish desires.

Memories crowded in of a hundred rumors Williams had retailed. He had scarcely troubled to listen. He knew that there was no word printed about Eulalia which Williams did not read with avidity, for the hotel proprietor had conceived an extraordinary fervor for the actress that was scarcely credible to a normal man; he could not have worshiped her more had they been lovers. Prompted by torments of unrequited passion, he had memorized every word about her he had read in the newssheets. These anecdotes he repeated at every convenient opportunity, with a masochistic anguish that had made Duncan wince with anger and disgust and would have precipitated a personal assault but for anxiety not to cause a scandal that inevitably would have resulted in embroiling Margaret.

"It is reported, says our Bath correspondent, that the reason for Lord D——'s suicide a week gone by was due to a state of regrettable, not to say extreme, penury, a fact which cannot but surprise a number of his less intimate friends, who remember that Lord D—— came into a magnificent inheritance of forty thousand pounds less than a year ago. Among those who will regret to hear news of his death will be E——a, that bewitching, bedeviling young lady whose charms are the toast of London Town. Gossip has it that E——a had been very friendly with my Lord until two weeks or so before his death.

> "This is the Cock that crow'd the Dawn,
> That woke the Vallet all Shaven and Shorn,
> That 'tended His Highness all Forlorn,
> That loved a Maiden *not* Tatter'd and Torn,
> That *mulct* the Prince with a Brimful Horn,
> That paid the Rates,
> That built the House of E——a.

As Duncan stared across the few yards that separated him from Margaret he knew that the gibes of the gossip writers were not unfounded. The face was Margaret's, but the soul was Eulalia's. The Margaret he had known was dead.

Eulalia was the first to step ashore. The other passengers moved aside as the gangplank was hoisted aboard, and obsequiously made a passage for her. Some men aloft raised a ragged cheer, which was echoed by the rest of the crew on deck. The master hurried to her side, as she moved with a regal carriage. At the head of the gangplank she halted, looked about her, and smiled condescendingly at the small group of clustering people.

"I should like to thank everybody for a very happy and comfortable voyage," she announced. "You have been most charming to me. Particularly Captain Johnson."

She spoke with studied effect. Duncan winced; he could scarcely recognize the voice that once had teased, enticed, raged at, soothed him. Margaret's voice had been warm, natural. Eulalia's voice was as artificial as her words. He had a feeling that every word was carefully chosen before being used, and inflected to give it the utmost dramatic effect.

"It's been a pleasure to have you, ma'am," the master acknowledged. "'Tisn't every voyage we have the honor of having someone with us." He raised his voice. "Hi, you men up there, and you on deck. A cheer for Miss Eulalia."

The men cheered lustily. Eulalia waved her hand and began to descend the gangplank. She stared at the people on the quay. For one moment her glance met Duncan's. Then it moved on. *She had not recognized him!* Had he changed so much? His hair was sun-bleached, his skin was burned a deep bronze, the contours of his face had lost the softness of young manhood, but surely he had not altered beyond recognition? How could she forget her own foster brother? How could she forget the face of the young man who had loved her, and whom she had pretended to love? He had recognized her immediately. Why had she not recognized him? More than ever he was shocked by the change which had taken place in Margaret.

She made her way slowly down the gangplank. A whisper traveled among the onlookers as the women observed the splendor of her jewels and the magnificence of her gown; the men commented in guarded undertones on her dazzling beauty. When she stepped down upon the wooden quay she was immediately surrounded by a number of beaux who hopefully angled for an introduction to her or at the least maneuvered to receive one of her dazzling smiles.

Somebody spoke to her. Duncan did not know who the man was; nor did he care. He was nauseated by her demand for adulation and by the sparkling vivacity with which she received it. He turned away and walked slowly toward the end of the quay. Upon reaching the farthermost point he halted and stared down into the clear, blue water. Seeing the rainbow-colored fish darting incessantly among the deeply colored coral, he was reminded of the jewels she wore; they too had flashed and scintillated in the sunshine. From where had they come, those jewels? Not from Mrs. Anderson, who had worn only pearls. Eulalia wore pearls, diamonds, rubies, and emeralds, in execrable but startling array. Mrs. Anderson could not have given her those jewels. Anderson would not have done so, for he could not abide a woman who wore too much jewelry. Had her earnings as an actress bought them?

> That loved a Maiden *not* Tatter'd and Torn,
> That *mulct* the Prince with a Brimful Horn . . .

He picked up a small stone close to his feet and hurled it into the water. For an infinitesimal moment the water blazed with flashes of brilliant light as the fish fled from unknown danger. Then all movement ceased. Duncan knew that his journey to Jamaica was fruitless. There was no love in his heart for Eulalia. Nor could there ever be. He wanted no wanton to share his marriage bed, no gilded strumpet to be the mother of his children.

CHAPTER SIXTY-THREE

ON THE twenty-second of October Leclerc fell ill of yellow fever. He died ten days later at one o'clock in the morning. He was mourned by few. Even his widow, Pauline, chose the handsomest among the officers to escort her and the remains back to France.

One morning Williams entered Duncan's bedroom in a flurry.

"Mr. Stewart!" he gasped and ruffled his thinning hair. "A Captain Staveley is below. He wishes to speak to you."

"I have never heard of him."

"He comes with a message from His Excellency the Governor."

"What does the Governor want of me? We have never met."

"How can I say? Perhaps Captain Staveley will be able to tell you more. Shall I say that you will be down soon?"

"I suppose a request from His Excellency is a command."

"Yes, yes, Mr. Stewart." Williams hurried to the door. "I shall reply that you will be down in five minutes."

"Fifteen, my dear Williams. I must look my best upon such an important occasion as the visit of a messenger from His Excellency," Duncan mocked. "Will you let Jonas know that I want him?"

Barely within the promised fifteen minutes Duncan entered the drawing room into which Captain Staveley had been shown. A tall man, in the uniform of the Sixteenth Regiment, rose quickly to his feet and saluted.

"Mr. Duncan Stewart?" Duncan nodded. "Captain Reginald Staveley, at your service, sir."

"I am sorry to be late, Captain, but I was not properly attired when informed of your visit."

"I can well understand, sir. It is indeed early, but I am acting upon the instructions of His Excellency the Governor. General Nugent desires me to express his compliments and to request your immediate presence at Government House, if same is convenient to you, sir."

"It is a strange request on General Nugent's part, Captain. I was not aware that His Excellency had knowledge of me, or my presence in Kingston. Why does he wish my presence?"

"I regret, sir, that I am not at liberty to speak. I am afraid that I know no more than you of the reason for the Governor's request."

The two men rode to Government House on horseback. Once the journey had begun Captain Staveley dropped his official attitude. The time passed pleasantly enough until they were within sight of their destination, when Stavely again became stiff and formal.

Within five minutes of his arrival Duncan was shown in the Governor's study, a large, airy room lined with bookshelves. The windows afforded a charming view of the town, the bay, and the encircling mountains. The far end of the room was occupied by a large polished mahogany table behind which sat Major General George Nugent.

As Duncan crossed the polished floor toward the table the Governor rose to his feet and held out his hand.

"It was good of you to come to Government House at so short a notice, Mr. Stewart. I am much obliged. Will you sit down?" He indicated a vacant chair which stood beside the table.

Duncan sat down. The Governor did the same and leaned back against his chair in a relaxed attitude.

"No doubt you are puzzled by my request," the Commander in Chief began. "I shall acquaint you fully with my reasons later, but first I must ask your indulgence while I ask you a few personal questions. Naturally, you are under no obligation to reply, but whether or no you choose to answer, I do ask you to take no umbrage, for my reasons are good and sufficient. Is it true that you have resided in Saint-Domingue for a considerable number of years, that you practiced there as a physician and surgeon, and that you were on intimate terms with many of the Negro leaders?"

"You are remarkably well informed concerning my past, Your Excellency," Duncan replied. "I must reply yes to all your questions."

"Ah! Then the history of that turbulent country must be, as it were, an open book to you?"

"Yes." Duncan smiled mockingly. "I was there during the years when an expeditionary force from Jamaica made such a dismal failure of adding the Colony to British possessions in the West Indies."

"An unfortunate and costly affair," General Nugent agreed dryly. "Toussaint l'Ouverture should have joined forces with us. Had he done so, he would not now be in a French prison."

"And the Negroes of Saint-Domingue might still be slaves, like their fellow Negroes in Jamaica. Toussaint l'Ouverture did not fight for the French against the English. He fought for the Negroes, and their independence, against all nations that still recognize the principles of slavery. I do not want you to gain the impression that I am either a renegade Briton or a renegade white man. I am neither. But I am not ashamed to admit that I am entirely sympathetic to the Negroes' struggle for independence."

The Governor nodded understandingly. "One last question. Why did you leave Saint-Domingue and come to Jamaica?" Before Duncan could reply, General Nugent went on: "Your face is very expressive, Mr. Stewart. I can see by your smoldering eyes that you consider that question a personal one. I shall word it differently. Is there any reason why you should not return to Saint-Domingue?"

"I have not considered doing so. I may go to America—"

"But there is no reason for your not returning if you should wish to do so?" the Governor continued.

"None that I know of," Duncan replied in surprise.

"Ah!" General Nugent seemed relieved. He leaned forward and smiled disarmingly. "I am relieved to say that I need ask you no further personal questions, Mr. Stewart, and that I may now acquaint you with my motive for asking you here. But first I wish to speak in the strictest confidence of certain matters of state. May I rely upon your discretion that nothing of what I am about to tell you passes beyond the four walls of this room?"

"You have my word, Your Excellency."

"Thank you. Now I wish to refer to the warfare in Saint-Domingue. You are probably aware that the command of the French forces has devolved upon General Rochambeau. What is your opinion of his prospects of subduing the Negroes?"

"The Negroes both fear and hate Rochambeau. They know him as more successful than any other French general. They also know him as one of the cruelest and will not forget that he devastated their villages and massacred their women and children. They will, I think, fight him with fervor and determination."

"I see. Then you do not think Rochambeau will crush the Negroes?"

"That is my opinion, Your Excellency."

"Contrariwise, do you think the Negroes will defeat the French? By defeat I mean, will they drive the French from the island? Cap François, the Môle Saint-Nicholas, and St. Marc are, I understand, difficult strongholds to storm."

"Not if yellow fever continues to be a Negro ally."

"I have information that Bonaparte intends sending further reinforcements to Saint-Domingue."

"In that event the French may eventually master the Negroes. If they can hold out long enough the Negroes will quarrel among themselves."

"A house divided, eh? Now let us be quite clear as to your opinion, Mr. Stewart. You believe that the situation in Saint-Domingue is likely to result in a stalemate, in which time will prove of advantage to Bonaparte."

"That is my opinion, Your Excellency, but I am not a military man.

"Perhaps you have a clearer vision on that account. What do you think would happen if the Negroes were to receive help?"

Duncan was startled. "Help, Your Excellency! From whom?"

"From the British." The Governor laughed shortly. "Your expressive face betrays you, Mr. Stewart. The suggestion shocks you. But remember that war is no longer a kingly sport. In Europe a madman, lusting for power, plans to dominate that continent; and afterwards, who knows? Perhaps the world. Rest assured that Bonaparte does not intend to pass England by. His most cherished dream is to invade and subjugate England. Once this is recognized it is not hard to realize that England is fighting for her existence. When a man is threatened with death he does not stand still and tamely await the threatened doom. He fights back with every weapon at his disposal. Nations are like men in that respect. They fight for life. England, thank God, has never been afraid to fight for her life.

"Now Saint-Domingue is a weapon England could well use in her fight against the Frenchman. The more reinforcements that are sent from Europe to Saint-Domingue, the more he weakens his home forces. For that reason, Mr. Stewart, we welcome the present warfare in the French colony." He laughed. "You may think that adversity makes strange bed-fellows. Certainly, for slave-owning Jamaica to encourage a Negro revolt in a neighboring island is a paradox. But to continue speaking in meta-phors, Necessity has no law. Which, at last, brings us to you, Mr. Stewart."

"To me!"

"To you. If you are willing to work for England there is a task for you to do."

Duncan was filled with laughter. That he of all people should be asked to do something for England; he, who had had to flee from England to avoid hanging from the gibbet at Newgate—surely no greater joke had ever been perpetrated!

"What is there I can do for England?" he asked dryly.

"Become her secret agent. Or if you prefer another description—liaison officer. Return to Saint-Domingue and contrive to meet General Dessa-lines, a task which should present less difficulties to you than to any man I know of. Make him appreciate that he has England's unofficial sym-pathy in his fight for independence; and also, that if he needs assistance in the matter of finance or arms and munitions, he will have our un-official backing."

"And what price is Dessalines to pay for such backing?"

"Price, Mr. Stewart?"

"Dessalines has a suspicious nature. I shall have difficulty in making him believe that England's motives are purely altruistic."

The Governor laughed. "You are a cynic, Mr. Stewart."

"I have studied history."

"In that case it is no use my arguing with you. But I will be frank: I give you my word of honor that England has no designs upon the terri-tory of Saint-Domingue. We have learned one lesson from our costly experiment—not to repeat it. Nor have we designs upon the independ-ence of the Negroes. On the contrary, England was the first country to raise the cry for abolishing slavery. Forces are at work at home which convince me that slavery will shortly be abolished throughout the British possessions. No, Mr. Stewart. We should have one motive, and one mo-tive only in assisting Dessalines, or any other Negro, to fight the French: that of embarrassing Bonaparte. Now, sir, what is your decision?"

"To go," Duncan replied promptly, as he thought of François, of Christophe—and of Phebe!

A long, rough journey, a long, uncertain time lay between them. Phebe was in the stronghold that would be defended by the French to the very end of their ability. If the insurgent armies should, against odds, reduce the town of Cap François, he might hope to reach her within weeks; to reach her, that is, if he could get in ahead of the victory-mad soldiery. But if the French held out until dissension ate into the insur-gent strength, then— He refused to think of it: the indeterminate months or even years, and Phebe always in the proximity of those French officers. No, he must believe that the Negroes could conquer; that Fran-çois would guard her.

He set out for Jérémie, the point farthest from his destination. All the nearer ports were in the hands of the French.

CHAPTER SIXTY-FOUR

EARLY in January, Duncan landed at the tip of the long southern peninsula to begin the arduous journey westward and northward. No sooner had he gone ashore than Christophe knew of his coming. The news traveled by the thumping of drums. When Duncan arrived at Bonnet-à-l'Evêque, he found Christophe anxiously awaiting him.

"Why did you leave me, Ti Rouge?" Christophe asked, immediately the two men had exchanged greetings. "When I arrived at the Cap to meet General Leclerc I learned that you had left Saint-Domingue and sailed for Jamaica."

"I left a message for you, Henry."

"Which I received, Ti Rouge. But I did not understand it. I was sad when I heard that you had gone away and knew that I had lost my good mascot."

"From all I have heard you did not need one."

"But you are wrong. I did. Nothing has prospered for me."

Duncan had no answer for Christophe's rebuke. It was beyond reason to assume that Fate had decreed that Duncan Stewart, Scots farmer's son, should be the mascot of a French Negro fighting for the liberty and independence of half a million black men, but how else could one explain the events which had persistently controlled his life by setting and keeping him in a groove parallel with Christophe's?

Duncan explained the British offer and the two went to Dessalines who glowered at Duncan. "What do you want, Ti Rouge? This is no time to ask favors."

"Patience, General. Ti Rouge is not here to ask favors but to give them," Christophe advised.

"Bah! I seek no favor from any white man. I hate all white people."

"Ti Rouge has just arrived from Jamaica—"

"I know that."

"But do you know that Ti Rouge brings us a message of help from the English?"

"What is that? Help! What kind of help?"

"The kind we most need, General; muskets, ammunition, powder."

Dessalines's eyes gleamed with fanaticism. "With enough muskets and ammunition I could force the Negro generals to carry out my commands. If I had all the arms I need I would sweep the French dogs into the sea."

"The English will supply you with all your wants."

"The English! The English are white like the French, Henry," Dessalines blustered, as he stormed up and down the tent. "Why should they help the Negroes to fight the French? I don't trust the English. They own slaves. I'll have nothing to do with white men who still have slaves. If the English are ready to help us it is because they have made plans of their own to seize Saint-Domingue. I can smell their scheming even if you can't, Henry. You are too trusting. Ti Rouge has touched you with his white magic—"

"Why not listen to what Ti Rouge has to say, General?" Christophe soothed.

Dessalines tried to control his raging temper, which, of late years, had become ungovernable.

"Very well. I'll listen to him. It shall not be said that General Dessalines was unwilling to accept arms. Why are the English ready to help us Negroes? Do they expect half our land in payment?"

"You are overlooking one fact, General," Duncan pointed out quietly. "Your enemy is also England's enemy."

"Bonaparte?"

"Bonaparte. The war in Saint-Domingue is only a skirmish compared with Napoleon's war in Europe. Every country in Europe fears what his next move will be. England knows that sooner or later she will have to grapple with him. Whoever tries to conquer Europe by force must count England among his enemies. This has always been the case in the past, is now, and will be in the future."

Dessalines waved an impatient hand. "How does England's quarrel with Bonaparte affect us Negroes?"

"In this way, General. Every French soldier killed in Saint-Domingue means one less French soldier to fight in Europe."

"You mean that England would like the Negroes to fight her battles?" Dessalines sneered.

"England asks nobody to fight her battles," Duncan retorted angrily. "She is quite capable of doing that for herself."

Christophe intervened. "Do you not see, General, that England looks upon us as an ally? That is why she is willing to supply us with all the arms and ammunition she can."

"She will exchange arms against merchandise and the right to trade here when you have made peace with the French," Duncan explained.

"The picking of coffee and cocoa beans would cost us little," Christophe urged. "The proposition is an attractive one."

"It would be to a trader like you." Dessalines strode up and down the tent. "Yet I begin to like the sound of it. Guns for coffee, powder for sugar! Why not? But how could the arms be imported? The cursed French frigates control the surrounding sea. They would seize the arms for themselves."

"If they knew that the arms were destined for us. But why should they know?" Christophe asked. "I have thought of a scheme, General, by which we could exchange our produce for English arms without interference from the French men-of-war. We would build a fleet of flat-bottomed barges that could travel farther up the shallow waters of the river than the French ships. These barges could be sailed out at night to the English ships in the bay and make the exchange of goods."

All trace of rage and suspicion vanished from Dessalines's ugly face, which gleamed with admiration. "That is a scheme to appeal to me,

Henry. Arms for coffee and sugar! By God! The coffee trees are loaded with cherries. I will make the cultivators and peasants work as they have never worked before."

His voice rose with fanatical enthusiasm. "You have brought me hope. With arms from England I could control the other Negro chiefs. Then, with their aid, I should sweep the cursed French from the face of Saint-Domingue. By Damballa! I will do all that or die. I swear it by the gods of Guinea."

Red-flecked eyes blazed with frenzy. Frothy saliva trickled from the corners of his thick-lipped mouth. Coarse, ham-like hands clawed at the air. For a moment Duncan believed that Dessalines had become possessed—no rare occurrence among a people who could lash their minds into a trance, or their bodies into convulsions—but he gave abrupt proof of his sanity. With a pounding stride he moved to the far end of the tent, where the colors of the Thirteenth Colonial Brigade, captured that day, were draped across a French drum. With a violent gesture he picked up the tricolor, tore it into three, and let the white portion flutter to the ground. As it settled there he stamped his heel down upon it and ground it into the soft earth.

"So shall we stamp out the white men," he screamed. "We will tear them from Saint-Domingue as I tore out the white portion that lies beneath my heel. Saint-Domingue shall be a land of free Negroes; for Negroes alone. And this shall be our flag." He held up the red and blue strips of the flag. "Liberty or death!" he bellowed. "Liberty or death!"

CHAPTER SIXTY-FIVE

"LIBERTY or death!" The words traveled through the land from coast to coast. It began as a reverberating whisper, and finished as a thunderous echo. Saint-Domingue for the Negroes! Liberty or death! Rousing words that stirred the slumbering emotions of the Negroes and spurred them into a frenzied determination to drive all white men from the Colony.

"It was a wise move of Dessalines's, to make a flag of our own," Christophe admitted to Duncan one day with grudging admiration. "Every Negro camp in the country is flying our flag, and our warriors are fighting better for having something to fight for."

"Haven't they always had something to fight for? Liberty—freedom—"

"Liberty! Freedom! Those are just words to the peasants, A flag is something for men to look at." Christophe laughed with childish pleasure. "When Rochambeau first heard rumors about the new flag he refused to believe them."

"How can you know that?"

The Negro shrugged with impatience. "We have our spies, Ti Rouge. Since we established our own flag, and Dessalines has arms and ammunition to spare, Rochambeau loses men every day by desertion. Nothing happens that we do not hear about." Day by day the Negro general boasted of further successes.

Duncan was on one July day gazing out over the bay, when he observed white sails appear over the horizon. The sight was no unusual one, so he paid no particular attention to them other than to reflect idly that another blockade runner was on its way to the Cap. But when, shortly afterward, he saw a second, a third, then a fourth, he realized that something unusual was happening. Soon the horizon was sprinkled with shimmering white dots that were beating a course for the Cap. The white dots grew larger as they approached land. Soon he was able to distingush them as British ships of war.

The English squadron left the fighting to the Negroes, but engaged themselves in intercepting all ships entering or leaving the Cap, and in supplying the black men with a steady flow of arms and ammunition.

The plight of the French grew steadily worse as their food supplies dwindled. Horses, mules, and asses were slaughtered for meat—even the dogs that had been imported for killing Negro prisoners. This meager, unnatural food weakened the stamina of the soldiers; in ever greater numbers they fell victims to the dread scourge which had already ravaged their ranks so cruelly. The Negroes, on the other hand, strengthened from day to day. As it became increasingly apparent that the hated French were destined to lose the war, Negroes who had hitherto hesitated to side against the whites now hastened to fight under the red and blue flag.

Dessalines decided upon a frontal assault. He made his disposition, and gave the command: "Advance!" Wave upon wave of fanatical Negro warriors surged forward against the French in an irresistible tide of hatred. The white troops fought valiantly, but ineffectually. One by one outposts fell and batteries were silenced. L'Habitation d'Estaing fell to Christophe and Romain; Charrier to another general; Dessalines captured Vertières and Pierre-Michel. When night brought an end to immediate hostilities, it was plain to both sides that the Negro armies were everywhere in a victorious position. With the eventual fall of Cap François inevitable, Rochambeau, defeated, dispirited, was forced to ask for terms of capitulation.

The evacuation of the Cap within ten days was demanded and agreed to. On the eleventh day watchers from the heights above the Cap—Duncan among them—watched the French fleet sail out of the harbor and mingle with the blockading British ships. Broadsides were fired; tricolors slowly fluttered down from the mastheads, to be replaced by white ensigns. Then the entire fleet headed westward and slowly disappeared. From the jubilant watchers came a turbulent, full-throated roar of triumph.

Bonaparte's soldiers had been defeated, but the fear of Bonaparte had traveled across the ocean. Bonaparte might yet organize a bigger expedition against Saint-Domingue. So cannon must be mounted against their coming; new forts must be built. Christophe rode ahead, for the black general had less interest in watching the French ships sail than in being among the first to enter the Cap as conqueror. Duncan, on edge with haste to look for Phebe, used Christophe's name as a password, but, for once, without effect. The Negroes either grinned at him because they could not themselves move aside in the jumbled mass of carts, wagons, oxen, horses, and mules, or else purposely closed their ranks and pointed their muskets at him to prevent his advancing. The color of his skin was responsible. They saw no triumph in driving an army of white men off the island and then being compelled to give way to a solitary white horseman. These soldiers he had to circumnavigate with some care, not wanting a musket shot in his back.

The nearer to the town, the greater became the press of people, for the soldiers were joined by the communities of outlying villages, hundreds of deserters who were no longer afraid to reveal themselves, and refugees from the Cap itself, who had lived for many months in mountains and forests. The din was terrific. Witch doctors were everywhere, exhorting—the gods must be told of the great victory over Bonaparte, of the victory of the Negro over the white man; the gods must be thanked for their aid in sending yellow fever to kill the white men in their thousands.

At last Duncan saw the walls of the city. Progress was still slow, but Duncan gradually worked his way through the town toward the Casino François. He might not have passed through the gates but for the fact that he was recognized; the entire staff of the Casino lined the railings at intervals for the purpose of mercilessly beating, with the long staves with which they were armed, anyone whose exuberance tempted him to try to climb into the grounds.

Duncan dismounted and passed into the cool shade of the building.

CHAPTER SIXTY-SIX

FRANÇOIS was waiting for Duncan, for the old soldier had been directing defense operations from the house and had seen him enter through the ornamental iron gates. He embraced him warmly.

"So you cannot keep away from the island, my boy?" he said gruffly, holding Duncan at arm's length and using his one, bleary eye to subject his visitor to an embarrassing scrutiny. "You have come back to this fever-ridden, blood-soaked land; and for why? There are a million people in this world who could not answer that question. But François knows the answer. He warned you, years ago. He knows. Now you will never be able to leave Saint-Domingue."

Duncan was shocked by François's appearance. The man seemed worn weak. He looked on the point of weeping. Suddenly Duncan dreaded to ask the one question tormenting him.

"I must live somewhere," he said with a poor attempt at a smile. "Does it matter?"

François waved his hand at one of the tapestry-covered chairs which lined the long wall. "Sit you down, lad, so that we can talk in comfort."

Taking Duncan's agreement for granted François pulled another chair nearer to the one he had indicated, and sat down.

"I will tell you why it matters," he continued. "Saint-Domingue is no longer a French colony. It is no longer a land where white people will be tolerated. The defeat of old Bony's expedition, the victory of the Negroes over the whites, has changed everything, my boy. From now on this will be a land of black people; as much a country of Negroes as parts of Africa still are. It is not good for a white man to live in a black man's country, on an equality with him."

Duncan shifted uncomfortably. "Do you propose to leave Saint-Domingue, François?"

"Me!" François revealed his stained, broken teeth in a pathetic carica-ture of his old grin. "Years ago I told you that I was too old to leave. Look at me! Can you see a corpse like me settling down in a French village?" His single eye glinted moistly. The blustering boisterousness of the past had entirely disappeared.

"Look at the swine," François continued loudly, this time meaning the crowds milling past the Casino railings. "I find it hard to believe that good, honest Frenchmen have been defeated by a rabble like that. Cor-nered like a colony of rats, starved, and driven out of the island. I didn't believe it, lad, until I saw the French ships strike their colors to the Brit-ish."

"Don't listen to the miseries of an old man," he pleaded huskily. "Tell me of yourself, lad. It's a tonic to hear your voice again. I suppose I should look upon you as an enemy. But there, I bear you no grudge. No soldier ever bears a grudge for his enemy when the battle is over. Talk to me, my boy."

But Duncan had no heart for recounting his experience in Jamaica or his part in the Negro advance. Making his voice as gentle as he could, and very distinct, he asked:

"Where is Phebe?"

François shook his head, with a look of bewilderment and vague re-gret. "She's gone, my boy. There has been neither sight nor word of her since the day you left. I thought she had gone to the French head-quarters in the hope of finding a new protector, but she did not return here with General Leclerc. I questioned some of the French officers, in the hope of learning her whereabouts, for if I could have traced her, I should have offered her good money to dance for me again, but none of them had heard of her." He turned and stared dismally in the direc-tion of the road. Presently Duncan realized, from François's expression, that the old soldier's thoughts were wandering. Perhaps he was dwelling upon the happy past. If so, it would be a pity to disturb him.

Toward evening Duncan, utterly dispirited, made his way through the crowded town to the quays. There he saw Christophe. The black general was surrounded by a group of officers who appeared to be engaged in a heated argument.

For a while Duncan remained unnoticed, but presently Christophe's sharp eyes caught sight of the familiar red hair against the foliage of the bush behind. Christophe stormed for silence when he had achieved this he shouted. "Ti Rouge!"

Duncan advanced toward the group of officers.

"Toussaint is dead."

Christophe scowled. "We have only just heard the news. Magny found a copy of a Paris journal dated the twenty-seventh of April which announces Toussaint's death in prison."

"In prison? Poor Toussaint!"

"Yes, in prison in France."

Christophe asked impatiently: "What is your opinion, Ti Rouge, of our argument about Bonaparte?"

"What is your own opinion, Henry?"

Unmistakable fear gleamed in his dusky eyes as he answered Duncan's question.

"The pride of the white man will not allow him to acknowledge that he has been defeated in battle by the black man."

"Bonaparte may be defeated in Europe," Duncan said.

"Then Spain might send a force to Santo Domingo. Besides, Magny, do not forget that there are still many French in Santo Domingo."

"England might want to add us to her empire," Bigaye added, with an embarrassed glance at Duncan.

Christophe slapped his huge right fist into the palm of his left hand. "I say we must fortify ourselves. We must make an armed camp of Saint-Domingue. Above all we must build at least one fortress such as the world has never known; an invulnerable fortress capable of withstanding any attack."

"And where would you propose such a fortress could be built?" Magny asked.

Christophe indicated the mountains behind him. "There, on La Ferrière."

The officers gazed up at the cloud-capped peak, and concluded that General Christophe was mad. He must be. He was a man, not a god. Only a god could build a fortress on Le Pic des Ferrières.

CHAPTER SIXTY-SEVEN

ON THE first day of 1804 the following document was signed by the 35 Negro generals and superior officers under Dessalines:

"In the name of the people of Haiti, we, generals and chiefs of the Island of Haiti, grateful for the benefits received from the Commander in Chief Jean-Jacques Dessalines, the protection of the liberty we are enjoying; in the name of liberty, independence, and the people he has made happy, proclaim him Governor General of Haiti for life. We swear entire obedience to the laws he shall deem fit to make, his authority being the only one we acknowledge. We authorize him to make peace and war, and to appoint his successor."

CHAPTER SIXTY-EIGHT

ONE morning Duncan was awakened earlier than usual by a commotion near at hand. He rose from his bed and opened the flap of the tent that was his temporary home. Together with two others, serving as surgery and kitchen, it had been set up on the site of the house in which Dr. Deschenel had lived. Immediately across the road a gang of laborers was setting about the task of clearing the site. What made the doing of it so noisy was the fact that they were still in the initial stage of discussing how and where to make a start.

Later that day Christophe visited Duncan, who observed that the Negro's expression was unusually abstracted. Duncan asked Christophe whether he was feeling unwell. Christophe roughly contradicted the suggestion.

"I am perfectly well, Ti Rouge. I bring good news. Dessalines has divided Haiti into four military divisions; the North, and the South, and two of the West. I have received the command of the North."

"Excellent," Duncan congratulated him. "Now you will have the opportunity of putting some of your ideals into practice."

Christophe's face was turned toward the open flap; his expression was one of fervid determination. "I mean to make the most of that opportunity, Ti Rouge," he said presently. "And one of my first acts shall be to rebuild Cap François—which Dessalines has renamed Cap Haitien. You know how I have always loved the Cap. I love it still, even though it is in ruins. When I first came to this city, it was the most beautiful and the most prosperous in the New World. I mean to make it that again, but more beautiful, more prosperous than ever." Unexpectedly, the gravity of his face gave way to eager laughter as he waved his hand at the workmen across the road. "Among the first orders I gave was one to have that site cleared. Do you know why?"

"No."

Christophe chuckled with naïve anticipation of the surprise he was about to give. "On that site is to be built one of the finest houses in Cap Haitien, when it is finished do you know who is to occupy it?"

"His Excellency, Governor General Dessalines?"

"No."

"Monsieur le Général Christophe, Commandant of the Department of the North?"

Christophe wriggled with excitement. "No," he shouted.

Duncan shook his head. "I cannot think who else is destined to occupy so important a house."

"Dr. Duncan Stewart," Christophe exploded, as he leaped to his feet with exuberant pleasure. "It is to be your house, Ti Rouge. Yours."

Simulating a surprise he did not feel—for Christophe's manner had, to some extent, enlightened him—Duncan made a vigorous protest against such unwarrantable and unnecessary extravagance. "Why should I need one of the finest houses in the city, Henry? As commandant of the department you should live in such a house—"

Christophe smiled cunningly. "I shall live in fine quarters, never fear."

Duncan ignored the interruption. "I am only a doctor, a white man—"

Again Christophe interrupted, this time sternly. "The debt we Negroes of Haiti owe to you, Ti Rouge, is beyond repayment. You have saved hundreds of Negro lives. Besides that number many more hundreds were saved by the Negro doctors to whom you passed on your great knowledge of surgery and medicine. There is no man, save only Toussaint l'Ouverture himself, to whom we Haitians should show greater honor. And perhaps Dessalines," he added as an after-thought, speaking with a strange note in his voice that made Duncan look up in surprise.

Welcoming the opportunity to change the trend of the conversation he asked: "How is Dessalines settling down to his new responsibilities?"

Christophe answered heavily: "Well enough. He has made Geffrard commandant of the South. To Pétion he has given the division of the West, formed by the limits of the Artibonite department, which is a pity, for Pétion is a mulatto, and I don't trust him." Christophe laughed sarcastically. "I think you can guess, from all I told you of the meeting at Gonaïves, the name of the fourth commandant."

"Gabart?"

"Yes, Gabart! Gabart, who was so hasty in demanding that Dessalines should be made governor general for life. Now he has his reward. Oh, yes, Ti Rouge, Dessalines is settling down. He is going to live in the Artibonite, where he plans to found a new town on the site of the Marchand camp. The town is to be called Dessalines, and properly fortified. Zénon has already designed its fortifications, and Lavelanet is to begin their erection as soon as possible.

"There is one rule to follow in the building of the perfect fortification, Ti Rouge: to see the besieging force without being seen, while obtaining cross fire and defilade. I have taught Dessalines this rule; he sees the wisdom of it. That is why he has instructed his commanders to build their fortresses, not along the coast of Haiti, but inland, on the highest mountain peaks, which are already, in themselves, a natural line of defense against the French; as Toussaint, Sylla, and Dessalines himself all discovered to their advantage."

"On La Ferrière, for instance?"

Christophe jumped to his feet; with an impulsive sweep of his arm he flung the tent flap to one side and stepped out into the white glare of the afternoon sun and stared up at the stark volcanic mass that formed a shimmering background to the scene of havoc and desolation that had once been a beautiful city. The nearer peaks stabbed the blue dome with a challenging gesture, intimidating in their immensity, yet one knew that behind, unseen, rose other, vaster heights.

"Think of the invulnerability of a fortress built on the summit of La Ferrière. No force could approach it unseen, no sappers could tunnel beneath its outer walls, for the mountainside is solid rock; no earthworks could be raised to menace its bastions, for there is not even enough soil for trees to root themselves; nor, for that reason, is there cover for an attacking army; no cannon could be mounted to enfilade the upper defenses; no man could approach the steep base below the walls without becoming an easy target. Such a fortress could not be invested by a thousand thousand men, nor in a thousand days. Against such a fortress Bonaparte might hurl his armies in vain."

"If Bonaparte could march his army to the walls of such a fortress he would have no need to hurl them against it."

Christophe frowned. "I don't understand you," he muttered sulkily.

"It is simple, Henry. Bonaparte, or any other enemy, would march his army against the fortress only if he possessed the intervening country, but with it in his possession, why should he risk the lives of valuable soldiers to capture a useless mountain summit? A fortress on La Ferrière might serve as a safe retreat against capture, but it could not defend the country against invasion. It would protect no important road or junction, no essential mountain pass, no town vital to the interests of the invaded. It would protect nothing save itself."

Christophe obstinately shook his head. "A nagging tooth does not threaten a man's life, Ti Rouge, but does he leave it festering in his jaw or pull it out? To an invader the fortress would be such a tooth; to prevent its festering he would have to besiege it, which would take a large force, so weakening himself elsewhere; perhaps dangrously. On the other hand, should he fail to besiege it thoroughly, then the defenders could harry him continually by making use of the guerrilla tactics which we Negroes used so successfully against the French. Multiply the one fortress by many, six, ten, perhaps a score, and tell me how many soldiers it would take to keep our land in subjection?"

Remembering to what good purpose the Negroes had previously put inaccessible mountain districts, miasmal swamps, and impenetrable jungles, by using them as natural fortresses that the white soldiers had found it impossible to invest, Duncan realized that there was some justification for Christophe's arguments.

Presently the anger left Christophe's face, to be substituted by the same expression of grave anxiety which Duncan had already observed.

"Why are you worrying?"

"At the meeting of chiefs this morning Dessalines reopened the subject of avenging what he calls the inhuman massacres perpetrated by Leclerc and Rochambeau," he explained, in a somber voice.

"Why? Leclerc is dead; Rochambeau is a prisoner of the British. How can Dessalines avenge himself on those two men? Besides, what they did was done in the heat of a war that is over and done with."

"Dessalines has hated the French from the day he was sold in the slave market," he mumbled. "He was so strong that he was expected to do double the work of other slaves. If he had been more docile in spirit no harm would have come to him; he might have become an overseer, or even freed. But Dessalines is a human bull. You know that, Ti Rouge. I would not say that to anyone except you, but I know you would not betray me."

Duncan did not like the deliberate way in which the other man averted his face. "What is Dessalines planning to do?" he asked.

Christophe continued to ramble on. "If only he had not been flogged! He was flogged again and again. You have seen his back; you know that he will bear the scars until the day of his death. The thongs did more than cut his flesh; they flayed his spirit. He is a mad bull, where the French are concerned. Only it is not red that maddens him, but white. It is good that he has that spirit, for it has helped us Negroes to attain our independence. But a bull is only safe when it is tethered by its nose ring; when it breaks loose from that it becomes dangerous."

Christophe's words did nothing to check Duncan's growing alarm. "Stop babbling nonsense, man," he demanded. "By what means is Dessalines proposing to avenge the massacres of Leclerc and Rochambeau?"

"You know what he said about killing any native of France who dared to soil the shore of Haiti by setting a sacrilegious footstep upon it—"

"He referred to invaders, soldiers—"

"He does not restrict his hatred to French soldiers—or even Frenchmen—"

"Good God! Is he proposing to massacre all the French who are still left in Haiti?"

With the back of his black, hairy hand Christophe wiped away the beads of sweat that were making his forehead shiny. "That was the suggestion he made to us chiefs."

"You did not agree to that, Henry? You, or Pétion, or Clervaux, or Gabart? You have always professed a liking for white men. They have been your enemies in battle, but, individually, the white men have never ill-treated you. They were kind to you; they gave you your freedom, they came to your hotel, they took you into their confidence, they made you rich, they were once your allies—"

"Peace, Ti Rouge, peace!" Christophe shouted. "When have I ever denied my liking for the white men?"

"And Pétion? Is Pétion a Judas Iscariot to a people whose blood runs in his veins? What has Clervaux ever suffered from French women? Has any French child ever lifted a hand against Geffrard, or Vernet, or Romain?"

"Listen to me, Ti Rouge," Christophe appealed thickly. "Not one of us supported Dessalines. We have no quarrel with the families who remain in Haiti. We want to live at peace with them and co-operate with them, so that trade can be restored, and the country become prosperous again. There is a lot we can learn from them—"

Duncan laughed his relief. "Why didn't you say so earlier? I began to think that the new era in Negro history was to be blackened in its beginning by a crime as foul as that of the Massacre of St. Bartholomew. What did Dessalines say when you opposed his wishes?"

"There is no opposition to the wishes of the Governor General. He is in supreme authority. We have sworn obedience to him."

"God! Christophe—"

Christophe slowly raised his head. In his large, black eyes there was a light of compassion and pity.

"I knew what you would have had me do, Ti Rouge. I did my best to make him see reason and to show mercy, but he is a vicious bull. The only concession I could wring from him was a promise to restrict his massacres to the French, so as to save the lives of other white men."

"Take me to him—"

Christophe shook his head. "It is too late. He started off for the Mole an hour ago."

CHAPTER SIXTY-NINE

DUNCAN planned to spend that evening at the Casino François. All the Frenchmen, the few white men of other nationalities who had remained in the Cap through all its vicissitudes, the richer mulattoes, and the more important of the Negro leaders—all still congregated there. His horror at the coming tragedy was not lessened by the knowledge that only French people were to be victimized—in his imagination he saw bloody sabers thrust into the soft bosoms of helpless women and heard the shrieks of innocent children as they were speared and mutilated.

Memories crowded in upon him of the horrors he had witnessed when he had fled with Christophe across the Plaine-du-Nord, on the night of the first insurrection. Were all those ghastly deeds to be repeated? In circumstances still more appalling, because they would be committed in cold blood?

In the faint hope that Dessalines's evil purpose might be prevented, he tried to evolve a workable scheme. Might there still be time to ride after the Governor General and demand the lives of the French people as repayment for the hundreds of Negro lives which he, Duncan, had saved in the past? This idea he dismissed, because it was foredoomed to failure. He had known Dessalines too long not to realize that any appeal to the Negro's finer feelings would be useless. Dessalines had never shown mercy to his fellow Negroes; was it to be expected that gratitude for the saving of lives in which he had no interest would prevent his putting to death other lives in which he had the interest of unremitting, merciless hate?

There was one thing he could do, Duncan presently decided. If he could not save the majority of the French people in Haiti from massacre, he could, at least, warn the inhabitants of Cap Haitien. There were sure to be some Frenchmen at the Casino; an alarm would spread rapidly. With this thought to ease his troubled mind Duncan lit a candle, filled a basin from the ewer, and immersed his head in the water. Its coolness refreshed him considerably.

The Casino was in a chastened mood compared with its state six months previously. Many things contributed to this change. The French had little heart for frivolity. They could not forget that their soldiers had been decisively defeated in battle, and that they were no longer living in a French colony but in a land now owned and governed by triumphant Negroes who made no secret of their jubilation at having overcome the power of the white man. Besides, the present was overshadowed by the uncertainty of the future. It was not easy for one to enjoy wholeheartedly the passing hour, when the morrow might bring calamitous news. Then there was the question of money. Money was scarce; only the fortunate ones had succeeded in saving from the wreckage of their fortunes sufficient for bare living purposes. This lack of money in a town where great fortunes had been commonplace applied equally to all white inhabitants of Cap Haitien. There was no trade, therefore there was no surplus money to waste in riotous enjoyment. Lastly François had lost the power of invention. The entertainment supplied by his mulatto girls was but a shadow of past performances whose familiarity bred a mood that verged upon boredom, although half a loaf was better than none, and the war-weary white men would have been lost without the Casino to lighten their troubles.

Upon his arrival at the Casino Duncan saw Webster with a party of Frenchmen. He made his way across the ballroom toward a vacant table at the far end of the room. He was halfway there when Webster noticed him.

"Hey, there, Mr. Stewart!" the American shouted. "Come and join us. There is room for one more at this table."

Duncan hesitated, as he saw the Frenchmen give polite but reluctant nods. He knew that he could scarcely be a welcome addition to their party; he was, after all, a Briton, a national of that detested country which had allied itself with the Negro army. By joining the party he would have an opportunity to pass on the first warning of Dessalines's intentions. He proceeded to Webster's table.

Webster rose from his chair, somewhat unsteadily. "You know Mr. Stewart, messieurs. Mr. Stewart, Monsieur Gérard, Monsieur d'Artes, Monsieur Lussac, Monsieur Ramlot, Monsieur Berges, Monsieur Charbonneau."

Duncan had no faith in rum to thaw out the atmosphere. He resolved to state his mission boldly.

"Messieurs, I will not mince my words. A few hours ago I learned that His Excellency, General Dessalines, is planning to execute all French people who remain in Haiti. I give you this information in the hope that you will benefit by the timely advice. In return, I ask you to circulate the same warning to all people of your nationality."

A strained silence held the small group who sat round the table.

Lussac shakily wiped the moisture from the corners of his lips. "I am not sure that I understand, monsieur," he said unsteadily. "You cannot mean that the Governor General is planning a—a massacre of Frenchmen?"

"I hesitated to use that ugly word, but it represents my meaning. But I did not say Frenchmen. I said French people."

"Not women—children—"

"I fear so."

"Mother of God!" Lussac whispered. "Mother of God!"

D'Artes caught hold of Duncan's arm. "I have a sister living in Port-au-Prince. She went there two weeks ago to marry Leconte."

Charbonneau folded his arms on the table in front of him and buried his face. Ramlot blasphemed, then drained his glass.

"I have a niece at St. Marc. She is only eleven but the prettiest child one ever saw. She is to go to her grandmother in Tours. That is why I came to Saint-Domingue three weeks ago—to take her back—" He broke off and stared at Duncan with agonized eyes.

"No man could be so vile—a massacre of women and children—" Gérard began.

"The Negroes have studied French history," Duncan interrupted sourly. "They know why the great bell of Saint-Germain l'Auxerrois tolled on the eve of Saint Bartholomew."

"Mother of God! Mother of God!" Lussac whimpered.

"That was more than two hundred years ago, when the world was less civilized," Gérard pointed out in scorn.

"The subjects of Charles the Ninth were a hundred generations removed from barbarism; the Negroes of Haiti not yet one."

"Perhaps he is bluffing," Webster said, his face pale.

"I wish I could believe you."

"What can be done to stop him?" D'Artes appealed in an anguished voice. "My sister is not yet twenty; a bride—"

"We whites must throw ourselves upon the mercy of Dessalines," Berges suggested in a trembling voice. "Let us go to him in a body, tonight. You are a friend of General Christophe's, Monsieur Stewart. For God's take, pray him to intercede for us."

"I know Dessalines. The word mercy is not in his vocabulary," Webster said unsteadily. "Your own Leclerc described him as the Butcher of the Blacks. He has massacred mulattoes and Negroes. Why should he stop at white men?"

"Mother of God! Mother of God!" moaned Lussac.

"He has already issued orders to his chiefs that all French people must be massacred. He started today on a tour of the country to see that his orders are carried out. There is no hope of their being countermanded. The only chance of saving life is to see that everyone of French nationality flees from Haiti while there is still time."

"There are no ships to take us," D'Artes pointed out. "The world does not seem to have realized that the country is now at peace."

"At peace!" Webster laughed grimly.

"I have reason to believe that Americans, and the homes of Americans, will be safe, messieurs. I am sure that you will find American citizens who will gladly hide you until the arrival of ships."

"Two of you can come to my home," Webster offered promptly. "I have no room for more."

"There are not enough Americans in Saint-Domingue to shelter all the French people who still remain here," Berges pointed out.

"Then some of the Negroes will do so. The massacre is solely Dessalines's responsibility; the other chiefs deeply disapprove of his proposal."

"Why do they not prevent their leader from carrying out his bloody plan?"

"They would do so had they the power, but Dessalines, by the oath of the chiefs, is now supreme."

"I shall go to Port-au-Prince tomorrow," D'Artes cried out wildly. "Perhaps my sister may know somebody who will give her and her husband shelter. Pray God that I am not too late."

Ramlot's eyes filled with horror. "My niece," he gasped. "I have just remembered—her father was proposing to visit a friend's plantation—he told me so in a letter I had yesterday, brought to me by special messenger."

"Follow them," Duncan insisted urgently. "St. Marc will probably be one of the first towns Dessalines will visit."

"I do not know where they were going; Jacques did not mention his destination."

"Then go to St. Marc first and find out his whereabouts from his friends there."

Lussac's shaky hand knocked over a glass of rum. "Mother of God!" he moaned.

Charbonneau raised his head. "For God's sake say something different, Lussac," he shouted out in an unnatural voice.

"Are we not all being too dramatic? Are we children to panic at what may be nothing but a false alarm?"

"A false alarm, monsieur?"

"Yes, Monsieur Stewart. I repeat the words. A false alarm! We are no longer living in the sixteenth century. For my part, I cannot help believing that a mountain is being made out of a molehill. I cannot and will not believe that even a Negro would be so monstrous as to order the massacre, in cold blood, of thousands of men, women, and children. Perhaps he spoke in a moment of anger; perhaps he means to select as his victims a few men who may have been guilty of cruelty to their slaves—but to order the death of thousands, as though he were thinking in terms of cattle—" Gérard obstinately shook his head. "It could not happen in the nineteenth century."

"It was the nineteenth century when your countrymen massacred thousands of Negro prisoners in the bay of Acul. Dessalines does not forget that fact even if the other Negro leaders try to."

"Bah! I do not believe half the stories I hear of supposed atrocities. Besides, war is war. The French and the Negroes of Saint-Domingue are at peace. Dessalines wants to win the respect of the world. He would not dare to begin his rule by horrifying all mankind."

Charbonneau looked more hopeful. "I think I agree with Gérard," he said shakily.

Ramlot rose abruptly from his chair. "False alarm or no, I take no risks. I love my niece. Tomorrow I ride for St. Marc."

Duncan rose, too. "I have warned you, messieurs." Now I must leave you. There may be other Frenchmen here who have a sister or a niece in St. Marc." With a curt nod to the Frenchmen and a muttered, "See you later," to Webster, Duncan moved on.

CHAPTER SEVENTY

ONE day, toward the middle of February, Christophe visited Duncan. "Is there news from Dessalines?" Duncan asked anxiously.

Christophe shook his head. "He will not listen to pleas for mercy. He wrote: 'Nothing shall ever avert our vengeance from those murderers who have delighted to bathe themselves in the blood of the innocent children of Haiti.'"

"Have you received information of any executions?"

"Not yet; the chiefs are reluctant to carry out the orders to kill the white men. But it is useless to hope that Dessalines will spare the French. Unless they escape in time they are doomed. What effect did your warning have?"

Duncan laughed shortly. "Little enough. Some of the men have taken what precautions they can to save their women and children, but many think me an alarmist. Some have even accused me of trying to spread a false rumor."

"The senseless fools!" Christophe exclaimed hotly. "Their blood must be upon their own heads. Enough of this subject. I came to ask you to come with me on an expedition, Ti Rouge."

"Where?"

"To Le Pic des Ferrières."

There was little need to ask the reason for the expedition; apparently Christophe was obstinately intent on investigating the possibilities of building a fortress there. Duncan decided not to encourage Christophe, but on the point of replying, he changed his mind.

"I will accompany you, Christophe, if only to prove the impossibility of doing what you contemplate."

Christophe laughed joyfully. "Do not speak too confidently, Ti Rouge, lest the boot should prove to be on the other leg."

At daybreak the following morning Christophe and Duncan, accompanied by a retinue of soldiers and the necessary paraphernalia, left Cap Haitien for the distant mountain peak.

Christophe was in his gayest mood; he talked incessantly; frequently his boisterous laughter drowned even the wordy price bickering and the noisy quarrels between competing vendors.

"This is one hour of the day which always makes me feel happy, Ti Rouge. When I ride through the streets of the Cap at this hour, I tell myself that the tens of thousands of Negroes who have lost their lives in the past twelve years have not died in vain. See how quickly the people have adjusted themselves to independence. Already they realize what it means to buy and sell on one's own account, instead of for a master. Listen to their laughter, look at their smiles. Could any man ask for a better reward for years of struggle and misery? And what will it be like a few years hence when trade has revived and the plantations are once more in full production?"

He gave Duncan no opportunity of replying, for he flourished his arm toward his right. "There is the spot which I propose to reserve for the foreign consulates. At first, the British and the American, and later, perhaps, the French. They will appoint consuls to Haiti, will they not, Ti Rouge?" he continued eagerly. "As soon as they realize that we are a new country and mean to take our place among the nations of the world, Britain and America will want to trade with us, won't they? They must. They need our coffee, sugar, and rum; we need their manufactured goods."

He flourished his arm again, this time to the left. "We must have a hotel there. No, two hotels; one for the rich merchants, and the other, more modest, for the sea captains and traders who choose to spend a night or two on land. And there, I think, the theater; or would it be better to have the theater in a different quarter of the town? For if we put it too close to the foreign residents they would be able to walk instead of taking a fiacre, which would be poor business. Every fiacre hired means more money spent; we want as much foreign money as we can get, to buy ammunition for our cannon. Look to your right again, Ti Rouge. An ideal situation for fine shops—"

The road seemed endless; they passed many side roads leading to more distant estates, large fields of cane, more plantations of coffee rioting in rank luxuriance, groves of guava that filled the air with a sweet, suffocating perfume; yet the blue mountain range that was their objective still seemed to remain beyond the next bend. But at last they arrived at the edge of the prairie, which was also the end of the good road. Before them rose the lower slopes of an outpost mountain and a rough lane that was no more than a horse track.

Here they met Barré, the engineer, whom Christophe greeted joyfully. "Have you explored the peak already?" He waved his hand at the round, flat summit that crowned the chain of mountains ahead of them. "What of my project?"

"I was delayed, General; I have not been here many hours. I had time to reach the top of the nearest height, but on looking back, I saw you at a distance, so I returned to this spot."

"So much the better; we shall be able to ascend together," Christophe glanced at the sun, which was low in the sky. "We can camp here for the night."

"I can suggest a better plan, my general. Up there—" he nodded at the height behind him—"is a view of Haiti that I can promise you is unsurpassed. There is just time to reach it before dark."

"Excellent; let us go." Christophe spurred his horse forward.

The gradient of the slope proved less than had appeared from a distance; the animals slowed down to a walking pace, but beyond having to pick their way because of the roughness of the track, they seemed to find no difficulty in carrying their riders to the top of the rise. There the travelers saw, below them, a broad, bowl-shaped plain that looked as if it had been scooped out of the mountains by a giant spoon and then covered by a rich carpet of verdant green.

The men had no time to admire the promised scene, for the sun was already below the horizon, so they made their arrangements for the night, which was barely completed when the swiftly graying sky darkened into black velvet. Two large fires were lighted; the bodyguard of Dahomeys sat round one; the second was reserved for Duncan, Christophe, Barré, and a colonel by the name of Cézar. They ate a meal prepared for them by a soldier cook and washed it down with rum. Afterward, Cézar went off to the other fire to appoint the men for guard duty; Christophe and Barré began a long and technical discussion concerning the refortification of Fort Picolet, which Barré was superintending. Duncan wandered into the darkness, and reflected that the night was the most beautiful of a thousand beautiful nights he had known in Haiti. In the velvet dome above him the stars shone with incomparable brilliance as if releasing in a few short hours the stored-up light of a thousand years. Behind him sparkled the twin fires of Christophe's camp, and weird, chanting notes came from one of them as black shadows leaped and postured round the flames in a barbaric dance. Below, more flames stabbed the dark mystery of night; the fires of many communities of peasants brewing tafia—the air was pungent with the sweet fumes of the boiling liquid. Nearer to, fireflies twinkled and flashed. A wild dog howled in the far distance; drums strummed a throbbing obbligato. The peace was sublime, the beauty majestic, but Duncan became restive, for the night unreasonably reminded him of Phebe. Phebe was complimentary to such a night. Possessed with the desire to fold his arms round her pliant, yielding body, he asked silently —miserably—Where are you? Where are you? His only answer came from the wild dog, which howled again.

Duncan awoke early the following morning. Judging that the rest of the party would soon be stirring, he rose from his bed and went to a near-by mountain stream, which ran swiftly. He stripped and plunged into the cool water of a deep, green-shadowed pool that tempted him irresistibly. Afterward, he went in search of Christophe.

At first he was unable to find him. He was not in the camp, nor anywhere near it, but on looking about him, he saw a figure standing on a distant elevation that was unmistakably Christophe's. He crossed the bowl-shaped plateau in that direction; as he approached Christophe, he realized that the Negro was staring into the distance with rapt concentration. Not until he was ten yards away did Christophe speak.

"Look," he said briefly, sweeping his arm round in a semicircle.

Duncan did so and experienced a deep sense of awe as he gazed upon the outstretched panorama. His feeling was one of being no longer earthbound, for a world was below him; a glorious world of unbelievable color and beauty. Green mile upon green mile of palm trees, coffee bushes, plaintains, bounded on one side by a mountain wall of blues, grays, and purples, on the other by a scintillating, expanse of lapis lazuli ocean, and above, by a boundless dome of cerulean blue. Barré's promise of an unsurpassed view had not been made without reason.

"Have you ever seen the like before, Ti Rouge?" Christophe asked in a solemn voice. He turned slowly in the opposite direction; the mountains rose up, tier upon tier, all but the highest peaks hidden beneath impenetrable jungle. "Is there another spot in the wide world with a more superb vista and a more majestic background? If one lived here, on this plateau, one could boast of being king of the world—king of the world—" His words tailed off, but his eyes were filled with excitement as he turned back to survey the valley again.

He spoke again. "If I were king, I should build a palace here, the most beautiful the world has ever known. I can see it in my imagination—there, on that elevated mount—" A pause, but only a brief one; he continued, stammeringly: "Over there, Ti Rouge, where every window should frame a prospect, different from its neighbors yet not less beautiful; where the decoration of every room should vie with the beauty of nature, and yet not overpower it. And there, beneath that star-apple tree, I should dispense justice; there, I should build a church; and there, barracks, servants' quarters, stables—" His voice rose to a high pitch and a half shout. "What king of Europe could boast so fine a palace as the one I see? What white king would not exchange all his palaces for the one which I would build there? Tell me the name of any monarch who would not envy his Negro brother a home built in this garden of paradise, and I will say to you that he is blind. Aye, Ti Rouge. Blind!" He paused, breathless, and soon his enthusiasm waned. "If I were king," he added morosely.

"Build your fortress here, Henry," Duncan suggested.

"Here!" the Negro repeated in scorn. He gripped Duncan's arm with one hand. The other he flourished at a near-by hill. "From that point an enemy could mount cannon to command the upper defenses of the highest fortress." He pointed at the encroaching jungle. "There, an entire army could conceal itself without its presence being suspected. There, one could build earthworks. From there, one could direct a cross fire and defilade upon every bastion. No, Ti Rouge. It is up there, where we now go, that the fortress should be built. But you will see. You and Barré, and all those fools who laugh at me for a madman. I will prove to you all that it is possible to build an invulnerable fortress." Muttering beneath his breath, Christophe released Duncan's arm and began walking swiftly back toward the camp.

After breakfast, the camp was dismantled, the luggage roped onto the pack mules, and a start made. Christophe led the way back across the plateau to the trail they had been following the previous day. This skirted the mound, which had enraptured Christophe by its possibilities as a site for a palace, and curved away to the right. For some distance they were warmed by the rising sun, but there came a sudden change when the trail plunged into the jungle, and from brilliant sunshine the party found themselves in a steamy, green twilight.

Above, the huge branches of ageless trees interlocked and formed a leafy canopy. Beneath, the ground became boggier with every step their nervous animals advanced. Strange, noisome smells offended their nostrils; the thick walls of undergrowth on either side flung back at them such distorted echoes of their voices that the cheerful chatter of the Dahomeys behind them gradually ceased, and the only sound to be heard was that of the squelching plop of the horses' hoofs as they were withdrawn from the glutinous mud.

Progress became increasingly difficult because of the low-flung branches that forced them to bend almost double, and undergrowth that laced across the trail. At last Christophe halted and ordered two of the soldiers to precede him and use their machetes to clear the trail. While the men were doing this Duncan spoke to Christophe.

"Is this the only trail to La Ferrière?"

The Negro mistook the inference behind this question. "It is the only one I know of, but if there are others, they are probably no easier than this, for the jungle covers the entire range. Now, can't you see how the jungle could be used as a first line of defense? When the fortress is built, I shall establish a special brigade of sharpshooting scouts, whose employment shall be just to know the jungle like the palm of their hands and to blaze their own secret trails so as to harry an enemy trying to reach the fortress. Behind that screen of undergrowth one man should be a match for a score. What chance would an army have of penetrating the jungle without suffering crippling losses?"

Duncan could not contradict this argument. "I agree, Henry, but I was not thinking of defense when I spoke of the trail, but of the building of the fortress. How are you to get your building materials to the fortress? Not along this trail."

"Why not?"

"It is not wide enough for us to get through in single file with ease. Look at the legs of the horses. Some have fallen into bog holes up to their bellies. If a lightly mounted man cannot proceed without the greatest difficulty, how do you expect wagons to do so?"

"The trail can be widened and drained, the bog holes filled up, and the ground paved with stone."

Duncan shrugged. "Words can always smooth out difficulties, but what does Barré say? He has studied engineering."

"Well, Barré, what do you say?" Christophe demanded.

Barré gazed behind him along the trail, then before him. "It might be possible, General," he admitted, with some hesitation.

"It might be!" Christophe bellowed furiously. "What is impossible about making the trail usable? There are enough axes in Haiti to chop down the trees, are there not, and men to wield them?"

"Yes, General."

"Ditches can be dug to drain off the water, can they not? Or is that a feat beyond the capabilities of a man who studied engineering?"

"It is not, General," Barré denied in a sullen voice.

"There is enough rock in any of these mountains to pave the trail, is there not?"

"Yes, General."

"Well, then—"

"One could not widen, drain, and pave the trail in a week, nor a month, nor in six months."

"Why not?"

"Even to make it usable as far as this would take months, and there are probably at least three leagues still to be traveled before we arrive at the foot of the summit," the flustered engineer argued.

"How many men had you in mind when you estimated that it would take months to reach this spot?"

"Between fifty and a hundred."

"There are thousands of laborers in Haiti not yet at work."

Barré was startled. "Thousands, General? But think of the cost of employing so many. When the French made the existing roads they had the use of slaves. There are no more slaves in Haiti." His voice rose in pride. "We are a free and independent people."

"Yes, yes, of course. Who should appreciate that better than I, who have fought so long in the cause of freedom?"

"Your pardon, General, I did not mean to infer—"

"Of course you did not, otherwise I should order your punishment." Christophe's face was grim, and Barré trembled. But the expression passed. "It would be folly to quibble about the cost of building fortresses to defend our freedom and independence. If everybody works hard, Haiti will become prosperous again; the fruits of that prosperity can be used for the purpose of protecting it." He impatiently tapped his boot with the hilt of his sword. "It will be your task to build the fortress, Barré, not to worry about paying for it, which is the business of His Excellency the Governor General."

"Yes, General," Barré murmured.

The trail grew steadily worse. The horses were unable to keep to any sort of even gait; they advanced upward in a kind of leapfrog motion as they picked out footholds with their forelegs and scrambled up with their hind legs. At last the trail became so rough and steep that Christophe ordered the party to dismount. Meanwhile, Barré's expression had become increasingly worried.

More than two hours later the riders emerged from the jungle; with the green canopy no longer concealing their ultimate destination they were able to see La Ferrière in all its stark, naked grandeur. It rose before them, higher and still higher, its extreme tip being hidden by a bank of fleecy cloud that clung obstinately to the mountainside. Barré gasped; so did some of the soldiers. Duncan glanced quickly at Christophe's face, but he surprised no indication of dismay or weakening; only obstinate determination.

The sun blazed down upon them, but nobody felt its fierce heat, for it was tempered by a keen wind that swirled round the sheer mountainside that faced them. The sight of this rock face caused Barré's face to lighten. He moved nearer and waved his hand at the obstacle.

"We can go no farther, General. We should need ropes to mount the escarpment."

Christophe glanced with contempt at the engineer. "There is a trail there," he said, nodding his head to the left.

Barré stared at the spot. "A trail—" he whispered.

Duncan sympathized with the engineer. What Christophe had optimistically called a trail was no more than a rough footpath precariously overhanging a precipice.

"Leave four men in charge of the animals," Christophe commanded Cézar. "The rest are to follow me." He strode resolutely toward the footpath, with his spurs jingling and the tip of his scabbard rattling against the surface of the rock. His broad figure, brilliant uniform, and martial bearing were majestic. Duncan was not alone in gazing at the Negro with respect; there was devotion in the eyes of the Dahomeys.

Duncan followed Christophe along the footpath, with Barré immediately behind him and the soldiers in the rear. In a rash moment he glanced at his left where, far below, was stretched the green carpet of jungle through which the party had already passed. He was glad to feel the firm surface of the cliff behind him as he stumbled back against it. After that he kept his gaze fixed upon Christophe's confident back—he experienced a moment of mean satisfaction when he heard Barré suddenly gasp with fear and begin to babble a prayer for safety.

The footpath curved round and upward. Duncan was glad to leave the unwelcome vicinity of the precipice, but the way grew steeper till here and there it was only possible to continue the ascent by using the trailing branches of some hardy mountain plant deeply rooted in a pocket of soil. Then the path curved. Once again Duncan found himself close to the precipice, now more sheer than ever.

Up and up. Everyday sounds of life ceased, except for the moaning of the wind, the panting breath of the soldiers, and the jangle of their accouterments. When they paused for a moment, and these noises ceased, Duncan experienced a sensation of having stumbled into a dead world, made up of flat blues, somber greens, and depressing grays.

Duncan heard a shout from above; it seemed to come from a long way off. He looked upward. Christophe had disappeared among the clouds. Duncan continued climbing. He reached the first fringes of the clouds; white, clammy, mystic. And frightening; for he could see nothing, hear nothing. A few paces farther on his head emerged from the clouds into the fierce glare of the sunshine—the strangest sensation he had ever experienced. He chuckled, then realized that Christophe was but a few feet above him, standing on the extreme summit of La Ferrière. Duncan scrambled up to join him. As he did so the wind suddenly swept the clouds away from the magnetic attraction of the mountainside; the fleecy bank split into two and sailed serenely off.

Christophe did not speak as Duncan and then Barré joined him. He merely waved one arm in a comprehensive sweep, and Duncan, at any rate, appreciated the reason for his wordlessness. All Haiti seemed beneath them, not just the valley they had seen from their camp. In the far distance, to the northwest, they saw the Atlantic Ocean; and the island of Tortuga dancing in its bed of shimmering blue. Farther off still, to the southwest, beyond league after league of verdant green, the pale blue surface of the Caribbean Sea merged into the burnished blue of the horizon. To the north, almost hidden by Morne du Cap, were to be seen the sloping streets of Cap Haitien and its roadstead in which tiny ships floated, fairylike, at anchor. To the east spread the wide estuary of Massacre River, where it flowed into Manzanillo Bay, and beyond, like a collection of colored pebbles, the Santo Domingo town of Monte Cristi. Nearer to, an undulating floor of mountains that was scarified in places by bleak, bare cliffs and summits and beautified by deep valleys of rich green and the scintillating rainbow flashes of tumbling silver cascades. Nearest of all, two other mountain peaks, almost as high as the one they were on. Bonnet-à-l'Evêque to the southwest, Morne-Ramiers to the southeast.

Barré was the first to speak. "Beauty unsurpassable!" he breathed in ecstasy. "Truly are the gods blessed who live in the celestial heights above our land. I feel godlike myself, General."

Christophe said dryly. "You will be able to appreciate all the more readily the advantages of celestial heights for the building of a fortress."

The engineer's enthusiasm waned. "I see your meaning, General. If it were possible to build a fortress here no artillery could cannonade it; infantry could only attack a few at a time. A thousand men might well hold this height against the weight of the mightiest army."

Christophe scowled. "*If,* Barré! If! Did I hear you say *if?*"

"But, General—" Barré could not conceal his uneasiness. "It would be impossible to build a fortress here. A fortress cannot be built of bricks; if it is to be solid its foundations and lower walls must be constructed of solid blocks of stone capable of resisting the attacks of sappers and bombardment. How could one such block be conveyed here? The trail is too precipitous for animals and wagons to be used."

"As an engineer, Barré, you must have read of the Egyptian pyramids."

"I have read of them, General."

"Then you know how one block was placed on another?"

"It is believed that each block was rolled on to the block below by pushing it on rollers along a raised roadway. As the walls rose in height so was the roadway lengthened, and raised to the new level."

"Then can you not read a lesson from past history?" Christophe demanded with impatience. "If the masonry cannot be brought to this spot on wheels it must be pushed up here on rollers, with the help of human labor."

Barré was aghast. He waved his hand toward the steep trail below. "It would take the muscles of a thousand men to move one block of stone up that slope, my general."

"And I have told you already, a thousand men shall be available if needs be." Christophe frowned. "We waste too much time in words. It will take deeds, not words, to build a fortress here, on top of the world. Look about you and consider this. If the delivery of materials be my business and not yours, can you design me a citadel that no living army could invest? Or do I have to shame the Negroes of Haiti by commissioning a white man to draw me the plans?"

The engineer swallowed. "I will design your citadel, General," he replied shortly.

CHAPTER SEVENTY-ONE

THE first information that Dessalines was putting his threat into effect reached Cap Haitien toward the end of March. Duncan and Webster were the first to hear it, for the bearer of the news was Silas Underhill, an American friend of Webster's. One night when they were at the Casino François, they were watching the marvelous antics of a Hindoo juggler, when Webster felt a touch upon the shoulder. He turned round.

"Silas!" He thrust out his foot, and expertly guided a vacant chair nearer to the table. "Sit down. What's happening in Port-au-Prince?"

"You haven't heard?" Underhill snatched at the bottle of rum in the center of the table. "Give me your glass, Bob, for God's sake! I need a drink. Three weeks ago, about four o'clock in the afternoon, a Negro officer informed me that Dessalines had given orders for a guard to be posted outside my house to see that none should enter or leave. I was indignant and told the man that I was an American citizen. 'That is why the guard is being posted,' he answered. 'His Excellency wishes you to come to no harm.'" Underhill swallowed what remained in his glass and wiped his damp forehead.

"I suspected what was in the wind. For a week or more a rumor had been circulating in St. Marc that Dessalines intended to massacre all French people living in Haiti. A few of the sensible ones took the precaution of escaping while there was time; others begged their American and English friends to give them shelter until the danger was over. Lamothe and his wife came to me. I thought they were alarming themselves unduly, but I didn't mind giving Lamothe what assistance I could; he had been very kind to me when I first arrived at Port-au-Prince.

"Poor Lamothe and his wife hid in a cellar, because they didn't trust the guard who had been posted outside my place. I went up on to the first floor balcony, but for the next hour nothing happened. Then I saw a platoon of soldiers coming along the street. They stopped outside the door of Delma's house. A moment later I saw the whole damned crowd of them running toward the house, yelling like fiends. They burst open the door, dragged poor old Delma out into the street, and shot him down like a dog. His wife was next; I think she must have swooned, for when I saw her the devils were pulling her along the ground by her hair." Underhill's voice broke. "I wish to God I had not gone out on to the balcony. I would give five years of my life not to have seen Delma and his wife butchered before my eyes."

Webster filled Underhill's glass.

Underhill said wildly, "The Delmas were not the only ones to die. There were the Juillacs, the Méranies, the Donnay kids—those hell-fired swine disemboweled them—God Almighty! I can't go through the list. Besides, Dessalines is a torturer. He didn't kill off everybody in one night. He took weeks to finish off the bloody work. It wasn't until the eighteenth of March that he stopped. By then there wasn't a damned French soul left alive, except the Lamothes and a few others who had found shelter with white people of other nationality."

"What about the Lamothes? Are they still safe?"

"Dessalines left Port-au-Prince as soon as his devil's work was completed. I made arrangements to ride here so as to give the French people warning of what to expect if they stay in Haiti. When the Lamothes heard I was proposing to leave Port-au-Prince they pleaded to accompany me. I warned them of the risks, but they said they were prepared to face them. None of us was molested; it seems that Dessalines is the only man mad enough, or bloodthirsty enough, to massacre the French; he only went to Port-au-Prince because the local chief had neglected to carry out his orders to massacre the French."

"Are the Lamothes here?"

"No, I left them near the Place de Clugny, where some French friends of theirs are occupying one of those wooden houses. They are going to help me warn everybody of that black devil."

"Dr. Stewart warned them weeks ago," Webster said. "It was because of him that the rumor of Dessalines's intention reached St. Marc."

Underhill stared, wild-eyed, at Duncan. "You warned the French?"

"Yes."

"Are there still any left in Cap Haitien?"

"Too many, I'm afraid."

"Then why in the name of God don't they leave? If they had seen what I saw at Port-au-Prince they wouldn't wait for the morning before making arrangements to escape to Jamaica, or America, or Cuba, or anywhere else they can get to. Damn money, possessions, and property! What good are they to a man with a musket shot in his belly? Let me talk to them."

Underhill's visit to the Cap was not entirely unfruitful. Several waverers—among them Charbonneau—acted upon his advice and prepared to sacrifice worldly possesions for the sake of their lives, and the lives of their families. These people left the island during the next few weeks; some aboard an English vessel en route for Mexico, some aboard a man-of-war from Jamaica, which was paying a courtesy visit to the Cap, and some aboard a German ship bound for Cuba; others escaped across the border into Santo Domingo.

But there were still many who refusd to leave Cap Haitien. Christophe would protect them, argued some; Christophe had always been at great pains to show that he liked white men, and wanted to remain friendly with them. It was in vain that Duncan pointed out that Christophe had no power to turn the Governor General from his purpose. Others, because Dessalines was traveling southward, reckoned that by the time he returned to the north, he would be sated with his blood purge. The pious were equally obstinate; God, Who had always listened to their prayers, would protect them from danger. Lastly, there were the gamblers who were prepared to take the chance of being overlooked rather than face a penniless future in a foreign land.

As the second week of April drew to a close, word reached the Cap that Dessalines was nearing Limbé. In spite of its inevitability, the news caused consternation among the French, for Limbé was distant from the Cap little more than twenty-six of the newly established kilometers—a day's journey!

Dessalines arrived two days later. That night the only white person in the Casino ballroom was François. The other whites remained in their homes, or in the homes of the Samaritans who were sheltering them. But the following day, the nineteenth of April, they were heartened by a proclamation, which stated that His Excellency the Governor General was satisfied that the murderers who had bathed in the blood of the innocent children of Haiti were now sufficiently avenged; in consequence, all those fortunate people who had escaped execution under the military decree were invited to parade the following day, in the Place d'Armes, when each person present should receive a ticket of protection, which thereafter would entitle him to live in perfect security.

That night the Casino was more crowded than it had ever been throughout its career as a place of entertainment. Many Frenchmen who had remained hidden for the past few nights ventured into the streets as soon as the night rendered them inconspicuous, and made their way to the Casino. They crowded into the ballroom in such numbers that there was not a spare seat to be had. Movement became impossible, so tightly packed were the people between the tables. No one fussed or grumbled; everyone kept his glass on the nearest table, irrespective of who sat there; or if he were beyond reach of a table, then he held the glass. Conversation and laughter were joyful, as was to be expected of a community that had been granted a reprieve from death. With light hearts many appointments were made for families to meet at the Place d'Armes the following afternoon.

Duncan was away from the city these two days, attending a patient through a difficult crisis. When he returned, he proceeded to the rue St. Joseph by way of the back streets. On three occasions he was greatly surprised to see parties of French people parading openly; on the third occasion he was tempted to remonstrate with the men of the party for their rashness in reminding Dessalines, through his legion of spies, of their presence in the town. He desisted, because he was tired, and because it was no business of his what the foolish people did. He had done everything within his power to save their lives. If they persisted in risking those lives because Dessalines had so far withheld his vengeance, that was their affair.

He entered the rue St. Joseph, a hundred meters from his temporary home. All sleepiness disappeared when he saw that five Negro soldiers surrounded his house; if posting the soldiers was a measure to protect his life, then it must be a sign that Dessalines contemplated a massacre of the French that night.

He rode up to a lieutenant, who stood by the main entrance. "What are these men doing here?" he demanded.

The lieutenant recognized him, and respectfully saluted. "I was ordered to post them here, citizen."

"Why?"

"To see that nobody leaves or enters the house, citizen."

Duncan thought of the hundreds of French people who were living at the Cap. "God save their souls!" he exclaimed in a husky whisper.

The Negro's mouth widened in a broad grin. "There is to be no killing of the French here, citizen."

"What do you mean?"

"Have you not read the proclamation of His Excellency? The French are safe; they will all receive tickets protecting them from execution."

Duncan's relief was very sweet, and he realized why he had seen so many French people in the streets. Christophe had promised to intercede for the French; evidently the plea had succeeded. He dismounted, tethered his horse, and ran up the steps to the door of the house. As he did so he heard the rattle of musket shots.

"What was that?"

Fear made the Negro wide-eyed. "I know not, citizen. Perhaps—" His words were interrupted by a second, ragged volley, followed by the faint echo of a shriek.

Duncan stepped toward his horse, but the lieutenant pulled out his sword. "Where you you going, citizen?"

"To General Christophe. There's devil's work going on near the Place d'Armes." A third volley punctuated his words.

The Negro shook his head. "You must stay where you are. My orders were to see that you did not leave your home on any account, citizen."

Duncan ignored him and took hold of the halter, but the lieutenant raised his sword so that its point rested lightly on the lower part of Duncan's throat.

"I would not wish to hurt the doctor; he is too much loved by all us Negroes; but I must carry out my orders or be executed. Step back into the house."

There was a determination in the man's eyes that warned Duncan that he would risk death if he insisted upon trying to mount his horse, but he made one more effort.

"Women and children are dying. I might be able to save their lives," he urged. "You know how many Negro lives I have saved; let me save some white ones for a change."

The lieutenant hesitated; Duncan was certain that he recognized pity in his expression. Then the man's resolution hardened.

"Into the house, citizen," he ordered harshly.

Duncan stumbled into the house.

Volley succeeded volley; as the pile of corpses rose higher, the Place d'Armes swam with blood, and the clear stream that ran through the town was stained with crimson. One hundred, two, three, four—and still the night was made hideous with the crackle of musketry and the shrieks of the women and children as they were forced to walk to the place of execution. Five hundred, six, seven—

Some were spared; priests, physicians, and white men who had a reputation for kindness to the Negroes. The rest died, whether they were men, women, or children.

As the sun touched the rim of the horizon, the figure of a white man stamped into the Place d'Armes. He was dressed in a French military uniform of ancient design. He had but one eye, half an ear, and two fingers of his left hand were missing. His face was burned the color of black-brown leather, his draggling mustaches were greasy. The moment he was seen half a dozen soldiers ran toward him, yelling their hatred of his uniform. He had a thick stick in his hand, with a heavy knob at one end. This he reversed; then struck with it at the head of the nearest black man. The heavy knob cracked the temple wide open and sent the man reeling to the ground. Before François could strike again the stick was wrenched from his grasp. Not yet was he helpless. He produced a dagger from a mysterious source and plunged it into the chest of a second Negro. This man, too, slumped to the ground and did not move again. Before François could do further damage the remaining four soldiers had him in their grasp and were marching him toward the huge pile of white corpses. Before they could reach it, they were halted by the loud voice of their governor general.

"Come here, you four men," Dessalines bellowed.

The soldiers dragged their captive in front of the Governor General.

"What are you doing with that man?"

"Taking him to die with the others, Your Excellency."

"Fools, that is François. I gave orders that he was to be saved."

The soldiers became terror-stricken. "We did not know him. Besides, he has killed two of us," quavered the man who had first spoken.

"I saw, and I shall execute the rest of you for allowing an old man to kill two out of six. Your deaths shall be an example to our soldiers to fight with more energy."

"But, Your Excellency—"

"Silence!" Dessalines raved. To an officer of his bodyguard: "Take them away and shoot them."

The order was quickly carried out. As soon as the four black bodies had been pitched on top of the hundreds of white corpses Dessalines turned back to François, and bellowed with laughter.

"Why did you come here, old François? Did you think we would shoot you? By Damballa! You are the only white man I have ever liked. Now, be off to your Casino and sleep peacefully. You are safe; you have the word of Dessalines."

François stared steadily at him. "You black bastard!" he said coldly.

Dessalines's fist knotted; his face became malevolent. "Be careful what you say, old man," he roared. "There are still bullets left to kill more whites."

"Then order the muskets to be loaded, Dessalines," François growled. "I have been a French soldier all my life; do you think I wish to live knowing that you have murdered my countrymen?" He leaned forward and spat: the tobacco-stained saliva dribbled down Dessalines's brilliant uniform. "Now order your men to shoot, you black-skinned son of a bitch."

Dessalines did not order his men to shoot; he snatched a musket from his nearest bodyguard and aimed it at the leathery, sneering face.

"*Vive la France*," François choked as he fell forward, his hand at the salute.

CHAPTER SEVENTY-TWO

DISPATCHES arrived from Europe at intervals. From one Dessalines learned that Napoleon Bonaparte had become emperor of the French on May 18, 1804.

Emperor! Dessalines ordered his secretary Boisrond-Tonnerre to read out that particular dispatch again and again. Emperor Napoleon! Emperor! Dessalines began to ask eager questions. This Napoleon Bonaparte was not born of royal blood, was he? He had lived his earlier life as a commoner, had he not? At an early age he had become a soldier, had he not?

"Yes, Your Excellency."

"I was not born of royal blood; I am a commoner, but I, too, have become a great soldier, have I not?"

"Indeed you have, Your Excellency."

"As great as Bonaparte? No, greater than Bonaparte, for he is the vanquished, I am the victor. Surely, the vanquished is a lesser man than the conqueror?"

"Of course, Your Excellency."

"Before Bonaparte became emperor he was appointed first consul for life, wasn't he?"

"He was, Your Excellency."

"I have been elected governor general for life. Does it seem to you that Bonaparte's life and mine have run side by side?"

"It does seem so, Your Excellency."

"But now Bonaparte has become emperor of the Fernch?"

"Yes, Your Excellency."

Dessalines's eyes shone. "As the gods have made the lives of Bonaparte and me run side by side, isn't it a divine command that I, too, become an emperor? Jacques the First, Emperor of Haiti!" Eagerly he awaited his secretary's reply, but Boisrond-Tonnerre remained silent. "Isn't it?" Dessalines demanded sharply.

"I think so, Your Excellency," the secretary agreed suavely. "But will the generals and chiefs agree?"

"They have sworn to acknowledge my authority. I shall order them to elect me their emperor, under penalty of my disapproval, which each chief will interpret according to the value he places on his safety. Besides—" The Governor General's expression turned cunning. "An emperor must have a court, and a court must have courtiers, and courtiers usually have titles—"

"Why, of course, Your Excellency," the secretary agreed with eagerness. "When you use that argument—"

"When you use it," Dessalines interrupted.

"I? But of course, Your Excellency, I understand. There will be dukes and counts—perhaps even princes—" The secretary looked inquiringly at the Governor General, who nodded. "And honorable posts for those who have served you well—"

"To Boisrond-Tonnerre, secretary of state, a barony."

"Your Excellency is too generous," the secretary murmured. "The generals and chiefs will appreciate the advantage of being the subjects of an emperor—Your Majesty!"

The secretary's shrewd opinion was justified. When he first suggested that Haiti would be more respected by the European nations, all of whom were kingdoms, if she were to have an emperor for ruler rather than a mere governor general, the chiefs were suspicious; but the secretary's cunningly offered bait, in his veiled references to dukes, barons, and counts, enabled them to see the project from a different aspect. Gabart saw himself as the Baron St. Marc; no, the Count St. Marc! Geffrard decided that Baron Jérémie sounded more attractive than Baron Miragoane, or Baron Jacmel. Pétion trifled with the dukedom of Port-au-Prince, but decided eventually that the Duc de Mirebalais was less cumbersome.

In August, Dessalines became Jacques I of Haiti. The ceremony of coronation took place on the eighth of October in the Champ de Mars, where his generals, chiefs, and jubilant subjects had assembled in vast numbers. When the ceremony was over the new emperor was given a royal salute, and acclaimed by the army and the public. Then the Emperor, at the head of his cortege, passed into the cathedral, where Corneille Brelle celebrated Solemn High Mass.

In due course the generals and chiefs approached their emperor with reference to the matter of the promised honors.

To their requests, desires, and hints the Emperor gave a bland refusal. His was to be the only title in the land. If the chiefs were enraged by this setback to their personal ambitions, they were careful not to let the Emperor suspect their true feelings. Whoever opposed the ex-slave did so at his peril.

The constitution was promulgated: the empire of Haiti was decreed a free, sovereign, and independent state; slavery was abolished forever. Ships arrived in Haiti in increasing numbers. Merchants came from several countries, particularly from America and England.

One day it occurred to the Emperor to ask whether there were any figures relating to the export of produce. He wanted money to pay his large standing army, for the upkeep of his palace at the Cap, to pay for the fortifications that were in the course of erection in every part of the country, for the maintenance of his many mistresses, to keep his supporting chiefs from becoming too restive.

Approximately one hundred and eighty-five thousand pounds of sugar exported from Cap Haitien during the first six months of 1804! The Emperor grunted his satisfaction. The amount sounded formidable. Then, in a moment of misguided zeal, he asked how much sugar had been exported from the Cap during the first six months of 1791. The secretary informed His Majesty that the total for six months was probably more than twenty-two million pounds. Even Jacques could appreciate the vast difference between one hundred and eight-five thousand, and twenty-two million. His expression became thunderous. In harsh, ominous language he demanded further comparisons. Syrup, none, as compared with five thousand *boucauts*. Indigo, none, as compared with nearly one hundred thousand pounds. Coffee, two and a quarter million pounds, as compared with fifteen million. The Emperor's expression was brutal.

"Enough! Haiti must produce more. We will organize labor for the benefit of the state. We will pass laws—"

The cultivators groaned and sweated to fill the treasury; the laborers groaned and sweated to construct fortifications and divert watercourses for the use of the garrisons; gangs of convicts groaned and sweated to make roads. The Emperor's rule became daily more tyrannical.

His suspicions, jealousies, caprices, and tyrannies at last destroyed the reverence in which his subjects had once held him. Just two years after his crowning the Emperor was informed that nationwide dissatisfaction had, in the South, assumed the more alarming character of armed revolt. He acted immediately, by calling upon the chiefs to join him in crushing the insurrection. In particular he addressed Pétion, who governed the neighboring department of the West. The answer he received was that Pétion had joined the insurrection.

The Emperor did not underrate the seriousness of the situation, but he did not lack courage. Accompanied by only a few officers, he rode to Port-au-Prince, where he proposed to conduct measures for the suppression of the revolt. On the outskirts of the town he encountered a detachment of troops who refused to receive him with the customary military honors. Enraged by this act of insubordination he galloped toward his soldiers, and angrily demanded an explanation for their mutinous conduct. His only reply was a musket ball, which struck him down. His body twitched spasmodically, then moved no more. With callous disregard for the remains of their dead emperor the troops turned and shuffled back into Port-au-Prince.

Jacques I of Haiti might have done better for himself by making Pétion the Duc de Mirebalais.

CHAPTER SEVENTY-THREE

FOR three days a courier from Port-au-Prince sped north, changing animals at every military garrison. Toward late afternoon of the third day he arrived at Cap Haitien and proceeded directly to General Christophe's headquarters. One hour later Jonas, who had returned from Jamaica with Suzanne, announced to Duncan that Christophe was calling on him. Duncan knew from Christophe's unmistakable elation that something of extreme importance had taken place. He wondered if the Emperor were involved, for strange rumors had been circulating in the town of the South's growing restiveness. Christophe's first words answered this reflection.

"The Emperor is dead!" Christophe announced dramatically. "Gérin's troops assassinated him."

The unexpectedness of the tragedy surprised Duncan. "So the tyrant is dead! I doubt that anyone will regret his death. Who is to rule in his place? Did he appoint a successor?"

"I do not know. Probably not, for he had no thought of dying so soon. But what he did or didn't do makes no difference; forty-eight of the leading revolutionaries have sent me this dispatch: 'With joy and unanimity we proclaim you the supreme chief of this island, under whatever title you are pleased to choose. Our hearts are yours; we swear before God to be always faithful to you."

A score of questions rose to Duncan's lips, but as he glanced at Christophe he suppressed them and remained silent. Christophe's face was softened by a light that was reflected from his soul; his eyes glowed with pride, a fanatical zeal, and also gratitude for the opportunity to realize his dreams. As in a trance he moved across to the window and gazed out. The sun was sinking rapidly toward the western horizon; soon the country would be cloaked in the velvet infinity of night; but for the moment the scene was warmed and softened by the last minutes of daylight.

"The ruler of Haiti!" he murmured. "After all these years! I thank Thee, Gracious Father in Heaven, for Thy boundless kindness in granting me this honor, and swear to Thee that I will faithfully and dutifully fulfill that sacred trust."

Duncan said nothing, for the man was thinking aloud.

Presently he spoke again. "I swear by the Father, the Son, and the Holy Ghost; I swear by the Virgin Mary, the Mother of God; by my patron saints, Bruno and Marcel; I swear by Damballa Ouedo, by Erzulie Freida, and all the gods of Guinea; I swear that I will restore Haiti to its past prosperity; that I will make it respected among the countries of the world; that I will defend it against the French to my last breath; that I will remain friendly with the white men, while respecting the constitution of Emperor Jacques; that I will encourage the arts; that I will employ whites to bring into Haiti all that is best of their lands, and keep out the worst; that I will restore happiness to the people of this land; that I will give them learning and education—" His voice sank to an unintelligible whisper, which was soon followed by a long silence. The sun disappeared; Christophe became a black shadow outlined against the darkening background of the night.

At last Christophe turned. "Will you light the candles, Ti Rouge?" he asked in a voice in which there was no note of embarrassment. He made his way to the center of the room and sat down, while Duncan fired a sulphur-tipped splint and lighted the candelabra on the table.

"Do you remember the night when you told me of your wish to help and strengthen the new nation of black men that was born on the first day of eighteen hundred and four?"

"I have tried to forget."

"You are bitter, but I cannot blame you. When Dessalines massacred most of the French inhabitants of the country you thought of leaving Haiti for good—"

"Not only then, but several times since."

"I know. Why did you remain here?"

"Heaven alone knows!" Duncan replied shortly. "Because Haiti is *le pays des revenants*, I suppose. Every time I thought of leaving I wondered where in the world I should find another country like it, with its mountains and its plantations, its mystery and its cruelty, its seductive perfume and its pestilent smells, its monotonous drums and its threatening silences. I didn't think I should find another land so glamorous, and yet so cruel. That is why I stayed. As poor old François used to tell me, Haiti is like a capricious mistress; she hurts you, torments you, ruins you until you come to hate her, but the more you hate her the stronger are the chains of passion which bind you to her."

"Poor François! We both loved the old man. He was kind and wise. *Le pays des revenants*. He was right, but Haiti's caprices, cruelty, and mystery were not what kept you here, even while you cursed the black men for being bloody murderers and pagan savages. You see, Ti Rouge, I know your soul as you know mine. You stayed on in Haiti because you hoped for the miracle to happen."

"Well?" Duncan challenged.

"The miracle has come about. The Emperor Jacques is dead; I am the supreme ruler of Haiti. I can do all those things that he should have done, but I shall need your help and advice more than ever before. You heard me make an oath to the gods. You can help me keep that oath." His anxious eyes pleaded with Duncan. "Do not interrupt me, Ti Rouge. If I am to sleep tonight I must talk myself out of the state of excitement I am in. Look!" He held out his hand at arm's length; it trembled visibly. "I am thirty-nine years of age this month. How many more years have I left to me? Ten? Twenty? Perhaps more. Fifty would not be too many, for the white man is hundreds of years ahead of us, and we must catch up soon.

"We must encourage foreign merchants to establish themselves here; they will not be permitted to own their warehouses, but for those who come first I shall build warehouses and offices to their own requirements, which they will be able to rent at moderate rates. I shall have a special clubhouse for white men; it shall be for their sole use; no black man shall go near it except as a paid employee. Do you think the merchants will come here if my intentions are made known to them?"

"Merchants will follow wherever trade leads, Henry, even at the risk of their lives, but they like to be quite sure that the trade is worth while before taking risks."

"To the first six merchants to come here I promise all the trade they care to handle. Tell me, have you news of your friend Nathaniel Martin?"

"I have not heard from him for several months; I suspect that his mind is occupied with thoughts of marriage."

"Why doesn't he come back to Cap Haitien? I liked him; it would give me pleasure to have business dealings with him."

"He was proposing to come back, but his assistant Webster advised him not to, saying that the amount of trade likely to be done did not warrant his employer's return."

"Then do me the honor of writing to tell him of the promises I have made. Promise him that before another twelve months have passed, many of the derelict plantations will be in production again. Tell him that Haiti is in sore need, from America, of salted beef, pork, hams, codfish, salmon, herrings, pickled mackerel, flour, biscuits, butter, candles, lead, soap, tar, pitch, rosin, turpentine, cheese, vinegar, gunpowder, copper, all kinds of oils, shingles, staves, seersuckers, nails—" Christophe broke off, with a shrug of his shoulders. "Both you and he know what we must import from America. If Martin will establish himself here, I swear that his work shall be rewarded."

"I'll send him a dispatch by the next American-bound ship."

"Thank you. But I have other favors to ask, Ti Rouge. I am making plans to build a special clubhouse for foreign residents, but until it's ready, I shall make use of the Casino. With the death of old François Cap Haitien was deprived of one of its landmarks; but the building is still there, untouched, just as it was in his day—"

"Except for the stained walls, Henry, where they were spattered with the blood of the French people to whom François offered shelter before the massacre."

"I did my best to save them when Dessalines learned of their presence. But if I cannot restore their lives, Ti Rouge, I can erase their blood-stains by dedicating François Casino to the benefit of the Cap's foreign residents. I have a man in mind to organize and manage it—an Englishman. Do you think that the Williams you told me about would leave his inn in Kingston and come here?"

After some reflection Duncan nodded his head. "I do not like the man too well, but I think that he would come if he were given the opportunity. His inn in Jamaica is too small for his soaring ambitions."

"Then will you write to him?" Christophe took Duncan's consent as granted, for he continued: "The school, which Laborie opened early last year, is flourishing, but it is only one; many are needed. I mean to establish schools in every town in Haiti; I want my black people to learn the white man's learning—grammar, arithmetic, religion, English, and science. From the London journals Dupuy has read out to me I know of the experiments going on in England with two new systems of education; I want to know more of them so that I may decide if either will be useful to Haiti. Is there anyone in London whom you could ask about this, Ti Rouge?"

Christophe's request surprised and shamed Duncan. He had regularly scanned the copies of English journals (all too few) that Williams sent on to him at irregular intervals, but he could not recollect having paid any attention to the subject of education. He knew nothing of the two systems referred to, and was amazed by Christophe's knowledge of them.

"What are the systems?"

"The first has been invented by Andrew Bell," Christophe explained with alacrity. "While Bell was in India he accepted the post of superintendent to a Madras orphan asylum, where he discovered that the school was making no progress because the half-caste children were not amenable to ordinary methods of teaching. One day he picked out one of the cleverer of the pupils and placed him in charge of the lowest class. The experiment was a complete success; thereafter every pupil was alternately master and pupil, and the school made rapid progress. If his system is so excellent for the colored children of Madras, should it not be equally good for our Haitian children?"

"It should be," Duncan agreed, "but if Bell is in Madras—

"He is not. He returned to England, where he published some years ago a pamphlet entitled something like this: 'An Experiment in Education, suggesting a system by which a school may teach itself under the superintendence of the master.' The system has since been introduced into the charity school of Saint Botolph's in Aldgate."

"I can write to the school," Duncan interrupted. "I am sure the principal would ask Mr. Bell to send me a copy of the pamphlet. What of the second system?"

"That, too, has been described in a pamphlet published by its inventor; an Englishman, by the name of Joseph Lancaster. He sounds like a good man, Ti Rouge. When he was a boy of fourteen he ran away from home, with the intention of teaching the word of God to the black men of Jamaica. Some years later he established a school in the Borough Road, where parents might send their children to be educated free if they had no money to pay the fees. But lack of money interfered with his plans for teaching; he had many free pupils, but too few who paid, so he had no money to pay teachers. He taught the elder scholars so they could teach the younger." Christophe's expression darkened. "Money!" he exclaimed irritably. "It is always the lack of money that ruins the fulfillment of one's dreams. But here in Haiti, thank God, we have the means of becoming rich. Here, we have hot sunshine and rich soil toiling unceasingly to produce coffee, sugar, cotton, cocoa, tobacco, and castor oil, all of which we can turn into money if our peasants work hard enough. That they will do," he continued with confidence, "when they realize what their work will mean to them; schools for the education of their children, hospitals for their sick, better houses for themselves, clothes for all." Emotion strangled his voice.

"I must go now. I have carried out my errand. A vessel will be leaving for New York within the next few days. If you would send a dispatch to Martin—" He glanced questioningly at the white man.

"I will write Nathaniel tonight," Duncan promised, as he tinkled a small silver bell.

"Thank you, Ti Rouge."

When Jonas opened the door Christophe strode toward it. "So little time, so much to do," he muttered, as he strode out of the room.

Christophe had an uncanny knack of judging and appreciating ability in other people, irrespective of the color of their skin. The death of Emperor Jacques I gave him the opportunity of displaying this faculty. Influenced by a strong conviction that his was the helping hand that was predestined to lead the black man from out of the jungle of slavery and ignorance into the fertile plains of freedom and industry, he began to assemble about him a body of talented men.

On October 24, 1806, Christophe addressed a proclamation to all nations, inviting their traders to resume relations with Haiti, promising all such traders adequate and even ample facilities, and guaranteeing all transactions on the good faith of the government.

CHAPTER SEVENTY-FOUR

DUNCAN and Williams were both silent as they rode in a fiacre to the Casino; the visitor, because he was a man of tact and appreciated that Duncan was in no mood for conversation. At the same time, he welcomed the opportunity of inspecting the city that was to be his future home. His first impressions were unfavorable. He had heard so much of Cap Haitien that his imagination had created a town that could scarcely exist outside paradise; in contrast, Cap Haitien was a city of ruins, many of which looked as if they would remain there, untouched, until the crack of doom. Then he saw traces of the past; and a hint of the future. The past was represented by the house that had once been the home of the Comte de Saramon. He stared at its lovely, graceful lines, at its size, at its ornamental stonework, at the gardens surrounding it, and began vaguely to realize what the city must have been when it was the pride of the West Indies. Of the future Cap Haitien he was permitted a glimpse as the fiacre passed across the Place d'Armes. The Place, dominated by the palace of Pauline Leclerc on one side and the cathedral on the other, was slowly rising to new glories. He was not an imaginative man (he was calculatingly practical), but he did realize that if the rest of Cap Haitien were to achieve the architectural beauty of the Place d'Armes, then one day the town would be entitled to reassume its proud claim to be the most beautiful in the New World.

For his part, Duncan was morose at the prospect of having to show the smooth-tongued Williams over François's Casino, every room of which would remind him of the old fellow whom he had loved, and still missed. Besides, the building was certain to be a dismal sight. Madame Vroux had been in bed when the news of his death was conveyed to her. At first she had refused to believe it, being convinced that it was beyond the power of any mortal to kill her François, but when the sad news was impressed upon her, her sunken eyes had filled with tears. Then she had turned her head away from the window and died—with such serenity, with so little effort, that the spirit of François himself was credited with having blown out the flame of life. Her death had preceded the slaughter of the unfortunate refugees by a few hours; later, Dessalines had sequestrated the property. He had been unable to find a buyer with courage enough to face the ghost of François, who, it was never doubted, inhabited the place. During the intervening years the place had become derelict.

The fiacre came to a stop before the wrought-iron gates. They were in sad condition and badly rusted; lianas had rooted themselves close by and had intertwined themselves so thickly as to make a screen through which it was almost impossible to see. It was quite obvious that the gates had not been opened for many months.

Duncan glanced with dismay at the gardens which had once entranced him. Gone were all the lovely flowers; the fountain no longer cooled the air; the loggia was screened with lianas. When Duncan turned the handle of the door and pushed, it opened protestingly.

The bright sunshine streamed into the hall through the open door; as the two men stepped in, their boots stirred up slight puffs of dust from the floor, which filled the hall with specks of gold. There were scurryings and squeakings behind the skirtings; some bats fluttered round their heads. The air was filled with the smell of decay.

Duncan was anxious to complete the inspection of the building as quickly as possible, but Williams refused to be hurried. Regardless of unlimited opportunities soon to be his of examining the tapestries at his leisure, he lingered by every panel, extolling the beauty of the female form that was characteristic of each one, and identifying it with a scene from mythology.

Williams at last joined Duncan, who waited by the doors leading into the ballroom. For a time the two men surveyed the ballroom from the door. Then Williams spoke again. "An excellent room; a truly excellent room, but more tables can be placed in it," he commented briskly. "I estimate another six at least. Perhaps a dozen."

Duncan's curiosity was momentarily aroused, for he remembered many occasions when guests had found difficulty in pushing a way through the tables; it was not easy to see where another six were to be placed. "Where will you put them?"

Williams pointed to his right. "At that end of the room."

"That space is used by the entertainers and dancers."

"They do not need so much room," Williams said carelessly. "Besides, I do not believe in giving people too much entertainment; they drink less while they are being entertained. After all, the Casino should be run as a business proposition, not as a philanthropic institution."

Duncan shrugged his shoulders. He would not speak to such a man what he remembered of François; who, indeed, had not been any kind of businessman but only an old soldier.

Christophe never doubted his right to be the logical successor to Jacques I. He was the sole survivor of the original leaders in the struggles for emancipation and independence (Clervaux having recently died); he was now the most powerful chief in the island; he had earned and won the respect of the population of the Department of the North and of the valley of the Artibonite. This conviction, allied with his preoccupation in encouraging commerce and industry, led him to overlook the existence of rival claimants. He was not unduly perturbed, therefore, when he learned that the military council which had named him Provisional Chief of the Nation had summoned a Constituent Assembly (the first of its kind in Haiti) to meet at Port-au-Prince on the following eighteenth of December, for the purpose of adopting a new constitution and electing a chief magistrate. Christophe believed that the Assembly was being summoned merely to confirm his appointment as chief magistrate. As for a new constitution, no doubt the Assembly would draft one on the lines he intended to indicate. In this comforting belief Christophe sent delegates to the meeting of the Assembly instead of attending it in person.

For once his judgment was at fault. The alliance between mulattoes and Negroes had never been other than uneasy. Christophe's old enemy, Pétion, resolved to use this traditional hostility as a steppingstone toward his own advancement. As leader of the mulattoes, who were strongest in the South and West, his first move was to propose election to the Constituent Assembly of mulatto deputies from districts which were not only opposed to Christophe but which, hitherto, had never been accorded representation in any of the island's political assemblies. This motion having been carried, despite energetic protests on the part of Christophe's deputies, Pétion found himself the most influential member present at the meeting of the enlarged Assembly. Supported by mulattoes and self-seeking Negroes, also those Negroes who were inimical to Christophe, Pétion succeeded in having himself elected chairman of a committee appointed to draft a constitution.

Pétion was a masterly tactician. By the use of honeyed words the mulatto chief persuaded his fellow committeemen to ignore completely the suggested constitution that Christophe's delegates had brought to the Assembly, and to draft instead a constitution that practically confined all executive, legislative, and military powers to the senate, and left the chief magistrate no more than commander in chief of the army, without even the power to confer title or rank, or appoint officials.

Having brilliantly maneuvered his initial victory, Pétion cleverly allowed matters to take their course without further exerting his influence. He did not oppose the election of Christophe to the chief magistracy because he was astute enough to realize that Christophe was unlikely to accept an office stripped of every vestige of executive power. Christophe was therefore duly chosen as chief magistrate by the votes of fifty-three members of the Assembly, and couriers were dispatched to Cap Haitien to advise him of his election.

There was only one answer Christophe could make to this invitation. He issued a proclamation accusing Pétion and other leaders of being conspirators and traitors, for having so drafted the proposed constitution as to place the real power of the country in their hands and called upon the black people of the northern province to take up arms in defense of their liberties. In case those same people might pause to wonder what liberties they had enjoyed in the past two years, Christophe promised them unlimited plunder in the event of an outbreak of civil war. A few days later he marched south at the head of a powerful, well-equipped army.

In the meantime, the delegates of the West and South still assembled at Port-au-Prince, having promulgated the constitution that Christophe had scornfully rejected, now declared Henry Christophe to be an outlaw and appointed Pétion and Gérin to maintain order in the West and South respectively.

As he half opened his eyes, Duncan wondered why Jonas was making such a fiendish noise. "Mist' Duncan, suh! Mist' Duncan, suh!" The voice grew louder as Jonas burst into the bedroom without knocking and stood by the bed, his mouth spreading from ear to ear.

"Mist' Duncan, suh! Mist' Duncan, suh!" he panted. "Wake up an' lissen."

"What do you want?"

"Ah sure got some news fer yo'. A ship has jest put in por'."

Duncan raised himself on one elbow. "Have you awakened me just to tell me that, you black-skinned sinner?" he demanded angrily.

"Yes, suh! Dat's jest what Ah have done." The smile grew broader.

Duncan was still too sleepy to realize that Jonas, with the familiarity of one who is as much a friend as a trusted servant, was deliberately teasing him. "Then I have a mind to give you a dose of senna with your coffee," he shouted testily. "Haven't I had the busiest morning for years, after rising before the sun was up, and yet you must come and wake me just after I had fallen asleep to tell me a ship has arrived? What of it, you woolly-headed limb of Satan?"

"Dat's whut yo'll will fin' out fer yo'sell, Mist' Duncan, ef yo' will jest step in de fron' parlor."

"The parlor! What on earth are you talking about?"

"Dere's a pusson dere whut says he mus' see de doctah widout fail, 'cause his hairt ain' beatin' like it sho', his breaf am all lil' breafs instead of one big one, an' one of his ribs am all bus' up."

"For the love of Heaven!" Thoroughly alarmed, Duncan sat up. "Why didn't you tell me that at once instead of wasting time?" He hurriedly slipped on his jacket. "And why did you put him in the parlor, instead of showing him into the surgery? You know as well as I that all patients must be seen in the surgery."

"Ah've put de pieces of his rib in de surg'y, Mist' Duncan."

Duncan started. "The sun must have made somebody crazy, and it isn't me. Pieces of his rib in the surgery!" Unable to understand what had happened, he hurried from his bedroom, ran down the stairs, and entered the principal salon, which Jonas insisted upon entitling the front parlor.

A lanky form uncoiled itself from the chair and stood up.

"Hullo, Duncan!" Nat Martin drawled as he seized Duncan's hand in a crushing grip.

CHAPTER SEVENTY-FIVE

DUNCAN felt inexpressibly happy to see the American back again in Cap Haitien. To Nat he could talk as to an equal, and in his own blessed mother tongue, which, in itself, was joy after years of the bastard French spoken by the Negroes.

"Nat! When did you arrive?"

"Not half an hour ago, on the *State of Ohio*. Just time enough to land, pass through the customhouse, and be driven here."

Duncan remembered Jonas's strange message. "What was all that nonsense about your heart and ribs? Was that your idea or Jonas's?"

"I have been suffering from trouble with my heart for some months past."

"Have you been suffering from giddiness or sickness?"

Nat reflected. "I have not been sick, but I have been dizzy on several occasions, and my appetite has suffered."

Duncan began to feel worried. "If you are not suffering from sunstroke—"

"I am not."

"Then I must question you more extensively before I can diagnose your complaint. But first, tell me more about your ribs. Jonas gave me a garbled message that he had put a part of your ribs in the surgery. What was he talking about?"

"Would you care to see for yourself? You can examine me afterward."

"I should." Curious and excited, Duncan led the way to the surgery. Jonas had opened the surgery window shutter; the room danced with shadows that rippled in the golden sunshine, for a crow outside the window shook the leaves of a palm tree. There were two chairs in the room; one was in a shaded corner and was occupied by a woman whose face was unknown to Duncan.

"Mademoiselle—" he began. Before he could put the question to her Nat had covered the intervening distance with his long strides and was standing by her side.

"My dear, this is Dr. Duncan Stewart; Duncan, meet Mrs. Nathaniel Martin."

"You are fortunate, Nat," said Duncan sincerely, taking the mittened hand advanced toward him—so all Nat's nonsense about his heart trouble simply meant that he had fallen in love and married! He took the hand within his own and inspected the dainty figure. She looked no more than twenty years of age, and in her high-waisted dress of buttercup-yellow muslin, rather fragile. Her hair was corn-colored, gathered in a heavy chignon and held in place by a fine tortoise-shell comb; her eyes were, like Nat's, blue, but warmer; they smiled, twinkled, and were shy, in turn. Her complexion was creamy, her lips rather pale. Beside Nat's long, lanky form she looked very tiny; rather like an oversized doll with a wistful human face.

"Nathaniel has told me so much about you, Dr. Stewart, that I feel you are just as much an old friend of mine as of Nathaniel's," she began shyly.

"I am lucky, Duncan. I asked Bella whether she would care to hasten our marriage and accompany me to Haiti instead of going to England with her father, whose one idea of visiting Europe is to write a biography of the Emperor Napoleon. Bella said yes, so we were married before the Judge sailed, and here we are, all ready to begin a new, happy, and glorious life." He turned to her. "It will be happy, dear?"

"Yes, Nathaniel," she whispered demurely. "How could it be otherwise?"

Nat kissed her, then sat upright again. "Well, Duncan, how is the new governor general progressing?" he questioned crisply. "I liked his proclamation. He should do well now that he is the supreme ruler of Haiti. Even

309

in the old days he impressed me as being more far-thinking than most of the other black men here."

Duncan waved his hand in the direction of the window. "On your way here, Nat, you must have seen something of the building work that is going on." Nat nodded. "Christophe is responsible. He has dreamed of a city, rising from the ruins, that is to rival the old Cap François. So, voilà—that new city is rising!" Duncan chuckled. "Slowly, I admit; much too slowly for the peace of Christophe's mind. He is impatient for quicker results.

"Christophe has other dreams, most of which are assuming concrete character. Some of them are fantastic—for instance, the erection of a fortress on the summit of La Ferrière—"

Nat laughed softly. "Fantastic is too generous an adjective, Duncan. Why, the man must be crazy if he imagines that it is humanly possible to build a fortress there. Does he think he is a magician?"

"The Egyptian pharaohs were not magicians, but they built pyramids."

The American stared at Duncan. "You are not trying to suggest that Christophe's dream is possible?"

"One day, I'll take Mrs. Martin and you on an excursion, Nat, so that you can see for yourself."

A week after Nathaniel Martin's return to Haiti Christophe temporarily abandoned his atack upon Pétion's forces and marched his army back to the Cap. This move was unexpected, for neutral observers had considered his chances of crushing further opposition more than good. Like Dessalines, he had never lacked courage (though he had always been a cautious man), so it was inferred that his real reason for returning north was to try to locate the considerable treasure his predecessor had amassed during his two years of office.

During the subsequent weeks Christophe busied himself with preparing a constitution for the country, less than half of which was under his immediate authority. He convoked an assembly of thirty military officers and civilians and two members of the Catholic Church and charged them with preparing the constitution. This they did, to Christophe's complete satisfaction, for he was named President of the State of Haiti and given orders no less dictatorial than those that Dessalines had possessed. On the seventeenth of February this constitution was promulgated, amid the jubilation of the common people, who were pleased to welcome any fete day as a rest from arduous labor. The Army, in particular, expressed their joy by firing at dawn a salvo of cannon from the fortifications, attending the cathedral to assist at a solemn Te Deum, and later, assembling in the Champ de Mars to hear a speech from their new president.

In the streets the common people danced the night through. Why not? They were happy to be told once more that they were free and independent.

Three weeks later the West and South elected Pétion President of the Republic of Haiti; and Pétion took the oath.

The comon people danced the night through. Why not? Was not their liberty and their independence doubly guaranteed by having two presidents?

CHAPTER SEVENTY-SIX

CHRISTOPHE'S dreams of a flourishing Haiti were doomed to delay; he had planned to set every available man and woman to work restoring the derelict plantations. Unfortunately, the splitting of Haiti into two separate states almost entirely ruined his scheme; as each state was inimical to the other, the first concern of both was the maintenance of a standing army. With a sense of bitter disappointment the President of the State of Haiti had to face the fact that complete restoration of trade must wait upon the subjugation of the West and South. In the meanwhile, he determined to put his own house, the North, in order.

Slowly, steadily, Christophe's projects began to prosper. Cap Haitien grew. Many more white faces were to be seen in the streets than had been the case since the occupation of the French troops under Leclerc. More British ships arrived in Cap Haitien than ever before.

American ships arrived, too, in greater numbers than British, for the American states, wanting coffee, sugar, and cocoa, had many surplus products to dispose of in exchange.

Haitian money began to circulate; silver pieces of six, fifteen, and thirty sols. The first national school was opened and was attended by a few pupils, mostly mulattoes.

One day Nat pointed out to Duncan that the proposed excursion to Le Pic des Ferrières was long overdue. The reason for Nat's reminder was chiefly on Bella's account. Bella was recovering from several weeks' indisposition, for the tropical heat had hastened an event that both welcomed. The morning sickness having passed off, Nat wanted Bella to take advantage of the hiatus, particularly as the rainy season was shortly due. When that was at its height roads turned into quagmires, trickling streams into raging torrents, and traveling was a chancy matter.

What with teaching more than a dozen pupils, treating his numerous patients, and dancing constant attendance upon Christophe and his family, Duncan hesitated to accompany Nat and Bella on their excursion to La Ferrière. That he eventually did so was due to Christophe. When the President heard that Nat wanted Duncan to visit the mountain, he insisted upon Duncan's accompanying the American. So one day Duncan, Nat, Bella, and Jonas set off for the interior.

The journey was uneventful, but Duncan, not having traveled to La Ferrière for more than a year, was interested in the changes that had taken place since then. There were now no deserted plantations to be seen; all were being cultivated; though no great progress had been made in arresting the encroachment of wild vegetation, yet it was evident that a start had been made. There were many more cailles, for the peasants could not be persuaded to sleep in the deserted plantation houses for fear of duppies. Also to be seen at intervals were Legba voodo shrines, which proved not only the presence of Negro communities, but also their constant faith in the gods of Guinea.

As they approached the end of the plain they saw evidence of the building operations that they had come to inspect. Just off the road there were *cailles* and lean-tos in great number, around which played hundreds of naked pickaninnies in charge of a few toothless, bent old women. On the road were a number of mule- or ox-drawn wagons, which proceeded in the same direction as themselves; these were filled with bricks, sacks of lime, rough-hewn timber, ropes and poles, and square blocks of stone so large that each one took a team of oxen to move it.

They reached the first upward slope. Duncan remembered that here, three years ago, the road had ended; from that point further progress was along a trail. That trail had disappeared; a paved road had been laid in its place up which some of the more lightly loaded wagons were slowly moving, though not without human assistance. Ropes had been attached to the wagons, and each was pulled by a gang of laborers who moved forward step by step as an overseer chanted a long wailing: "Pull! Pull! Pull! Pull!"

As the party proceeded up the slope Duncan pointed with his whip at the surface of the road. "This is all new since Christophe's time," he told Nat. "This was nothing but a trail some years ago. Now look at it. Not so finished as the French roads, but efficient enough."

Nat agreed. "I have seen many roads worse than this in America. Where is that plateau you told me about; the one you slept on? Just there—" he nodded at the top of the first rise, "or higher up?"

"Just the other side of the first brow."

The horses found no difficulty in breasting the slope, which was easier than it had been when Duncan, Christophe, and Barré had made their first journey up it; every meter of uneven surface had been leveled and paved. But when they reached the top of the slope and saw the plateau outstretched before them, Duncan gasped his amazement, for everything had so altered since last he saw the plateau that it was practically unrecognizable. One corner of it was occupied by a village of *cailles*; another by huge masses of building materials. It was almost impossible to see the greensward for the hundreds of black bodies, male and female, moving restlessly about, engaged on a score of different tasks. Yet it was none of these things that had startled Duncan, but the change in the physical aspect of the plateau as a whole. It was so much larger, and, despite the disfiguring collection of *cailles* and building materials, more majestic, because it was rounded and shaped.

Nat, who had heard Duncan's exclamation of astonishment, asked, "Is anything the matter, Duncan?"

"It seems to have grown overnight; I could swear it was only half this size."

"So it was, Dr. Stewart."

The voice came from behind Duncan, who turned and recognized Henri Barré.

Duncan introduced the engineer to Bella and Nat, then asked, "How could it have doubled in size?"

Barré flourished his left arm. "Do you remember the small hill that rose up just beyond those three trees forming a triangle?"

Duncan did; from the top of that hill he had looked down into the dark night and seen the fires of the peasants.

"What has happened to it?" he asked in amazement.

Barré smiled with pleasure at Duncan's surprise, but instead of answering he pointed to his right. "Do you also remember the slight ravine where we erected the latrine?"

Duncan thought he remembered a ravine there, but he could not see one. He said so, and this time Barré laughed.

"You cannot see it, Doctor, because it is no longer there. The hill has filled up the ravine. That is why the plateau has grown in size; within certain boundary marks every rise has been leveled and every ravine filled."

Nat whistled. "That must have been an immense undertaking."

"It was, monsieur."

"Why has it been done?"

"Because His Excellency has ordered a palace to be built here."

"A palace!" Once again Nat whistled.

"Yes, monsieur," Barré said proudly. "A palace to rival the finest in Europe."

"If I were king!" Duncan recollected Christophe's reverie upon the occasion of his first visit to this plateau. "If I were a king I should build a palace here, the most beautiful the world has ever known—"

"Your pardon, Doctor." Barré looked puzzled; he had seen Duncan's lips moving, but the words had been unintelligible to him.

"Nothing, Barré. I was remembering the past." Duncan gazed round the amphitheater. A garden of paradise. Christophe had not misnamed it. It was difficult to imagine more beautiful surroundings for a palace. So Christophe intended to fulfill yet another of his dreams. He was not king; he was only president of a state less than one half the size of Ireland, yet he was determined to have the palace of his dreams! A resolute dreamer, Christophe. But at what cost! There were sweating black bodies wherever one looked. One could count them not in dozens, but in scores.

Presently the four travelers resumed their journey to the mountaintop. They crossed the plateau toward the trail that was to take them to the summit. As they approached its beginning, where it joined the newly made road, their amazed eyes were greeted with an astonishing scene. Like the road, the trail had been improved beyond recognition; it no longer crossed over a slimy bog, nor was it shaded overhead by a green roof of overlapping branches and trailing plants. The encroaching jungle had been cut away to leave a clear pathway, the boggy ground had been drained, smoothed, and cobbled. Bordering the edge of this trail stood a long line of Negro men and women, who were spaced, irrespective of sex, at regular intervals of a meter. Along this human chain traveled a continuous, never ceasing procession of the materials needed on the summit above; bricks, sacks of lime, ropes, and poles.

They halted to watch with fascinated gaze the slow, rhythmic movements of the countless black bodies, many nude to the waist, men and women alike. The laborers dipped to the right, to reach for the brick that was being passed on to them from below, turned to the left, and stretched upward as their lithe, muscular arms passed the brick on to the one above.

Then they turned again, back to their right, and dipped to take the next brick. Dip, turn, straighten up, turn, stretch. Dip, turn, straighten up, turn, stretch.

There was one brick that Duncan noted particularly; it was lighter in shade than its companions. His eyes followed this one up the trail as it passed from man to man, man to woman, woman to man, woman to woman, ever traveling upward until at last he lost sight of it, where the trail curved out of sight. Later he saw it again (unless his imagination deceived him), this time much higher up the mountainside, as the trail curved again to the left. It was still traveling from hand to hand, still traveling higher, until for the second time it disappeared from sight and did not reappear; although still higher, and yet again, still higher than that, he could espy a snakelike line of dipping black specks.

"That is one way of shifting bricks," Nat commented in admiration.

His wife asked, "Where are they taking the bricks to, Dr. Stewart?"

Duncan pointed to the mountainside, stark before them. "Up there," he replied, as he waved his hand at the sky.

She gasped. "Not above the clouds?"

As if to save Duncan the necessity of answering, the clouds parted; the sun shone down upon the summit of La Ferrière, and they saw a colony of tiny black objects silhouetted against a dazzling dome.

"Now you can see for yourself, dear," Nat told her.

"I cannot believe my eyes, Nathaniel," she whispered. "There must be hundreds of people lining the trail. Hundreds."

"At least. But what they are doing now is easy enough. What I want to know is, how do they propose to get up there those solid blocks of stone that we saw in some of the wagons?"

Nat was soon to have this question answered. When they were satisfied with watching the monotonous chain of dipping, turning figures, the travelers urged their horses forward toward the trail; soon they too were ascending the mountain. The Negroes who lined the trail gazed at them with incurious, emotionless eyes. In much the same way had they looked at the whites during the period of slavery. In those days they would have felt the sting of the lash if they had paused from their labors for a moment to stare too attentively at passing whites. They had no lash to fear now, but old habits die hard.

Up and up, with the trail becoming steadily steeper. Soon, Nat thought, they must arrive at the clearing that Duncan had mentioned; where they proposed to dismount and leave Bella to rest. Just as this thought occurred to him he became aware of loud noises ahead.

"Pull! Pull! Pull! Pull!"

The travelers rounded the bend, and halted their animals when they saw that further progress was barred by a crowd of black-skinned men spread across their path. Upwards of sixty men were engaged in moving one of the solid blocks of stone that the travelers had noticed earlier. It was mounted on large wooden rollers, and was wrapped about with a network of ropes. Some thirty-six men strained at the ropes; another sixteen levered underneath the stone block with immense poles, four men to each pole; four men manipulated huge wooden checking blocks; the remaining men stood by to take up the rollers as they were released behind, and move them to the front.

"Pull!" At the overseer's bellowed command the sixty men strained at their task, the muscles of their arms and legs bulged in knots, the sweat poured off their naked shoulders, their breath burst from their heaving chests in choking gasps. The block moved fractionally up the cobbled trail.

"Pull!" The ropes tautened; the men on the levers tightened their muscles. The block moved fractionally forward.

"Pull! Pull! Pull!" With each shout the block moved farther up the steep incline. By the side of the trail the bricks passed on. The Negroes who dipped and turned, and turned and dipped, ignored the upward progress of the stone. Why should they be interested? They were lucky to be tossing bricks about, instead of twisting their belly muscles pulling and pushing a massive piece of rock up the side of a mountain. It was tomorrow that they would become interested, for then it might be their turn.

Presently the overseer gave the order to rest. The Negroes sank to the ground, giving the white travelers the chance of passing them. But with quivering lips Mrs. Martin pleaded for a return to the Cap. She no longer wanted to visit the mountaintop upon which Christophe's invulnerable citadel was beginning to rise. So they returned home; Duncan in time to receive a shakily written note signed: "Armand de Saint Just."

CHAPTER SEVENTY-SEVEN

MONSIEUR DUNCAN STEWART,
The receipt of this note, subscribed by him whom you know always to have been your enemy; him, indeed, whom you must have believed long since dead, cannot be other than a disagreeable shock to you, yet I pray you to desist before acting upon any justifiable impulse to rend this paper to pieces, and to read on. Know, therefore, that, although as yet alive, it is a dying man who addresses these words to you, so spare him a trifle of that sympathy which you have so freely bestowed upon the Negroes of this unhappy land.

I am dying, slowly but inevitably. Perhaps I may live one more week, or one more month, but longer than that is as unlikely as snow in Saint-Domingue (I cannot, even now, force myself to use the hated name by which this country of revolted slaves is now recognized by an indolently tolerant world). This emaciated body of mine is racked with an unceasing, searing pain that is beyond all human concept, beyond human bearing. Each night I pray to God to receive this unhappy, erring soul of mine, but alas! It is not for such as I to expect Celestial Grace. Would that I had the courage to anticipate the Call, but I have some Christian belief; with death so near I have deep fear of the burning fires of Hades that await the soul of a suicide. So must I await God's own time for my happy relief. But is it a sin to ease my miserable body of the tortures that hourly convulse it? I do not believe so; willingly, therefore, would I do anything that would relieve me even of the pain that I can no longer endure.

I am told, by a faithful woman who attends me, that Negro witch doctors know of divers strange brews and concoctions that would quickly banish my torments, but I spurn to demean myself by applying for help from men whom I refuse to regard as other than savage barbarians. Besides, I have no belief in the claim of such people to perform miracles unknown to the scientific skill of their cultural superiors, the white races of the world. But surely, if such ignorant black men know of concoctions to relieve pain, white physicians, also, must possess similar knowledge? I cannot believe that white men are less knowledgeable than black, particularly as I have read, in a recent issue of this country's *Gazette*, your article on the use of narcotics for the easing of pain, in which you mention the researches of two countrymen of yours, Priestley and Davy. My pride, while it has not descended so low as to seek the resources of a Negro devil's brew, has yet sunk low enough for me to humble myself before a fellow white man. So if it be true, as Humphrey Davy maintains, that nitrous oxide is capable of destroying physical pain, I pray you, monsieur, to forgive and forget the enmity toward you that I never ceased to nourish in the past, and haste to my side, so that the few remaining days of life that are still mine may be spent in peaceful prayer that no diabolical agony shall disturb.

If, in the goodness of your heart, you can do this last service for me, monsieur, there is no reward that I can offer you, for I have long since been penniless; I can do no more than ask the good Lord to bless and prosper you. Yet perhaps I could give you sight of a jewel that has no intrinsic value, but is more precious to you and me than all the precious stones of Solomon's treasure—the jewel of your mercy and forgiveness! If, I repeat, you will act toward me in a Christian spirit, then the Negro who carries this note to you shall bring you to my poor abode. But haste, I beg of you.

Duncan gazed at the spidery handwriting. Had he wanted confirmation, either of the veracity of the note's contents or of the identity of its writer, the handwriting supplied it. It was obviously that of a sick man; at the same time, behind the straggling, shakily formed letters there was an immaculate quality and ostentatious flourish that was characteristic of De Saint Just.

It was a shock to learn that the Frenchman was still alive. So many years had passed since last the two had met. No word of him had ever reached the Cap; it seemed unbelievable that some mutual acquaintance had not heard of him and passed on the information. It was even more incredible that Phebe had heard nothing, neither of nor from him. When she had first come to live with him, Duncan had anticipated intrigue on the part of the Frenchman; either to wean Phebe away from her new lover, or to avenge her desertion. With the passage of time, lack of any news of De Saint Just had convinced him of the other man's death. Nothing had happened since then to throw doubt upon that belief—until the arrival of the letter.

He felt that a ghost from the past had risen up before him, and the knowledge was unpleasant. He had hated De Saint Just perhaps as much as the Frenchman had hated him. He had always felt ill at ease in De Saint

Just's presence, for the exquisite Frenchman had made him experience the disagreeable sensation of being an intellectual inferior. Now that their positions were, in one sense, reversed, he felt no happier at the prospect of meeting the other man again. It would give him no satisfaction to crow over De Saint Just's misfortunes. In fact, he was extremely sorry that the note had ever been delivered to him. Ghosts were best left where they belong—in the oblivion of the past.

In reality, he had but one question to answer: was he prepared to forgive his enemy, and visit him with the idea of trying to ease the remaining days of life? To a Christian and a physician there was but one reply: yes. He was not a good Christian, but he was a physician.

Duncan turned to Jonas, who had been patiently waiting. "Who brought this note?"

"A field nigger, suh," Jonas replied with contempt.

"Where has he come from?"

Jonas looked aggrieved. "Ah kain tell yo', Mist' Duncan, fer dat nigger shu' am stupid. He jes' won' say nuthin' ter nobody nohow."

Duncan rose abruptly. "I will speak to him, Jonas."

As Duncan approached the tree under which De Saint Just's messenger was sprawling, fast asleep, he appreciated the reason for Jonas's contempt for the Haitian. The man was dressed in trousers and shirt, but both garments were so torn and tattered that there was scarcely enough material to hang together; what there was of it was incredibly dirty, the man himself was caked with filth.

Jonas stirred the man with his foot. The Haitian opened his eyes. When he saw the white man he scrambled to his feet and stared at Duncan with vacant eyes. His thick lower lip hung down from his open mouth.

"Did you bring me this letter?"

The man nodded his head.

"Where do you come from?"

The Negro pointed his arm toward the west.

"There," he replied, in an adenoidal mutter.

"Where is there? L'Acul? Limbé?" Duncan demanded in a voice sharp with irritation.

"Not L'Acul, Limbé. There!" The Negro waved his arm again; this time more to the northeast.

"In a town or village?"

"In a caille."

"Where is the caille?"

For the third time the Negro pointed his arm; but even more toward the north. "There."

Duncan frowned. He felt suspicious that the Negro was being deliberately stupid in order to keep secret the whereabouts of De Saint Just's caille.

"What is your name?" Duncan demanded sharply.

"Jean Goutte."

"How far away from here is the caille?"

"A few kilometers."

"How many, man? One, three, six?"

"Maybe four, maybe eight."

317

"How long did it take you to get here?"

Goutte shook his head to indicate his ignorance. In this reply, Duncan thought, the man was probably sincere; time was of no consequence to the majority of Negroes. It was evident, however, that Goutte had no intention of revealing any information of value; it was hard to understand why. As likely as not the man was under the influence of a spell. Or he might be a genuine idiot.

"Shall I be able to get back here before darkness?"

Goutte nodded. "Yes."

"Then I shall accompany you at once. Will you bring my horse round, Jonas?"

"Yes, suh, an' mah own?"

Before Duncan could answer Goutte interrupted. "No. The white man will not let Negroes approach near his *caille*."

Jonas knew enough French to understand what had been said, "What are you, and who are you giving orders to, you field Negro?" he asked indignantly, in the same language. Then in English to Duncan: "Huccome you listen to such trash, suh?"

Duncan, impatient to be off, raised his hand. "I don't want any arguments, Jonas. What Goutte said was probably true; since the revolt, Monsieur de Saint Just has possessed a rabid hatred of ex-slaves. I will go alone; if I can be back before dark, the *caille* cannot be far away. Probably it is somewhere in the mountains between here and Limbé."

Jonas was disposed to argue; he was reluctant to let his master go off unaccompanied to an unknown destination, but a glance at Duncan's face closed his lips; he had learned from experience to respect that particular expression.

Duncan packed into a bag all medical necessities that might be needed, then mounted his animal. Goutte gestured to Duncan to follow and set off in a loping motion for the western gate. Duncan followed at an easy walking pace.

For a short distance beyond the boundaries of the city Goutte followed the road to Limbé, but when they had proceeded a distance of nearly half a league Duncan saw the Negro turn off unexpectedly into the thick forest that bordered the road. From there a narrow trail leading through the trees in the direction of the coast.

Soon the trail began to rise; Duncan believed that they were making for the mountains that bordered the coast. Later, when they turned to the right again, the trail rose so steeply that his horse began to labor. Then, unexpectedly, he found himself in a clearing with a *caille* at the far side. A fat mulatto woman sat on a stool outside against the wall, with her head hanging sideways at an awkward angle.

"There," announced Goutte, as he nodded at the *caille* and caught hold of the horse's bridle. Duncan dismounted and began to walk across toward the *caille* when a strange impulse prompted him to glance behind him; he saw Goutte pat the horse's sleek neck and look at the animal with a particularly gloating expression. Duncan was tempted to return and halter the horse to the side of the *caille*, but he desisted, because it seemed ridiculous to harbor suspicions. At the same time, he was comforted by the feel against his body of the pistol without which he never traveled, for small gangs of robbers still roamed the countryside despite all Christophe's efforts to capture them.

He resumed his walk to the caille. By accident he trod on a dead branch, which broke with a snapping noise. The mulatto woman awoke with a start. A weak voice inside the hut called out: "Who is that?" He recognized the voice as De Saint Just's. The woman answered, "Monsieur le docteur, Armand. He comes."

Armand! Duncan was astonished to hear the colored woman calling the finical Frenchman by his Christian name. He gazed at the woman; her face was vaguely familiar. Each step he took nearer to her made him more convinced than ever that they had met before.

At the entrance of the caille he said to her, "I have seen you before. What is your name?"

Before she could reply a mocking voice from within did so. "You have met her dozens of times, my dear Stewart, but I am not surprised at your failing to recognize her. It was many years ago when you last saw her. Then she was a sylphlike creature for whose favors two gentlemen of France have fought a duel. Now, as you can see, she is much too fat and bloated for a lover other than a Negro. Is that not so, my Clémentine?"

Clémentine, once De Saint Just's mistress! But the girl for whom De Saint Just had built a special pavilion, had been a slender gazelle; one of the most beautiful mulatto women in the Colony!

Clémentine saw no insult in De Saint Just's brutal words. Her round face parted in an indulgent smile. "Yes, Armand," she replied tranquilly. "Come in, Dr. Stewart, come in. I have been anxiously awaiting your arrival."

Duncan entered the caille. When his eyes accustomed themselves to the semidarkness he glanced about him. The hut consisted of one room, approximately five meters square; the windowless walls were of wattle plastered with a mixture of mud and ashes, the roof was thatched with palm leaves and cane straw. The floor was of earth, pounded to a concrete hardness. Not a stick of furniture, nor an item of decoration relieved the bareness of the room. All that occupied the hut was the large bed of straw on the floor, in which the Frenchman was stretched out, full length, on his back. Only among the most destitute of Negro peasants had Duncan come across more miserable surroundings. To see De Saint Just, once among the wealthiest of the planters, and certainly the most fastidious of them all, living amid such squalor was pitiable.

When he looked at De Saint Just himself his pity intensified. The patient was naked, but a tattered blanket covered his body from the waist downward. Both arms were stretched out alongside his wasted body, but his hands were beneath the blanket. His hair was ill-kempt, dirty, and so long that its straggling ends reached the shoulders. He wore a beard and mustache, which were as much in need of attention as his hair. His eyes were sunken, black-rimmed, his lips gray, his cheeks gaunt, his tight-stretched skin alarmingly translucent. Save in one respect, he was as unrecognizable as Clémentine, but the expression of the eyes had not changed. They were still the eyes of the old De Saint Just, mocking and contemptuous.

319

"How are the mighty fallen!" De Saint Just gibed. "This is different from my home in the rue de la Fontaine, no? It has not, I think you will agree, the same commodious ease, nor the same luxurious appurtenances, but there, who am I to carp at mere surroundings? I am lucky to have remained alive these last few years, since so many of my compatriots were butchered some years ago, not far from where my house once stood. Besides, my dear Stewart, my loss will be somebody else's gain. I hear that a very grand house is to be built on the site of my old home. It will be a comfort to die, since some black plutocrat will soon be living there."

De Saint Just came to a breathless pause; Duncan shifted uneasily as he tried not to hate the other man, and to ignore the old familiar sensation of feeling like a schoolboy before his usher.

"You sent for me because you are ill," he reminded the Frenchman.

"My dear fellow, there will be plenty of time to talk of maladies and complaints after I have had an opportunity of talking for a while. Surely you would not begrudge me that pleasure? It is many years now since I had the privilege of conversing with a white man, and—an—" He paused in malice. "An equal," he concluded.

"Let me examine you—"

"Later, later," De Saint Just interrupted, with a slight rasping laugh. He gazed reflectively at his visitor. "You have not changed overmuch, monsieur. Of course, you are a little older. Who is not? And a little plumper, I think. You are not like me in that respect." He patted his stomach with his hand; the noise was like that of a drum being knuckled. "Yes, and you are definitely looking prosperous. With so many patients you must be a very rich man." He observed that Duncan was about to interrupt again, so he continued quickly: "But otherwise you have not changed. Your clothes, now! Look at them. They are unworthy of you, Doctor. So bourgeois. Surely that vest is far too square-cut. And, 'pon my soul! Stewart, do I see that your vest is buff? And the cut of that lapel! I refuse to believe that Paris ever shaped such a lapel. And your hat! It horrifies me. What is it? It reminds me of a chamber pot."

"It is called a beaver," Duncan told him irritably. "It is the latest fashion. According to European journals it has come to stay."

"Journals are printed for the bourgeoisie," De Saint Just sneered. "Those dull pantaloons, have they also come to stay? But there, I forget. I hear that London is becoming the center of men's fashions, thanks to—what is his name? Ah! Yes! Beau Brummell. To think that, had I still been wealthy, I might not now be asking you news of the latest fashions. Well, well! There seem to be compensations even in death."

Duncan had to remind himself that De Saint Just was a dying man. "I came here to treat you for your pains, De Saint Just, but I cannot diagnose your illness until I have examined you more closely," he said harshly. He advanced toward the bed. "Let me feel your pulse."

The Frenchman's attitude changed; the mocking light vanished from his eyes. "Keep away from me, Stewart," he shouted in a frenzy. "Keep your cursed hands away from my body."

Duncan halted. "Are you, or are you not, ill? If you want me to ease you of your pain it is necessary for me to examine you."

"No," De Saint Just raved. "God knows! I wrote nothing less than the truth when I told you that I suffer constant agony, and that I may die any day now—I do not need a physician to tell me that my end is near. But I would rather suffer all the torments of hell than allow you to touch me, Monsieur l'Ami des Noirs! Do you know why I sent for you? Because—because—" His words were lost in a spasm of choking coughs that racked his body. For more than two minutes the seizure doubled him up; the sweat poured from his attenuated body. By the time he had recovered sufficiently to speak again, Duncan had subdued the violent fury that the old taunt of L'Ami des Noirs had threatened to precipitate.

"Well?" he prompted calmly. "Why did you send for me?"

"To see that you die before I do," De Saint Just wheezed. His left hand appeared from under the ragged blanket, holding a cocked pistol.

CHAPTER SEVENTY-EIGHT

DUNCAN realized that his danger was real. The vicious hatred in the Frenchman's eyes was proof that he was serious in his intentions, and the hand that held the pistol was steady, although the rest of his body still shook with the aftermath of his coughing spasm. Duncan comprehended that his one chance of life was to remain calm and alert, in the hope that he might catch him off his guard.

"What good will it do you to kill me, De Saint Just? Are you prepared to die with murder on your conscience?"

"Murdering you, my dear Stewart, would not lie heavily upon my conscience. On the contrary, I am quite sure my soul would never rest in peace if I were to reach the other world without having just sent yours to purgatory. I have only to think of the Negro lives you saved to remember that, had you saved less, many thousands of my countrymen might now be alive; and this country might still be a French possession."

"I do not follow your reasoning."

"No? Then I will explain. But please sit down; you look most uncomfortable standing up, and there is still much I want to say to you." De Saint Just raised his voice. "Clémentine!"

"Yes, Armand?" Clémentine appeared in the doorway.

"Give our visitor your stool."

"Yes, Armand." The mulatto obediently fetched the stool and set it down just behind Duncan. Then she turned to leave, but the Frenchman halted her.

"One moment, Clémentine. It occurs to me that our visitor might have taken the precaution of arming himself before coming to visit me. It would be a good idea, I think, to search him."

Clémentine ran her hands lightly over Duncan and discovered his pistol in its concealed holster under his arm. She placed it on the straw beside De Saint Just; then she slipped noiselessly out of the hut.

"I was fool enough to believe in the sincerity of your letter," Duncan said bitterly.

"Why?" De Saint Just asked, with a sneer. "I have hated you, Stewart, from the moment you betrayed your birthright and befriended the Negroes. When you stole Phebe from me I swore to kill you."

"I did not steal Phebe from you. She had deserted you first."

The Frenchman shrugged his shoulders. "No matter; she went straight from my bed to yours. Had she not been convinced beforehand of your protection she would not have left me."

"She could not have had that conviction. After your departure from the Cap I did not see her again until she danced at the Casino."

"Then why did she threaten to become your mistress if I did not give her my last gold livre?"

Duncan did not reply; not for the first time he suspected old François of having played an important role in the matter of Phebe's transfer.

"Friends brought me news of Phebe's whereabouts some few weeks after she had joined your household," the Frenchman continued. "I vowed then to kill you. With my last gold pieces—some that Phebe had no knowledge of, otherwise she would have remained with me for a few days longer—I purchased this pistol, intending to kill you as soon as I could travel to the Cap. Fortunately for you, I fell ill of yellow fever. A miracle saved my life, but by the time I was well enough to make new plans, you had left this country for Jamaica. You see, my dear Stewart, I was well acquainted with your movements. At that time I still possessed a few friends. Particularly Clémentine. You would not think that that woman had a heart of gold, would you? But she has." He shook with laughter. "Do you remember the command to cast thy bread upon the running waters, for after a long time thou shalt find it again? Clémentine has taught me how profitable it is to obey that particular command. I found my bread again."

"You lived on Clémentine's—Clémentine's charity?"

"Charity! Trust an Englishman to conceal his true thoughts! The word in your thoughts, my friend, was not charity but earnings, was it not? But the answer is yes. Why not? I once kept her in every luxury that money could purchase. Why should she not show her gratitude by keeping me? Though I can scarcely claim that she has done so in luxury! In fact, had I not promised myself the satisfaction of destroying you, I should probably have joined my friends in the Place d'Armes when they were butchered to make a Roman holiday for Dessalines."

De Saint Just started to cough again; Duncan hoped that it was a prelude to another spasm, and tensed his muscles so that at the first sign of the pistol hand wavering he could leap for safety beyond the door. Perhaps the Frenchman sensed this, for he struggled to check the spasm, and succeeded, though the effort forced more sweat from his racked body.

He lifted himself up on his free elbow. "You should feel honored to know, Stewart, that only my hatred of you, and my determination to be avenged, kept me alive through many years of excessive misery. I contemplated suicide on several occasions, but each time I told myself, 'Avenge yourself upon Stewart first, and then die.' The anticipation of seeing your dead body was the medicine that cured me of the yellow fever, the food that kept me alive when I was starving, the liquid that refreshed me when I was dying of thirst, the buoy that kept me afloat when I was drowning. Oh! I have been through many adventures in the past few years, in both the French and Spanish territories. I lived quite well in the Spanish territory; the Spaniards liked Clémentine until she became too fat even for their taste."

He paused and relaxed upon the straw. "Now the time has come to kill you. Not quite in the manner I had hoped. If it will interest you to hear, I had planned to await an opportunity to kill you in the Place d'Armes, before the eyes of Christophe and the Negroes of the town. A picturesque avenging of Dessaline's massacre, no? But this cursed illness ruined my plans; it brought me to this filthy *caille*, which I shall never leave. When I realized I was doomed I had to make other arrangements, for I refused to die without having killed you first. Are you ready for death, Stewart?" De Saint Just's eyes burned; he sighted the pistol.

Duncan saw from the Frenchman's expression that he was as surely doomed to death as De Saint Just himself. He did not want to die, especially in this gloomy hovel. Life was far from perfect, but it was still very sweet. He tried to think of some stratagem to escape, but De Saint Just's burning eyes watched him too carefully; the pistol never wavered. A chill spread from his spine to his heart as he saw from the Frenchman's eyes that the crisis was upon him.

But it was not! De Saint Just laughed. "I was forgetting my promise to you, Stewart."

"What was that?" Duncan asked, with a feeling of relief. The critical moment was to be postponed; even seconds were precious.

"To show you a jewel more precious to you and me than all Solomon's treasures. Is that not what I said in my letter?" De Saint Just pulled his right hand from beneath the blanket; to Duncan's amazement the wrist was encircled by a narrow iron band to which was attached a light chain, the other end of which was buried beneath the pile of straw to the right of the Frenchman.

"You can see how precious the jewel is to me," De Saint Just continued conversationally. "For several years now the chain has been attached to my wrist so there could be no fear of my losing the jewel, or of having it stolen from me. Would you like to see it?"

Because there was a faint possibility of the Frenchman's attention being distracted for that precious second, Duncan said, "Yes."

De Saint Just's gray lips parted in a diabolical smile; his malicious eyes continued to watch Duncan closely while he used his right hand to part the straw. Then the jewel was uncovered; Duncan rose to his feet with a shout. Phebe lay there, her arms fettered, her mouth bound round with a length of cotton cloth.

"Sit down!" De Saint Just threatened.

Duncan sat down and gazed with pity at the woman who had once been his mistress. He forgot his own danger in thinking of the years of torture to which the fiendish Frenchman had subjected her.

Her face had changed; it revealed all too vividly how much she must have suffered from the torment of being dragged along at the heels of her captor. Her dazzling beauty was scarcely discernible, for her face was filthy. So was her hair. The glorious eyes, which had once had the power of quickening a man's heartbeat to suffocation point, were dull and stupefied with misery. Her body, however, looked much the same; it still possessed that sleek catlike quality that had always fascinated him and revealed no sign of the ravages of rape and starvation. It was still slender, despite her added years; he could not think why, when he compared it with Clémentine's shapeless obesity. Perhaps the cause was mental, he thought. Or perhaps partly mental, and partly starvation.

Divining something of Duncan's thoughts, De Saint Just chuckled with spite. "I pride myself on devising original but apposite retaliation. Fate has robbed me of the pleasure of killing you in the Place d'Armes, which would have been a truly apt revenge, but that fickle lady treated me less scurvily in the matter of avenging myself on charming Phebe. When you left her to go to Jamaica, I sent her a message to say that I was again rich enough to take care of her. She came to me as quickly as she could."

"You damned fiend!"

"Why? I gave her warning long ago, when first she became my mistress, that I should make her suffer if ever she betrayed or deserted me. She has no reason to feel aggrieved because I fulfilled my promise to her. On the contrary. I had threatened to kill her, but you see, she is still alive. In the circumstances, she has reason to feel grateful to me for sparing her life. Of course," De Saint Just continued with a caustic laugh, "she might have preferred death to her life with me these past few years, for whatever suffering I have had she has been compelled to share, not being able to escape from these marriage shackles." He waved the chain about; it tinkled musically. "When I starved, she starved; when I nearly drowned, she was by my side and nearly drowned with me. Can you imagine what it meant to our luxury-loving little tigress, Stewart, to have to sleep in filthy hovels, to exist on plantains for week after week, to be deprived of any man's company save mine? Not but that should have sufficed her," he added, as he stroked Phebe's left breast with his long fingers. "I have always been a satisfying lover." He laughed. "I have felt very much the Turk these few years; after all, it is not every Occidental who has the privilege of traveling in the company of two such loving mistresses. I think there is something to be said in favor of being a Mussulman."

"Good God! Do you say that Clémentine was an accomplice in this damnable crime?"

The Frenchman smiled scornfully. "Of course! You have never understood women, have you, my ignorant Englishman? Or do you forget that it was Clémentine whom Phebe supplanted? She was very glad to be able to avenge herself on the woman who had turned her out of her own special pavilion and deprived her of the jewels and luxuries that I had previously showered upon her. Indeed, Clémentine had found that revenge is very sweet. It was she who, sleeping on my left side, guarded me against any attack from Phebe, who slept on my right. It was she who snatched the food from Phebe's hands, that I might have more. Yes, and it was she whom I caressed, whenever I had to punish Phebe for being too unruly. Of course, I have not always kept her bound and gagged as she is now; that measure was merely precautionary, to prevent her spoiling the surprise I prepared for you. There is no reason why she should not be freed." He stretched out his arm again and released the cotton material from her mouth, the fiber rope from her arms.

"Duncan!" Phebe raised herself to her knees and held out supplicating arms.

"Do not move, Stewart," De Saint Just warned sharply.

"Take me away with you, Duncan," she sobbed. "Please take me away from him, and let me come back to you. I swear I will never leave you again."

"Of course she would not; you are a prosperous man," the Frenchman mocked. "But I did not bind your ears as well as your mouth, my little brown gazelle. You heard me say that I intend to kill the Englishman. You will get your freedom upon the day you wake up to find yourself shackled to a corpse. Then you can find another man to buy your kisses; I shall not kill you, I have punished you enough. Now the comedy is ended." His voice grew tired and lifeless. "I have talked enough. Are you ready, Stewart? Are you saying your last prayer?"

For the second time Duncan saw the Frenchman's pupils dilate behind the pistol butt; he breathed a short prayer, the first for many a year. With slow deliberation De Saint Just pulled the trigger. As he did so Phebe leaped before him. The flame scorched her breasts, the bullet scored a line across the flesh beneath and was deflected, by her rib, through the open door. She staggered, screamed, then fell across the Frenchman's legs. Duncan gave a sobbing gasp, fearing the worst, but as he bent down she gave a convulsive twist. There was a second explosion as she pointed Duncan's pistol at the Frenchman's heart. An expression of disappointment passed across De Saint Just's face as he closed his eyes. His body twitched, his lower jaw fell open.

Phebe stumbled to her feet. "Swine!" she spat out viciously, as she kicked the dead man.

Duncan snatched his pistol from her hand and reloaded it. He stepped outside as Clémentine and the sulky guide came running toward the hut. They fell back at the sight of his pistol. "Bring my horse here!" he commanded.

As Duncan rode toward Cap Haitien with Phebe held firmly on the saddle before him, the loud lamentations of Clémentine rose over the body of the man to whom she had given complete loyalty all her life.

CHAPTER SEVENTY-NINE

ONE day Christophe convened a meeting of all his chiefs.

"My generals," he began, as soon as the formalities had been complied with, "it is now a little more than four years since you proclaimed me ruler of Haiti. What has been done in that period? Little or much?"

"Much," some of the sycophants murmured.

"Wait!" said Christophe, holding up his hand commandingly. "Let us analyze the position of our state. First, the war! Not yet is our war against the Republic at an end. It cannot be considered as finally ended until the so-called Republic has been overthrown, and our brave soldiers occupy every town and village from Fort Liberté to Aux Cayes." He stared at the assembled company with challenging eyes.

"Hear, hear!" halfheartedly agreed those who were unlucky enough to meet his glance.

"But that, my generals, must come in the fullness of time. Meanwhile, we have driven the enemy forces out of our towns one by one; we have battled well and valiantly; none can deny us our victory."

"Of course not," said Yacinthe loudly. "Who would dare deny credit to His Excellency, our heroic leader?"

"Thank you, my dear Yacinthe," Christophe acknowledged, reflecting silently: Yacinthe is going to ask me for a command for that son of his. "So much for war, my generals. Let us now inspect a more pleasant picture. Trade! We have not done as well as I had hoped, but how could we? Were not the cultivators of our plantations bravely fighting for their fatherland instead of continuing their natural work? But nevertheless, my generals, in 1809 we produced more than eight hundred thousand pounds of muscovado sugar, as compared with five hundred thousand pounds the year before."

There was a general murmur of approbation. "A wonderful yield," congratulated Corneille Brelle, enthusiastically and sincerely.

"Ten million pounds of coffee were produced, in comparison with less than seven million the year before," Christophe continued triumphantly. There were fresh murmurs of approval. "With cotton we were equally successful; instead of thirty-eight thousand pounds, we produced one hundred and seventeen thousand pounds."

"Incredible," muttered Prévost, who was interested in cotton.

Christophe looked pleased. "Cocoa, I regret to say, did less well, dropping from forty-four thousand pounds to thirty-two. Dye woods did badly; three thousand pounds instead of twenty-four thousand. But," he hurried on quickly, "tobacco jumped from seven thousand pounds to ten, and rum from three hundred gallons to seven hundred and sixty. How excellent this last item is you will be able to judge for yourselves when I tell you that no rum at all was exported from the Cap during the French possession."

"They drank it all themselves," Romain declared. Everyone except Christophe laughed heartily. He was annoyed, for the interruption was not of his choosing.

"Other products increased similarly," he continued shortly. "But no more of trade; I have said enough to show you, my generals, how well we did under my leadership, despite the civil war. I might add," he went on, apparently as an afterthought, "that there are many plantations that now lack an owner."

He paused in studied deliberation; the chiefs became unusually interested, and Christophe smiled his satisfaction.

"I think I can rightfully claim that I have done well by the State of

Haiti, can I not?' Christophe demanded. "Have I done all that man could have done, or have I left undone things that should have been done? Give me the answer to those questions, for it is important that I should know how I stand with the generals and chiefs who supported me."

"No man could have done more, or better, Your Excellency," Vernet said quickly. "I think we are all agreed upon that?"

"Yes, yes," the chiefs chorused.

"Have I made Haiti a country of importance?" Christophe persisted. "A country respected by England and by America, with whom we are doing increasing business?"

"Yes, yes," they confirmed.

"I am glad to hear you say so," Christophe looked grim. "I have a proposal to make. I want a new title."

There was an awkward silence. "A new title?" repeated Magny. "We do not follow your meaning, Your Excellency."

"It is simple. An important and internationally respected Haiti deserves a more dignified ruler than a president. Haiti deserves a *king*."

Some of the chiefs gasped, but none spoke.

"Well?" Christophe demanded, thumping on the table with his fist. "Have none of you tongues?"

Father Corneille Brelle pressed finger tip to finger tip but did not lift his head; he had no wish to look into Christophe's eyes. "There can be no praise too extravagant truthfully to describe Your Excellency's rule," the priest murmured. "But—"

"*But*—my reverend father," Christophe prompted, when Brelle paused.

"Your people are no less grateful than your generals and chiefs, Your Excellency, but they do not forget what happened to them when they were ruled by an emperor."

"I am not Dessalines," Christophe pointed out with impatience. "But I am building a palace, and what use has a palace without a king?" There was no reply to his question. He leaned forward. "I might further add: what use has a king without a court; what use has a court without courtiers?"

"Courtiers!" Romain repeated.

"But of course, my dear Romain. Which do you think the people would cheer more loudly: General Paul Romain—or His Highness the Prince of Limbé, Grand Marshal of Haiti?"

"The Prince of Limbé," Romain murmured as his eyes sparkled.

Christophe turned to his left, where Vernet sat. "What does His Highness the Prince of Gonaïves say?"

"A real court would undoubtedly bring us to the respect of England," Vernet whispered.

"But not of America," argued Jean-Pierre Richard, who was jealous of Christophe. "The American states are ruled by a president; what is good enough for them should be good enough for us Haitians."

"Indeed, Monsieur le Comte?"

Richard appeared to be surprised. "Le Comte?" he queried in a slightly husky voice.

"Le Comte de la Bande du Nord, shall we say? Would you, Father Corneille Brelle, refuse the Dukedom of Anse, and the Archbishopric of Haiti?"

Brelle touched his lips with his handkerchief and said nothing; he was thinking: As Archbishop, I could do much good for Mother Church. I should be answerable solely to the Holy Father; I could ordain Jean de Dieu as Bishop.

"And who deserves the Dukedom of Plaisance more than our dear General Magny?" Christophe continued slyly. "Who would dare to say that Prévost should not become the Count of Limonade, Yacinthe the Count of Borgne, or my esteemed secretary, Dupuy, Baron Dupuy? What do you say, my princes, my dukes, my counts, my barons, and my chevaliers? Or should I say: my generals, my chiefs, my secretaries?" he finished on a scornful note.

The Negroes glanced uneasily, one at the other, none caring to be the first to speak. The silence became embarrassing. Then Dupuy called out: *"Vive le Roi!"* There was a full-throated chorus: *"Vive le Roi!"* and only beaming faces and glowing eyes were to be seen.

CHAPTER EIGHTY

CAP HENRY—Cap Haitien, once more renamed—was *en fête*. For weeks past the drums had throbbed without cessation as they beat out the story of the coming rejoicings. Never had the checkered history of Haiti known so exhaustive a program of pomp and ceremony. The people were delirious with anticipation. From far and near they made their way toward the city, men, women, and pickaninnies; feet bare, shoulders bare, their small piles of possessions balanced dexterously on their heads, they plodded along little known trails over mountains, through thick forests and jungles, along valleys.

They poured into the city; poor peasants, with their single wives and children; richer peasants, with as many wives and children as they could afford to keep; deserters with other people's wives; laborers; soldiers who had served under Pétion, but had willingly transferred their allegiance to the stronger man—they poured into the city in a shuffling, laughing, excited throng until it seemed impossible for the inelastic streets to hold another soul. But they did, when the officially invited visitors arrived: representative civil officers from every district in the state; officers and men from the navy and the army who carried with them the three flags of each regiment.

Foreigners, too, visited Cap Henry. In the roadsteads lay the British frigate *Rendear*, commanded by Captain Douglas. Another vessel, which flew the Spanish flag, had come from Monte Cristi, bringing with it Don Raphael de Villars, Don Ramón Villa, Don Vicente de Lima, Don José Tabares, and other notabilities from Santo Domingo. There was also a

German, a Dutch, and a Colombian vessel, but these were merchantmen with cargoes for disposal, whose crews were not hurrying about their business because the laborers were on holiday and refused to work.

The day before the first of the official celebrations preceding the Coronation was noisy, but the early hours of that night were worse. People swarmed everywhere. Every plot of land not covered by a building was occupied by as many sweating black bodies as could crowd together on it; there was scarcely room to walk along the quays; even the roads were choked with sprawling people who endeavored to rest while they might. Yet room was found to light fires, and as the sky darkened every quarter of the city glowed with leaping flames around which shuffling dancers revolved unceasingly, noisily. From a hundred throats came the full-throated roar; again, again, and yet again:

"*Oui, moins! Oui, moins! Oui, moins! Oui, moins! Oui, moins! Oui, moins! Oui, moins!*"

Round and round the fires they moved, feet shuffling imperceptibly, hips and buttocks swaying, mouths frothing, eyes white-rimmed. Round and round and round and round; and as the tafia circulated, the throbbing of the drums deepened; the throaty voices grew more excited. Presently the rhythm changed.

Zin zin zin zin zin zin. Ba yan min oh! Say a Pimba. Zin zin zin zin zin zin. Ba yan min oh! Say a Pimba.

There was no sleep for black man or white. The noise deafened their ears, the acrid smoke from the fires choked their nostrils and made their eyes smart. The white seamen from the ships explored the towns in groups, drank raw tafia, fought rival seamen of different nationalities, and slaked their passion in the arms of the sex-lusting women who staggered out of the weaving serpentine chain of dancers.

Tom-tom-tom-tom-tom-tom-tommity-tommity-tommity-tom-tom-tom-tom-tom-tom. For hour upon hour the throbbing drums beat out their barbaric rhythm, and did not cease until the last dancers collapsed and the fires expired for want of attention. Then, and not before, Cap Henry slept the few remaining hours before cockcrow.

The day was not yet dawning when Suzanne entered Duncan's bedroom; the hand that held a flickering candle quivered with excitement and made her bulging shadow dance a fantastic fandango on the wall behind her.

"Wake up, Miss Phebe; wake up, Mist' Duncan." Phebe opened her eyes lazily, but Duncan slept on. Suzanne leaned over him. "It am time ter git up, Mist' Duncan. Wake up, wake up," she called, and shook him by the shoulder. This had less effect than the spot of hot candle grease that splashed down upon his neck. He sat up hurriedly.

"De time am gone nearly four o'clock, Mist' Duncan. Ef yo'-all is gwine ter git yo' seats 'fore it am too late yo' bes' be rousin' yo'self mighty quick."

"All right, Suzanne, I will see that he gets up at once," Phebe told her.

"Very good, Miss Phebe," Suzanne replied, as she lighted the candles

329

beside the bed and waddled back to the door. "Jonas am layin' de table fer de coffee."

Phebe, no less excited than Suzanne, rose from her bed, and with one of the candles hurried into the bathroom. Duncan heard the sound of splashing as she emptied the waiting ewers of water into the bath; he heard more splashing as she sat in the bath and dashed the water against her body. The noise was punctuated by trills of excited laughter; presently she began to hum a strange, lilting melody.

The humming ceased. "I am getting out of the bath, my sweetheart," she called out.

He groaned his misery before he could force himself to sit up in bed; he was convinced that less than an hour had elapsed since the noise in the streets had allowed him to fall asleep. He had never felt less like exposing himself to the hot sunshine for a number of hours, and envied Phebe her simple elation.

He entered the bathroom. She stood on tiptoe on the wooden floor, with her arms stretched high in the air. Though his eyes were still misted with sleep, he thought that her taut, slender body had never looked more perfectly molded, or her face happier. Suddenly she began to dance; with almost imperceptible movements her stomach and buttocks swayed in a sinuous *danse de ventre*. In a cooing voice she sang:

> Bah day, bah day, oh man jah ee!
> Bah day, bah day, oh man jah ee!
> Bah day, bah day, oh man jah ee!
> Oh bah day, oh way, oh man jah ee!

"Phebe!"

The sharpness of his voice brought the dance to an abrupt end. Her arms dropped to her side; she looked at him with reproach and asked, "What is the matter, sweetheart? Don't you want to see me dance?"

"It is time for you to dress," he muttered, ashamed of his outburst.

"I dance because I am so happy," she told him. She threw her arms about him and forced him to encircle her with his arms. When she saw his eyes beginning to flame, which they always did when he held her close to him, she laughed contentedly, and instead of kissing him on his waiting lips, she raised herself up on tiptoe and kissed him lightly on the forehead, just below his red hair. Before he could prevent her she wriggled out of his grasp, and ran back into the bedroom.

When he returned to the bedroom, Phebe was dressed. He halted as he stepped within the doorway; for the second time that morning he wondered whether he had ever seen her look more beautiful. That this could be the wretched, ragged creature whom he had found five years ago literally in chains was almost incredible. How amazingly she had responded to months of patient care—and years of happy luxury! She had on a dress that had arrived from France only two days previously; brought by Captain Beard. The gleaming white satin of the underrobe fell from a high waist, above which a small bodice was cut low on shoulders and bosom; the fullness was draped at the back, and its folds formed a graceful train that swept the ground. A sleeveless redingote, the lines of which followed those of the gown, was of crimson brocade, to match a fantastic turban, which was decorated with rare osprey plumes, clasped with a diamond buckle. The crimson of her dainty slippers was of the same bright color as redingote and turban. The ensemble was completed by court-length white kid gloves and the ruby and emerald necklace, her favorite piece of jewelry, which had been his first gift to her after that day when she had leaped between him and De Saint Just's pistol.

She clapped her hands and laughed with joy at the effect her dress had upon Duncan. "You are going to be proud of Madame Stewart today," she called out gaily. "Do you think I look lovely?" she pleaded, yearning, as always, for adulation.

"You look charming," he replied sincerely. "More lovely than Cleopatra." He paused. "I wonder what Bella will say," he mused.

"It is not what her lips will say, but her eyes." Phebe's own eyes twinkled with sly amusement. "Dear Mrs. Martin! Sometimes I think she is very shocked with me."

As five o'clock struck, Jonas announced that a small company of soldiers had arrived to escort Duncan's party to the cathedral.

"Is the barouche waiting?"

"Yes, suh," said Jonas, whose face was one huge smile of joy. "Everybody am ready an' waitin'."

The Place d'Armes was only a stone's throw from Duncan's house, but the journey took several minutes, for the dense mass of people clustered in the neighborhood of the Place made progress, even at walking pace, almost impossible. Many people were clubbed by the musket butts of Duncan's escort, and the escorts of other notabilities who journeyed to the Champ de Mars by way of the Place d'Armes; some of the poor unfortunates were not clubbed once but many times, because they were unable to escape from so dangerous a spot. Several men and women died from repeated blows; at least a score of young children were trampled to death.

As Jonas guided his animals past the fountain the occupants of the carriage gazed eagerly round the Place, which was transformed. Every building facing the square was decorated with festoons of tropical flowers, colored lanterns, garlands, flags of all nations, and plaques of the royal cipher. The Palace itself, which was situated on the west side of the place, had all four façades similarly decorated, and in addition bore the ciphers of the Queen, the Prince (François-Ferdinand had died in Paris some years previously), and the two princesses. Between the Palace and the fountain a huge column had been erected, eighty feet high; it was surmounted by an eight-foot-high transparent globe, which had the royal ciphers in its middle and a crown above.

The carriage passed from the Place d'Armes into the rue Bourbon, which had been specially leveled, repaved, and sanded for the occasion. Both sides of the road were guarded by several lines of troops; all buildings were decorated with festoons, flags, and the inevitable royal cipher.

The Champ de Mars, too, was transformed; for what had once been a tree-bordered empty space, used for outdoor assemblies, was now partly

331

occupied by a church, erected especially for the occasion. On the right was a large canopy surmounted by two flags, decorated with the royal arms, and divided into three partitions by hangings of green taffeta decorated with fringes of gold thread, a gold phoenix, and stars. Beneath the canopy was a carpet of crimson velours on which were seats decorated with the royal ciphers.

When Phebe and Duncan entered the church they were received by His Grace the Duc de la Grande-Rivière, whom Duncan had known, not long ago, as General Toussaint-Brave. With a solemn bow the Duke took the tickets that Duncan handed to him and escorted the guests to their allotted seats, which they found were next to those of Bella and Nat.

"You are late," Nat greeted. "You are the last of our contingent to arrive."

"Good day, Mrs. Stewart," said Bella.

Smiling to himself, Duncan watched her. It was a harmless prevarication he had foisted on her, and how well justified time had proved it! The first day he had taken Phebe to the Martins' he had introduced her as his wife. He had known it to be a necessary lie; Bella's straightlaced Boston morals might have wrecked the friendship had she been forced to accept Phebe as Duncan's mistress. As it was, this minor fiction served to make life bearable for all of them.

Duncan suspected that Nat did not believe him; he had seen his quizzical eyebrow at the time. It seemed to say: "You're not fooling me, but I won't give you away. I like you too well to let Bella's New England conscience close my doors to you and Phebe."

Sometimes Duncan wondered, too, if he had really succeeded in deceiving Bella. Something in her glance now and then intimated that she knew this was a pretense. But obviously she was willing to let sleeping dogs lie. And thank heaven it never entered Phebe's beautiful head to question her status—as long as the presents were forthcoming in satisfactory quantity.

Duncan sighed and glanced about him. Captain Douglas of the British frigate sat on the other side of Bella. In the seats behind sat Webster and his wife; Williams, whose clothes made Duncan conclude that the Casino must be doing very well; Captain Beard, unfamiliar in his Sunday best, and looking as though he half expected the devil to whisk him away from such a holy place; the masters of the other foreign ships anchored in the harbor; and the foreign traders who had established themselves in Haiti during the past few years.

Captain Douglas indicated the church with a movement of his head. "What do you think of the decorations, Dr. Stewart? Somebody has imagination, or else a remarkable knowledge of European coronations."

"Christophe has both, sir. I have met no other Negro with a better developed imagination. As for his knowledge of Europe, I can assure you that it is very extensive, particularly as to foreign royalties and royal courts. Since he has achieved power his secretaries have read many books to him on the subject, and he has spoken to many Europeans; having a retentive memory, he seldom forgets what he hears or has read out to him."

"Extraordinary chap, begad!" Douglas murmured.

A pause in the conversation gave Duncan an opportunity to inspect the church, which was magnificently decorated with azure silk ornamented with gold fringes and sprinkled with golden stars. The route of the royal procession was covered with sumptuous carpeting that bore the King's arms set amidst the ubiquitous golden stars. The throne was set under the cupola, beneath a baldachin of crimson, gold embroidered, strewn with phoenix and stars. On the left of the altar was the accommodation allotted to the Queen and her household, similarly decorated. On the right, in the sanctuary, was the raised archiepiscopal throne, hung with violet silk to match the small canopy above.

He then inspected the people; the women, in dresses designed and fashioned in the dressmaking establishments of Paris and London; the men, in the ceremonial uniform of their noble rank or order, as stipulated by a decree of the previous April; Their Serene Highnesses the princes and Their Graces the dukes, in white tunic, black mantle embroidered in gold, silk stockings, square buckles of gold, gold-hilted sword, and round hat braided with gold, with raised front brim and five black and red plumes; messieurs the counts, the same, save that the mantle was of azure blue, and three red plumes in the hat; messieurs the barons, in red coat, long and full, embroidered with gold, waistcoat and breeches of blue taffeta, and two white plumes; messieurs the chevaliers, in blue coats, waistcoat and breeches of red taffeta, white stockings, square gold buckles, green leather shoes, green baldric, and two green plumes; the members of the Royal and Military order of St. Henry, with their azure enameled gold crosses—grand crosses with wide black ribbon, commanders with red ribbon, and chevaliers with no ribbon.

Duncan's inspection was interrupted by a distant salvo of artillery. An agitated murmur traveled round the church; Phebe whispered excitedly: "The Queen has just left the Palace." The murmur became a hum; there were outbursts of shrill, hysterical laughter, barely suppressed. Soon the noise within the church was drowned by that from without—the musical jingle of accouterments, the rumble of wheels, the rhythmic clop-clop of hoofs. A second salvo of artillery greeted the Queen as her coach entered the Champ de Mars. The procession came to a halt; the Queen, the Prince, and the princesses entered the church, where they were received by the Grand Marshal of the Palace and the Grand Master of Ceremonies and escorted to the tribune reserved for them. For a time the church was hushed; only the Queen spoke. She whispered to her children, and frequently glanced at the throne as though she were trying to explain the meaning of the ceremony; her expression was one of loving pride. The minutes passed, and the church became noisy again.

With every minute the hum of conversation grew louder. At last Duncan glanced at his hunter; the hour was just seven o'clock. About time Henry was starting off, he thought. A salvo of cannon announced that the King was keeping punctually to his program. A few minutes later, magnificently uniformed, he swept imperiously into the church, followed by a brilliant cortege. He was received at the door by the Archbishop and members of the clergy, and paused long enough to be sprinkled with holy water. Then the Archbishop escorted the King to his throne and celebrated Solemn High Mass.

The oath of allegiance followed the Gospel. At a sign from the Grand Marshal, His Serene Highness the Prince of Limbé raised his arm. "I swear obedience to the constitution of the kingdom, and loyalty to the King." Romain was followed by Vernet, now Prince of Gonaïves. Then followed the dukes, the ministers, the counts, the barons, and the chevaliers. Then the King rose and, addressing himself to the representatives of his army and navy and to the civil officers, commanded them to swear obedience and loyalty. With uplifted arms, and in one voice, they swore the oath. "*Nous le jurons.*" The three words rumbled round the church like a muffled clap of thunder, and were followed by the booming of the artillery in the square outside. The King sat down; high officers of the army marched forward carrying new flags and standards for the archiepiscopal blessing.

Duncan's thoughts grew reflective. Was this church in Cap Henry, principal town of a small black country? Surely it could not be; surely it was in some backward European country, and the king that had just received the oath of loyalty from his assembled subjects was no black monarch but a petty princeling, descendant of a long line of hereditary rulers. This pomp, this circumstance, this pageantry; these richly appareled princes and nobles and barons and counts and chevaliers; these members of a royal order; this archbishop in his state robes; these military officers, each in the brilliant, specific uniform of his regiment; surely these things belonged to a German state or a Balkan duchy.

Captain Beard leaned forward. "To think he was nothing but a scurvy waiter when you first came to this place," he whispered.

CHAPTER EIGHTY-ONE

THE celebrations continued. On the day following the taking of the oath of allegiance, Their Majesties and the members of the Royal and Military Order of St. Henry attended the parish church. Afterward the Order attended a banquet at the Palace; a gay affair, thanks to Christophe's unremitting efforts to please his guests, most of whom had known Christophe only as a military leader. Those who remembered the graciousness and cordiality of Toussaint l'Ouverture whispered that Christophe was another Toussaint, which was good. But even Toussaint had not been quite so imperial in his manner; he had been a true governor general, but Christophe, now, was a real majesty, which was better. It made a man feel more important, they said, fingering their enameled gold crosses. These feelings manifested themselves during the banquet; they cheered and applauded when Christophe toasted: "To my faithful nobles, grand crosses, commanders, and chevaliers of St. Henry; to the valiant representatives of my armies." Then they sang the Haitian hymn with enthusiasm.

334

On the third day Christophe was crowned at the Champ de Mars amid scenes of pageantry that far excelled those of the previous days. Only one incident marred the ceremony; the King neglected to kneel before the Archbishop when the time came for the crown to be placed upon his head, and remained seated. This omission astonished most of the white people present, for, until that moment, Christophe's observance of the forms of ceremony had been remarkably correct, and paid credit to the coaching of an émigré from the French Revolution, whom Christophe had attracted to Haiti from Monte Cristi. The Negroes, however, did not recognize the slip; to remain seated when everyone else stood was the prerogative of majesty. Then Christophe proclaimed: "I swear to maintain the integrity and independence of the kingdom; never again, under any pretext, to permit the return of slavery or other feudal measures contrary to liberty and the exercising of civil and political rights of the people of Haiti; to maintain the inviolability of the revenues and sales of produce of the kingdom; to govern solely in the interests, well-being, and glory of the great Haitian family of which I am the chief." Upon which King of Arms proclaimed sonorously: "The Very Great, Very August King Henry, King of Haiti, is crowned and enthroned."

The celebrations finished where they had begun, in the Champ de Mars. The King reviewed his army there, on the site of the church where he had taken the oath a few days previously. During the intervening days the church had been removed en bloc. This was a prodigious feat, and it evoked the admiration even of the stoical Douglas.

The following day the gracious, affable majesty of the coronation celebration disappeared, like the church. In his place appeared a new Henry; a man whose soaring ambitions had been whetted by success. From a personal aspect he was fully satisfied with the progress he had so far achieved; he was absolute monarch of half a million subjects; he was surrounded by a number of able and intelligent men who respected him; he owned one palace in his beloved city that was now named after him, another was in the course of being erected in one of the most beautiful spots in the world; a massive, invulnerable citadel, symbol of his power, was making slow but certain progress; he was looked upon with friendly eyes by two great countries, one on either side of the Atlantic; he had a loving wife and three survivors of his four legitimate children; he had a loving mistress or two, and some bastards, one of whom, Blésine, was reaching marriageable age. But Henry was equally ambitious for his country. Haiti must become one of the great countries of the world, like Great Britain, the union of American states, and France—for Henry, never having had an opportunity of comprehending land distances, had little conception of the comparatively vast size of the white countries. Yet he was not blind to the fact that first there was much to be done. Haiti must prove herself worthy of that equality. She had a king and a court and increasing trade. So far, so good, but it was not enough. As a king he must prove himself a worthy brother of the white monarchs.

CHAPTER EIGHTY-TWO

DUNCAN inspected himself in the mirror. There was a pensive expression in his eyes. His hair was as unruly as ever. As unruly as ever, maybe, but was it quite the flaunting shade it had been, say, five years previously? He tried to persuade himself that it was, but here and there, particularly about the region of his ears, were some scattered hairs that were colorless. The first gray hairs!

"Duncan, my sweet!"

He turned. Phebe sat up in bed and beckoned to him. "Come here, my little one." She patted the coverlet.

He sat down on the bed. "What do you want?" he asked, although he knew perfectly well what the answer would be. She would demand that he kiss her, not solely because she craved his kisses, although she was still insatiable, but also that she might arouse his passion, and having done so, tease him by pretending to become too languid to continue the embrace to its logical conclusion. It was a game that they often played; she, because she never tired of displaying the strength of her hold upon him; he, because it kept her happy, and because he still enjoyed her kisses.

"Kiss me," she commanded.

Suzanne knocked upon the door.

"Mist' Duncan. Here am a note frum de King," she called out, for Duncan had at last succeeded in making her understand that she was not to burst into his bedroom without warning.

"All right, Suzanne, you can bring it in."

Suzanne entered; as she waddled across the room she first glanced at Phebe, and then, with mischief-filled eyes, at Duncan; she appeared disappointed at seeing him undisturbed. Duncan read Vastey's note, which was brief; His Majesty the King would be obliged if Monsieur le Docteur could see his way to attend at the palace as soon as convenient.

In these days Henry's wishes were commands; but Duncan experienced no resentment, for however inconvenient these impatient commands were at times, the King remained a generous taskmaster.

Upon the arrival at the Palace Duncan proceeded directly to Henry's bureau; none of the guards questioned him, for instructions had been given that the *blanc papaloi* was to enter the palace unchallenged. The guard outside the *bureau*, one of the King's Royals-Bonbons, rapped upon the door as Duncan approached. Vastey opened the door and beckoned him to enter.

Henry was striding up and down the thick carpet; he glanced absently at the white man. "Sit down, Ti Rouge, I shall keep you no more than a few minutes." He turned back to his secretary, who had reseated himself at a table. "Lastly, my dear Vastey, write to Peltier" (Peltier was the

King's London agent) "that he is to purchase, for shipment by the next merchantman outward bound for the Cap, two violins, one cor, and one bassoon for our royal orchestra; also the compositions of the young German composer, Franz Peter Schubert. I understand that he has written a pianoforte fantasia which has attracted some attention in Vienna." (This was an aside to Duncan.) "While you are on the subject of music, remind Peltier that he neglected to send flute parts for Beethoven's Overture to Coriolanus. Why was this? He is to supply an explanation, and avoid similar carelessness in the future. Lapommeraie is a capable *chef d'orchestre*, but I am sure his idea of orchestration would not meet with Beethoven's approval. He is also to order six Wilton carpets of seven meters' length, five meters' width, to be woven in dark blue and black, patterned with a crimson phoenix, in the design which Peltier has already acknowledged receiving. He will also purchase one carpet two meters square, of azure blue and black, spangled with golden stars, and patterned with the royal coat of arms; also a similar carpet patterned with the arms of Her Majesty."

For several minutes Henry continued to dictate to his secretary. He spoke crisply, effortlessly; in spite of the concise details of the articles that he desired should be shipped from England, he did not once falter or consult any papers. Fifteen carpets; eight tapestries; four Staffordshire teapots; a set of six Wedgwood Blue Jasper vases; six bedroom suites to be ordered from Mr. Sheraton; two carved, gilt bedsteads with azure blue silk damask hangings, with the inevitable phoenix motif; one dozen gilt mirrors, two meters ten centimeters by one meter forty centimeters; a complete printer's font; ten sets of leather harness—the list continued for longer than the few minutes he had promised.

Duncan inspected the King; with surprise he noticed that Henry's hair, like his own, was turning gray. He wondered why he had not realized this sooner, for on thinking back, he realized that the King's hair must have been gradually turning gray for several months past. No doubt the discovery of his own gray hairs had made him more aware of other people's. When he, then, glanced at the King's face, he was shocked. He had not seen Henry for several weeks; in that time he had changed. His face was drawn; the flesh beneath his eyes was pouchy.

Henry stopped dictating, and turned abruptly. "Why are you staring at me, Ti Rouge?"

"How is your health? Good?"

"Yes, yes, excellent," Henry replied impatiently. "Why should it be otherwise? Do I look ill?"

"You look overtired."

"I have been busy lately; we all have; Vastey, Dupuy, Limonade, all my ministers. We have been working on a new constitution. It is to be known as the Code Henry." The King spoke with enthusiasm. "What Napoleon has done for France, I am doing for Haiti. The people shall be told what is to be expected of them, what punishments will be meted out to them if they disobey the laws of the land, how they can best serve the kingdom." He paused, shook his head reflectively. "I did not bring you here to tell you about the Code Henry, but to ask if you are free to accompany me on a journey to Sans-Souci. It is some weeks since I visited my new palace."

"When are you planning to go?"

"At once. Can you come?"

"Of course. Will you stay there the night?"

"Yes, yes." He turned to Vastey. "See that everything is made ready for us to leave within thirty minutes.

"Yes, Sire."

As soon as his secretary had gone, Henry turned back to Duncan. "I am not ill," he said harshly, "but I am finding many things to try my patience, Ti Rouge. I am working hard; you know that, for I have had to deprive myself of your company for several weeks—even when you visited the palace the other night. I work all day, and half through the night; some of my friends are loyal to me and do the same, but others—" He shrugged his shoulders in despair. "There are some who will not realize that to achieve success one must work. Work, work, work!" In a spasm of temper he banged Vastey's table with his clenched fist. "To the devil with them, I say! They are no patriots; they deserve punishment, and by Damballa, I will punish them if they do not heed my warnings." He paused; became calmer. "Perhaps the publication of the Code Henry will help. Now for Sans-Souci. Meet me outside, Ti Rouge." He strode from the room as though he were an enemy of Time.

Well within the half hour Duncan and the King left the palace for Sans-Souci, attended by a substantial body of Royals-Bonbons. Some considerable time had elapsed since Duncan had ridden to Sans-Souci. The changes which had taken place since then were marked: for instance, the brickyard outside the walls of the town seethed with industry; the road by which the party was traveling was in first-class condition, for its surface had been leveled, and repaved where necessary; ditches had been cleaned out; culverts repaired.

Although Duncan could see all these changes for himself, nevertheless he had them pointed out to him by the King, who was too proud of his handiwork for the least aspect to go unnoticed. See this, Ti Rouge; see that, Ti Rouge; what do you think of that? Look over there! For an hour Duncan strove to find different ways of wording the unceasing expressions of congratulations, for Henry liked to hear his triumphs praised. Presently, when there were no more triumphs, Henry changed the conversation.

"You visited the Royal Academy of Arts on several occasions, didn't you, Ti Rouge?" he asked unexpectedly.

Duncan had done so, but it must have been many years since he had mentioned the fact to the King; certainly he could not remember the occasion. "Yes," he admitted. "I knew a young fellow of about my own age who exhibited at the Academy. His name was Edward Dayes."

"Did Dayes paint portraits?" Henry asked eagerly.

"Not when I knew him."

"Was he a good painter?"

"I thought so."

"Why did he not paint portraits?"

"The art of portraiture is somewhat different from that of painting landscapes," Duncan explained awkwardly. "Like that of prose from poetry."

"Most kings have their portraits painted, don't they?"

Duncan masked a smile as he realized the drift of the King's questions. "Yes."

"I want my portrait painted, Ti Rouge, to hang at Sans-Souci," the King said. "A palace that does not contain a portrait of its sovereign is no palace. Besides, I want the future kings of Haiti to see what kind of man the founder of their house was. I should like several portraits, one to send to your king of England, another to President Madison. Who is there in Haiti capable of painting my picture?" Henry testily answered his own question. "Nobody! Do you think Peltier could find an English painter who would come out to Haiti to paint my portrait, and act as professor at our Academy?"

"I see no reason why some young painter should not welcome the honor of painting a king," Duncan confirmed. "If Peltier communicates with the President of the Academy I am sure he would be given the name of a suitable man to approach."

"Vastey shall write to Peltier tomorrow."

When the horsemen reached the rise to Sans-Souci, Duncan saw more changes, more improvements. Gone was the trail he remembered; also the paved road. In their place was a wide, stately avenue bordered with lovely palm trees, which the incredible fertility of the soil had already nourished to grow to noble proportions.

"This is a kingly avenue, Henry," Duncan commented sincerely.

When Henry said nothing, Duncan glanced at his companion. He was smiling broadly, with an expression that was more one of mischief than pleasure. The Scot wondered why, but the summit of the knoll revealed the answer. His exclamation of astonishment produced a delighted burst of laughter from the King.

There was good reason for the white man's amazement. The palace was still far from completion, but it was sufficiently advanced to give one an idea of its ultimate size and beauty. Already the main building, the palace proper, had risen three stories; above that, in the center, was rising a domelike structure that appeared from a distance to be a belvedere. The two upper stories consisted of a noble façade of twenty-three French windows; the rez-de-chaussée below was mostly hidden by an imposing horseshoe staircase leading up to a balcony and terrace that stretched the length of the building. Beneath the balcony there welled out a bubbling spray of water, which first tumbled into an iron bowl and then overflowed into a wide marble basin. Above this rainbow-hued jet was a carved black sun, surrounded (as Duncan later discovered) by the inscription: "I see all, and shed light on all things throughout the world."

The keynote of the architecture was simplicity; there was no evidence of the sculptured pilasters, corner towers, battlements, entablatures, or minarets that were a feature of French châteaux. Henry's palace lost nothing from this lack of ornamentation; the vivid green of its forest background, and the silver rain of cascades, supplied all deficiencies. Accepting it as a perpetual monument to the genius of a Negro slave who had battled his way into kingship, Duncan could find no fault with it.

The palace, though predominant, was only one of many buildings, all in different stages of completion. To the left of the palace was rising another, nearly as large, and connected with the palace by a covered passage. To the right was a smaller building. Farther off were other buildings large and small; one was obviously to be a church. As he saw Duncan's gaze wander from one building to another, Henry laughed happily and answered Duncan's unspoken questions.

"That building on the left is to house the Council Chamber, with bureaux for the different Ministers of State. The building on the right will become the barracks for my Royals-Bonbons. Farther away to the right is the Petit Palais for the apartments of the Prince Royal; in front will be the Treasury; the smaller buildings in front of the Treasury are the stables, and the grooms' quarters." He pointed to his right. "The building near the church is to be the Archbishop's residence; farther away are more barracks. The building behind the Gardens is the arsenal and foundry. The gardens on the right of the route to the Citadel are the Queen's Gardens; behind are the printing works, and farther on, the military hospital."

Duncan stared at the amazing collection of buildings. "Sans-Souci will become a small town in itself," he commented at length.

"A royal town," Henry corrected proudly. "I plan to spend much time here, Ti Rouge. I shall hold courts here, and councils of state, and lawsuits requiring the King's judgment." He broke off with an excited laugh, and pointed to a small house set in the midst of the royal gardens. "Do you see that house there? Can you guess its purpose?"

Duncan could not, and said so.

Henry's laughter was exultant. "That is to be your house, Ti Rouge. Whenever I come to Sans-Souci, or whenever you need a change, that house will always be ready for you and Phebe. Do you like it?" he asked naïvely.

How could one not like a house situated in this Garden of Eden? Duncan turned and surveyed the superb panorama; the green miles of rolling jungle, the avenue of gently swaying palm trees, the distant splash of lapis lazuli, the majestic background of mountain, the shimmering housetops of Cap Henry, the toy ships riding in the roadsteads. What color, what magnificence, what peace!

"You do like it?" Henry asked again, anxiously.

"I am trying to find words that will tell you how much I like it; and how deep is my gratitude—"

Henry raised a hand. "You have no need to do that, Ti Rouge," he interrupted. "Do you think I am ever likely to forget that, were it not for you, I should not be King of Haiti, and that there would be no Palace of Sans-Souci? Besides," he continued, his voice taking on an authoritative note, "I shall need you near me just as much here as at the Cap."

"When the palace is finished, I must have a housewarming," Duncan mused. "The Martins, the Websters—"

"No," Henry interrupted. An ugly scowl distorted his face. "Naturally, you may bring Phebe to Sans-Souci with you—she is a mulatto—but not the Martins or the Websters. They are white."

"But—"

"No, I say," Henry shouted as he waved his hand in the direction of the palace. "That palace is being built by black men for a black king of a black country; it is to be a monument to the future greatness of the black nations, and a warning to the whites that this century has seen the birth of a new race of black men. No white man shall ever visit Sans-Souci save you. Is that understood?"

"You are King of Haiti," Duncan acknowledged dryly.

Henry scowled again, and sought to excuse himself. "I like and respect the white people. You know that better than anyone, Ti Rouge. I want to do business with them, meet them as friends, employ them for the good of my country. At the same time I fear them. I know them as clever men who will worm their way into this, then into that, if they are given the opportunity. My subjects are still a simple people; if I allow the white men too much rope they will exploit my Negroes; perhaps in twenty, thirty, or forty years' time they will have almost as much power in the country as the French had in colonial days. Where the whites were concerned Dessalines did many foolish things, but he was right to prohibit white men from ever again owning property in this country. Haiti is a black man's country, and is going to remain a black man's country. Is that understood, Ti Rouge?" he shouted. "You will come here, but no other living white person. Is that understood?"

"It is," Duncan agreed quietly, and decided to prescribe a cooling draught for his companion; never had he seen Henry in such a mood; it was quite evident the King had been overworking.

CHAPTER EIGHTY-THREE

DURING the first weeks of 1812 the production figures compiled for the past year proved beyond all measure the success of Henry's unflagging efforts to revive the country's prosperity. But if further evidence had been necessary, it was supplied by the increasing numbers of white faces to be seen in Cap Henry. Henry spared no expense in his determination to make Haiti the envy of the world. Scores of experts were attracted to the country by the promise of generous rewards; engineers, architects, builders, printers, wheelwrights, ship repairers.

Among those to arrive at the Cap was Richard Evans, a young man still in his late twenties. He was a portrait painter, first a pupil of, and later an assistant to, Thomas Lawrence. Clever, subtle Peltier had made no mistake in approaching a pupil of the principal portrait painter in ordinary to George III; Evans shone in the reflected glory of his late employer, and Christophe, in commissioning the young man to paint his portrait, felt that a bond had been established between himself and the British sovereign.

In July the Code Henry was published. At Henry's request Duncan conscientiously read every one of its 1,517 articles on civil law, 86 articles on criminal law, 421 articles on judicial procedure, 133 articles on agricultural law, 500 articles on military law, and articles relating to civil procedure, commercial law, and the law of prize. He marveled at a colossal task successfully undertaken by a man who, even now, wrote his signature with difficulty and could not properly read. True, Napoleon had codified French law, which was a sharp spur to Henry to emulate his white rival; true, the Code Henry had for its model not only Napoleon's Code and the Constitution of the American States, but the groundwork of Dessalines's constitution; none the less, it was a stupendous work that lost nothing by being Haiti's first written code.

Perhaps the most interesting of the sections was that relating to agriculture, which was subdivided into eight heads: the duties of proprietors and farmers, and the obligations of laborers; the supply of equipment; obligatory crops; payment to laborers; public works; punishments; and two sections dealing with breeding farms and with cattle grounds. To Duncan's amazement and gratification he read that it was the legal duty of a proprietor or farmer to provide every plantation with a midwife, and a hospital which was to be visited once a week by a physician at the expense of the proprietor. He paused in his reading, to blink absurd tears of gladness from his eyes. Months ago, at Sans-Souci, he had believed that Henry had given him the ultimate proof of gratitude. He realized now that the house at Sans-Souci was a widow's mite in comparison with the indirect reward that the pages of the Code Henry offered him. The house was the man's reward, but this provision for the well-being of the cultivators was the physician's, and the man in Duncan was no more than a cloak for the physician, as had always been so from the moment he had heard from Elspeth of the manner of his mother's death. At last the complicated pattern of his life was clear; all the pieces fitted into a composite whole. Because his mother had died in giving birth to him, hundreds of Negro lives were to be saved in the plantation hospitals; because medical attention had saved the life of the then king-to-be, the King intended future medical attention to save the lives of hundreds of his subjects. This was why Fate had guided a Scotsman's footsteps to this tropical island—to inculcate appreciation for the white man's medicine and surgery into the minds of an ignorant, backward black people.

At last Duncan laid down the thick pile of paper which comprised the Code. Henry, whose impatience during the previous fifteen minutes had become increasingly pronounced, leaned forward.

"Well, Ti Rouge?" he questioned eagerly. "What think you of my code?"

"It's a prodigious feat of work," Duncan replied with sincerity.

Henry made no attempt to conceal his pleasure at this praise. "I knew what your answer would be; it could not be anything else. The Code is prodigious; we have worked many months preparing it." His eyes shone brightly. "Did you read about the provisions for every plantation to possess its own hospital and midwife?"

"I did. That article alone marks you as the greatest legislator in Negro history."

"You really mean that?" Henry laughed his satisfaction, and in his anxiety to miss nothing of Duncan's praises, moved his chair nearer. "My subjects have you to thank for that; it was you who made me understand that the more I care for the health of my subjects, the better work they will be able to perform."

"I realize why the article was added; I can scarcely begin to thank you, Henry—"

The King was too full of the Code to listen to thanks. "You read, too, that all field laborers were to be attended by one or two women water carriers?"

"I have read every word—"

"And one or two nurses to look after suckling babies? And the article that insists upon the workers' being paid properly, with ultimate appeal to myself if they are not? And the article in the military laws that obliges every barracks to maintain a free elementary school for the instruction of soldiers in reading, writing, and arithmetic? And the obligation of a domiciled Haitian to make himself responsible for the frauds of merchantmen selling cargoes in Haiti? The Code Henry will guard the financial interests of rural workers, care for their welfare, protect the community from foreign exploitation, increase and maintain the prosperity of the country. Do you blame me for taking pride in the Code Henry?"

"Yes."

The abrupt answer surprised Henry. His forehead puckered in a puzzled frown; he glanced at his companion with an expression that put Duncan in mind of a dog from which a tasty bone had been snatched. "You misunderstood me; I asked whether you agree that I should be proud of the Code?"

This time Duncan's reply was unequivocal. "It is not entirely something to be proud of, Henry."

Henry became angry. "Why not?"

"Some years ago you fought for the emancipation of the Negroes. They looked upon you as their savior, and believed you when you swore never to sheathe your sword until every slave in Saint-Domingue was freed. Later, when you became President of the State of Haiti, you swore an oath to maintain the new constitution. Do you remember the articles of title one, Henry? That every person residing on the territory of Haiti is free, in the fullest sense; that slavery is forever abolished in Haiti?"

"Well?"

"The Code Henry repudiates the very essence of title one of your constitution, and condemns the laborers of Haiti to the state of slavery that you swore should be forever abolished."

Henry scowled. "Those are hard words, Ti Rouge."

"They are true," Duncan maintained. "What else can you call an existence that forces men and women to work from sunrise to sunset, and orders them to be flogged at the first signs of slackening work?"

"Does it hurt to work so many hours?" Henry demanded curtly. "I work from sunrise to sunset, and usually much longer; so do Vastey, Dupuy, Limonade, and some of the ministers. So, too, do you, Ti Rouge. How often have you worked fifteen hours a day? Many times. If you, and I, and Vastey, Dupuy, and many others, can work so hard, why should not the laborers on the plantations do the same?"

"The circumstances are different. There is nobody to compel you or me to work—"

"Nonsense, Ti Rouge. The welfare of my country compels me to work, just as the necessity of operating on your patients compels you to work."

"You and I are well paid for our labors," Duncan dryly commented.

"The cultivators are paid for their work. Is not a fourth part of the crops they produce theirs by legal right of the Code Henry? If it is not paid to them they have the right to appeal to me, their king, for justice. Of course," Henry added ironically, "they do not receive as much as you or I; but do you place the work of a cultivator on the same level as that of their king, or Dr. Stewart?"

"There is nobody to order your punishment, Henry, if you choose to rest for a few minutes in midmorning, or midafternoon."

"And how long would the rest last if the cultivators were permitted to take one whenever they pleased? Not for ten minutes, or twenty, or thirty: it would last until the next mealtime."

"Would you have admitted that years ago, before you had fought for that freedom which you are now denying others?"

"I have always been a hard worker," Henry maintained sullenly. His mood changed; he looked depressed. "What you say is partly justified, Ti Rouge. Years ago I believed that the Negroes could achieve a mighty country for themselves if only they were given their freedom."

"And now?"

The King waved the question aside, with an impatient wave of his hand. "Have you any other objection to the Code Henry?"

"Why can't a cultivator choose his own place of employment? It's not freedom in its fullest sense to prevent a man's leaving one place of work to go to another; or to give a plantation a lien on the lives of all souls born within its boundaries. If, years ago, you had faith in the ordinary black man, what has happened to change it?"

"Experience!" Henry replied bitterly. "If you wish for proof that my way is the best, compare my kingdom with that cursed republic of Pétion's. My kingdom becomes wealthier every year, foreign countries are anxious to trade with us, our money is good, and with it we can import machinery for the improvement of commerce and goods for the improvement of our standard of living. What of the republic? Pétion affects to promote industry and agriculture, but his subjects work harder at achieving idleness. His exchequer is so bankrupt he has had to debase his coinage; neither his exports nor his imports are a tenth of ours; crime is rampant in the republic, so is licentiousness."

Duncan knew that Henry spoke nothing more than the truth, and was silent.

The year 1812 drew to a close, a fateful year for the French Emperor, who had marched an army of over half a million men into a snowy morass and there suffered his greatest defeat. When the news of the debacle reached Haiti, there was great rejoicing. That is the end of Napoleon, said the people. Now we shall never need the Citadel, for Napoleon is no longer strong enough to invade us.

Sans-Souci neared completion. Early in 1813 Henry announced the date of his housewarming party (though, as Nat said as he fanned himself, it was neither a house, nor did it want warming!). Later, Phebe and Duncan received an official invitation from the chamberlain to attend the celebrations there. So did Bella and Nat, Evans the painter, and others, so Duncan concluded that Henry had waived his intention of forbidding any white people other than his physician to visit the palace. Williams, to his bitter chagrin, was not invited.

When Jonas brought the carriage to a halt in front of the palace gates, Duncan and Phebe alighted, and waited for the Martins to join them; all four entered the gates and walked down the avenue toward the palace.

"This place is colossal, Duncan," Nat remarked. "Henry had my admiration even before today, but now—well, frankly, I didn't think a Negro was capable of achieving a tenth of what Henry has done since his rise to power. I believe that the nineteenth century is destined to be an epoch. What other century has produced at the same time two such geniuses as Napoleon and Henry? White Napoleon and Black Napoleon!" He chuckled, and turned to his wife. "What do you think of the palace, my dear?"

"The colors are dreadful, Nathaniel, but the situation is heavenly. Duncan, I am almost envious of your having a house of your own here. If once I were to live here, I should never want to leave."

"That is Henry's idea; he plans to spend most of his time here. The place is a small town in itself." Duncan paused and pointed out the buildings as he remembered them. "The foundry—do you know, by the way, Nat, that Henry is now manufacturing his own gunpowder?"

"Bad for American trade!" Nat commented.

"That building is the arsenal. The military hospital is over there, then the printing works, and the cutlers." He turned, pointed to some buildings outside the palace grounds. "Next to the stable is a carpenter's shop, where the royal carriages were made, and beyond, the distillery. In addition he is establishing a goldsmithy, a sewing school, a school of art, and a royal orchestra. The park over there is reserved for any dignitaries who want to erect houses—but the houses must be of masonry."

"I don't blame him for making that regulation. Can you imagine this view being spoiled by wooden houses?"

Phebe pouted. "I should not want to live all my life here. I cannot think why the King is not satisfied with his palace at the Cap."

"But then you are fond of pleasure, my dear," Bella pointed out in a not unkindly voice. "As a mother you would come to welcome the peace of home more than the excitement of the Casino."

"I never want to be a mother; my figure would be ruined."

345

Bella had long ceased to be shocked by anything that Phebe did or said. She smiled and turned to Duncan. "Where is your house?"

"Behind the palace. We must go there later."

The quartet ascended the stone staircase, passed by the sentries, reached the terrace, and entered the palace. They found themselves in a large audience chamber in which guests, sentries on guard, and pages in gold and blue livery jostled one another in every direction. The room had been modeled on a European audience chamber; lovely tapestries, oil paintings, and immense gilt mirrors covered the walls, heavy silk curtains draped the windows, carved mahogany furniture stood soundly on a polished floor of the same wood.

"It is beautiful," Bella gasped.

"So madame likes His Majesty's audience chamber?"

They turned; Vastey bowed low with elegant taste.

"May I be permitted the honor of escorting you round the palace?"

They accepted gladly, for everyone liked Vastey. "This room, as I have already said, is the audience chamber," the King's secretary began.

"Say, where did all these decorations come from?" Nat asked.

"Mostly from Europe, monsieur. Everything save the furniture had to be imported from either England or France—the tapestries and mirrors from France, the oil paintings and those lovely hangings from England. The furniture was made on the spot," he added with pride.

"Here, in Sans-Souci?"

"Yes, monsieur, by our own woodworkers, from our own unrivaled native timber."

Nat ruffled his hair. "It's marvelous," he muttered.

The compliment pleased the mulatto. "Come this way, if you please, messieurs et mesdames, to the Throne Room."

The amazed white people followed him from room to room: the Throne Room; four banqueting rooms; the library, stocked with a great number of elegant and erudite volumes imported from Europe and America; the King's private apartments; the Queen's private apartments; several remarkably modern bathrooms; the King's bureau; rooms of the household staff. Lastly, Vastey showed them the system by which the palace remained cool on the hottest day; through trapping the water from natural cascades behind the palace, passing it through the palace by way of hollow walls and of culverts beneath the principal floors, and so out again into the fountain at the foot of the horseshoe steps outside.

"That finishing touch puts even White Napoleon into the shade," the astonished Nat whispered in Duncan's ear.

CHAPTER EIGHTY-FOUR

THERE was general rejoicing that day in Haiti when the news arrived that Napoleon had abdicated the throne of France, which was restored to the Bourbons. No Haitian would ever forget that evil trinity:

346

Leclerc and Rochambeau, and behind these two, Napoleon. The people rejoiced and danced round their fires; the King held a concert at Sans-Souci, to which all the notabilities were invited. Christophe was more affable that night than he had been for many months.

Life in Haiti proceeded serenely. Duncan often visited the palace and remained there as long as the King wished, or his duties at the Cap permitted. He was working harder than he had ever worked before; besides attending the King and the King's family in addition to his own practice, he was charged with directing the body of physicians and surgeons attached to the army and military hospitals. These doctors were grouped into classes and given corresponding military ranks. Even more work faced him in the future, for the King was contemplating the creation of a chair of medicine and anatomy at the big hospital that was still in the course of erection at the Cap; the chair, naturally, to be occupied by Duncan.

Henry was busier than ever in his desperate attempt to accomplish in years a culture which had taken white nations centuries of heartbreak and endeavor to achieve. Under the direction of their tireless leader everyone in Haiti was busy. But not busy enough for Henry, for the production of sugar, coffee, cocoa, tobacco, rum, indigo, and molasses had dropped during the previous year. True, not to any great extent; and to make up for decreases there were increases in cotton, dyewoods, and castor oil. Production must not be allowed to drop, Henry thundered. Production must increase, not drop. Increase, increase, increase! That word was rarely absent from Henry's lips. Increase! Production must increase. The proprietors must insist upon greater production from the laborers; if it were not forthcoming, well, forced labor was needed for the Citadel. . . .

One day Vastey received news, through his spy in the French cabinet, that Louis XVIII was sending emissaries to discuss the question of a treaty of alliance between France and Haiti. The emissaries traveled by a circuitous route: from France to England, from England to Jamaica. There they remained for a time, while couriers traveled back and forth between the emissaries and Pétion. Vastey smelled a rat and gave fresh instructions to his spies. Later a courier arrived from Jamaica with a letter for Henry, which Dupuy conveyed to Sans-Souci, where the King had assembled his council of state in anticipation of Dupuy's arrival.

At the appointed time Dupuy arrived at the palace and made his way to Council Chamber. "Well, well, Dupuy," Henry greeted him excitedly. "Is there news from France?"

"There is, Sire."

"Is it good news, Dupuy? Has France recognized Haiti as a great country? Is there a possibility of an alliance with us?" Henry's eyes shone as he faced his ministers: this was a great moment for Haiti, and a great moment for her king, Henry I; an alliance between France and her one-time colony; an alliance between His Very Christian Majesty Louis XVIII of France, and His Serene Highness Henry I of Haiti! History was in the making; a new epoch was in the throes of labor.

"I will read you a paragraph from the letter, Your Majesty—"

"Never mind one paragraph, Dupuy. We want to hear the complete letter. Who wants a tail without the dog to wag it?" Henry concluded jovially.

"Because it is indicative of the whole." Dupuy ignored Henry's frown and read on:

". . . For I know that you have too sound a judgment, too enlightened and lofty a mind not to be satisfied to become a Grand Seigneur and General under this ancient dynasty of the Bourbons, which, despite all human machinations, it pleases Providence to perpetuate on the Throne of our dear France: you will prefer to become an illustrious servitor of the Great Sovereign of the French rather than choose a precarious fate as the leader of revolted slaves—"

The rest of Dupuy's words were drowned by a pandemonium of rage from the council of state; the members shouted out incoherences, swore pagan oaths, hammered clenched fists on the table.

"Canaille!" Henry raved. "Pig! I spit on him! God damn him! He dares to describe King Henry the First as a leader of revolted slaves—" He choked over the hated words, but what he said next was not heard, for a renewed howl of rage went up from the assembly. Hate-filled eyes under scowling foreheads glanced about the ornate, bemirrored, tapestried room; these princes, dukes, barons, and counts, these generals and admirals, richly dressed in their silks and taffetas and gold braid—We, the nobles of Haiti, sitting in the council room of a palace built by us, by our own elected king—revolted slaves! Curse the French! Curse them for their lying insults! Curse them for their supercilious arrogance!

The disorder continued until Henry rose from his chair and hit the tabletop with his cane; the noise echoed about the room. "Quiet," he rasped. "Quiet." The noise died away in sullen defiance; white-rimmed abominating eyes stared at the letter.

"Shall I read the remainder of the letter?" Dupuy asked.

"No. Tear it up. Burn it."

Henry hammered on the table. "I command silence," he shouted. "Dupuy, who dared to address that letter to the King of Haiti?"

"Dauxion Lavaysse, Your Majesty, one of the emissaries of France. His postscript adds that Colonel Franco Médina is en route for Haiti, to discuss a proposition with Your Majesty—"

Henry interrupted harshly. "Médina! We shall know how to deal with him when he arrives." His words were greeted with acclamation. He glanced along the line of tempestuous faces and smiled significantly. There was no minority present. In their hatred of France, the council of state were as one. He turned back to Dupuy. "What is the meaning of that letter?"

"I can give you full information as to that," Vastey interrupted. "I received news about it in a dispatch from France, which arrived this morning. I was only awaiting the opportunity of informing Your Majesty of its contents. Malouet is at the root of King Louis's attitude toward us."

"Malouet!" In spite of the King's repeated injunctions for silence, the name, well known to the older members of the council, caused renewed exclamations of anger.

"Malouet has organized the planters who escaped from this country in the years preceding Dessalines's massacre," Vastey related quietly. "They have gained the King's ear; he is sympathetic to their cause because he is anxious to add Haiti to the French Empire again."

"The damned French are preparing another invasion," the Duke of Plaisance shouted.

"Not if more subtle methods will gain them their objective. Your Grace," Vastey corrected. "My information is that the agents who are on their way to Haiti have been instructed to intrigue among the chiefs and urge them to rise against His Majesty—"

"What!" The deep-throated exclamation was more like an infuriated bellow than a word. "The canaille would dare to try to incite my chiefs to insurrection!" The scowling lines deepened, the threatening glance traveled about the table and rested quickly, but none the less definitely, on each man in turn. The members of the council shuffled uneasily, but not one spoke. Henry laughed shortly. "They would be wasting their time, those agents," he commented unpleasantly. "I should know how to deal with anyone who is not satisfied with my rule. Continue, Vastey: what further orders have their agents been given?"

"To sow dissension between Your Majesty and Pétion—"

"Ah! They should have no difficulty in achieving that object, but I have no fear of Pétion."

"To persuade all Haitian chiefs to renounce independence, return to the regime of seventeen hundred and eighty-nine, become faithful subjects of Louis the Eighteenth, and restore slavery to this country, by disposing of all people hostile to France, and importing Negroes from Africa to take their place."

This time Henry's shouts to restore order were in vain; the fury of the Haitians was beyond restraint. The King relaxed, smiling; it was better to see his subjects express rage than mere indignation; it was safer. Then the smile relaxed and was replaced by an expression of uneasiness. The efforts of the French agents to win back Haiti by methods of intrigue would fail—he would make certain of that—but afterward, what would be the next move on the part of the French? Invasion, as suggested by Magny? Possibly, for France was no longer at war with Europe; after a year or so to reorganize, the French army could well be in a position to spare time and effort for the recapture of the old colony. To meet this danger Haiti must be put in an even better state of preparation. Above all, the Citadel must be finished. The Citadel, that invulnerable pivot of defense, must be completed and fortified.

The nobles stared at the ferociously determined face of their king and were satisfied that he would leave nothing undone in defense of their independence.

Sans-Souci saw little of the King during the weeks that followed Vastey's disclosure; he was constantly on the move, visiting every part of his kingdom in turn to inspect the country's fortifications and issue instructions for defense. One command was paramount: in the event of another invasion every town and village in danger of capture was to be fired, after its inhabitants had retired to the fortresses that had been built, or were being built, in the mountains. Day after day Henry spent in the saddle; night after night he dictated in the late hours to his secretaries. At last even his magnificent physique revealed signs of strain. After one especially long journey Duncan warned the King to rest.

"I need no rest, Ti Rouge. I am as strong as a bull."

"There are limits even to a bull's endurance. Your eyes are puckered; have you been out in the sun?"

"Naturally."

"You would do well not to expose yourself too often to the sun."

"I am a Negro, not a white. It is only you whites who suffer from sunstroke. The sun cannot hurt us Negroes."

"Do not be too sure of that, Henry. It is true that the white man has to be especially careful to protect his head and neck against the direct rays of the sun, but of late I have concluded that, in some circumstances, one can be affected without necessarily exposing one's head. I believe it is possible to absorb poison from sun-impregnated air; also, that the sun sometimes affects Negroes. I have examined many Negroes whose illness I have been unable to diagnose, but whose symptoms are those of sunstroke. What is more, I believe that the sun is responsible for the many cases of 'possession' that affect Negroes from time to time."

The King looked uneasy. "The gods possess us sometimes; you can't be referring to those occasions?"

"I can. As a Christian I do not believe in the Guinea gods."

Henry seemed disposed to argue, but then he shrugged. "Sun or no sun, there is work to be done. I have told you what the French intend, but they shall not succeed. I swear by everything I hold dear in this life to prevent the French reconquering Haiti."

"Are you quite sure you are not misjudging the situation?"

Henry smiled craftily. "I am more certain than ever since Médina crossed the Spanish frontier into our territory."

"Why?"

"I gave orders for his arrest and search; he was carrying enough documents with him to prove all that Vastey has said. There will be no rest for me until I know that every fort in Haiti is finished and ready for defense."

"You must have visited most of the important centers; why not rest for a week before starting off again? I feel quite sure that no French army will land here before then," Duncan concluded dryly.

Henry reflected. "Perhaps I'll take your advice. I am visiting the Citadel this afternoon, Ti Rouge. Come with me. It must be many months since you were last there."

"Years, not months," Duncan pointed out.

Later the two men left the palace and proceeded along the road leading up the mountainside to the Citadel above. As they neared the beginning of the ascent, a not unfamiliar scene greeted Duncan's eyes: the endless chain of dipping bodies that bordered the steep winding road as far as the eye could see, and the sweating, straining groups of men who pushed and hauled at blocks of solid rock, heavy balks of timber, small cannon, trunks of trees. When they began to ascend the road to the Citadel, Duncan realized that the laborers were even more numerous than before, and that a far larger proportion of them were women of all ages, from fifteen upwards. There appeared to be more overseers; but whether or no this was the case, Duncan was convinced that both the voices and the attitude of the overseers were more threatening. The most important change of all was in the expression of the workers. Almost every black face at which he looked was morose, sullen, bitter, hopeless. There was none of the badinage and carefree laughter usually associated with a group of Negroes; the only talk to be heard was the harsh commands of the overseers.

The two men's routes were repeatedly obstructed by one or another of the many hauling gangs, but such stops were brief, for as each overseer in charge saw the King, an order to cease work was given so that a path could be cleared. The overseers obsequiously saluted their sovereign, but the only greeting given by the laborers was a glowering stare that Duncan sensed long after they had passed on; he could not ignore the hundreds of burning, hate-filled eyes. Henry seemed unaware of them; he was impatient to reach the summit of the mountain, and every delay served to increase his irritation.

On one occasion their upward progress was halted by an exceptionally huge block of masonry. More than fifty men struggled with it; their taut muscles looked like knotted whipcord beneath their flesh. The overseer was unaware of the presence of his king; to the accompaniment of lurid oaths the man bellowed at the gang to pull harder; at the same time he sought to encourage the gangers by flailing with his cocomacacque any naked backs within reach of his restless arm. "Pull, you lazy, pot-bellied swine. Pull, you sons and grandsons of bastards! Pull, you filth from a goat's tail."

One of the gang stepped back from the block of masonry. He straightened his back and stretched his limbs. Then he bent double with a choking gasp, fell against the King, and sprawled full length upon the cobbles. The overseer used his foot to stir the man and shouted: "Get up there, you seventh son of a pot-bellied bitch." The body twitched and was still. At that moment the overseer saw the King beside him; he hastily commanded his gang to relax. The men flopped on to the road and stared at their sprawling comrade. Duncan kneeled down and felt the man's pulse. He turned the sweating body over and placed his hand over the man's heart.

"Has he fainted?" Henry asked in a curt, angry voice.

"He is dead."

"Dead! Of what?"

"Heart failure."

The overseer, having overheard the conversation, burst into a torrent of abuse. "May his bones rot, the weak-kneed pig! That is the third man to die upon me this week."

"The third!" Duncan repeated, startled. "Did you say that three men have died in six days?"

The overseer looked astonished, and, aware of the note of criticism in Duncan's voice, was immediately on the defensive. "That is nothing to grumble about; three gangs lost four of their men last week; three weeks ago six men died on one journey up to the top. Six!" he repeated in an aggrieved tone.

"Do many die?"

"Of course they do. What else can you expect? How many chicks live from a hatching of eggs? How many fish die in a single spawning? It is natural to die."

"How many die?"

"How should I know? I don't count the bodies. Hundreds in all. A score every week, perhaps, no more. I don't know. I can't count. What do you expect?" the overseer repeated. "Some just die, like this canaille here. Some fall down the mountain. Some are crushed to death." He pointed at the block. "Two days ago, one only half that size rolled off the trail and tumbled down the mountainside, taking five men and a couple of women with it. Work was held up for nearly half an hour." His voice turned apologetic. "It is things like that which hold up the work, Your Majesty."

Henry frowned. "The work must not be held up. Not even for half an hour. The Citadel has to be finished. Do you understand? Finished soon."

Duncan looked up at the King. There was an unhealthy glare in Henry's eyes; his forehead was a mass of throbbing muscles and veins; his thick neck seemed pinched in his tight neckband.

"Can nothing be done to prevent so many deaths, Henry? It is a bad record, if what the man says is true."

"Nonsense!" Henry rasped. "Would you have me order all work to cease because a few men have lost their lives?"

"A few!"

"What are a few hundred lives compared with the thousands whom the Citadel will save if the French invade Haiti?" The King's voice rose. "Good God! Are you trying to criticize me, Ti Rouge? Your heart is soft because you are a physician. But I cannot afford to have a soft heart. I am a king. The safety of my kingdom depends upon the Citadel's being built. Isn't that worth a few lives? Besides, most of them are convicts who have refused to do their share of work in the fields." His voice continued to rise, as though he wanted all within sight to hear his words; his expression grew wilder. "If a few of you die it will be a lesson to the rest. Do you hear that, all of you? We've got to work, all of us, not sleep our lives away. We've got to make this country one of the greatest in the world, and the envy of the white men whose slaves you were. We Negroes are going to prove to the whites that we are as good as they are. Do you understand?"

He paused, and glared at the rows of staring eyes. "If you were fighting the French in battle some of you would die, and none of you would look twice at a handful of dead bodies on the ground. Well, you are fighting the French now, by building the Citadel. When it's finished no Frenchman will dare to set foot in this country, nor any other man, white or black. It will make us unconquerable; a great nation. And by Damballa, the Citadel shall be completed in spite of tens of thousands of lives. Do you hear me?" he shouted. "The Citadel's got to be finished soon. If it isn't I'll execute some of you as traitors to your country; you, and you, and you—" His rigid arm pointed to a number of men in turn. "Take your choice. Work or die. Which is it to be? Work or die?" His words tailed off in a strangled gasp; he plucked at his collar, loosening it from about his neck. The rows of laborers stared expressionlessly at him; not a man spoke.

At last Henry turned, as though he was satisfied that he had tamed his convict subjects. "Come, Ti Rouge, now we can continue our journey," he said thickly.

"Why not some other day? Tomorrow it may be less hot."

"Hot! It is always hot," Henry sneered. "Come." He started off up the ascending road at a fast, grueling pace. Duncan followed, leaving the body of the dead laborer to be dealt with by others. When he had gone no more than a dozen paces he heard the overseer shout: "Pull, you sons of bitches, pull, you asses' filth, pull—" The harsh voice died away as Duncan turned a sharp corner—nearly to trip over the motionless body of the King.

A quick examination of Henry's congested eyes and vascular engorgement confirmed what Duncan had feared; Henry was suffering from a seizure induced by sunstroke.

Henry was slow to recover, for the attack had been a severe one. Besides, he made a bad patient; he would not believe that he, a Negro, could sustain sunstroke, and took elaborate steps to conceal the disgrace. He also fretted constantly in his anxiety to proceed with the work that he sincerely believed was so urgent and imperative. Nearly two weeks passed before Duncan allowed his patient to be up and about, and then he was far from satisfied with Henry's progress. He would not have given permission had not the King announced his firm intention of ignoring his doctor's orders. So Henry resumed his duties, but not as a healthy man. Three days later he brusquely ordered Duncan back to the Cap, saying that he was not going to be fussed over any longer.

Within a half hour of his return Duncan was walking along the rue St. Simon; Nat had sent a message asking him to call as soon as possible, to see some mysterious spots that had appeared on Junior's chest. As he passed by Tellier's, the jeweler's, his glance was attracted by a jeweled brooch likely to appeal to Phebe. He paused to inspect it more closely; it was a peacock's feather, of silver filigree, set with diamonds, emeralds, rubies, and pearls. Should he buy it for her? he reflected. He had not given her an expensive present for several months, and her manner lately had been somewhat distrait, usually a significant indication that it was time to buy her something new. The peacock's feather, or a jeweled comb? If he were to please himself, then the comb, for it was simple and elegant; but the gift, after all, was for Phebe, and Phebe liked her jewelry to dazzle. As he toyed with the problem, there was a gasp to his right. He turned quickly.

Elizabeth Anderson was by his side.

CHAPTER EIGHTY-FIVE

THERE was no mistaking Elizabeth. Although he had last seen her when she was sixteen, her plump, dimpling cheeks, her good-natured mouth, her twinkling, serene eyes, and her deep red hair seemed scarcely altered. Her figure, of course, was plumper than ever, though not unpleasantly so; her well-pronounced bosom was quite matronly, and, together with her broad hips, suggested motherhood. Dear, dear Elizabeth! She was a ghost from the past, but what a substantial, what a dear, delightful ghost!

For an agonizing period they stared unbelievingly at each other; as though afraid that the least movement would banish the happy vision, neither stirred. But the crisis was too poignant to be long sustained, and Elizabeth relaxed. She sighed as her eyes misted with tears, and her cheeks crimsoned with embarrassment.

"Oh! Please forgive my staring at you, monsieur," she said in a confused whisper, and speaking in indifferent French. "For a moment I mistook you for someone else."

A spirit of mischief possessed him, a lighthearted spirit he had believed dead and buried in the grave with Armand de Galinière. This moment was too precious to be wasted by a premature revelation.

"For somebody in Haiti . . ." He glanced down at her left hand, but it was gloved. "Madame?" he risked.

"No, monsieur, for somebody in England who was very dear to my family."

Duncan's resolution faltered. Somebody very dear! No sweeter words had ever been spoken to him, but he was acutely embarrassed for fear she should continue in that strain.

"I am sorry, madame," he said huskily.

"Not more than I, monsieur." She glanced at him, and shook her head in perplexity. "It is incredible." She sighed again. "I must not keep you, monsieur," she regretfully concluded.

He bowed. "The pleasure is mine, but perhaps Elizabeth would permit me the honor of escorting her to her hotel?"

She reddened, as she glanced shyly at him. "I would not dare, monsieur. I am already incurring my husband's displeasure—" She paused abruptly; her hand fluttered to her heart. "How did you know my name was Elizabeth?" she whispered.

Duncan imitated Miss Frilby's shrill voice and tart manner when she was in one of her "black bear" moods, as the children had entitled them; he spoke in English. "If you do not swallow that rice pudding immediately, Elizabeth Anderson, I shall ask Mr. Blodgett to bring your father to the nursery—"

Elizabeth's face whitened; she stretched out a shaky hand and steadied herself against the window of the jeweler's shop. "Dear God!" she whispered. "You are Duncan." She laughed; there was a shrill, unnatural note in her voice. "I still cannot bear rice pudding," she told him hysterically, as she threw herself into his arms.

Between laughing and crying, and threatening to succumb to hysterics, several minutes elapsed before Duncan could calm Elizabeth sufficiently to disentangle her from his arms; by that time a small group of giggling, nudging black people had gathered round to stare at them.

"Be off with you," Duncan told them irritably. "Be off with you."

None of the Negroes made any attempt to obey his instructions, but fortunately, at that moment, an officer of Henry's bodyguard of Royals-Bonbons approached. Duncan beckoned to the man.

"You will oblige me, Captain, by moving these people on."

"But certainly, Doctor," the captain promptly agreed, and saluted. "Move on! Move!" he called out, as he smote the Negroes with the flat of his sword. They shuffled away.

Duncan thanked him. "My pleasure, Doctor." The officer saluted, and passed on.

Still holding tightly to Duncan, Elizabeth said: "So you are a physician! I am so glad. And we all thought you dead. Oh! Duncan, my dear! Whatever has happened to you all these years?"

"It is too long a story to tell you now. Shall I take you to your hotel?"

"Not yet," she pleaded. "My legs feel too weak to walk yet a while."

"I didn't intend you to walk. We can wait for a fiacre to pass."

"Not yet, please. I cannot wait to talk to you. Is there no other place near by to which we could go?"

"There is a café across the road—"

"The very place," she interrupted quickly. "Take me there, darling Duncan."

He took her into the café. A mulatto girl, one of his patients, greeted him. "Good afternoon, Doctor. Here is a little table for two. Shall I bring you coffee, and some pastries for madame?"

"Please."

Elizabeth glanced dubiously at some Negroes who were occupying other tables, but she made no other comment than: "You seem to be well known, Duncan."

"Yes," he agreed shortly. He stared at his foster sister. How lovely, how fresh, how sweet she was! The passing years had touched her but lightly, and then only to turn the pretty bud into a charming blossom. "I have so much to ask you, Elizabeth—"

"And I, you."

"Who shall begin?"

She did not hesitate. "You must answer all my questions first. I saw you first; besides, it is my womanly privilege." She leaned forward across the table. "Did you kill poor Armand?"

"Yes," he acknowledged. "I was mad with jealousy, and drunk. I went from inn to inn, looking for him. When I found him, we quarreled. I struck him with a chair. Then there were shouts; somebody said that the

355

watch had been sent for, somebody else caught hold of my arm and took me away from the place. It was all a horrible nightmare, Elizabeth, which even now is not very clear in my mind. When I recovered I found myself aboard a vessel bound for Haiti. I asked the master to put me ashore, but he refused, saying that I should be hanged for murder."

"Poor Duncan!"

"Poor Duncan! I cannot make up my mind whether one should say poor Duncan or lucky Duncan! I decided to remain in Haiti. I have been here ever since. As I've achieved wealth and fame, perhaps one should call me lucky Duncan."

"Have you also achieved happiness, Duncan?"

He replied after giving the question thought, "I don't know, Elizabeth. I can't decide. I have had better opportunities here to practice surgery than would have been possible in any other place in the world. Circumstances have forced me to experiment with operations far in advance of any performed in Europe, where no surgeon would dare to risk the lives of his patients as I have done in Haiti. Life is cheap here, so when my experiments failed, as they sometimes did, nobody thought the worse of me, when they were successful the natives regarded me as a magician. American doctors acknowledge me as one of the leading surgeons of the New World."

"But are you happy?" she persisted.

"How could I be absolutely happy knowing that I was dead to you and Jean, and the dearest foster parents man ever had?" he asked with bitterness.

"And Margaret?" she whispered. "Why have you not mentioned her name?"

His reply was caustic. "I still read the London journals. I followed the career of Eulalia with interest as soon as I discovered her identity. Besides, I saw her in Jamaica."

"Have you spoken to her?"

"No. I saw her from a distance, and lost any desire to let her know that her one-time fiancé was still alive."

She sighed and squeezed his hand. "Poor, dear brother! But why did you not write to us to let us know what had happened to you?"

"Because I was too ashamed of myself," he explained, still in bitter mood. "When I thought of all that your family, and particularly your father, had done for me, and how I had repaid that kindness, I hadn't the courage to write."

"Poor Father!" she exclaimed sadly. "Your disappearance broke his heart. He thought you must have accidentally fallen into the Thames and been drowned."

"But—but didn't he suspect that it was I who had killed De Galinière?"

"No. Why should he? As far as he knew you two were the best of friends. Of course, we heard of Armand's death, but none of us connected your disappearance with it."

"You must have done so, Elizabeth. You knew about his letter to Margaret."

"I did, Duncan, but I—I said nothing about it to anyone else in the family. I—I thought it better for Father to think you had died by accident rather than that you had fled because of a crime."

"God bless you, Elizabeth, for that! And Father, is he still well?" he asked, thinking that Anderson must be growing old.

"Father—" She bit her lip. "Father is dead. He had a stroke after you disappeared, from which he never properly recovered. But it was Margaret who really killed him," she accused with passion. "When she told him of her wish to become a play actress, he forbade her to contemplate such a disgraceful act. She pretended to comply with his orders, but one day she ran away to join an actors' company. Father died two days later."

Duncan turned away. He had often recalled the stern, kind face, but not for many years had every detail of it been quite so sharply etched in his memory; he supposed Elizabeth's presence was the cause. Elizabeth brought everything back so clearly; Anderson's blue eyes, so disconcertingly steady, his strong, straight nose, firm lips, prominent, square chin— features which had given his face an expression of righteousness and strength.

"And Mother?" Duncan asked huskily.

She wiped away the tears that rolled down her cheeks. "Mother died three years ago."

He attempted no words of comfort, for his own agitation was too great. Time stood still for nobody, of course, but he was shocked to hear of the death of his foster parents; he had never given thought to their dying; whenever he had thought of them he had always seen them in the family sitting room; the doctor in the big chair on the right-hand side of the fireplace, which was sacrosanct to his person, Mrs. Anderson in the left-hand corner of the settee, needleworking and listening with close attention to her husband's sage words of wisdom, or whispering with her children. And these two sweet people were dead! It seemed unbelievable.

"Tell me of yourself, Elizabeth," he said presently. "As a guess I should say that you are happily married, and the mother of—three?— children."

The tears vanished from her eyes; they shone with happiness. "Four, Duncan darling. Three girls and a boy. Girls run in our family, you see. I began to think that I was never going to present poor John with a son and heir, but, thank heaven, the last was a boy. I am Mrs. John William Willowby," she announced with pride.

The name conveyed nothing to him, but he tried to look impressed. "How long have you been married? Tell me all about the wedding. I wish I had been present; I am sure you must have made a beautiful bride. Where did you live after your marriage? What are you doing in Haiti?"

"My! What a lot of questions to ask in one breath. John and I have been married twenty-two years. Dear me! How time flies. I am almost sorry you asked me that question." She smiled with tenderness. "Those twenty-two years have been happy ones, my dear. Every one of them, without exception. John is the dearest man in the world. He is just as kind as Father, and not nearly so strict. He had proposed to live in the country, at Acton, but Mother was so lonely that she begged us to live with her in Leicester Fields. We have been there ever since. And now for your last question; what are we doing in Haiti? Well, my dear, we are on holiday. John has worked hard all his life, as the head of a banking firm, so he retired at the end of last year. After a few months of doing nothing he became bored, so, when that horrible Napoleon abdicated, and peace with France was declared, we decided to visit America by way of the West Indies. We arrived in Jamaica three weeks ago. While there we heard so much about Haiti and its black king that John made up his mind to spend a few days at Cap Henry, in the hope of seeing some-thing of the country. So here we are." She squeezed his hand. "And I, for one, will never cease to be grateful for the impulse that brought us here."

"Nor shall I, for another. And now, how is Jean? I suppose she, too, married some nice person, and has a family?"

"Jean!" There was a rising note in her voice as she repeated the name. "No, Duncan dearest," she continued slowly, "Jean is still unmarried."

He frowned. "Jean an old maid!" Elizabeth winced. "Good heavens! I can't see Jean as an old maid. The idea isn't right."

"It isn't," she agreed, in a tense voice.

"Damn those young men of London! Why, Jean was worth two of any other woman. Are the young sparks in London blind, or mad, or what? Why, I always thought young Callcott, for one, was sweet on Jean."

"Jean had three offers of marriage, but refused them."

"Refused three offers of marriage. Whatever for?"

"For the obvious reason that she was not in love with any of the men who made the offers."

Duncan made a wry face; the Elizabeth he had known was not often tart. He thought he knew the reason for her present mood. She had al-ways loved her eldest sister with unusual passion, and was distressed at Jean's singleness.

"Where has she been living?"

"At home, with Mother, John, and me. She has been a dear companion to me, Duncan, and the children worship her. Their chief regret at our departure was our not leaving her with them."

"Where did Jean go?"

"With us," Elizabeth gurgled happily. "She is waiting at the hotel for me."

Duncan jumped to his feet. "Why didn't you say so before, you little wretch? Come along, we are going to your hotel as quickly as a fiacre can get us there."

On the way to the hotel Elizabeth placed her hand over his. "There is one favor I want to ask you, Duncan darling: let me break the news to Jean before she sees you."

He scowled. "I want to surprise her."

"That would be a selfish pleasure. You should know the danger of shock. Besides, you can still have the pleasure of seeing her surprise with-out her seeing you. Wait until we reach the hotel; I will show you."

At the hotel Elizabeth led Duncan to the public sitting room and ex-plained her plan. One corner of the room was enclosed by trellis-work, 'bright with clusters of flowers growing from large earthenware pots. He squeezed in behind the trellis and made a peephole for himself through the flowers, while Elizabeth sent a chambermaid to fetch Jean.

When Jean arrived, he warmed with happiness at the sight of her tall, willowy figure, still youthfully virginal. On the other hand, the lines in her face were conspicuous; yet they improved her. She had always had character in her face, but the lines emphasized this and enhanced the serenity in her eyes. She resembled a piece of statuary of classic days that had had warm life breathed into it; perhaps Cleopatra, with virtues instead of vices.

"Why did you send for me to come here?"

"I have something to tell you; it was more convenient to tell you here than in one of the bedrooms."

"More convenient here?" Jean glanced round. "Elizabeth dear, you are so funny, I shall never understand you."

"I am so excited, Jean. While I was out looking at the shops, I met somebody I know."

Jean was instantly interested. "Who?"

"Somebody we both know, Jean darling; somebody we have not seen for a very long time."

"Male or female?"

"Male."

Jean puckered her forehead. "Who might that be? Mr. Jollybois? We have not seen him for nearly ten years."

"No."

"I know! Mr. Carstairs? He came out to the West Indies about seven years ago."

"No."

"Tell me who, Elizabeth dear; I am much too excited to think."

"Somebody we knew very, very well," Elizabeth explained slowly. "Somebody of whom we were both very fond; somebody we believed—dead!"

There was a long silence; Jean's face whitened, her eyes filled with a stark expression. "Not—not Duncan?" she whispered. Then she shook her head. "No, it could not have been Duncan. I am being too foolish. Duncan is really and truly dead. Please tell me who it was," she pleaded, close to tears.

Elizabeth placed her hand in Jean's. "It was Duncan, Jean darling."

With an abrupt movement Jean buried her face in her cupped hands. Elizabeth reddened, and slipped her arms about her sister's waist. "You mustn't cry, Jean. Duncan is here now, in this room—"

Jean lowered her hands. "Here?" she asked in a strained voice.

Duncan answered for himself, by stepping out from behind the trellis. Jean rose to her feet; Duncan moved quickly forward, gathered her into his arms, and tried to kiss her with boisterous enthusiasm. But Jean's reception of his embrace was different from Elizabeth's. She avoided his lips, kissed him sedately on each cheek, then gently but firmly pushed him away from her. Duncan stepped back from her, chilled.

"What is the matter, Jean? Aren't you glad to see me again?"

"Of course I am, Duncan," she said sincerely, "but you were crushing my dress."

"Your dress!" This was a nice reception for a long lost brother, he thought bitterly; evidently her dress was of more importance to her than the joy of reunion. "A thousand apologies," he said frigidly. "For the moment I had forgotten that you have grown up since I last saw you."

"Duncan! Jean!" Elizabeth stared from one to the other in perplexity. "What is the matter with you both?" Tears gathered in her eyes. "I thought you were going to be overjoyed to see him again, Jean. Oh! You have spoiled everything. I cannot understand you."

"Why should I be overjoyed at seeing a brother who deserted his family without a word, and has remained dead to them for all these years? I think you are the cruelest man I have ever known, Duncan Stewart, and I shall never forgive you for the way you have acted toward people who loved you as one of their own. Are you aware that your cruel disappearance was indirectly responsible for Father's death?"

"It was not," Elizabeth flashed out. "It was Margaret's becoming an actress which killed Father. Besides, this is the first time you have ever told me you hated Duncan. You have always led me to understand that you—"

"Please, Elizabeth," Jean interrupted sharply.

Duncan scowled. "If you harbor feelings of that nature against me, Jean, I am very sorry I returned here with Elizabeth. But, as I am here, allow me to inform you that I did not desert your family. It was no fault of mine that I had to leave London without a word to anyone."

"Whose fault was it then, may I ask?"

"Jean! Duncan!" Elizabeth appealed. "You are horrible, the two of you. I thought this moment was going to be one of the happiest in my life, and all you are doing is to quarrel with each other."

Jean and Duncan were too intent on their own affairs to pay heed to Elizabeth. They gazed at each other with bitter, accusing eyes.

"It was my misfortune, not my fault," Duncan pointed out sullenly. "I had to leave London; if I had stayed, I should have been dead to you in real earnest."

"I do not understand."

"I should probably have been hanged at Newgate for the death of Armand de Galinière."

Jean stared at Duncan with horror. "You killed Armand?"

"Yes, during a fight. I did not mean to kill him—I was intoxicated and mad with jealousy. Didn't you suspect it was I who killed him?"

"Why should we have done so? You and Armand were friends."

"So I thought at the time. But would you call it the act of a friend to steal Margaret's affections from me?"

Jean looked confused. "Armand did not do that, Duncan. I told you once that Armand's attentions to Margaret meant nothing to him, nor to her. Besides, did he not act differently toward her directly you spoke to him of your engagement?"

"Yes," Duncan admitted. "But that was before I knew of the note

Armand sent to Margaret, making an assignation at nine o'clock in the evening."

"Margaret received no such note from Armand. I am sure of that," Jean denied firmly.

"I saw the note for myself. If you still do not believe in its existence, ask Elizabeth. She read it, too."

"Elizabeth!" Jean turned. "Did you see a note from Armand to Margaret fixing an assignation?"

"Yes. I showed the note to Duncan." Elizabeth tossed her auburn curls defiantly. "Margaret never really loved you, Duncan. She only thought she did, because she was in love with being in love. She was not capable of loving anyone sincerely. Her subsequent life has proved what Jean and I always suspected. You were a thousand times too good for Margaret. That is why I showed you that note; I had hoped to make you stop loving Margaret."

"But you couldn't have been certain," Duncan protested; like Jean's, his own thoughts were bemused. "If Margaret had married me, her entire life might have been different."

"Nonsense!" Elizabeth contradicted with unshakable confidence. "From the moment Margaret played a part in *Bajazet* she had but one interest in life, to become an actress; she would have ruined half a dozen lives to achieve that ambition. Am I not right, Jean?"

"You are a wicked woman, Elizabeth," Jean gasped. "Now go, please, please go."

Elizabeth's eyes twinkled. "Not until I have finished all I want to say. I had a second reason for trying to make you mistrustful of Margaret, Duncan. I hoped that, once you had finished with Margaret, your eyes might be opened to the truth."

"What truth?"

"That another member of the family really and truly loved you."

Jean gasped, and again hid her face in her hands. Duncan turned toward her.

"Dear God!" he exclaimed.

CHAPTER EIGHTY-SIX

FOR a long time there was silence in the hotel sitting room. Not one of the three wished to be the first to speak. Jean kept her face concealed; Elizabeth sat down and gazed affectionately at Duncan; he glanced first at the elder sister, then at the younger.

Jean broke the long silence. She lowered her hands from her face with a pitiful, despairing gesture and looked remorsefully at her sister.

"Why did you tell Duncan? You have humiliated me; I shall never forgive you, Elizabeth."

"Nonsense, my dear! There is nothing humiliating in loving a man, is there? I love John, and am not ashamed to admit the fact. Indeed, I am quite brazen about it."

"But John returns your love, while Duncan—"

"There is still nothing to be ashamed of, Jean. You have loved him from the time you were old enough to know what love meant. That is why you turned down the three men who proposed to you—"

"Elizabeth! Please!" The hot blood flooded back into Jean's cheeks.

Duncan glanced angrily at Elizabeth, then drew a chair closer to Jean's and sat down. He took one of her hands into his own.

"Elizabeth is embarrassingly frank, Jean dear, but she is right. There is no reason to feel ashamed of love. I always knew you loved me; you told me so yourself—"

"That was at a Christmas party," she murmured. "Children always say silly things at Christmas parties."

"Did it make any difference to our lives, your making that admission to me?"

"We were both children. Now— How can I face you in the future, Duncan? Every time we meet you will think to yourself: Poor Jean! She loves me so much, and I do not love her in return. And I shall know you will be thinking that, and everything will be horrible, beastly—" She snatched her hand away from his, and turned her flaming face away.

"What nonsense you talk," he said testily. "I shall think nothing of the kind. You have had three proposals of marriage, haven't you, Jean?"

"Yes," she whispered.

"Didn't you guess that they loved you long before the proposal?"

"Yes."

"Did that kind of thought pass through your mind every time you met them? Of course it didn't. Listen, Jean dear, tragedy has parted us all these years; don't let a ridiculous embarrassment spoil the rest of your stay here in Haiti."

She smiled wanly. "I promise." Her voice was steadier when she continued: "And now you must tell us about yourself, Duncan; how you came to be here, and what you are doing."

Elizabeth laughed with mingled relief and pride. "He is a physician, Jean, and a very famous one."

Jean's eyes shone. "Duncan! Oh! I am glad for your sake, for ours, and for Father's. He will be happier—there—knowing that you are continuing his work. When did you begin?"

Once again he told the story of his flight from London, of his arrival in Haiti, of his first operation, and of subsequent events. He then went on to relate something of the Negroes' desire for emancipation, and later, independence; of Toussaint l'Ouverture, Dessalines, and Christophe; of his own dilemma when faced with the choice of black world or white; of his treatment of the Negro wounded; and lastly, of his subsequent reward.

Neither of the sisters once interrupted him; they were too enthralled. Then Jean stated, with conviction: "You were right to take care of the Negroes, Duncan, and I am sure that Father would have done the same. Oh, dear! You have made me so happy, I want to cry."

"You have already cried enough for one day," Elizabeth pointed out. "Didn't I always tell you, Jean, that Duncan was probably alive, and practicing medicine?"

"You knew why he disappeared from London; the rest of us had no reason for believing that Armand's death and Duncan's disappearance were connected."

"Of course not," Duncan agreed soothingly. "What I want to know is how long you will be staying in Haiti."

His words caused a bleak expression to cross Jean's sensitive face as she glanced at her sister. "I cannot say," she answered in a toneless voice. "It depends upon what John decides."

"John spoke of staying here for about a week, and then going on to Santo Domingo by the first convenient ship."

"How long have you been here already?"

"Two days."

"Then you may be here for another five days only?"

"Yes," Elizabeth agreed miserably. "Unless we can persuade John to stay longer. Unfortunately he prepared an itinerary, and Jean knows how obstinate he is about keeping to itineraries. John has one of those tidy, precise minds; everything must be found in its proper place, everything must be done at the right time."

"Perhaps the very special circumstances of our reunion may persuade him to relax his usual habits just for once. In case not, we must make the most of what little time we have."

"Yes, yes," Elizabeth agreed with enthusiasm. "Have supper with us tonight, Duncan." She clapped her hands. "Four is just the right number for a dinner party. Oh! I am so anxious to see you and John together; we have spoken about you so often." She rose to her feet. "I am going up to the bedroom to see if he is awake yet; he always likes a long sleep in the afternoon."

"Wait, Elizabeth! We do not know yet whether we have the right to ask Duncan to come unaccompanied." Jean turned toward him. "Surely you are married?" she asked in a steady voice.

"Oh!" Elizabeth exclaimed, and then again: "Oh, dear!"

The unexpected question ruined his happiness; and yet, Duncan thought, how else could he explain Phebe to them? Besides, Bella believed him to be married; he could not very well tell his foster sisters one thing and his friends another. But Jean—she looked so beautiful, she recalled the London of long ago. There had been a time when he had thought of Jean— That was before Margaret.

He drew a deep breath. "Yes," he said. "I am married."

Elizabeth gave another tremulous "Oh!" and her eyes misted as she glanced at her sister. Jean's expression remained composed; the only indication she gave of what effect his reply had upon her was the unconscious tightening of her hand round a tiny lace handkerchief.

"Then you cannot ask Duncan without his wife, Elizabeth," she pointed out with tranquil detachment.

"Of course," Elizabeth agreed tonelessly. "You must bring Mrs. Stewart with you."

"But—but—I'm not sure—"

"Not sure of what, Duncan?" Jean asked.

The unhappy man glanced from one sister to the other. "Before you extend your invitation to—to Phebe—I want you to know—" Once again he paused in embarrassment.

Jean smiled wistfully. "Phebe is a pretty name. Does it suit her?"

"Helen or Aphrodite would suit her better," he muttered, glad of any excuse to postpone the inevitable moment of revelation. "She is a beautiful creature—"

"A creature! Duncan! That is no way to describe your wife."

His eyes turned bleak. "Before you invite Phebe, you must know that she is not a white woman," he rasped.

Elizabeth's guileless face was eloquent of her feelings. "Duncan! How could you have married a black woman? Oh! How horrible!"

"She is not black. She is a mulatto; in appearance, as white as you."

"But she—she is still part Negro?" Elizabeth accused, with a pathetic hope that he would contradict her.

Duncan glanced miserably at Jean's drawn face. "Haiti is not England," he pointed out. "Ever since the Negroes obtained their emancipation, and all citizens, irrespective of color, were declared equal and black, marriage between white men and mulatto women has been rcognized socially, and generally practiced; many of the permanent white inhabitants of Haiti are married to colored women. Besides," he continued on the defensive, "a man living in the tropics needs a wife, and when there are no white women to marry, he selects a mulatto instead."

"You do not have to explain, Duncan," Jean told him bravely. "It is not for us, who have led sheltered English lives, to criticize the manners of other countries. How—how many children have you?"

"None," he announced; never had he felt happier at Phebe's sterility. Then he added inconsequentially: "She saved my life . . ."

Jean sighed with relief at hearing Duncan's emphatic answer; warmth flowed back into her cheeks.

"I want to meet your wife, Duncan. You must bring her with you tonight."

Elizabeth was more doubtful. "I don't know what John will say, Jean, when he learns about Phebe's being a—a mulatto; you know how prejudiced he is about such matters."

"If Phebe really looks white, perhaps it would not be necessary to say anything to John—"

"You must tell him the truth, Elizabeth darling; he would never forgive your deceiving him."

Elizabeth continued to protest. "He is so obstinate—"

"Nonsense, you know very well that you can twist John round your little finger whenever you wish. Now run along, dear, and see what you can do with that husband of yours."

"Very well." On her way to the door Elizabeth stopped to hug Duncan. "I am glad we have found you again," she whispered. Then, with a loving smile at her sister, she hurried out.

Elizabeth successfully overcame her husband's objections to meeting a mulatto; at any rate, she soon returned to the public room with both the invitation and John Willowby himself. Duncan and John soon formed a mutual liking for each other, even though John was a man who was rigorously and righteously English in all circumstances and possessed all the Englishman's instinctive prejudice against anything foreign. In spite of this failing, he was goodhearted and cheerful.

Later in the day they all met again round the supper table, this time with the addition of Phebe. The meal was an unqualified success. Phebe was at her best; her conversation was trivial but sparkling, her laughter infectious. She looked ravishing in a dark green dress that had been designed for her by Evans, and made locally by a French seamstress whom Henry had brought from Paris to make dresses for the royal household. Duncan was amused to notice how often John's eyes strayed toward her, once his initial frigidity had thawed. Jean, also, was fascinated; on one occasion she whispered into Duncan's ear: "She is charming, Duncan. I could not blame any man for marrying her. She must have made you very happy."

He nodded, smiling, and Jean, her attention on Phebe, did not observe the quizzical look that outlasted the smile. There is a half-happiness that is as much as most mortals can expect, he had long since decided.

That night was the first of several; the following night Duncan held a party at his home in honor of the Willowbys and Jean. He asked the Martins, the Websters, and Evans. Bella took Jean to her heart. The night after that Duncan took John and Nat to the Casino, while Bella entertained the sisters and Phebe at her home. John thoroughly enjoyed himself; he drank enough to encourage him to dance with one of the girls there; having led an exemplary life, he found it highly satisfying to become a wicked, dashing fellow for once.

On another occasion Duncan, having received Henry's permission, took his visitors to Sans-Souci, where they were graciously received by the King. Once again Jean made a conquest; she remembered how much Duncan owed to Henry's generosity, and was so charming to him that Henry exerted himself to be equally pleasant. John, of course, was his usual reserved self (a charming mulatto woman was one thing but dammit, a full-blooded Negro was quite a different matter, even if he was a king!) but presently he got to talking business with Henry, and his attitude changed. During the return journey to the Cap, John admitted his wholehearted admiration for the Haitian king. "And begad! I am going to see that my old firm does business with him, too," he added. "I always like to do business with a man who knows his subject well, which that man does, begad!"

John extended the period of their stay at the Cap by another week—he did this upon his own initiative, which both Elizabeth and Jean agreed was a compliment to Duncan and Duncan's friends. But the second week seemed to pass even more quickly than the first. On the eve of the Willowby's departure Duncan held the final party at his home. It was a simple affair. Besides the Willowbys and Jean, the only guests were Bella and Nat. It also tended to be gloomy, in spite of the efforts of everyone to act as cheerful as possible. They had had a jolly time, all of them, and the knowledge that it was to end was depressing in itself; but chiefly the gloom was on Jean's account. Phebe, alone, was unaware of Jean's love for

Duncan; the rest could imagine the extent of her sorrow in leaving the man she had adored so long and so loyally. Jean herself wore a brave air; her laughter was the most spontaneous, the most cheerful. Nevertheless, behind her eyes was a stark expression that she could not entirely disguise.

The meal was over; Jonas served coffee and filled the liqueur glasses. Nat raised his glass and gazed at it with regret.

"Well, folks, it seems that the time has come to wish you bon voyage. I'm sorry you aren't staying here instead of returning to that foggy old England of yours."

"I am sorry to be going," John announced sincerely. "I did not think it was possible to meet so many nice people in so short a time, or to have so much fun. Still, Elizabeth and I have the consolation of knowing that we are returning to our children."

The remark was unfortunate in its tactlessness; there was a significant pause, followed by a hasty jumble of voices, as Nat, Duncan, and John all spoke at once. Jean bit her lip and glanced down at the table. Bella's eyes filled with sympathy, to sparkle, immediately afterward, with excitement.

"Nat, Duncan, Mr. Willowby!"

"What is it, dear?"

"Oh, Nat! I have just had an idea. Mr. and Mrs. Willowby are going on to America for two months, aren't they?"

John answered for himself. "Yes, Mrs. Martin."

She turned to Jean. "Are you particularly anxious to go to America, Jean, my dear?"

The question confused Jean. "I—I am not sure."

"Why?" John asked.

"If Jean would rather remain here in Haiti, instead of going on to America, Nat and I would love to have her stay with us for two months; or even longer, if she should wish. Junior adores you, Jean, and if you would teach him to play the pianoforte, why, all of us would be very, very happy."

Elizabeth turned to her sister. "Jean darling, that would be lovely for you. Don't you think so, John?"

"Yes," John nodded his head. "Yes, I do, my dear, if Jean would care to remain in Haiti. What do you say, Jean?"

As Jean turned from one to another in perplexity, they saw that her eyes shone with excitement. "Oh! I do not know what to say. In many ways I—I should love to stay here, and yet—" She paused, and carefully avoiding Duncan's glance, looked at Elizabeth with inquiry and doubt.

"There isn't a reason in the world why you need hurry along with us, Jean darling," Elizabeth answered promptly.

Bella laid her hand upon Jean's arm. "Snatch your happiness while you may, my dear," she urged in a low voice. Then she added: "You would be happy, wouldn't you, Jean?"

"Yes, yes."

"Then, will you stay?"

Jean nodded her head; there was a lingering, happy smile on her lips. But Phebe, next to her, frowned. It was not strange that Bella should want Jean, of whom she was so very fond, to stay on; nevertheless, instinct warned Phebe that something had happened which was not in her own interest. Perhaps her sharp observation had caught something in Bella's expression that went beyond simple pleasure and was more like—triumph.

CHAPTER EIGHTY-SEVEN

INSTEAD of returning to England at the end of a further two months Jean remained at Cap Henry. The suggestion came from Elizabeth. A week before she and her husband were due to return to England she wrote:

Jean darling,

John has at last announced the date of our departure for England; we are to sail next Wednesday week, or thereabouts, from Boston, aboard the *Flying Fish*. I must confess that I welcome the news. John and I have enjoyed a most wonderful time in America. . . . I have so enjoyed your letters; I cannot tell you how much I enjoyed having news of dearest Duncan, and those sweet Martins, and that funny Mr. Evans. John and I have missed you sadly, but we are happy to know that you do not regret your decision to stay in Haiti.

My heart is pining to see all my dear children again. So is John's. . . . Not that I do not like the Americans. I do. They are so hospitable, and so warmhearted. There is no trouble they will not take if it is for the sake of visitors to their beloved country.

Now, dearest Jean, there is something I wish to say to you. As long as you are happy in Haiti, why should you return to England? Of course, we should all miss you terribly; the children, John, and myself. We all love you so. Yet your happiness is of more importance than ours; you have only yourself, whereas we are so many.

I have spoken to John about this suggestion, and he thoroughly agrees with everything I say. You are financially independent, thanks to Father's will. You could stay at one of the hotels, and now that you have made so many, many friends at the Cap, I know that you would never be lonely. Besides, you would still be able to see Duncan, and I know how much it must mean to you to be near the dear man again, despite the circumstances. Do consider this idea very carefully, darling, and do not hurry about making a decision. Discuss it with dear Bella and her charming Nathaniel, and with Duncan, too, for I know what *his* choice would be.

Jean's first reaction upon reading this letter was to sigh and fold it up. Until now, somehow the adventure of reacquaintance with Duncan had submerged the fact of unequal affections and dulled the sharpness of her disappointment. But if this mingling of joy and pain were prolonged, would not the balance inevitably be reversed? To anchor her life upon the man she could not have—it was unthinkable.

For twenty-four hours she was able to keep to her resolution; but when she met Duncan the following day, once more she was caught up into the movement of life in this strange, colorful land; into the satisfactions of his work; into his questioning yet lively hopes for the firm establishment of a free Negro state. Now it was the prospect of having to leave the island that seemed unthinkable. Here not only the best of friends but something in her own gypsy spirit called her. In a stir of eagerness and doubts she hurried back to the Martins before there was need to, and in the privacy of her bedroom she reread the letter several times. Then she showed it to Bella. As Elizabeth had suspected, Bella proved herself a stanch ally. Of course Jean must stay at the Cap, she asserted vigorously; what was more, there was to be no thought of staying at a hotel. Jean was to stay with them as long as she wished. Bella's eyes moistened with tears, which was unusual. With unexpected emotion she explained that Jean's presence, among so many black people, was very, very precious, especially in the circumstances—

Jean's decision to settle at the Cap delighted Duncan more than he dared admit; at the same time there were unexpected repercussions, as he discovered when he passed on the news to Phebe. In caustic tones she asked why Jean was not returning to England. When he attempted to explain that Jean was remaining in Haiti by her own desire, Phebe again asked why; in a shrill voice she pointed out that most white people resided in Haiti because of business interests, or from the hope of making money. In Jean's case it would cost her money, therefore she must have some other motive for living in Haiti. As question succeeded question, and Phebe's voice sharpened, he realized that his mistress was suspicious of his foster sister. What had aroused these suspicions it was impossible to say; perhaps her womanly instinct had read danger from Jean's attitude toward him; perhaps rumors had traveled to her ears via the Martins' servants. Whatever the cause, he was left in no doubt that Phebe was acutely jealous of Jean, and that unless he acted with circumspection, his domestic life would quickly lose such felicity as had, so far, characterized it.

Because of Phebe's jealousy Jean and he saw less of each other; even so, a week seldom went by without their meeting at least once; at the Martins', in Duncan's own home, at the theater, at a soiree given by one or another of the other white inhabitants at the Cap, occasionally at the palace. These encounters were a source of increasing happiness to them both.

The months passed. One day Napoleon left his tiny kingdom of Elba and sailed for France, where he reclaimed his abdicated title and once again plunged Europe into war.

This news, following the French efforts to overthrow Negro independence, drove Henry to increasing precautions against possible invasion. He could not rid himself of his fear of the French emperor; it flourished in his breast like a rank weed that threatened to choke and strangle his finer disposition. More and more laborers were put to work upon the Citadel, which already rose starkly from the summit of the mountain like a vast granite tumor—an Olympian landmark for the seafaring, an imposing warning to the French, a frowning incubus to the Haitians. His ministers and chiefs remonstrated with him as much as they dared; the Citadel was costing too much money, they argued, and for what purpose?

Henry overbore all opposition. The Citadel had to be finished; it was not only a means of keeping Napoleon, or Louis XVIII, or any other enemy at bay, it was also a symbol of Negro might; an imposing and perpetual memorial to Negro culture and capacity; a challenge to the white world to produce a modern, comparable edifice; a new Wonder of the World. The Citadel had to be finished! When the groaning people heard of this inexorable decision, they turned their sad faces to the south and thought enviously of the happy, slothful existence led by the Republicans.

Some of the bolder spirits attached to the busy plantations deserted their masters and furtively made their way toward the Republican border. Many were captured by the vigilant Dahomeys and sentenced by the judges to forced labor on the King's works; but there were others who reached safety and under Pétion's mild rule settled down to the idle life of their dreams. The population of Henry's kingdom slowly decreased. He was not unaware of the southerly drift of his subjects; for a brief spell he was prevailed upon to relax his severity. Within a few months he had reason to regret his weakness; a preliminary survey of crops revealed a definite drop in production, with a corresponding fall in revenue. He immediately restored the measures against laziness, and the figures improved again.

Money flowed into the Treasury but quickly vanished. Whispers circulated that a considerable proportion of the national income was disappearing into secret coffers beneath the immense Citadel, but nobody was able to produce proof in substantiation of this rumor. On the other hand, there was evidence that much of the revenue was being used for the betterment of the population. Schools, modeled upon that of the British and Foreign School Society's Central School in the Borough Road, London, were erected at Cap Henry, Sans-Souci, St. Marc, Gonaïves, and Port-de-Paix; new reservoirs and bridges were built; experts from England arrived in Haiti to build and equip a weaving mill at Cap Henry; ships were purchased to form the nucleus of Haiti's own mercantile fleet; a golden coach (the replica of Henry's state coach) was built in the royal stables at Sans-Souci as a gift from Henry I of Haiti to the Prince Regent of England.

"Is it true that Henry is building another palace at Plaisance?"

Duncan nodded.

"How many palaces has he now?" Nat went on. "The number must be seven or eight."

"Nine."

Nat whistled. "Nine palaces! This king business has gone to his head." Nat had the American's contempt for anything savoring of royalty. "Is it my imagination, Duncan, or is Henry changing?"

Jean looked up from her tatting. "He has a very stern face."

"That's the point, Jean. He has, but when I first met him he had quite a pleasant expression. He was always ready to laugh—but then, of course, that remark applies to most Negroes—and his manner suggested that he was very glad to welcome you. If there was anything you wanted, all you had to do was to mention the matter to him and he saw that your want was satisfied. He was the most affable and intelligent Negro I've ever met, but he's not that now. Nowadays, he's beginning to wear an expression—" Nat hesitated. "I should describe it as tyrannical, only Bella would accuse me of exaggeration."

"You do exaggerate dreadfully, dear," Bella confirmed serenely.

"He is severe, but he is not a tyrant." Duncan stared out of the window. "But what you say about his changing is true, Nat. Since his attack of sunstroke he has become increasingly impatient and intolerant. He is such a hard and willing worker himself that he cannot understand why others are not as enthusiastic about work as he is."

Phebe joined in the discussion. "He is a dirty Negro," she exclaimed viciously. "What else can you expect from a Negro but tyranny?"

Her remark was ignored in discreet silence; they were accustomed to hearing disparagement of the Negro race from Phebe and had learned the wisdom of paying no attention to her outbursts.

Jean asked: "Is it usual for Negroes to suffer from sunstroke?"

"It is not unusual, although it is commonly accepted that they are immune. In some circumstances they are as vulnerable as the white man."

"What circumstances, Duncan?" Nat asked.

"Disease, for one. Severe mental strain or protracted worry are subsidiary causes."

Phebe's shrill laughter was scornful. "Have you ever known a Negro to suffer from mental strain?"

Duncan frowned; he had frequently asked Phebe not to identify herself with the mulattoes by insulting the hated Negroes. "It would be no surprise in Henry's case," he said quietly. "Few men use their brains more than he does. For that reason I'm worried."

"Worried?"

"Yes, Nat. Each late afternoon Henry goes for a walk through the countryside round about Sans-Souci. His only companions are a page and a few military officers, who follow him at a short distance. Ostensibly he takes these walks for the sake of exercise, but his real reason is to spy upon his people. Woe betide any workers who are not hard at work, from the owner down to the youngest cultivator on the estate."

Bella was indignant. "How mean!"

Duncan nodded. "Power usually leads to mistrust and petty tyranny. These solitary walks of Henry's do him little good; they lend themselves too easily to introspection, which is a dangerous habit for a man of his mentality. Every day he thinks of some new scheme to make his country great, unfortunately he lacks the sense of proportion which would warn him not to compare Haiti with Britain, or France, or America."

"Why does his habit of introspection worry you, Duncan?" Jean asked.

"I am afraid that his constant brooding, and his intense impatience to realize his boundless ambitions overnight, may, sooner or later, warp his judgment, and then—"

"Trouble?"

"I am afraid so, Nat."

Nat looked worried. "Almighty God! As if Haiti hasn't had trouble enough to last her a century! Was Henry glad to hear of Napoleon's second abdication?"

"Naturally he rejoiced over the downfall of a man he regarded as his bitterest enemy, but Louis the Eighteenth's return to the throne has not relieved him of his anxieties. Spies from Paris have reported that France is still determined upon recovering her old colony. More commissioners are supposed to be on their way here."

"France seems to possess more commissioners than a dog has fleas," Nat grunted. "Now, I suppose, he will be keener than ever to finish that citadel of his?"

"Yes," Duncan somberly agreed.

Rumors spread upon the wings of the wind which nightly blew down the slopes of the mountains and cooled the baking earth of the Plaine-du-Nord and the torrid streets of Cap Henry. As soon as nightfall cast its black velvet cloak upon the uneasy island, the air was charged with sibilant whispers. From the heart of jungles and forests, and the summit of distant mountains, the throbbing drums beat out strange stories in broken rhythm that made the eyes of the uneasy peasants open wider in alarm as they stared through the darkness at the distant, flickering fires ringing La Ferrière, King Henry's citadel of freedom.

The source of these rumors none knew; but they persisted; and nothing of the original horror was lost in the constant repetition. In hushed murmurs men spoke of tyranny, of torture, of floggings, and of death. They spoke of straining men who tried in vain to haul enormous cannon up the precipitous trail to the Citadel; of the *cocomacacque* which unmercifully flailed the naked backs of human beings who could not do what was beyond human endurance; of the execution of each tenth man in every squad; of the cannon that, after all, reached the summit of the mountain. No man nor woman was to be found who had heard the sound of the musket shots or had seen the black bodies slump to the ground; but there were few who did not mourn the death of someone who had worked at the Citadel. What other explanation was there to account for the death of thousands? What but fear of death could force human endurance to perform what human endurance could not perform?

The pounding drums and the furtive mutterings also spoke of cells deep down in the bowels of the earth, into which many enemies of the King vanished. They told of shrieks and groans that often mingled with the sharp wind whistling through stone corridors; they told of the strange disappearance of anyone privy to the secrets of the Citadel; they told of the mysterious underground passage that ran from La Ferrière to the palace of Sans-Souci—though none knew where the entrance to the passage was, and none knew of any man who had helped to excavate it.

The rumors spread. The mutterings grew louder—but not loud enough to reach the King's ears. Life was precious; even to men who slaved in the broiling sun from cockcrow to sunset, and twisted their bodies out of human shape in their efforts to haul immense cannon up the side of a mountain.

The rainy season arrived, revitalized the fertile soil, and died away again. One year merged into another, bringing little change to the people of Haiti. Henry's widespread building operations continued; one could not proceed far without passing a royal estate, a royal palace, or a royal château. The King's personal fortune mounted to a fabulous total, but so did the national wealth. It almost seemed as if the soil of Haiti were trying to prove its gratitude to the King for his wholehearted appreciation of its potentialities. Early in the new year it was learned that more than six million pounds of coffee had flowed into the warehouses at Cap Henry during 1816: nearly six times the average yield for the past four years, or twelve times that for the reign of Emperor Jacques.

CHAPTER EIGHTY-EIGHT

PÉTION dead!" Henry rejoiced with Vastey, who had brought him the news, then thrust his chair away from the table so he could rise to his feet. "That damned mulatto has gone to join his friends in purgatory." His heavy tread sent a tremor along the polished mahogany floor and caused a loose window frame to rattle. "Do you realize what the news means, Ti Rouge? That cursed republic is without a leader."

"The revised constitution of the Republic entitled Pétion to name his successor," Vastey warned the King.

"What of it?" Henry demanded. "There was only one man capable of holding the Republic together, and that man was Pétion. With him dead, the Republic is a plum ripe enough to fall into the first pair of hands." He spread his fingers and held out his huge, ungainly hands. "Vastey, send a special messenger to Port-au-Prince tonight; he shall take with him a message to the petty chiefs of the Republic demanding the immediate incorporation of the Republic with the Kingdom of Haiti. Then this country will really be worth ruling." His eyes glowed with enthusiasm; his voice boomed louder with every sentence. "With the entire country under my control Haiti will produce crops which not even the best years of the colonial era could boast. Think of the Cul-de-Sac, Vastey, as it will be after two or three years under my rule. By that time it will be producing threefold, fivefold—no, name of God, tenfold the miserable crops of the past years! But by Damballa, the peasants will have to work as hard as our peasants here in the north are working; there will be no more idling their days away like drones." His face was ruthless; he snapped his fingers with impatience to get to work. Then, unexpectedly, he halted. "Well, Vastey, why don't you answer? What are your thoughts, man? Carping, by your expression. Speak up."

"I was wondering whether Your Majesty would find the Republicans willing to join the Kingdom of Haiti. The prospect of working as hard as their northern brothers might not attract them."

"Are you presuming to criticize my rule, Vastey?"

The secretary was unable to disguise his uneasiness as he stared at the King's turbulent face, but he manfully held his ground.

"Your Majesty is aware that I have frequently warned him of the growing discontent among his subjects."

"You think my rule too severe, do you?"

"The peasants think so."

"They do, do they? Perhaps they call me a tyrant." Vastey was silent. "If I have become a tyrant it is their own fault," Henry stormed. "I fought for their freedom, and won it for them, but what would they have done with it if they had had their own way? They would have slept and danced it away again; they would have impoverished themselves; all the whites would have deserted us; by this time Haiti would have been no better than a community of African savages. Instead, we are a rich country, respected by the white nations; we are the foundation stone of a new Negro civilization. I have done this." He slapped his chest. "I, Henry the First of Haiti. I have made Haiti what it is today, because I have made the peasants work. And when the western and southern provinces join us, Haiti will become greater still. I swear that by all the gods there are."

Vastey obstinately shook his head. "Next to yourself, Your Majesty, there is nobody keener than I to hear of the union of the Republic with your kingdom, but I must counsel caution. General Boyer is not a man to be easily intimidated—"

"Boyer, Boyer! What's all this about Boyer?"

"Has Your Majesty forgotten that Pétion named Boyer as his successor?"

"Boyer!" Henry gnawed his nails, a habit into which he had lately fallen.

"General Boyer has considerable influence and is very popular," Vastey continued swiftly. "I have no hesitation in asserting my opinion that the West and South will not voluntarily agree to incorporation in your kingdom, Your Majesty."

The veins in Henry's thick neck throbbed. Duncan felt uneasy as he gazed at his scowling features, for Henry was shaking with a ferocity that looked dangerously like the prelude to a fit.

"You should try to keep calm, Henry," he cautioned the King.

"Nonsense, Ti Rouge," Henry shouted. "Nowadays you fuss over me like an old sow with her litter. Because I have been ill once, is that any reason for me to nurse myself for the rest of my life?" He began his restless pacing again; his voice rose. "How can I keep calm when every day I have a hundred problems to perplex me? One would think I was king of the world, instead of only a portion of it. By Legba! Keep calm, when so many tremendous issues are at stake! I'd like to see the man who could. Damn that Boyer! If the West and South will not incorporate voluntarily, then they shall be made to do so. Do you hear, Vastey? Be made to do so! Is that clear?"

"Do you mean war, Your Majesty?"

"Of course I mean war. It would not be for the first time in our lives that the North has warred with the West and South—but this time I shall see to it that the North wins."

Vastey pursed his lips. "The Republic has a strong army," he murmured. "If Your Majesty wishes to raise an army of equal size, it will be at the expense of work on the plantations and the Citadel." His eyes filled with cunning. "Why not finish the Citadel before declaring war on the Republic? Meanwhile, Sire, you could proceed with your plan of buying Santo Domingo."

Henry's eyes flamed as he turned to face Duncan. "I have not told you of that plan, have I, Ti Rouge? I have opened negotiations to buy Santo Domingo."

Duncan was startled at the suggestion of buying a country, until he recollected the modern precedent set by France—the sale of Louisiana to the American states. Henry's ambitions became more comprehensible. Certainly it would be an effective method, and might well prove a feasible one, of adding to the kingdom.

"Have you sufficient money in the Treasury to make the purchase?"

"Not yet, but soon—if Haiti continues prosperous—"

"Which is a good reason to conserve your resources, Sire, and not fritter them away in war," Vastey interrupted opportunely. "Once Santo Domingo is in your hands your army would be far larger than that of the Republic; you would also have the strategic advantage of being in a position to attack the enemy from the rear. In such circumstances the Republic would find itself unable to resist your might."

"Do you think so, Vastey?"

"I am sure of it, Sire," the secretary replied.

"What do you say, Ti Rouge? Do you agree?"

"I think war at the present time would be greatly to your disadvantage."

"The devil!" Henry chewed at his nails. "I shall give the matter further consideration. Meanwhile—" His expression turned grim. "The Citadel must be finished; it has already taken too many years in the building. It must be made ready for instant use." He glanced at the golden timepiece on his desk. "Is there any more business to be discussed, Vastey?"

"Nothing that cannot wait, Sire."

"Then I shall pay another visit to the Citadel; I have not been up there for more than a week. It seems that little progress is made if I am not constantly watching to see that nobody slackens. Will you come with me, Ti Rouge?" Duncan nodded. "Meet me outside the gates in ten minutes' time," the King ordered brusquely.

As the two men toiled up the ascent, Duncan was uncomfortably aware of the hundreds of burning eyes which stared at them; he seemed unable to avoid them, they were to the left, the right, in front, and, even more horribly, behind him. He could particularly sense those behind him, and although he knew that a small bodyguard of Bonbons was but a short distance away, he experienced a prickling sensation in his back that was extremely unpleasant. Two years had passed since Duncan had seen the Citadel from close quarters; he had not climbed the ascent since the day of Henry's sunstroke. Even then he had not reached the top. Along the same trail, nothing much had changed since then: the long, sinuous line of naked, dipping bodies was the same; so were the straining, heaving masses of men who struggled to haul up the bulkier, heavier objects necessary for the erection, the furnishing, and the fortification of the Citadel.

Only the eyes were different. Before the majority had been vacant. Only a few had been resentful; of these not one pair had dared—nor, probably, desired—to express hatred of the man who was their leader and hero. Now there was no mistaking the sullen hatred that followed the King during every moment that he was in sight; it did not vary from face to face, whether on that of man or woman, boy or girl.

Duncan began to hate the Citadel. It was absurd to claim that the great fortress alone was responsible for transforming respect and obedience into threatening hatred; there were the many palaces, and royal châteaux, and other fortresses, that had to take their fair share of the guilt; but the Citadel Henry was, as it were, the embodiment of all those other places. To the people, whose blood and bones had supplied the cement that bound the massive walls together, the Citadel was not a symbol of Haitian independence and Haitian culture but a living monument of despotism and oppression. Who among them did not believe that the Citadel was a curse which distorted the King's vision and prostituted his ambition?

The Citadel rose up before him, one hundred and forty feet high, an irregular pile, shapeless and unsymmetrical. It conveyed no sense of beauty, only one of might; a gargantuan might of walls of incredible height and depth, of bastions wherever danger might be anticipated, of countless gun emplacements. He whistled as he gazed about him, below him, above him. Henry had sworn to build an invincible fortress; and had done so. It was not possible, it could not be possible, for man to capture this stupendous, mountaintop fastness. How could men scale unscalable walls in the face of the murderous enfilading fire which could be directed upon the attackers from above? How could cannon batter a breach in the walls, when for many leagues roundabout there was no site for even a single gun emplacement? A resolute army inside the walls of the Citadel could defy the armies of the world.

Henry was not unaware of the effect that the Citadel had upon Duncan. His grim expression vanished, and he laughed his gratification; with something of a shock Duncan realized that he had not heard the King laugh for months.

"What do you think of my fortress, Ti Rouge? Is it not an achievement to be proud of?"

"It is terrifying."

Henry nodded understandingly. "You are not the first to say so, and if it is terrifying to my friends, how much more so is it to my enemies—as some of them have already found to their cost," he added with an unpleasant chuckle. "Do you think the French could capture the Citadel?"

"Citadel Henry has nothing to fear from the attacks of men," Duncan stated with confidence.

Henry looked apprehensive. "Do not emphasize the word men."

"I was thinking of starvation, lack of water—"

"Ah! I thought you were referring to the gods." Henry glanced about him with uneasy eyes. "There are times when I seem to hear the sound of deep rumbling from the bowels of the mountain—probably it is only the wind howling along the corridors, but it makes me think of earthquakes, Ti Rouge. And sometimes the lightning up here frightens me—"

He made an impatient gesture as though shaking off his despondent mood. "I am not afraid of any lack of food, or water—"

"There is no water within miles."

Henry laughed boastfully. "You will see what you will see. I'll be your guide."

The King led the way toward the tall opening in the wall of the main bastion. "The only entrance to the fortress," he explained. "Later, we shall hang an iron door here for protection."

For the next two hours Duncan followed his guide along endless labyrinths of corridors and passages, which turned first to the left, then to the right, and then, to Duncan's bemused imagination, seemed to double back on themselves as if part of an intricate maze. Before long he had lost all conception of distance and direction and number. He saw batteries to the north, to the south, to the east, to the west; he passed pyramids of cannon balls beyond counting, pile upon pile of small arms, barrel upon barrel of gunpowder. He was taken into innumerable storehouses; along galleries that never saw the light of day; into empty dungeons that dripped with moisture and smelled fetid.

From the deepest depths of the Citadel he was conducted to the uppermost walls. Here he saw, as Henry had promised, the ingenious method which had been evolved to combat the absence of water— the thick walls had been utilized to hold eight huge cisterns: four covered, for drinking purposes, and four uncovered; the roofs had been designed to collect rain water; tanks had been constructed as reservoirs.

Then down again to ground level, and into the large courtyard within the walls of the fortress. Here, as elsewhere, hundreds of laborers were at work completing the fortress; here, too, were the barracks to hold ten thousand men, and a basement capable of housing another two thousand; Henry's palace of forty rooms; quarters for the governor of the fortress; and other buildings to be used, if necessary, as places of refuge for the population of Cap Henry and Sans-Souci.

Even here Duncan was not allowed to rest; there was still more to be seen—the room set aside for the manufacture of gunpowder, the hospital, the treasure chamber, the bathroom, and lastly, the billiard room with its fireplace. By that time Duncan was weary, physically and mentally. He should have explored the Citadel in sections, he reflected. It was too vast, too amazing a phenomenon, to be appreciated in two short hours.

CHAPTER EIGHTY-NINE

HENRY chewed his nails and glowered resentfully at Duncan. "Why must you always lecture me every time we meet? I haven't heard one cheerful word from you for months. By the gods of Africa! One would think you were one of my ministers. Pétion found out to his cost what happens to a ruler who betrays weakness. Do you know how Pétion died,

Ti Rouge? Vastey told me yesterday. That damned mulatto committed suicide by starving himself to death."

"Are you sure? I was told that he had been ill for many weeks previously."

"Yes, he had been ill. But he starved himself to death, nevertheless. And for why? I'll tell you. Pétion died because his heart was sick. When he was chosen president of that damned republic, his one idea was to make himself popular. Well, he was popular. I'll not deny that. But why was he popular? Why? Because he let them do as they pleased, instead of telling them what to do. Hell! What happened? You know what the present state of the Republic is. The cultivators spend the days doing as little as they can; all they think about is satisfying their sexual appetites. No wonder they are diseased and poverty-stricken! As for his money, I can tell you this: his treasury only issued about five million dollars, but there are more than twelve million dollars circulating in the Republic." Henry laughed. "What do you think, Ti Rouge? There is actually more silver in the counterfeit than in the official money."

Henry was talking on one of his favorite topics. He went on: "Pétion was just as anxious to improve the Republic as I am to improve my country. But where I have succeeded he has failed, just because he used the wrong methods. He tried to be humane, where I am severe. Poor devil! He realized this fact when it was too late. Weary of life, tormented by public annoyances, and disillusioned, he decided to die and allow someone else to try to carry on."

Henry's strange fear of the association of lightning with the Citadel was shortly justified. Just three weeks after Duncan's visit the building was struck by lightning that penetrated to the powder magazine and caused a tremendous explosion. Immense havoc was caused to the buildings in the immediate vicinity of the magazine, and as one of these was the Treasury, part of Henry's fortune was scattered to the four winds. Over and above the damage to property, Prince Noël, many of Henry's bodyguard, and some laborers were killed. In spite of the violence of the explosion, the outer walls of the fortress received no damage from a calamity that would have destroyed a building less strongly constructed.

The storm had strange repercussions. The superstitious Negroes looked upon the disaster as a warning from the gods that the hated Citadel was accursed. The cultivators looked up at the frowning mass with frightened eyes, and worked with a heart more unwilling than ever as they wondered what form the next visitation of the gods would take; the malcontents among them dared to raise their voices more loudly than hitherto. The convicts, the soldiers, and the pressed laborers who toiled at the Citadel itself could not be persuaded to resume their work until the cocomacacques had battered some of them into insensibility.

Henry angrily brushed aside arguments and informed his sulky followers that the damaged part of the Citadel was to be repaired and the remainder completed as soon as possible. When this decision became known, the drums throbbed with added emphasis, calling upon the people to attend secret voodoo ceremonies so that blood sacrifices might be made, to placate the wrath of the gods. During the night following the explosion the darkness was relieved by the twinkling lights of a thousand fires; deep in the heart of the forests, the jungles, the valleys, and the ravines, high up among the hills and mountains, they glowered like a thousand rebellious eyes. From his palace at Sans-Souci, Henry saw the fires and understood their portent; he stormed, raged, and threatened, but he knew there was nothing to be done; even if his Dahomeys and Bonbons were to track down the offenders, they would melt away before the soldiers could make any arrests. By degrees the King learned of the indirect effects of the voodoo ceremonies; from one plantation after another came news of mass desertions; from across the border his spies informed him that hundreds of northern subjects were flocking into the Republic. That was not all. Other spies reported that Boyer boasted of his intention to invade the Kingdom of Haiti. Henry's face wore a perpetual scowl.

Christophe's fame spread; the white nations were eager for news of the black king who was molding a colony of revolted slaves into a small but prosperous nation. Books dealing with the history of Haiti were published in London, in Paris, and in Mexico; copies of Vastey's works, printed at Sans-Souci and Cap Henry, reached America, where they were widely read. The stream of white people who hoped to make a living from the island swelled perceptibly; those who could add to the country's welfare or culture were allowed to remain, but the majority were discouraged and politely shown aboard outgoing vessels.

England, particularly, betrayed an increasing interest in King Henry. Lord Liverpool's government sent orders to Rear-Admiral Sir Home Riggs Popham, commander in chief of the Jamaica station, to pay King Henry an official visit. This Sir Home did, and in admiration of the industry and energy of the King formed a sincere liking for him, which liking was reciprocated.

But hidden behind the record of success and triumph was another story, of which few foreign observers had any inkling. Those few whose ears were attuned to the heartbeat of the country were alarmed by Henry's increasing despotism and ungovernable rages. His cane, without which he rarely moved, became an object of consternation to his subjects, who could never be sure that it would not whack their shoulders in a moment of fury. Even his nobles were not immune from this indignity. Cabals were formed within court circles; conspiracies were mooted, only to dissolve at the first suggestion of active participation—fear of the King was still deeply implanted in the breasts of the Haitians. Yet many were arrested upon suspicion of intrigue and punished by a sentence of labor upon the King's works. Among these latter was Jean-Pierre Richard, Duke of Marmelade. Queen Marie Louise, once more risking Henry's displeasure by interfering in matters of state, reminded her spouse of Richard's past zeal and loyalty to the monarch and secured his release, but not before the iron had bitten into the soul of the Duke.

The fog of intolerance, distrust, and suspicion spread and thickened throughout the early months of 1820, until finally it enveloped the person of none other than Corneille Brelle, Archbishop of Haiti, Duke of Anse:

one of Henry's most sincere and loyal friends. One day Brelle disappeared. Haiti speculated in hushed whispers; but nobody knew the truth of why he had been arrested or what had happened to him. There were the usual rumors; the most persistent was that Brelle had conspired with French colonials—but nobody knew for sure. Then it was whispered that he was dead, that early one dawn Gattie, Henry's bearded executioner, had struck off Brelle's head (at the first blow, said rumor, meaning that the victim's fee to Gattie, for the privilege of being executed, was a substantial one, for Gattie, it was said, inflicted more or less torture upon his victims in proportion to the amount of the fee paid). But nobody knew for sure. The only sure and certain fact was that the Archbishop had vanished.

In the jungles, forests, and mountains the drums throbbed and zoomed with a note of deep unrest.

CHAPTER NINETY

ONE night, after he had snuffed out the bedside candles, Duncan heard the soft pattering of naked feet and felt the bed move as Phebe crept in beside him. He gathered her into his arms, but when his lips sought hers, she turned her head aside so that he could only reach her cheek.

"Please, Ti Rouge—no! I want to talk to you."

He was surprised by her request; it was unusual for Phebe to prefer conversation at such times, particularly on serious matters such as the tone of her voice suggested.

"Well?"

She did not reply. He realized that her body was unusually taut and that her heart was beating abnormally. He felt uneasy, for an unwelcome thought occurred to him. The possibility that Phebe might become a mother had grown daily more distasteful. He could not think why. His thoughts were a confused jumble, in which Jean played a prominent part. What connection had she with any child of Phebe's? None; yet he had a feeling that, if Phebe were to bear a child of his, the sincere, comforting friendship between Jean and himself would be spoiled, all the deep, warm beauty of it would wither; a bleak prospect indeed. He realized, for the first time, how much her selfless companionship meant to him.

"What is the matter?" he questioned shortly. "What do you want to talk about?"

"Listen," she whispered.

He listened, but heard nothing unusual. "To what?"

"The drums."

He listened again. The drums were insistent, but they had been noisy for many nights past.

"They are somewhat busy," he agreed absently. "What do you want to talk about?"

' The drums, Duncan; they frighten me."

He laughed with relief.

"Why are you laughing?"

"At the idea of your being alarmed by the drums, Phebe." Relief gave way to astonishment. "Good heavens!" he exclaimed.

She caught hold of the arm that enwrapped her. "I am not being stupid, Duncan," she defended herself, speaking swiftly in a voice sharpened with anxiety. "The drums are so angry, they terrify me. The Negroes are becoming rebellious—I am afraid—"

"What have you heard?" he interrupted.

"It is not what I have heard; it is what I feel and what I see."

"See?"

"The faces of the Negroes. They are so sullen; and haven't you seen the way the peasants whisper among themselves? When they look at me, they leer, just as if they know something terrible is going to happen and are planning to avenge themselves upon me because I am white."

"You are worrying yourself needlessly, Phebe. It is true that Henry is making them work harder than they would choose—"

"Harder!" she laughed scornfully. "The peasants are worse off than the old colonial slaves."

"That's not true; they are paid for the work they do."

"How much are they paid? Not much; there are too many people to dip a finger into their profits. Besides, they would rather earn less money and have their lives."

"You have been listening to fantastic stories."

"The stories are not fantastic. Do you know how many people have died while working at the Citadel? Thirty thousand—"

"Nonsense! Besides, suppose it were true, why should you be frightened?"

"In case the people revolt again."

"Henry will know how to deal with them."

"Dessalines thought he could deal with them, but he died."

"Let's hope Henry does not suffer a similar fate," Duncan muttered somberly. "But why feel nervous? Nothing happened to you when Dessalines died."

"I was not yours, Duncan."

"So you are nervous because you are linked to me?"

"Yes. Oh! Please, please, listen to me. If the workers revolt, there is no knowing what may happen. There might be another massacre—"

"Always assuming that the revolters gained the upper hand, of course."

"You are a fool!" she exclaimed in a high-pitched hysterical voice. "Last time you were saved from massacre because you were a friend of Henry's. If there is another massacre you will be one of the first to die, for the same reason. There will be nobody to save you this time. Not even your nationality. Many Negroes hate the whites, never mind what nationality they are."

She pulled him closer to her. "You do still love me, don't you, Duncan?"

"Yes," he muttered.

If there was a hint of insincerity in his voice, she was apparently not conscious of the fact. "And you are rich, aren't you? Very, very rich, I mean."

"You should know," he replied dryly. "I have been able to satisfy even your extravagance without beggaring myself."

"Where is most of your money, Duncan?"

"Why do you ask?"

"Is most of your money in England or America?"

"That is my business, and I would thank you not to worry your head about matters that do not concern you."

He felt her body tremble. "Please, please, let us leave Haiti and go to England or America," she pleaded. "Let us go soon, by the next ship, before it is too late. Please, Duncan, please!"

He was amazed by the intensity of her emotion. He knew her to be a good actress when the occasion demanded, but he realized that, for once, she was not acting. She was genuinely afraid.

He stroked her arm and spoke more gently. "You are talking nonsense. I cannot leave Haiti. I have my patients to consider, also my work at the hospital, my lectures at the medical school."

"Work, work, work!" she cried shrilly. "You think of nothing else but your work!"

"My work is me. You know that, Phebe; I have often explained to you that life would mean nothing to me if I could not practice medicine and surgery. How can I make you understand—"

"You don't have to. I understand quite clearly that your horrible work is more important than me."

"That is not true," he contradicted. "If I had to choose between you and my work, then, naturally, my dear, you would come first. But there is no question of having to choose. I do not deny that there is unrest among a section of the peasants, but that's all. You are making a mountain out of a molehill."

"You would be able to practice medicine just as easily in England or America."

"No doubt!" he exclaimed, nettled. "But I don't intend to. As long as Henry is alive, my place is here in Haiti, and here I am going to stay, so please do not let me hear another word of your absurd fears."

"But Duncan—"

"Enough!"

She freed herself from his encircling arms and slipped out of the bed. He heard the pattering of her feet on the floor as she returned to her own bed. Then he heard her sob once or twice. Presently there was silence in the bedroom.

There was nothing in Phebe's attitude the following morning to suggest the disagreement of the night before. Duncan was surprised, for she possessed a smoldering, sullen temper that was usually slow to subside. She was her customary gay self, inconsequentially happy and cheerful. He was glad, for his conscience was none too easy; he felt that he had been too severe with her. In the light of Dessalines's treatment of whites and mulattoes alike, she was scarcely to be blamed for fearing the consequences of another revolt. Besides, although he had made light of the matter, he was not blind to the fact that the peasants were restive; the increasing desertion of some of the petty chiefs proved that. One by one they were making their way across the border into the Republic, where Boyer gladly received them.

Later that day his equanimity received a second jolt. Nat was the cause. He called at the hospital.

Duncan greeted him with surprise. "Hullo, Nat! This is an unexpected pleasure. Have you come to see me at work?"

There was no answering smile on Nat's face. "I have come here to talk to you, Duncan. I have some news for you—bad news, I am afraid."

"Bad news?"

"In the first case, old man, Bella has just learned that she is to become a mother again."

"But Nat!" Duncan stared at the American in amazement. "That is not *bad* news!"

"Good God! I should say not!" A lingering smile transformed Nat's long face. "I don't object to having any number of children; sometimes they are pesky little devils, but I love 'em, Duncan. No, that part of the news isn't bad."

"Then, what is?"

Nat ruffled his hair, embarrassed. "I have decided to take the family back to America, Duncan."

Duncan looked bleakly at his friend. Bad news! It was the worst possible news! Haiti would not be the same place without Nat and Bella and the children. And Jean? Would she accompany the Martins?

"But why?" he asked huskily. "I thought you intended to remain in Haiti until you were ready to retire from business."

"That had been my intention. If I had only myself to think about I should not change my plans. I like Haiti as much as ever I did. But I'm not trusting the lives of Bella and the children to a matter of chance."

"What do you mean?"

Nat paced restlessly up and down the surgery. "I don't know how much you know of what's happening in Haiti. You meet more Negroes than I do, so you should be better informed than I am. But are you? I wonder if the Negroes are cautious when they talk to you, because you are a friend of the King's. I believe they are, otherwise you would not have been so surprised by my decision." He gave Duncan no opportunity to interrupt, but hurried on: "As you know, I meet a number of Haitians in the course of business; some of them are owners of big plantations, others are small holders. I also have indirect contact with the peasants, through the workers employed by Roncin's. I am therefore, to some extent, in touch with current opinion. That's why I think that Haiti is about due for another eruption. Don't ask me for concrete evidence; I could not give you any. It's been a matter of a word here, a hint there; a glance of fear or cunning or embarrassment, a general reluctance to enter into future commitments."

Nat had never made a longer speech, for he was inclined to be sparing of words. As soon as he finished speaking he mopped his damp forehead with his handkerchief and glanced at Duncan with an apologetic, self-conscious expression. "I suppose you think I'm crazy," he muttered.

"What about your business interests, Nat?"

"They can go hang for all I care, if it's a matter of choosing between them and the safety of my family. But Webster is staying on; his roots have dug too deeply into the soil of Haiti to be transplanted. He's quite capable of carrying on, especially since I made him a partner."

"And Jean? Have you told her of your plans?"

"It is about Jean I want to talk, Duncan; that is why I came here, where we shall be safe from interruption. Yes, I have told her. I suggested that she should accompany us to America. She was terribly upset, but you can guess her decision."

"To stay here?"

"Yes. She will never willingly leave you again, Duncan, even though she thinks you are the husband of another woman. By God! I never believed any woman could love a man as much as Jean loves you."

"Please, Nat!"

"She is not ashamed of her love, so I don't see why you should be, or why, for that matter, you should try to act like an ostrich, by pretending that your feelings for her are brotherly. Pah! You are pretty nearly as much in love with her as she with you."

Duncan reddened. "You are talking damned nonsense, Nat."

"That's what you think; being an ostrich you may not realize the truth. But I do; I have seen the way you look at your 'sister' when Phebe isn't around. Still, that is not what I wanted to discuss with you. I know it's no business of mine, but if it is not safe for Bella to stay in Haiti, then it is equally unsafe for Jean to do so. Do me a favor, Duncan; a favor to yourself as well, and to Jean, and the whole darned lot of us. Come back to the house with me now, and persuade Jean to sail for America." He chuckled dryly. "Or perhaps I should have said, try to persuade her."

Duncan went to the window of the surgery and stared down at the sun-splashed street. His thoughts were chaotic; he wanted time to sort them out so that he could consider the situation in its proper perspective. So much had confused him in the past fifteen minutes: Nat's fears, his decision to leave for America, his conviction that he, Duncan, loved Jean, his plea for assistance in persuading her to leave Haiti.

The thought of bidding her good-by, perhaps forever, was too dismal for contemplation; so was the possibility of seeing her mutilated, violated body in the Place d'Armes, as years before he had seen the bodies of other white women. His thoughts traveled in a vicious circle: it was absurd to contemplate danger—but parting was better than massacre; he did not love her—but life without her would be empty, detestable.

"Well, Duncan?"

"I will come," Duncan agreed wearily.

But Jean proved obstinate, as Nat had anticipated.

"No, Duncan, I will not go to America with Bella and Nat and the children."

"But you would love America."

"I know I should, my dear. I have always wanted to visit there, and I shall be sorry to part with Bella and the darling children." She turned her face away, that he should not see the tears gather in her eyes. "I have been so happy living with them; I never guessed two such dear people existed. But I will not leave you again. We have been parted once; it shall be through no act of mine if it happens a second time."

"Think of the possible danger—"

"I have thought of it," she interrupted evenly. "If there is danger for me, there is also danger for you. You must go, too."

Duncan shook his head. "I cannot leave Haiti. Henry has been a good friend to me; would you want me to desert him just when he might need friends more than at any time in his life?"

Jean did not answer, but he saw her lips quiver.

"Would you, Jean?" he persisted.

"No, my dear," she whispered. "No, it is your duty to stay here, at least for the time being. Perhaps the situation may change for the better. You must see the King and warn him of his danger. But if you stay, so do I."

"Jean—" he began angrily.

She shook her head. "Please, Duncan," she appealed.

He had not the heart to continue the discussion; in spite of his better judgment he was delighted to know that she would not leave the island. He determined to act upon her suggestion of warning Henry. If Henry relaxed his tyrannical rule of government the Haitians might settle down again to a contented, peaceful life.

Henry must be made to see the chasm toward which he was heading. Duncan decided to visit Sans-Souci without delay.

CHAPTER NINETY-ONE

THE following morning, as Duncan rode through the countryside at a steady pace, it seemed to him that the air was charged with brooding discontent. The only sound that disturbed the peace was the echoing clop-clop of his horse's hoofs. There was no other traffic about, though, as a rule, there was not a busier road on the island; apart from the normal agricultural traffic there were usually many vehicles transporting goods to the palace and building materials to the Citadel. Today there was nothing, and Duncan was puzzled until he recollected having heard a rumor to the effect that the Citadel was finished. Its three hundred and fifty cannon, its huge pyramids of ammunition, its immense stacks of muskets—everything needed in a fortress was there. Even its billiard table had been set up, he had heard, so that the King could indulge in his favorite recreation whenever he stayed at the Citadel.

Citadel Henry was finished; to the last stone the colossal, miraculous undertaking was complete, and now stood above the world, arrogantly defying not only the puny forces of mankind, but the elements themselves. A sigh of relief traveled the length and breadth of the kingdom, but it was soon followed by bitter curses when it became known that the King was already planning other buildings to absorb convict labor and forced levies.

Duncan unconsciously shook his head in confirmation of his own conclusions. Discontent might be rife in the country, but it was not likely to develop into open revolt so long as Henry retained his fighting vigor. Although his head was now plentifully streaked with gray hairs, he was still physically powerful; a fact that could easily have accounted for the rumors that said that, in his impatience to have the Citadel finished, the King had frequently lent a hand in its erection. No man among the army of workers could, it seemed, lay bricks either quicker or better than he. All the same, Duncan reflected, it would be a gracious gesture on Henry's part to express his gratitude to the people who had built his palaces and his fortresses by relaxing his severity and becoming more constitutional in his rule. He was glad to reach the palace and note the usual bustling and scurrying of the people there; the scene was cheerfully normal.

He soon found Vastey. "Is the King about?"

"He went up to the Citadel early this morning."

"In this heat? It feels hotter than usual to me."

"I agree." The secretary shrugged. "But you know how obstinate the King is, monsieur. He said that he did not intend to be away long; so he should soon be returning."

"How is His Majesty?"

Vastey looked about him with uneasy eyes. "Not too well, Doctor," he answered in a low voice. "He has not been the same man since he ordered the execution of Corneille Brelle. The Archbishop's treachery preys upon his mind. Now he is suspicious of everyone about him. Even of me," the secretary concluded, nervously.

Duncan frowned. "Then the King cannot be well, for I am sure that nobody is more loyal to him than you, Vastey."

"Quite true, quite true, monsieur; and I thank you a thousand times for your kind words. I have always been a loyal follower—"

There was a heavy step behind them. "Whispering again, Vastey," Henry shouted. "Damn! Wherever I go I hear the sissing of whispered voices, or see skulking figures trying to hide from me."

"I was telling Dr. Stewart that you would be returning soon, Sire."

"Does that information need your personal assertion that you are a loyal follower? Of whom are you a loyal follower? Of me, or that damned General Boyer?"

"Does Your Majesty need to ask that question?"

Henry glared at his secretary. His mood changed. "Perhaps not. You are a good friend, Vastey, and I love you. But in these days one cannot be too careful. There are too many people who are jealous of my power, or hate me because I refuse to allow them to sleep all day." He turned to Duncan. "What are you doing here, Ti Rouge?"

"I came here to see you, Henry."

"To see me! I'm not ill."

"That is a matter of opinion," Duncan said dryly, for there was a light in Henry's eyes that was far from healthy. "I want to talk to you."

The scowl slowly left the King's face. "That is different; as long as you do not start fussing me— Come along to my study." Henry turned and led the way up the marble staircase to the upper floor; the King walked with a dragging step and leaned heavily upon his cane. Duncan's lips tightened; Henry looked ill. He decided to ignore any objections the King made and make a medical examination.

"Now, my friend?"

The beginning was not auspicious; there was a suggestion of condescension in Henry's manner that irked him.

"Martin has decided to return to America," he announced abruptly.

"For a visit?"

"No. Permanently."

The King was startled. "Why? I understood that Martin had settled in Haiti."

"Circumstances have forced him to change his plans. He intends leaving by the first America-bound vessel."

"What circumstances? He has the pick of Cap Henry's export business. Isn't he satisfied? That is the worst of those American merchants; they are never satisfied with doing well, they always want to do better and better."

"Martin is quite satisfied with his share of Haitian trade. He is returning to America for private reasons."

"Is that why you have come out to Sans-Souci, to give me that information?"

"Yes, because it concerns you."

"In the name of the gods! How can his private life concern me?"

"He is afraid to trust the lives of his wife and family to the future." A scowl returned to Henry's face. "What do you mean?"

"To be brief, Henry, Martin is convinced that, unless you adopt a milder form of rule, your subjects will revolt against you."

"Hell!" Henry shouted furiously. "Has Martin dared to send me that message?"

"Of course not. He knows it is no business of his to try to teach you how to rule your country. I put it that way for the sake of directness. I might add that he is not the only foreigner who is nervous of what the future holds for you and them."

"Damn all your white men! What business of theirs is it how this country is ruled, so long as the trade is there for them to handle?"

"They do not concern themselves with your internal affairs, except where their legitimate trade interests are concerned," Duncan explained with as much patience as he could muster. "At the same time, they are businessmen who have to keep their eyes open to the future. That is why some of them are taking precautions to protect themselves; they recognize that you are sitting on a volcano that may erupt at any moment—if you do not take steps to prevent that calamity."

"Good God! Do the canailles think they know more about the country than I, the King? Let them clear out of the country, your Martins and your other damned merchants. I spit on them! Tell them that from me, Ti Rouge. I spit on them!" He spat into a convenient spittoon.

"There are plenty of other merchants to take over their trade. If the Americans and English are too cowardly to settle here, I will do business with the Germans, the Poles, and the Hollanders."

Duncan watched the King with anxiety. "Please listen to me, Henry," he said quietly. "I didn't come here to plead on behalf of the foreign merchants. They don't interest me, with the exception of my friend Martin. I came here as your friend, to beg you, for your own sake, to reflect upon the course you are pursuing."

"Stop that, Ti Rouge," Henry shouted. "I will not be lectured, do you understand? Do you think I don't hear enough from those idiot ministers of mine, to need your advice as well? God damn! Am I King of Haiti, or am I not?"

"You are."

"Then stop interfering with me, damn you! You stick to your medicine, and let me look after my throne. I know how to deal with my people better than you do."

Duncan's temper flared. "Maybe you do," he taunted. "Maybe Dessalines knew. He thought he did, but what happened to him? Had he listened to your advice he might still be alive today. Have you become as blind as he, that you cannot see the chasm opening out before your feet?"

The King raised his cane and lurched toward Duncan. "Get out of here, you filthy canaille!" he screamed. "Get out and stay out, you damned white!" The cane swished through the air and thudded against Duncan's left arm and shoulder. Once, twice, thrice. Then Duncan wrenched the cane from the King's hand, threw it aside, and hurried from the study while he still had some control over his own rage.

"Damned white!" Henry screamed, as he hurled a porcelain inkpot at the door.

Duncan's temper did not abate until he was more than halfway back to the Cap. Even then it did not entirely die away; it merely changed its form. Livid heat turned into ice-cold resolution. He mentally excused the blow, but could not forgive the indignity. That Henry was in ill health had been obvious before the interview began; ill health caused by overwork, worry, and overexposure to the Haitian sun. Henry had not been his normal self; his keen brain had been temporarily unbalanced. All this Duncan could understand, for he believed that a normally sane Henry would have given away a quarter of his kingdom rather than have behaved so.

But understanding and excusing were not forgiving. Their friendship could never be the same again. Those three blows would rise up between them, an insurmountable obstacle, for his own fierce pride would never let him forget. The same pride would make it impossible for him to withhold the hand of friendship while accepting the King's favors. The solution to the problem was obvious; to do as Phebe and Jean and Nat had urged—to leave the island. This he resolved to do. During the latter part of the journey he began making plans for his departure; there would be a thousand and one ends to tie up if he were to be conscientious in his last duty to King Henry.

Jonas met him at the door and led the horse to the stables. He hurried into the house; Phebe, he knew, would be delighted to hear of his decision; since that night when she had appealed to him to leave the island he had noticed several indications to confirm that her mood of alarm had been no passing one.

"Phebe! Phebe! Where are you?"

Suzanne waddled in from the kitchen.

"Does yo' want Miss Phebe, suh?"

"Why do you think I'm calling her, my big-bellied angel?"

Usually Suzanne was receptive to his chaffing; he often indulged in it for the pleasure of seeing her big round face divide into halves, and hear her delighted, high-pitched, squealing laughter. On this occasion no responsive smile appeared on her face. She stared expressionlessly at her master.

"Miss Phebe done gone out, Mist' Duncan."

"Shopping as usual?"

"No, suh."

"To Mrs. Martin's?"

"No, suh."

What was the matter with Suzanne? Duncan wondered. "Then where has she gone, Suzanne?" he demanded, irritated by the Negress's unusual taciturn mood.

"Miss Phebe done gone fer allus."

"What in the name of God are you trying to say, woman?"

"Miss Phebe, she done gone 'way frum Haiti to Sou' 'Meriky. She ain't neber comin' back hyah, 'gain, she say ter Suzanne jes' 'fore she leabe fer de boat. She say fer ter tell you', Mist' Duncan, she doan want ter be kill' by dem Haitians, so she go while she wus still safe."

Gone! Phebe gone! It was not possible; Phebe would not desert him like that—not while he was still rich!

"Did she take anything with her, Suzanne? Parcels, boxes, anything—"

"Yes, suh. She done take all her clo's an' jools an' everything whut she cou'd git inter dat big bag o' yours."

Duncan felt the muscles of his face twitch as he stared at Suzanne; no longer could be believe that she was making any mistake. Phebe had gone! Why? Alarmed by her fear of being involved in a possible revolt against the King, had she deserted him to seek safety in South America? The story sounded too fantastic to be credible. There must be some other explanation to account for her secretive departure; she had neither the intelligence to plan such a momentous step nor the courage deliberately to leave a rich husband.

"Isn't there something else to tell me, Suzanne?" he pleaded. "Didn't she tell you to tell me that she would be returning in a week's time?"

"No, suh. She done gone fer allus."

"Then hasn't she left a letter for me?"

"Ah doan know of one, Mist' Duncan."

"I can't understand what made her do it, or how she did it. Did you know she was planning to leave me?"

"No, suh," Suzanne denied emphatically. "Ah doan know nuthin' till disyere morning."

"Why did you let her go?"

"Ah did mah best ter stop her, Mist' Duncan. Yo' know how Ah loved dat honey chile, but ah loved yo' more, an' Ah wouldn't lift a han' ter help her do sech a mean, pesky trick. No, suh."

"But who made all the arrangements with the captain of the vessel; who took her to the quay, who helped her aboard—my God! I cannot make head or tail of this."

"Ah doan know nuthin' 'bout seein' de cap'n, but Ah specs Ah knows who took her to the boat."

"Who?" he asked sharply.

"Dat dere Mist' Willums."

"Williams!"

"Yes, suh, Mist' Willums."

"But why him? Why Williams?"

" 'Cause he's done gone wid her, dat's why," Suzanne replied, spitting her disgust of the man. "He been sending his money there, Ah heard."

If there had been the slightest possibility of Duncan's revising his decision to leave Haiti, that chance was destroyed by Phebe's desertion. Within an hour of his return to the Cap he began making preliminary arrangements for accompanying the Martins to America. Later he visited them. They listened to his news with a stupefaction that changed to joy when they learned of his plans to sail with them to America. Nat jumped up and wrung his hand with such vigor that he felt it turn numb with the pressure of the grip. Bella's eyes filled with tears of gladness. Jean slipped out of the room, and did not appear again that night. For once her superb poise was destroyed, by sheer happiness.

The days passed, busy days for all concerned. The approximate date of sailing, the twentieth of August, steadily approached. On the afternoon of the fifteenth, Duncan was at the Martins', where he had spent all his spare hours since Phebe's departure. Thither came a lieutenant of the Royals-Bonbons. His face dripped perspiration, his uniform was streaked with dust from the road, he breathed hoarsely.

He looked alternately at Duncan and Nat. "Monsieur Stewart?" he inquired between gasps.

Duncan nodded. "Well?"

"Can you come at once to His Majesty, monsieur? He needs you urgently."

"I cannot come," he replied abruptly. "I am too busy."

"But monsieur—" The lieutenant stared at Duncan with amazement. "His Majesty is ill."

"Ill?"

"Yes, monsieur, at Limonade. He is suffering from a seizure. Monsieur le Baron de Vastey said for you please to come quickly."

Duncan hesitated.

"You must go to him, my dear," Jean urged. "He is your patient."

"He was."

"He is," Jean insisted gently. "He was also your friend. Will you allow one irresponsible act to offset years of friendship?"

"I am ready to accompany you," Duncan told the lieutenant.

Something in Jean's eyes made him wish with all his heart that he had never told her the lie—never told her Phebe was his wife. And yet that same expression told him that when the time came he could explain, could make her understand how Phebe in running off with Williams had freed him, Duncan, of all obligations to her for all time.

CHAPTER NINETY-TWO

ON HIS way to Limonade Duncan learned some of the details of Henry's seizure from the lieutenant, whose name was Clérié. The King, said Clérié, had ordered the transfer of the court from Sans-Souci to the Cap, for the celebration of the Feast of the Assumption, which was the patronal feast day of Cap Henry, and the anniversary of the Queen; a doubly important day for the Haitians.

"But last night, Doctor, on the eve of the fête, His Majesty, unexpectedly issued an order to the court that the fête was to be solemnized at Limonade instead of Notre Dame du Cap."

"Why?"

The officer of the Bonbons shrugged his shoulders. "Nobody knows. Doubtless it was a whim on the part of His Majesty." He lowered his voice, although there was not another person within a kilometer of them. "It is said that Her Majesty the Queen protested, saying that the fête should be solemnized at Notre Dame, the church dedicated to the Holy Virgin, to which His Majesty replied: 'If Our Lady wants her fête to be celebrated, she can follow me.'" The officer paused; Duncan had no need to glance at his companion's face; the hushed, shocked tone in the officer's voice told its own story.

"But His Majesty persisted?" Duncan prompted.

"Naturally, monsieur, so this morning the court set off for Limonade in procession, attended by a large bodyguard of light cavalry and a military band. Upon arrival at Limonade Their Majesties were received by the Queen's chaplain, Father Jean de Dieu Gonzales. Presently mass was begun." Clérié paused and turned toward Duncan. "I was inside the church, so I know what happened," he explained in a dramatic but uneasy voice.

"What did happen?"

"Mass had been celebrated up to the Credo, monsieur; so Father Jean de Dieu went toward the altar for the Offertory. Halfway there he came to a halt. I was near enough to see his face; there was a terrible expression upon it as though he were seeing a ghost. I followed the direction of his glance—"

The officer paused, obviously intending to achieve the greatest possible dramatic effect from his story. Duncan masked his irritation and played up to the man. "What did you see?" he asked patiently.

"Nothing," Clérié replied. "I looked again at Father Jean de Dieu, thinking that he might be ill. Then something made me look at the King. As I did so His Majesty rose to his feet. 'Corneille Brelle,' he called out in a choking scream, pointing his arm toward the altar. Then, monsieur—" Once again he paused.

"Well?"

"He fell to the ground as though he had been hit by a musket ball. Mass was forgotten; everybody crowded round the King. Monsieur le Baron de Vastey rubbed the King's hands and ordered some water to be thrown in his face, but he did not open his eyes, nor did he move. At last Monsieur de Vastey turned to me and said: 'Ride to the Cap and ask Dr. Stewart to attend the King immediately.'"

That was all the information Clérié could pass on concerning Henry's seizure, but it was enough to inform Duncan that the strain of the past few years had, at last, taken toll of the King's mental and physical strength, which had already been weakened by disease and sunstroke. This conclusion was confirmed when he arrived at Limonade. He found Henry still unconscious, lying on the floor of the church, surrounded, at a distance, by groups of anxious nobles, and, more closely, Vastey, Father Jean de Dieu, and Dr. Massicot.

Massicot welcomed Duncan with relief. "I am glad you have arrived, Doctor." He indicated the King. "As you see, His Majesty has not yet recovered consciousness."

Duncan kneeled down beside the King. Somebody had loosened Henry's clothes to leave the throat and neck free, and had inserted a soft pad in the patient's mouth to protect the tongue. A calabash of water, and a handkerchief soaking in it, stood beside his head.

Duncan glanced up at Massicot.

"An epileptic fit?"

"Without doubt," Massicot confirmed. "In the midst of the service His Majesty sprang to his feet, gave a terrible scream, and fell down. He hit his head against that pillar, but the wound is superficial, as you can see, and will do him no harm. I bathed the wound, head, and face, and inserted the plug in his mouth. Now that he is breathing easily I suppose it will be safe to take it out."

"I think so." Duncan gently forced open the patient's mouth, pulled out the pad, and felt the pulse. This appeared to be little faster than normal. He frowned.

"Has the King perspired much?"

"Not for the past hour. I have been expecting him to recover consciousness at any moment."

"He should have come round by now," Duncan glanced at the head wound, but, as Massicot had pointed out, it was superficial. "I am afraid he is in a trance."

"How long will it last?"

"There is no knowing; perhaps for an hour or more, perhaps for two or three days."

"What shall we do with His Majesty? What is the treatment?"

"The treatment is absolute rest and quiet until recovery is complete. Meanwhile, he must not stay here. Is there anywhere locally where he can be taken?"

"His Majesty's château, Bellevue-le-Roi, is the nearest convenient house," the secretary replied promptly.

"Good. Have some of the soldiers secure an armchair and form a party to convey the King to Bellevue."

A small party carried the King to the château, where he was put to bed and made comfortable. Duncan dispatched a messenger to the Cap, to inform Jean that he intended to remain until the King was well enough to be moved. Vastey then issued orders for the immediate killing of all poultry in the parish, and the removal of all livestock capable of making a noise. Dr. Stewart had prescribed quiet, so Vastey was determined to see that this command was strictly carried out.

The hours passed by, but Henry remained stricken in his trancelike sleep. The surrounding parish was quiet. Only in the far-off distance was there noise to be heard—the muffled pounding of drums that telegraphed the news of the King's seizure to every parish in the country. Before long every village knew that the King had been struck down by a mysterious malady.

As soon as the new day dawned Duncan and Massicot made a fresh examination of the King, who still had not recovered consciousness. The two men applied every known method of inducing consciousness, but without success. Henry might have been a corpse but for the faint pulse.

Soon after dawn the following morning, the two doctors again entered the King's bedroom in the hope of finding Henry conscious. They found him still asleep, still unmoved, as far as they could judge, from his original position. Yet it seemed to Duncan that there was a slight change in the patient; a firmer pulse, a more regular breathing. They repeated the treatment of the previous day, and presently Henry's eyelids fluttered. Within a short period of time the King was fully conscious.

"What are you doing to me, Ti Rouge? Why are you here, Massicot?"

Duncan answered: "You have been ill, Henry."

"Ill!" Henry frowned. "When? How?"

"When you were at church. You fainted unexpectedly."

"Damn! Why should I have fainted? I do not remember anything happening to me. Father Jean de Dieu solemnized mass, didn't he? Yes, of course he did—I remember that much, but after that—nothing. Have I suffered another sunstroke, Ti Rouge?"

"No, a fit."

Henry frowned again. "Why should I have suffered a fit?"

"From overwork, probably. Didn't I warn you of the danger of living at a persistent high pressure of mental activity?"

"What are we given brains for, if not to use them?"

"Man is given horses to ride, but he doesn't ride them to death.'"

"How long have I been here, Ti Rouge? One hour, two hours?"

"Today is Tuesday."

"Tuesday! Hell!" An uneasy expression flashed across his face. "The gods must have taken possession of me. I don't feel as though I have been lying here nearly three days." He then added: "But I feel rested. So I should, I suppose, after three days' rest." He began to laugh loudly, but the laugh died away to an anxious whisper: "Three days! By Damballa! What has happened in that time, Ti Rouge? Anything?"

"Nothing extraordinary. What did you expect to happen?"

"A hundred things, without me to keep an eye open," the King replied testily. "Three precious days! My God! I am going to get up. There is work to be done; I must see about my business."

"Do you feel well enough—"

"I have told you I feel rested, Ti Rouge, Massicot, help me."

The two doctors, one on each side of the bed, turned down the blanket that covered the patient, then each held out an arm. Henry made no move.

"We are ready, Your Majesty," Massicot indicated respectfully.

Still Henry made no move. His eyes filled with terror.

"Ti Rouge—Massicot—"

"What is the matter?"

"I can't move my arm. I can't move my arm. What has happened? I can't move my arm."

"Which arm?" Duncan thought that the King must have broken an arm when falling on the ground during his seizure.

"Neither arm! What have you done to me? You have poisoned me. You are killing me—"

"Nonsense. You are either weak from sweating too much or stiff from your long trance. Probably the first explanation is the more likely. Move your right hand, Henry; not the entire arm, but just the hand."

He stared down at the big coarse hand, and waited for it to move. It remained stiffly motionless. His gaze traveled slowly up the body to Henry's face. There were beads of sweat on the black forehead; there was anguish in the white-rimmed eyes.

A shriek burst from Henry's lips. "I have no hands; they are gone. You've cut them off, you white devil."

Duncan lifted Henry's right arm into the air so that it could be seen by its owner. Upon releasing his arm it fell lifelessly back upon the bed.

"Good God!" he muttered. He looked round for his bag.

"Pass me my bag, Massicot. Quick."

The alarmed Massicot passed it over. From it Duncan extracted a scalpel, the fine point of which he thrust gently down the quick of Henry's forefinger; a drop of blood welled up. There was no reaction from the flabby hand.

"What is the matter with me?" the anguished King demanded. "What are you doing with that knife? Leave my hand alone."

"Wait!" Duncan stripped the blanket completely off the bed and bent over the King's feet, where he repeated his experiment with the scalpel. As in the case of the hand, there was no reaction from the nerveless foot. When he straightened up he saw that the King's glance was pleading and terrified. He ignored the tortured eyes and continued with his examination of the body; he pressed a nerve here, a nerve there, and pierced the black flesh with his scalpel in a dozen places. Not until he reached the neck did the King experience pain.

"Tell me the truth, Ti Rouge. What has happened to me?"

Duncan knew it could serve no purpose to hide the truth from the stricken man. "You are paralyzed from your neck downward."

"My God!" Henry whispered. "My God!" His eyes sought Massicot's, but the black doctor turned away. "My God!" he whispered for the third time. Presently anguish vanished before an expression of grim resolution. "How long shall I remain like this?"

"I cannot say."

"You must have some idea, Ti Rouge. Will it be a week before I move again? A month?"

"I can promise nothing."

"You must promise. You've got to cure me soon, before my people know I am ill. You must make me well again, as you have in the past. I am relying upon you, Ti Rouge. There is still so much I must do before I can be sure of Haiti's future. I must get back onto my feet again. You must make me well, very soon."

Duncan could not face the King's questioning eyes. He turned his head away. "I cannot promise that you will ever walk again."

The shock of Duncan's announcement temporarily robbed the King of speech. His eyes filled with tears. After a long interval he whispered: "So much to do! So much to do; so little time!"

Later that day Duncan returned to the Cap, to learn that the ship which was to carry them all to America had anchored in the roadstead.

"You will have to make haste if you are to complete your preparations in time," Nat told him jovially. "Only three more days to go."

"I am not coming with you, Nat."

Silence greeted Duncan's announcement. Bella and Nat stared at him in astonishment; Jean glanced down at her needlework to hide the gathering tears.

"Why not?" Nat demanded at last. "Surely you are not going to spoil everything just because that black despot is ill?"

"He needs me, Nat, more than at any time since my first year on the island."

"What if he does? Are you forgetting the way he treated you?"

"I am trying to."

Nat was annoyed. "I think you are crazy."

"Nathaniel!" Bella reproved. "I think Duncan is being gallant."

Nat grinned. "That is a woman's description of downright craziness. I am darned if I see any sense in your staying here. What has happened makes it more imperative to get away quickly."

Jean gasped. "Why?"

"If I know anything of the Haitians they will look upon Henry's seizure as a direct sign from the gods that divine protection has been withdrawn from him. When the news gets around they will lose their superstitious fear of him and attack him like a pack of ravenous wolves."

"How horrible!"

"Horrible, but true. Ask Duncan; he knows the mentality of the Haitians better than I."

"It is true, Nat, which is all the more reason why I should do my best to restore Henry to health."

"I thought you said he was paralyzed."

"He is."

"Then what can you do to restore him to health?" Nat demanded.

"I can try. The illness might possibly yield to treatment."

Both manner and answer were unconvincing, and Nat was disgusted. "I liked him well enough until he changed from a benevolent monarch to a tyrannical despot, but you are doing more for him than I would."

"You are not a doctor. Doctors owe a duty to their patients."

Nat grimaced. "Give me trade."

Duncan turned to his foster sister. "Thank you for understanding, Jean darling."

She smiled wistfully. "I hope you will reciprocate."

"In what way?" Duncan asked her.

She busily plied her needle. "I am not going to America, either."

"You are," he stormed. "You've heard what Nat said, about Henry's illness possibly precipitating a revolt. You are to go; I insist."

"I thought you were going to be equally understanding," she pleaded.

"No, Jean, not if it is a question of your remaining in Haiti. She must go with you, mustn't she?" Duncan appealed to the Americans.

"Of course she must," Nat promptly agreed.

"But Duncan—" Jean glanced up at Duncan, and choked back the remainder of the sentence, for she saw that argument would be useless. "Yes," she said submissively, "I will go."

When he had collected a supply of medicines from his surgery Duncan returned to Limonade to superintend the removal of the King from Bellevue to Sans-Souci. As soon as Henry was installed at the palace Duncan worked upon the King's malady. He treated the patient with purgative medicines to rid the body of its poisons, and then, with Massicot and Turlin, who was the King's first physician under Duncan, took turns to massage the thick, ebony-black limbs. The treatment proved useless; the muscles did not react, the nerves remained insensible. The work continued without cessation, day after day, but there was no sign of improvement, although the doctors wore themselves out with their efforts.

Theirs were not the only gloomy faces; Henry's loyal followers grew increasingly worried. As news of the King's continued helplessness spread, insurrection raised its head. At first, passively; no one could be certain that he would not soon recover and take vengeance on all who had dared to defy him. Even helpless in bed he was still feared. So the malcontents proceeded cautiously. There is no need to work so hard—said the whisperers; the King is in bed. He cannot spy upon us now with his telescope. Nor can he ride about on horseback, to watch that we slave all day long for a crust of cassava bread while he lives on the fat of the land. Work on the plantations slowed down, though the cultivators kept their ears and eyes alert for the first sign of the King's coming. But when each passing day brought no news of that, the Haitians grew bolder; the rebellious spirit spread from cultivators to soldiers, from plantation to proprietors to nobles. More and more tongues spoke openly of the benefits to be derived from associating with the Republic in the South.

Duncan did his best for Henry, and in one respect his labors were selfish, for they gave him little time to dwell upon personal matters. Whenever he did have a few spare minutes for introspection he tried to analyze why, with the departure of Jean and the Martins, life had become particularly depressing. Life had not changed to such an extent after Nat's first return to America, although the loss of Nat's cheery personality had been a matter of sincere regret. Still, he could not believe that Nat's second departure was any worse than the first. Therefore, Nat was scarcely to be held responsible for his present gloom. Nor Bella. What of Jean? Had her going made so much difference to him? He missed her, of course; missed her terribly. But what of the years he had spent in Haiti without her? Those years had been by no means melancholy. However much a man might love his sister, her absence was unlikely to affect his happiness. And yet— No, the idea was preposterous. Jean's love for him was passionate, but his feelings for her were those of brotherly affection.

What of Phebe? Could it be, Duncan reflected, that her absence was the cause of his unrest? The obvious answer was yes, for now that he had recovered from the first shock of her callous desertion he appreciated the real happiness that she had brought to him. But was it she he missed or her beautiful, panther-like body, her passionate kisses, her wholly satisfying embraces? A year or so ago the answer would have been beyond doubting, but now—he was not sure. He was sometimes tormented by sexual cravings, but he was not sure that his desires were wholly physical.

Haunted by these dreams, Duncan did not spare himself to put the pleading, anxious Negro king back on his feet. August passed, then September. With the coming of October the situation approached its climax. The Haitians were convinced that their king would never spy upon them again. What need to work? What need to fear the King's wrath? Weren't all Haitians free and independent?

On the first of October the torch of insurrection burst into flame. The Eighth Regiment of St. Marc revolted against their military commandant, Jean Claude, whom they killed in the street.

CHAPTER NINETY-THREE

HENRY was too shrewd not to realize the danger of the revolt. He called his three favorite secretaries to his bedchamber; loyal Baron Dupuy, loyal Baron de Vastey, and loyal Chevalier Prézeau. These three men had served him faithfully in the past. What of the future? He inspected each face in turn; and in turn each pair of eyes steadily returned his own searching glance. The King sighed his relief; these men would not betray him; with three such devoted officials to serve him unquestioningly, the crisis might yet be halted before it developed. If only he were not chained to the bed!

He signaled the three secretaries to approach.

"You have heard the news. I am not blind to the consequences of the insurrection. Let us calmly examine the present situation so that we can put the necessary plans into operation to stop the spread of trouble. Vastey, have you had any reports upon why the Eighth revolted?"

"Yes, Your Majesty. The Eighth resented the imprisonment of their colonel, Paulin, at the Citadel."

"The man was insubordinate to Claude and irreverent to me."

"He richly deserved his punishment, Your Majesty," Vastey hastened to confirm. "But his soldiers believed Jean Claude to be responsible for Paulin's punishment, so they killed him in revenge."

"Then the insurrection was directed against Jean Claude, not against me?" The question embarrassed the three secretaries; not one of them dared to face the King's questioning eyes. "I see," Henry said grimly. "Claude was the excuse, not the reason."

"I am afraid so, Your Majesty. That is why President Boyer is planning to send help to St. Marc."

Henry's uncontrollable temper flashed into existence again. "The canaille!" he shouted. "May that damned Boyer rot in hell!" The mood quickly passed. Calm once more, he made a jerky movement of his shoulders which the secrtaries took to be a shrug. "For years I suspected that advantage would be taken of any weakness I revealed, not only by the cursed Republicans but by my own people as well. Now this cursed illness of mine has crippled me I must expect trouble. Is Prince Romain dealing with the revolters?"

"He is, Your Majesty. He and the Count Mirebalais. Prince Romain is occupying Fort Diamant and menacing St. Marc with his cannon, while Count Mirebalais attacks the town."

"Then the situation is not so bad as your face suggests, Vastey?"

Vastey said nothing. Once again Henry found that none of his secretaries was willing to face him frankly.

"Well?"

"I am afraid the insurrection will spread whatever may happen at St. Marc," Vastey declared unsteadily. "Ever since Your Majesty's illness the country has been very—very restless."

"Then send orders to the Duke of Marmelade to march against the revolting troops; his loyalty may persuade the younger hotheads to think twice before defying their king."

"Is His Grace's loyalty beyond suspicion?" Dupuy asked hesitatingly.

"Why shouldn't it be?"

"He has not forgiven you for making him work on the Citadel, Sire."

"Loyalty seems a questionable asset among Haitians," he muttered. "We must take a chance on his honesty; after all, he is a relative."

"That makes him the more dangerous enemy," Prézeau pointed out.

"Why?"

"He is in the better position to claim the leadership of the Haitians."

"God damn! He would not dare."

"Not in normal circumstances, Sire, but—" Prézeau paused.

"But now that I am helpless— Oh, God! If only I could move! If I could show myself the danger would disappear." In that moment of desperation Henry tried to raise himself up, as if he believed that will power would achieve the miraculous, but the effort proved as vain as hundreds of similar attempts before it; his head fell back upon the pillows. "The chance must be taken. Send a message to Marmelade to join Prince Romain and Mirebalais, for the purpose of crushing all insurrections and revolts against us."

"Very well, Sire."

"And send Dr. Stewart to me, Vastey. He must get me well. He must."

That Prézeau had good reason for fearing Marmelade's loyalty was shortly proved. As October 7 dawned a messenger arrived at Sans-Souci with news from the Cap. After forcing the captain of an Austrian vessel in the harbor to sell the ship's stock of arms and ammunition for five thousand livres, Jean-Pierre Richard, Duke of Marmelade, governor of the capital, had joined the ranks of the insurgents; his followers were already burning the King's private plantations.

A melancholy expression settled upon Henry's face when Vastey told him the unhappy tidings. "Why did he do this to me, Vastey? Once he was my friend and a loyal follower; why does he turn against me now?"

"Because he envies you your wealth and power," the secretary replied with sincere wrath.

"We cannot all be kings."

"Haiti would be a happier country if its leaders would realize that, Your Majesty. The more wealth the nobles have, the more some of them aspire to take your place."

"Then there are others besides Richard?"

"There have always been some who have been jealous of you, Sire."

"Yes, Vastey, I know," Henry agreed wearily. "One of my reasons for severity was because so many of my subjects were too willing to step into my shoes. I liked Richard, I was grateful to him for his past services to me, but I've been suspicious of him for some years. That's why I seized upon the excuse to imprison him in the Citadel. Now he is seeking to avenge himself upon me, is he? Very well, we must deal with the menace, and crush it. This time Richard shall die, even though he is a relative. Vastey, send a message to Prince Romain instructing him to move against Richard."

"It is too late, Your Majesty."

"What?"

"Soon after the messenger from the Cap arrived, another came from St. Marc. Prince Romain and the Count of Mirebalais are joining Richard, Sire."

A stricken expression contorted the King's face. "Romain as well! Isn't there any loyalty in Haiti?" The next moment he was remorseful. "That is unfair of me, Vastey. I'm still surrounded by a few faithful followers. And my Bonbons, and my Dahomeys? Are they still loyal to me?"

"As yet, Your Majesty."

"Good!" Henry's face grew brighter. "We must make plans to defeat my enemies. To the devil with them! I've fought and won battles before. I'm not defeated yet. My people shall learn not to defy their king. Vastey, order all troops at Sans-Souci and the Citadel to parade tomorrow, for review."

Vastey looked startled. "For review, Sire? By whom?"

"By their sovereign, of course."

"But, Your Majesty—" Comprehension dawned. "From the balcony, Sire, where you can remain seated?"

"No, Vastey. I'll review my troops on horseback; our soldiers and subjects shall see with their own eyes that their king is still able to maintain order."

"But, Sire—" Vastey began stammeringly, for he wondered if the King were suddenly mad.

"Those are our commands," Henry said sternly. "And Vastey—" he added, as the secretary moved slowly toward the door.

Vastey halted. "Sire?"

"Send to the mountains for Tio-Tio."

"The houngan!" The confused Vastey appeared even more startled and uneasy than before. "What will the good fathers say?"

"I do not care what they say," Henry snarled. "The white man's God has failed me; why shouldn't I turn to the black man's gods?"

Henry said nothing to Duncan of the message to the houngan, or voodoo priest, but it happened that he was massaging the King's legs when Vastey entered the bedroom, accompanied by a soldier.

"This man has returned from Tio-Tio's caille, Sire."

"Is he coming?" Henry asked eagerly.

The messenger's eyes gleamed white with fear. "Papa Tio-Tio was not at his caille, Your Majesty."

"Then why didn't you wait for his return?"

"I spoke to his woman; she said that the houngan was already on his way to the palace to see Your Majesty."

"How did he know I wanted him?"

"That is what I asked her," the man replied, as he glanced fearfully over his shoulder as if expecting to see an unpleasant apparition behind him. "She said that the gods had let him know that Your Majesty wanted him."

The King laughed his joy. "It is a good omen, Vastey. The gods are with me; with their help I shall overthrow my enemies." He spoke to the messenger. "Did she say when the houngan would be here?"

"Half an hour before sunset, Your Majesty."

"Why not before?"

"He is gathering the simples for an ouanga, Your Majesty."

The King laughed again, as though the news was heartening. "Good, good. You can go now, man. Tomorrow you shall be rewarded."

An awkward silence followed the soldier's exit. Neither the King nor his secretary had the courage to face Duncan's accusing eyes. He moved away from the bedside, approached the window, and stared out at the beautiful panorama. He had seen it often, but not often enough for its glory to fade. For once, he was blind to its ever changing beauty; he was shocked that Henry would return to his people's superstitions. Then doubt crept into his mind. He realized the *houngan* was the King's last hope. But even so, this was a bitter blow to his own pride. Even now, he hoped he could cure Henry, doubtful as he was of this possibility.

His reflections were interrupted. "I have sent for an *houngan*, Ti Rouge," Henry mumbled in an aggressive voice.

Duncan turned. "So I understand."

"Do you blame me?"

"It is not for me to criticize Your Majesty's acts."

"I don't speak to you as His Majesty, Ti Rouge. I have never been His Majesty to you. You know that. You are my friend; the best friend a Negro ever had."

"I am also your physician. You've sent for the *houngan* hoping that he will prepare an *ouanga* that will cure your illness. That is no compliment to my professional skill."

"You do not understand, Ti Rouge," Henry argued in a pleading voice. "The blood still flows in my legs; they are not dead; they are as alive as my head and shoulders, which can move. Look at my arms; I can now move them a little, as you know. If they can move, why not my legs also? They must move, I tell you. They must, so that I can put myself at the head of my army and show myself to my people." His voice strengthened in confidence.

"When I do that, the cursed rebels will flee before me like dead leaves before a hurricane; Haiti will be saved from another blood bath."

"But your legs are not alive. True, the blood flows through them, but the nerves which should make them move are as dead as the branches of that tree out there, which lightning struck a year ago. Half of that tree still lives, but has the other half recovered? You have always been a brave man, Henry, and now you must face the truth with your usual courage. Your legs, like those branches, will never live again."

"Perhaps they have been charmed by a *bocor*, paid by one of my enemies to cast an evil spell upon me," Henry suggested with a fearful glance that reminded Duncan of the messenger. "If so, Tio-Tio might be able to exercise a more powerful charm, for he is a great *houngan* and noted for his magic."

"Magic!" Duncan cried. "No magic can cure paralysis."

The King gave a nervous shout. "Don't say that, Ti Rouge, you might anger the gods so much they'll refuse to cure me." He appealed to Duncan. "You have been in Haiti long enough to know the power of the *houngans*. Do you deny that they have cured illnesses where white men have failed; where even you have failed?"

Duncan would have denied the charge could he have done so with sincerity, but this was not possible. He had seen many strange and fantastic happenings; such as healthy men who had dropped dead because, many leagues distant, some *bocor* had charmed away their lives by spell and incantation; he had known barren women becoming pregnant after drinking the appropriate philter; he had seen love *ouangas* act with unaccountable efficiency and speed; he had seen dying people restored to health after drinking secret potions. Even the dead had been known to live again in Haiti.

Precisely thirty minutes before sunset a bent and wizened old man, who called himself Tio-Tio, appeared at the palace gates and demanded admittance to the King. His hair was snow-white, his face was so puckered that his beady eyes were scarcely visible; when he grinned he exposed hardened gums from which the last tooth had long disappeared. His arms were long and gangling, his feet were splayed, his flesh was covered with the filth of years, and he smelled more offensive than a mangrove swamp. Yet the sentries, with averted eyes and trembling lips, hastened to open the gates to him, for the fame of Tio-Tio was widespread; some claimed him to be a *houngan*, or a voodo priest who confined himself to beneficial magic; others said that he was a *bocor*, or priest of evil magic; whichever he was in fact, his name was a password.

Tio-Tio shuffled into Henry's bedroom and grinned at the bedridden King; his toothless, whitened gums made his face repulsive.

"I wondered how long it would be before you sent for me," he mumbled familiarly in a cracked, high-pitched voice. "You should have remembered before that your skin is too black for white man's magic." He glared galefully at Duncan, who stood beside the bed. "Now it may be too late; the moon is in the wrong quarter for a complete recovery."

"Can you make me walk again?" the King asked eagerly.

The old man sniggered. "That depends upon whether the gods are pleased with you or not, Henry."

"You will intercede with them?"

"Why not? You are as good a man as the one who hopes to take your place."

"Who is that?" the King demanded angrily.

A cunning expression made Tio-Tio's face more hideous than ever. "The gods know." He flopped down upon his haunches, crossed his knees, and produced from inside his shirt a small, dirty bundle. The contents of this he emptied upon the floor to his right; the square piece of material that held them he spread flat upon the floor in front of him. Then he picked up the contents from the floor one by one, placed them in a pile on the center of the cloth, and repeated in a singsong voice after each article some words in an unintelligible language.

"A piece of root from the *bois chica* tree—a piece of rag soaked in blood from a virgin, not yet moon-afflicted, to renew your blood, Henry —the toenail of a babe newborn today so that your legs, too, may be reborn, and a piece of the umbilical cord to join you to Mother Earth —the pollen of orange blossom to remarry you to life—a silver piece with your head, Henry, for the gods to recognize you—a thunderstone for luck—a piece of granite to make you strong—three feathers from the tail of a cockerel victorious in a fight, to give you victory in your fight— salt and pepper to keep away the evil duppies—incense from the church and a chip from a wooden cross, to please the white man's God—dirt from the four corners of your palace—the leaves of verbena, and seven *cachimenta* leaves—" He nodded his head many times. "Good, good! I have forgotten nothing."

He lifted his head and glanced at the King. "Now four articles from you, Henry, to complete the charm. Parings from the little toe of your left foot and the big toe of your right; a tuft of hair from the crown of your head; a square bit of a shirt soaked with your sweat; and lastly, twenty-four drops of blood, one for each hour of the day."

Henry glanced, shamefaced, at Duncan, for there was no other person in the room. "Will you cut my nails and my hair, Ti Rouge, and draw the blood?"

Duncan was saved the perplexity of deciding whether or not to assist in what he was convinced was useless hocus-pocus, for Tio-Tio gave a high-pitched cackle of laughter.

"No, no, Henry; no white man's hand must touch the *ouanga*, for the gods would be angry." He rose to his feet, produced a knife from one of his pockets, and shuffled toward the bed. He drew back the cover, his puckered eyes stared—with envy, it seemed to Duncan—at the King's naked limbs. Presently he began to stroke them with his filthy hands.

"Fine legs, fine legs!" he mumbled. "The legs of a bull."

"Can you make them walk again?" Henry demanded impatiently.

"Wait, wait! We must await the rising of the moon. Tonight, when the moon is at its height, Tio-Tio will pray to the gods to restore life to these lovely bull legs." With apparent reluctance he removed his hands from Henry's legs; while he proceeded about the business of paring the nails of the little toe of the left foot and the big toe of the right, he droned a prayer to Papa Legba: "*Papa Legba, Papa Legba, ouvri baisière pour li; tout mystère 'gides li.*"

The nail parings, the hair, the piece of shirt, and the drops of blood were added to the other ingredients that comprised the charm. These the *houngan* stirred up with his hand as he muttered another incantation to Papa Legba and the gods of Guinea. When he had finished he gathered up the material by the four corners and transferred the contents into a leather pouch, which he passed on to the King.

"Wear this round your neck tonight, Henry. Tomorrow I will give you a bath in rum and pimiento, and massage you with the dust of the charm; if the gods are pleased, you will walk."

The old man made his way out of the bedroom as Henry, carefully avoiding Duncan's eyes, hung the pouch round his neck.

During the earlier hours of the night Duncan slept fitfully; for once he seemed unable to close his ears to the booming of the drums, which were louder and more turbulent than usual. Again and again he awoke with a start, as if something had disturbed him, but he heard nothing but the persistent drumming that seemed to echo from every direction, as if the entire country were awake and restless. This atmosphere grew more intense as the hours passed; at last, moved by impulse, he rose from his bed and went to the window. The blackness of the night was silvered by the light of the waning moon; the mountains were alight with the twinkling flames of a hundred fires. One, two hundred meters off, attracted his attention, for it was unusual to see fires within the palace grounds. He saw, silhouetted against the leaping flames, a bent, wizened figure that squatted on the ground and swayed unceasingly to and fro. The *houngan* was praying to his gods. Each time his arm moved toward the fire, there was a shower of tiny sparks.

CHAPTER NINETY-FOUR

AS SOON as he had eaten, Duncan went to Henry's bedroom. The King was in a more lighthearted mood than for many weeks past; since the day of the seizure that had confined him to bed.

"Good morning, Ti Rouge; have you seen anything of that *houngan* this morning? He should soon be here."

"I have seen nothing of him. I came directly here from my house."

"He should be arriving soon; he knows he must get me up in time for the review." Henry glanced at Duncan's face. "Do not look so solemn, man; this day may prove to be a day of blessing, not of gloom."

"Supposing Tio-Tio fails, Henry?"

An expression of dismay flashed across the King's face, but quickly passed. "He will not fail," he stated with confidence. "During the night I dreamed I walked again; that dream was a sign from the gods that Tio-Tio will be successful. He has never failed, Ti Rouge. He is the greatest priest in Haiti; that is why I sent for him."

"I hope you are right, but, as your physician, it is my duty to warn you that I do not think he can succeed; there is no cure for complete paralysis. God knows, I wish there were."

"He *will* succeed; he *must* succeed." Henry said somberly. "Did you hear the drums last night?"

"They kept me awake."

"I listened to them. They are plotting mischief against me, but once I am on my feet I shall crush the revolt as easily as slicing a coconut with my machete. Look at my arms, Ti Rouge. Have you seen me lift them as easily as this before?" Henry exultantly lifted his arms shoulder high; it was quite true that the limbs were infinitely more flexible than they had been for weeks. "That proves the *ouanga* is beginning to take effect."

"Can you also move your legs?"

"Not yet, but I shall later on this morning. As surely as night will come again, I shall walk today." Confidence transfigured the King's face as he stared challengingly at his physician; Duncan had not the heart to disabuse him further.

Five minutes later Tio-Tio appeared, dressed in a red and yellow garment that Duncan knew to be the robe of a voodoo priest; a red handkerchief round his head, a red belt round his waist. He leered at Duncan, chuckled malevolently, addressed himself to the King.

"I prayed to the gods last night, Henry, and they answered favorably. In one hour's time you will walk again."

"Then hurry, Papa Tio-Tio, for I am to review my soldiers in one hour's time. Everything is ready for you."

"I, too, am ready, Henry."

The King signaled to a soldier who stood on guard by the door. The man knocked upon the door, whereupon it was opened from the outside, and several servants appeared. Four of them carried a hip bath, which they placed on the floor beside the bed; other servants carried large ewers of steaming rum, which they poured into the bath. At Henry's command all but four of the servants retired; the remaining four stood by the bed awaiting further orders.

The *houngan* stirred into the rum a quantity of ground pimiento, muttering an incantation while he did so; soon the room was filled with a pungent steam that made Duncan's eyes and nose prickle. Then Tio-Tio gave an order in his high-pitched voice to the servants; after they uncovered Henry and removed his shirt, they raised the helpless King from the bed and lowered him into the bath.

For thirty minutes Henry sat in the bath, while the *houngan* pounded the ingredients of the *ouanga* into powder and muttered propitiatory prayers to Papa Legba and other beneficent gods. When he had finished he ordered the servants to lift the King from the bath and replace him on the bed. Then he sprinkled the powdered *ouanga* over Henry's belly, thighs, and limbs, dipped his hands in a pitcher of fresh rum and then into a pot of ground pimiento, and began to massage the helpless limbs.

"Fine legs," he mumbled. "The legs of a bull; fine and strong. You must walk again, my beauties; you are too fine to waste lying in bed."

The bony hands proceeded methodically about their task. Taking one leg at a time, they worked down from the hip to the thigh, thence to the knee, and finally to the sole. Duncan watched with derisive but curious eyes; were he not being given the opportunity of seeing for himself, he would not have believed that the withered hands could be so vigorous and expert. With swift, circular movements the yellow palms raised an angry rash upon the black flesh, while the pointed fingers traced out and vibrated each nerve and muscle. Soon the sweat poured down the *houngan's* face and splashed upon the patient's body, but the old man neither paused nor flagged. Duncan became dazed from watching the circulating hands, Henry's breathing became hoarse and labored from the pressure of the hands upon his stomach, but Tio-Tio continued tirelessly, monotonously. After fifteen minutes' massage he stopped, but only to order the King to be turned over onto his chest; whereupon he leaped upon the bed, straddled the black body, and pressed his rum-impregnated palms down upon the King's back and spine. The King gasped, but the old man ignored his victim's distress.

Meanwhile, from the direction of the parade ground came the noise of shouted commands and the steady tramping of feet, as the Household Troops assembled for review. From where he stood Duncan could see line upon line of black, stolid faces, probably a thousand in all, and here and there officers mounted on restless, stamping horses. They looked, and were, a fine body of men, these Household Troops of Henry's; he had seen to that, for each man was picked and under oath of loyalty; as a body they had been drilled and disciplined under his personal supervision. Led by a competent general, these men, Duncan was sure, would give a good account of themselves even against many times their number, for, besides being well disciplined, they were well armed and well accoutered. As he gazed at them through the bedroom window it occurred to him that Henry was probably justified in claiming that the revolt would soon be crushed if he could place himself at the head of his Household Troops. If still hesitant subjects were to see their king, mounted, resolute, well guarded, all but those already compromised would quickly shout their loyalty to the monarchy, and Henry would then be able to deal with the rebels at his leisure.

If! That fateful word! That fateful condition! How could a paralyzed man place himself at the head of his troops? A malignant fate had struck the King down, and chained him forevermore to his bed. When that news was confirmed, when the people became convinced beyond all doubt that their dreaded sovereign was a helpless invalid, when the King failed the Household Troops who now awaited his appearance and his leadership—what then? It was not fair, he thought, that a man's throne, and a man's life, should hang so precariously in the balance, to be saved or sacrificed according to whether that man could or could not move his legs. He might be less a man for not being able to move them; but was he less a king? He was not; on the contrary, perhaps adversity, by inducing the exercise of patience and tolerance, might even make him a better king. Poor King Henry! God help him when he failed to hold the promised review!

Duncan's reflections were interrupted by Tio-Tio. "Stand up, Henry. Stand up."

He turned quickly. The *houngan* had moved away from the bed and now stood, trancelike, in the middle of the room, with his two arms, stiffly outstretched, in the direction of the King. "Stand up," he repeated in a deep, unrecognizable voice. "Stand up and walk."

The silence in the bedroom was in strange contrast to the noise from the parade ground. Outside, drums were beaten, underofficers shouted orders, fat Prince Victor-Henry, the Heir Apparent, who commanded the Household Troops, galloped his horse up and down the lines. The only sound to be heard within the bedroom was Henry's gasping breath and the uneasy breathing of the four terrified servants.

Henry's naked body, in spite of the inevitable wasting of the past weeks, was still enviously magnificent in its muscular development and splendid proportion, but it was as immobile as something dead. His head, likewise, seemed to lack life, for it was turned toward the voodoo priest in a rigid, unnatural pose. His eyes alone refuted the impression that the ebony body was a corpse; they were brilliant with hope and determination.

"Walk, Henry; stand up from your bed and walk!" the priest chanted in a deep singsong. "Papa Damballa, the Great Source; Papa Damballa, the Good, the Powerful; Papa Damballa, the God of Gods, commands you to walk! In the name of Damballa Ouedo, he who lives in the sky; walk, Henry, King of Haiti. In the name of Papa Legba, Keeper of the Gate; in the name of Papa Loco, God of Medicine and Wisdom—walk!"

In dread that he would see the hope in Henry's eyes changed to agonized despair, Duncan tried to look elsewhere, but he was unable to resist the somber triumph of witnessing the failure of Tio-Tio's black magic. He stared at the motionless body. Not a ripple of a muscle, nor the twitch of a nerve disturbed the still form; but Henry's forehead ran with sweat as he strove to compel his paralyzed limbs into movement.

"Walk! Damballa Ouedo commands you! Walk!"

The first movement was no more than a convulsive twitch, but it was distinct, and was followed by a second, a third, a fourth, and presently a succession of movements. With painful deliberation Henry raised his right foot in the air, held it there for several seconds, turned it from side to side, and finally let it fall back on the bed. Then he did the same with his left foot.

A joyful shout broke the long, tense silence. "I can move my feet! Look, Tio-Tio; I am well again! Look, Ti Rouge. I can move my feet!" Henry's eyes glowed with happiness, triumph, exultation, determination. Peal after peal of gusty, excited laughter rang through the bedchamber. This stopped as abruptly as it had begun.

"Bring me my uniform, help me to dress. Hurry, hurry!" he shouted at the four servants.

Duncan dried his forehead, which was damp with perspiration, and marveled at the miracle that had happened. What had restored life into those thick black legs? The *ouanga?* The prayers of the voodoo priest? The rum and pimiento? The massage? Henry's own terrific will power? Who could say?

With each minute the King's movements grew easier. He sat up, and later, with the support of two of the servants, stood. As soon as he had accustomed himself once more to being on his feet he advanced a tentative step away from the bed. His limbs collapsed; only the strong arms of the servants kept him upright. But his face never lost its determination; he moved a second, dragging pace forward, then a third and a fourth, and with each pace he grew stronger, more assured. He crossed the bedroom to the window, stared at the assembled troops, and laughed confidently.

"Let go of me," he ordered the men supporting him.

"Be careful, Henry," Duncan warned, fearing the consequences of a possible fall. But Henry laughed again, challengingly. Tio-Tio, speaking once more in his own high-pitched voice, muttered scornfully: "Walk, Henry, for Damballa is with you." He leered at Duncan. "Now, white man, what do you think now of your white man's God? Your God could not help him to walk, because he isn't as powerful as Damballa Ouedo, the Source."

Duncan was to intent upon watching Henry to make any retort to the sneers of the voodoo priest. The King swayed unsteadily as the servants let go of him, but he stiffened his muscles and carefully moved one foot forward. As he did not fall, he walked, with stilted but resolute movements, back to the bed.

"In a few minutes you will hear my soldiers hail their king," he predicted with confidence, as he gestured to the servants to begin dressing him.

As soon as he was dressed in full military uniform, he ordered a servant to warn Prince Victor-Henry of his coming, and moved slowly toward the door. His jerky movements were those of a wooden puppet, but they carried him forward, pace by pace. After refusing assistance, he passed through the door out of Duncan's sight.

Duncan turned toward the window and looked down upon the distant parade grounds. He saw the servant convey Henry's message to Prince Victor-Henry, saw the Prince give orders to his aides, heard shouted commands from the officers, saw the troops coming to attention. Some anxious minutes passed, but then, below him, he saw the broad figure of Henry appear on the palace veranda.

There was a wild, enthusiastic burst of cheering from the soldiers. "*Vive le Roi! Vive notre Roi! Vive le Roi Henry!*" There was no stopping the men of the Royals-Bonbons and the Royal Dahomeys. Their king, whom rumor had declared ill—dying—dead—was none of these things. He was alive and well, ready to lead them against the insurgents. *Vive le Roi!* He was their king, their general. He would teach those insurgents not to raise the flag of revolt. *Vive le Roi!*

The cheering died away as the King marched stiffly toward the white horse that was stationed in the middle of the parade ground—a magnificent beast of fine mettle, seventeen hands high. The distance was too great for Duncan clearly to see Henry's face, but the bond of sympathy with the Negro warned him that each pace was more deliberate, more measured, because Henry was finding each step more and more of a physical effort, which only a stupendous exercise of will power was enabling him to sustain. Then the King half turned, as if to see how far he had walked, and the physician glimpsed the set face, the black flesh wet with perspiration, the hard, determined mouth, and the white-rimmed eyes that were aflame with resolution.

The soldiers began to cheer again. They did not know that they were witnessing a miracle; that the man who moved across the parade ground with spectacular deliberation had risen, not fifteen minutes previously, from a sickbed to which paralysis had chained him for the past few weeks. But, all the same, they cheered him. *Vive le Roi!* Some called him a tyrant. What if he were? He was a good general, wasn't he? By Damballa! A fine figure of a man! *Vive le Roi!* If he were walking more slowly than usual, wasn't it to give everyone a good view of himself, just to let people know he was not a sick man?

The cheering continued spasmodically as Henry moved nearer to the horse, for as the cries died in the throats of one company, they were carried on by another, just to let the King know that his soldiers were glad to see him back again. It was all a game, but why not? The King liked to be cheered, didn't he? And he was well worth cheering, wasn't he? Ill! An old woman's tale! The King was as strong, as healthy as the next man. He would show the rebels a trick or two.

Duncan heard the cheers, and understood the reason for them, but he was not happy. All was proceeding well. The King was infinitely better than he, Duncan, had dreamed possible, for had he not declared, and believed, that the King would never walk again? Yet Henry was walking; ten more paces would see him safely by his horse. But Duncan could not feel happy.

Ten more paces. Nine more. Eight more. He prayed, but was not conscious of saying a word. His only feeling was one of intolerable strain, which instinct told him was not a twentieth of that which the King suffered. He stared down at Henry with anxious eyes. Henry was a big man, but he looked very small, very alone, in the center of the big parade ground.

Six more paces. Four. Two. One. Henry caught hold of the bridle of the horse with a sigh of relief. He had been so near to failing: each step he had taken, from the moment of leaving the palace, had robbed him of some of the stimulus that the *houngan* had rubbed into his legs. With each pace forward his limbs had seemed to grow heavier, more wooden. But he *had* reached the horse! He had only to swing himself onto the saddle to save his kingdom, for himself, and for posterity. That was as sure and certain as that, later on, the sun would sink and the moon would rise. One more effort; one last supreme endeavor—

Sweat blinded his eyes, his head swam in dizzy circles, but he lifted one leg and slipped his foot into the stirrup. Now up! he whispered hoarsely. Up on to the saddle. Up, for the end of the rebellion; up, for the retention of his throne; up, for the foundation of a dynasty; up, for the new Negro civilization! Up, the gods helping! Up!

The soldiers shouted: *"Vive le Roi!"*

The supreme effort! But not even Henry's tremendous will power could lift his heavy bulk up those few vital feet. He fell back upon his feet, which collapsed and let him sprawl on the ground. When he tried to rise again, he could not move his legs.

His troops stared at him with stolid eyes, and the cheering died away.

Henry was carried back to his bedroom by four servants. They sat him in a chair and hurried off. There were tears in his eyes.

"Where is the *houngan?*" he asked tonelessly.

"Gone," Duncan told him. "I did not see him go. He was here just before you tried to mount your horse."

"He did his best; he promised to make me walk, and I walked. I should have been satisfied with doing that. Now I shall never walk again."

"Nonsense! What you have done once you will do again. Rest—"

"I shall never walk again," Henry repeated with finality. "Did you hear the soldiers cheer me when they first saw me? They were glad to think that I could still lead them. They would have followed me anywhere, Ti Rouge. With those men behind me the revolt would have ended with the first battle." The old fire chased away the tears of mortification. "Even now it may end quickly. In my stead, Victor-Henry is leading my soldiers. Tomorrow, I may hear good news; perhaps today, for Richard's army is not far off—" He caught hold of Duncan's arm. "If anything happens to me, Ti Rouge, will you see that Her Majesty and the princesses escape from Haiti?"

"Nothing is likely to happen to you. You are still king; you have still many loyal followers."

"You must promise, Ti Rouge; for the sake of the past, for the sake of our friendship," Henry insisted in desperation. "There is money in London to keep them in comfort for the rest of their lives—I have seen to that. You are to put them safely aboard a vessel to England, Ti Rouge. Swear to be responsible for the safety of my wife and children, Ti Rouge, swear!"

"I swear."

The King sighed his relief. "Prézeau and Dupuy and Vastey will aid you; they still love me. Now go; make all the necessary preparations, see Dupuy—" He wiped the sweat from his forehead and shook his fist in the direction of the Cap. "The dogs!" he snarled. "If my legs had remained strong—"

With the departure of the household troops a brooding crisis descended upon the palace. The royal family, the secretaries, the servants, and the remaining troops all sensed that the future of the King depended upon the news of the impending battle. There was not a man or woman in the vicinity of the place who dared, or cared, to raise a cheerful voice. Most of the long corridors of the palace were deserted; silence reigned where usually one heard snatches of exuberant singing and loud, giggling conversation. The servants went about with tight lips and frightened eyes; the sentries, posted about the palace, wore sullen expressions and neglected to ogle the female staff.

Duncan shared this pervading spirit of despondency. He had admired Henry from the first, but never to the same extent as now. He could still marvel at the iron determination, and the unconquerable spirit, that had carried the King from a sick bed to the center of the parade ground. For all the incantations to the gods, the rum bath, and the *houngan's* massage, a lesser man would not, he was convinced, have moved one step from the bed, still less a thousand. Sheer will power had enabled the King to reach his horse. The pity of it lay in that final moment. The pity of it!

The fateful hours passed with demoralizing slowness. There was little movement in the palace. Everyone waited for news. Henry sat in the bedroom. Thither, at intervals, came his wife, his daughters, his secretaries, and Duncan, but he listened to all that was said to him with little attention. His eyes stared down at the empty parade ground, and everyone knew that his thoughts were leading his household troops into battle against the Duke of Marmelade and his rebels.

Then news at last, when it was least expected. An officer of the Dahomeys galloped toward the palace from the direction of the Cap; horse and rider alike were dirty with sweat and grime, but the officer, whose name history has failed to record, wasted no time in formalities. He flung himself off the heaving flanks of his animal, clattered up the stone staircase, rushing past the sentries, and grabbed a passing servant.

"Take me to the King," he gasped.

The servant took the officer as far as the door of the King's bedroom, which Dupuy opened.

"News for His Majesty," the officer announced.

Dupuy motioned the man to enter, and closed the door. The sentry outside, and the servant who had conducted the officer, each pressed an ear against the panel of the door.

"Well?" Henry cried eagerly. "What news, man? Have we won?"

"When we sighted the Duke of Marmelade's army, we saw that it was a large one. Nevertheless, we were in a favorable condition, so we prepared to fight—" Anothing fit of choking interrupted the story.

"What then? What then, man?"

"The insurgents raised their hats upon seeing us and cheered: *Vive l'Indépendance! Vive le Général Richard!*"

"The canaille! Did you shoot them down as they deserved?" The officer made no reply. "Did you shoot them down, I say?" Henry shouted. "Have you taught the dogs not to rebel against their king?"

"Your Majesty—" The officer's lips began to tremble. "I swear I am a loyal subject of Your Majesty's."

"I know that, man. I am not asking about you. What of my Bonbons and my Dahomeys? What did they do?"

"They shouted back 'Down with the King!' "

"You mean, there was no battle?"

"There was no battle, Sire. The household troops have joined the forces of General Richard. Now they are on their way here to Sans-Souci to kill you. May their bones fester in hell. Curse them, the rats! Curse them." The officer wept.

Outside the room the servant and the sentry exchanged glances. Then they straightened up, and ran as fast as their feet would carry them away from so dangerous a place as the king's palace. "*Vive l'Indépendance! Vive le Général Richard!*" they called out as they passed other servants and other sentries.

There was no time to waste. Henry looked at Duncan. "It is time to carry out your promise," he said in an even voice. "Vastey, Marie Louise, and my daughters are waiting for you in the courtyard."

"Good God! You cannot ask me to desert you now. A fine friend I should be if I scuttled away like a rat from a sinking ship."

"You promised. Now go quickly; it will not take long for the insurgents to reach here."

"What about you, Henry?"

"I have made plans—" Henry became impatient. "Go, go, for God's sake, Ti Rouge," he shouted testily. "Go while there is still time."

The two men, white and black, exchanged a long, understanding glance. A smile crept into Henry's black eyes.

"One day the whites will pay tribute to you, Ti Rouge."

"Rubbish!"

"By saving my life, Ti Rouge, you helped to found Haiti. You helped to make me like and respect the white people, and make Haiti prosperous. You tried to advise and guide me— If I had followed your advice—" Henry shrugged his shoulders, held out his hand.

"Good-by and godspeed, Ti Rouge! May the gods protect you!"

"And you, Henry."

The Negro smiled; the sad wistful smile was Duncan's last, and most lasting, memory of Haiti's king.

Duncan galloped with Vastey ahead of the carriage bearing the Queen and her daughters to Cap Henry. Together he and the faithful aide had laid plans for making a secret approach and locating, among the vessels lying in the harbor, one bound for England, to which he could deliver the royal family, and another to speed him to America.

Ahead lay the future, Duncan knew. But he could not leave the past without a knot in his throat, though already it was fading as London had faded. This Haitian countryside would never entirely leave his dreams, Duncan knew, but it would never beckon him back .A lifetime was over for him, a new lifetime lay ahead.

François and Phebe and De Saint Just and Henry himself—Henry with his great dreams and his great strength—these all lay behind now. They had made a different man of him from the one who had landed in Saint-Domingue so long ago, but Duncan was glad it was a man no less acceptable to Jean than the first had been. His sadness was swallowed up in an overwhelming surge of longing; at last his truer life would begin, at last he would again be the Duncan whom Jean had loved and remembered. He urged his horse forward impatiently.

Henry sat alone in his bedroom and listened to the drums. The exterior of the palace was silver in the moonlight, but within the building no more than half a dozen rooms glimmered with candlelight. The remainder were in darkness, because the palace was deserted. All the lesser nobles, the staff, and the sentries had gone, shouting, "Vive l'Indépendance, à bas le Roi!" as they went. Only Dupuy, Prézeau, Vastey, the officer of the Dahomeys, and a handful of others had remained behind to face the music.

The King was no longer dressed in uniform. His last order to his chamberlain had been for water, soap, towel, clean nightclothes—and a certain casket. With the assistance of the trembling chamberlain he had washed and changed into the clean nightclothes. Now he sat in his chair, solitary and helpless, and contemplated the casket, which stood on a small table, close to his hand. A tear welled slowly up into his clouded eyes; a tear not for himself, or the fate in store for him, but for a dream that had become a Stygian nightmare.

He had no false optimism about what would happen to him when the advancing horde of insurgents, under the Duke of Marmelade, reached Sans-Souci. The white man's God had said that he who lived by the sword should perish by the sword; he recognized both the justice and the inexorable application of this rule. His enemy and kinsman, Richard, would know what to do—Richard, whom the King had struck with his cane and imprisoned at the Citadel. Richard would not hesitate to claim his revenge; he would not be clement because the King was paralyzed and deserted. He would hang his enemy from the highest battlement of the Citadel, and rejoice, claiming that he had rid Haiti of another tyrant.

But Henry smiled, for the contents of the casket would rob Richard of that ultimate satisfaction.

The smile died away; his glance moved away from the casket to the nearest of the dark windows that faced him. Somewhere out there, in the silver night beyond the window, was his Citadel, the Fortress of La Ferrière, which had been fourteen years in the building, and which he had prepared and fortified for just such an emergency as had arisen. He had built it at the cost of millions of silver pieces, and tens of thousands of lives, and now, just when he had most need of it, it was useless to him because Fate had made him incapable of movement.

He smiled again, in grim irony. If, soon after paralysis had seized him and while his kingly commands had still been respected and obeyed, if he had ordered his helpless body to be transported to the Citadel instead of Sans-Souci, he might now be defying the insurgents, and challenging them to dethrone or harm him. By the gods! Up there, with his bodyguard of a thousand Bonbons and Dahomeys to guard him, Marmelade, and Limbé, and Miragoane, and the whole cursed crowd of insurgents, could no more have touched him than reach the moon. Besides, in those circumstances, the British authorities at Jamaica might have been persuaded to send an expeditionary force to rescue him and restore order. The British might have done this because they liked his trade with them —weren't the British always ready to protect their trade? Even now, indeed, it might not be too late to reach the Citadel. The three secretaries, the officer of the Dahomeys, and the handful of people who remained at Sans-Souci would convey him up there somehow. There was a company of the Household Troops there who would hold the Citadel against assault.

For some minutes Henry contemplated this possibility; but gradually the hope in his eyes died away. He no longer desired to live. What was the use of living if he were but half a man? As half a man he would be even less than half a king. Besides, who could say that the troops in the Citadel would obey his orders and hold the place against Richard? Likely as not they would desert him as readily as their fellow soldiers had; why imagine that they would remain loyal to half a king?

His people no longer wanted him! This was the bitter reflection that destroyed his desire to live. His people had turned against him! And this after he had fought and struggled for them, had worn himself out for them, had given them hospitals, medical attention, schools, a standard of living such as no other black nation had ever known, a navy, and an army to be proud of! He had made their country rich beyond imagination—and they had turned against him! The realization was as gall and wormwood.

The guttering candles flickered and dulled; they required snuffing. But there was nobody to snuff them; and in any case, he was not aware of this as his glance strayed back to the casket beside him. Therein lay the finish of his dreams—dreams more far-reaching than he had dared to voice to any other living soul, dreams in which the complete conquest of Haiti and Santo Domingo was to be the steppingstone to the creation of a Negro empire, built up with painstaking effort and courage. It was not for his own aggrandizement that he had dreamed this dream, but for the glory of the Negro race. The glory of the Negro race! This had been the goal for which he had striven so passionately; the birth of a Negro era, the glory of the Negro race. And the people for whom he had planned this greatness were the people who had betrayed him. By their carefree indolence, their incurable laziness, they had challenged, defied, and, finally, defeated him.

One of the candles flickered just before it died out; a long shadow on the floor danced a fantastic jig, which attracted Henry's gaze and held it. He sucked at his lips, for the shape of the shadow was that of a lean figure wearing a soutane. Corneille Brelle! He whimpered a little, for he had never succeeded in wiping the picture of the Archbishop from his memory. The ghost of Corneille Brelle terrified him. Many other ghosts began to crowd in upon him; the ghosts of Frenchmen whom he had killed in hand-to-hand combat, opposing Negroes whom he had hanged as enemies, friends whom he had later executed for treachery, and the ghosts of the laborers who had died in their thousands so that the Citadel might be built; magnificent, blood-built La Ferrière, the most useless of all man's colossal achievements.

He willed away the mocking images; why should the last minutes of life be tormented by specters of the past? Soon he would be one of them, and then they would be able to wreak their supernatural vengeance upon him. Until then he was ready to defy them, as once they had defied him by refusing to co-operate in his plans for Negro glory. What he had done had been done for them, for Haiti. If they had given of their best, as he had given of his—

But had he? A new specter materialized from the shadows and mocked him. Conscience! He had begun well, but how had he finished? He had forced his subjects to work for the good of the state; he had robbed them of the liberty for which they had fought, he had compelled them to build palaces and fortresses; he had, indirectly, killed many thousands who might otherwise have lived. He had become a despot, and a tyrant, his conscience accused. He nodded his head. It was true. He had become a tyrant. But not willingly. The people themselves were to blame—all those people who had been unwilling to work for their own salvation. Compare the two Haitian states: the Kingdom and the Republic. The first was a thriving, prosperous community of healthy, hard-working men and women; the second was bankrupt, indolent, and dissolute. Which was the better country? He made no attempt to reply to his own question, for he had no doubts about the right answer. Yet had he been less tyrannical, he reflected pensively, perhaps Sans-Souci would not now be a deserted palace, and himself, a deserted king. Had he been less a tyrant, perhaps he would now be more loved.

The beat of the drums grew louder. Henry lifted his head to listen to their angry note. The throbbing boom was beating out a message of death. Death to the king! Death to the tyrant! *Vive l'Indépendance! Vive le Général Richard!* The insurgents were on their way to Sans-Souci, to kill the king who had dared to make them active instead of indolent. Death to the King! Death to the tyrant! Death! Death!

413

He stretched out his arm and lifted the casket lid. Inside was a pistol, which he lifted from its handsome setting and loaded. With slow, deliberate movements he raised it up toward his forehead. The drums throbbed. Death! Death! Death! Death to the tyrant who made us work! The crooked finger tightened—an orange-blue flash paled the glimmer of the candles—